Annette Motley is the author of two previous novels, MY LADY'S CRUSADE and SINS OF THE LION, which were acclaimed on both sides of the Atlantic. She currently lives in Ireland.

Also by Annette Motley

MY LADY'S CRUSADE
SINS OF THE LION

Annette Motley

THE QUICKEN- BERRY TREE

Futura
Macdonald & Co
London & Sydney

A Futura Book

First published in Great Britain in 1983
by Macdonald & Co (Publishers) Ltd
London & Sydney
This Futura edition published 1984

ISBN 0 7088 2518 4

Typeset, printed and bound in Great Britain by
Hazell Watson & Viney Limited,
Member of the BPCC Group,
Aylesbury, Bucks

Futura Publications
A Division of
Macdonald & Co (Publishers) Ltd
Maxwell House
74 Worship Street
London EC2A 2EN
A BPCC plc Company

For Carol McCarthy

Part One

Tower Hill, 12 May 1641

It is an alarming and tremendous thing to be a small girl in a crowd of nearly 200,000 people. The great mass mingled and swayed, trampling anything that was dropped, as Lucy dived down into the airless forest of legs. A sea must be like this, she thought, a sea choked with coloured weed. She fought sturdily among the breeches, stockings and skirts, trying to keep clear of the boots.

'Lucy! God save us, what is the child doing now? Do you want to be kicked to pieces, girl?' Her father's voice rumbled above, her mother's murmur breaking vaguely over it.

'I've dropped my orange!'

Her cropped yellow head bobbing against the backs of knees, she stretched her fingers until they ached. An inch more – then a sharp wrench hauled her rudely upright and her brother Tom, unsympathetic, had lost her the precious fruit. He shook her. 'We're here to see an execution, not a play. Show some respect.'

'Everyone else is eating oranges,' Lucy protested, rubbing a sore spot and avoiding her father's eye. Sir George did not like his daughter to appear a hoyden in public.

'Everyone else,' pronounced Tom clearly and savagely, 'apart from the few who have the wit to comprehend the history of this case, might just as well *be* at the play. They are only here to gratify their desire for entertainment; to see a great man die in response to their own ignorant baying for his blood!'

He squared his shoulders and glared about as if to challenge disagreement. No one gave him satisfaction. There was no need. It was Jack Straw of Shoreditch who would have his will, for once, on Tower Hill today, and not Thomas Heron, courtier, nor yet Sir George Heron, Bart MP, the King's loyal servants, gathered with their family in sad black, as much an embarrassment to the gaudy day as a flock of crows at a convention of popinjays.

Lucy was sorry that Tom was upset, but she was sorrier for the loss of her orange. Her second brother, Jud, had given it to her and she could see from the smooth set of his jerkin that there were no more in his pocket. His expression, too, was unpromising as he looked at Tom in disgust at his unnecessary self-publicity. Lucy sighed. She hated it when they were out of temper. She hoped they wouldn't begin to argue here, as they did on the rare occasions when both were at home.

The whole day felt uncomfortable, though she knew it was a great and solemn event and that she should think herself lucky to be here. But she couldn't help remembering the last great and solemn event she had attended. It had been the wedding of their Lincolnshire cousins. Tom and Jud had been in fine spirits then, joking and singing and drinking too much ale at breakfast. They had all worn their best clothes, not this fusty black, and the little ones had been invited too. There had been *dozens* of oranges and wine flowing in bucketsful and flowers everywhere and dancing on the grass. None of this miserable *waiting* that they were doing now.

This noisy, tight-packed crowd pushed and shouted and stank worse than anything she could have imagined. She had never seen more than a thousand bodies met together before, and that only at the Michaelmas Fair. She felt her heart squeezed and wrung out like her own facecloth as her father suddenly lifted her to his giant's shoulders and said with his great booming laugh, 'There. You shall see the cohorts of the Philistines, come to jeer at Samson in chains.'

The crowd spread about them, both moving and still, from Tower Street, near to where they stood, down past All Hallows Church and backwards into Crutched Friars, covering the hill with coloured figures all the way across to the Victualling Office and up to the crusty old walls of the Tower itself. Her first sensation was a simple terror that the whole of the world that she could see was filled with people, none of whom had a name she knew or a face she could recognize. They pressed inwards upon her, closer and closer, their voices babbling and meaningless, like the sounds inside her head when she had the fever. Such myriads, and all wanting one man's blood! For a second she felt herself to be that man and fear engulfed her. Then, gazing about, she saw that individual faces expressed only pleasure or impatience and that they were men and not wolves. There were even other children, aloft like her, who waved and shouted. As she waved back, her fear subsided. She saw too that there was order, of a sort, prevailing at the hands of the Tower Guard who had cordoned off various gangways to a saner world, one of which was nearby.

Almost directly in front of her, at a distance of about sixty feet, raised on a platform before the Tower wall, stood the block, a tiny, black-draped gravestone upon yards of scarlet cloth. Lucy suddenly felt very lonely and struggled to be back on the ground, very respectful of the silver lace on Sir George's funeral suit.

Now the long wait was over. Though she could no longer see the block itself, she was tall enough on tiptoe to watch the solemn procession of noblemen who were the prisoner's escort. Something between a sigh and a growl went up from the crowd as their man came before them at last.

Her father cried out deeply, 'God be with you, my lord!'

Their neighbours looked at them unkindly and one of them spat. Straining to see the man whose trial had set their household on its ears, Lucy was disappointed in the Earl. If this were Samson he would pull down no temple. His great height was stooped and he walked with difficulty. His beard and hair were very grey and his expression severe. She could not see how he might be called Black Tom Tyrant. Only his clothing was black, like that of his few friends in this great congress. He came to the scaffold with an everyday composure and waited while his name was called.

'Thomas Wentworth, Earl of Strafford, sometime Lord Lieutenant of Ireland.' Found to be a traitor by means of a Bill of Attainder, after all existing laws had failed to find him one. The King's highest servant, fallen most low.

He began to speak to those who had brought him to these depths. At first they would not listen, but increased their grumbling roar as though to cast their grievances at last in his face. He spoke on regardless and eventually, damming every breath, that enormous throng attained a silence that seemed unnatural. All of them wanted to be able to say, afterwards, that they had heard his last words. The Herons were among the few who did.

He began clearly and simply. 'I am come here to pay that last debt I owe to sin, which is death. I offer to all the world a forgiveness that is not spoken from the teeth outwards, but from the heart. I never had anything in that heart but the joint and individual prosperity of King and People. If it has been my luck to be much misconstrued, that is the common portion of us all.'

He paused and looked about him and then with deep gravity continued. 'I wish that every man in this great concourse will lay his hand on his heart and consider seriously whether the beginning of the happiness of a people should be written in letters of blood.'

His words frightened Lucy. They seemed to be meant for her too. What did they mean? Why did this man make himself such a willing sacrifice? Was he a tyrant and a traitor, or not? He did not sound like either as he expressed his devotion to the Church and the Protestant religion. Then he went on with a tranquil sureness that made Lucy feel the truth of his heart as a swift stab in her own breast.

'I desire heartily the forgiveness of every man for any rash and unadvised word or deed, and desire your prayers. And so my Lords, farewell; farewell all the things of this world . . .' The silence that fell seemed to fill with the presence of the waiting block.

The pain in Lucy's chest became an even less supportable sensation. She wanted to be sick. Even more, she wanted to get out from this hateful crowd before she would have to watch this courageous and dignified man be degraded to the two pieces of a bleeding carcass. She didn't care what he had done. What he *was*, at this moment, was what he ought to be remembered for.

Lucy looked at no one as she ducked past her family and dived again into the human forest. The gangway that should have led to Tower Street was obliterated by now, but those with a sense of where it had been let her through rather than miss, by argument, the moment for which they had come. She emerged from the thickest part of the crowd quite quickly and reached Tower Street with a sense of relief. There were only a few people here, running up from the river lest they were too late. Nausea compelled Lucy also to run; that and dread of the sound which her instinct expected at every second.

She had flung herself down on the flat stones of the wharf, and was lying with her head hung over the familiar Thames, when it reached her – useless to cover her ears – the great groan of pain and pleasure of the mob that has sated its most demeaning appetite. She retched into the clear water, then sat trembling in the mild sunlight, wiping her mouth on her best handkerchief and trying not to weep.

Her chief feeling was that she did not understand anything about people any more, not even her own father and brothers. Her mother, she knew, was present only because of Sir George's insistence that as many of his family as had reached the age of discretion should be there to honour the Earl in his extremity. Lucy did not see that they had done him honour to be a part of so unchristian a multitude. Nevertheless, she expected a beating for leaving it. In some strange way she would be glad of it, as if her small suffering might, instead of her witness of his death, be offered to Strafford in expiation of that unchristianity.

But Strafford was dead now, so how could that profit him? She frowned and sniffed. It was all difficult and incomprehensible. She didn't *want* any of these new and uncomfortable feelings and didn't know what she was supposed to do about them. She wished she could have stayed at home with the younger ones.

She got up and walked a few aimless yards along the quay, then sat down on a stone bollard and stared glumly towards London Bridge. The river was choc-a-bloc with traffic, most of it motionless because of the execution. She could see the barge that had brought them down from Chelsea, lying snug between two others close beneath the jetty. She detested its cheerful bunting now. The greater part of the web of rigging and furled sail that filled her immediate horizon was strung with gay banners in celebration of the day. The only sober vessel in sight was a spanking new three-masted merchantman some ninety feet long, her timbers still bare of decoration. Her only lustre was added by a wicked row of gleaming mouths in her gunports. For no particular reason Lucy counted them; ten on the lower deck, five on the upper. That would make thirty in all. Trade was a dangerous business these days. She was just wondering what further embellishment the shipwrights would add in the way of carving about the stern galleries, whose impressive windows were still empty of glass, when a faint twitch of her skirt made her spin round.

A tousle-headed boy, knife in hand, was making off with the purse he had just cut from her belt! With a yell of fury she was up and after him along the wharf, her feet in their soft slippers tingling on the cobblestones. The boy looked back once, judging her distance, then raced on. She saw that he must turn off up one of the side streets if he was to lose her, so she veered away from the water's edge and kept close to the walls opposite. Back at Tower Street she made a heart-thudding effort and gained on him before he could make his turn. For a split-second he stopped, then feinted and would have run back the way they had come, only to sprawl headlong over the foot she had thrust in front of him.

Making full use of her advantage she threw herself upon him, pummelling him with her fists as though he were the executioner himself, making him the recipient of all the sadness and puzzlement of her morning, translated into firm physical statements. She made every blow count, as Jud had taught her. It was an enjoyable release. In very little time, however, she realized she was no longer meeting with any resistance.

She stopped punching the boy's chest and sat up, astride her enemy, victorious and triumphant for a full second before it occurred to her that the urchin was somewhat undersized and very probably she had killed him. Apprehensive, she examined him. He did not seem to be breathing. She bent closer. All of a sudden *she* was the one on her back on the hard stones, her arms pinned to her chest and her head horribly sore where she had hit it. Tears sprang but she shook them away and spat straight up into the grinning dirty face.

'Let me go, you poxy misbegotten thief! And give me back my purse or I'll holler so loud the Tower will fall down!'

Whether or not she could accomplish the fate of Jericho without the aid of trumpets would never be tested, for before the boy could answer this interesting threat he found himself torn with shocking suddenness from the body of his victim and hoisted into the air, where he dangled a second, and then, from an unkind height, was dropped.

'Shagamuffin! What the devil are you at, you witless, gutless, gallows-bait?'

'Gawd's hooks, sir! I thought you was at the toppin'!'

Lucy sat up, rubbing her head, and stared and stared. Any rescuer was welcome but this one presented an extra dimension that stunned her reactions for the moment.

Was it a trick of the sun or did the man really shine like that? He was tall, perhaps as tall as her father, and appeared to be made of gold from head to foot, as if he wore armour like Sir Lancelot or St George. But even as these professional deliverers of damsels dashed across her mind, she saw that the sheen was that of satin rather than steel, and that the fine-cut features expressed amusement rather than chivalrous concern. She was helped to her feet in a kind enough manner, however, and dusted down with a proficient swipe of his leather glove. The boy, crouched with his grubby paws over his ears like a bad dog discovered, fared less well at the toe of an exquisitely gilded Spanish boot.

'Get up, you fool, and make your apologies to the young lady!'

Lucy detected a trace of sarcasm in his reference to herself and was suddenly conscious of her fever-cropped hair and disordered dress. She stood tall and did her best imitation of her elder sister, Jane, who had beautiful manners.

'Thank you, sir, for your timely assistance. To whom have I the pleasure of addressing my gratitude?'

His demeanour became suddenly grave.

'My name is William Staunton, merchant of this city.' How disappointing. She had thought him at least a lord.

'And *this*,' he added, taking the risen cut-purse painfully by his goblin ear, 'is Robin Whittaker, of a bad beginning and a predictably worse end. Who, for his sins and mine, is one of my apprentices. What do you say, mistress? Shall I keep him on, or turn him out to beg his living where he can get it?'

Lucy considered. The boy's face was scarlet with discomfort but it was a nice face, she thought, all pointy and alive like a fox's. And he had freckles like hers. She scuffed a toe in the dust, avoiding his furious look. He must hate her. 'If you turn him out,' she told the bold, clear countenance above her, 'he will spend *all* his time stealing instead of only some of it.'

His roar of pleasure made her jump.

'There's wisdom in that, as well as kindness. Your name, mistress?'

'Lucy Heron. You'll keep him then?'

'I will. I can't have a minx of a dozen summers show me up for a cruel master. You may grovel at Miss Lucy's feet, Robin.'

Robin looked shamefaced but openly relieved. He liked his work. Thieving was only his pastime. He nodded at Lucy, showing crooked teeth in an amiable grin. It was clear that he had forgiven her his embarrassment. He took her purse from his pocket and handed it back to her. She exchanged a smile for it.

'A mistake, miss.' His accent was pure Thames water. 'Won't 'appen again.'

'I should think not, ungrateful cuckoo's child!' A hearty cuff on the head underlined this, then Lucy had all the resplendent merchant's attention.

'A Heron, you say? Of Sir George's family at Heronscourt?'

'My father, sir.'

He seemed pleased. 'I'm acquainted with your father. He'll be up at the business on Tower Hill?'

'Yes, sir.' She looked down.

A hand touched her shoulder. 'Not to your taste? No, nor to mine neither. But all's done now if I'm not mistaken. Your father will be worried about you, thinking you swallowed alive by the mob. I'd best get you back to him.' He waved a dismissive hand towards the stream of people now pouring down Tower Street and along the dock.

'No use to look for him in such a press. I'll take you home. I believe you stay at Chelsea? We may have to wait a while for my bargemen. Their tastes are bloodier than mine.'

'Thank you, but we came by barge ourselves.' She turned and pointed. 'One of those. My family will come back to it if I wait.'

'Then I'll wait with you. I don't want you gone astray again. Robin, you shall wait too, and explain yourself to Sir George. It will serve to make your sins indelible to your memory.'

'But, sir, the ship's carpenter –' Fox eyes, sharp with hope, narrowed on the fine new ship.

'– will do very well without your company.' Hope was abandoned.

'Keep your eyes skinned for a very tall man with a red face. He'll be dressed in black and walks as if he'd rather be on horseback.'

Lucy laughed. It was true.

'If you see him first you shall have a lighter beating.'

Robin raked Tower Street with an alert and beseeching gaze.

'D'you like my ship?' Staunton asked Lucy, seeing her scan the water.

'What, *that* one, the new one? Is she truly yours? She's wonderfully beautiful! My brother Jud will love her. He's always wanted to go to sea.'

'Has he now? And what does your father say to that?'

'Nothing. That is, Jud's at his Inn at present and is supposed to study.'

'And does he?'

'Not as much as father wants. What'll you call your ship? Is she a warship or a merchantman?'

'She might be either,' said Will Staunton diplomatically. 'I'm naming her the *Gallant Lady*. D'you like it?'

'I do indeed. It suits her very well.' Lucy looked longingly towards the lovely vessel, wondering if she had the courage to ask if she might go aboard. She had more or less decided that she had when Robin cried out, 'There he is, sir!' and was seconded by a bull-like noise to which Lucy's tender ears were only too well accustomed.

Sir George Heron hastened towards them, walking feet asplay precisely as Master Staunton had described. She was careful not to smile as he bore down on them. He was a tall, broad, bulky man, built like an oak.

'Lucy!' he roared. 'The devil is in you today, you nasty imp! If we were not in public view I'd whip you here and now until my arm ached, by God! Be sure of it when we reach home, you saucy little trollop. Yuh servant, Will Staunton! Glad to see you! How came you into the company of this graceless want-wit? I would you might keep her, for I get no good of her! Sharper than the serpent's tooth!'

Lucy, hearing love in his anger, was unperturbed.

Staunton moved his left foot six inches and bent at the waist some thirty-five degrees. 'Yours, Sir George! As for the matter of whippings, I doubt your daughter deserves one, but this knave apprentice of mine has one to beg of you.' He pushed Robin in front of the Baronet's surprised and frowning face. 'Speak your piece, sirrah!'

Robin groaned. He wondered whether to bring up his indigent mother (true) and his seven (true) starving (untrue) siblings, or just to make a plain case of it and take his beating. A beating more or less was nothing to him; his back was already scarred as though he had served seven years in the galleys. But his trained seventh sense, the one that made him the best of his living, felt, sniffed, almost *touched* on some advantage here, if he could hang on to these silken coat-tails. Beside, the girl was a good'un and he fancied more of her company.

'I cut your lass's purse, sir,' he announced, the poor to the rich without shame, 'but she give me a run for it, and I gave it 'er back willin' enough.'

This doubtful précis seemed to satisfy Sir George, who growled and turned his whiskered frown on his daughter. Lucy admired Robin's brass face too well to dream of adding further substance. She lowered her eyes. Will Staunton continued to look, about *his* eyes and the corners of his mouth, as if life were primarily a matter for amusement.

The arrival of the rest of the family, to everyone's satisfaction, created a timely diversion. There was the inevitable flurry of introductions. Mary Heron, a fair, softly attractive woman with the bloom of fulfilment about her, inspired Staunton's most elegant courtesies. Then he turned to the tall, whip-thin figure of Tom, saturnine and withdrawn, who returned his bow with a soldierly punctilio; and made an acknowledging leg to the stockier Jud, who beamed back from a cheerful, open countenance in which mischief waited on manners.

In the midst of their pleasantries Lucy found herself as usual surrounded by giants who talked above her head, and so eased out from among them and edged closer to Robin who had effaced himself near the brink of the quay. 'They'll forget all about us now,' she said comfortably. 'Do you think your master would show us his ship, if I were to ask?'

'Your father may forget, but not Silken Will. I'll have my beating before my dinner. But, aye, he'll show you sharp enough,

17

I'd say. He's as proud as a pig in breeches of his fancy frigate.'
He sounded proud himself.

'Why d'you call him that – Silken Will.' Lucy stared again at
the elegant sunstruck figure in its vibrant reproach to the family
black.

'I'd have thought it was obvious, ninny!' was the jeering reply.

It was. Lucy grinned, unoffended.

'Butterfingers!' she retorted pleasantly.

'How old are you?' he asked, overlooking the insult in honest
recognition of its truth.

'I'll be thirteen in July.'

'Cancer or Leo?'

'Leo. Who'd be a scuttling scaredy crab! And you?'

'I'm near sixteen and Gemini like my master.'

'Two-faced! Sixteen! I don't believe it!'

'And only five foot high. I know,' he grinned. 'I can only grow
upward – meanwhile it's useful; more'n you'd think.'

She had a vision of him slipping fox-quick and nimble-fingered
through the holiday crowd on the Hill, just another child in a
hurry . . . Catching her thought, he nodded and patted the breast
of his shirt. 'I don't *need* your purse, but I reckoned you was
invitin' me. There's enough here to see us right for a week or
two.'

'Who's us?'

'The family. Mother, brothers, sisters, little 'uns mostly.'

'Like us Herons. But no father?'

Like them? His smile twisted, strange to her. 'No. Not
permanent anyway. We do 'ave one from time to time, but they
don't stay. Too many of us.'

Lucy did not understand but felt that there was cause here for
sympathy. She had just heard her own father insist that William
Staunton accompany them to the inn where they would eat
dinner, and now ran to tug urgently at her mother's arm.

'What is it, Lucy?' Lady Heron was reminded that she should
be angry with her daughter. 'You're a very naughty and inconsiderate girl to run off like that! How could we know what was
become of you? You might have lost your way and never been
found.'

'How could I lose my way when there is the river?' Lucy calmed
her. 'But listen, dearest mother, I have invited Master Robin
Whittaker to dinner also. I was sure that is what I should do,' she
added virtuously.

Mary Heron, distracted from her homily and knowing nothing

of purses cut, agreed at once, nodding benignly towards the astonished Robin. 'Of course the child shall come along with us. Who is he?'

'He isn't a child. He's sixteen and he's Master Staunton's apprentice.'

'Well, he looks as though he could do with his dinner.'

A couple of hours later, Robin had done everything in his power to prove her right. The meal had been a pleasant one, though not *too* merry, in consideration of the day. The host had served some excellent teal and a fine fresh leg of mutton, as well as a salmon and some spiced beef. There were side servings of beans, salsify and pumpkin sliced with apple; then custards and flummeries to follow, all washed down with old-fashioned hippocras, a warm red wine fragrant with cloves and cinnamon.

Now they were seated about a companionable blaze in the innkeeper's best chamber. Will Staunton and Sir George toasted on opposite sides of the hearth in the two most comfortable chairs, long legs asprawl amid a heap of dogs. Lady Heron occupied the settle before the fire with her eldest son, while Jud lounged in a windowseat and Lucy sat tight and quiet beside Robin on an old hope chest. Though sensible of the honour of being allowed to sit with the adults, she hoped that the conversation would exclude them so that they could slip away to the stables and look at the horses, and perhaps beg a few tit-bits of crackling from the kitchen. She also wanted to hear more about this mysterious life which was so abundant in fathers, and what it was like to work for the gilded merchant. Anxious for the friendship that she felt in him, it did not occur to her that Robin might have more sophisticated tastes in pleasure. Jud did not and he was older than the undersized apprentice.

'I had thought your brood larger than this,' Staunton observed, his eyes travelling the arc of handsome faces and lingering to flatter Lady Heron, whose rose and cream beauty was full blooming and fresh at forty.

'Twin lads, a moppet and a baby at home,' supplied the Baron. 'But we don't bring 'em much to town. We've enough sticky fingers here, with Lucy.' He disturbed his red and white striped beard to grin at her as she sat with the box of walnut suckets they had handed round. It looked as though she was forgiven today's misdemeanour. She licked her fingers and grinned back. 'You forget Jane, Father.'

He grunted. 'She forgot herself, I'd say, when she married

above her brains and beneath her common sense! The elder girl, Will,' he expanded, 'wed a stick of a scholar. They live at Oxford, in college, stuffing themselves with learning till they puke Latin and shit Greek! Poxy fellow can't ride a horse nor shoot a gun nor tell a dog from a dumpling! Can't get children, neither, as it seems.'

'They've been married only a year, husband,' Mary Heron protested.

'One year or ten! The fellow's a capon! Mark my words. Jane'll not make me a grandsire.'

'With seven other children you've no fears on that score,' Will said smiling.

'With Tom fishing in the Pope's pond, Jud half a wild thing and the rest too young, it won't come soon.' Sir George glowered at his sons, Tom answering with a faint repressive smile, Jud with a scowl deeper than his father's. Staunton steered for clearer waters.

'You appear to have a poor opinion of scholarship,' he suggested.

'Not so. I've a poor opinion of my son-in-law,' said Sir George cheerfully. 'Scholarship is an excellent thing, though I've too little time for it myself. Leave it to my wife who shames me. But I like a balanced man. One that has a use for his body as well as his books.'

'A man such as Thomas Wentworth, perhaps?' Staunton said softly, knowing that sooner or later they must speak of Strafford. It was his day though he was dead.

There was a little silence. Sir George cleared his throat and deepened his frown, nodded sadly but did not speak.

'It has been a bad business, this trial,' Staunton pursued.

A vein stood out on Sir George's pink temple. 'I'm glad to hear you say so, Will Staunton. It is not, I think, the opinion of some of your friends.' The tension in the room, strung taut at first by the mere fact of the family's being together, now stretched further to include their visitor. Lucy and the dogs, sensitive to the shift, pricked up their ears. A setter bitch got up and came to sit with her nose in Lucy's lap.

'I won't presume to speak for friends,' Staunton said carefully, 'but I think there are very few among them who do not regret the sad necessity of this day.'

'Necessity! Parliament has committed murder and you'd have it a necessity!'

'It was a *judicial* killing.'

'Bah! A trumpery coward's way that hasn't been used since the

Wars of York and Lancaster. A Bill of Attainder isn't law, it's barbarism! They couldn't prove him guilty by a fair trial so they *voted* him guilty by statute! He had committed no treason. They made a mockery of the law when they sentenced him by the wilful misunderstanding of his written words as to the use of the Army. "I will use this army to subdue this land!" How could that be any other land than Ireland? They knew it and they used it to destroy him. A fine thing for England, to have such judges; a fine thing for His Majesty!'

'His Majesty is the one who really brought him to his death.' The protest came from the windowseat where Jud sat pushing his feet against the embrasure as though trying to transfer unwanted energy into the stone. 'If he had refused to sign the Bill there could have been no execution.'

'You know it was not the King's will he should die,' Tom said quickly before his father could take breath to blast his brother from the room.

'Then why did he sign? He is the King. He may surely do his will. "Rex is Lex" as they say.'

'Because, booby, he had no choice. He didn't believe the Lords would pass the Act. God knows his speech to them was plain enough. When he said that *he* was unsatisfied as to Strafford's guilt, it was as good as to say that *they* should find likewise. They didn't. They voted to please themselves and be rid of Strafford. They put the onus back on the King.'

'With respect, His Majesty gave them no *legal* directive. And still he might have done as he wished.' Jud's look was mulish.

'What! While that misbegotten mob of Puritans and potboys was roaring for their ignorant notion of justice and snapping at the heels of the Lords as they went in to vote?' Sir George was, as it seemed he must do every time they met, losing patience with his second son.

'He is but one man, though he is the King, and must have support. Besides, he thinks it is his duty to consider the wishes of his subjects, even if they are knuckle-headed and graceless enough to belabour his palace walls and utter foul threats against his Queen.'

'You mean he's afraid of the mob,' said Jud matter-of-factly. Jud had, as a matter of fact, been part of that particular mob. Such experiences, he found, made for a wider education than musty Lincoln's Inn could ever give him. No member of his family was aware of this.

'God damn you to hell for your insolence, you stupid young

puppy!' Sir George's face counterfeited a complete thunderstorm, dark clouds of wrath massing portentously above lightning eyes and sunset cheeks. 'You're not too old for a whipping and you'll have it soon enough if you show disrespect to His Majesty.'

Jud sighed and pushed at his wall. 'I intended no disrespect,' he said truthfully, though he didn't feel, when he thought about it, anywhere near as much respect for King or Lords or Court as either his father or his brother appeared to do. But then, Sir George had been the King's liege man from birth, and Tom had his way to make at Court. They were enjoined to their respect by their circumstances. Jud, at present, had no circumstances. He was a younger son, with no particular prospects in view. He didn't know what he would do or be, but he knew, when he looked at Tom's tense and preoccupied face, that he didn't want to be a courtier. This perception gave him a sudden feeling of lightness and liberty. He smiled at his father from this excess of cheerfulness and Lucy let out the breath she had been holding on his account. The boy had a peculiarly engaging smile which portraits suggested he had inherited from their grandfather, Thomas the Pirate. It had a hint of cutlass and earrings about it, particularly attractive to the female of the species.

Its only effect on his father was to deepen his scowl.

'You're too hard on the boy, Sir George,' drawled Will Staunton, drawing the paternal fire. 'The King does well to fear the disquiet of citizens, who in their turn, are fearful lest *he* release the might of Strafford's Irish forces upon them and afterwards perhaps dissolve Parliament – as he has done before – and rule without it – as he has done before. Since he has not disbanded the army the people fear violence, therefore they fend it off by a violent show – like any animal that feels itself threatened.'

'You are apt in your estimation of them,' growled Sir George, shifting so that the fire could comfort a numb buttock. 'That mob is John Pym's mad dog – and Strafford was the bone he threw to stop it turning on its master. He knew the King could not choose but make the sacrifice. The man's a menace, a manipulator, an Iago!' His voice had risen to his House of Commons bellow. He had all of old Will Shakespeare's plays in print, and much of them by heart. This did not count as scholarship but gave him considerable satisfaction. If *he* was ever without an answer, old Will was not. His bright blue eye glinted now with something resembling love of the chase. He knew that John Pym, the subtle and relentless politician who was emerging as a leader of the

22

Commons, was a particular friend of Staunton's. Pym was the secretary of their New Providence Company, that select band of merchant adventurers founded by the great Earl of Warwick, Puritan and Privateer, whose kin young Will had the good fortune to be. In the directors of this Company, men of great influence, largely Puritan, this present Parliament had found the nucleus of the organization that had, for the first time in history, disputed the franchise and successfully laid open the vote beyond great landlords and local oligarchies. Not *far* beyond, it was true, but progress had been made – so much so that even Sir George had found himself challenged quite closely by the most reprehensible Puritan in his own Hundred. Remembering this, he wondered why he found Will Staunton such good company, particularly as the elegant merchant seemed to be laughing at him.

'Poor sober John. He'd be cut to the quick if he could hear you . . . He does not deserve such reviling, truly. His aim is not to discomfort the King but to keep his Parliament safe in their seats. You will have to admit that His Majesty has put on a pretty show of force these last weeks – what with that abortive attempt to fortify the Tower and rescue Strafford, and then all the rumours of Roman Catholic plots, and of the army's plotting to seize London and rule by martial law – all very uncomfortable. The army *is* very restless – you can't walk an inch without running up against one of Strafford's bully-boys looking for trouble.'

'Looking for a square meal, more likely,' said Tom shortly, 'The troops haven't been paid for longer than they can remember. It goes hard with some of them. At Court we get 100 petitions a day from officers whose credit has run out. It's a disgrace that gentlemen should have to be embarrassed in such a way.'

'Well then, if you were John Pym, what would you do?' persisted Will quietly. 'He simply could not afford to let His Majesty follow his inclinations and fall into armed strife. The citizens of London would not take kindly to the sight of your embarrassed gentlemen's steel – there'd be blood shed, and plenty of it, blue, bad and indifferent! And the King blaming Pym for failing to keep the peace, and doing God knows what with Strafford's army. Pym can't allow it and the people won't have it – they know they have his ear – but they're no mad dogs, just averagely determined to keep what they have, a voice to speak for them – your own voice, Sir George, in your own Hundred.'

The Baron looked surprised at this peaceable red herring. 'The people? What have they to do with it?' He queried vaguely, knitting his brows over an imagined picture of his own enraged peasants, disporting themselves over his land in the manner of the Assyrians at Sennacherib, screeching themselves hoarse over his new enclosures. It had already happened in certain areas and these contentious London Puritans were of the same nasty breed and required the same treatment – a shot or two up their backsides and a good stiff sentence at the next assizes. Sir George was also a JP for his Hundred.

Will thought better of a reply, continuing instead, 'I agree that Tom Strafford has been sacrificed, but on the altar of the continued existence of the Parliament, not on that of the rage of the mob. Call them Pym's dogs if you will, but they are not so mad that he cannot control them. John has used them to win above the King in this matter; *they* have not used John, though some of them may think so.'

'It's plain you share Pym's cast of thought. I wonder you don't join us in the Commons. Your tongue's as tricksy as a leveret.' Sir George was only half-complimentary.

Will smiled and stretched, tired of the conversation. 'Not I. There isn't a politicking bone in my body. I like my life easier. The House gives John Pym the belly-ache and he's the chief master of its arts. God knows what it'd do to me! I much prefer,' he purred, turning towards Mary Heron with the admiring and modest appreciation of the studied courtier, 'by bringing them rich and strange goods from the further reaches of the Orient, to satisfy the desires of beautiful women.' If he could have reached it, she felt he would have kissed her hand. She would have enjoyed it. He was a very handsome young man, tall and strong with a rich animal presence, as Sir George had been in youth; and more than that, when Will spoke of the desires of women, he did not bring silks and spices to her mind. Not at all. As he flashed fine teeth at her from a sunburned face, she felt an odd half-forgotten fluttering, much much lower than her heart.

Surprised at herself, she sought cover for confusion. 'Lucy! Stop eating those comfits or you'll be sick,' she ordered, a trifle breathlessly.

'I've only had three!' Lucy's love of sweets was legendary.

'Quite sufficient. When you eat too many it always makes you irritable. Hand the box around again.' Her eyes sparkled at Will as she bit into one, her lips curving about it as though it were a lover's mouth.

Tom, who had been brooding, cut across this irrelevance. 'For all your glorification of John Pym as the people's wet-nurse, I do not think it was the violence that decided His Majesty at last, but the logic used against him. You'll have heard of the bishops' defection?'

'I know the bishops refused to vote on the Bill of Attainder – they have their own skins to save. I suppose the less they are seen to meddle in lay matters, the more chance they have of holding on to their seats in the Lords?'

'I was thinking of Bishop Williams. The King called him in, with Archbishop Ussher, to advise him after the Lords had let him down, whether there was any way he might yet save Strafford. Ussher said he shouldn't go against his conscience; but Williams was a smooth philosopher in Parliament's cause, discoursing gravely on the dual nature of kingship – how Charles Stewart the *man* may do one thing but Charles Stewart the King, God's anointed, shepherd of his people, must do another. He must not take on his royal conscience the responsibility for the bloodshed which threatened if Strafford did not die. It almost unmanned the King to hear it. He wept, I tell you. But it was the logic that did it – the appeal to his conscience was all he has ever considered, mob or no mob – and once it was proved to him that he had mistaken the conscience of a King for that of a mere man, they had him at their mercy. He wept, and cried that Strafford was in a better case than he, who thus betrayed him.'

'But he signed,' said Jud contemptuously, impatient of Tom's emotions. 'And Strafford is dead and the House may proceed to its next business.' He was restless. He had disliked Strafford, who had been too rich, too powerful and too blunt an instrument in the King's hands, but he had disliked even more the manner of his taking off.

Tom swore.

'Your pardon, sirs, but won't the King dissolve this Parliament?' piped up young Robin suddenly. He had listened carefully and thought he had followed their argument.

'He can't,' said his master, with a sympathetic nod towards Tom. 'While Charles was consulting his conscience, Pym rushed through a Bill by which Parliament can only be dissolved by its own consent. Neat. It was presented to His Majesty at the same time as the Act of Attainder. I don't know why he signed it. I suppose he thought he could have it rescinded later.'

'He signed it because he was so distressed that he didn't know what he was doing,' Tom said bitterly.

'None the less,' was the thoughtful reply, 'now your father is a Member for life. How will you like that, Sir George?'

The Baronet grunted. He suddenly felt very depressed. 'His

Majesty must have Parliament, God knows. But there would have been a time for such a bill when he was less driven and distressed. I don't like Pym's underhand ways and never will. A cold fish. No heart to the man. Why at this very moment he is back in the House, reinstating old Coke's book of Laws. Can't wait a day to be at his machinations again.'

'I suppose that is better than if he were dancing in the streets, as most people will be tonight,' suggested Jud.

'Dancing?' Lucy's cry betrayed unseemly interest. Her mother's face reproved her.

'Better? Who knows?' Sir George ignored his daughter. 'I remember when the King forbade old Coke to publish. Thought he'd have an apoplexy – but Old James wouldn't stand for all that shouting about Magna Carta under the "common law" – and Charles won't stand for it either.'

'But now he may have to?' enquired Robin, brightly. 'No more Rex is lex then!' He tried not to sound pleased, out of consideration for the company. Where he came from, the King was a tyrant.

'So you've long ears as well as long fingers, eh boy? Mind you don't find them pruned like lawyer Prynne's.' His host was unimpressed by Shoreditch Latin.

'My ears will be my good servants, sir, seemingly, if only I can learn to master my tongue.' Rob tried to make amends.

'It's ready enough to answer for itself, by jove! Where did you get the lad Will? He's sharp enough to cut himself.'

'They breed them like that in the stews – they need to be sharp to survive. I expect to make a half-decent factor out of him one day, if he can keep out of Newgate.' He looked doubtfully at Robin. 'I'm teaching him to read and he already has an instinct for numbers – especially if it's coins he's counting.' The dig did not offend the boy who nodded and grinned at him.

'I look to be in business for myself one day, if God wills,' he told them with all the pride and determination of his knowledge of his own world and his ignorance of theirs.

Sir George's grunt could have been approval. It became a testy cough when his eyes fell on Jud, whom he saw much in the same light as this precocious urchin. If Rob Whittaker made free with other people's money, that was the way of the world, but young George was making free, too damn free, by God, with his father's! There had been painful scenes between them every time the lad had come home, as he occasionally did, for a square meal and to borrow from his mother, or Tom if he could. Sir George had never been known for his patience and it was more than time that the insolent wings were clipped.

'Tell ye what, Will,' he said abruptly, slapping his thigh in the manner of one who's conceived a capital idea, 'I'll give you an apprentice who can read and figure and knows something of the laws of trade into the bargain, not to mention his excellent pedigree, blue blood, no diseases – and his vices only half-formed – you can catch him before they turn criminal. You have my leave to use whatever methods you choose.' He waved a lavish arm towards his son.

Mary Heron, noting Will's flicker of amusement, and herself well-accustomed to hear her children described in terms of the stable, wondered if he realized that this was a serious offer. For herself, she hoped it would be accepted, as only last week something had been said about putting Jud into the Church, which she felt would do no favour to boy or Institution. She had also noticed what Sir George had not, the look of interest that had replaced the sulks on Jud's face. It might be the very thing for him.

'Jud has been tiresome these last months,' she said quietly, smiling at Will, 'so my husband has forgotten his good points – but I assure you he has them. Can you do with another apprentice, Master Will?'

'I can do with a dozen – provided they are all intelligent, painstaking, pleasing in dress and manner and honest in their dealings with their master and his customers.'

Lucy squeezed Robin's hand. *That* was for him.

'Would you take Jud on the *Gallant Lady* if he worked for you, Master Staunton?' she enquired.

'Indeed I would, and you too, if you've a mind,' said Will kindly. She was a funny little maid, with her thistledown hair and her huge green eyes watching like those of some candid animal – not a kitten, there was nothing domestic about her. She made him want to laugh for no reason at all – and then, as he looked closer, and saw the passionate commitment to her brother, remembered her instant championship of Robin, he sensed that there was something in her that might start tears as much as laughter. One day, when she was a woman, she'd be worth a great deal of trouble to some man.

Meanwhile here was her mother, as handsome a woman as ever he'd seen, looking at him with the same big eyes, hers very blue and unexpectedly innocent. He would please her in this, if the boy was willing – and then, perhaps later, when they were all

27

better acquainted, she would want to please him. The thought was mischievous, but as instinctive in him as a desire to eat or to sleep. He loved women, that was all. They knew it and usually reciprocated in kind. He turned to Jud, who had already seen his opportunity. To get away from the dingy Inn and its dusty books, to be in the company of fine men like the merchant and amusing youngsters like Robin, it was like a reprieve to a life-prisoner. He swung his legs off the window ledge and stood respectfully before Will, his smile studiously grave and intent. 'You mean it, sir? You'd try me out? I'd never thought to be a merchant but – '

'You'd never thought to be anything but your father's pensioner!' came a growl from Sir George. 'Give him little money, Will, and I'll give him less. It trickles through his fingers like shit through a sheep's tail. A merchant! You'll be lucky if Will will let you fetch and carry in the warehouse. Well, so be it, so you be off my hands – your brother was a soldier at your age and came home an officer.' Tom sighed briefly and looked out of the window.

'You wouldn't let *me* go! You said I was too young,' Jud protested.

'So you were. And now you're older you've even less sense.'

Tom's war had been in Holland with Prince Rupert, the King's nephew, in the cause of the Protestant Dutch against the armies of Spain. He had also distinguished himself at Oxford and at his Inn and had visited those parts of Europe that were not torn entirely into rags by war. Tom was a paragon. Jud knew better than to pursue the cause of justice further.

'I'll be glad to serve you, sir, if you'll have me,' he said simply to Staunton. This was a man he could admire. There was something of the sea about him even in his court attire, a challenging, farsighted look to him, such as Drake might have had, or Raleigh, or any of the old sea-dogs who had been his early heroes.

The merchant stood to shake his hand. 'That's settled then, Jud. You'll come to me at the Merchant Adventurer's Wharf tomorrow. Anyone will tell you where to find me. I'll have your indentures already prepared. And if you care to bring Miss Lucy, I'll show you both my ship.'

'Lucy must stay at home tomorrow, sir,' said Mary Heron firmly. 'She has not behaved well today and must be punished.'

Strangely, Lucy did not mind. She was happy for Jud and happy for Robin, for they would, she foresaw, become friends. She would escape her beating and it was not so bad to stay at home in the little house at Chelsea. She had her books and her virginals and the garden. Besides, she thought she had probably had enough of Will Staunton's rarefied company. Who was he to walk into their lives like some tiresome Duke at the end of one of Shakespeare's plays her father was so fond of, distributing smiles and largesse in all directions? 'Too big for his boots' was what Margery Kitchen, at home at Heron, would have called him. Lucy muttered the phrase to herself with some pleasure as the splendid merchant took his leave. Oh but the boots were a marvel, though! Could that be real gold, or was it just paint?

Heron, Summer 1641

The execution over and her duty done, Mary Heron began to pine for home, as she always did in London. The Chelsea house, though pleasant and pretty enough in its way, was a doll's house to a woman who had the running of a manor such as Heronscourt. She had nothing to do at Chelsea and she did not enjoy either idleness or the pleasures of the city. She missed her busy, full life and above all she missed her gardens, fretting for her seedlings and cuttings and wondering if her instructions had been well carried out in her absence. Gardening was her private obsession. So it was that after delivering a hopeful Jud to Master Staunton's imposing Strand mansion, and regretfully leaving Sir George to the problems of Westminster and Tom to those of St James's, Lucy and her mother set off in the best family coach behind its four matched chestnuts, bidding John Coachman get them home as soon as he could. He set a spanking pace almost all the way to Oxford, where they rested shaken bones overnight at the college of Christ Church where Jane lived with her James.

The visit, though brief, was very enjoyable, perhaps the more so as Lady Mary neglected to pass on her husband's parting quips upon James's progenitive abilities. Jane was an excellent cook, indeed this was her eccentricity, just as her mother's was gardening. No lady should do either of these things for herself; but both did as they pleased, and were pleased by the results.

They spoke mostly of these pleasures, while the gentle scholar James retired, smiling, into his books, and Lucy, finding no entertainment in such ordinary domesticity, slept like a dog on the settle, never waking when she was carried to bed.

Coming home to Heronscourt was always a special pleasure to Lucy, greater even than going away. Of course, it was a different kind of pleasure. Going away was a time of adventure and excitement and looking forward to new things, while coming home was a softer, more certain feeling, with odd tears at the back of your throat, and then a tremendous, ridiculous sense of relief to find that it was all still there.

The feeling began when you rattled across the border from Oxfordshire into Gloucestershire. Then you were in your own country and all its soft hills, and harsher moors, and fields and forests in five hundred shades of green silvered by hidden streams were somehow a credit to you as well as to themselves.

An impatient ten miles further and you were among Sir George's own acres, 4,000 of them, and the best pasture for sheep and cattle anywhere in England. Lucy had sometimes thought that they ought to have a sheep as the family device rather than a heron, for it was the sheep who were the foundation of their fortunes, while the local siege of herons merely looked decorative and even escaped from providing the occasional Sunday roast because their namesakes had become sentimental about them and it was forbidden to fly a hawk at them. However, the rights of history were with the herons, for they had given their name to the house that sat at the heart of the broad demesne 200 years ago when it was first built as a Cistercian priory. Cistercians are known for their excellence with sheep. The monks called it Heronsiege, or Heronsedge, after the birds' untidy nest of sticks and rushes, but when that bold ambitious soldier, Sir Humphrey Heron, had had gratified his royal master Henry VIII by his enthusiastic liberating of the monasteries, it had amused the jocular monarch to bestow upon him the priory that carried his name. Sir Humphrey, having thus come up in the world, decided that Heronscourt had a nobler ring to it and so it had remained, though its present inhabitants generally called it simply, Heron.

The journey through the demesne to the house was a little short of five miles. You entered it just south of the village of Northleach near where the carriage road from Oxford to Gloucester crossed the rougher track from Stow to Cirencester. You were up on the hill then, on one of the southern spurs of the Cotswolds where the creamy-white sheep ambled, heavy with fleece now, along their accustomed daily paths. Next month they would be shorn. Lucy enjoyed watching that. Now they rolled down the moorland into the valley whose other end held the house, through eerie Hangman's Wood where her brother Humpty said he'd seen the ghostly Green Lady, past the ancient wreathed shrine of the Virgin where the footpaths met, and the spring at the end of the wood that never dried up, and then out at last into a long tract of ripe farmland, the lush fields where the brown herds were at pasture, and the full grainfields where the women were weeding the autumn-sown corn.

The women worked in the old way, using two sticks, the righthand one hooked for dragging out the weed from the corn and the lefthand tined for pinning down the head of the weed while they swung the hook strongly behind them, pulling out the roots and dropping the plant in line. There were two rows of women, mostly labourers' wives and daughters, their skirts brought up between their knees and tucked into their girdles for ease, moving as rhythmically along the furrows as though they followed the steps of a long-learned dance. It was harder than it looked, Lucy knew. She had tried it for herself last year and had made a fool of herself until she had got the hang of it. Even then, she had not been able to keep up for long.

'There'll be plenty of weeding out for you and your brothers to do, never fear,' her mother said, seeing her admiring gaze.

'Oh, burrs and chickweed and bedstraw! It's not the same.'

'It has to be done.'

Lucy grinned. Everyone at Heronscourt was well aware of that. Weeding was regarded on the estate as Lady Mary's private madness. No one could understand it, since it patently did not work and the same insolent weeds appeared each year.

They were coming into Heron village now. This had grown from a few homesteads huddled in the protection of the priory to a well-established centre with two main streets, both cobbled as befitted the dignity of the wool trade. One being set some twenty feet above the other, they were known with laconic simplicity as Highgate and Lowgate. Highgate accommodated the richer businesses, the inn, the bakery, the saddler, the house-carpenter, while Lowgate housed the more humdrum tradesmen, the smiths, the wheelright, the cobbler and the fine new dairy. At the top of the town stood St Michael's Church with its tall belfry and its tidy rows of tombs and at the bottom of the double slope, near the river and the millhouse, was the village green. This sported three ancient and untidy oaks, the communal pump, the pillory (unoccupied) and three public benches, occupied to overflowing by the village elders, gossiping, dozing and trying to remember to keep an eye on their grandchildren who rolled and rollicked on the grass. These stopped what they were doing to run after the coach in a body, calling greetings and squealing when they got too close to the wheels. Lucy leaned out to wave to them but was hauled back by her skirts and slapped for being a hoyden. This was a word of which she heard a good deal.

At this moment, however, she didn't care if she heard it every day for a month. She was home and she was happy. She tried hard not to bounce with unladylike joy as they racketed up Highgate and took the turn to the right past St Michael's that led to the walled and wooded grounds of Heronscourt itself.

One of the nicest things about the house was that it took the traveller by surprise. The carriageway, after winding through the thick woodland and shrubbery that protected the southern side of the estate, came out into fine parkland, ascending slightly, with copses of trees at a distance on either side and only the smooth patchwork of the hills to be seen above the horizon. Then the horses, scenting the stables, would make an excited dash to the top of the slope and there you would see it in the dip, a firm confrontation of solid stone, as sudden and arresting as a highwayman.

Yet Heronscourt was not one of those houses that stand grandly against their setting, making a spectacle of themselves and demanding attention. Its stones were quarried from the same rock upon which it stood and they were as comfortable in the landscape now as they had been before they were hewn. They showed the same mellow tones from amber to grey as did the hills beyond.

The house was roughly L-shaped. The short stem, heading north from the east wing, was a single-storey cloistered series of rooms that had once been monks' cells, with a graceful chapel at the north end of the row. The long stem, the main part of the building, was in two storeys and consisted of four generations' improvement upon the original Plantagenet pattern of hall, great chamber, parlour and domestic offices. Soldier Humphrey had done little to add to its comfort, being well enough pleased to trust to the taste of the Prior. Sir George's grandfather, Thomas the Pirate, however, had some notions about ease and the exclusion of draughts. He had divided the lofty hall horizontally, thus giving more warmth beneath and creating the fashionable long gallery, as well as a couple of good-sized bedchambers, above. If it was not as cosy as his galleon, it was considerably more ship-shape than before. His son, a rectitudinous wool-baron who disliked the very smell of the sea, took up the new trend for getting away from one's inferiors, especially at meal-times. Having converted the pantry and buttery into a small family dining room and built new ones, he then built an additional suite of family rooms onto the west wing. There was a parlour, smaller and warmer than the great parlour next to the hall where guests were received. Above this were bedrooms and next to it, that distinguishing mark of the civilized New Man, a library. It had always nettled his father and somewhat tickled Sir George that many of the books were part of Pirate Thomas's booty – and since most of them were in English it was wiser not to consider how he may have come by them.

Sir George, finding no excuse for further extensions, confined himself to refurbishment, with his wife's heartfelt blessing. His first exercise was to renew all the floorboards. Then came a passion for panelling, in the interest of insulation as well as beauty. For months the house reverberated to the bang and tap of carpenters and one went everywhere knee-deep in sawdust. Then a multitude of carpets and hangings were brought to cover the boards and the panelling and flaunt their rich stained-glass colours in every scrap of sunlight. There was new furniture; tables whose sheen seemed to come from deep within the wood, chairs whose upholstered velvet kindness was especially welcome after their disciplinary predecessors. There were even new soft win-dowseats in the oriels, covering the cold stone. There was very little trace left of monkish deprivation, even in the servants' quarters, for they too benefited from the changes when the old leather carpets, the unwanted stools and bench-seats and the old but soft mattresses came their way.

As far as Mary Heron was concerned this was all just as it should be, nothing less than was expected of a man as prosperous as the Baronet or was due to her as a member of an ancient and well-respected family, the Laceys. The house was very well now, and she was pleased with it, but her life's great interest, when her family had been served, would always be the gardens and grounds. Indeed, she would worry more deeply about an ailing seedling than a sick child. The child, once it had got through the first few taxing years, was wont to recover from all ailments, whereas the seedling's system was far more delicate. Now, therefore, her ladyship was hanging out of the coach in the very manner for which she had reproved her daughter, tutting and clucking over the long herbaceous borders beside the driveway, spying unwanted weeds and diseases where Lucy could only see the first stirrings of what would soon be a tumult of colour. Irises, phlox, foxgloves and delphiniums stood guard behind evening primroses, verbena, scarlet flax and huge flat daisies that opened to the sun.

'I wonder if Jack has remembered to cut back that deadwood in the rose arcade. It's late, I know, but it's the only thing to do –'

'You'll see tomorrow, or this evening if you must,' comforted Lucy. 'Only you must not try to see 300 acres at one glance from the coach. It simply cannot be done.'

Mary Heron smiled and ruefully accepted the good sense of this. 'I don't know about that, but oh, I am so glad to be home!' she sighed happily. Then, frowning, 'If only I could have persuaded Mr Tradescant to visit us.' John Tradescant was the King's own gardener, and Lady Mary had spent one of her days in London harrying him round Lambeth Palace with merciless question after question.

'Well, you have your notebook. That will doubtless keep us all busy for a while. Apart from that,' Lucy sniffed, preparing to leap out as they circled before the front door, 'I can't see why we had to go to London at all.'

Luckily for Lady Heron's passion and for her children's tempers, the summer promised to be a good one. Everyone spent as much time as possible out-of-doors. The children even obliged with the weeding, as long as the sheep-shearing, the haymaking, or flax-gathering did not hold them, or a hundred other occupations.

At the end of June a letter came promising them a visitor. Lady Valora Grey was an heiress of twenty and Tom wanted to marry her. As Tom was in the King's good graces and Valora was a Ward of Court, this might have seemed a simple matter to arrange. But there were problems. The largest of these was the stout person of Sir Horatio Bulmer, an elderly courtier to whom the King had given the guardianship of Valora and of her valuable manor of Spindlesham in Surrey, in the expectation that they would one day marry. Sir Horatio, like Valora herself, was a Roman Catholic. The faith was despised by the majority and was, indeed, illegal, but the Queen, too, was a Catholic and the illegality was largely ignored by everyone except the most exigent Puritans, of whom there were none at Court, though there were many elsewhere.

Valora enjoyed a position as one of the Queen's ladies-in-waiting. That is, she *had* enjoyed it until she had met Tom Heron.

Now, both were in a fever of passion and indecision, for though Tom, mortally in love, was prepared to overlook his beloved's Catholicism, Valora herself could not. She did not wish to see her children brought up as members of the heretical Church of England, while naturally neither Sir George nor Tom himself could envisage Heron as a recusant seat.

However, Tom was a positive young man and always tried to work towards an objective rather than stand still and contemplate its insuperability. He treated Valora as though she were expected to be the next chatelaine of Heronscourt and hoped that she herself might fall into the way of it through custom. The coming visit was his next strategic move. Tom loved his home and could not conceive of Valora doing otherwise. He confidently expected that her stay would undermine her doubts.

When the bell sounded for morning prayers at seven o'clock on the day that Lady Grey was due to arrive, Lucy had already dressed and dispatched her younger sister, Julia, downstairs. She had curled back onto their bed in a patch of sunlight and was deep in her beloved book world of giants and dragons with the intrepid 'Sir Bevis of Southampton'. She had dressed but had left off her corset which she detested. It was not a very tight one. Mary Heron had forbidden both Jane and Lucy to wear the terrible old-fashioned iron bodices when Tom had reported from Court the case of a girl whose ribs had *grown into her liver* from tight-lacing! Lucy's was made of soft leather, boned and laced; nevertheless she left it off whenever the occasion did not demand it. Today *was* something of an occasion. Would it, she deliberated, make much difference to the lady if she were not to wear it? She would be used, after all, to the fashion and manners of the most civilized court in Europe. She pondered, scuffing a stockinged toe on the rush matting. Then the prayer bell stopped and she grabbed her slippers and raced for the hall.

The last of the servants were scuttling into the long, tapestried room as she slipped to her knees between Humpty and Julia, behind the bench at the top table. She hoped her mother would not notice her lateness. Mary's prayers were shorter than the absent Sir George's but her discipline was far more determined. Lucy proclaimed the responses with extra vigour in atonement.

Eyes tight shut, the smell of new-baked bread a worldly temptation, she felt a sharp kick on her left ankle. 'We're going fishing; you coming?' Humpty was feeling friendly.

Eyes, startled open, caught the disapproving gaze of Master Davies, the tutor, so she did not reply until she saw his long head bent once more. 'Can't. Something else to do,' she muttered quickly, adding a loud and fervent 'Amen' to the prayers for the King and Queen. The exchange had been noticed however, and as always, Lady Mary's punishment came immediately and without anger.

After they had breakfasted the two long rows of servants, dismissed with their tasks for the day, departed towards kitchen, brewery, bakery, laundry, farmyard and forge and the children followed, all but Humpty and Lucy whom their mother restrained with a single severe glance.

'No, Kit. You may go,' she told the other twin who was hanging back, it being unheard of for the two to be separated for a second. Kit vanished, to flatten himself next to the doorway and wait.

'Lucy. Humphrey. I will not have you offer such a bad example to Julia and to the servants, nor such discredit to your mother and upon your own characters. Your hands, if you please.'

Lady Mary did not enjoy the physical punishment of her children but knew it to be for their general good. She detached the short, pear-shaped ferula from her belt where it reposed between the keys and the small hornbook of family prayers that had belonged to her grandmother. She struck quickly and effectively upon both extended forearms. The blisters would rise almost at once. She would not use the instrument upon the lips or even the hands as most people did, feeling that the pain was sufficient without causing difficulty in eating or moving the fingers. She sighed as the two made their apologies and Humpty shook his wrist so that it would hurt less. Lucy merely hid the hand behind her back and the pain behind a smile.

'What time will Lady Valora arrive, madam?' she asked.

'How can I know, since I don't know when she starts or how fast her pace? Be patient, Lucy. I expect she will be here in time to dine with us.'

No mention was made of corsets. Relieved, Lucy made her curtsy and her escape, Humpty hard on her heels. Her mother left the room by the other door towards the kitchen. She would spend her morning encouraging the servants very energetically to sweep, dust and polish the house until it shone.

It was all quite unnecessary. It was already as clean as it needed to be, and besides, the mere sight and scale of Heronscourt was so impressive that there was every reason why Lady Valora, whose own manor of Spindlesham, though graceful, was of modest proportions, should be not only impressed but overwhelmed by the prospect of succeeding to such splendour.

Nevertheless, the preening would continue until each of Heron's feathers had reached its full lustre.

The tutor being occupied that morning with Julia, who at six was a poor scholar, slow to read and figure, there were no lessons for Lucy or the twins.

'Why won't you come fishing? You always want to come and then, when we say you can, you won't, just like any silly girl. We're taking Maggots, to see if he will catch us worms and things.' This was the half-grown magpie the twins were trying to tame. Even the possible fascinations of watching the bird at work did not persuade Lucy, who had far more delicate business on hand. She became quite irritable when Kit joined his brother's call. 'Come on Lucy – you'll be keen enough to eat what we catch.'

'Be *told*, won't you. I'm not coming.' She frowned. 'But you mustn't *say* I didn't come, if you don't mind. We needn't tell lies, but we could just sort of, *look* as if we'd been together. Just in case. Where will you be? I'll find you later.'

'Where are you going?' Kit scented intrigue.

'None of your business.'

'It is, by Jove, if we're to cover up for you.' There was no suggestion that they might not be willing to cover up. The twins had generous natures.

'I'll tell you later. It's something I want to do by myself.'

Humpty scowled. 'If you don't want to satisfy curiosity you shouldn't arouse it.' He hoped adult pomposity would do the trick but soon saw it was no good. 'Oh well, probably some stupid *girl's* rubbish. Come on, Kit.'

Lucy waited until they would have become bored with hanging about if they planned to follow her, filling her time by picking flowers from one of the borders on the south side of the house. Thinking of their recipient, she made up her bouquet of lavender, scabious and cornflowers. It was not eyes she was matching but a certain misty quality. Then she wiped her green fingers on her tawny dress and ran them through her hair. Her preparations complete, she left the garden and made her way briskly down through the grounds to the village. She did not pass through the main gates which were imposing as far as their rose brick construction went, but rendered less so by the pair of herons which surmounted them. These were rather ridiculous and therefore lovable, but not quite dignified. Sir George often threatened to replace them with lions but never did. Lucy went instead by a backway which she knew and emerged from the bushes some way down the road to the village.

She was going to visit a witch.

Martha Knyvett's cottage stood back from the road on the outskirts of the village, near enough to it to be included and protected by it, but not near enough to feel it breathing down its neck. Lucy let herself in at the wooden gate whose purpose was to keep out sheep and cattle and walked approvingly through humming borders of Damascus roses, flat petals sunbathing bravely. At Heron some of the flowers shrieked rather; these only sang quietly to themselves and made one feel peaceful. There were rosemary bushes and a rowan tree near the door. As these were popularly supposed to prevent the Devil's entry, Lucy thought they might be inconveniently place for witch's work. But perhaps Martha only met the Devil on blasted heaths – or not at all. She did not seem as if she might enjoy his company.

Lucy knocked firmly three times. The door was opened by a young woman of strange and absolute beauty. There was no one else who looked like her. It was a matter of colouring and fragility. Like Lucy she was blonde, but the difference between them was that of sun and moon. Where Lucy shone with robust gold of wheatfields at noon, Martha's illumination was all within, her glow that of primroses by moonlight. Her hair was long and pale and heavy, her face small and piquant, her eyes foreign and aslant, her mouth wide and generous, her skin translucent. Lucy had met her before but still found the unexpectedness of her unnerving. Witches are more comfortably envisaged as old, ugly and ill-natured, their houses dark and foul-smelling, hopping with toads and scuttling with spiders, and properly entered only with one's clothes turned inside-out.

Martha, serenely unaware of her professional shortcomings, looked pleased to see her visitor. 'Lucy, how are you? Won't you come in?' She held the door wide but Lucy thrust the offering of flowers towards her before entering.

'You have plenty, I know, but it's all I could think of.'

'I couldn't have too many, and these are especially lovely.' Martha did not say that she thought it a sin to cut flowers and take them from their most necessary element. Her small room was decorated only with double-daisies growing in pots on the window ledges and an earthenware jug of honesty on the dresser, an echo of herself with its pearly, insubstantial gleam.

'Sit down and I'll fetch us some milk and honey. And I've new-baked lardy cake. How are they all at Heron?'

Lucy, at home in the bare comfortable room, chose the settle rather than the stool and sat, feeling greedy and apprehensive until Martha returned with the feast. While she ate and the witch sipped milk to keep her company, they discussed the health of Sir George and his lady and each of their children, then the unusual pleasantness of this summer and the particular industry of Martha's bees. Then Lucy wiped her mouth on her hand and plunged into the real business of the day.

'I need a spell – only it must work first time and it mustn't *show* at all.'

Martha waited and looked interested.

'It's for Tom.'

'Indeed? You said he was well.' A wisp of worry was in the ascent of her voice.

'Yes, but he's in love.' According to books this was a similar condition to that of sickness.

The quality of Martha's attention changed indefinably.

'There is this lady, Valora Grey. She's coming to visit us today. Tom wants to marry her; she is very suitable.'

'I see.'

'Except she is a Catholic and isn't sure she wants to marry Tom.'

'Ah.'

'So I thought, if you could give me something to put in her wine – to make her love Tom or love Heron so much that she can't bear to leave it . . .'

'That would certainly seem to make matters tidy.' Martha smiled, very small. 'You say your brother loves the lady – ?'

'He was ill-tempered all over Christmas and Easter and madam my mother says that is why.'

The witch's pale hair quivered a little. 'Then we had better do something about it as you suggest. I will make up something for you – a charm I think, not at this stage a potion. I will write down what you must do with it.' Martha, apart from her other talents, was valued in the village for her ability to read and write.

'Thank you. I'm most grateful. Only I hope it will not cost more than half a sovereign, for that is all I have.'

It was the one redeemed by Robin Whittaker.

'I don't care to take money for this, Lucy,' said Martha gravely. 'You've already given me these flowers.'

Lucy flushed. 'That isn't the same. They were a present.' Now

39

she felt she should not have offered money but was still weighted with an obligation. 'I'll think of something,' she grinned. 'Do I take the charm now?'

'No. It takes time. Will you come back for it later, perhaps after noon?'

This was agreed, though Lucy would have to evade Master Davies and the wars of Julius Caesar. Their interview was ended and, satisfied with its business-like formality, Mistress Heron took her leave.

Martha stared after the small departed figure, seeing a certain family likeness in the confident gait, the proud set of the shoulders. She shook her head and went off to pick the herbs she would need to make Lady Valora Grey fall a victim to Aphrodite and Tom Heron. Privately, she had doubts as to the necessity of any such thing.

The summer crowded her with its scents and sounds as she considered, chose, discarded, chose again. Its sensations were too strong to be ignored. It touched her skin and ruffled her hair with infinitely gently fingers, made her close her eyes for an instant while memory ached and showed her things she did not want to see – pictures of Tom Heron sure enough, but pictures that did not include any Lady Valora Grey.

Just as one of the interminable Roman chariots came hurtling down upon yet another plain littered with hapless Gauls, Lucy, head bowed, stuck her fingers down her throat. She then rushed from the library under Master Davies's surprised brows and was sick in the passage outside.

'Mercy on us, child! You'd better go and sit quietly somewhere,' said the startled tutor, fearing for the Turkey carpet. The twins, left to struggle with *De Bello Gallico*, glared at the door, resentful but prevented by loyalty from voicing their suspicions, even as their sister had been prevented by honesty from a downright lie, preferring actual physical discomfort.

In the deep cool kitchen, she had a drink of water and as she drank she remembered the last time she'd been sick, at the execution of the Earl of Strafford. She thought she might tell Martha about him and how brave had been his last speech. She sensed that Martha would understand, better than any of her own family had done, why she had had to avoid seeing him die. There was a *connection* that her instinct made between them, the dark, dead Earl and the gentle, lively woman. She thought then of Foxe's *Book of Martyrs*, with its horrid retributions. There was a connection there too, but she didn't know what it was. Shivering, she ran out of the kitchen and back into the comforting heat, which hit her in the chest like a wave and dispersed her sad fancies with a single thud. She had to visit Dickon in the stables. He had just the currency with which to repay Martha's professional services. One of Heron's legion of cats had recently given birth to a fine strong litter, one of which was jet black all over, with huge yellow eyes and a long-haired, heraldic tail. Dickon, a gentle giant whose job it was to drown all unwanted animals about the place, had saved and tended this one for Lucy, knowing her passion for cats. She loved it but was willing to give it to Martha on the grounds that every witch should have a cat and this one seemed eminently suitable for such a post.

'Here 'tis, Mistress Lucy. I've swaddled 'un like a babby so he don't scratch.' Dickon proffered a greyish bundle, furious-eyed and struggling. Catching the eye, Lucy decided against setting the creature free. She thanked soft-voiced Dickon and, with the joyless parcel in the crook of her arm, set off back to Martha as fast as she could. She tried to ignore the heart-rendering howls which went with her but nearly bit her lips to pieces in the attempt. 'Be quiet, puss, *please!* You're going to an excellent home. You'll like it, you'll see. Then what will all the fuss have been about?'

Martha's gate was open when Lucy reached it. So was her door, the roses now crowding into it as though curious. There were voices. One was Martha's, the other a man's. Strong, resonant, pitched as though policing a crowd rather than addressing one gentle woman, the soft accents of Gloucestershire had hardened in its custody. It was the kind of voice, Lucy thought, that enjoyed waking people up on a frozen winter's morning when they were deep and warm in sleep. She had recognized it at once. It belonged to the Dismal Puritan.

She hesitated at the step. Should she go in, or not? If she stayed here she must eavesdrop which, though impolite, might also prove interesting. Also, the Dismal Puritan was no friend to Heron or its inmates. Born Nehemiah Owerby, he owned his latest christening to the contempt of Sir George. The two were enemies for a number of reasons, not the least of which was that Owerby had had the temerity to stand against the astonished baronet at the last Parliamentary elections. Even more galling, he had succeeded in gaining a very respectable number of votes. He had also managed to get himself appointed JP for the area, Sir George himself being the other. Their battles at the Quarter Sessions were a favourite local entertainment. Each detested all that the other stood for, whether in matters of church, state or justice. In addition they loathed each other on a purely personal basis, as any man might loathe, did he not love, his opposite. Lucy's hesitation, therefore, was based upon an acquired distaste. And then there was the disgraceful behaviour of the twins . . .

The voice, insistent, interrupted her decision-making.

'It is much marked and therefore much talked about that you do not attend a regular place of worship.'

'My ways of worship are *not* your concern.' A world of patience was in Martha's neutral tone. 'But I do go to St Mary's, since you mention it.'

'You were not seen there last Sunday.'

Now she was irritated. 'I would have thought you'd be occupied in more holy and more useful work on the Sabbath, Master Owerby, than in harking and marking after my whereabouts. I don't care to be watched and I don't care to be admonished by one who has no place over me.'

'You know why I do it, Martha.' Lucy was puzzled by the notes of humility and anger which she recognized but found odd bedfellows, together with another emotion which she didn't know but which she sensed to be responsible for both the others.

'I know why.' Martha's patience sounded stretched and tired. Would it last? 'But I don't know why you keep it up so. You have had my answer – both my answers – why do you not accept them and leave me in peace?'

'Peace! Peace? What is your peace to me? Unless it be the peace of God given to a godly life there is no virtue in it.' Lucy groaned. He was off! But the next words revived her interest.

'You know what I feel for you. If God sends me that grace do you think he intends me to ignore his bounty for the sake of your trivial peace? Come to Him through me and you will know peace such as you could not now believe to exist. We hold a meeting in my house every Sunday. Come. God is making a new world, here in England, Martha. I implore you to let Him make you part of it.'

His harsh voice broke but Lucy sensed a power of certainty and persuasion in him that made her afraid in the sunlight. And yet he spoke only of God and goodness. Tensing, she stood back against the wall. A loud and affronted howl transfixed her there, then another. She had forgotten the cat. She clapped her hand over the small muzzle and was bitten. Further complaint issued but the pain became insignificant as a tall figure loomed in the

doorway. Unsuitably framed in the weaving roses, Nehem.
Owerby, dark-suited, plain-collared and frowning though he wa
did not appear to correspond to Sir George's views of him as
dismal. He was broad and well proportioned for his considerable
height, his complexion ruddy-dark and healthy, and his face with
its fine liquid eyes and fleshy mouth might be supposed to appeal
to women. He was certainly not disposed to appeal in any way to
Lucy however; his eye, as it fell on her, was terrible to behold. It
narrowed, it glinted, it loosed arrows of steel, while a bruising
hand leaped for her arm.

'You! You shaven imp of mischief! What brings you here
poking and prying into others' business?'

'Mind the cat. He bites.'

'If he does, I'll break his neck.' She shuddered. She knew he
meant it. 'Answer me, mistress, if you please.'

'I'm waiting to see Martha. I didn't want to interrupt.' Her
dignity was reduced by the continuing feline struggles as the
animal became successful in loosening its bandages. 'I think I'd
better get him inside,' she said, grateful for the excuse.

'Bless you child, what have you there?' Martha replaced
Owerby in the doorway.

'It's for you – for a present.' Lucy did not wish to mention their
business transaction in front of the enemy.

Martha took the kitten by its nape, supporting it with her free
hand. 'Why thank you. I've been needing a cat.' Ignoring an
exclamation of impatience from beneath Nehemiah's tall black
hat, which he had replaced in reproof to the sunlight, she
motioned Lucy inside and nodded briefly as he turned to face
her. 'It was civil of you to call, Master Owerby. And now I bid
you good day.'

He regarded her dourly. 'Civility, it seems, is not what was
necessary. I shall call again, Mistress Martha.' He inclined his
head in a parody of the unnecessary quality and shouldered off
down the path, knocking petals about him in a helpless shower.

Inside, Martha finished unwrapping her present and gave it
some milk. She liked the company of animals and it was several
months since her last cat had died. She established male sex and
strong limbs and was pleased, though not surprised, when after
turning three circles the creature settled happily in her lap, raised
its huge yellow eyes once to her face, then slitted them and cosied
down to doze.

'He likes you.' Lucy was gratified. 'What will you call him?'

'Sir Topaz. Because of his eyes.'

This was approved. *Sir Topaz* was one of Lucy's favourite books by Chaucer.

'Shall you use him for your magic?'

'I can't imagine any use I could put him to.'

'But won't he be your familiar?'

Martha looked disapproving. 'That is silly talk, Lucy.'

'Oh, I'm sorry. But you *are* glad I brought him?'

'Very glad. He is beautiful. And now you will like to have your charm for Lady Grey.'

'If you please.'

'It is in the drawer of the dresser, if you will get it. Then we need not disturb Sir Topaz.'

It was a very small packet sealed with beeswax.

'The instructions are written on the wrapping.'

'Thank you. And now I must go. I want to be sure to be home before she arrives. I do hope Master Owerby has gone. He looked as though he hadn't finished.'

A fine brow lifted. 'I think he has gone. Why don't you like him? Because of your father?'

'Yes – and then the twins did something dreadful, but –'

'What was that?'

'During the election. You know how the Dismal Puritan thundered about on that great black horse, looking important and telling everyone to vote for him? Well, one night the twins got into his stable and painted the horse yellow. They mixed some saffron dye with the stable whitewash. Nehemiah was so angry we thought he'd burst. But he didn't hit Humpty or Kit or tell father or anything.' Her voice broke. Martha waited.

'He said . . . he said . . . it was not always ourselves who suffered from our misdeeds. And he shot the horse before our eyes.'

'Merciful heaven!' Martha's whisper whitened the golden light.

'I don't think God can love a man as cruel as that, do you – despite how much *he* tells us he does.'

'I don't understand God's love, Lucy. We none of us do – though certainly, as you say, Master Owerby seems to be confident of it . . .' she broke off, her mind still stunned, thinking of the loves he had offered her, not once, not twice, but it seemed a hundred weary times – his own and God's, all in one neat package. She made a small sound of pain and shook her head.

'Don't think of it, Lucy. Put it from your mind if you can. Dwell on your visitor instead. You'll enjoy new company. Come and tell me about it whenever you like.'

It was good advice and Lucy would try to take it but she would hate Nehemiah Owerby for ever and nothing could change that, nor her firm conviction that God hated him too. She walked home with a purposeful speed, half singing, half muttering as she made up one of her fast walking songs.

> N.O. spells NO!
> Dismal Puritans must Go!
> Help us, Lord, thy faith keep free
> Lest Ne-he-mi-ah's ho-ur be!

It was not one of her best but it relieved her feelings.

Valora Grey had more than a touch of bravado about her. Blessed with the stigmata, or cursed with the stigma, of Roman Catholicism – it depended on your viewpoint – she had made an early decision to carry it off with a dash. Protected by letters patent from the King allowing her father (for a large sum) to practise his illegal religion and by the personal favour of the Queen, she enjoyed a double indemnity. At Court, Catholicism was clothed with the glad rags of fashion as well as the garments of righteousness, a bold rosary of gold and garnets swung from her waist in place of a chatelaine. It was the first thing that caught Lucy's eye as she stood with the family at the main door of Heron to welcome the visitor stepping down from her spanking new eye-catcher of a coach. It was much moulded and gilded and hung about with lamps. The coach and coachman were predominantly azure, the horses white and Lady Grey herself was dressed in silver grey, much of it Bruges lace. The heavy cross of the rosary swung at her knees as she descended and Lucy, seeing that Humpty's eyes were also riveted upon it, hoped that he had not yet managed to train his magpie. He had just learned that they were attracted by the glint of jewels.

The children watched their mother, in her best daytime gown, go forward to greet the guest. Mary Heron was a bountiful woman, all her outlines inclined to softness and roundness. As she embraced Lady Grey and kissed her on both cheeks it was as though a cloud enfolded a bright, clear-etched mountain top. Valora was tall and straight and hard, her whipcord body yielding to femininity only so far as the possession of remarkable breasts and heavy ringlets of very black, very shiny hair, which showed her skull, very white, along the parting as she bowed her head to return the greeting. Lucy, so recently come from Martha, was struck by the fact that here was the witch's physical opposite. Going forward in her turn to curtsy, she became aware how much *more* physical this scented presence was. Whereas Martha seemed to have been part of the summer afternoon, like some companionable haze, this Lady Grey, who must be about the same age, seemed to draw it all in towards her, so that it could make her gleam the brighter. She was a little overwhelming.

'And this is my daughter, Lucy,' her mother said affectionately. Lady Grey smiled as if she liked the look of Lucy and printed a kiss with warm lips which surely *must* leave a stain. She nodded in a friendly, rather mannish way to the twins, thrilled Julia by twirling her round thrice in the air, and took baby Edward from Jouncey the foster mother to tickle him under the chin and produce delighted gurgles.

Everyone was smiling as they entered the house.

Later, as they dined in panelled splendour, the talk was all of the Heron menfolk and of the news from Court. This was disturbing; a stunned inactivity had followed the cold realization of what Strafford's death had meant. Many who had not previously done so felt an aghast sympathy for the King they had driven to that extremity. There was a general instinct to seek middle ground before the twenty-year-old dissension of King and Parliament should erupt into further violence. His Majesty himself showed an inclination to befriend those whom he had once avoided. The Queen underwrote her husband's activities by canvassing many Catholic officers of the army. The King should be able to draw upon military strength if necessary, in the event, for instance, of a Puritan demonstration against the Queen or her mother, or even the simple over-exuberance of the London mob. There had been bloodshed in the streets on a number of occasions. Henrietta Maria did not believe in middle ground.

'And now,' continued Lady Grey, biting into her spiced apple and warming to the incessant questions of her hostess, who had not heard from husband or sons for a month, 'There is a new cat snarling among our pigeons. A plot has been discovered by some foolish young bloods to take over the army on behalf of His Majesty, even, can you credit it, to capture the Tower in his name! Mere boys' games if you ask me – but dangerous games. The world grows serious. There was more to it; some talk of taking the main ports. I don't know the ins and outs of it, but Tom will tell you more when he comes. But you see how black it looks for the King, as though he were conniving behind the nation's back . . .' Seeing that Mary Heron at last showed signs of being unable to digest further information she broke off and admired the roses in the bronze bowl at the centre of the table. She was unaware that this was to unleash a ravenous obsession, and soon became a little dazed herself as she was treated to the history and difficulties of the cultivation of each separate species of rose yet known in England.

It was under cover of this familiar discourse that Lucy, having long since mislaid Martha's careful instructions, slipped the contents of a small phial into Valora's wine cup. She was noticed only by Kit who at once relayed the interesting event to Humpty. They waylaid their sister as she prepared, dinner disposed of, to join the ladies in the long gallery and display her skill on the virginals.

'Why are you poisoning her? What has she done? Don't you want her to marry Tom and live here, is that it?'

Lucy, forgetting she no longer had curls, tossed her fluff. 'Don't be ridiculous. And mind your own business.'

The twins consulted each other's faces. 'We aren't sure. Perhaps we ought to tell –'

She knew they never would. They wanted only to drag the secret from her. But she would not give in to blackmail. 'There is nothing to tell. You would only look silly.' She pushed past them and went off to enjoy her own music.

She played Dowland's *Lachrimae* first, in tribute to the mood of the court, then jollied things up with *The Earl of Essex, his Galliard*, one of her favourites. She played well and was glad of it as she need never be afraid to play in public.

Valora Grey was the first to show her appreciation. 'Your brother has told me how well you play – but, brothers' praises being so often partial, I expected anything between pleasantness and purgatory! How delightful to hear something so much better.'

'Thank you.' The remarks were so obviously genuine that Lucy felt no embarrassment. 'Do you sing?' she asked. 'Shall we have a duet?'

Valora pulled down her mouth. 'Not well, I'm afraid, but let us try by all means. Do you like *The Nut-Brown Maid*?'

They did well enough together, Lucy thought. Valora, who when speaking sounded rather husky, as though she had a slight cold, produced an uncertain but pleasant contralto to complement Lucy's higher tones.

'Good Heavens, child – do you know you have the voice of an angel? I suppose you *must* know by now. It is quite lovely. What a surprising family you are.' She gave Lucy a hug because she felt like it. Lucy, feeling a little guilty, suggested another song.

As they sang she glanced several times, apprehensively, at

Valora. Her ladyship appeared perfectly normal and was obviously enjoying herself. How long would the charm take to work? How would its success reveal itself? Would Valora throw herself upon Tom's breast when he arrived and refuse ever to leave Heron? Would she beg him, in tears, to marry her at once, dragging at his ankles and wrapping her hair around his boots? Though Lucy did not hesitate as she trilled her way through their duet, her voice was enlivened by the pictures with which her imagination replaced the music she no longer needed to read.

It was not until much later that night that her curiosity was, in a manner, satisfied.

It had been difficult getting to sleep. She had eaten too much and Julia was restless and full of questions about 'the pretty lady' so that Lucy was forced to threaten violence to quiet her. When sleep *did* come, it brought a series of frightful dreams associated with cheese tart, and Lucy started up twice in a sweat just in time to escape the clutches of witch-prickers who thought she was Martha and were going to drown her and Sir Topaz.

When she sat bolt upright a third time, to the accompaniment of hollow groans, she was certain it was no dream and she was about to answer for her meddling in magic. So she was, but not at the hands of witch-prickers.

The groan was repeated. It, at least, was no dream. It was coming through the wall to the left. A second's expectation of some horrid ghoul bursting through the painted panels was followed by the realization that this was the guest chamber. The groaner therefore must be Lady Grey.

'Oh mercy! Oh St Catherine, please don't let her be dying!' Lucy scrambled out of the bed and made for the next room. There, while her maid slept heavily on the truckle bed, her ladyship moaned and threshed and made a froth of black hair and white sheets, her face pale in the light from a single open shutter.

Lucy's conscience raked at her. 'Please – where does it hurt?' She half-hoped it might be an ankle twisted in a nightmare.

'Who is there? Lucy? It's my stomach, my child. I'm sorry if I woke you. The pain is so strong.' Valora pulled herself up and leaned on the pillows. 'But it is probably only wind and will go away. I must have eaten too quickly, and then the singing . . .' She clutched at her side as another spasm took her, eyes widened and surprised at the pain.

'You must have physic,' Lucy could see. She thought quickly. Should she tell Lady Grey about the charm? What would be the use, if she could not also tell her of the antidote? She knew that witches always *had* an antidote. She would therefore have to visit Martha again, and quickly! This time, however, it could not be done secretly. Authority must come to her aid.

'I'll tell madam my mother. She will know what to do,' she comforted, her heart wrung by the evident awfulness of Valora's suffering and her own wickedness. If she had known! She would never in the world have used the potion. What had Martha been thinking of? Or had she perhaps used too much of the stuff at once? She scrambled down dark passages to her mother's room, dived between the curtains of the great bed and shook her awake without ceremony.

Mary Heron, twenty years the mistress of some thirty souls and as many crises, understood almost before her eyes were open.

'A physician you think? Dr Grace is twenty-five miles away – he'd not be here before noon. I could try my own skill meanwhile. But what can it be? Is anyone else afflicted I wonder?' Wrapped in her padded chambergown, Lady Mary clapped on a lined cap and went to view the damage. She wasted no time in apologies to her guest but put several sharp questions. There appeared to be no culprit in Valora's recent diet unless it was wine and cheese she had taken at an inn on her way to Heron. But this was unlikely. A concoction of rue and cuckoo-pint was hastily produced and the patient took it gratefully. It also contained poppyseed, in the hope that sleep would outwit the pain. Valora looked very ill. Out in the passageway, where by now three house servants hovered with lights, Mary gave her opinion that Dr Grace had better be fetched. Lucy nodded soberly, then asked with a proper deference, 'Might not Martha Knyvett be able to help her? She was very good with Kit's rheum.'

'I'd forgotten Martha. She is no trained physician but the villagers would sooner go to her than to Dr Harvey himself. You may be right Lucy. She can be here and gone in an hour and then Dr Grace can come if she can do no good.'

Dickon in the stable was woken and dispatched on Moonlight, Sir George's fastest pacer, and Lucy offered up silent prayers to St Catherine, St Jude and St Cecilia to the rhythm of beating hooves.

It seemed a very long time until Dickon was back with Martha, hair flying over her fallen hood, clinging to his back. There was no chance for Lucy to speak to her, so she could only follow in the busy wake of her mother as the witch was escorted to their victim. She did think however that Martha looked at her strangely when she caught her eye across the small circle of torch-light about the bed. She wondered miserably whose fault it was. It was, she sensed, more than likely to be her own. Her confidence in Martha was not, she noticed, diminished at all. It had not occurred to her *not* to call Martha out. There was no evil in Martha, witch or not. It *must* then, be her own fault. Things often were. She felt ill herself now from regretting so passionately being the cause of pain. She looked imploringly at Martha from across the bed. Touching the distended abdomen with cool hands and well aware of Lucy's dilemma, Martha asked without lifting her head, 'Has she had anything to drink, do you know, apart from what she has taken here?'

It seemed to Lucy that she lingered on the word 'drink'.

'Only wine she took at an inn,' answered Lady Heron.

'She *could* have taken something,' Lucy said, begging to be understood, 'and not *known* she was doing so – or at least not remember it,' she amended as her mother's concerned look turned impatient at such nonsense.

Martha looked at Lucy and smiled, nodding kindly as though to a younger child. She put her face down to Valora's pillow for a moment, sniffing delicately.

'Is there poison on her breath?' asked Lucy, horrified.

'No. It is only a little tainted as one might expect.' She straightened and spoke reassuringly to Lady Heron.

'She has perhaps taken bad wine. It is uncomfortable but not serious. Dickon told me how it was. I have everything with me to make up a draught. It's mostly wormwood, nothing too strong. But she should be purged daily until all the discomfort is gone – and she must eat lightly – no spiced meat or bacon. Wine is good and plenty of eggs and milk.'

'Then there is nothing more I can do,' said Mary briskly, aware of a thousand morning tasks and her few remaining hours of sleep. 'You'll sleep here Martha, if you please – and tend to Lady Grey while it may be necessary.' It was a command and Martha, as one of Heron's outer ring of dependents, would naturally obey it.

Mary Heron emptied the room of all but the physician and patient and the house resumed its slumbers; all but Lucy, who sat up in bed worrying into the dark and biting her nails.

Alone with Valora, Martha did not go to lie on the truckle from which the defective maid had been ousted, but stood for some time looking down on the sick girl whose still face lay in a shaft of dawning summer light crossing the pillow. Without envy, but by no means without interest, she reflected upon the differences of birth and fortune, dispensed by God, according to His most precious will.

He had endowed Valora Grey with beauty, lineage and riches, adding to these the priceless gift, as far as it might come to a woman, of independence. The face, moving in uncomfortable sleep, was strong as well as lovely, as were the limbs now thrown about the bed as though their owner wished to get rid of them. All in all, the contents of the bed were much to offer any man. Tom Heron would doubtless find himself a contented husband if his little sister could leave the lady alive long enough. The thought of Lucy had the apparent instant effect of one of the spells Martha was popularly supposed to weave, for the child appeared in the doorway, her face imploring, and was bidden in by a whisper.

'Good. Just so we are sure. You put it in her wine, yes?'

'Yes, but I didn't know . . .'

'*Sh*, quietly. Don't worry, she will soon recover. Didn't you *read* my note?'

'I lost it. I didn't think it would matter.'

'Well, it did. Had you read it you would have sprinkled the liquid on her pillow not tipped it into her drink!'

'Oh sweet Jesu!'

'Yes, indeed. Now go to bed and try to grow up a little. I would have thought I could trust you, Lucy, not to be so foolish.'

Hangdog, Lucy scuffed slowly off, turning once to see if she would ever be forgiven.

'I have the remedy. I thought this might be the case. She'll be well in a day or so,' was all Martha would say. Then she relented a little. 'And I shall say nothing to anyone of how she came to be ill – though I would much prefer to do so on my own account.'

'Oh thank you, Martha. You are good!'

But Lucy determined not to sleep any more that night. She did not feel she deserved to.

In the morning Valora awoke from a sleep which seemed to slump over her like a great dog. Her head was full of bread dough and there were crickets walking about among her eyelashes. She sensed sunlight and treated it cautiously, rubbing her eyes open. Ah yes, she had been – was still? – most unpleasantly ill. Her stomach felt sore and her whole frame knew lassitude. Still a little ill, certainly. She raised her head towards the heap in the truckle bed. 'Pru, are you awake?'

A strange young woman reared up, yawning amid a stream of

very fair hair. 'Good morning, my lady. How do you feel this morning?'

'I'm not sure yet. Who are you? Where is my servant?'

Martha rose as tidily as she could and shook out her grey gown and her hair. 'My name is Martha Knyvett. I am a tenant of Sir George's. I have some small skill with physic and Lady Heron sent for me to attend you last night.' While she spoke she helped Valora to sit up and straightened the dishevelled bed.

'Indeed? Then I was by no means well. I imagine Lady Heron is herself well acquainted with herbal cures. But you are something more advanced?' She was staring at Martha, taking in her beauty, her obvious rarity, with frank curiosity.

'I have read a great deal, and I have the knack for growing things.'

'And patience? You'd need it,' remarked Valora who was conscious that, however she had felt last night, and she could not quite recall just how that was, she now felt very much better.

'Do they call you a witch, for your trouble?' she enquired conversationally, gesturing automatically for Martha to fetch the lace chambergown hung from a shutter.

Martha paled, though it would have been hard to notice. 'Some do,' she said. She wrapped the gown around its owner and was astonished by a low laugh.

'They say the same of me, some of them; witch or Catholic, it's all the same to a certain turn of mind.' She stopped and considered looking about for her comb. 'Even though *you* minister to the bodies and *I* would save the souls, if I could – we must not expect gratitude.'

Martha found the comb and began to work on Valora's black tangle. She did not speak.

'I speak to you like this because I sense something in you which is like something in me. I have very strong instincts. They are never wrong. You have them also, I think.'

'I do.' A small prohibitive silence built itself around Martha. 'You should not talk so much, Lady Grey,' she said neutrally. 'Save your strength. You are not well yet. If you have no objection, Lady Heron wishes me to remain to tend you.' Against her will Martha felt she owed her patient something in return for the easy friendship flung at her so unguardedly.

Valora grinned and stretched her tired abdominal muscles, followed by all the others in her body. Then she licked her lips and took the comb from Martha. 'Not an objection in the world,' she declared heartily as she commenced to return the favour of playing hairdresser. She meant it to make them equal, for she had spoken the truth concerning her instinct and she knew that in several ways as yet undiscovered, equal was what they were. She did not mind if Martha was silent. She herself had words enough for a regiment.

In the next room, as Valora's comb glissaded down its fall, Lucy was struggling out of her own treacherous sleep. The sound of voices through the panelling brought instant and sober recollection. She listened. Only a low murmuring up and down and a little warm laugh. Not, certainly, her mother. Good! Because this morning she knew without doubt what she had to do. After that, everything was up to Lady Grey. She edged out of bed, careful not to disturb the series of curves that was Julia, and opened the shutters and looked out to see what the day was doing. Freshness raced towards her. The essence of summer lay distilling in the grass, sweet and scintillant in this early stage, to become mulled and heavy and spiced with scents as the sun aged and warmed it. Lucy smiled generally at everything in the garden, with a special grin for her favourite oak, and got her green dress out of the aumbry. She loved outdoor colours best. She often played Maid Marion in this dress with the twins taking scrupulous turns to be Robin or Little John. However, before any such pleasure could be planned, she had an uncomfortable duty to perform.

She dressed quickly and neatly and presented herself, before she could start thinking it over, at the door of the guest room. Valora's voice, huskier even than usual, invited her in. She took instinctive pleasure, despite her nervousness, in the scene presented by the two young women, the dark and the fair, set against the velvet and satin and the old glow of the wood. Martha sat on the edge of the bed, her body turned towards Valora as the comb did its work. The light fell upon her own hair and turned her into a saint, it was as though some mediaeval artist had completed one of those gentle Dutch pictures that Tom had brought back from his war.

'Good day, Lucy. Come in properly. Don't hang by the door. You look delicious; green is your colour.'

'Thank you. Good morning, madam; good morning, Martha. I'm sorry to come so early but there is something I have to tell you.'

Martha made a small movement as if to rise.

'No, please stay. You know what it is, anyway.'

'A mystery,' drawled Valora, settling back into her pillows, 'I love a mystery.' Then, having looked more carefully at Lucy's set face, 'Hurry then, child,' she said kindly. 'You look as if it is not a pleasant secret. You'd better rid yourself of it.'

'No, it isn't. And I don't know how to say it. But it is my fault that you have been so ill. I have poisoned you.'

'God's boots!' Valora sat up and stared at her.

'I didn't *mean* to,' Lucy added quickly. She looked at the floor. The next bit was harder. 'It was a – a love potion – so that you would like us and Heron and want to marry Tom!'

An explosion of mirth shook the bed.

'My dear child! What an intrepid step to take – but what in heaven's name did you use?' She rubbed her stomach ruefully.

Martha stepped in. 'The mischievous element was dog's mercury.'

Valora gasped. 'Then I'm lucky to be so blithe today.'

'There was very little of it.' Martha was sombre. 'Or I should have been hung for a murderess at the next assizes.'

Valora looked as though she had suffered too many shocks. 'You?' She was bewildered.

Very dryly, Martha explained. 'It is unnecessary, I think, for us to tell you how very much we regret this. Luckily I was able to contravert the effects of the mercury. But you have been quite ill and must be a little careful for a few days.'

'Hades! I shall be well enough.' Valora's smile had returned. 'My sweet Lucy! Tom has a faithful sister, that's sure. How he will laugh when I tell him!'

Lucy looked miserable.

'Why, cheer up, my chicken. All's well that ends well!'

'Tom will not laugh. He will never forgive me, *never*!'

Valora considered certain past attitudes in her suitor. There was no denying that Tom could be severe. His sense of humour was not his most obvious characteristic, though she hoped to alter that a little, in time. 'Ah, I see. In that case I think I had better *not* tell him.'

Lucy's face brightened.

'In truth,' continued Valora thoughtfully, 'it would be best if we did not tell anyone. I have come to no harm. I have the constitution of a horse. And I have gained a pleasant new acquaintance out of it.' She looked at Martha with spontaneous affection.

Martha, grateful for her generosity, gave in return her faint rare smile that was like the last few seconds of a rainbow. This offer of friendship, too sudden, disturbed her. It was neither fitting to her station nor accustomed to her temperament. Valora Grey was evidently a person to whom convention meant little. To Martha, for reasons not of her own choosing, it had to mean a very great deal.

Lucy, however, had no reservations about Valora. From this moment she was more her ally than the absent Tom's. She had started out on her project more to provide herself with incident than for her brother's sake. Now she began to think that God's hand was in it somewhere. Tom and Valora were obviously meant to marry. Such a ready desire to laugh in a woman would do Tom the world of good! Though she admired him deeply, Lucy always found her brother's presence a trifle rigorous. In fact, there was something of the beloved Jud in Valora, some fine carelessness which was yet not careless of others. Both Tom and Jud, who avoided each other as much as possible, would have been astonished to hear it.

Lady Grey was an unwilling invalid and insisted upon getting up that afternoon, dressed in cream silk and the rosary. She was still tired and sore but more able to make the effort which would bring her into company than that of resting alone according to Martha's stern counsel. As it turned out, she would not have missed the evening's entertainment for a Barbary mare.

When Sir George was absent at Parliament, Mary Heron transacted any necessary business on his behalf. Born into a large estate herself, she was an excellent steward and had an exact eye for costs and values. This, added to a pleasant manner with the tenants and farm workers, the weavers, fullers and dyers who lived, as did the Herons themselves, off Sir George's sheep and cattle, made her a popular and respected figure in the countryside. She was not surprised, therefore, when as she relaxed with her daughter and her guests after supper, her major-domo puffed up to the gallery with the news that Master Nehemiah Owerby was asking to see her on a matter concerning the estate.

Tibbett was sixty, two and a half yards high and fatter than he liked. Stairs no longer suited him.

Mary groaned. 'Take your breath, man. I'm tempted to refuse him. Nehemiah's opinions do not agree with my digestion. But, best to see him now, I think. He's a determined man and will only return to plague me later. What new dereliction of duty can he have discovered in us now? Please God he will not lecture me a couple of hours and end with a sermon on my husband's probable difficulties with the eye of a needle!'

She was about to rise from her chair when Valora stayed her. 'No. Why should you leave your comfort? We are very snug here and I confess to an outrageous curiosity concerning this puritanical paragon. Let him come up and entertain us all.'

'What has Lucy been saying?' Mary demanded suspiciously, but she gave the order nevertheless to show up the visitor to the gallery.

At this Martha, taking no leave, glided unnoticed from the room.

'I said he was cruel and cold-hearted,' began Lucy warmly, only to be silenced by her mother's frown as steps were heard and Owerby entered. Still in his well-cut black, but with the addition of a many-pointed collar of enviable lace, he uncovered his fine black curls for Lady Heron's benefit and bowed almost as creditably as Tom could do. His expression, however, was grim with disapproval.

'It was my hope to find Sir George at home, madam, but as he is absent, I will merely deliver you a message for him. It is on behalf of some friends whom I have persuaded against delivering it themselves, in a manner you might find – less than courteous.'

'Indeed?' Mary's brows perished the thought. 'How so?'

Nehemiah smiled. 'It is difficult to persuade men to behave well when they feel themselves threatened.'

'Threatened? I have no idea what you mean. Don't speak in riddles. Who is threatened and by whom?'

'Many of your husband's tenants fear for their livelihood, Lady Heron,' he said abruptly. 'Their taxes are increased beyond their capabilities and the common land taken from them for Sir George's own use.'

'Insolent!' gasped Valora Grey.

Owerby had already noted the new presence. His admiration for beauty being far surpassed by his loathing of rosary beads, he offered her a scowl, which, caring nothing for his opinion, she ignored.

'How dare you enter Sir George's house and speak so to his wife in his absence!'

'I have spoken no insult nor do I intend any,' he returned her his bleak stare. 'Nor do I take direction or correction from a treasonable papist. I wonder you parade that bauble so openly, madam, or that *you* permit it in your house,' he challenged Mary.

'My God, sir, I'll tell you what I will not permit! I'll not brook such impertinence to a guest under my roof. Apologize to Lady Grey and go your way as soon as you like.'

'I make no apologies to papists. I am truly sorry to see you harbour one.' Nehemiah was intractable. 'My business here is brief enough. I come to speak for the tenant farmers, the wage-labourers, itinerants and poorer sort of this honour who demand – with respect – ' he added sardonically 'that Sir George remove all the fences, hedges and ditches with which he has lately enclosed certain lands, a list of which I will leave with you.' He took a small scroll from his pocket and dropped it onto a table.

Mary Heron was on her feet. 'Nehemiah Owerby, you were always too big for your breeches and you'll burst them yet! It's a disgrace that you, a JP and a would-be member of the Parliament, should take the side of the common sort in these matters!'

His slight smile showed no bitterness at that 'would-be'. 'I dare say I'll unseat Sir George yet,' he supposed genially. 'Or join him in the House. There are souls enough in this part of Gloucestershire to require more than one MP to speak for them.'

'Heaven forbid it!' Mary said roundly.

'It is heaven desires it – for the good of those for whom you care so little,' said Nehemiah softly.

The eye of the needle, thought Lucy, but no sermon was forthcoming today.

'If our matter does not receive prompt attention, then you will hear from me again – and although I can *speak* peace for these people, I have no influence over their actions. Your husband would do well to remember this. Good day to you, madam.'

'So now, it is *we* who should feel threatened? A swift turn about!' Mary was mulling over several of Sir George's less savoury expressions, desirous of hurling them after his black, departing figure but decided she was too glad of his leaving to delay it further.

'Sweet Saviour! The man has a voice like the crack of doom and a presence as heavy as a tombstone,' said Valora, fascinated and repelled. 'And yet he's a well-looking man and well-enough-to-do, I'd say. Why can't he be content to tend his own garden? A JP and a contender at the elections; he should be your good neighbour surely?'

'He's a Puritan of deep conviction. He sides with the mischievous in the honour at every opportunity. He gives Sir George apoplexy every time they meet.'

Lucy considered remarking that he wanted to marry Martha but decided that this was Martha's business.

'He's certainly no lover of Catholics.' Valora said. 'He looked at my rosary as if he thought it would burn if he touched it.'

'So he did, and it disquiets me a little to have him notice you. He is a leader in these parts and though he's pesky he has a power, of sorts. I only hope he may do you no harm.'

Valora looked amused. 'Harm? What is he – a yeoman farmer with a fast tongue and a Bible beneath his belt? How could such a man harm me?' A gentlewoman, she implied, endowed with blue blood and yellow gold from the Conqueror's kist, beloved of the Queen, protected by the King, how could Nehemiah Owerby's prejudice possibly affect her?

'I know, I know,' said Mary gently, 'and yet – you yourself have said it – the world grows serious.'

And they were serious for perhaps half an hour thereafter, trying to digest Nehemiah Owerby's unpleasant food for thought. Then Valora asked Lucy to play. They would disperse the heaviness with the most popular songs they knew. They were exceedingly frivolous and Lucy half-hoped, half-imagined, that Nehemiah could hear them as he pounded down the road on the dun mare that had replaced the great black horse. There was that in Nehemiah that brought out all the challenge in her nature. It was not just that he was a Puritan and horse-murderer. He was the opposite of all that she would wish to become, or to see in those about her. He killed joy, and that, too, was a kind of murder, perhaps even the mysterious sin against the Holy Ghost that Valora had once spoken of, but not defined. Lucy played very hard for the rest of the evening.

After a week of idle, golden days and melodious evenings, their even rhythm was disrupted by Tom's homecoming. Rooms that had harboured peace, music, needlework and gentle conversation, lit by the occasional brilliance of Valora's wit or Martha's smile, were now filled with dogs, oaths, tobacco smoke and long legs. It was astonishing that one man could make so much difference. Doors and windows were left open; the passages seemed always to be full of lounging serving men. Ale and wine flowed non-stop into the systems of an equally constant flow of young, male visitors, all with dogs and horses and serving men of their own. Valora whose own establishment was as orderly as a convent, though by no means so austere, considered Heronscourt to resemble an inn, but Mary Heron to her surprise, seemed to bloom under the demands of the guests saying that Sir George always loved them to be hospitable. Her usual, rather somnolent gait stepped up to a brisk pace and her cheeks were often attractively flushed under the extravagant compliment of some young blood of the country. Valora, seeing her preoccupation, sought female companionship in Martha, when she could persuade her, and in Lucy.

As for her lover's own preoccupation with the friends of his youth, she saw that they came unsought and forgave him. They were, in a way, convenient to her present frame of mind which was more confused than she allowed to appear. She already loved this family and Heron was a heart-catching house, but – she did not *want* to think about marriage, not yet! She had prayed over it incessantly during the months she had known Tom, the prayers of a desperate soul seeking its duty, alternating with the wily traps a spoiled child sets for its God – 'if you wish me to give him up, Lord, show me a sign' or even in a passionate combination of the two – 'I will go down to hell, willingly, if only I may have him here and now!'

Now that she was here with him, away from Court where they lived in a state of continual excitement heightened by their own intrigue and the heady possibility of stolen meetings, she longed just to be simple with him, just to enjoy the beautiful fact of their attraction. Not to look forward. It did not help matters for Tom to point out how near this attitude came to dishonesty. The fact of their attraction might be simple but the depth and power of it rendered the simple approach impossible. What had taken them both by storm was the unequivocally physical aspect of that attraction. It might be something she would prefer to ignore, but her body reminded her of it every time she came in sight of him. She did not doubt that she loved him and that this love would do all that was needed to provide healthy heirs and a contented household, but equally, if she married elsewhere, *duty* would provide the same; and her duty did not and could not, unless he were to turn Catholic, lie with Tom Heron – no matter how much her body burned to do so.

Sir Horatio Bulmer, rake, foppish and stupid as he might be, was the King's friend and a Catholic of unimpeachable lineage. The King wanted her to marry him, and presumably Christ wanted her to marry him. To go against both Christ and King for her own selfish and fleshly pleasure would need a special kind of cold courage. Valora was unsure whether she had it, but every time that Tom took her in his arms she began to think that she might have. It was not at all that she loved him only in the carnal way; it was just that her situation forced more emphasis upon Eros than on Agape. In the normal way of things, unless one positively disliked one's partner, one might confidently expect the Agape, while Eros might grow or not, as the case might be. Here, they were already ambushed by Eros.

Another unfortunate aspect of the problem was that Valora *did* dislike Sir Horatio quite decidedly and in a very physical way. The thought of lying beneath his drunken bulk tormented her every time she smiled and took his arm into supper at St James. It was apt to tease her in the midst of even the lightest conversation with him, usually on his favourite subjects of dogs or how to get hold of a really good claret – though how to hold it once he had *got* hold of it was not in his wisdom, alas.

Another favourite subject was how to keep the peasants in their place. Some of his methods were cruel and she preferred to avoid that particular discussion. Sir Horatio, in short, was like a thousand other men in England, a good solid landlord who enjoyed his life with all his senses except good sense, and who might end up making an excellent husband if the right woman were to take him in hand. This last was what the King had opined to Valora. Sir Horatio, as though to mock His Majesty's solemn opinion, had tried, when drunk, to get her to take him in hand in quite a different fashion and had been mortified and then embarrassed at her refusal. He explained later, sober and shame-faced, that he had taken her in the dim light after dinner for another dark-haired lady of more lenient habits known as Sharon Sharealike. She was, it seemed, one of the Queen's sewing maids. Valora had forgiven him because she had a sense of humour, but the experience made marriage with Horatio seem less attractive than ever.

Nevertheless when Tom asked her with mischievous casualness, as they walked in the walled garden, Heron's most private place, 'So now then, my lady; tell me how you like your children's inheritance?' she replied without hesitation, 'I like it very well – as long as they also inherit the true faith.'

His reaction was first to rage, and then to kiss her until she begged for breath, and lastly to offer his latest idea of a compromise, conceived in desperation at her stubbornness. 'My heir shall belong to the English Church, and all the boys. You may make papists of the girls if you must.' Perhaps God, hearing, would send them no girls.

'You would have me save the souls of the girls at the expense of their poor brothers? A cruel father you'd make!' Her voice was light but she stared at him resentfully. They were nearly of a height and she wore French heels, so that their eyes were level. 'When will you learn that there can be no compromise on this? It is unkind in you to make a mock of it, when you know it is as real and serious a barrier to our marriage as though it were made of iron and set from heaven to earth between us.'

He closed his eyes for an instant, teeth set. He made a sound as though those teeth ached. 'God's sweet mercy! Am I not aware of it every waking hour?' He snatched at a rose and tore it to shreds. The impotent gesture drew blood because of the thorns, alleviating nothing. 'And it is *not* as though the Catholicism of one female of independent mind were one of the eternal verities, fixed and immutable forever! People change. Men *have* changed their faith, and women too, in both directions. It happens often; why, in God's name, not to you?'

'Because there *is* one, true, fixed and immutable faith.' She dropped each word quietly and separately like the soft forms of sweetmeats into boiling sugar. They seethed in the hollow of his skull and he wanted to hit her. The worst of it was that he knew his own religion burned with no like fire in him. It was a part of him, like his boots or his gun, but if he were not to be the master of Heron, he would snuff it out without a qualm and light the Roman candle for her sake. Because she could not do the same, he respected her, but there were times when he almost hated her for it. Now he felt weary, flat, enervated. It had all been for nothing, her coming here. Her manner of worshipping the same God who stood over them all counted more for her than his love, an empty form more than all the fulfilment of a lifetime's purpose.

'You should become a nun – if you're so hot for the Pope and so cold for me!' He flung at her venomously, hurt in his manhood and his pride.

'I sometimes think,' she said fiercely and with the same sense of failure, 'that I will do exactly that.'

Then she left the garden. But half an hour later the memory curled in her of his lips on hers and his hands upon her breasts. Saying the rosary did not drive it away.

Her place was taken in the garden by Lucy, who wanted a private space to re-read her letters. She checked, conscience racing, when she saw Tom. He was frowning. 'Hello imp! What mischief are you up to?' This was the tiresome way he had of speaking to her. He treated her like one of the twins, and even they resented his lordly assumption that their entire reason for occupying the earth was to add to its mischief. In their case, however it was more true than otherwise.

'Nothing,' she said, her voice going up at the end, making it sound as though she were lying. She clutched her letters more firmly for moral support.

'What have you there? A recipe for corn candy?'

She sighed. He was trying to be friendly, she could tell. Only he didn't know how. She was often teased for her passion for corn candy.

'No. The letters from Father and Jud.'

Tom's frown lowered again. 'What does Jud have to say for himself? I've seen him but once since the execution and he asked me for money. And now he has made me his courier. A fine brotherly gesture – to call at my rooms and leave his letters in my absence.'

'He couldn't see you if you were not in,' said Lucy reasonably.

'He could have left word.'

Lucy found it politic to return to the letter, censoring it carefully, and leaving out a good deal. 'He says he is much happier working for Master Staunton than he was at Lincoln's Inn, that there have been a lot of riots and that the papists are becoming very unpopular with the citizens. And that he hopes we are all well here and not troubled with the Puritans.' That was about right, she thought. There's nothing there for Tom to object to. 'I saw Valora going into the house just now,' she volunteered, by way of changing the subject. 'She looked,' she added, judiciously or not she couldn't be sure, 'as if she had been crying.'

Tom grunted, rudely, considering how careful she had been of his susceptibilities about Jud, and gave her her privacy.

She was used to his sudden exits and entrances. They were part of his tension, which was very much a part of him.

What Jud had said was this.

Dearest Lucy,

I hope Tom will bring you this when he rides home. Be careful not to lose the top sheet which is intended for Mother. She would only worry if she read of the times I've had these last few weeks! Will Staunton is a splendid fellow in every way and the work is not heavy as yet, though he threatens an increase. Young Robin – you remember *him* I daresay – is amazing good company when you get to know him. He has the wit to grasp the chance he is given and though he's only one of the common sort, and horribly poor, he'll make something more of himself one day, I'll wager.

As for me, though I care as little for my ledgers as I did for my lawbooks, I do care to please my master, for if I do well he has promised to send me off on the *Gallant Lady* when she sets sail. It's what I've always wanted, to go to sea! Meanwhile I live in hope and amuse myself with Robin. Last week we had a very jolly time, gingering up the mass-takers at the French Embassy. Now, I don't care if a man is a papist, but I can't abide those stuffed-silk, prosy frog-eaters who hold a kerchief to their noses whenever a lesser mortal comes by. Anyway we bloodied a few of the noses to give them good use of the kerchiefs! No harm done and to the tavern after, with a few coins that shook loose in the proceedings. Good ale and the serving girls friendly. There was one that put me in mind of you; pretty lass, name of Marion . . .'

There was more, much in the same vein, together with some careless comment upon the King's lack of love among his London subjects. Then Jud reverted to the subject of his master.

'I think Silken Will is the best-set-up man that ever I knew. He knows how to be easy with every man, yet he is never bested by any. He makes our duties as pleasant as he can, saying that all things have an interest if only one will look at them in the right light. I confess that even *he* cannot enter any charm into the dreadful ledgers, but he has made me see that the figures stand for other things; work, men, voyages, goods, in short – prosperity. He is much keen on prosperity, and not only upon his own as most men are, but upon that of the whole nation, which he says comes to the same thing in the end. He takes me about with him a good deal and I have met many other merchants.

'One of his friends is that John Venn whom Father so loathes for his leadership of the multitude against Strafford. He has been a captain of the Trained Bands and a member of the Common Council of the city and has now entered Parliament. Father will like that even less! He is a very cheerful man for a Puritan, not like our own Dismal species, and treats all as equals though he is rich as Midas.

My master has other friends, more dedicated to pleasure than good causes. I had to fetch him home recently from the house of a certain lady – as beautiful as Venus and with such a wicked look in her eye! Will was singing drunk and walked as though he were still at sea. I had to sober him quickly for the Justices were waiting to accuse him of piracy in the morning! I need not have worried; he was more than able for them, dressed like a prince and his excuses falling upon their ears like birdsong. By the way, Silken Will says I am to enquire after you, Lucy. He hopes you are still "pert and pretty" and asks when you will come up to town and go aboard the *Lady*. I tell him it will not be yet, but one day you will come for sure.'

Lucy felt a restlessness. She loved Heron and the country but she had been cheated of her exploration of the lovely ship. As for Silken Will, she had thought him a fop herself – so sure of himself in that smug purring tom-cat way! And if he was easy with every man, he was probably a hypocrite. He must be, if he was both a merchant and a pirate. She shrugged, bored with Will Staunton. Jud, she decided, was at an impressionable age. Girls, she had noticed, matured earlier in this respect, and had better judgement – unless, some patient saint preserve her, they were silly and twittering like Isabella Stratton.

She sighed and folded the letter. She would have to entertain the witless Isabella this afternoon, as her family were to visit Heron. It was a compliment to Valora, for the Strattons were an old Catholic family. Sir Joseph, although a dozen years his elder, was one of Tom's greatest friends. Isabella knew nothing about music or the natural world and cried if her hands got dirty. She liked to play foolish guessing games or 'I spy' like Julia who was half her age. And she was *ridiculous* about Humpty whom, she had confessed after swearing Lucy to a lifetime of secrecy, she wished to marry. Lucy, having sworn, did not reveal this to Humpty, though she thought longingly of the things he would do to Isabella if he knew. She had a morbid terror of all insects and arachnids! Lucy had contented herself with the observation that Isabella could not marry Humpty because she was a Catholic. At least, she hoped not. She would welcome Valora as a good sister – but Isabella! That would be to carry broad-mindedness far too far!

Her afternoon was every bit as tedious as she expected, but she was rewarded for her boredom by permission to join the adults at their evening entertainment after supper. Several near neighbours, those within twenty miles or so, had joined the party, and the new dining room and withdrawing room were put to full use. As usual Lucy's virginals were brought. She played and was praised and then allowed to play cards until bedtime. Lucy was good at card games and won three pins from Mistress Stratton and seventeen from Isabella, who sulked and said she would play no more. She moped off to a windowseat and sat gazing out, curling the ends of her exquisite brown ringlets round her fingers, loathing Lucy and suffering pangs of despised love. Humpty had taken no notice of her all afternoon, apart from a grunt of welcome forced by his mother's frown.

'I can't think what we shall make of her,' said Susannah Stratton ruefully. 'She has no head for figures, scarcely reads, and her hands may as well be hooves! She'd ruin any man with her housekeeping in a week!' Lucy thought a good secluded convent suitable, but did not say so.

'Well, God be thanked, she's pretty enough,' comforted Lady Mary. 'Men seldom marry for wits and some of them have little enough in that quarter themselves.'

'That is an opinion I have never heard you express when my father is at home,' said Tom, overhearing and grinning at her. His good humour had returned with the advent of his friend Joseph Stratton.

'No,' allowed Lady Mary equably, 'but I dare mention it in *your* company I suppose?'

'Unkind! What's a man to do, Jo, if his own mother won't stand up for him?'

'Tell her he gets his wits from her and his looks from his father, pass the claret to his friends and give in with a good grace to the ladies! Dammit Tom, we're outnumbered. What can we do?' This was true of their table at least, where Lucy and her mother were supported by Valora and also by Martha, whom Valora had summoned imperiously from the village by sending her carriage for her.

Martha had been embarrassed by the flamboyant equipage but had got in without a murmur when the coachman had said, with a chamberpot face, that her young ladyship 'had need of Martha's talents'. She had been doubly embarrassed, even angry, to find that it was her talent as a social companion that was required.

Valora's penchant for her nurse and saviour was even becoming a faint embarrassment to Mary Heron. Martha was, after all, by no means a lady, but then she was not quite *not* one either; indeed she seemed to have created a status of her own. Mary had no objection to her company as a general rule. They shared a very satisfactory reciprocal relationship on the matter of plants and herbs. Martha was a gentle soul and the children liked her, but Mary questioned the wisdom of Valora's sending for her in this highhanded fashion and sitting her down to cards among their guests. It may have been intended kindly but it was not a kindness all the same. It was not that Martha couldn't pick up the various games with ease, nor that she could not or did not answer when spoken to. Yet somehow her presence, undemanding and tranquil as it was, created a strange point of gravity in the humming, populous room. This being so, her very simplicity, incapable of standing out in any way itself, made their persons and their speech seem somehow overdecorated, even foolish. They did not know that this was what they felt; only that something in the composed, cool-haired girl made them uncomfortable. Except for Valora that is, and Lucy.

Tom Heron was the most uncomfortable of all. For him Martha's presence was a small personal outrage. He could not look at her over the table without recalling a certain afternoon in another summer, when he had kissed her many times and told her that it was the saddest thing in all the world that they could not marry. He had been entranced, besotted by her then. She had been his first passion and because she would not give herself for love alone, needing to keep her own respect, it had been an innocent love and had come into his mind often, during the wars in Europe, like sweet remembered music. There had been nothing to regret. It had not endured because it could come to nothing, and besides, he had gone away. But now, in sight of her, so soft in her grey dress and with her few words, her eyes meeting his unafraid, unchanged, all he could feel was a fierce guilt.

He swaggered a little, making a fool of himself, drinking too much and talking nonsense to Jo Stratton. The room struck him as hot. He opened the window, absently passing his hand over the head of Isabella who still sat there brooding. 'Why so solemn, chick? Will you not play too?'

'I'd sooner look out of the window,' she said repressively. Couldn't he see that she was a lady left and lorn?

Tom followed her mournful gaze without much interest. He noted Kit and Humpty dashing about out there, no doubt engrossed in one of their complex games involving unseen henchmen.

Martha looked up from her cards as he turned towards the table again and a trap caught both their eyes. This time she did not merely look at him but smiled a little and inclined her head with an odd graciousness.

'She's letting me go!' he thought, outraged. What right had she to feel so much in command? Had she thought to own him because he had given her an ignorant boy's first love? He did not frown or show his reaction in any way, only smiled at her with empty courtesy. But Martha, who spoke so little because she was accustomed to listen to what was unspoken, heard and understood this overdue betrayal. She was only sorry that in his lack of chivalry it was himself whom he betrayed. As for her, she would never change. She loved him. She would always love him. And she would use her rather peculiar powers to protect him, as much as it was permitted.

Valora was playing to her. Obediently she laid down a card. It was the winner. When she saw this her smile became mischievous. Beginner's luck for her, in this at any rate! Valora, delighted at her new friend's success, leaned to kiss her affectionately. Martha lifted her cheek and suffered the refined torture of those who are too generous of nature to feel jealousy, while Tom swore to himself and pretended it was because he had lost the game.

Half a mile from the scene of these delicate emotions, something far more robust was moving purposefully towards Heron. Nehemiah Owerby, astride his dun mare and with twenty picked men of the militia riding behind him this time, was bringing the will of God and the might of the law to Sir George's door. The baron might be absent but his heir would serve equally well for Nehemiah's purpose, which was that of pointing out clearly and unmistakably Sir George's bounden duty in the matter of his tenants and of the local papists. There was a job to be done and by rights, Tom should assist him to do it. It was quite unlikely that he would; Nehemiah knew that, but he proposed to make him uncomfortable by asking him to. Nehemiah had discovered that Joseph Stratton was a guest at Heron and his business concerned that gentleman. He had chosen to go about it in this public fashion as he sensed it to be high time that the proud and lazy brood of Herons were brought to recognize their responsibility to those about them and beneath them. If this should prove to be the outcome of his visit, that would be all to the glory and honour of God; if not, as was almost certain, the attempt would do much to point out to all men the direction in which their leading family now leaned. It was *not* the way the wind was blowing, and it was better they should be made to see this.

The men behind him, Puritans every one, were all Sir George's tenants, holding their land by copy of Court Roll 'according to custom of the manor'. The custom in the manor of Heron was that the tenant held his estate as an inheritance and his heir had the automatic right to succession. This put him in a happier position than a life tenant or a man whose tenancy was only for a fixed period after which the rent was lawfully subject to a thumping increase. These were known, somewhat ironically, as tenants-at-will. At Heron, the rents were fixed, an excellent thing for the tenants. The fines, however, were arbitrary and provided a subject for endless negotiation, brow- and breast-beating on the part of both landlord and tenants. Sir George, like many another in his place, spent much time and ingenuity trying to prove that certain tenants did *not* have the right to copy-hold. A useful law of James I invalidated any tenancy created out of old wastelands or forest or the demesnes of a manor. The tenants in question were those who had become well-to-do yeoman farmers over the years at, as Sir George saw it, his and Heron's expense, battening and fattening on his grass, his sheep and his time. The richest of these, and therefore the chief offender, was Nehemiah Owerby. The fact that he was also an educated man, articulate to the point of eloquence, who saw fit to waste his gifts in puritanical rabble-rousing, underlined the injury of the relationship.

So too did the fact that Sir George and Nehemiah's father, a man of unexceptional ways and tastes (very like the baron's own) had been the best of friends, tumbling up as boys together, learning the countryside and human nature with a shared curiosity and a healthy competition. Andrew Owerby had been a God-fearing man and a good one but he'd also loved a joke, his ale and his horses. Sir George had always understood him, loved him, relied on him. Now he was dead of some unknown swift fever and his only son was an enigma to the world he had lived in. Misunderstanding had gradually turned to dislike and this had augmented on both sides until it was commonly pondered about the county which pig-headed man would harm the other most. Sir George had all the wind in his favour by birth and circumstance but Nehemiah was making a good shot at circumnavigation and his recent attempt to enter Parliament had brought him a great deal of local approval. He was a tenant and a farmer and stood for the men who worked the land rather than those who owned it. He seemed to the lesser tenants, the labourers, the wage-earners, to represent some bolder future when their financial situation might not gnaw at their stomachs and thieve their sleep but might give them, like those above them, the right to the incredible luxury of peace of mind. They did not expect to *own* anything; only to know that they should go on renting it without paying with every shred of their skins. It was not, men like Nehemiah gave them the courage to know, such a very great deal to ask.

So the horsemen at Nehemiah's back thought on the ancient miracle of the Magna Carta and were heartened as they entered Sir George's ornithological gates. They were unimpeded as they covered the driveway, and surprised at this. When they reached the imposing iron-bound doors of the house their hearts betrayed them a little. They suffered a strong sense of being uninvited. Nehemiah, having no such qualms, strode up the shallow steps two by two and hammered boldly on the oak. There being no immediate reaction from within he turned the worn ring and pushed. The door opened. Nehemiah walked in. Each of his followers fell back slightly while firmly shoving his neighbour forward. One Sam Hudson, recently enlarged in confidence from discovering that he could read well in church, found himself at the top of the scuffle and was precipitated suddenly into the hall. In the internal gloom, the monumental Tibbett materialized. He held a loaded carbine, aimed unequivocally at Nehemiah's belt.

'You trespass here, Nehemiah Owerby, and unless you turn yourself and your pack of unruly dogs about, I shall be forced to lose control of my hand, which is itchin' on this 'ere catch.'

Nehemiah, three inches shorter but in higher boots, grinned pleasantly into the grizzled, scowling countenance and unhurriedly cast up the business end of the gun with his right hand while seizing it determinedly with his left. Thanks to Tibbett's good sense it did not go off. It had made its point and he was more or less prepared to give it up. He neither liked nor disliked Nehemiah, and was interested to see what was up this time. This is not to hint at disloyalty. Had he thought Nehemiah intended any danger to a Heron he would have shot him without the courtesy of first explaining that he was going to. As it was he was satisfied with sarcasm.

'I take it you wish to speak with Master Thomas? He bade me say he may not leave his guests for the present, but if you care to wait . . .'

What Tom had actually said was, 'Sling the bastard-boots down the steps for all I care! He shall learn thus, not to interrupt a gentleman's leisure. I don't care if he *has* twenty men with him. They are all our tenants and can do us no hurt beyond inconvenience – and I'll not have even that from them!'

'I won't wait.' Nehemiah laid the gun against the wall and gestured the major-domo towards the sound of voices. They entered the company just at the point when Tom Heron's impatience with Valora, Martha and himself had reached the necessity of some expression other than wine and pretence.

Inwardly angry and feeling himself made in some way ridiculous by the presence of the two women, he was delighted to see his father's old enemy. He had not expected Tibbett to delay him so long.

'Master Owerby craves the honour of an interview,' Tibbett was still enjoying his sarcasm.

'He does, does he? It must be a mighty serious business, Nehemiah, that won't wait on courtesy. Is something afire? Was there some insult you forgot to offer my mother?' The tensions of Tom's day heightened his tone. The general talk faltered and fell.

'Neither.' This boy gave the same stiff welcome as his mother. On the whole Nehemiah preferred the father, whose aggrieved roaring was at least amusing. He looked round the room, noting the cards, the wine, the identities of the players and drinkers. Excellent. Then he saw something that did not please him.

'Mistress Martha? What do you here?' his tongue betrayed him inadvertently.

She flushed with anger to be singled out. 'I please myself!'

His eyes moved to Valora. 'In such company?' She should not have been here. It was not what he had expected. He was disconcerted. Why was it that she was the only area of his life where he could not be sure of his control? He felt anger rising in him and tried to put it down. 'Are you not a little out of place here?' he asked quietly. He turned away from her cold look and his eye fell on Joseph Stratton.

'As others are,' he continued, lifting his pulpit voice, confidence flooding back now that he had assimilated the surprise of Martha. Newly refreshed in his purpose he turned to Tom.

'It is reported, with much credence, that the papist rebellion is underway. It is therefore our duty under God and as His Majesty's faithful subjects to do all in our power to circumvent it. I charge you therefore in His Majesty's name, aye and in your father's too, as the chief protector of these parts, to accompany me together with the gentlemen of the Trained Bands to the home of the notorious recusant Sir Joseph Stratton, there to search for arms and any evidence as to their intended use.' It was as though Sir Joseph were invisible to him.

A kind of protracted gasp bounced about the room. A few men laughed out loud and Valora Grey cried, 'The man's a lunatic!' Sir Joseph, whose main interest in life was lepidoptera, looked as though he had just met with a new species. There were shouts of 'Oh, I say!' and 'Tip him out of the window!'

Only Tom, it seemed to himself, had the wit to be properly angry. He found he panted slightly when he spoke. It was important not to lose his grip in the face of Owerby's matter-of-fact calm. 'To mention my father's name in such a circumstance is a confounded liberty! To mention the King's is something more like *lèse-majesté* – knowing as you do that Queen Mary is a Catholic! To insult my guests before my face, though something less than either, is becoming habitual in you and that in itself is reason enough for me to have you thrown out of this house.'

Sam Hudson, skulking at the door, now slipped hastily away.

But Nehemiah had not come for drama. 'There'd be danger to the glass ware. It doesn't surprise me that you are derelict in your duty, seeing that you provide a haven for those who would undermine our State. His Majesty is poorly served by such as you.'

Tom sprang to his feet. 'My God, if I'd my sword – !' His face flamed as he made for Nehemiah. Jo Stratton was also on his feet. Nearer to the Puritan than either, Valora kept them off with her imperious voice, lounging back in her chair and holding up her glittering rosary. 'Is it this you fear, Master Owerby – do you see it as a yoke of fire to sear the necks of your unborn children? Do you see the Pope sit at St James? The mass said daily throughout the land? I think not. Though you lack manners you're not without intelligence. What is it brings you here? I do not think it is fear of rebellion and love of duty – such clarion calls.'

She leaned forward and swung the beads beneath his face. 'My family has been Catholic since there have been Catholics in England and I have a sixth sense of such things. It tells me that what inspires you, Nehemiah, is hatred; the pure and simple bloodlust of the strong for the underdog. Your own religion, though God knows it has nearly bored half the country to an early grave, is not proscribed; it thrives; can it be because there is a little more to it than sermons and sanctity? Something of a more political nature, perhaps? And do you believe that a man of your faith, that has nurtured such traitors as Burton, Prynne and Bastwick, has the right to accuse anyone of seeking to undermine the body politic? No, you don't fear us; you only hate us. You yearn to light the fires of Smithfield again.'

Nehemiah, interested, examined his conscience. Then he shook his head. 'No. That was a cruel way. But Prynne and his friends were also cruelly treated. They did but speak their minds, and write them, according to their consciences. You are right, Madam, to say I hate the popish faith. With all my bone and sinews, I do hate it! But I'd not have you burn.' He looked at her gently, surprising her, and put out a hand to push her beads aside. She was right to think him afraid of them. Perhaps it was folly, but there *were* objects of evil power in the world, even as there were objects of virtue.

It was at that moment that Isabella opened the window. Then she screeched as though all the devils in hell, both papist and Protestant, had hold of her. A flash of blue, black and white bisected the room and Valora gave a sharp cry as her rosary departed heavenwards from her fingers!

Maggots, trained or otherwise, had deposited his beakful of juicy spiders upon the luckless Isabella's breast and swooped for the glitter of garnets. He made one wide triumphant circuit, then flew out whence he had come. A cry of young male delight was heard in the shrubbery. Laughter and anger trembled and clashed in his wake.

Isabella screamed and screamed, her mother and Mary Heron scrabbling frantically at her chest. The whole room was bemused and boggling, unable to say quite what had happened and what difference, if any, it might make to what happened next.

Lucy, the first to recover, clapped her hands in delight as though at a travelling play. Valora slumped with a gesture both defeated and amused. Nehemiah gasped, undecided whether he had witnessed the devil at play or a *Deus ex machina* at work for Puritans. Tom, though, was nearly driven to hysteria by the ludicrousness of the event and became suddenly and stubbornly determined to keep his given word. 'Tibbett!' he roared, in excellent imitation of his father. 'Throw this damn fellow out. At once!'

Tibbett measured his man. Help was at hand in the form of two footmen and Tom's valet, Josh Pye, a slender man who did not like to disarrange his curls.

Before they could attempt to obey their master however, Jo Stratton rushed forward with a cheerful yell, followed by several other young bloods, and Nehemiah found himself propelled through the house by the whole pack of them, howling as if manners had never been invented. When they got him to the front door, they opened it and swung his inert, gigantic body three times, counting loudly each swing, then out into the waiting mass of his followers, now huddled at the foot of the steps as if taking refuge in each other's warmth. No further word was spoken but the message was clear enough; Magna Carta would not be signed anew today.

*

The excitement was over and the world grew still more serious. Tom was back at Court, his stubborn heart more than ever bound to Valora after a stormy reconciliation and Valora was extending her leave at her own manor of Spindlesham, where she could rage and pray and be herself, when the officers of Parliament descended on Stratton Hall, their way conducted by Nehemiah Owerby. They did their duty very thoroughly. The house was stripped of its arms, its plate and any other article of value that might have been sold, as they said, to fund the cause of the rebellious papists. The pleasant artifacts of several centuries had gone far towards making Sir Joseph's house a hospitable and comfortable home. Now it was bewildering to him, to his wife and children, to find themselves standing about in cold and naked rooms in as wooden a way as the empty cupboards and denuded dressers themselves. Such strangeness and loss made them quite unable to understand what had happened to them.

'They left me my butterflies; they thought them worthless,' Sir Jo comforted himself when they came to Heron to rest and recover. His wife Susanna forbore to remark that 'they' were only too right, and wished that anything could comfort her for the loss of her dishes and sheets and household dignity and her children's portable heritage. Isabella was inconsolable; they had taken her Venetian looking-glass.

The Strattons, after the first instinctive flight thither, would not stay long at Heron, for Nehemiah sent up constant ominous messages about the harbouring of recusants which, though Mary Heron ignored them as they deserved, caused Sir Joseph to fear that Heron itself might be favoured with an official visit. It was vain to point out that Sir George was *in* the Parliament and must therefore be immune to its excesses of zeal.

'You are a good Protestant family. Have nothing more to do with Catholics,' was Sir Jo's advice as he took his family back to the large and echoing house now tenanted only by the insubstantial forms of butterflies.

It was excellent advice, for the fear of rebellion was feeding greedily on its own flesh, and fear breeds cruelty, especially when the majority is afraid of the minority.

King Charles, alarmed at the rumours which had him harrowing his own kingdom with the help of rabid Irish and Scots, fell in hastily with any plan John Pym might have to allay suspicion. A treaty of mutual aid was signed with the Scots Covenanters and various unpopular royal servants were dismissed.

Pym took advantage of this acquiescent mood to insist that

henceforth all appointments to the royal household should be made by Parliament. In July he put through a bill to abolish the detested Prerogative Courts; it was the end of the King's direct judicial power.

Sir George was unimpressed with events. He wrote indignantly to his wife,

'Is King Charles to be a mere blob of sealed wax and King Pym to rule the land? By Jupiter, he goes too far! He'd have the government in ruins in a day, and the Church too, if he were let. He is now very busy concerning the swarm of *plots* that buzz about our burning, weary ears. Indeed, if Pym were *not* so busy, the people would hear less of the plots and the King be less blamed for them, traduced as he is, poor gentleman, by those who should be his best help. Pym is as slithy as an elver and has the Covenanters in his pocket to grease him further.

A curious letter has come from Scotland, purporting to be from His Majesty to young Montrose. It is written in code, a preposterous thing, full of inexplicable nonsense about serpents, elephants and dromedaries! They would have us believe that it concerns a plot by Montrose in which the King may take the government of Scotland directly into his hands. The next thing is that Argyll and the Covenanters, jealous of their power and hot for Montrose's blood, have sacked his house and without benefit of a trial, have flung him into jail on suspicion of conspiracy. God knows what truth, if any, lies beneath it, but Tom goes north with the King next month and will doubtless seek it out. You remember he befriended Montrose when they met last year in Edinburgh?

The frenzy against the papists increases daily. There are two priests from the Jesuit College in Douai just sentenced to the traitor's death, and one of them Chaplain to the Venetian Ambassador who complains to His Majesty and demands the fellow's right to his protection. Damned if Secretary Vane (whose name is like to overtake his character) does not up and lecture the King on the evils of reprieving a priest. T'other, having none to speak for him, was hung, drawn, etc. They say he made a good end; but I doubt his blood will appease the mob for long . . .'

Mary Heron, deploring the doleful contents of her husband's

letter, wished she had better news for him than the sack of Stratton Hall. She took great pleasure, however, in describing how the Dismal Puritan had been routed from the house. As she wrote she remarked to Lucy how glad she was that they were no longer in London.

It was upon the very next day that they learned that London's tentacles were long and strong.

Father Dominic Lacey of the Society of Jesus, lately from the Seminary at Douai, had just completed the most gruelling journey of his life. He had travelled from London to Heron in record time and discomfort. Neither his horse nor he himself was at all sure they could manage the last few furlongs from gate to door. Drenched in foam, sweat and mud, legs aching, breathing racked, eyes streaming, they collapsed in an undignified lather of waving limbs upon the very spot where the large body of Nehemiah Owerby had recently been slung like a sack of turnips. There being no friends present to break *his* fall, Father Dominic, winded, lay still and thanked God that the stones now bruising his ribs belonged to his cousin's husband. The horse explored the possibility of a broken leg, then, reassured, rose and stood trembling.

'We'll not be 'aving t'shoot 'im, then?' remarked a lugubrious voice, all but tinged with regret. Tibbett, finding his carbine unnecessary once again, descended to pick up this unceremonious and decidedly dirty stranger and see what manner of man he might be. When set upon his feet and dusted down, he proved to be a young man of a slight and nervous build, all bones and planes and awkward angles. His face was good-humoured under the dirt. His eyes sparkled, though partly with the tears of the road, and his voice, when he could get his breath, was low, liquid and rather beautiful.

'Tibbett, you old rogue! How are you? I'm glad to see you. Tell me, is my lady at home?'

Tibbett's craggy face broke open in his gap-toothed grin as his memory provided the picture of a slight boy giving an eloquent exposé of God's desire that the figs on the south wall vine should be free for all to take at any time.

'Master Nick! The Devil take me, I'd not have known you! You've grown out of all recognition. 'Tis good to see you, sir!' It seemed ridiculous that the boy was a priest, so Tibbett ignored the fact. He felt more comfortable that way. Dominic clapped him unsteadily upon his shoulder, then Lady Heron was searched for and found in the dairy where she was introducing Lucy to the mysteries of making curd cheese. Dominic, if he had any doubt of his welcome, was at once reassured by cries of delight followed by the immediate transference of a blob of cream from Lucy's nose to his own. 'Merciful heaven, how have you reached us, with this pestiferous militia looking out for papists behind every tree?' Her mother was content to kiss his cheek. He laughed a little shakily, pushing away certain recent memories.

'I don't have "priest" burned into my brow – though I don't doubt there are many who think I should have – and it's a good few years since I've been to Heron –'

Indeed the last time they had met was at the Lincolnshire wedding when Dominic, newly ordained, had performed his first nuptial mass. Catholics had generally been left to practise their religion in peace at that time. It was hard to believe it was only three years ago.

'You look ill, cousin, and tired to death. A good meal will set you on your feet.'

Mary's idea of a good meal proved to be so rich and generous as to make the setting upon feet impossible, but Dominic did begin to feel very much better. He realized, as he lay stretched upon the settle after he had eaten, that sleep was what he needed above all. He struggled to keep his eyes open long enough to ask the all-important question.

'Can I stay here, Mary? Would it put you in danger? No. Don't tell me now. Think it over while I sleep, for sleep I must whether I will or no.'

'Well then, get you to bed. Lucy will show you where.'

But his eyes were closing, his limbs dissolving. 'If you had seen where and how I have slept these last days,' he murmured, 'you'd know that this is bliss; the epitome of comfort. Let me be. We'll talk by and by . . .' Claimed by exhaustion he was gone from them, leaving only his pale effigy for their contemplation.

'It needs but a dog at his feet, poor lad,' whispered her ladyship, her heart wrung by the picture.

'Shall we say yes?' demanded Lucy anxiously but her mother put her finger to her lips and they tiptoed out of the room.

'I have to think what your father would say, for there's not time to write. In the two weeks it takes the carrier we could have Nehemiah and his ruffians down on us and all cleared out in a day. Come child. I can't think unless I'm occupied. We may as well finish the cheese.'

Back in the cool dairy, stone-flagged and grey-walled, its very air heavy with the thickness of cream, Doll the plump dairy maid was dispatched to the common to examine the cows for soft hoof, while Sir George's probable reactions were surmised. The curds were set and Lucy fed plum suckets to Huw, the little Welsh pony who turned the great churn.

'Sir George has always been fond of Nick, ever since he took him to the play as a boy,' Mary remembered.

'Father likes anyone who likes Shakespeare,' observed Lucy truthfully, stroking Huw's rough neck.

'And he bears no malice towards the papists. God knows half of my family would be unwelcome here if he did. But the affair of Stratton Hall disturbs me deeply, and I doubt that if Nehemiah were to get wind of Dominic's presence here –' Mary's brows wrinkled, making her look for a moment like the older woman she had not yet become. 'We must hide him, Lucy. The house is large enough. He can range about within a certain distance, but should not go outside.'

Lucy thought. 'But does anyone here *know* him? The last time he was here he must have been a boy. I know he came when I was three but I don't remember.'

'Perhaps not. No, I don't think anyone outside the house would recognize him and precious few within.'

'Who?' Lucy had conceived a plan. 'Which of the servants, apart from Tibbett, who has been here the longest? Master Davies or Margery Kitchen?'

Mary considered. 'Not Davies, no, nor many of the women. A lot of them have changed. And even Tibbett says he knew him only by his voice. But what's your drift, child?'

'Only that it seems a pity to be mewed indoors in such a lovely summer. If no one knows him, we can just say he's cousin Nick and let him live an ordinary life. No one could possibly know he's a priest. I suppose Nehemiah doesn't know him?' she asked anxiously, checking her enthusiasm.

'They have never met to my knowledge. But Nehemiah could sniff out a priest at half a mile I shouldn't wonder!'

'No, don't worry. We don't need to disguise his face, but we'll disguise his character.' Mary looked doubtful but Lucy would say no more until Dominic woke up.

'I haven't said yet that he may stay,' she said slowly.

'No, but then where is he to go?' asked Lucy simply.

Her mother sighed. 'There is nowhere. If he goes to the Catholic Laceys, he will be suspected at once if he's seen. Any new member of a Catholic household is suspect now. No, I think you're right – the intelligent thing to do is *not* to make a secret of it.'

'So cousin Nick stays?' said Lucy slyly.

'Yes. He stays. But don't be too happy about it, not yet, Lucy. It is a dangerous step for us to take and I confess I wish your father were at home.'

Dominic, awake and refreshed and told of the decision, followed a brief instinctive prayer of thanks with a whooping 'Hosannah'. 'By God, Mary, I knew you'd not let me down. I'll not be discovered, I promise you. I'll live in an aumbry if you like!'

Mary waved her hand towards her daughter. 'That is not what we have in mind for you, I believe.'

His eyes were alert with interest. 'Tell me! Am I to be disguised as a sewing girl?'

'No – as one of our cousins,' said Lucy.

'Forgive me, but I . . . ?'

'Well, more as one of Father's cousins, I should think,' Lucy developed her idea. 'I don't think Mother's are unpriestly enough.'

'Be careful, Lucy! I'll not have rudeness.' Mary's lips thinned a little.

'I didn't mean to be rude, Mother. But I was thinking of perhaps, Uncle Drew. If Father Nick were to behave as though he were Uncle Drew, then no one could ever take him for a priest!'

Mary, as so often where Lucy was concerned, was torn between the desire to slap her for insolence and hug her for honesty. It was uncomfortable to have a child who always spoke the truth. But Lucy's idea was undeniably a good one. Her cousin Drew, though, was a reprobate, however close of kin.

'Your Uncle Drew drinks too much, hunts too often and takes the name of the Lord in vain – how is *Father Dominic* to manage to emulate him?'

But Dominic's face showed approval and a trace of mischief. 'Excellent scheme! Couldn't be better. I shall practise my oaths every evening before prayers. I'm sure that God will forgive me. All is in His cause. I'm certain no one hereabouts will take a hard-drinking, hard-riding squire for a priest. But there's one thing I have to say, Mary, and that is that first and above all *I am* one of God's priests and my greatest duty is not to save my own insignificant skin, but to serve him in this world as long as I am in it. That means that, despite this flaring up of persecutions, I *must* say mass for those who wish to hear it. Even here. Do you understand this, Mary, because it's all-important? I have a list of Catholic families in the country whom I may serve and it is my duty to make converts if I can – yourself perhaps?' He grinned boyishly, taking the weight of his words from her.

'Too late for that, Cousin Nick – and I'll thank you to leave my children to their English faith. As for your duty as you say it is, do not endanger our lives by it. That is all we ask of you.'

'I won't, Mary, I promise you upon my faith, and thank you, my dear. You don't know how many blessings are stored up for you for this.'

'Never mind blessings. Just put a word in your prayers about my Quickenberry tree. You're nearer God's ears than I am, for all you're a papist and a priest.'

He was content to change the subject, knowing that Mary was comforting herself for the unhappy changes in the world outside her by turning to the things she loved best in her own.

'Won't it grow? You've fine soil here?'

'The best, but the tree is not a native and so it's hard to rear. The King's gardener John Tradescant has one at Lambeth. He has given me sheets of advice on its feeding and welfare and yet it tarries.'

'It is like a rowan tree, is it not?'

'Much like, except that it bears larger berries. It is very cheerful. But I cannot get it above four feet. Are you fond of gardening, coz?'

Father Dominic marshalled his thoughts. Mary's passion for her garden was reputed to have worn down many strong men whether in the field or in conversation, but a garden *is* a pleasant thing and Heron's was one of great beauty. 'I'm ignorant but willing to learn,' he said modestly. Mary beamed. 'Then stay forever, if you wish,' she said, all doubts swept away by the possibility of another green hand. 'I'll start you on the bed-straw. Horrid stuff, it gets everywhere – but keep all the roots; we need them for their dye.'

But if Mary Heron was satisfied to speak no more of priesthood or popery, this was by no means the case with her children. One splendid afternoon shortly after his introduction to the household, Dominic found himself upon his knees not to his Maker, but to the bed-straw which was romping in one of the shadier corners of the 'Italian Garden'. This, naturally, was where the more flamboyant and self-conscious flowers were found, bordering an elegant avenue of pines and cyprus which provided a guard of honour as one walked the hundred yards or so to the 'vista', that point on the estate where the chief beauties of all the county were set out before the viewer as though they and not the gardens had been laid down precisely for the purpose. So they should be; the landscape artist had been internationally famous and he had cost Sir George's pirate ancestor a great deal in Spanish doubloons and Jerez wine.

There was a certain amount of marble statuary about and Dominic, looking up occasionally, was never sure whether he caught sight of a sculpture or a child, for both had a tendency to lurk behind foliage. The twins had been playing some bloodthirsty games involving the Romans and the Gauls. Lucy had spoiled it, they said, by electing to be Boadicea. They would not have minded if they had been at that point in history but their war was Gallic, not British. Lucy, bored with both game and argument, came to sit on the path behind Dominic as he worked. He did so slowly and methodically, his movements different now from the swift stabs at the air he made in conversation. She imagined that this was how he might be when he said the mass, but the other way perhaps, when he gave a sermon. She herself hated sermons for she had never heard a good one and hoped that Father Dominic would not overtake Cousin Nick so far as to give one in her presence. 'Were you in great danger when you had to leave London?' Her father's letters had made her curious.

'Very great. I nearly lost my life.' He went on weeding but his concentration was no longer on the bed-straw.

'How?'

He sighed. It was not an edifying tale for a child, but these Herons seemed hardy-minded enough, raised on Roman atrocities and Foxe's *Book of Martyrs*.

'I would have died a traitor's death had I been taken.'

'Like the Earl of Strafford?'

'No. The King commuted his sentence to the block. A priest must pay the full penalty.'

'He'd be hung, and his entrails pulled out alive and burned before his eyes – and then, when he'd died in agony, they'd cut his body into quarters and take it to four different places!' Kit, who had an exact memory for all unsavoury information, had crept up behind them.

Dominic turned to him, wishing he could distance himself from the awful description as easily as Kit could do. 'It is a horrible death. It is because you cannot yet imagine it you can speak of it so lightly. But men *have* died that way, one of them very recently.'

The sober tone did not deter the boy. 'Did you see it?'

'Yes, I did.' His patience was finished. 'He was a very dear friend of mine.'

'Oh, I'm sorry. Who was it?'

At this point there was a shriek from the shrubbery and the three turned, startled, to see a triumphant Humpty emerge, dragging Martha, laughing and dishevelled, with him. He had waylaid her on a mission to Lady Mary with a healthy juniper plant to replace one that had died. She approached shyly. She was a party to Dominic's identity and had been sworn by Lucy to an awful secrecy, but she felt awkward with him as yet.

'She's a Catholic and I'm the captain of militia. I've just captured her and I'm taking her away to be questioned.'

'Why can't she be a Gallic chieftain's wife – then we shall all be in the game?' demanded Humpty.

'I'm sick of Roman stuff. I want to be something modern.'

' "And violent sorrow a modern ecstasy",' murmured Dominic, sighing.

'What did you say?' Humpty didn't like to miss anything.

'From Macbeth. A Celtic chieftain lamenting the times.'

'What times?'

'Oh *you* know,' said Kit, 'the one where he keeps on saying tomorrow and tomorrow and tomorrow'.

'And there are witches? And "Lay on McDuff"?'

'That's the one.'

This was not at all interesting to Kit. 'Now tell us about your friend who was hung, drawn and quartered,' he said firmly to Dominic.

'Sweet Jesus!' said Martha. 'It's never true?'

'I'm afraid it is.' The priest spoke gently. 'It seems impossible to make these bloody-minded children understand the difference between their games and hideous realities. Perhaps it would be salutary if I were to try.'

'Oh – no thank you very much,' said Lucy hastily. She had managed to avoid Strafford's last moments and didn't really want to know about anyone else's. Besides it was only natural for the boys to play war games. Their cousin had to realize this. But it was as though Dominic could not stem the words that came out of him now.

'It was a sultry day. We hadn't believed it would come to this. The ambassador had saved Father Green but none came forward to save my friend. They drove him in a cart to the place, where they had already set the fire. The executioner was waiting on the scaffold with his instruments. My friend asked him if they were fine and sharp and they joked a little. He was told he need not die if he abjured the faith but would have none of it. Then he prayed for the man and spoke to the crowd, but they would not hear him.

'Then the terrible business began. They hung him and then cut him down as he struggled in agony. They gave him a little time to recover – oh, cruel time. Then the executioner slit up his belly as the butcher does his meat and his blood flowed and flowed. Unspeakable. He tried to make no sound, only moaned a little and prayed steadfastly, as I did, as many did by now though not of our faith. I dare swear by this moment, seeing the living man gaze at his bowels displayed to the disgrace of humanity, that more than half of that vast assembly asked themselves in shame what it was in *them* that brought him to this pass. Now was the worst moment of all, when the intestines were drawn from his body in agony so exquisite as to make him faint with pain, then cut away and burned as he died. He had wept the whole while, but silently, his lips moving in prayer. It was his silence which set him apart. They had taken his dignity as a man, they were taking his life; but he would not let them take his courage. Well, he is in heaven now and I'll make no doubt his voice is heard often enough, as he pleads with the Lord God for the poor fools left behind in England.'

'It was Father Ward, wasn't it,' whispered Lucy, shaken. 'Father wrote to us about it. You had to get away because you were his friend.'

'Yes.'

'Or – or the same thing could have happened to you!' As she made the inevitable deduction Lucy's face expressed a horror that told her cousin that here, at any rate, he had succeeded in breeching the gulf between imagination and reality.

'But you must not think of it any more,' he said, repentant now that his aim was reached. 'I'm safe with you and all is well.'

'No.' It was Martha who spoke, her look intent, more as if she were listening than speaking. 'All is not well, nor will it be well in time to come. The persecution will go on – as it has always gone on – and soon it will no longer be only the witches and the priests who pay for all our sins, but our brothers and ourselves. All will become scapegoats of each other's fear.'

Dominic sat back on his heels and stared up at her pale, haunted face. She was gazing into the distance, seeing nothing but her own fearful visions. He had to know *what* terrible phantom it was that caused that look or he would not be able to help her. And he wanted to help her. As soon as he had set eyes on her he had recognized something lost in her, something the lack of which she concealed with that detachment, that total privacy which she carried about with her as though she inhabited a glass box. Others saw her as reserved, serene, whole in herself. Only Dominic saw that she was lost. 'What is it that you see, child, or have seen?'

Her eyes ceased to fathom space and refocused on him. 'I'm less a child than you are, I think,' she said gravely.

The twins, seeing that this would turn into yet another boring adult conversation, with no action in it and no juice at all, nudged each other simultaneously and raced off. Lucy, her instinct and her curiosity strained to an intense pitch, scarcely breathed, hoping that they would not notice if she remained. Nor did they, or if they did they felt her presence less than a butterfly's.

Martha, though reluctant, sensed the kindness in Dominic's question. As there had been with Valora, so with him she felt the existence of a bond. She disliked human contact in general and would have liked to deny it. Valora, with her imperiousness and her fierce affection had simply overwhelmed her. It had been easier to make her happy than to deny her. Dominic's case was different. He made no demands; his voice was gentle and hesitant, his manner shy and nervous. He seemed to have to summon the courage to speak to her, indicating what they shared without naming it, perhaps even without being able to name it. She was not quite able to do so herself, though she knew that if she tried to see what it was, she would be able. She was cursed with the seeing, as her mother had been . . . and though she would let it tell her no more, she already knew that part of her fate was linked with that of this gentle priest. She sensed also that there was heaviness in it and did not want to give him a further burden, knowing that his was already no ordinary load.

'It is memory that disturbs me, as it does you,' she said slowly, looking into his eyes so that he would hear only what she told him and ask for no more. 'Like you I have watched someone die who was very close to me.'

He nodded but would not release her yet. 'How close?'

'It was my mother. I was twelve.'

'How did she die?'

'She was burned. A man died. She had given him physic. They would have given a physician his pay; but they said *she* was a witch.'

'Oh no! Please! Don't say that. Oh Martha, I'm so sorry –

please forgive me!' Lucy now threw herself upon Martha in a torrent of tears and self-loathing. Its suddenness broke Martha's bitterness.

'Hush! sweetheart, hush! Whatever is the matter?' Martha cradled her, feeling the small heart throbbing as loudly as her own.

Dominic made a helpless gesture as Lucy sobbed convulsively. At last she sniffed wetly and made some attempt to speak. 'What I said that day – that *you* were a witch. I didn't mean it. I didn't know . . .' Her eyes were despairing.

Martha patted Lucy. 'Of course you didn't know. How could you?' How could she have known, for no one knew, that the other face of Martha's calm was that of ever-present fear, that every time a sheep or a cow died in the village, she was a prey to blank, unreasoning terror. She had not cured it; would they say then that she had killed it? 'Ah now, be quiet my lambkin. It doesn't matter. I thought no harm.'

'I think', said Dominic delicately, 'that there is too much emotion in this garden. It must be the Italian influence.' He stood up, knees creaking, and held out his hand to them. 'Come, let us remove ourselves into a more English atmosphere.'

Martha checked for a moment, looking at him as she rose. His words had opened a window in her mind. She did not want to look out, but it had opened and invited her.

'What now – a goose walking over your grave?' Dominic smiled, trying to lower the tension with the homely proverb.

She shook her head. 'Not mine,' she said. 'Come, we'll take Lucy to the still-room and see if Alice has made anything this afternoon that might cheer her up. Treacle toffee perhaps?'

But there are some things, Lucy was learning, that cannot be cured by sweets. She was growing up, and it hurt.

Something of Lucy's late tearfulness and excessive emotion was very soon explained, to her mother's satisfaction if not to her own, when in the course of that month she experienced her first menstrual flow.

To Lady Heron who wrote of it proudly to Sir George, it meant that Lucy was now a woman of marriageable age and should begin to take more seriously the tasks involved in the running of a household. To Lucy, it was simply the most painful, disgusting and embarrassing thing that had ever happened to her. She was bewildered by the pain, which was different in quality from any she had suffered before, and she loathed and resented the bloody clouts that she had to wear in a thick, revolting wodge between her legs. She worried intensely lest they smell and spent three days washing and changing them almost constantly. At first she determined to sit on the close-stool until it stopped, but was laughed out of it. She just could not accept that she had to put up with this horror for the rest of her life.

Her mother gave out that it had something to do with having babies. Lucy therefore determined *never* to have any. She was evil-tempered all week and fought viciously with the twins whom she now regarded as having got away with something in life at her expense. She passionately wished she were a boy. The boys were much amazed when, instead of reproving Lucy for her ill nature, Lady Heron told them not to plague her more than they could help. Having a great deal on her mind at the moment, as the pear trees were not all setting as they should, she made sure of this by dispatching Lucy to Martha for something to lessen her pains.

Glad to escape from her lessons, and her unfinished pillow lace as well as the twins, Lucy dragged off towards her private woodland path. She soon found that walking dulled the ache in her belly and this cheered her a little. The repulsive flood seemed to have abated since yesterday and she no longer needed such heavy cloths to absorb it. Nevertheless she was still strongly conscious of the horrid layers and longed to tear them off and bathe her body which felt as hot and cross all over as her mind. Her mother had said she was not to have a bath until the foul thing was over, which she might expect by Friday. It was not healthy to do so before this. When asked why, she had replied vaguely that she did not know exactly but that her own mother had said so, therefore it must be true. 'Some say it's because the devil, loving women's discomfort, is more busy about them at this time and might fly into their private parts with the bath water.'

'He'd have to make himself pretty small,' Lucy protested. Nevertheless she was very impressed with this threat and walked about with her legs very close together until she forgot about it. The walks in her native forest did much to unjangle her nerves. Every summer she saw again with gladness how many and how fresh were the shades of green in the grass and the trees, how startling the scents of their secret fluids, how heady those of their flowers. She walked softly upon spongy mosses and tiptoed to avoid the shepherd's purse, the speedwells, the scarlet pimpernel and all the tiny things that grew in her path, only to commit vegetable murder every time her eye wandered upwards.

When she reached the place that she knew in the middle of the wood she stopped and sat down in the dark, strong grass. She listened. Nothing.

The unhuman stillness here was what made it the centre of her most private world, far more personal than the chamber that she shared with Julia, more sacred even than being alone in the chapel.

She could sit here, in a place roofed by sun-dappled interlacing branches, carpeted by fern and moss, pillared by these ancient trees in their brave young foliage and feel herself to be at the very heart of England. And she, Lucy, was part of it, her breathing mingled with the sweet air, her body quiet, her spirit part of the spirit of the place. She did not think of God here, as she tried to do in the chapel, not even of the Child Jesus as a boy of her own age. He did not occur to her here. And yet it was amid this green stillness that she knew herself best, not because she searched her conscience and tried to analyse what was good and bad in herself, as she had been taught to do by the chaplain, but because she found this was a place where all questioning stopped and she became unaware of self except as an infinite part of something vast and old and necessary. It was not required of her to be good or evil, simply that she *be*. It was a great relief. She came often. This was her sanctuary. No matter what happened to her in life, she would always be able to come back here and find herself. The place would be unchanged and she would know that she was too.

She was quite cheerful again by the time she reached the cottage. Martha was in the garden at the side of the house and Dominic was with her. Lucy hung back for a few moments. She felt particularly embarrassed before males just at present. Then she told herself not to be silly. After all he couldn't *know*, not just by looking at her. She wished, in fact, that she could ask him if it were true about the devil, but couldn't imagine how she might find the words. A pity. As a priest he'd be bound to know.

Dominic had become very fond of Martha. His instinct to seek out and try to allay her fear of her mother's terrible fate had overcome his natural shyness and her own.

Now they were very companionable together, behaving, though they could not know it, like a couple who have been married for a long time and do not regret it. In Martha the priest found a friend who did not treat him as though he were different from other men. She seemed to have no special respect for his cloth or his faith. She simply respected the man he was and made allowances for his ordinary humanity. Martha found that she could relax with Dominic in a way she had never done with any man, certainly not Tom, whose presence had always kept her as taut as a lute-string. Though she would never seek out Dominic's company, nor indeed any, other than perhaps that of children, she was glad when he came to her and talked freely with him, finding as she did so that some of the pain and fear that had been instilled in her at her mother's death was beginning to purge itself.

Lucy opened the gate and they waved a welcome. 'Lucy – how nice! Your cousin Nick has just asked me to show him the village church. Come with us.'

'St Michael's?' Lucy frowned. 'He won't like it.'

'Well, they haven't destroyed *everything*. There are still the tombs and some brasses and all the fine carvings.'

The church of St Michael and All the Angels had by now changed its form of worship five times. Catholic until Henry, Protestant, then Catholic again for Mary; Protestant for Elizabeth and now, purified of all its portable ornamentation, as Puritan as was possible. By now, the greater part of the local gentry, those who preferred the Anglican form, attended St Mary Major's in the next parish, Sir George and his family among them, unless they used the family chapel at home.

The dark cool of the building was welcome after the half-mile walk in the sun. Each of them was aware of very different feelings as they entered the straight and solid nave with its Norman pillars and later Gothic superstructure of graceful clerestories and delicately boned roof tracery.

As Martha had said, the Puritans had found it impossible to reduce such an elderly and determinedly glorious stone prayer to the undistracting nullity they thought more fitting to their form of worship.

For Dominic, however, they had been completely successful; this was no longer the house of God because His Presence no longer resided upon the altar in the form of a wafer of bread within a gold monstrance. He loved the old building for its own sake, however, and brooded happily among the ancient, marked graves and family brasses, too secure to have come off the walls without disturbing the dead.

Martha, as always, was uncomfortable in the church. Was it because she was a witch's child, unable to bear the contact with holy ground? She did not think so. Rather it was an irritation that she felt, as if, whatever was the answer to the mystery of God's love and of His whole creation, it would not be found here, where human argument had taken such demeaning and ludicrous toll. Nehemiah had been right; she rarely attended church. Even St

Mary Major caused impatience in her, especially if Vicar Archbold delivered one of his interminable sermons on human weakness and divine forgiveness. He made God a most unattractive character.

Lucy too had observed this and felt much the same about churches. She suffered in addition the fearful physical restlessness of all healthy children who are forced to sit still for three hours and look pious. She loved their own chapel at Heron for its lightness and simplicity and the bright wooden statues carved by the monks who had once lived there. Her family must be seen at St Mary's as an example to the tenants, otherwise nothing would have persuaded her to go there. When she did, she was careful to sit at the end of the pew where she could see the relief of St Hubert and the Stag and all the other forest animals, at the back of the stall in front. She amused herself, while the Vicar droned on and on, by making up stories about them. She looked for something similar here, but the carved stalls had all been replaced by plain wooden benches. She made do with the enamelled brass representing the prolific family Peachey, whose sixteen children knelt in decreasing size and age behind their parents, who faced each other hands together, doubtless praying that the fat baby in swaddling bands at the end of the boy's row would be the last. Lucy wondered for a moment just why babies kept on coming so fast, but saw no prospect of an answer just then. When they made a tomb for her father and her mother, she reflected, it would look very similar, with Jane and herself and Julia on the girls' side and Tom, Jud, the twins and Edward on the boys', with poor little John, Elizabeth-Eleanor, and Celia lying at their feet packaged in their grave clothes like fat little chrysalids.

As they mooched about the empty church, Martha and Lucy wanting to leave and Dominic becoming more and more fascinated with parochial history, the plain oak doors were flung open in a forthright manner and Nehemiah Owerby strode down the aisle, the rowels of his boots clanking against the silence. Sensing the church to be occupied he checked and peered hard, unable to make out their faces in the gloom. Whoever they were, lurking in the aisles, they were not engaged in prayer. 'Who goes there? What is your purpose in God's house?'

'Looking at it, that's all. God give you good day, Nehemiah,' said Martha cheerfully, his disadvantage making her mischievous. Recognizing her voice, he was delighted.

'Mistress Martha? I'm right glad to see you here.' He made

towards her, warmth flooding him. Surely his prayers were beginning to be answered.

Then he saw Dominic beside her. 'I have a friend with me,' she said quietly. 'This is Master Nick Heron. It was he who desired to see the church.'

Nehemiah's face fell. He looked closely at Dominic, noting the frivolous dress, the languid stance. The name of Heron did not please him. 'You are not here to pray then?' he asked Martha regretfully.

'Why should you think so?' she replied.

He smiled and sighed despite his disappointment. Just to see her was a gift. His smile, thought Lucy, spying from behind the pillar, was very nice when it was for Martha. He looked at her as Tom looked at Valora – sort of pleased and angry both at once. It seemed odd in a man she knew to be so hard and cruel.

'Whether you pray or not I'd rather see you here than up at Heron Hall in a nest of traitors,' he said baldly, the smile giving way to reproof.

'Now hold you, sir,' Dominic drawled, waving a limp paw within a foam of lace. He had had very little opportunity to practise the role of the worldly lordling and was now improvising the character of worthless Cousin Nick with a great deal of innocent pleasure. 'I'll not hear the lady insulted, damn me!'

'God's body, man! It isn't the lady I insult, it's your lack-lustre family of Herons, who have no better notion of their duty to God and King than to harbour the Harlot of Rome!'

'Faith! I hope you do not refer to Lady Valora Grey, sir, with such an objectionable epithet. If so, I shall be forced to call you out!'

Nehemiah's look was withering. 'The man's a fool,' he said in disgust. 'I spoke of the Catholic Church, sir, as everyone must know.'

Dominic considered, still flapping an idle hand, his face bland as a baby's, revealing nothing of an almost uncontrollable impulse to throw this long, strong, self-satisfied man to the ground and beat the satisfaction out of him.

Martha, sensing this, hastily intervened. 'I should have thought you'd had your revenge on the Catholic Church to the fullest possible measure, sir. As for duty, do you call what was done to the Strattons a Christian act?'

'Revenge?' asked Nehemiah blankly, ignoring the rest. There was no use arguing with a woman. The heart ruled the head; it was as simple as that, and all as it should be.

Martha looked him in the face. 'For your humiliation at Heron.'

A slow flush coloured his dark cheeks. 'Humiliation is too large a word, mistress,' he said tightly. 'I suffered little and was not hurt. I have done my duty as I saw it – and since I could not persuade Tom Heron to do the same, I took the law into my own hands – and will continue to do so. They are safer hands than a Heron's. There are many hereabouts who think so too.' His voice became softly urgent. 'Have no more to do with the brood, Martha, I beg of you.'

By this time Lucy, her face scarlet with repressed indignation, could no longer control herself. She dashed out from behind her pillar and stood sturdily in front of Nehemiah, puffing a little with sincerity. 'We're the oldest and best family in the county, Nehemiah Owerby, and my father and Tom are as well respected as ever they were – which is a hundred times as much as you would ever be! *We* don't steal from people's houses just because they belong to a different church – and we don't shoot innocent horses for our own cruel pleasure either! You're a stinking hypocrite, Nehemiah Owerby – and I hope you go to hell when you die!' This was the worst thing she could think of to say and she enjoyed saying it.

Nehemiah's retort was short and sharp and painful. As the imprint of his hand began to flame on her cheek, Lucy staggered back and stared at him, incredulous. 'Impudent brat! The devil take you for his own!'

'Not I. He'd rather have you!' The slap had been hard and tears of pain sparkled in her eyes but she was by no means cowed.

'By Our Lady, this is too much!' Dominic stepped towards Nehemiah, his face like thunder. 'Do you make war on children too?'

Nehemiah's face registered a flicker of puzzlement before he shook his head. 'Be quiet sir, you know little of your relatives if you don't know that this little hell-cat and her brothers are known and feared throughout the honour for their tricks. My fingers have long itched on her account, and I regret nothing – lest that it could not be her behind!'

Lucy gasped, mortified. He didn't know that he was speaking of a woman not a child, but nevertheless her pride would never forgive the indelicacy of his remark.

Martha, reading the three furious faces, decided it was time to call a halt. She stepped a little in front of Dominic and brought Lucy into the protection of her encircling arm. 'Master Nick, it is not worth your trouble to make anything of this. Nor is it fitting that you should do so in this place,' she said firmly. Then she turned coldly to Nehemiah. 'Mr Owerby, I'm disappointed. This was unworthy of you. Lucy is my friend and I would have you apologize to her.'

Nehemiah glowered at Lucy. 'Certainly not. She deserved it. So, you'd bring up children to address their elders with no respect? That would be unworthy of *you*.'

She knew this was an oblique reference to his courtship of her and the marriage he wished for between them and something hardened in her eyes. 'I'd bring them up to think kindness of greater importance than what is called duty,' she said. 'If you have nothing further to say to Lucy I wish that we will all take our leave.' She swung Lucy around with her and led her away down the aisle. Just before she reached the door she turned with an afterthought, 'I hope you will *not* call on me again, Mr Owerby. Good day.'

Her disembodied voice echoed to him between the old walls as though from the other world, angelic, clear, detached. He cursed his own ungovernable temper and cursed the Heron child even more thoroughly. His eyes narrowed as he saw Martha take the arm that the dandified young sprig offered her. If *that* were the way she was looking . . . the idea flamed up and consumed him with hatred. He almost shook with the violence of it. He *must* know. Martha was his destiny and he hers. He was as sure of it as that he stood in the right hand of God. He must find out how close was her friendship with this elegant nothing who treated God's meeting place with as much careless contumely as though it were no better than a common tavern.

He would speak a word with his friend Master Tim Davies, a good and conscientious man, who, besides doing his utmost to instil some knowledge into the thick skulls of the pestiferous Heron brats, was a sincere and fervent member of the lower Anglican Church and had recently found himself turning with more sympathy towards the Puritan persuasion. Nehemiah was his mentor in this and it might be that he could give Nehemiah a great deal of assistance in return. A little knowledge could be a very useful thing these days, and dangerous, yes dangerous too, if necessary to God's almighty purpose for this kingdom.

August, the harvest month, brought Sir George home from Westminster for the Parliamentary recess. Lucy was the first to see his coach as it rumbled past the cornfield where she and the twins were binding sheaves with blissful faces and blistered fingers. 'It's Father!' she yelled unnecessarily as the red face and gesticulating arms thrust out of the window of the swaying vehicle and Walter Rollins, Heron's chief steward, stumbled through the stubble to report on a fair to middling crop which he had tried to balance, financially, by hiring fewer day labourers.

Sir George, who knew that Rollins was not responsible for late summer storms, cursed him in a friendly fashion and grumbled that he'd seen some cows in among the clover back down the road. 'That's the sort of work for you, miss; if you must meddle,' he growled as a greeting to Lucy, who was panting towards him, her brothers close behind. 'Chasin' cows is ladies' trouble, not doin' field work like a peasant, you dirty doxy!'

Lucy, who could tell by his tone that he was pleased to see her, wiped her hands on her dress and clambered up to be kissed, inhaling the heady mixture of claret, tobacco and horses that made its home in the baronet's wiry beard.

'Good girl, that's the way. And you, sirs!' He frowned at the twins. 'What devilment have you been up to since last I saw you, eh?' Kit checked and looked as if he might be counting, but Humpty grinned and delivered his most filial bow. 'Nothing, sir, just bookwork, sir, and helping with the harvest. You said we might,' he reminded.

Sir George did not remember giving any such permission, but it had been taken for several years now and he was not about to question it. Besides, he needed as much labour at as little cost as he could get, and the boys were strong and willing. Lucy was a different matter though. He glared at her, taking in her ragged hands, her dusty dress and the stork's nest of her hair.

'See you here, mistress,' he said peremptorily, waving a thumb backwards down the road, 'I have brought guests home with me, hard on my track. I do *not* wish their first impression of my family to be that of my draggle-tail daughter disporting herself in the fields like the gipsy changeling I often think she is! D'you hear me, Lucy? Now get you up here this instant, and you too, you grinning imps of Satan, and you shall all be combed and curried and stuffed into your best gear before Will Staunton sets eyes on you.'

'Will Staunton! The one Jud says is a pirate?' cried Humpty gladly, leaping through the door that his father held open for them.

'Be fair,' cried Lucy, seeing Sir George's brows draw together, 'he only said he was *accused* of piracy, not that he was guilty.'

She stepped nimbly into the coach, helped by the clasped hands of John Coachman who had descended to help her.

'But isn't he related to the Earl of Warwick? It's known *he*'s piratical; you said so yourself, sir,' said Kit stoutly.

His father grunted. 'You'd better not let your mother hear you say so. She's of the opinion that the Earl's reputation is exaggerated by those who dislike him for being a Puritan.'

'Do *you* dislike him, Father?' asked Humpty, greatly daring.

'No, I do not, though I dislike his religion. But Warwick's a good man and a good sailor, and there's no nonsense in his noddle. Nor in Will Staunton's neither,' he added cheerfully, pleased with the prospect of his guest.

'Maybe we could be pirates, when we're older – if we don't have a war to go to,' suggested Humpty hopefully, 'like Grand'fer Thomas.'

'It isn't an ambition I'd recommend, if you want to keep the end of my belt off your backsides,' replied their parent amiably.

Something occurred to Lucy. 'You said there would be more than one visitor,' she reminded him. 'Who else is coming?'

Sir George beamed. 'Master Staunton is breaking his journey with us. Then he goes on to Warwick, where he has business with the gentleman whose name you are so free with; he is also escorting his cousin, Lady Elizabeth Hartley, who will spend some time at Warwick Castle with the Countess.'

'What is she like?' Lucy asked.

'Bide your time and you'll see. But she is a great lady and will not expect to find herself in a menagerie, so spruce yourselves up and look lively about it, as soon as we're home!'

Before they went their separate ways to accomplish this transformation, Kit pondered again on the nature of their second guest. 'She might be like Valora,' he said hopefully. Valora had often been their champion at ticklish moments.

'A widow!' declared Lucy scornfully. 'She'll be old and ugly and covered from head to foot in black veils. And there's *no one* like Valora,' she ended loyally.

Her mother had told her to take herself to Alice Jouncey, the younger ones' nurse, to be suitably cleansed and brushed and dressed, but Jouncey was not to be found. After a desultory search, Lucy ran her to earth in the stables, where she was enjoying a warm reunion with John Coachman. John had had the misfortune, brought about by last year's harvest festival ale, to father a child upon Alice, and she had ever since been after him to marry her. Sir George had almost decided to enforce the match, in the name of decency, when the baby had died, making it unnecessary. So John was left to his own conscience and Alice, conveniently, became baby Edward's wetnurse. Their relationship continued much as before, with the rest of the servants laying bets as to whether or not Alice would land her fish, who was, as he said, willing enough to be played but not so keen to be eaten.

Also in the stables was a very handsome equipage which bore a crowded coat-of-arms with a black hart in one of its quarterings and the bear and ragged staff of Warwick in another. By the time Lucy had examined this, caressed her favourites among the horses and questioned John about his visit to London, she had left the blushing Jouncey very little leeway in the matter of her grooming. Their hasty preparations in Lucy's bedchamber were hurried even further by the familiar sound of the baronet roaring for his dinner. 'That will *do*,' insisted Lucy, tired of having her hair pulled and her clothes twitched. 'Let me go, or I'll be late.'

'You still 'ave wheatears in your 'air,' Jouncey hissed after her as she thudded downstairs. Lucy felt but couldn't find them; she hoped no one would notice. She slowed down to get her breath for a dignified entrance to the parlour where the guests would be taking claret-cup with her parents. She suddenly felt self-conscious at the prospect of meeting Silken Will again. He had been the very glass of fashion on that day in London and she was uncomfortably aware that even the dress into which she had changed had grass stains upon it. True, her hair had grown out a little, but she still looked more elvish than human – and there was this grand Lady Hartley to contend with too. Oh Hades, what did it matter what they would think? She lifted her chin and marched into the room.

They were all talking nineteen to the dozen and at first she was not noticed. Her father, standing characteristically, feet astride before his fireplace, was puffed up like a turkeycock beneath the attentions of the exceptionally beautiful young woman who sat beside Mary Heron on the fine new soft settle. She was long-legged and slender, dressed to the utmost point of fashion, just this side of vulgarity, in poppy-red silk. Her hair, in superb challenge, was a rich, ruby-lit auburn, piled high with side curls. There was a good deal of striking and expensive jewellery about her otherwise naked neck and bosom but her fine dark eyes outdid all of it for sparkle.

She gave a long, low chuckle at something her host had said and turned towards the other settle, opposite, to demand lightly, 'What do you say, cousin, shall we allow Sir George to describe

Her Majesty in such disrespectful terms, merely because she has hurt him sadly in his pocket – or shall we proclaim him guilty of *lèse-majesté* and fine him another thousand livres for his wicked tongue?'

Will Staunton was lounging as much at ease as the field hands at their lunch, though with considerably more elegance, very handsomely dressed in a dramatic white doublet slashed with blue at the sleeves, and narrow black breeches. 'I think,' he drawled, 'that the Queen would be flattered, rather than otherwise, to hear herself described as "a game, thievish little vixen". She would not deny all the qualities of the mate who will see her family fed and protected though it cost every rabbit in the warren.'

'At a thousand livres a head we are tasty rabbits indeed,' grumbled Sir George, 'But there. I don't grudge it, when all's done. This time next year, I may not have it to give, if we have another harvest such as this one is like to be.'

'Never fear. By then my argosy will have come home laden with riches, and you will be a minor Croesus.'

'And if your ships go to the bottom of the sea?' grinned the baronet.

'Then the Queen will probably ask for a pound of your flesh in lieu of your livres.' It was then that Will noticed Lucy, still standing in the doorway until she might make her curtsies.

'Come in, come in. Why Lucy, I'd hardly have known you. You have grown at least half an inch since last we met.'

Lucy ignored this pleasantry and looked at her mother.

'Yes, yes, you may come in and greet our visitors. Lady Hartley, this is my second daughter, Lucy.'

As she rose from her practised obeisance, Lucy was aware of a wide smile upon a wide, red, mouth, but somehow the width was not matched by warmth. The lady beckoned her and she was enveloped in a cloud of spicy, oriental perfume and kissed glancingly upon the cheek. 'Take no notice of my cousin, Mistress Lucy. He is known for a rogue and a tease,' the throaty voice declared, addressing Will rather than Lucy.

Lucy smiled politely and moved to dip before Staunton. 'What, do I not share a kiss also?' he laughed. 'You look like an infant Ceres,' he informed her, holding out his hand. She went forward and he gravely removed the wheatears. 'It is not that they do not become you mightily, but that they were in danger of dropping into your dinner.'

'Thank you, sir.' She tried not to scowl. Then a happy revenge came to her. '*You* look,' she said innocently, 'rather like Humpty's magpie. It's the sleeves.'

It was perfectly true. Will threw back his curled head and shouted with laughter. Sir George, after a doubtful second, did the same. 'Damme, I want my dinner!' he rediscovered as the mirth died down. 'You shall meet the other pestiferous brats when we have eaten!'

The meal was accompanied by a great deal of wine and banter between the adults. The children, including Lucy, were banished to the second table with Master Davies. They noticed that Sir George twiddled his moustaches a great deal when he spoke to Lady Hartley and laughed inordinately at her jokes, while Dominic, who avoided company as often as not, practised his witless manner upon her with such admirable success that she demanded his arm as her escort when the meal was over.

After dinner they all trooped upstairs to the gallery where they could take a turn up and down to aid digestion while Lucy played soothing tunes on the virginals. She had done so for perhaps fifteen minutes when Silken Will came to stand at her shoulder. 'You play very well. Too well to be ignored. I am very fond of music and so is Cousin Eliza. Best of all I like to sing. I feel like singing at this very moment. Will you try a duet with me? I'm sure you have a charming voice.'

'How can you be sure when you've never heard it?' asked Lucy ungraciously.

'Because your speaking voice is particularly well controlled for someone of your age. This suggests that you know how to breathe properly and therefore you have begun to take your music more seriously than the usual mincing performer.'

Lucy grunted.

'What do you wish to sing?'

'Do you know Ferrabosco's *Drown my tears*?'

'Yes. Begin and I'll follow you.'

He struck a chord to give the key. She knew the song well. It was one of her own favourites. She played without thinking, concentrating upon the timbre of his voice, considering how she might weave her own pattern within its warp and weft. He had a pleasant light baritone, with darker tones that gave it depth and poignancy. He was very sure, touching each note exactly in the middle so that Lucy, after a few hesitating notes, was able to pitch her own descant as truly as she could have wished. She used the attractive device of singing the whole air in a minor mode, always three notes below Will's lead. It had a plaintive effect very suitable to the lament for an absent lover which they sang. She did not see the astonished tilt of Lady Hartley's elegant head as her full rich voice rang out, nor her father's satisfied nod at her compliment.

Pure enjoyment carried her away from them all. Will's resonant and darkly masculine tone was just what was needed to match her soaring purity. There had never been such satisfaction in singing with either of her brothers; Tom's tenor was too light, too sophisticated, while Jud had a drone like a bagpipe. This was different; this was truly making music.

The two voices dipped and climbed, Lucy following Will in his flight as a swallow trails its mate across a warm evening sky. The effect so nearly approached the sublime as to create a pool of silence at the end of the song into which no one wished to be the first to cast a pebble of applause.

Eliza Hartley was the first to recover. Bestowing her wide, bright smile like a gift, she cried, 'My dear child, you are a very nightingale. Who taught you to sing so beautifully?'

'I'm afraid she has had no tutor save myself,' Mary Heron said. 'There are few to be had in these parts. Our Master Davies, though he does his best, is no musician. But Lucy does very well by herself. She has all the books and practises a great deal.' Mary smiled at Lucy. 'But I am sure that you have a delightful voice yourself, Lady Hartley. Shall you not let us hear it?'

Eliza considered. Her voice was good enough but it was not of Lucy's quality. It was not her policy to take second best. 'I think not, if you will forgive me.' She raised a white hand to her throat. 'I have had a slight cold lately and am a little hoarse –'

'Then I shall not be deprived of my nightingale quite yet,' said Will agreeably, searching among Lucy's music sheets. Lucy, embarrassed now that she had come down from her flight, stared at the keyboard and said nothing.

Eliza frowned at her very slightly. She herself had been accustomed to sing duets with her cousin ever since they were children together. She did not take kindly to being replaced by this tow-headed young virtuosity. It was all very well to be pleasant to children for the sake of one's host but there was no need to turn the girl's head. They had sounded quite superlatively well together and therefore she was in no haste to hear them again. Her interest in Will was deeply proprietary and more than cousinly. She did not lend him out if she could help it, even to skinny chits of twelve or thirteen. 'It is such a mellow evening,' she declared appealingly. 'I had hoped that we might see something of your famous gardens before dusk.'

Seeing Mary Heron light up as though she'd been given an unexpected present, Will rose at once to add his own request. He touched Lucy's hair as they left the gallery. 'Let us sing together again very soon. We make excellent music.' Lucy nodded. No one had asked her to go with them so she bent over the keyboard again, content to be left. The twins had already disappeared. They would not be seen again until dragged in to bed by Tibbett, who was the only one among the servants for whom they had sufficient respect to obey.

She began to toy with a song of Dowland's. She didn't know why it should be but she felt suddenly rather sad. She decided she did not care for Lady Hartley. She did not seem to be sincere, only emptily courteous, as far as the younger Herons were concerned anyway. She neither looked nor behaved, Lucy thought, much like a widow. Perhaps she had been widowed for a very long time. She certainly couldn't imagine her wearing black veiling, unless perhaps to create a dramatic impression.

The visitors were persuaded to remain for a week. It was an unusually festive week. Sir George left the greater part of the overseeing of the harvesting to the steward, Walter Rollins, who was given the ancient title of Lord of the Harvest, enabling him to keep good discipline in the fields so that everyone worked unstintingly towards the 'largesse', the bonus they could expect when the last grain was in. It was not like the baronet to trust this valuable work entirely to another, and he did find time to go out and encourage or curse the workers as he thought fit, choosing hours when his guests were still abed or engaged on one of the long rides they took alone together, a habit much discussed in the household.

'I guess he be courtin' her,' Tibbett remarked to Margery Kitchen.

'Get away with you, you girt lummox,' mocked large Mistress Margery. 'Any woman'd tell you as it be her as is courtin' him!'

Certainly there was a spark between the cousins that made them as lively a presence as any dozen others could have been. It seemed to Lucy that there had rarely been so much gaiety at Heronscourt, and that sustained at such a high pitch. Surely so much drinking and laughing, dancing and playing of cards had never been attempted by a mere four persons. Her father's cheerful thunder filled the house and her mother was more animated than she had been for many a month, her eyes sparkling like a girl's at some compliment of Will's over a table, her steps about the house still in the rhythm of the dance. Once, when he had praised the soft bloom of her skin, Lucy had seen Lady Hartley's eyes snap at her as though she were dry twigs to fire. She began to be of Margery's opinion.

It was some days before Will sought out Lucy again at her virginals. Eliza seemed always to discover something else for him to do. But one morning, while the lady still slept, he heard the sound of the keyboard and presented himself in the gallery. 'No, don't stop. It is a fine piece. You have it a little differently, I think.'

Lucy took him at his word and finished her experiment. 'It was just for a change. Master Byrd's way is better.'

'I don't think I prefer it; yours is more complex.'

Lucy was pleased. 'But I couldn't have made it so if he had not already suggested the possibility,' she said honestly, 'Listen; here –' She played the phrase that had led to her variation.

'Of course!' he cried. 'Or, you might take it like this –' He sat beside her on the long bench and executed a swift improvisation of his own. They finished together, both smiling at the accomplishment.

'Have you written anything of your own, Lucy?' he asked. He spoke to her as an equal, a fellow music lover. Like this, he was good company and she could not help being flattered. Also, he played as well as she did and his enthusiasm was as great. Lucy began to like him. Shyly, she showed him the songs she had written.

When they had sung them all as duets, followed by a very rowdy rendition of a haymaking song that Lucy had just learned, they stopped for breath and she took the opportunity to ask after her old friend and adversary, Master Robin Whittaker.

'The scapegrace does little better than before, except that now he has your brother to aid and abet. They have a good deal in common, those two – let us hope it does not hang 'em both!'

'Mercy! Is it really as bad as that?' Lucy was dismayed. Her father would have no more patience with Jud if he ruined his chances with Silken Will. She told him as much and he was instantly solicitous.

'Never fear. Jud loves a pickle as well as the next high-spirited lad of his age – but he has the sense to see where is his advantage. He may set London by the ears with Rob Whittaker in his spare hours, but in *my* time he is quick with the figures and charming with the customers, and I think, enjoys his work. I ask for nothing better: Do not worry, little Lucy. Time and patience, both mine and his, will make an excellent merchant out of Jud.'

'I am very glad to hear that. My thanks to you,' said Lucy, relieved. She had once met Jud's old tutor at Lincoln's Inn, a craggy scholar with a cynical eye. He had told her father in her hearing that Jud was as like to turn to crime as to concern himself with its prevention or punishment. Jud had been beaten raw.

Her mind at rest, and finding Will so ready to talk, Lucy satisfied her curiosity on various other points. Was the *Gallant Lady* finished yet, and where would she sail, and would Jud go with her?

'She is very near done. There is a small matter of gilding and painting, that is all. She will sail for various eastern ports and return laden with silks and spices and make us all rich. What shall she bring back for you – a monkey, a Turkish slave, a bolt of Damascus silk?'

'The monkey, if that's my choice – but I'd sooner have another instrument of some kind, a strange pipe or a zither.'

'You shall have one. I will give instructions,' he promised. 'You are almost a member of our company, now that your father has done us the honour to invest in our voyage.'

Lucy wanted to ask Will if he were a pirate, but this seemed impolite and ungrateful at this moment. Instead, she thanked him prettily and, to cover her embarrassment at so much attention, asked him if he was really in the habit of importing monkeys in his cargoes.

'Indeed, yes. I have brought two of the creatures from the north coast of Africa, for Her Majesty the Queen, who loves anything small and quaint, probably because she is so herself. However, at present her needs are rather greater, as you will have gathered from your father. I shall have to cough up my thousand livres like a loyal servant, or she'll accept no more monkeys from me.'

'But *must* one give one's monkey to the King and Queen? I do not think it very fair, if it is not a tax.'

'It is a tax, in a manner of speaking,' Will said. 'For if Parliament will vote no money to the King, how else is he to get it?' Lucy felt ill-equipped to go further into these matters. Instead she asked him if he often went to court.

He grinned. 'As infrequently as possible. Every time I meet His Majesty he offers me a knighthood, which I most ungraciously refuse. This too, as you know, is a costly business.'

Lucy nodded disapprovingly. Almost everyone spoke of the King's habit of selling knighthoods and fining their refusal as unworthy. 'I am glad you refuse. I think it is foolish. One cannot buy an escutcheon. It has to be built up by years.'

'Quite so, mistress. Alas, if only my blood were as blue as a Heron's,' he added mischievously.

'Oh dear! I am sorry. I didn't mean it to sound like that. What a prig you must think me.'

'Not at all. I think you very honest and sensible. If you maintain these qualities until you are grown you will be a very unusual woman.'

Flustered, Lucy continued hastily, 'Anyway, your blood is probably much bluer than ours. You are related to the great Earl of Warwick while father has only a baronetcy.'

'Nevertheless, I am a commoner. My mother, though she was born a Rich, and a Viscount's daughter, married for love and not family.'

'How lucky she was,' said Lucy with grown-up gravity. 'Such things are not easy, I know. My brother Tom cannot persuade his chosen lady that it is the right thing to do. Though her problem is not family, exactly, but faith,' she added sadly.

'Valora Grey is known for a strong-minded woman. He'll not find it easy to school her to his way of thinking.'

'No indeed, but she is kind and loving too . . .' On an impulse Lucy told Will about her unfortunate 'spell' and its dire effect upon Lady Grey.

So it was that when Eliza Hartley wafted into the gallery in a great deal of perfume and an enticingly tight green riding habit, she found her cousin chuckling mightily, with his arm thrown around the shoulder of that damnable little musical minx, and obviously enjoying her company. Will, she knew, had a very great gift for enjoyment. It was a major part of his charm and one which she had long been delighted to help him to develop. She was planning to do just that this very morning. She came to their side and stood a second or so until she was noticed, a forbearing smile affixed.

The perfume did its work and Will swung round on the stool. 'Forgive me, my dear. I didn't hear you come in. We have been singing like two birds in a nest. Will you join us for a round?'

'I thought we were to go riding.' The delightful smile lessened.

'Ah yes, indeed. I had quite forgot.' His eyes teased her. He had not forgotten at all. 'I'm afraid I must leave you, Lucy. It has been a most pleasant time. *A la prochaine!*' He rose and stretched his long legs.

Lucy's education did not extend to French but she did not wish to prove this before Lady Hartley, who was tapping her foot with obvious impatience at Will's gallantry. 'Yes. It has been very pleasant,' she agreed. 'I hope that you will enjoy your ride,' she added courteously to Eliza.

'Make no doubt of it,' replied Eliza, her words for Lucy, her look, which was loose-lipped and inviting, all for Will. They went out, walking very close together, Lucy quite forgotten.

Lucy wondered what she would do now. She was tired of playing. It would not be so much fun, alone again. She crashed a chord or two in a sudden irritation then flung off to a windowseat. She kicked her heels there for a while, then fetched a deep sigh and went downstairs. She would go to her private place. She felt the need of its peace. There was too much going on at Heron these days.

As always, the way through the wood laid a calm approbation upon her spirit as though she were given a blessing. It was a hot day and the heat had collected between the trees so that it was like wading through warm water as she trod the spongy moss and grass. There was a great deal of light too, like that in a church when the stained glass is new. Lucy felt warm and welcomed and caressed. She hummed to herself in tuneless contentment for a while, then stopped so that she could listen to the silence.

The quiet was as heavy as the heat, its presence as deeply felt as her own. The sounds of the brook, of the few birds taking the shade, of the intermittent conversation of leaves, were all parts of its being, rather than of its opposite. Then she heard another sound, a stranger. She listened again. It was the chink of metal. Then came the soft snuffing of a horse. Not far away. Not near either.

Lucy was annoyed. Whoever it was, he might be in the way of her path. She never met anyone on these occasions and did not wish to now. She sat down, thinking she would wait until she heard the horseman move on.

Again the chink of harness, the horsey snuffling. The rider could be asleep. He might remain for an hour.

She longed to get to her private place. It was still a considerable distance away. She might as well pass him by. She would try to avoid coming too close to him.

She walked on with instinctive stealth, her feet hardly bruising the grass. She followed her usual path, listening for the sounds that would guide her out of the way of the intruder. She was coming very near to him now. The horse stamped and snickered, making her jump. They must be almost on top of the path. Lucy muttered one of Jud's favourite oaths. Then she stopped short, brought up by a sudden different sound. It was a giggle. And it was female.

Disgust and disappointment flooded over Lucy. She recognized that self-satisfied tone. It could only be Cousin Eliza. She stood hesitating, uncertain whether to turn back or try to pass them unseen. It would be difficult. There was no undergrowth here, only the beeches, elms and birches and a carpet of ferns. She had half decided to go back when she heard more laughter, Will's too, this time.

She stood, curious now. She could get a little closer if she struck off to the right. She didn't question the rightness of her instinct. She had followed too many hapless quarries with her brothers to remember parlour manners.

She flitted between the trunks, certain of invisibility in the worn green dress. She could see the horses now, standing contentedly, browsing the grass. There were no human figures to be seen. And then the voices came again, soft, intimate, and surely not far away from the horses.

Where were they?

Of course! She had it. They must be sitting down. They would not be easy to see among the ferns. She moved forward, aware now of her own noisy heartbeat. Then she nearly leaped out of her skin as Will's voice, dreadfully close, said lazily, 'M'mm. Delicious! I've been wanting to do that.'

Lucy clapped her hand to her mouth in case she let out a sound. She could see them now, much nearer than she had thought them. If she had continued she might well have tripped over them. For they were not sitting but lying in the soft grass, canopied by the waving branches, cradled in fern. Will, supporting himself on one elbow, hung over Cousin Eliza's supine body, his fingers moving dexterously among her laces.

'You look particularly fetching in that gown,' he murmured, his voice muffled as he concentrated on what he was doing.

'Then why are you removing it?' asked Eliza, with creamy anticipation.

'So that I can show you what it has fetched.'

There was further laughter and no more talk for the moment. Lucy wondered what to do. Half of her wished Humpty and Kit were with her to share the fun, as they had when they once tracked Dickon and Alice Gibb from the village to the hay barn; the other half knew she was both too old for such a pastime, and also too young.

She could hear them breathing now, harder and faster, just as Dickon and Alice had done. She would go. This was unworthy of her.

Just as she was turning away, Will stood up, pulling Eliza with him. 'It's no use. I can't get the confounded thing undone. Turn round and keep still, damn you!'

Lucy dropped to the ground, thankful that she had her own share of greenery for cover. Since she must stay, she may as well look.

What she saw was quite unnerving. Cousin Eliza stood limply entwined in Will's arms. Her brave green habit hung about her waist with the top of her shift, while the corset that had pushed up her breasts was relieved of its duty by Will's large hands which weighed and stroked them as if they were summer plums whose ripeness he tested. Lucy's eyes were riveted by the breasts. They were startlingly white, even whiter than the rest of the exposed, milky flesh, but what drew her eye was their flaunting, russet tips which stood out like Jouncey's when she fed baby Edward. Even as she thought so, Will bent his own lips to one of them, with every evidence that his enjoyment was as great as Ned's.

By this time Lucy could not have ceased to watch.

Will scooped up Eliza to shoulder height, kissed her long and thoroughly then slowly bent to lay her on his cloak. She was soon completely naked apart from the itinerant covering of his hands. Into Lucy's mind came the words of one of Dean Donne's forbidden poems – 'What need thou better covering than a man?'

The Dean, despite his latter saintliness, would perhaps have approved of Eliza Hartley's state. She seemed larger when naked. There were light, fading lines about her where her dress had been tight. Her hair had come undone and was falling about Will's dark blue cloak in a tangle of deep crimson curls. Her face looked quite different now. In public it had seemed superior, sardonic and watchful. Now it was relaxed and somehow heavier, her mouth swollen and very wet, her pale lids weighted over slitted, expectant eyes.

She rubbed her breasts against the silk of Will's shirt which she had pulled out of his breeches, though he was still clothed, apart from his boots, which he had pulled off and flung exuberantly into the brake. She made an impatient movement and he tossed the shirt after them so that now she could press herself against his skin.

He had a healthy sunbronzed body, well-muscled, his chest golden-haired. He looked as if he spent a lot of time without his shirt. Eliza moved her hand over him in caressing waves, from the curled chest to the opening of his breeches, but though he ground down her hand into his groin for a moment, he shook his head after, rolled a little way from her, and smiling, drew his hands slowly down each successive curve of her body, lingering a very little in certain places, but only a little.

'It's so much better if we wait,' he suggested, stretching like a spoiled cat who knows the cream will be waiting.

'Tantalus –' But she lay back on her elbow in imitation of Will and in turn drew one delicate finger across the hills and valleys of his own private geography, coming, after prolonged and determined circumnavigation, to an impassable ridge which apparently required a more geological investigation.

Lucy had seen naked men and women before, but never quite like this. She began to realize that on the occasion of Dickon and Alice she had, in fact, seen very little, and imagined not much more. Their two bodies were much closer now, though Will still seemed to hold back from something that Cousin Eliza evidently wanted very much. She was still running her fingers all over him, though rather feverishly now, making grand impatient sweeps of his golden skin, her eyes glittering as though with greed, as she whispered huskily, 'So it is for this they call you Silken Will? And I had always thought you christened so by men, not women.'

Staunton gave a brief forbearing laugh, then seemed to come to some decision. He gathered in his body like a man who has work to do and putting madam firmly on her back, swung himself astride. There was elegance and control in all his movements and from here on it was evident that, though his mistress might have initiated a good deal at the start, he was now her master and intended to treat her accordingly.

What happened next seemed to Lucy very much like what happened in the farmyard. The horses and cows, however, being unable to smile, had never displayed the enjoyment that shone so beautifully upon Will Staunton's blazing face. His eyes sparked like a tinder box; his smile was that of a pirate taking a prize. His single earring jiggled in participatory glee. All in all he looked so astonishingly pleased with himself that Lucy had to laugh.

She froze in the instant she stifled the sound, cramming her fingers, shaking, into her mouth. Her eyes had closed in fright.

When she opened them again the lovers lay relaxed and inter-twined, silent and motionless for the moment. Lucy felt that she had been there for a century and wondered if she was going to get away as easily as she had come here. They would hear any extraneous sound more acutely now that they were less preoccu-pied.

All desire to laugh had left her. She felt more like crying. Time dragged itself, wounded. The enormity of her behaviour hit her sickeningly. She was conscious of having done something so hugely unforgivable that she would have to spend years in purgatory for it. She knew that the 'sins of the flesh' were the extremity of wickedness, if not made blessed by marriage. She had taken part in such a sin by being its witness. She was sure Dominic would think so. Lady Hartley and Will Staunton must be very wicked indeed, but she was almost as bad.

She wiped her eyes with her knuckle to stop the tears trickling. She tried to pull herself together and think. She had better leave the scene now, before they had got dressed again. They were hardly likely to follow, even if they heard her. If she kept low, they might not even see her.

Unable to bear another second, she dashed suddenly back along her path. It sounded to her as though she made enough noise for a disturbed herd as she missed the way and crashed into the bracken.

At any rate it was enough to make Will Staunton prick up his ears. 'What the Devil – ? Here, I say – you there – ! God's boots, I'll not have this! Get dressed Eliza.' He flung this good advice back at her as he ran, fastening his breeches, after the peeping Tom he expected to catch. He was a swift runner, as accustomed to do without shoes as shirt, if necessary, and soon gained on the unfortunate Lucy who by this time had lost all sense of direction and was entirely given over to panic. When the iron grip took her arm she shrieked as though it were the Devil's pitchfork, quite beside herself.

'Lucy! Great heavens, child, hold your peace! There's no need to howl like that. I won't hurt you.' He gave her a little shake and waited until her eyes lost their wild, uncomprehending look and filled with shame.

'Now then, stay calm and tell me what you were doing here. Did you follow us? Are your brothers with you?'

'N-o, no,' she hiccuped. 'I *didn't* follow you. I was going to my private place – and you were in the way,' she finished, sniffing tragically. 'I didn't want to – see you. I couldn't help it.'

Will wondered shrewdly just how long she had been there, but decided that this was not a question to ask. He did not want to humiliate Lucy any further. He could see that she was suffering quite enough to punish her for any childish curiosity which she might have indulged. 'Very well. There is nothing to cry about. I had thought you more grown up than that . . .'

She stared at him dumbly, wishing she could disappear from the face of the earth.

'I'd lend you my kerchief if I had one about me,' said Will cheerfully. 'But as you see, I am temporarily at a loss.'

The effect of this reminder of his semi-naked state was to start the tears again as she thought of what she had just witnessed. She turned her brimming eyes away from his chest as if it were an obscenity and blushed to the roots of her being.

'Oh, sweetheart! Come, I assure you it isn't as bad as all that.' He put out a hand to touch her shoulder and she flinched and stepped backward with a gasp. Then she gave a different kind of desperate sound and he saw that she looked behind him into the wood.

He turned to face Eliza whose expression resembled that of the famous basilisk. She thrust past him, full of purpose and took Lucy painfully by the arm, glaring into her face. 'You filthy little trollop! You will have a beating for this that you will remember all your life! I will see to it.' Lucy, though now doubly miserable, reacted with her normal logic to this injustice. 'I scarcely see how *you* may call *me* a trollop. As I understand the word, it is more correctly applicable to yourself, madam.' This earned her a resounding slap that made her grit her teeth so as not to cry out.

'Hold hard, Eliza,' said Will quietly, releasing Lucy's arm from the bruising grip. 'There is no need for this. The child meant no harm. She was merely walking in the wood.'

'You're a fool if you think so,' said Eliza with contempt. 'And she is no child, as I make sure you can see. She is old enough to wish you would do with her what she has seen you do with me. Have you not seen her cow's eyes follow you wherever you go?'

Lucy stared at her in horror for a burning second, then she could bear the awful moment no longer. With a stifled wail she burst past Will Staunton and fled through the trees, sobbing as though her world had ended.

'That was cruel, Eliza,' Will told his cousin, looking regretfully after the running figure. 'And unnecessary. Why, in God's name, did you have to do that? And that last remark? She *is* a child still, and an innocent one. But perhaps you do not like to be reminded of a quality so long lost to you? If indeed you ever possessed it, my dear.'

'I possessed it until you relieved me of it,' she said fiercely, 'you forget that.'

'Not I,' he replied with a smile. 'I remember it with great pleasure. It was, as you suggest, a relief to you. You had no desire to remain a virgin, as I recall.'

'I was a child then, as young as that little draggle-tail.'

'You were never a child, Eliza,' he said, weary of the argument.

'No, perhaps not,' she agreed, coming close to him, her whole body indicating a change of mood. 'I was a woman from the first time I met my handsome cousin. I wanted you then, and I still do.'

'Well, you have me,' he said with faint irritability, 'so why the need to torment young Lucy. You can scarcely regard her as a rival.'

'I regard her as an impudent brat who must be taught her manners.'

'You still plan to get her a beating? I'd be interested to know how.' He smiled coldly. 'You can hardly explain the situation to her father and beg a whipping of him.'

'Why not? I may say simply that she was spying on us.'

'And saw what, a chaste kiss? Do you think she will not tell the truth if she is asked?'

'Hades, no! How could she, for very shame?'

His look was ironic, 'I do not think you have quite got Mistress Lucy's measure, dear cousin. She is accustomed to tell the truth, even if it shames her as well as the Devil. She *would* tell, make no mistake about that.'

She stared at him, mutinous. 'Why don't you finish dressing,' he suggested coolly, 'then I will help you to put up your hair and we will continue our pleasant ride.'

When Lucy got back to the house she raced upstairs and threw herself on her bed in a tempest of tears. She hated herself and could not bear the feeling. There was nothing worse than a sneaky, peeping eavesdropper! If only she had turned back the moment she had realized who they were.

She finished crying, sat up and pushed back her hair, wiping her eyes on the coverlet. Then she got off the bed and washed her face in the water that always stood in the ewer. She looked doubtfully in the mirror above her little dresser. She didn't *look* any different, but she felt nasty and grubby in her soul. She wished Will Staunton and his odious cousin had never come to Heron.

To make matters worse, the silliest thing she could have done was to have run away; it meant that she would not learn the outcome of the misadventure perhaps until some dreadful public moment. Would Lady Hartley complain of her, and if so, to whom? She imagined her mother might feel it discreet, however severely she punished her, to keep such scandalous behaviour to herself, but her father would hammer it out to the whole household in his choicest Shakespearean language. She would never be able to hold up her head again. She despaired. The rest of her life would be shadowed by this horrible morning.

As for what she had seen, she could hardly bear to think about it. She knew that she could never face Will Staunton or that horrible woman again as long as she lived. Nor could she erase from her mind the disgusting thing Eliza Hartley had said – that she herself wanted Will to do with her what he had done with his cousin. It had been an enormity that she had not known how to deal with. It had made her feel more dirty and uncomfortable than all the rest of it together, not because there was any truth in it; how could there be? But because Will might have thought there was, and she had been beginning to like Will and to trust him. And now he would despise her, and quite rightly, and maybe think other, worse things of her, things that Lady Hartley understood how to hint at, and from which Lucy had no means of defending herself. No, she could not see either of them again. Somehow, she must find a way to avoid their company until they left Heronscourt. It should not be too difficult. They would leave in the early morning two days from now.

The only problem was the dancing.

Tomorrow her parents were giving an entertainment, with dancing, for the gentry of the whole county, in honour of the guests. They would certainly expect Lucy to attend, and though she might easily make herself scarce during an ordinary day without its being much marked, she could hardly do so upon such a rare occasion.

Unless she were ill. She examined herself in the mirror again. She did look rather flushed, and she truly felt far from normal. Perhaps she would take a fever and be allowed to keep to her bed. But it was not really very likely, she saw that, however convenient it might be.

She sighed and sat down hopelessly on the bed. There must be a way out, but she just couldn't see it. She must just take it hour by hour, keeping well out of the way and waiting to see whether Lady Hartley complained of her. She would soon know if this were the case; nothing so sure as that. Very soon she found that, since she was not ill at all, keeping to her chamber was an impossibility; she was far too restless. Accordingly she decided to filch herself some bread and cheese from the kitchen and then seek out Dominic in the garden where he usually spent part of the afternoon. She would be safe enough there. She knew that Will and that woman were to ride over to the Strattons' with her father.

She found Cousin Nick seated on a bench at the end of the vista in the Italian garden, energetically discussing a book, which was open on his knees, with the pale-faced tutor, Master Davies.

At the sight of Lucy, Davies rose. 'I am expecting a dissertation upon virtue from you, Miss Lucy. I trust you will have it ready at the appointed time.' He never could bear to see her in the sunlight.

'I trust so, Master Davies,' she said sweetly. Virtue! Holy wounds! The tutor bowed stiffly to Dominic then made his way between the borders without once turning his head to look at a flower or a tree. As for the statues, he had made it quite clear that he considered them lewd, though most of them were clothed in a wonderful selection of drapery held up by, presumably, the will of God.

Lucy pulled down her mouth. 'I often see you with him lately, Dominic; how can you stomach such sad company?'

'Oh, he's well enough. He seeks me out, I don't know why. He likes to discuss morality and religion. I have to be very careful with the religion. It's a tax on my mind, I can tell you; I have to avoid the pitfalls of popery and still give him opinions.'

'Be careful, won't you? Though I don't suppose he matters. He's such a dry old stick.'

'He's a young man, Lucy,' Dominic smiled. 'His problem is that he seems to have forgotten it.'

'Well, I am glad he's gone, because I have a problem too. I'd like you to discuss morality with *me*, if you would.'

He noted her sober tone and turned sympathetically towards her.

'What would you do,' she demanded, 'if you had done something wicked, but it wasn't your fault – well, not altogether – and you were expecting to be punished, only nobody seems to know you should be?'

Dominic considered the implications and gave them deep thought. 'If it really was not my fault,' he said decidedly, 'then there is no real wickedness involved, merely – a mistake, perhaps?' he suggested with a query of the brow.

Lucy thought it over in this light. 'It certainly *began* as a mistake,' she said sadly, 'but I think it went on as wickedness.' She looked so depressed that he wanted to smile but sensed the seriousness of her purpose.

'Ah. Well, in that case, I think I would say that to the just man – or woman – his own repentance is the greatest punishment.'

Lucy's face cleared a little. Then she remembered. 'But if one is expecting another punishment, eventually?'

'Then I imagine the *waiting* is an even greater penance.'

She nodded glumly.

'Lucy, my dear child, just what is it that you think you have done?'

She blushed. 'I couldn't possibly tell you, not ever.'

'Of course not, if you don't want to, though people of my faith find the father confessor a most merciful relief. I don't know what you can do, apart from to put yourself in the way of those whom you think should punish you, and wait and see. But you are obviously penitent, and therefore God has already forgiven you. You should draw your strength from that.'

Lucy was doubtful. 'Thank you. I will try to, only I hope it is enough. I don't feel very strong about it.'

He put an arm affectionately around her shoulders. 'It will be enough, you'll see. And now, though I am not your confessor, I will give you a penance among the weeds, and I, for my own sins and your mother's kindness, shall share it.'

The afternoon thus passed without too much agonizing, and Lucy found later, a source half of relief, half of further tension, that the visitors had remained at Stratton Hall and would stay the night, bringing the Strattons back on the morrow for the ball. So it was that, even had she wished to 'put herself in the way' of her punishment, it was not possible. There was no sign of them at either breakfast or dinner and she was forced to spend most of the afternoon standing still, stuck all over with pins, while Jouncey and the sewing maid finished the new dress she was to wear that evening.

Normally she would have been delighted to have something new but today she simply felt like St Sebastian, prickling with arrows like a porcupine, and it was all she could do to keep her temper with those who wanted to help her.

'You're goin' to look a real treat, miss,' Jouncey beamed, pinning down the lace that framed the neckline.

'That's too low. I usually have them higher.'

'You don't want it no higher'n that, Miss Lucy. This is a real grown-uppity gown. You want to show them what you got, not hide it away. Just look at this waist, Mog; 'ave you ever seen a smaller? 'Tis as tiddy as a babby's.' The maid cooed agreement.

'Ow! You're cutting me in two!'

'Get on with you. Just you take a deep breath and keep quiet.'

The dress was the colour of ripening apricots, its lace dyed to match the silk. There was a little gold fan to dangle at her wrist. Even though it meant wearing the despicable corset, so tight that at first she thought she might faint, she could see that she did look very nice and her shape seemed almost new to her.

'I think we'll put your hair up, miss,' suggested Jouncey.

'There isn't enough of it to put up.'

'No, but I can make it look as though there is. Trust me.'

So it was that when she descended to the great hall to welcome the guests with her parents, even they beheld a different Lucy from the elfin child they had expected. There was a good deal of murmuring about it. Lady Stratton told her that she had grown, and carried herself so beautifully these days. Ribs cracking, Lucy smiled her thanks. Her new shape was remarked upon in various ways. Her father, staring her pointedly in the bosom, declared to anyone who wanted to know that his daughter was developing nicely. Isabella Stratton said enviously, 'You've got titties; are they real?'

Perhaps the person who most noticed her appearance was the one before whom she would have wished to be invisible. Elizabeth Hartley, this night, was dressed to enslave. Like her silken cousin on the occasion of his first meeting with the Heron family, she was gilded all over like some brilliant statue to herself.

The effect was superb, from the dyed osprey plumes in her tiara to her narrow gold kid slippers. Even her pale skin had taken on the tint of sunlight. She carried herself like the Queen of Sheba, very much aware of her own grandeur. It was just as well she did not hear Kit's whispered compliment which was that she reminded him of a specially good pork pie – all luscious golden crust. Around her neck were her dead husband's rubies, worth a tenth of his barony, and on her arm, worn with as careless an air, was Silken Will, gleaming in his favourite scarlet, wearing earrings he had won from an Indian prince.

As this grand procession of two crossed the hall towards their hosts, the crowd parted as though before royalty. The county was got up in its best to do honour to Heronscourt, but their silks and satins faded into mere daytime things before the glitter and panache that were Will and his Cousin Eliza.

Her ladyship was not best pleased, therefore, to find before her a small, proud figure in peach silk, with a wealth of fashionably dressed golden curls and a waist that could be spanned by a couple of glad hands. So mortified was she by Lucy's transformation that she almost forgot her duty to her hosts. Recovering quickly, she murmured soft compliments to Mary Heron upon the appearance of the hall, whose lambent candlelight blessed the guests with their best looks. Then she turned sweetly to Sir George, flashing him a flattering eye, and totally ignored his daughter.

Not so, Will Staunton, who had shown an appreciative smile the moment he had set eyes on Lucy. 'My dear, you look ravishing,' he told her quietly, with no hint of teasing in his manner. 'All of a sudden the elf has become Titania.' He took her hand and kissed it to underline the homage.

Lucy flinched and withdrew her hand, her mind in a welter of apprehension. This was by no means lost on Eliza who gave a peal of laughter, its bells faintly out of tune. 'And to think that only yesterday, she was romping through the woods like a gipsy, playing her childish games.'

Lucy's stomach took a downward plunge. Surely the creature could not be about to expose her here and now, in front of all the people? But no.

'Much as you were yourself, my dear,' Will suggested pleasantly. 'I seem to recall a decidedly gipsy quality about your own behaviour at certain moments, though I'm sure your games were not at all childish,' he finished with an innocent air. 'Now come with me. I believe we are to start the dancing.'

He took her firmly by the arm and led her away into the crush in the great chamber, where the local gentry thronged and buzzed, exchanging news for rumour and bewailing the state of the nation. Lucy, reprieved, continued to greet guests automatically, and allowed the sweet realization to sink in on her – no one was going to complain of her behaviour, because their own was every bit as scandalous, more so in fact. Staunton had made that quite clear, perhaps had even intended to reasure her, for he indeed had shown no anger at her spying, had rather seemed angry with his cousin. And yet none of this had occurred to her, so concerned had she been with her own guilt.

This sudden release was too much for her. She no longer knew what she felt. She would not be punished, because she was not to be found out; but her wrongdoing was not altered, nor was her supreme embarrassment. Will Staunton was a kind man, but she still could not look him in the eye without recalling how she had seen him in the bracken. And Lady Eliza was not kind, and would be her enemy if they ever met again. All that Lucy could hope was that they would not meet again, and that Will Staunton would conduct his business with her father in London and come no more to Heron.

These hopes cheered her a little. After all, they would leave tomorrow and she need not see them again tonight, not at all if she were careful. She may as well, therefore, enjoy the ball. It *was* her first grown-up occasion and she had promised dances to several partners, some of them as old as Tom. She would not forget Kit and Humpty either, forbidden the dancing chamber on pain of whipping and ordered to bed at ten; she would take them some of the nicest things to eat and a good slug of punch to make them drowsy and not think of mischief.

Lucy loved dancing and after her first few turns about the floor, where there was no sign of those she wished to avoid, she was flushed and happy from music, movement and her first genuine masculine compliments – if you didn't count Will Staunton's. Ralph Stratton, awful Isabella's seventeen-year-old brother, had even began to murmur sweet nothings into her hair until she told him to stop or it would all fall down.

This pleasant state of affairs might have lasted till dawn had not Sir Jo Stratton brought his grandmother to the feast. This ancient and autocratic dowager was a byword in the county. She had an iron constitution and a will to match and was generally to be found reorganizing some hapless underling's life to suit her fancy. Informed of Lucy's new good looks, she expressed a desire to view the phenomenon. Lucy was commanded into her presence.

She found the old lady, encased in black velvet and what seemed to be crow's feathers, domineering a small group who stood about the fireplace in the large parlour. This consisted, unfortunately for Lucy, chiefly of her parents, the Strattons, Will and the glittering Eliza, who stood fanning herself with languid boredom.

The next half hour passed like the submerged and illogical

events of an early morning dream where the sleeper tries to awake but cannot drag herself towards the light. Greeting old Lady Stratton was the easy part; Lucy was welcomed with a bristly kiss and a fierce examination of shrewd short-sighted eyes. 'She's going to be a beauty,' was the prognosis, 'not in the usual way of things – her face is all wrong for that – but in her own way, which is better. *I* have always looked my own way, done things my own way, and *got* my own way, and I can recommend it,' the beldame finished triumphantly.

'Thank you, madam. I hope I may follow you in that,' said Lucy politely, keeping her eyes unwaveringly on her advisor.

'I think she is already well set upon *that* path, Lady Stratton,' Eliza Hartley said softly, 'though some of her ways are passing strange.'

'Eh? What'd'ye mean by that, my gilded peahen?'

Will stepped in before feathers should become over ruffled. 'My cousin has spent her time in London and at court; she is not versed in country ways,' he said, looking hard at Eliza.

'Alas no,' said the unrepentant lady, 'but I may always apply to young Lucy if I wish to learn more of country matters.'

'Eh, what?' puzzled Sir George for whom Hamlet was sacred. Lucy, who knew the quotation as well as her sire, blushed furiously.

'Are you too hot, child?' enquired Mary Heron. 'Sit down awhile.' The only seat was a footstool next to Lady Stratton's chair. She took it and hoped they would forget her.

For a time, they did. Her octogenarian ladyship, who was an indefatigable royalist, born in the early years of Elizabeth's reign and possessed of many of her less feminine qualities, now considered it her duty to lend her aid and support to the present incumbents of the throne. She had watched the struggle for supremacy between monarch and Parliament across three reigns and was no fool as to where the advantages lay. Her concern tonight was with Sir Henry Gurney, King's man and candidate for election as the next Lord Mayor of London. Her aim was to open as many fat purses as she could in his cause. 'Who rules London, rules England,' she reminded them, banging her ebony cane. 'If you want to see the King made powerless in his own capital, let them put a Puritan in the Mayor's office.' There was a murmur of agreement. All were loyal here.

'Very well, then – you, sir, Will Staunton. I've heard ill as well as good of you. Will you prove yourself an honest man and the King's loyal servant by forsaking that monstrous friend of yours for once in a way and lending your good right arm to Sir Harry's election?'

'I'll give you my good right arm gladly, madam – for I am left-handed and it would cost me little and allow me to fight shy of swordsmen! But my good yellow gold – now there is quite another matter!'

She allowed him to tease her but did not budge an inch. 'Your arm would not grow out again, should you be so asinine as to remove it – but your money might well return to you much increased, with your monarch's gratitude. With trade in the sick case that it is, you should be able to use such golden thanks. Are you so lukewarm an investor? And you so ready to take other men's money.' She looked knowingly at Sir George, who was uncomfortably aware that he must have told her more of his affairs than he had meant to do.

Will needed no advice from this quarter to know that it was as well, in these turbulent times, to butter one's bread on both sides. He had also some personal respect for Harry Gurney, whom he knew. John Pym and his other partners in the New Providence Company would not grudge what they did not know about. He turned a brilliant smile upon the old witch in black. 'How much am I to be – allowed – to invest in the gentleman?'

Lady Stratton was delighted with her victory. 'Oh, I must leave that to your generosity. But they do say,' she said airily, 'that you have a famous hoard of Spanish doubloons that was once a duke's ransom.'

'If only it were true!' he sorrowed.

'Then you would be one of the richest men in England as well as one of the wickedest,' her ladyship cackled happily.

'Dear me, is that my reputation. How can I have earned it?' Will pondered, looking rather hurt.

'A dangerous combination indeed,' drawled Eliza, wetting her lips as she remembered some of the wickedness.

'What he needs is a good wife, to keep him in good sense,' declared the old lady, startling them. 'He should not be left to dally about, breaking reputations.' She gave Eliza an extremely searching look, but if she expected a blush she was disappointed.

'Oh, aye,' agreed Sir George cheerfully, 'we must marry him off before he becomes a public nuisance.'

Eliza Hartley knew perfectly well that she was spoken of as her cousin's whore, though she did not relish the old bitch's putting it further about. She had long ago made up her mind to marry Will. She had known since she was fifteen that to do so would

take patience and skill, and above all, time. He had left her under
no illusions when he had taken her young virginity, nor later,
when, shortly before her bedridden, ageing and very rich husband
had died, she had again become his mistress. He enjoyed her
body and her company; they were two of a kind, dedicated to
pleasure and their own advancement, but he did not love her.
Love was not a word he used. However, one day, like every other
man, he would require an heir. They had done very well together
thus far; why then, should he not eventually make her his wife?
He could never ask for a warmer bed. She was beautiful, cultured
and had more money than she knew what to do with. And then
there was her uncle of Warwick. This gentleman was as appreciative of Eliza's talents as she was herself. With him on her side, his
influence, his wealth, his supremacy in trade and at sea, she would
have a very heavy weapon with which to demolish any doubts in
Will. However, she was not yet ready for the assault.

'If you were to marry him off,' she said, all honey, 'he would
simply become a great nuisance to one woman instead of a small
one to us all.'

Lady Stratton grunted. She had taken a dislike to Eliza, of
whose strength and beauty she was retrospectively jealous. Also
she thought that she understood her game with her cousin. For
her own amusement, which was scarce and poor in quality
nowadays, she would try her out. 'Then he must marry a very
young wife,' she said craftily, 'one who will need his overseeing
so regularly that he will have no time to spend upon others. Let
me see,' she wondered, warming to her theme, 'whom shall it be?'
She looked about for a likely candidate. Anyone would do.

Her eye fell on Lucy. 'Why not your daughter here, Sir George?
She will need a husband in a season or two. From what my
wantwit great-granddaughter tells me, she has brains to match
her looks, and you'll not see her short of her portion. Will
Staunton can finish sowing his wild oats while he waits for her to
grow.'

Will shrugged and grinned apologetically at Lucy. Sir George
became suddenly more awake. To Lucy the evening seemed
suddenly transfixed, like a Gaul on a Roman sword; and herself
the bleeding heart of it. They were looking at her. All of them.

'Well, child, what say you?' Lady Stratton demanded, watching
Eliza Hartley whose face was a picture.

A voice that didn't seem to belong to Lucy gasped, 'Oh no,
madam! I couldn't possibly. That is I don't –' She could *feel* her
thoughts scurrying about inside her head, searching desperately

for a release. The awful voice that wasn't hers decided to continue. 'Besides,' it blurted, 'Master Staunton prefers more mature meat than I fear my meagre bones will ever supply!'

She stood her ground for a moment, meeting the baleful gaze of Eliza, then, vanquished by the total impossibility of her situation, bolted headlong from the room, a strong wash of interested whispers swishing in her wake.

'*Non tam praecipites*,' quoted Will Staunton who also was raised on Roman history. 'I think you have been unintentionally cruel, Lady Stratton. The girl is very young and must have felt that you were mocking her.'

'God's boots! I intended no such thing. Someone go and tell the child. No need to be so sensitive. Don't flatter *you* much, does it though?' she chortled, nodding her head at Will. Then she tapped her chin with a veined hand and nodded again. 'Not a bad notion either, when all's done. Presumably one day you will wish to marry? Why not the little Heron? She has spirit, as we have all witnessed.' She shot another glance of enjoyable malice at Eliza. 'And the match would set the seal on your business with her father.'

Will saw a thoughtful look come into the baronet's claret-clouded eyes and damned the woman for an interfering old she-goat. He thought very quickly. He was well content with his single state. But as the feathered crone had said, he needs must marry some day. He might have his pick of heiresses at any time, without the need to wait for Lucy Heron to grow up. The very fact of her youth showed him his way out. The thing to do was to maintain the light mood gracefully, without offending Sir George.

'Lucy is right to fly from me,' he offered, smiling ruefully. 'For I'm a sad rake, and would make her an ill husband. But perhaps I may reform – in a year or two.' His rolling eye made it clear that this was only half likely. 'What say you then, Sir George? Shall I come calling on your daughter, when I am reformed and she is grown? In a year or two?'

Sir George could also think quickly when it was to his advantage. He knew well enough that Will was not serious in his proposal, but such a marriage would be an excellent thing for the Herons. Staunton's connection with the Earl of Warwick, pirate or no, was one that any man would be proud to bring into his family, to say nothing of the merchant's own station and fortune. Therefore he clapped Will on the shoulder with a smile as wide as his own but several times more innocent and said, 'She'll be glad to welcome you, m'dear fellow! Capital notion, quite capital! Can't think of a man I'd rather have for m'son-in-law.'

Will, admitting himself beaten for the present, beamed back at him as though he longed for that happy day. Then he caught Eliza's look, which plainly said that she had suffered enough of this play-acting.

'I do think, however,' he said gravely to Sir George, 'that the subject should not be discussed with Lucy for a considerable time. She is a child still, for all her pretty looks tonight; let her wear out her childhood in peace.'

'Eh? Oh, anything you say, m'dear boy! I'll keep mum, never fear. And you too, madam,' he addressed Mary sternly, 'for it is women who must tittle-tattle of such things.'

Mary made a soothing murmur, as much to cover her own confusion as to aid her husband. She had no idea, she found, whether or not this had been a genuine proposal. Her best way, therefore lay in a pleasant-faced quiet, which would do for either expediency. She had given very little thought to marrying Lucy and certainly Silken Will had never entered her thoughts in this wise. But he was a man any woman might take with the utmost willingness; she had thought that long since. She found herself almost envying the possibility for Lucy . . .

Sir George, sensing that Will wished to be quit of this talk, turned the conversation back to political matters, whither Lady Stratton, realizing that she had, for once, gone quite far enough, was glad to follow his lead.

Eliza, making no excuse, left their company very suddenly. Will sighed, seeing that, if he wished for a peaceful night, he would have to follow her. As he did so, at his own pace, he reflected that he felt a little guilty about Lucy Heron. She had suffered real unhappiness for the old lady's foolish amusement, which could only compound the distress and embarrassment she already felt on his and Eliza's account. He had meant to tell her not to think of it any longer, to make a joke of it, perhaps, and cheer her that way. But his chance had not come now, he knew, he would not see the girl again, not upon this visit.

With an odd wryness in his heart, he went off to assuage his mistress. His last thought of Lucy was to hope that when her heartache and regrets had faded, the memory which would remain with her of that strange little episode in the woods would ultimately be one of pleasure – even if it was not her own.

London

Young George Heron was in love with London. He loved her many and various faces, young and old, beautiful and squalid; he loved the multitude of her scents and stinks; he loved the babble of her voices, her shrieks of laughter, her murmurs of invitation. He gorged himself on her flavours, he sank his body into hers with a daily sense of renewal and excitement.

In return, the gracious, knowing, filthy city bestowed on him an increasing sense of his own identity, his rightful place as heir to her bounty. What if there were, by now, close on 300,000 of her children, all with a similar claim? Somehow, because they were London's own, each and every one felt himself to be her eldest son and held his head high in consequence. This pleasant self-awareness had grown out of the great city's increasing prosperity. London was, despite the efforts of several of England's monarchs a self-governing city, managed, like all English cities by a freely elected mayor, aldermen and bailiffs. Her money was in her own hands. So was her militia. Her efficient trained bands were one of the few in the country to deserve that adjective. As the capital city now held ten times the population and ten times the disposable income of any other city in the kingdom, her temporal power, should she ever think of using it with an organized and single purpose, would be awesome to contemplate.

And now her citizens, through the organ of Parliament, which by possession they regarded as more their own than England's, had freed themselves, by their own insistence and by the advice of their own best men, from the restraints of both Whitehall and Lambeth. Freedom, at any time in the history of a nation or of an individual, is the headiest liquor of all and both London and Jud Heron, released from their dreary monitors, were a little drunk most of the time, these days.

There were, however, those who kept their heads. These were the men who were less interested in freedom *from* than in freedom *to* – to think, to plan, to be the architects of their own future and that of their great city. Even the London 'mob' which had so shaken the Court and the Lords was not composed merely of the rag-tag and bobtail from the noisy and malodorous Liberties or the masterless flotsam that haunted the quays but of honest traders and shopkeepers and a host of apprentices. They did not howl at the gates of Whitehall for their daily bread but for the bread of righteousness, their own religion in their own hands. They stoned the bishops and the Catholics, they cheered all shades of Puritans and sectaries and listened to their sermons; at home they read their bibles assiduously and taught their children to do the same.

Above all, they talked. Jud thought he had never heard so much discussion and disputation as went on around him no matter where he went. His ears seemed permanently bent beneath the weight of arguments, none of which interested him much at first, but none of which he could avoid. If the Inns of Court were places where the dust of all argument had settled long ago, the merchants' houses, the warehouses, the taverns, the theatres, the churches and every street corner were sounding-boards for every kind of religious and social dispute.

Many of his impressions came to him through the agency of Robin Whittaker. The two were firm friends. Though they had nothing in common beyond their apprenticeship they liked each other instinctively and uncritically. Jud appeared to have most of the advantages in the relationship, being a gentleman, a lawyer (almost) and a rich man's son, but it was Robin who was at first the leader in every way, despite being three years junior and a foot shorter than Jud. For one thing, he had already completed a year of his apprenticeship and would be a journeyman before his friend – if, as Will Staunton often doubted, he could keep out of jail. For another, he was born and bred of a London Jud had never seen, begotten by knavery on poverty, lusty and untrusting, taking both her kicks and her ha'pence for granted. He was raised in the stews of Southwark, the eldest of seven, where his mother plied whatever trade fell to her hand and was as law-abiding as she could afford to be. The only gift her children, all accomplished thieves, could give her was a kind of Sunday honesty. She had been a country girl, seduced by the town, and liked to remember that she had once been righteous every day of the week. Jud had not met her, though Rob spoke of her often with affection. He kept his private life fiercely to himself. He sent home the greater part of the money that was given him by open-handed Will and never stole from his master's house. Although the merchant had first met him in much the same manner as Lucy Heron, he had liked him and wanted to give him the chance that birth and fate had denied him. Rob had seized the chance with both hands and was making a good thing of it, but this did not prevent him looking about for other opportunities. He had found one today.

'I tell you, Jud, there's nothing underhand about it. We're offered good honest labour for good honest coin – and in a good cause too; from what I hear. Master Overton's customers are strong for the Parliament.'

'If he's such an honest man, your printer, why does he keep his office in such a damnable stew as this?' enquired Jud, stepping smartly to avoid the overflowing kennel in the middle of the narrow street, and banging his head for his trouble on an overhanging gable-end.

'The fewer men know your business, the more you get on with it in peace,' said Robin sagely, looking back avidly as a velvet dandy in lace boot-tops fell back from the steps of a bawdy-house waving a limp hand in farewell, his sword and his purse trailing side by side behind his belt.

'He'll be less troubled to find the rent, too,' deduced Jud, wondering why it was that, even in this city of a thousand stenches, the poor contrived to smell worse than the rich. Back in the Strand where they lived in Staunton's imposing mansion, much was done with rue and rosemary and a fleet of scouring servants to keep the air pleasantly fresh. Even the streets were kept relatively clean with the aid of rigorous by-laws; whereas here the slime of generations clogged the narrow alleyways, daily renewed by the discharge of the leaning, crooked houses and their pissing, crooked inhabitants.

They were in fact about a stone's throw from Rob's ancestral home but he swallowed all insults to his acreage in silence.

'Here, this way!' Rob dived suddenly off to the left. Jud groaned. It would have to be down a 'rose-alley', fragrantly named but noisomely endowed, where a man might 'pluck a rose' when he was far from his chamber-pot. Rob had already disappeared inside a low-browed house halfway down the mud and excrement lane. Jud followed him, slapping from one to another of the bricks that some kind soul had spread for those with a care for their boots.

An appalling clatter greeted him on the threshold together with the acrid tang of printer's ink. The gloomy room had an earthen floor and was rush-lit even at noon. The presses clapped to a halt as Jud entered and two gentlemen bent eagerly over the result of its labour, several quarto sheets closely printed in stark black. Robin stood to one side, looking respectful.

The younger of the men, his inspection done, slapped the

papers excitedly. 'Excellent! My thanks, Master Overton. You'd not go so far as to distribute them at your station I suppose?'

The printer smiled. He was middle-aged, grey and hunched from years of poring over his books, his machines and his pamphlets. 'No, I'm afraid not. Such matter as this would hardly do at St Paul's. I'd like to help you but I treasure my membership of the Stationers' Company.'

His customer, small and lightly built, unremarkable save for rather fine eyes, took no offence. 'Never fear. They'll sell in the streets like hot biscuits. It's stirring stuff!'

The printer sighed. 'I don't doubt it, Master Lilburne. Only so be as it doesn't land you back in the Fleet.'

Overton laughed and Jud joined in the laughter from the doorway. So this was 'Freeborn John', the young Puritan who had been imprisoned for importing Dr Bastwick's book against the bishops, and had later been whipped through the streets from the Fleet to Westminster pillory by order of the infamous Star Chamber. Nothing daunted, he had somehow managed to give out three copies of the offending manual from the pillory itself; from the Fleet prison he had issued a pamphlet calling on London's apprentices to rise against the promotion of the Scots War.

By this time, he was a popular figure and not only with the Londoners. The injustice of his sentence had attracted the notice of Oliver Cromwell, the sombre Cambridge MP with the corncrake's voice and the unshakeable convictions, who had raised his case in Parliament. As a result the sentence was quashed and Lilburne was free to become the people's hero.

'You are merry on my account, sir,' he said now to Jud.

'Oh, I'll be merry on any man's account,' replied Jud amiably. 'I'm right glad to make your acquaintance, Master Lilburne, though it is Master Overton whom I've come to meet.' He turned with a slight bow to the printer. 'I believe Robin has told you about me, sir?'

Overton turned a watery eye on him and appeared satisfied with what he saw. He pumped Jud's hand in welcome. 'He has indeed, Master Heron and I'll be mighty glad of your help. I'm to leave this side of the river to these two young men, Master Lilburne, so you must address yourself to them from today. I have too much to do with my books and my sermons to dabble overmuch in politicking.'

Lilburne looked shrewdly at Robin, nodding as if he knew him already, and then turned to Jud again. 'Merry on any man's account, eh? That's pleasant enough, but tell me this, Master George Heron, on whose account are you solemn and serious, what holds your heart and your mind?'

Jud felt uncomfortable, having no answer he could think of. 'Why, sir, I hardly know as yet,' he furnished lamely.

Lilburne looked doubtful. 'Then I suppose you care not what you may print – however, I'm astonished to find a son of Sir George Heron agreeing to work for a Puritan printer who is known to walk just this side of sedition in some of his pamphlets.'

Jud, who had no idea what Master Overton printed and, as Lilburne correctly estimated, cared less, was beginning to feel embarrassed by his lack of established beliefs. 'I am my father's son, sir, not his reflection,' he said, more firmly than he had the right. For although he disagreed with his father on almost any subject, it was as much out of habit as out of conviction, if he were to be honest about it.

'Ah so. Do you love your God?' was the next question.

'Certainly.'

'Do you love the King?'

Jud shifted his feet. 'As I am bound to do.' He thought that sounded about right. He did not, in fact, love the monarch especially, finding little lovable in a figure so far removed from those about him. Why, even Tom, who saw him every day, confessed that he hardly knew him.

Freeborn John laughed once, harshly. 'Well then, do you love your fellow men?'

'Aye, I do that.' It was true. Jud was full of goodwill these days, despite the broken heads.

Lilburne thumped his papers again. 'And would you do nothing more for him than share his merrier moments?'

For a moment Jud thought he was going to lose his temper. He was sick and tired of this catechism. Who was this jumped-up little jackanapes to tell him his duty to his fellow men? And then he remembered: Lilburne was someone who had truly suffered for his fellows and would again if need be. This earned him the right to question lazy Jud Heron and that was a fact.

The Puritan watched with satisfaction as the conflicting emotions sped across the boy's face. It was a countenance as clear as a mountain stream. He would make an excellent convert if he could be convinced. But Freeborn John had learned to be wary of sudden conversion, whether to ideas or to sects, and determined to take it slowly.

'I guess I'd help my fellow men if I could,' said Jud slowly, hoping it was true, 'but I do not see what power I have to do so.'

John opened his mouth and stuck out his tongue. 'There is your power,' he said, stabbing it with an inky finger. 'And here!' He tapped his head. 'God gave you a box full of brains. Shake it up and use it! Use it to think for yourself, not just to soak up what others tell you. Look about you, lad. Ask questions of yourself. You may surprise yourself with the answers.'

Jud was becoming increasingly uncomfortable in the company of this odd, excitable man who was perhaps only six or seven years his senior but who already had the air of knowing exactly how he would behave were the last trump to sound. 'If I cannot cudgel out the answers for myself, I'll be sure to come to you, Master Lilburne,' he said, though less lightly than he would have wished.

'We'll meet soon enough,' Lilburne said. 'And now, Master Overton, I'll bid you good day. I must put these broadcasts about before the city election campaigns are under way.'

Robin alerted himself at this. 'Please, Master Lilburne, sir,' he begged winningly, 'if you have good distribution for those, maybe you'd not mind, sometimes, taking a few for Master Venn, he's agin Gurney like you.'

John considered the small, serious face. 'Indeed he is. I know him well. Master Venn is a friend of mine, Master Goodfellow. Now tell me – what is in this for you, if I deliver his pamphlets? The money Venn gives you to pay your own distributors, I'd hazard?'

Robin, knowing himself caught, put on his shamed face.

'I thought so. Well, you've the makings of a man of business about you – but I do not care to do business with such men. Remember that.'

Robin sniffed. He was embarrassed but not much. Jud looked at him in disgust. He was not surprised but he did not, he found, want Lilburne to associate him with Robin's freebooting ways.

To everyone's relief Lilburne laughed and slapped Robin's shoulder. 'God bless you, lad. You must do the best you can. I know that. But it's as well to be honest with friends. It makes a start. Who knows but one day the world will follow suit?'

'I don't think so, sir,' said Rob quietly.

'Why not?'

'Because there is less profit in honesty than in t'other road, if you can get away with it.'

Lilburne nodded. 'And if each man had the same substance,

the same money in his purse, year in, year out – what then?' Robin smiled at the ludicrousness of it.

'Well?' John pressed him. 'Would you still be dishonest? There'd be no need of it.'

Robin considered, then said reluctantly, 'But 'tis natural for one man to want more than his fellows have, isn't it?'

Lilburne seemed suddenly depressed. 'Is it so?' he murmured softly. 'Alas, it must be so, since you think so. Do you think so too, Master Heron?'

'Yes I do,' said Jud.

'And so do I, John,' added the printer stoutly. 'We don't all have the ideals of the Greek philosophers, thank God. We'd have nought but crusts on our tables if we did.'

Lilburne's face hardened. 'I don't ask for or expect perfect equality in this world, Richard – but surely by God we could have a little less inequality? We'd all profit by it, the poor in their purses and the rich in their souls. None the loser. What could be better than that?'

'I notice you do not bother to distribute your pamphlets among the rich,' was Overton's reply.

'You are a cynic, sir. Time I left you. Yet remember my words, Master Heron. I've a use for such as you, when you've a use for me. You're not rich, not poor either. It's the middle sort of people I would enlist to our cause. The middle is a comfortable position to be in; it draws people because of that.'

He left them then, his pile of quarto sheets beneath his arm. Released from his powerful presence, Jud exploded. 'What the devil was all that about? Causes? Equality? When has such a thing ever existed? Whoever would *want* it to exist?' He was mystified.

'He doesn't really mean it as strongly as that. He just wanted to make an impression on you,' was Robin's shrewd judgement.

'Oh, he has, he has,' Jud allowed with a sigh. 'And now, Master Overton, will you be so kind as to introduce me to the operation of your printing press. It seems to me,' he added thoughtfully, 'that the real power of persuasion lies not in Freeborn John's magical tongue, but in this splendid machine; its reach is boundless.'

Overton chuckled. 'He knows that very well, Master Jud. And he knows how to use it; to him it is an extension of that tongue. And more and more people are listening to it every day.'

Jud did not doubt it. He was glad to have met the man, no matter how overbearing he had been. Though lazy, Jud was not a fool, and he had to concede, as he took in Overton's concise lesson on the use of the presses, that he might well learn a great deal more than the workings of mere mechanisms if he stayed long in the printing business.

Heron, Michaelmas

The end of summer was a busy time at Heron. The last of the harvest had been gathered in under Sir George's surveillance. The fruit had been picked, and the new-fangled turnips that Tom had insisted upon to feed the cattle in winter so that fewer must be slaughtered at Martinmas. The barns were full of hay, roots and apples. The brewery brimmed with cider and barley wine. The spinning wheels in the yeomen's cottages were clicking and whirring their woolly song. The smoking chamber tanged with lean hog flitches and the still-room glistened with preserves and sugared fruits – the figs, quinces, damsons and apricots that Mary Heron had tended with such skill.

The children eagerly helped Margery Kitchen to pack these away, dusting them with powdered sugar and putting them in little wooden caskets lined with paper. Margery could not count above her ten fingers and seven toes – she had lost three to her husband's scythe long ago while they were courting and she had crept up to surprise him in the field. She had forgiven him and married him, but her ability to figure had remained hazy from that day, so that the young Herons could be sure of a good number of fall-outs from the comfit boxes, gleaming as richly as jewels, and infinitely preferable.

It was just before Michaelmas. Both village and household looked forward to the coming day of sport at the annual fair. It was also a Quarter Session day, and the Circuit Judge, Sir Cloudesly Willows, would be paying them a visit, officially to inspect the services of Sir George and Nehemiah Owerby as magistrates, but privately to enjoy Heron's hospitality. There would also be another visitor, far less welcome, at least to one member of the household.

William Staunton was calling on his way from Warwick, for no good reason that Lucy could see. His letter had claimed the desire to discuss certain possible merchant ventures with her father; and they would hear of Jud's progress. If Sir George hoped that there might also be some mention of his second daughter, Lucy herself hoped heartily for the opposite, so much so that at dawn on the morning of Will's arrival she equipped herself with a book, a breast of chicken and some apples and made for her private place, leaving honest-faced Kit to explain to Master Davies that she was ailing again.

When asked tartly why it was that his sister suffered so many malaises this summer, Kit replied vaguely that his mother had said Lucy was becoming a woman. Kit had no idea what this might mean but it seemed to satisfy the tutor, who went puce and never again asked after Lucy when she went missing.

As Lucy did not plan to be back for a very long time, she thought it would be pleasant to take the long way to the wood. She avoided the front of the house in case her father should catch sight of her during his morning ritual of flinging open the window, coughing and scratching his chest while informing his waking wife what sort of a day it was.

On the southeast side of the house, in front of where the new rooms had been added, Mary Heron had made the prettiest garden of all. It was slightly sunken below the level of the house, giving it a queer, submerged feeling as though it might be the enchanted region of some underwater princess. Everything that grew in it was rather small and delicate, the only colours permitted were shades of rust, vermilion, crimson and rose, with a little white here and there to spike its luscious, sensual quality. The trees were all small and tender; a flowering cherry, an almond or two, a young copper beech and several mysterious oriental growths with unpronounceable names on wooden labels; waving, heavy grasses and luxuriant bushes with glossy damson leaves.

It was at the core of this peaceful and luminous place that Mary had placed the object of her special love and care, her precious Quickenberry Tree. It stood beside a small unevenly shaped pool so that it might admire itself and be encouraged to grow. It looked very much like the rowan tree or mountain ash, so common in the north country, but since it was not in fact a native was harder to rear. This year it had consented to produce its berries for the first time and they were large enough and scarlet enough to keep the whole army of Satan at bay, should this be necessary. They looked good to eat but were not, being poisonous.

Lucy sat down next to the tree and spoke to it for a while, telling it how much she admired the berries and the slender, pointed leaves that set them off. The berries reminded her of robins and of the painted beads her sister Jane had sent last Christmas.

'You are the same height as I am now,' she said. 'Perhaps we shall grow tall and graceful together. I should like that, although it seems more likely I shall remain small.' She looked with disparagement at her brief reflection in the pool, then bent, and cupped some water in her hands to give the tree a drink. It hadn't rained lately. She thought it looked grateful. The lovely, flaunting berries shone as though they had been polished and the leaves held up the water drops to reflect the rising sun. Lucy liked the tree; it had an indomitable cheerfulness like an heraldic standard or the flag on a maypole. It improved her mood and she smiled as she left it.

She decided to cross the deerpark to the woods. It was still too early for her father to be out hunting, and anyway he had lately taken to riding further afield than his own acres, especially if he had visitors with him.

The park consisted of some 800 acres of stretched-out grassland studded with ancient oaks and populated by the finest herds of deer in several counties. Lucy was fond of these animals and had helped the gamekeepers to bring up several motherless fawns. It had taken her some time to accept that the same timid, exquisite creature she had tamed to trusting might eventually end its days with the fangs of one of the hounds sunk into its neck. At one time she refused to eat venison. Her mother, losing patience had asked her whether she intended to go into the same mourning for the inhabitants of the dovecote, the stewpond, the chicken-yard, the grazing fields and the fowler's acreage. If so, said Mary tartly, she was liable to starve, for as the Bible rightly suggests, man cannot live by bread alone. Lucy still did not hunt, however, and doubted she would ever take pleasure in it. The twins dearly loved the chase and spent many happy hours training the hounds to sound the same peal as the bells of St Mary Major.

The dew was still on the grass and tickled her bare feet above her pattens with a pleasant chill. Even now, before seven, it was not really cold and the light that was spreading was soft and expectantly gilded.

On the first few hundred yards of parkland there were no deer to be seen. This was because they slept together in large groups and might be anywhere within the miles of paling that enclosed them. Lucy walked on, filled with that particular contentment that comes when sensing oneself as a part of a beloved landscape, half a sensual satisfaction and half a deep security. She loved her home best, perhaps, at this time of day, when the great household and all who depended on it were sounding the first notes of the rhythmic daily song that had lulled and comforted her all her life. From the pastures came the complaint of cattle ready for milking and the call of the shepherd to the cowman as he drove them in. Behind her in the farmyard the hens clucked disapproval of the theft of their eggs while the doves commented soulfully from the tall pigeon-house in which a thousand could roost at once. From the smithy she could hear the clear bounce and stop of the blacksmith's hammer, in turn with the resonant notes on the beak of the anvil. There would be the huffing of bellows and the hiss of steam, and the shifting of great hooves amid the plangent smell of singeing horn. The carriage horses were to be re-shod today so that Lady Heron could go visiting in style at Michaelmas.

Soon Lucy heard the sweet, authoritative clamour of the chapel bell, gathering everyone into the hall for prayers and breakfast. Her absence might be noticed there but it didn't matter. One punishment more or less wouldn't harm her, though her memory still smarted from the last one, upon Will and Eliza's departure, which her mother had delivered, very doggedly and with the intention of making it memorable. Her parents had been ashamed of her and that had quietened her spirit a little. She was trying to do better, but Will Staunton was more than she could manage quite yet.

She saw the deer now, still gathered together in sleep. She was surprised, for they were usually up with the sun which now gleamed confidently through transparent cloud. Afterwards she knew that she must have realized from the first that something was wrong. Animals, unlike humans, do not alter their habits for mere novelty. Unaware of it, she began to run, her heart prophetically sick within her.

She stopped when she reached the first little group and looked with agony upon their delicate bodies, unnaturally relaxed upon the reddened grass. Each one had had its throat cut. All were dead. Stunned, Lucy knelt beside the nearest one and uselessly caressed its soft, spotted hide. It had been a late fawn, one whose progress she had watched. She cried out in anger, hurt and raging at the unknown slaughterers. Who would do a thing like this? And why, for God's sake?

They had not even taken the bodies. It was not venison they had wanted, only the deaths. Stiff with shock and misery, she started back for the house, quickening her steps at the last so as to be able to share her horrible burden the sooner. And all the time she walked, she thought of Nehemiah the horse-murderer and wondered sickly if he had now turned deerslayer too.

Breakfast was over and the household leaving the great hall so that she was able to waylay her father with the news.

'Great Lucifer, child, what do you tell me? Is this true? How many dead, d'you say?'

'I don't know. I suppose there were about twenty where I was but I didn't seek any further—'

'No matter. Good girl. No tears now – I'll send the men out direct- ly—'

The mission was very swiftly accomplished, some two dozen men riding about the park at once. Their report, when they returned, panting and enraged, was grim. Almost the entire herd had been slaughtered, more than a thousand. Not a single carcass, it seemed, had been taken. Several of the wooden palings had been cut down. Tibbett, who had led the search, had discovered a message tied about the antlers of one of the larger stags.

'Restore the common land and you may raise your herds in peace.'

Sir George had greatly extended the park during the last year. He had paid no attention to the insolent, warning visits of Nehemiah Owerby and his followers. This, it might be supposed, was the result of that negligence.

'I'll hang them, every one,' he promised now, looking forward in sour pleasure to the approaching Quarter Sessions.

'Aye, if you can find 'em,' Tibbett offered morosely. 'They're not about to admit to it, you can be certain sure.'

'Then I'll hang enough of them to be certain sure I've got some of the villains amongst 'em! God's boots, Tib – I know well enough who they are. And so do you. You just recount to me whose faces you saw when that ruffian called on Tom that night – and I'll see them hanged in a suitable frame!'

'Sure as God's my witness, Sir George, I don't reckon I can rightly remember. It was a while back – and I'd not like to accuse any man unwarranted.'

'Then you'd better scratch in your mangy memory as hardily as a dog for fleas – for I am to hang a round half dozen of 'em no matter if they be the guilty ones or not! Maybe more!'

It was unfair but the idea did not surprise Tibbett who spent the rest of the day trying to work out whom he might mention. He had no desire to see the companions of his childhood dangling in the marketplace. He thought it best, therefore, if he were to mention the names of men that even Sir George could not lightly consider disposable, men who were widely respected about the hundred, men who, in some cases, had not even been present upon the occasion of Nehemiah's assisted descent of Heron's steps. He had said that his memory was poor, and he would prove it. He also begged a private word with Father Dominic, in the forlorn hope that the priest could exercise some mitigating influence on the baronet's unpleasantly wholesale intentions.

As for the children, they knew well enough whom to blame. 'It was masterminded by the dismal, Dismal Puritan, sure as the Virgin,' Humpty swore. 'By God's britches, if *only* father could hang *him*! Wouldn't we just all turn out to cheer!'

'Well, he can't, because Nehemiah is a magistrate too, and wouldn't agree to hanging himself,' Kit opined sadly.

'But he shan't get away with this. We'll find a way to make him pay for it. We'll punish him for this – and for the poor old horse too.' To the twins this was a debt of honour still outstanding.

'What can we do, though?' Lucy was practical. 'We can hardly even get near him now. His house is always full of his foul, beastly militia, as he calls them. And his dogs'd tear your throat out soon as look at you. Have you been up there lately?'

Nehemiah's house was set above the village, on the hillside, overlooking the church he had converted into a stronghold of Puritanism. It was a sturdy farmhouse, much improved with the increase of its owner's fortune and status. Surrounded by thick woods on three sides and the steep hillside on the other, it presented a constant challenge to the ingenuity of the twins.

'Well, we've had a look around, but you're right. Those dogs of his are a prime botheration. Most of them are new and he's obviously training them just as guard dogs, not for the hunt. One had a bite of my britches the other day – and I'm not too anxious to go back and give him what's inside!'

'Never mind,' comforted Humpty, 'Nehemiah's bound to come down to the village for the fair. We'll think of something then.'

For the moment they had to be satisfied with this as there were adult claims on their time. All of them must be washed, brushed and thrust into their best clothes in time to greet the company. For Lucy this meant the corset, but she minded less now and had a new taffeta petticoat to flaunt beneath the hem of her green dress. For the boys too, the discomfort of buckled shoes and velvet coats was balanced by the short swords they were allowed to wear. These were of excellent steel and could be employed if necessary; Sir George did not approve of useless weapons that were merely decorative, such as the jewelled toys sported by some of the courtiers. The twins, however, had been dared to fight with them at their peril and they generally hung upon the wall of the room they shared with Jud when he was home.

'I don't know why we have to bother with all this for old Sir Cloudesley,' Humpty grumbled. 'He always treats us as if we were a couple of dogs anyhow.'

Lucy thought of this, trying not to giggle, when the judge arrived, puffing like an old bull, after a twenty-mile gallop if his horse's condition was anything to go by. He was a large man, less tall than Sir George but of greater girth. His complexion and nature were choleric. He slid from his mount like a sack of grain down a barnshoot and engulfed Mary Heron in sweat and jollity.

'Dammit Mary, you're still as bedable an armful as I've ever laid hands on! Mornin', George! How do you all here? You're lookin' mighty prosperous.'

Sir George scowled in memory of the dawn's discovery. 'I am, Cloudesley – and so I intend to remain, begad!' He clapped his guest on the shoulder and ushered him towards his dinner.

It was then that Sir Cloudesley caught sight of the hovering children. After looking Lucy up and down and telling her she was getting more like her mother, he patted Kit kindly on the head and called him a 'good boy'. The family sartorial effort, however, was hardly on behalf of the genial judge, who always looked as if he had just been hunting and generally had, but for the appreciative blue eye of Will Staunton who arrived hard on the hooves of Sir Cloudesley, but at a pace that left his person and his clothing relatively spruce.

It was only when she saw him swing an elegant leg over his saddle that Lucy was reminded, most graphically, of her reason for wishing to avoid him. Now it was too late and Silken Will was amused to find her blushing as she greeted him with a few carefully chosen, dull, conventional phrases.

'Mistress Lucy, you have an excellent colour in your cheek. It is the exact shade of the wild woodland rose.' He was grinning like a dog and she hated him cordially.

'A species of which you have seen a good deal,' she said, flouncing her petticoat. Then she wished she hadn't said it, for now *he* would think about – all that – too!

'We are on our way to table,' she said brusquely, since she could hardly tell him to go to Hades, as she would wish. 'Perhaps you will like to follow me in.'

'It would be more friendly if you would allow me to walk beside you,' he said, sounding as if he would like to laugh. She sniffed and marched beside him without a word.

While her parents greeted him and held back the first courses on account of his odd desire to wash before eating, she made her escape. At table she sat as far as possible away from him, grumpily fielding the cheery gales of laughter from the more convivial end. Master Davies, glared at most horridly when he asked her for the saucer, wished she would hurry up and finish this business of becoming a woman and resume her normal, sunny nature.

After dinner the men retired for half-an-hour's hard conversation on the subjects of the slain deer and the probable culprits, and possible ways of bringing them under Sir Cloudlesley's jurisdiction. Meanwhile, up in the gallery, Mary Heron tried to rest while Lucy prevented her by fretting up and down the room tugging at the ends of her hair and refusing to settle.

'For heaven's sake, Lucy, what is the matter with you?'

Lucy preferred not to say. If she were to mention aloud the dreadful notion of her possible marriage to Silken Will, somebody might actually *do* something to make it happen. If she kept quiet, everyone might forget about it, or so she hoped and had recently prayed nightly. The merchant's presence at Heron was causing her a great deal of discomfort and she longed for the visit to end. She was made even more irritable by the fact that they would have to take Will Staunton with them to the villagers' Michaelmas Games this afternoon. It was an occasion she usually enjoyed, there being countless opportunities for fun and food, but today she felt miserable and uncomfortable and thought she might well not go.

She did droop in her room with a book for ten minutes, but in the event found it an impossible prospect to listen while the entire family and many of the servants set off in a jingling cavalcade, with a further rowdy gaggle on foot behind them.

Lucy threw the book at the wall and wished Will Staunton to the devil. She was double-damned herself if it was to be everyone's holiday except hers! Anyhow she had not seen Martha for some time; her friend seemed to be avoiding Heron at present and Lucy had been confined to the house and grounds for a punishment. But Martha would certainly be at the games. Everyone would. So, at the last second she saddled Beatrice, her fat pony, and trotted in the wake of the procession.

The Michaelmas Games were a famous and far-flung attraction;

there would be stalls and sideshows, hawkers, cooking-booths, trials of strength and fortune-telling as well as the organized games that traditionally took place on that day. With so many folk come together from far and wide, one had to have a particular care for one's possessions, particularly one's horse, so Lucy took advantage of her name to stable Beatrice safely in the Golden Ram, next to the landlord's own hunter, as every other inch of available space was taken.

Today the village was all but deserted. St Michael's, which one might have expected to be bravely dressed in honour of its patron, was sunk deep in puritanical gloom, its doors shut up like a disapproving mouth. Everyone was in the broad field behind Lowgate. The welcoming clamour made Lucy break into a run as a hundred sensations raced to meet her; the winner was the heavenly smell of Mistress Taverner's Kissing Candy. This was a soft toffee of astonishingly elastic properties. The idea was that a pair of lovers, consuming first the toffee and then each others' lips, would be rendered inseparable for life. Lucy had no time for such foolishness but homed like a bee on the candy stall and married her top jaw firmly to her bottom one with the added satisfaction of *not* having to share.

Then, clasping her hand firmly over her heart, not because she had well-deserved indigestion but because this was where her purse hid beneath her dress, she set about enjoying herself. It should be simple enough to avoid Will. The crowd was thicker than ever this year. Besides the regular stallholders, the sellers of pewterware, leather and lace, ale and food and good Gloucester-shire cloth, there were gipsy horse-dealers, an astrologer claiming descent from Nostradamus and best of all, a company of travelling players who were to give two separate performances of 'St Michael's Defeat of Satan'. Lucy made a note to save a groat for that. People were getting rid of their money as though it burned their fingers, and the careless ones even more quickly at the hands of the cutpurses, and this despite the loud presence of the balladeer who was bellowing Ben Jonson's famous warning:

> My masters and friends and good people draw near
> And look to your purses, for that I do say
> Although little money in them you do bear
> It cost more to get than to lose in a day.

Lucy grinned as she hummed the familiar words through her diminishing toffee. How Rob Whittaker would have profited from a fair like this! Still, he had probably made himself a fortune at

London's great Bartholomew Fair that was the subject of the song. This was a small affair in comparison but there must be close on 1,600 souls here all the same, at least a third of whom were personally known to Lucy, and half of those by name. She struggled through the crowd about the greasy pole and shouted herself hoarse when John Coachman clambered almost to the top and was presented with a squealing piglet as his prize. Unfortunately there was so much grease on John by that time that the creature immediately escaped him and mayhem resulted as everyone joined in the attempt to catch it. At the centre of the cheerful chaos Lucy bumped her head against the even more solid skull of her brother.

'Humpty! You fool! I'd nearly caught it!'

'So had I!'

They glared at each other furiously and then both fell over, giggling and clutching their heads.

'Come on – let's go and see the wrestling.' Humpty recovered first.

'But what about the piglet? John Coachman wanted it so badly – for his wedding feast with Alice.'

'Oh, someone'll catch it!'

'Yes, but will they give it back?'

'Father'll give him another. Come on! It's William Smith against one of the gypsies. My money's on William.'

'You promised not to bet.' Lucy believed in keeping promises.

'It was just a manner of speaking,' explained Humpty, who did not believe in keeping *foolish* promises, especially when there was money to be made. He had mooched about the caravans and had already seen the gipsy stripped; he was well-muscled but wiry and slender built, not up to the blacksmith's huge bulk. Honest John Taverner was holding all the stakes, happily aware that most of it would come back to him later on at the Golden Ram, either in celebration or commiseration of the day.

It was at the wrestling that Lucy found Martha, who was waiting resignedly, her face turned away, with her small sack of ointments and bandages, as ready as the innkeeper to minister to winner or loser. She was delighted to see Lucy and kissed her warmly.

Lucy returned the kiss but asked directly, 'Why haven't you been up to see us? Dominic's been worrying about you. He has called on you several times but says you didn't answer. I couldn't come; I've been sworn to stay within gates since halfway through harvest. Why didn't you answer Dominic? I thought you were friends.'

'We are.' Martha drew Lucy back from the crowd of roaring men and boys. 'You must not be so swift to think the worst. I have good reason for avoiding your cousin. Nehemiah has been asking questions. He waylaid me in the Highgate last month and asked me straight what Dominic was to me.' She reddened at the memory. 'I told him, a friend; he asked me how should there be friendship between a noble jackanapes and a witch's daughter.' She bit her lip. 'I'm afraid I was too hasty in my reply and now his suspicions, whatever they are, are deepened rather than set to rest. He made me angry. He is so sure of his *right* to question and order my life.' She had almost forgotten she spoke to Lucy as she brooded over the persecution of her unwanted suitor.

But Lucy was amused. 'Hades! He thinks Dominic is in love with you! The numbskull! If only he *knew*!'

Martha shook her arm, hard. 'Lucy, don't talk like that! He must never know! What do you think would happen to Dominic if Nehemiah were ever to learn the truth?'

Lucy was offended. 'I know, I know! I was the one who *thought* of Dominic's disguise.'

'Of course. I'm sorry. It's just that I'm so worried for him. He has too much courage for his own good. Going about the country saying mass in out-of-the-way farms and cottages—'

'He does that? I didn't know. He has never told any of us.'

'One day someone will let fall the wrong word in the wrong ear, and then—'

Lucy took her hand and squeezed it. 'You must not torment yourself so. It will not help. I will speak to my cousin, if you like, if you don't wish to see him yourself, and explain to him why.'

'It's best I don't see him. Then Nehemiah can have no cause to think us more than friends.'

But Lucy wondered, 'If he did, wouldn't *that* be an even better disguise? No priest,' she murmured, 'can have a sweetheart.' Martha smiled but remained doubtful. 'I think not. It would make him angry. He'd not stop his ferreting until he had discovered the truth.' How could she explain to Lucy the obsessive weight of Nehemiah's interest in her? Or the feelings it aroused in her, of suffocation and a dull, far-off premonition of fear?

'No, it is best I do not meet with Dominic alone again.' She sighed. It was a friendship she had come to value more than any before. Her instinct had allowed it, for once, and she had received great solace from their long discussions. But his danger was real and must take precedence over such luxury.

Lucy saw the wisdom in it and promised to explain to her cousin and to warn him to be more circumspect in his clerical duties. She felt sad suddenly.

Just then the cry went up: 'All fellows at football!' and the fairground erupted into a volcanic activity that shattered sorrow and suggested self-preservation as thirty able-bodied males, born in the village, set themselves against the same number of 'strangers' to dispute the eventual fate of an inflated pig's bladder. It could by no means be described as a *fair* game. It was never that, not even between the villagers only, on an ordinary Sunday. The only rules were these: that the game be kept out of the village streets; that one team played towards the church and the other towards the green; and that the game was over when all the players on one side had given in, be it from lack of wind or glut of wounds. The Michaelmas game was like no other and several sage cottars were already hurrying homeward with a care for their looms and their few pots and pans.

The twins, who had been strictly forbidden to take part, were well to the fore when the bladder was tossed into the air by Sir George, according to custom. Though he scowled at them, they only grinned and Kit even secured the honour of the first kick. It was a good one and the boys were off up the field before their parent could deliver himself of a 'damme'. The game appeared much like a preview of the war of the good and evil angels to be performed later; no form of battle was forbidden and both methods and injuries were often bizarre.

At one point the bladder became entangled in the upper branches of an oak, with both teams baying below while a representative of each climbed towards it. Heron's Dickon won the argument by kicking his man sturdily out of the tree; but sadly he landed on William Blacksmith, breaking one of his ribs and thereby considerably lessening the home team's strength.

This aroused a very natural indignation in the villagers. The game was abandoned in favour of an all-out battle in earnest, in which Heron attempted to pay back its visitors for such discourtesies as stolen purses, horses, sweethearts and the like. However Sir George, who was racing up and down on his hunter with the admirable aim of seeing fair play, would not countenance more than ten minutes of this. He saw that the village was not getting the best of the fight and had the bellringers stop it with the peal reserved for 'fire alarum'. As soon as he had explained himself the football was resumed and the whole pack, villagers and strangers, howled away across the fields again, led, somewhat surprisingly, by Father Dominic and Will Staunton, distinguishable, through the mud and blood that covered them, only by their shredded lace. It was said afterwards that the game had been stopped just when Heron had reached a triumphant peak of swiftness and accuracy and that the blasted Puritans may as well have been in league with the strangers, so plaguey inconvenient was their intervention!

Be that as it may, Lucy and Martha had a better view than most when, as Dominic Lacey, clutching the bladder, pounded up the hill with the rest of the pack on his heels, like Orestes pursued by the Furies, there suddenly appeared on the brow the black shapes of some three dozen riders. These, rather than dividing to let the game pass through them, as politely requested, gathered themselves determinedly and plunged downhill into the throng of players. Their faces were grim and set and Lucy thought she heard singing. Cries of 'Bloody Puritan scum!' went up and several riders were dragged from their mounts to the detriment of their Sunday suits. Martha and Lucy groaned in unison, gnawing their knuckles, as one figure, taller than the rest, stood in the saddle and attempted to rally his followers.

'Nehemiah!' they chorused.

'God rot him!' Lucy added vehemently. She stared round, wild-eyed. 'He shan't spoil everything, he shan't, the blackguard!' she yelled, beside herself. Where was her father? He would know how to stop the miserable canting kill-joy.

It took but a second to spot Sir George. Every bit as furious as his daughter, which in his case rendered apoplexy a severe hazard, he too stood in his stirrups, waving his whip and bellowing incomprehensible orders at the villagers.

It seemed that they understood him well enough, however, for there was a sudden rush toward the field where the majority had left their horses and Lucy caught sight of Silken Will, his blond head as dishevelled as a stormed haycock, sprinting ahead of the crowd. When they came back, mounted, there must have been fifty of them, all grinning like gargoyles and waving their arms and whips and digging in their heels. Cousin Dominic was well to the fore, holding his feathered hat aloft like a standard as he galloped past the two girls yelling, 'Run, Reynard, run! The hounds are on your trail!'

It was a resonant cry and a certain pair of small, pointed ears caught it and pricked up. Seconds later Kit and Humpty could be seen, galloping home to Heron at lightning speed, both on one 'borrowed' nag. Their cousin had flung them the inspiration they had sought all day. They were going home to let out the hounds!

The hunt was headed in exactly the right direction, as Nehemiah and his troop had turned, Christian feeling or good sense prevailing over the instinct for battle, and fled along the only path left open to them, back over the fields towards the eastern edge of Heron demesne. It was at the point where they passed the east gate of the deerpark that the hounds joined them, belling joyfully at the unexpected treat.

The twins had worked very quickly. It just so happened that they had secreted, in a very private retreat, one of the deer carcasses, from which they had been attempting to learn the fascinating science of anatomy. The carcass was partly dissected but that made its scent all the more appetizing to the dogs, who slavered after their young masters in expectant cacophony.

The boys, now on their own horses and having timed things nicely, were able to join Nehemiah's discomforted followers without undue exertion of speed. They kept well out of eyeshot of Owerby himself, imagining hideous fates if he caught them. As it was, they got the odd glance from their depressingly clad companions, both of them being dressed to rival the parakeet. But they simply smiled and nodded and looked like boys out after a bit of sport – and kept a close guard on their bulging, stinking saddle-bags. Behind them, closer and closer behind them, the dogs shrieked their ecstasy at the prospect of ripping those bags, or something, or someone, apart!

At a steadily decreasing distance behind the dogs, a similar joy was evidenced by the ebullient galloping of Sir George, his cousin and both his distinguished guests. Sir Cloudesley had so far forgotten his position as to join in without hesitation, though with great discomfort to his girth and his gout which coloured his language well beyond the biblical. Will Staunton was simply enjoying himself more than he had done for months, and Father Dominic was revelling in the novel sensation of being thoroughly bad for once. He knew there could be no excuse for one of God's priests to be hounding his fellow men across the fields like so many thieving foxes and yet, was that not exactly what they were, these prating, lugubrious Puritans – thieves of God's holy word, who changed and perverted it to their own misguided purposes and sought to take the minds and souls of the nation with them? 'View halloo!' bellowed Dominic, chuckling into the wind in sheer exhilaration. 'In the name of the Father, the Son and the Holy Ghost!'

It was a very good thing that Nehemiah couldn't hear him, thought Master Davies, riding unwillingly next to Dominic. It was no part of a tutor's duty to be part of this screeching, impious throng, but Sir George's eye had bidden him and he'd not dared to disobey. He stored away Master Dominic's strange dedication in his tidy mind and joined scratchily in the huntsmen's cheers.

The ground rose and the hounds gained. At the back of the Puritan party Kit and Humpty shot each other a look of complete understanding. Forcing effort from their horses they pulled slowly towards the front, until they rode just behind Nehemiah himself. They heard him bawl an order to stop and turn at the top of the hill. They even helped him to pass on the order. And then came their moment of glory. When they reached the top Nehemiah slowed, stopped and wheeled his horse, still shouting the order. Some followed; many overshot and had to turn later; some cravens did not turn at all but broke for home. Those who had pressed into some sort of order stood their ground and prepared to beat off the dogs, not to mention the men who were working towards them with such a will. Someone struck up a quavering psalm.

The twins waited until the dogs were salivating at the stirrups of the first of their companions and then, in unison, flung their bloody venison straight into the centre of the huddle of horsemen. This done, they tore downhill to join their father. Sir George hardly noticed them, so surprised was he by the prospect of the hounds after their well-deserved quarry. He couldn't for the life of him think what it was that had so excited them, nor could he stop laughing as the hapless Puritans tried to beat them off. All would have been well if Nehemiah's friends had realized it was deer flesh they wanted, but by now believing themselves persecuted by the hordes of Baal they were sure of being torn to shreds, they beat frantically at the dogs, and the dogs, in turn, leaped energetically at them, though really much more interested in the meat.

It was Will Staunton who worked it out. He had noted the emergence of the twins from the mêlée, their expressions smug and righteous. From there, it was simple.

Will rode in close to Sir George and roared in his ear. 'There's meat in there! We'd better call them off before they kill someone.'

'Whassat? Kill? Let 'em! Good thing. Goddam' Puritans!' But reluctantly he held up a hand to rein in the hunt. He had just remembered that Nehemiah, like himself, was a magistrate, and that both of them would sit tomorrow before Sir Cloudesley, now puce and stertorous behind him.

The fun was over.

Two strong lads were sent in to drag out the split carcass and the hounds were called off and given the ragged remains while everyone collected themselves.

Nehemiah, tight-lipped with control, faced the scarlet-faced, still grinning baronet. A hush fell, in respect for the confrontation. The pulpit voice rang clearly for all to hear.

'It may be, Sir George, that we should thank you for this; perhaps there remained, before today, some amongst your tenants and labourers who were unaware of the precise esteem in which you hold them. You have made it clear to them now that they are as little to you as the brute beasts of the field, to be hunted likewise for your sport. But remember what the Lord has said of the unrighteous – "they shall fall by the sword; they shall be a portion for foxes".' He sat very tall in his saddle, his granite face displaying nothing but gravity. His men crowded in on him and he raised his voice further. 'But these are men, Sir George, not hapless animals, and men will forgive many things, especially in one who has, in earlier days, treated them fairly, according to his lights – but they will not forgive humiliation, such as has occurred today, nor indignity to the spirit.'

Sir George made a disgusted noise. 'Oh come now, Owerby, you said yourself it was nought but a bit of sport. All's fair. You broke up our game and we took up another. There was no call for you to spoil the general holiday. As to huntin' and humiliation, 'twas you who first came at us on horseback – so who has the right of it there?'

Nehemiah raised a satirical brow. 'I would remind you, Magistrate, of the law you passed in Parliament which forbids the profanation of the Lord's day with games and sport. We sought to bring Heron back to its duty. But we did not come with hounds at our stirrups and we wished to hurt no one.'

Sir George scratched his head, unembarrassed by the reference to a law for which he had not voted. 'As to the hounds, I swear I know nothing of it; they ran with you, not us. Only knew 'em for me own at the last ditch. But it's all one, so far as I can see – no harm done and good sport for all. Better than football, I say!' He was seconded by a roar of appreciation from behind.

But Nehemiah was not to be placated. 'Is the pursuit of pleasure your only concern?' he asked contemptuously. 'Does the loss of so many deer speak to you of nothing more serious than the loss of your sport?'

The good humour left Sir George's face. 'Aye, it does. It speaks to me of a hanging. Of a dozen if I can get 'em! So I'll bid you good day, Owerby, and I'll see you on the bench tomorrow – when you may expect to lose a few friends.' He wrenched his horse about in high irritation.

Nehemiah let him go, seeing no point in a battle of words. He would save his further speeches for the courtroom, or rather for the largest room in the Golden Ram, which was where the Sessions took place. In fact he did not know who had organized the slaughter of the Heron herd, though he could make a shrewd guess at a name or two; whoever they were, they had his goodwill if not his approval. Sir George had stepped outside the common law in widening his enclosures. No one should hang if Nehemiah could help it.

That evening, when the Golden Ram came into its own and flowed down Highgate to the Green where well-wrapped gossips relived the day until dark, Heron Hall rounded off its own festivities with a visit from the players, who pitched their cart in the stableyard and made up for missing the day's performances by enacting St Michael's victory with a hastily edited script which compared it to the recent rout of certain Puritans. They acted with admirable verve, giving as lifelike an imitation of the heavenly and hellish hosts as could be given by six men, four women, three boys, a couple of mangy curs and a goat. The entire household crammed the courtyard to watch, and enjoyed it every bit as much as they had done every year of their lives, even Sir George, whose taste for such ancient mummery was not at all diminished by forty-five years' attendance on such sophisticated stages as the Globe or Blackfriars.

Sir Cloudesley, seated on a barrel, hooted and clapped with the best of them. Silken Will, reminded of scenes of his childhood in the great ward of Warwick Castle, chortled and snorted at jokes he'd heard a thousand times, blissfully unaware that he was all the time regarded with narrow distaste by a pair of icy green eyes.

Lucy was not enjoying the play. How could she? If her father *did* intend to mention the matter of marriage again, he would do it tonight while he was in such good humour, tomorrow being a day for getting people hanged. As she looked round the packed and happy crowd, she could not help thinking how silly every single male face looked – Sir Cloudesley nodding like a bountiful Bacchus on his barrel, her father wagging his head like the village idiot when he recognized the lines, the twins gawping and snickering and pushing each other, and worst of all, the elegant Master Staunton – catching flies with his stupid mouth grinning open and his collar all askew, just as daft as Dickon Stable next to him with his nose dripping. You couldn't tell them apart, not at the moment. If she had to marry either Dick or Will, she'd as soon have Dick and that was a fact. She had soon made herself so cross that she could not bear to stand in this pack of grinning simpletons another second. She struggled out of the crowd, kicking where she could not beg her way and stalked loftily back to the house. She would go up to her chamber and get on with her book. It was Sir Thomas Malory's tales of King Arthur, in which the knights all behaved in an exemplary fashion and were never caught with their mouths hanging open.

As she turned along the passage towards her room, she heard a sound from the chamber to her right, which now belonged to Dominic. She was pleased for she had not yet given him Martha's message – and besides, the priest was one of the few people she could stomach, just at present.

The door was ajar and she pushed it open and went in. 'Dominic, I'm glad you're here because – oh!'

The man bending over the desk was not Dominic but Master Davies. He straightened and looked annoyed.

'I thought you were my cousin,' said Lucy, stupid with surprise. 'What are you doing?'

The tutor looked even more annoyed. Then his expression fell back into its usual gloomy puzzlement. 'I am most anxious to find a copy of Pliny's *Letters*. I left it in the library but it is no longer there; I thought Master Dominic might have it.'

'I doubt it. Too stuffy for him,' Lucy said, staunchly upholding her cousin's reputation as a man of licence, not letters. Master Davies smiled thinly and shut the desk. Then he followed her out of the room. 'I trust he will not mind my looking for it. It really is most urgent. You see the book is not mine and the friend who loaned it to me wishes to have it back. I must find it if I am to catch the carrier.'

'I'll look out for it,' Lucy promised. 'I expect it will turn up.'

'Thank you. And I'll be sure to mention my search to your cousin. Just in case he does know of its whereabouts.'

'As you will,' she said as they went their separate ways. She decided that Master Davies was more interesting than she had previously supposed. She also decided that *she* would mention to Dominic that she had found the tutor going through his desk — just in case he forgot to do so himself.

Supper was large and festive that night but Lucy was not hungry. She put Julia to bed and told her a story. After a few quiet words with Dominic, she left them all to carouse in the dining room while she carried Malory out into the declining light beneath the Quickenberry tree. Wrapped in her green cloak with the folds cushioned under her, she was warm and comfortable as she leaned against the alabaster urn beside the little pool. She opened her book and prepared to slip into its other world. She read a few lines and then, realizing that she had not got the sense of them, read them again. The same thing happened with the next paragraph. It became clear that she would not be able to concentrate. She gave up trying and allowed herself to drift.

The tide of her thought was troubled. The fear of marriage floated uppermost like the carcass of something drowned and unrecognizable. Why was she afraid? Was it of marriage to Silken Will or of marriage in general? Would she ever change her mind about it? Most women did. Or had to . . . And anyway, she did not *want* to change. She wanted nothing to change, either in herself or in her life . . . yet she was forced to recognize that changes were taking place in both.

She, whether she wished it or not, was fast becoming a woman, while her life here at Heron, and those of all about her, were somehow sadly different this year. Things were happening that had never happened before. All this unrest and discontent in the countryside was of a new and stronger order than the old grumbling that her father had always been able to dissipate. Even Nehemiah had been a joke among the children, never the force among his neighbours that he was now. And he had not been cruel, once. And this killing of deer; she knew that it was an age-old thing, a tradition almost, among dissatisfied peasants; but it had been unthinkable that it should happen at Heron, until now.

Then there had been the foolish chase this afternoon. She wondered why her father found it so amusing, for in the chill of afterthought she did not find it so. Nehemiah had not been playing a game. He was a serious man. The chase itself had been the work of the overgrown schoolboy in each of her father's men, but it was undeniably underlaid by the fact that the hunters were bitterly opposed to the ideals and demands of the hunted. In Malory, if knights met with opponents they fought to the death. Oddly, it was in Nehemiah that Lucy sensed a strength of purpose

145

every bit as determined as that of Sir Galahad. Indeed, she was sure the Puritan would claim the same inspiration, that of Almighty God. It no longer seemed appropriate to call him the Dismal Puritan and laugh at him. This year, Nehemiah was not funny any more.

'You look as if you had reached a crossroads and found no friendly hermit to be your guide,' a deep voice informed her, making her jump. It was the one she least wished to hear.

She looked up, scowling. 'I was just thinking,' she said foolishly, feeling at a disadvantage.

'Not cheerful thoughts, I'll wager.' To her horror Staunton dropped easily to the ground beside her, offering his most engaging smile. 'But if you must be sombre, you have chosen a most delightful spot for it. I have not seen a garden as pretty as this at this time of year.'

Conversation being unavoidable, she said pointedly, 'It is where my mother comes when she wants to get away from us all.'

He smiled. Lady Heron had shown a similar desire, as far as her family were concerned, this evening; she had wanted to show him the garden herself but had been delayed by Sir Cloudesley who wanted her advice about gout. Will was relieved; he thought he had seen signs of a new recklessness in Mary's blue eyes and though he would have enjoyed encouraging this, he was now in too delicate a position with regard to the family to indulge himself.

However, he always found amusement in Mary's little cross-patch of a daughter. Not that she was always cross – he had seen her merry enough in her brothers' company – but he himself seemed to bring out the worst in her. Not that this was surprising, in the circumstances. It was not every young girl who had watched a man perform his masculine duties with a willing woman and then been told she might have him for a husband. Small wonder the chit had avoided him. He chuckled inwardly as he remembered the little white face staring up at him in disgust. 'Master Staunton prefers meat more mature than my meagre bones can supply!' Very true, and his more mature meat had not liked it at all. But Will had been tickled by the child's honesty despite her youth and her embarrassment. He had liked her for it. He liked her now.

'I'm sorry if you, too, wished to be alone, Lucy,' he said gently, picking up her last words. 'I'm glad I found you nevertheless. It seems to me that all is not as it should be between us.'

Her heart thumped. What did he mean? Was it something to

do with marriage? 'Oh? How should it be?' she asked jerkily. Sweet Jesus, surely they hadn't discussed it already?

'Why, as things are between friends, of course.' His look was reassuring but that need not mean anything good. She waited.

He saw her shiver as the night cold ambushed her, and reached instinctively to pull her cloak more closely round her.

She flinched and he checked in surprise. He had made a gesture to comfort a child and had been snubbed as if by a woman not wishing to be touched. 'I'm not cold,' she justified, seeing his puzzlement.

'But you are as twitchy as an unbroken filly. What's the matter, Lucy?'

She could not tell him the main truth, so she chose the lesser, putting her new fears into words for the first time. She spoke resentfully, not wanting to speak to him at all. 'Everything's changing,' she said bitterly, 'and I don't know why.'

It was the complaint of a child again.

'We used to live so peacefully here,' she went on, 'and now there's always some sort of trouble. It doesn't feel right anymore.'

He nodded as though she had asked for his opinion. 'You have a strong Puritan faction here,' he observed. 'There are bound to be disagreements. And with a man such as Master Owerby to organize matters, I'm afraid the troubles will multiply. He seems like a man to be reckoned with.'

She was interested despite herself. 'Yes, that's what I was thinking about. Nehemiah is strong; and he hates everything about Heron. He would destroy us all if he could.'

'I think – and hope – you exaggerate, Lucy. He is a man with a mission, that is all, and does not allow himself the luxury of letting any personal feelings he may have get in the way of his cause. I think your Nehemiah, whatever you may think him, is a man of principle.'

She told him a few choice facts about Nehemiah, just so that he should know that she was not in the habit of exaggeration. Then it occurred to her that here was a way to discover more about her own present predicament, since Will did not seem likely to mention it.

'Nehemiah does have some personal feelings,' she revealed. 'He wants to marry – a friend of mine. But of course, she wants him to leave her alone. He keeps coming to see her and following her about. She hates him. I don't think,' she continued stoutly, looking straight ahead, 'that people should be pestered to marry when they don't want to. Do you?'

147

Will, who had not yet given a single serious thought to the idea of taking this quaint little scrap in marriage, gravely shook his head. He had seen her fear. 'No, I do not,' he said firmly. 'Speaking for myself, I do not intend to marry until I am old and infirm and need looking after. Life is far too enjoyable in the single state.' He was rewarded by a sudden shining in Lucy's eyes. Hardly flattering, but he had come to expect that.

'Oh, you are absolutely right, Master Staunton! Nor do I,' she cried brightly. She stood up. She was suddenly very hungry. 'I think I should like to go inside now,' she said gracefully. 'Will you not accompany me, and perhaps take some wine to chase away the chill of the evening?'

Amused by the swift change from sulky child to dutiful daughter-of-the-house, he got up and offered her his arm. Lucy settled her cloak more comfortably on her shoulders. As she held up her slender arms to lower it, he noticed with a pang of male pleasure that the quaint little scrap was rounding out very attractively indeed. And her tiny waist was positively poetic. He discovered this with something very much like regret. Shaking his head at himself he escorted her very properly into the house.

During the rest of the evening he was attentive to her. They rediscovered their musical partnership and were soon very easy together. Will found in Lucy a ready wit and a sharp intelligence that were lacking in many ladies dozens of years her senior. Once more, she felt that he made her his equal and she responded to it. He had soon made it clear, very subtly, that he would never again refer to the incident of the tryst in the wood, and after an hour of his company, Lucy was able to relax as she had not done since his last visitation.

Sir George, seeing them playing cards and laughing in the corner, made victorious signals to Lady Mary. He'd have 'em wedded and bedded before long, or he was a Dutchman. He would have been even more delighted had he known, as he and Sir Cloudesley left for the Assizes, that Lucy would spend the morning as Will's willing escort. They rode out into the park, now cleared of its pitiful corpses, and across the autumnal countryside that Lucy told him held the roots of all England deep in its cinnamon-tinted soil.

'You love your home, Lucy. I envy you. I've no such feeling for mine.'

'I am a part of Heron, that is all; and when I am away from it, Heron is a part of me. But surely you like your home in London. Jud says it is very fine.'

'It's well enough, I suppose. I've not been there very often. I'm always off at sea, or in Holland, or France; at least I used to be. I'll have to stay home more now, if I want my business to grow as it should. And I should also attend more to my Norfolk acres. I've not been to Stanton St Paul for nearly a year.'

'Then you must have an excellent steward,' said Lucy.

'I do. But his excellence can't match my mother's. She rules him with an iron hand and a steel tongue.' He smiled affectionately. He was close to his mother, who had never reproached him for all the years spent away from her while he learned his trade and grew into a man whom she might recognize as the inheritor of her own spirit and strength. She was as formidable a woman as he had ever met, combining all the most laudable characteristics of the house of Warwick – good sense, good manners and responsibility for others. She suffered no fools, but was as renowned for the kindness of her heart as for the keen edge of her conversation.

'I should like to meet your mother,' said Lucy, seeing his smile. 'She sounds like the kind of person who could deal with Nehemiah.'

'Oh, she would. She does not subscribe to his principles. But I'm sure your father is equal to that task.'

Lucy was not so sure. At any rate she was not surprised when that day's dinner was eaten beneath the shadow of judicial failure.

Sir George had been unable to secure a single conviction, let alone a hanging. Not one man, except Sam Hudson's backward brother, could be found to admit that he had visited Tom Heron with Nehemiah. And Nehemiah himself would not give what he described as prejudicial evidence.

There was no hope of accusing the same men of deerslaying, if there were no men to be accused in the first place. Tibbett, when called to give his list, was castigated for poor eyesight and slanderous tongue, and warned that he would lose one or the other of them if he did not mend his ways. It was then suggested by Nehemiah in a helpful tone that the true culprits were most probably the gipsy traders who travelled to the fair, two of whom the baronet had indeed hanged earlier that year. They were certainly wily enough to have left the note concerning the freedom of common land, to give the suspicion that Sir George's tenants were to blame. It caused him great sorrow, said Nehemiah, as it doubtless did to the Lord, to know that the baronet was so swift to believe ill of his own.

Sir George was beaten. Sir Cloudesley could do nothing but

gloomily move on to the next case. In a rare wax, Sir George fined a pig-stealer thrice the price of the pig, and ordered old Ephraim Weekes to be locked up to keep his lecherous hands off the village maidens. An irreverent groan went round the court. Ephraim Weekes had been goosing young girls for at least sixty of his seventy-three years, and this one had not minded, only her mother had turned Puritan and thought the old devil needed a lesson.

'I don't know what is happening to this country,' grumbled the much disgruntled baronet over his venison. 'There's no sense of order or decency left!'

London, Winter 1641–2

It was the venison, as much as anything, that made Sir George more cheerful than usual about his return to Westminster. He was simply sick of it. They were all sick of it. They had eaten it fresh until it had become too high to go near. They had eaten it roast, boiled and stewed, with herbs and with fruit, in milk and in wine, hot and cold, tough and tender until each one gagged when it was mentioned. The prospect of eating it smoked and salted throughout the winter was not an appealing one. When Sir George announced that he did not like the unrest in the countryside and would take the family with him to London, there were no complaints.

Dominic remained at Heron as caretaker, with strict instructions to 'stand no nonsense from those pesky Puritans'. Sir George had added to his stock of firearms and a stone wall was going up in place of the disputed fences. 'If Owerby sticks his damned interfering nose over it, shoot it off!' was his parting advice to his cousin.

The baronet was not foolish enough to think that London was the place to escape either the Puritan element or a certain amount of unrest, but he rightly thought that very little disturbance would reach the small house in Chelsea. Even the plague, which had made its usual summer onslaught and was still billeted in the poorer areas, did not attack so far upriver.

In the House of Commons itself there followed one of the most uncomfortable months that Sir George had ever known. The atmosphere was gloomy from the start. Plague provided an excuse to augment the normal absenteeism and the Royalist ranks especially were thin. The King was not expected back from Scotland until 24 November and John Pym used every day of his absence to undermine his authority and increase that of Parliament against him.

On 1 November came the news that provided Pym's ammunition. His Majesty's Irish Catholic subjects, fearing the friendship between the English Parliament and the Scottish Covenanters boded ill for their religion and for their property, had risen in rebellion. They proclaimed however that they would restore King Charles to his rights and that they had the King's own warrant for their bloody actions. An army must be raised to suppress the rising, but the King must not be allowed to control it, in case he turned its force on Parliament in a bid to regain his losses.

To Sir George, the rebellion brought a double misgiving; his wife's cousin, Walter Lacey, had settled years ago on an estate not far from Dublin. The family was Catholic and likely to be in danger.

On 5 November, after due celebration of their deliverance from Gunpowder Treason, the Commons heard Pym's opinion that no plans, loans, arms or troops should be voted to quell the revolt unless the King agreed to rid himself of all advisors save those chosen by his Parliament.

This piece of insolence set off a small, uncelebratory explosion in Sir George's part of the House, and was treated with contempt in the Lords. Pym, who could wait a little, turned to other matters. His main preoccupation was the drafting of his 'Grand Remonstrance'. This was no less than a complete compendium, act by act, of every misdeed that the King was considered to have committed against his subjects. If Pym were to get it through, Charles would have no shred of reputation left. He did not force the issue; he had twenty days or so in hand. Fire was drawn from the ticklish Remonstrance by an intelligent proposal from Lilburne's old champion, Oliver Cromwell, the stolid Member for Cambridge. He moved that the Southern Trained Bands be placed under the command of the Puritan Earl of Essex, who was well respected by men of all shades of opinion. A less crude step than straightforward insistence that Parliament made all military appointments, it was nevertheless the thin end of the same wedge.

Sir George's days were spent in asperitive argument. He made several loyal speeches in which he reminded the House how far the King had already come to meet their demands and upbraided those who would greet his return with old complaints, dug over, as he said 'like vomit uncovered long after the feast'. Upon Pym's mild enquiry as to whether he were quoting his favourite Shakespeare, Sir George replied grimly that they would all do well to remember that

> More rest enjoys the subject meanly bred
> Than he who bears the Kingdom on his head.

and that they should not compound their sovereign's troubles by these shameless graspings at an authority which God had not intended them to have. He felt better after this and enjoyed his dinner without indigestion for once.

John Pym enjoyed his considerably less. For one thing there was the pain which consistently grumbled in his bowels. For another, it was by no means only Sir George Heron with whom he must deal if he were to get the Remonstrance through. The influential lawyer Edward Hyde, once his staunchest supporter, had now decided he could travel no further with his old friend and had set his considerable talents to organizing the opposing faction, assisted by the immensely popular Lord Falkland. Since these two drew about them all the most moderate men as well as the King's accustomed supporters, the situation began to look dangerous. In addition the Londoners, tiring of sermons, elected the royalist Sir Richard Gurney as Lord Mayor. These were setbacks, but Pym was not deterred. They meant only that he must work harder.

The pain gnawed away at his belly, and, ignoring it, Pym gnawed away at the opposition. The King was due home on 24 November. By 23 November he had gnawed hard enough to put the Grand Remon- strance, his compendium of the King's misdeeds, to the vote. He had left nothing to chance.

At one in the morning the House divided. The motion was passed by 159 votes to 148, a mere eleven votes. The pain let up a little. The House tottered out of the flickering candlelight and into the blackness at two o'clock, rubbing its eyes and uttering curses of relief or chagrin. Sir George woke up his bargemen and continued to curse all the way home to Chelsea. There he woke up the entire household with further curses and lamentations, with the exception of Julia and the baby who displayed their usual unfilial ability to sleep through general anathema.

'Don't worry, Father, it will be all right when the King comes home,' Lucy comforted, blearily offering mulled ale to which her mother, somewhat unhopefully, had added poppyseed.

'Home! He will scarce recognize his home! Pym has taken his reputation and that mongrel Cromwell has taken his army! His Parliament is divided as it has never been! What a homecoming that will be for His Majesty.' He groaned. They had never seen him so distressed. He had even worn out his anger.

'We have failed him. I am ashamed,' he said softly. He told them all to go to bed and he would follow. He did not do so but sat long before the fire, seeing pictures in it to which he could give no name but which he knew were very terrible.

By morning he had not slept but he had formed a resolution which would be welcomed by his friends in the House. At dawn he awoke the long-suffering bargemen again and they pushed off without sound, leaving the message that Lady Heron might expect them when she saw them.

The Baronet reached Westminster to find that Geoffrey Palmer, the member for Stamford, was already canvassing his own nightformed resolution; which was the lodging of a protest against the Remonstrance on behalf of the minority and in consideration of those forty members, the sick, indolent and selfish, most of them King's men, who were still absent. They had certainly entered Pym's arithmetic; now it was the turn of his opposers to count them. It was an appalling sitting.

Tempers rose and soon the House was in a ferment of enraged altercation, the protestors howling for their rights and their opposers roaring against them. Someone lost his head and unsheathed his sword. Others followed. Sir George, beside himself with shame and fury, found himself one of a row of bellowing members, each grasping his sword by its pommel and beating the tip upon the ground. They *would* not have the Remonstrance hawked about for every common jack to gape at. They would sheathe their swords in John Pym's bowels first!

It was Hampden who brought them to their senses. Pym could not have done it; not then; but the quiet sagacity of the victor of the Ship-money case was guaranteed an audience. He rose and waited. Gradually the tumult died, permitting him to speak.

He suggested that the proposal to print the bill should be laid aside for the present, as the cause of too much dissension. There was agreement. Tempers cooled. Apologies were made. But it had been an uncomfortable and disturbing experience. Every member was distressed and frightened by the extent of their differences.

As is human in such circumstances, a scapegoat was found. It was moved that Geoffrey Palmer be charged with inflaming the temper of the House to a point where violence was narrowly averted. The motion was carried by 190 votes to 142.

During the debate on this motion, when leashed resentment strained on both sides, John Venn, fearing his friends would get the worst of any further violence, sent home to his capable wife Judith to fetch out the Trained Bands and send them to Westminster. If the nobility and gentry must behave like schoolboys they must take their lesson, if necessary, from the honest traders and apprentices who formed this excellent militia.

Three hundred of them came at once; by the time the Houses rose there were 1,000. Amongst them were Jud Heron and Rob Whittaker, armed with stout cudgels in case there should be any fun.

There was not. The honourable members had frightened themselves quite sufficiently by their earlier display of steel and were not, after all, disposed to repeat it. No member regretted this. Neither did any serious-thinking citizen who stood quietly beneath the authority of his Constable in the falling darkness outside the House. Perhaps the apprentices did, a little, but they could always fight among themselves if they wanted a rumpus and there was something about this peaceful vigil outside the dim-lit windows of Westminster that laid a restraint upon even their ebullient senses. They were all, all the thousand of them, waiting for something; they didn't know what. And in the end they went away, puzzled and quiet, still not knowing.

The worst piece of luck fell to Jud Heron. When the House rose, not only peaceful but subdued, the crowd turned away and faded back home with its elected representatives. If Jud had not waited, just a few minutes more, to see if he could catch Master Venn, for whom he had a query concerning one of his pamphlets, he would not have come face to face with his father as the baronet strode, unhappy and unsatisfied, out of the House with a face like a glowing forge. Jud, who had been home only once since the family had come to Chelsea, foolishly ignored his parent's complexion and waved his cudgel in glad greeting. 'Father, sir! How do you? Well met, sir!'

Robin became invisible beside him.

Sir George's eye, enticed by the cudgel, fell upon his least favourite child; it took in both cudgel and the company Jud was keeping – still some 300 or 400 of them – and suddenly all the humiliation and frustration of the day and of the preceding days seemed to heap themselves into a single dark shape; that shape hovered a moment and then resolved itself into a cap that fitted one guilty and ignominious head. With a breaking, unstructured cry, Sir George charged at his son and seizing the cudgel, struck him with a single blow to the ground.

'Hold hard, sir! There's no need for that!' Robin rematerialized. He could see the old boy was past himself and he wasn't going to watch his best friend beaten senseless without reason, even by his own father.

Sir George's head felt muzzy. A moment ago it had seemed as though lightning had cracked inside it. He was giddy. He staggered a little and reached blindly for support. Robin gave it to him warily.

'What? What's that? Jud, is that you?'

Jud, whose head, it has been explained, was becoming accustomed to the occasional crack, was sitting up and shaking it experimentally. He felt it. No blood; good! Deuced sore, though! There'd be a fair lump, all right. 'Yes, this is me, Father,' he said ruefully. 'Didn't you recognize me?'

'I don't think that was the case,' Robin told him hastily. 'Your father's not well, I think.'

'Felt well enough to me,' grumbled Jud, getting up and peering closer. He took Sir George's arm and put it around his own shoulders. 'There, sir. Are you better now? Do you want to sit down? We could go back into the House—'

His father shuddered. 'No. Better now.' The miasma was clearing and he saw where he was and with whom. He remembered. 'What are you doing here – and at such a time?' he enquired, his voice regaining strength and his eye suspicion.

'Just watching the world, Father. You have to admit it is getting to be interesting.' He thought it better not to mention John Venn.

'You stupid young puppy,' said Sir George contemptuously. 'The world is becoming corrupt – and there is nothing that feedscorruption so well as mindless, useless, selfish puppydog ignorance! It's time you got yourself an education, George. God knows I've tried to give you one but you made your own muck of that. I did have half a hope that Will Staunton would knock some sense into you – but I see I was too hopeful by more than half!'

He broke off, wearied by his own repetition, by his disappointment in his son, in his colleagues and in his own abilities. He had talked himself hoarse in the House this day, this week, this goddam endless month and all to no avail. He was hanged if he would waste further words on Jud. 'I'm for home,' he said abruptly and turned away.

'Give my best love to my lady mother, sir,' Jud called after him, his voice a little lonely, 'and tell Lucy I'll come soon to take her to town.'

There was no reply. His father was already striding off towards the river, his head sunk deep into his collar.

'I'll tell you what, Jud, my old second son,' said Robin feelingly, 'there are times when I count myself extraordinarily fortunate to have been born a bastard!'

When Jud called as promised to take Lucy up to town, his father was at Westminster, which according to his mother was just as well, as he was still in no mood to be civil, either *to* his son or about him. Mary Heron, who had always, a little guiltily, found it easier to love Jud than Tom, missed him daily and was overjoyed to see him. When they left Chelsea at ten o'clock their barge was loaded with gifts of food and clothing and Jud's purse sat pleasantly heavy against his hip.

Lucy settled astern, slightly self-conscious in her new winter clothes, a gown in the new floral heavy cotton from Holland, quaintly called 'chintz' and a splendid orange-tawny cloak with a coney lining. Her hair was growing into little ringlets and Jud thought she looked very pretty in her rich colours, with her new air of being a young woman, which perhaps would not last all day but which suited her better than he would have expected. She was no longer play-acting, he thought wistfully; she really was growing up. Probably, in that mysterious way that girls have, she would leave him behind.

'Where shall we go?' she asked happily. 'You said you would show me the bear-garden. I should so love to see it – but only if they are not unkind to the bears.'

'The bears are their living,' he said evasively. 'But we won't go to Bankside today. I have a surprise for you.'

'Oh, that is even better! I won't ask what. I won't even try to guess. Do I have to shut my eyes?'

'No. Well, at least not yet. In a while, perhaps.'

They sped on the current between green banks overhung with foliage. They might have been on any river in England where the private lives of the rich hung reservedly back from the banks, betrayed only by tip of a turret or the shimmer of a shingle among the trees. As they drew into the city those lives became public and came down to the river; they got their feet wet and their hands calloused and they engaged in trade. There were docks and warehouses and a great many ships and boats and barges. There were still the great houses, no longer reserved but standing on the bank to be admired for their stolid or extravagant architecture. Great names were attached to them: Salisbury, York, Durham, Somerset. The river so teemed with craft of all kinds that Lucy had the sense, as she did only in this rare precise situation, of being part of the whole urgent flow of a life that was as much larger and wider than Heron as was the mighty Thames than the trickle of her morning washing water through her fingers.

It was exhilarating and a little frightening, and she was so happy that she sang aloud all the way down to London Bridge. She was silenced then by the stone splendour of the great piers that supported 350 yards of handsome houses and shops. They swung above the water, crowned with the ornate Renaissance cupolas of Nonesuch House and served by the water-wheel devised by the ingenious Dutchman Pieter Morice, which pumped up river water for the city's use. The arches were so narrow and the water so forceful that Jud would not chance 'shooting' the bridge. They landed and took another boat on the other side.

'Now you may close your eyes,' Jud said as they sped off again. Lucy knew at once what it would be but pretended otherwise to please Jud, screwing her eyes as tight as she could and looking expectant.

And indeed the sight of the *Gallant Lady* with all her paint and powder on, returned and resting from her voyage to warm seas and even warmer assignations, was more than enough to elicit a cry of pleasure and surprise from one who had last seen her in her shift with none of her jewels or finery about her.

They rowed alongside so that Lucy could take in her full magnificence. The fifteen guns, her sinister pearls, still gleamed in their ports, but their barrels were blackened now. There was a wealth of gilded carving about her and her beakhead carried the figure of a proud-breasted woman, her long hair flowing back, her profile fierce and strong.

Jud gave the hail and some sailors helped them aboard when they had landed. 'Follow me,' said Jud in a casual proprietary way.

On deck there was a swift impression of acres of scrubbed wood beneath a skeleton forest of ropes. Then they climbed backwards down a shaky companionway and into a narrow passage where the wood was not scrubbed but polished. At the end of this was a heavy stained-glass door depicting St George and the Dragon. Behind it were voices; opened, it revealed the master's cabin, a chamber of almost vulgar luxury, married to the utmost practicality, in which Silken Will did his business and took his pleasures in comfort. At present he was engaged in both; that is, the business – an extraordinary meeting of the shareholders of the New Providence Company – had by now devolved into pleasure – the consumption of dinner, with the addition to the company of Lady Elizabeth Hartley. Jud peered round the door, trying to judge his welcome.

Will saw him and signalled that he should come in. Then he caught sight of Lucy hesitating behind her brother. He rose and came to greet her.

He wore crimson satin and lots of gold chains and his teeth were whiter than she remembered. He pressed her hand, noting her elated look, and murmured, 'My dear Mistress Lucy; this is a pleasure.' In fact he had forgotten that he had said Jud could bring the girl today. He could feel his mistress' eyes snapping at his back. He hoped that there would be no unpleasantness – or, if there were, that it would be amusing. On the other hand, he did not want little Lucy made uncomfortable. He set about putting her at her ease.

'There are some gentlemen here whom you do not know. Let me introduce them to you. Jud, I think you have met everyone before.' Jud nodded and bowed to a general reception of grunts.

The gentlemen were taking their ease upon a three-sided green leather divan built into the bulkhead beneath a row of gleaming, diamond-paned windows. They held plates of meat and flagons of wine.

'But first – Cousin Eliza, you already know Mistress Heron.' Eliza rested in a nest of unknown exotic furs, sipping wine and eating nothing.

She met Lucy's eye mercilessly. 'I thought they had confined you to the schoolroom, Miss,' she said with no particular emphasis. 'I believe you have been in some disgrace.'

Lucy blushed. She thought, 'She thinks I cannot say why. It is very unfair of her to use her advantage so.' She looked at the circle of interested male faces and knew that she could make no reply that would embarrass Jud before his idol, Will Stanton.

'Your Ladyship is misinformed,' she said quietly. 'The disgrace was not mine.' She met the frosty eye with an excess of candour.

'I'm sure we are all pleased to hear that,' Will said affably.

Smiling at Lucy and turning his back on his cousin, he presented the first of his friends. 'Lucy, this is John Pym. You will have heard your father speak of him.'

'Yes indeed, sir.' As she dipped and inclined her head she tried not to think *how* she had heard him speak of this elderly man who resembled nothing so much as a bearded mastiff, heavy browed and jowled, with eyes that were moist, alert and kindly. He wore plain dark clothes and was the most confounded nuisance in England.

Pym's warm eyes twinkled. 'Mistress Lucy, your father does not love me, but I hope that you and I may do better together.'

Lucy smiled politely and reserved her judgement as Cousin Dominic had recently taught her. Ogres must, she supposed, possess a certain amount of charm or woodcutters' daughters and princes in disguise would not be so easily tempted into their fastnesses.

'And here is John Hampden—'

This was better. Even Sir George admitted the good qualities of Pym's nephew and righthand man; Hampden too smiled kindly at Lucy and remarked easily on the beauties of Gloucestershire before relinquishing her to the very different proposition seated next to him.

'—Oliver St John, for whose legal talents we all have cause to be grateful.' It had been St John's brilliant speeches that had swayed the judges in the ship-money case so that, at the end of that long drawn battle between King and subject, two of them were prepared to risk their wigs to uphold their doubts. A significant shareholder in the New Providence Company, he was also its solicitor. He did not appear to share in the general sense of ease and festivity. His dark face was drawn into long downward lines and there was a tightness about him which suggested discontent.

He gave Lucy a curt nod for Will's sake, but it was obvious that he did not understand why their colloquy should be interrupted by the admittance of a young girl and Staunton's apprentice.

'Don't mind Oliver, Miss Lucy. Never will be sociable. Come you and seat yourself next to me and I will prevent him from growling at you.' The speaker was a much younger man, of about Will's age perhaps, dressed in the height of fashion, a single lock of his hair curling down upon his breast and sporting a rosette.

Lucy caught the scent of something spicy and fruity, which she liked. She also liked his face which was ugly – a large nose and pale, prominent eyes in an irregular setting – but full of animation and pleasure.

'Harry Vane, Little Mistress, and yours to command.' His crooked smile was the most infectious of all, and yet she hesitated, genuinely taken aback for the first time.

This was the man whose evidence had procured the death sentence for Strafford. A real ogre and yet, see how he smiled! This was difficult. She wished to have nothing to do with him. Embarrassed, she hung back, but Vane had made room for her and Will evidently expected her to sit down. She did so, very gingerly.

'I have promised to show Lucy over the ship, gentlemen,' said Will in explanation of her presence, 'but perhaps she will forgive me if we defer the tour a little.'

'I could take her, sir, if you like,' Jud offered.

'No thank you, Jud. I look forward to doing it myself.' It was one way he might restore any self-esteem she might have lost to the account of his mistress. 'But first, you must eat.'

Will gave her wine and Vane produced a breast of cold pheasant and pickled cucumbers. A cunning table slotted out of the wooden base of the seat. Lucy took a deep swig of the wine. It was very good. Will had come by it aboard a Spanish ship he had pirated; el Capitano Ramirez had come by it similarly aboard a French vessel whose unfortunate captain had been a connoisseur of fine wines.

'Pray do not let me interrupt your conversation any longer, sirs,' said Lucy airily after her second draught. She was beginning to feel more at home. Eliza made a small muffled noise. Will rose to take her more wine and gave her a special, sensual smile that invited her to recall their night together. She ignored it and raised her goblet to John Pym.

'The matter is,' said St John who thought they had wasted enough time, 'that this Spanish business has changed the New Providence from a company with considerable assets to one with massive debts. Warwick could clear himself if he wanted; so could Saye and Brooke – you too, Will, have other ventures – but it will be all up with the rest of us if we are arrested for debt.'

'You're safe enough, surely?' Will questioned. 'An MP *can't*, legally, be arrested for debt?'

'Not so long as there is a Parliament of which to be a member.' There had, after all, been eleven years without one.

'Surely the Own Consent bill secures *that*, at least?'

St John looked gloomy. 'The vote on the Remonstrance was very near. It was not sent to the Lords, who support the King in all things. It is possible that the King, if he so determined, might persuade his misguided friends in both Houses to vote a dissolution.'

There was a silence.

Pym said softly, 'The King will not do that. We have tipped the balance too far in our favour. He may not do without us now.'

'The *law* must ascertain that he cannot,' St John asserted. 'We have a permanent King – why not a permanent Parliament?'

Hampden and Vane shook their heads at Oliver climbing onto his worn old warhorse and Eliza yawned. She had heard all this before.

This morning she had taken a strong interest in a depressing discussion of the losses sustained by their Company from the Spanish attack on Providence Island, a god-forsaken outpost where the English settlement had been totally obliterated. Will had put money into the Providence Company for her. It did not appear that she was likely to see it again. Happily it had not been much; unlike Will, she did not care to take risks. The talk plodded on. They seemed to get no further.

'You will hardly wish for permanence upon the grounds of our debts, Oliver,' grinned Hampden. 'There are many of our opposers who would make a great deal of capital out of *that*.'

'Naturally not,' said St John irritably, 'only we *must* secure the Militia Bill tomorrow. Once the army is under our control, His Majesty will have to take our advice concerning Ireland. And after that – the army is its own guarantee of our security. We stake high on this. If the King should win, he will rid himself of us if he can.'

'Try not to worry so much, Oliver,' Pym said, though he looked worried himself. 'I have done all that is possible and our chances are more than fair. The King helps us by making himself unpopular since his return. That foolish speech blaming all disturbances on "the meaner sort of people" will scarcely win the hearts of those so described. And they feel slighted by his removal to Hampton Court, so near to Christmas; it's bad for trade. And then, to replace Essex with Dorset as commander of the Trained Bands – so clumsy, and only to spite our own appointment. The Londoners love Essex and follow him gladly, but they've no stomach for Dorset's high-toned ways.' He sounded satisfied.

'The apprentices have tried Dorset's mettle already, I gather,' said Will who had come in on the ship only two days ago. 'I found several of mine the worse for wear. Jud here seems to have got off lightly for once.'

'I wasn't at the rough-and-tumble, sir,' said Jud virtuously, 'I was delivering the *Westminster Mercury* at the time. And we are collecting signatures to support your Root and Branch bill while we hand out the broadsheets. If they won't sign,' he added cheerfully, 'we offer to slit their throats: we tell 'em they're slitting their own if they allow the bishops and the Lords to do their thinking for them!'

'Hold hard, lad,' chuckled Harry Vane, 'we don't want the Lords out, only the bishops, though I must say, it ain't a bad notion at that! You've got a rare young politico here, Will. Didn't think you concerned yourself with such matters?'

'I don't. I was never quite sure what Jud was doing with his spare time. He seems to keep good company though. I found him at John Venn's the other day.'

'There's a sharp wit,' nodded Pym. 'His calling out the TBs the other night – a little excessive, but it demonstrates to our opposers that we are able to protect ourselves, and that London loves us, even with Gurney in office.'

Will looked sober. 'But do you not find it uncomfortable, to say the least of it, that so much must hang upon the command of arms and of armed men?'

Pym shook his head. 'We've no more time to consider comfort. Hear this – and it must not go beyond this room, not for the moment—' He looked severely at Jud, then at Eliza and Lucy. 'The C-in-C at Berwick, Sir John Conyers, has sworn before the House Committee that the King sent to him the Irish rebel, Daniel O'Neill, to persuade him to join him in a march on Parliament!'

Only Lucy was surprised by this news. She realized that she must be very ignorant and listened even more carefully. She was very confused. These were the King's enemies, and yet their voices, when they spoke of him, were respectful, even a little sad – apart from Vane who sounded as though he had lost patience with a fractious child. Would His Majesty really lead an army against them?

'So you see,' Pym was saying passionately, 'that we *must* have that control of the army and only the King's discredit can give it to us. Thank God Conyers was no fool.'

'Your famous Remonstrance will accomplish the King's ill name,' said Will rather ruefully. 'What does His Majesty say to it?'

'He has not yet graciously consented to notice its existence,' said Pym, 'though whether because he has no conception of its importance, or because he is playing for time, I don't know.'

'Perhaps he does not believe he can be thus called to account,' said Will quietly.

'He will learn soon enough,' said Vane grimly. Then, grinning, 'I'll tell you one man who is truly aware of its importance – your cousin Oliver Cromwell, Hampden. He said that if it had failed he would have sold all he had and gone to America!'

'A fine patriot!' said Will.

'Don't mistake the man. That is exactly what he is. He'd never have gone, not if I know him – but the idea explains just how crucial he thinks the Remonstrance to be. And he is right.'

'That was a good notion of his, to put Essex over the TBs,' Will allowed, feeling that he owed the unknown member a recompense. 'If only the King had let well alone.'

'This is no light matter, Will,' cautioned Hampden. 'God knows we wish for no lasting division between the King's men and ourselves. We had to make a statement for solidarity – surely you can see that?'

'Oh aye. I can see the statement. I can't see the solidarity.'

They were silent.

'It comes and goes,' remarked Pym peaceably. 'I vote we think in more positive terms and raise our glasses to the Militia Bill.'

'Here's to it – and may it prove the solution we all desire,' agreed Hampden readily.

'But don't forget the bishops – they can still outvote us in the Lords,' St John reminded them.

'Not for much longer – please God!' Hampden allowed himself a little joke. 'You keep on collecting those signatures, young Heron, and never mind what your father says.'

'He doesn't know,' said Jud with the innocence of one who has not seriously taken stock of what he is doing.

Will raised his eyes heavenward. 'He'll not find out from me, else I'll lose my skin. Take care not to sail *too* close to the wind, lad, or you'll capsize a promising career.'

This lightened their mood and by common consent they abandoned Parliamentary matters in favour of more general conversation, much to the relief of Eliza, who was bored, and Lucy, who had found their talk depressing. More and more, she felt that she should not be here; her father would be horrified if he knew. And look at Jud, sitting there with his eyes shining like some addled Puritan who'd just 'seen the light'! The fool! Will Staunton ought to give him a good talking to.

Her brooding was cut short by a determined movement on the part of Eliza, who rose and shook out her furs, bestowing her smile like largesse upon the assembled gentlemen. 'The time has passed so pleasantly and I have been so engrossed that I had quite forgot that I am engaged to visit the Countess of Carlisle this afternoon. You promised that you would go with me, Cousin. Had you forgotten also?'

Will frowned. He disliked the Countess of Carlisle, a powerful, meddling sort of woman whom he found very tiresome. Happily he had a ready-made excuse for avoiding her company on this occasion.

'I have no such recollection,' he said firmly. 'What is more I am engaged to display the *Lady*'s charms to Miss Lucy. Go without me if you will. We shall meet tonight at supper, in my house.'

Eliza knew him well enough not to waste time in empty persuasion; besides she would not cajole in front of his friends. 'I would not for the world deprive Lucy of your company,' she said, honey-sweet. 'I know how much she values it.' Somehow she managed to make it seem as though Lucy were a green-sick girl, languishing with love for Will, and all the more so when Lucy, furious, reddened with anger.

Pym then announced that he too was going in the direction of the Countess of Carlisle's house, and Eliza had perforce to go off on his arm, her backward glance promising a reckoning over the supper table. Lucy Heron was becoming the most damnable little nuisance.

'Come along, Lucy, let us walk about,' Will encouraged. He was glad that circumstances had relieved them of Eliza. She and young Lucy got on like two wild cats in a cage, but then their relations so far made that unsurprising. It was unfortunate that they had met today.

Just then John Pym called back to Jud, 'If you would walk with us a step, I have a proposition to put to you. I'll not keep you—'

Jud left off wondering how sore his head might have felt if his father *had* known him a seller of inflammatory matter and beamed at Pym, signifying willingness to be proposed to.

As she climbed back onto the deck, where Will said they must begin, Lucy felt suddenly shy of him again. The presence of Lady Hartley had brought back everything she wished to forget, and the fact that the woman had *referred* to it, however obscurely, doubled her humiliation. She had wanted badly to tour the ship, but now it was all spoiled. She wished she could just go home with Jud instead.

Will's voice breezed over her head, succinctly explaining the forest of rigging. Gradually she calmed and began to listen. She learned that the *Lady* was built after the Dutch style of three-masted frigate; that she was 120 feet long and twelve feet deep and her tonnage was 270. Her upper planking was clinker-laid, overlapping for maximum strength and maximum weight, a practice not yet employed by English shipwrights. A crew of 120 was needed to man her. She had cost nearly 6,000 livres to construct and was one of the most advanced vessels on the Thames apart from the King's own magnificent *Sovereign of the Seas*, which Lucy had once seen moored down river.

'I don't think I need to know what *everything* is called, thank you,' she said as they got into matters of shrouds and deadeyes, catheads and nunbuoys. 'I should only forget them. There is little point in knowing such things if one is not going to be a sailor. Jud knows most of them, because he *does* want to be one; but I don't need all those names to know that your ship is very beautiful and that I wish, most heartily, that I might sail in her.'

'Where would you like to go?' asked Will, sympathizing.

'I don't know. America? The Indies. Where *does* she go?'

'Lately she has ventured into Spanish waters.'

She caught a reminiscent kindling of his eye. 'I've heard it said you are a pirate,' she challenged.

'I have just paid the Justices a great deal of money to be rid of that stigma,' he said severely. 'You may call me a privateer.'

'And what is that?' She was suspicious of his grin.

'It is one who has his government's approval for his piracy.'

'I'm sure King Charles does not approve of piracy!' She was indignant.

'Don't be. The King's approval, like that of most men, is directed by expediency. I suppose you are too young to know of the famous pepper consignment?'

'Probably. What was it?'

'It was during the Scots Wars. The King pirated an enormous cargo of valuable pepper from the East India Company.'

'But did he not pay for it?'

'No.'

She digested this. 'I expect he had good reason,' she decided. 'Anyway, it does not absolve *you* from pirating, if that is what you do.' She was aware of taking a moral stance that she did not genuinely hold. She didn't give a button if he were a pirate or not, on the whole she thought it rather romantic if he were; but she wished, for some reason she couldn't haul to the surface of her consciousness, to disapprove of him.

'I do not do it very often,' he said, regretfully, she thought. 'I am chiefly a merchant, but these are hard times for merchants.'

'Are all those men pirates, as well as Members of the Parliament?'

'They are all members of the New Providence Company.'

'And my father? He shares some venture with you – is he also a privateer?' She recalled her great-grandsire.

Will laughed and gave in to the temptation to run his hand over her curls. 'No, never fear. There is none of Sir George's money lost in New Providence. It is safely tied up in silks and spices. I have some samples of both for your lady mother, if you will allow me to place them in your barge when you go back to Chelsea.' She did not object to his touch which did not feel patronizing.

He added, 'Soon, when you are older, perhaps your father may allow you to sail with the *Lady*.'

She sighed irritably. 'Everything seems to be going to happen when one is older,' she complained, 'but one never gets there. How long, I wonder, will it be?'

Will looked at her carefully, taking her point seriously. He thought how pretty she had become and how well she had herself in control today, considering the temptations offered her. 'Not long now. A year perhaps. But you will have to learn to be a little less abrupt in your speech. Ladies are not abrupt.'

'Lady Hartley is. She is downright rude,' said Lucy aggrieved.

The girl was right. He forbore comment and suggested they continue their tour. He gave her plenty of time and all his attention and answered her questions carefully. His cousin was not mentioned again but Will noticed that Lucy would do no more than put her head round the door of his richly furnished sleeping cabin, while the sight of the vast satin-clad bed made her flush to a splendid scarlet once more. This made him feel oddly fond of her and he found himself presenting her with a beautiful length of pale yellow silk and a fall of amber beads as well as the intricately carved guitar he had chosen for her from his Spanish prize. 'You see – I remembered my promise.'

Lucy was near to tears. 'It is so very beautiful. How can I thank you?'

Had she been older, he would have asked for a kiss. 'Play it for me, what else?'

'But I have not the fingering of it.' She caressed the deep golden wood, the pearl and satinwood inlay slipping beneath her hands like watered silk.

'You will soon master it. Play it to me when we meet again.'

She promised and began to make some preliminary discoveries upon the taut, clear strings. She was almost disappointed when Jud returned and offered to take her home.

Later, she walked with Jud along the busy quay towards Billingsgate. Great masts, cats-cradled in rope, towered beside them and they could hardly hear each other speak above the mechanical chorus of metal, wood and stone, counterpointed with raucous orders and scurrying obedient feet.

'Well, what did you think of it all?' demanded Jud.

Lucy sniffed, appreciative of the mixture of tar and strange cargoes. 'I thought the *Lady* magnificent – like a ship in a great legend. She should belong to Odysseus or Sir Tristan,' she said dreamily.

'The men, booby! What did you make of John Pym and the others?'

'I am not sure. They did not seem to be – wicked enough.'

'Stupiditas! Why in the name of Beelzebub should they be wicked?'

'She shrugged. 'I expected it, that's all. Father speaks of Master Pym as though he *were* Beelzebub, and St John as though he were a traitor, for his defence of John Hampden. I liked *him* – he was nice and ordinary. But I wish I might like Sir Harry Vane,' she concluded wistfully.

Jud hooted. 'Trust a female! Just because he preens like a peacock and likes women. But you must know he's almost as much of a fanatical Puritan as old Nehemiah, God rot him – though a far nicer fellow in all respects.'

'Don't mention the Dismal Puritan; not on such a lovely day. Master Vane is a *million* times more human.' Then she remembered something. 'Tell me why Pym wanted you, while we – I was looking at the ship.'

'Oh, it was just some speeches he wanted us to print and distribute – about getting rid of the bishops, and the proper control of the army.'

She walked without speaking for a space and then asked him, 'Do you agree with them, then, Jud? You seem most willing to aid their cause. You know what Father would think.'

Jud scowled. 'Why talk of causes? I'm making my way in the world, that's all. Father won't give me any money now, so I have to turn a penny where I can. Besides, I like the work. It's interesting. And damme, I like the men! I've heard more good sense spoken since I took up the press than it was ever my luck to hear at Lincoln's Inn – or at Heron either, for that matter,' he added belligerently.

'What kind of things?' Lucy was not sure what Jud would now consider good sense.

Jud frowned, concentrating. 'When I was at home I always used to disagree with Father and Tom; you know that. I don't think I even knew why, not then. I think I supposed it was just because I was the younger son and they always seemed united against me. But I was always more of a rebel than Tom. I would have been so even if I had been the heir. It's my nature to argue – and that's part of what is so good for me here. I meet men, every day, who argue every bit as much as I ever did, with purpose and conviction. And often about the same things as used to set Heron by the ears; I never understood, for instance, why the King should be able to tax us all at will; I thought Hampden and the others were right to refuse the ship money. You'll remember how sorely I was beaten for saying so? I didn't mind the disagreement, but I resented that beating – that bull-headed attitude that Father is right because he's Father – and the King is right because he's the King! I tell you, Lucy, it's a relief to be amongst men who think that only what is *right* is right – and that open to sensible dispute. I can respect such men for what they are, not for what power they hold over me. John Venn and John Lilburne; I work for both of them. You should meet them. They are the sort of men I mean. You'd like Lilburne. He's kind and amusing, though he has an odd way of talking until one gets used to it.'

'The one who was in the Fleet? The one Father calls a "scab on the nation's backside"?'

'Blast Father! Freeborn John is a fine man. He's a phenomenon.'

'Indeed. And what does he talk about, in his odd way, this phenomenon?'

'Oh the Devil – I can't put it all into three words like a pig's belly into a sausage skin! About freedom, I suppose, and power and how it should be used.'

'Like Plato?' Master Davies would have been proud of her.

Jud sighed. 'More like Plato than like King Charles, at any rate.'

But Lucy had had enough of the sung praise of Puritans, chiefly because she couldn't argue with it until she had acquired a sufficient ammunition of knowledge. She determined to do this, but for the present, in fairness to her ignorance, she changed the subject. 'Does Silken Will see a very great deal of that hideous woman?'

'*What* hideous woman?'

'Lady Hartley.'

'She isn't hideous. She's one of the most beautiful and sought-after women in London. She even has verse written about her, and has had her portrait done dozens of times. If you ask me, Lucy Heron, your nose is out of joint!'

'Well, I don't ask you,' replied his sister tartly. 'But if *you* were to ask *me*, I'd say London life has addled what few pitiful wits you possessed!' Then, after a suitable interval, she changed the subject again.

The Herons' house at Chelsea did not stand directly on the river, but one cannot have everything; they did have a private pathway down to the jetty, walled and scented with roses and honeysuckle in the warmer months, now, in this week before Christmas, floored with sucking mud, just stiffening into ice.

Once the Dower House of one of the great Thames mansions, built of rose brick and timber in the Old Queen's day, the house was small, neat and pretty, with a long, well-stocked garden crammed with colour when seasonally possible and even now celebrating the Saviour's coming birthday with a heart-lifting heraldry of green, gold and white. Near the house, so that it could be seen from the parlour window, stood the winter cherry, its broad sprays of white blossom standing guard over a young colony of aconite that gabbled, yellow and cheeky, around its roots. The long walls which sloped towards the river, were almost obscured by the interlaced skeletons of dead climbers, reminded of life by a bright network of jasmine, just coming into flower. In the borders a few brave lilies stood sternly amongst the laurel, ivy and hellebore, whose polished and poisonous dark green leaves were the perfect foil to their purity.

Near the kitchen door was a tiny, ridiculous maze of herbs which Lucy had planted for her Mother. Inside, the warm, compact rooms were filled with dried honesty and catkins and dozens of little pots of exotic plants that Mary Heron had begged from John Tradescant; and of course, there was holly; it came from a splendid tree at the front gate, thickly berried this year and reminding Mary of her Quickenberry, which she missed, though she knew Dominic would tend it as carefully as a member of his farflung flock.

They did not usually spend Christmas here, but Sir George would have only a few days leave from Westminster, and besides, he did not care to leave London now that the city was in such a turbulent mood, nor the Commons now that John Pym was pressing the King so closely towards disaster.

Since they were to stay, it was decided that they should be festive. They would eat, drink, sing and be merry. Margery Kitchen had been impressed from Heron to take care of the eating and drinking, and they could do the rest for themselves. It promised to be a happy time. Jud was now *persona grata* once more, for at least 'as long as he keeps his confounded nose out of the dirt', and Valora Grey was to keep the feast in their company.

On the afternoon that Valora was due to arrive with Tom from Whitehall, up in her bedroom Lucy passed the time in writing to Dominic and to Martha. She divided the news between them, giving her cousin the 'politicking' events, such as the King's reprieve of seven condemned priests, and Robin Whittaker's latest scrape – a spell in Newgate for taking part in the sack of a sectarian preacher's house – and saving the more domestic concerns for Martha. These included the advent of three new 'patchwork' kittens for her ginger female cat, of a parrot for Humpty and Kit, sent by Will Staunton to make up for the loss of the magpie, and a description of her own latest gown, grey velvet trimmed with red, and a red muff. She also told them that she loved them and worried about them and that they were to look after each other and avoid all contact with Dismal Persons.

She was just sanding and sealing her letters when she heard a flurry of noise from downstairs. By the time the wax was dry and she had added the superscripture there came a single impatient rap on the door and Valora was in the room. Lucy was enfolded in scented skin and crackling violet taffeta.

'Gracious child, how one misses people! Let me look at you.' Her swift critical scrutiny led to the judgement, 'Something has changed. It isn't just that your hair has grown. And there's nothing much physically – turn around – well, perhaps there is – but mostly, I think, it must be in your *mind*. Anyway, whatever it is, it suits you. You are not only very attractive but you look like yourself and no one else. See that you keep it that way. Now, sit down, here on the bed. I have so much to tell you—'

As she sat, Lucy noticed that the rosary still held its strategic position at her waist. The garnets were particularly striking against the violet silk.

'I've only been at St James three days – I had work for Her Majesty at Hampton Court – but already it promises not to be dull. Only I wish this cold and rain would stop and these *dreary* demonstrations against my faith. I was almost torn limb from limb when I stepped from my coach on a visit to the wife of the French Ambassador. Happily the gang of ruffians who surrounded me decided I was harmless, though only, I fear, because I most resoundingly denied being a "bastard, French-poxed catholic she-wolf!" Had they simply cried "Catholic" I'd probably be decorating the ambassadorial gatepost by now.'

'How horrible! You must take more care! Tom would be furious if he knew that you—'

'Tom is furious in any case. I can do nothing with him. He's simply a bear! A raging, senseless brute of a bear!'

'Why, what's the matter?' Lucy had no need to direct the flood; it found its own level automatically.

'Oh, glory, what is *not*? I haven't had a single quiet moment until now. Here, help me to unpack my clothes, there's a dear girl; they'll be creased to Hades else. Where am I to put my things?'

'Well, you may share my aumbry, and I've made some space behind this curtain – I hope you do not mind sharing the bed with me and Julia – only we are rather stuck for space; you could have a camp bed, Mother says, from the Tower barracks—'

'No, no, this is perfectly fine; we shall sleep like birds in their nest. Now what was I saying?'

'Tom. Being a bear.'

'Yes. Well, I suppose it is really Lunsford who is at the root of it – or is it Bulmer? Both – and the King, of course. Oh *why* do men have to be so damnably stiff with their own importance?'

'The King?' Lucy was startled.

'No, Tom. And Bulmer – and of course the wretched Lunsford. *He*'s known for it – and hated for it – all over London.'

Lucy took a deep breath, though it was Valora who ought to need one. 'Who,' she demanded firmly, 'is Lunsford? I know who Bulmer is – Sir Horatio, your guardian.'

'Yes, yes, and he's behaving like the foolish old goat he is, God forgive me. And Tom is not much better. He is shocking bad company when he's in the sulks. You see, it's all on account of the King's determination to put in Colonel Lunsford as Lieutenant of the Tower. He's one of the most unpopular men in England – and leader of that scavenging pack of marauders from Strafford's disbanded army. They have lean purses and long swords and spend their days picking quarrels with honest citizens, all supposedly in the King's name, poor gentleman! The people call him Butcher Lunsford. You know how they feel about the Tower: it stands for England, God and King all rolled into one! They didn't mind Balfour, the present Lord Lieutenant, because he scotched poor Strafford's attempt at escape. He's a good soldier and a good Protestant, if there can be such a thing. But Lunsford is a swaggering, unprincipled jackass – what's more Pym is putting it about that he's a Catholic, blast his sharp wits. The mob was incensed already and now, it seems, they have persuaded themselves that the King wants control of the Tower only to turn its troops on *them*. Or rather, Pym has persuaded them. He has tossed a lighted torch onto dry kindling. And you tell me that man is not a jackal!'

'I only said he seemed an ordinary sort of man. But why does the King *choose* such a man as Lunsford?'

'It was that angel-faced idiot Digby's idea. He has become His Majesty's chief friend and can do no wrong. Tom was man enough to say he thought it ill advice, and asked the King if he would reconsider the appointment. But King Charles does not like to be criticized once he has made up his mind. He was very displeased with Tom.

'Naturally, Horatio was delighted. He spoke to Tom, in front of me, as if he were his accuser on the Day of Judgement – saying that if Tom could not accept his Sovereign's will in all things, honour demanded that he should ask to be relieved of his duties at court.

'The barefaced cheek of it! My guardian imagines that if Tom were gone I would come to see our love as a foolish aberration and do my duty to God and the King by falling into his arms!' She grimaced.

Lucy worried. 'But cannot the King *make* you marry Sir Horatio? Especially if Tom is out of favour?'

Valora gloomed. 'Let us hope not. I doubt it. The Queen will speak up for me. But I can't be sure; Horatio has King Charles' ear. God knows, Lucy, I am His Majesty's most loving subject – but I must say he seems to find virtues in the most undeserving of his friends.' She sighed crossly. 'If only Tom would keep quiet and do as he is told. And he is so out of temper now that we quarrel every time we meet. Oh, Lucy, who'd be a poor bitch of a woman, I ask you?' She huffed again and gave the cross of her rosary a vicious swing. 'Love,' she pronounced, 'is hell.'

'Why, this *is* hell, nor are we out of it,' quoted Lucy who liked Kit Marlowe because he died young.

'It is beginning to look that way,' Valora agreed. 'There is a decidedly unpleasant glow about London these days.' She swished the rosary again.

'You ought not to wear that thing so obviously,' Lucy warned. 'It will be the death of you one day.'

'Strange that you should say that,' said Valora, reminiscing. 'Your charming friend, Martha, once said the self-same thing to me at Heron. She was staring into the fire in that faraway manner she has, and her eyes were full of tears. I don't know what had distressed her, and there is something about her, you know, that prohibits one from asking personal questions.'

'Martha is a very private person. And very independent. I only hope,' Lucy added anxiously, 'that if she ever needed help in any way, she would not be too much these things to ask it of her friends.'

'What kind of problem do you envisage?' was the practical query.

'Well, there is Nehemiah, for example. He will not stop pestering her. And some of the villagers think she is a witch.'

'Superstitious fools!' Valora was the enlightened kind of Catholic. 'But surely your cousin will look after her interest?'

'Dominic, yes. But he is not the best connection for her if there were any trouble – he is in danger himself.' Yet Dominic would do his best for Martha, Lucy knew, for she sensed that in some way, unlike other ways she knew, he loved her. She sighed. 'It is a pity he is a priest.'

Valora looked surprised, then disapproving. 'It is the highest calling to which a man may aspire,' she observed, severely. 'I hope that one day I may be privileged to meet your cousin.'

There was the sound of further arrivals downstairs.

'Oh Bedlam, that'll be Tom! He has been with the Scots Commissioners all day and will be dog-weary. Come, let's go join the company.'

They came down the narrow passage that traversed the back of the west wing of the house and out onto the long, broad landing that served as a kind of minstrels' gallery to what was surely the most attractive room in the house, the miniature 'great hall' with its tapestries, its fine panelling carved with Tudor roses and its wide stone fireplace, pounding out heat like a great oven so that even Sir George was standing to one side of it rather than sear the seat of his breeches. The rest of the family were distributed about the room in characteristic positions; Jud and the twins sprawling among several recently acquired spaniels; their mother sitting serenely with her sewing; Julia beside her with her own grubby handwork. Tom, looking worn-out as Valora had predicted, was helping himself from a jug of hot punch on the dresser.

'Why who is that?' asked Valora, peering over the balustrade. 'I didn't know you had another guest. What a handsome boy.'

'Nor did I.' Lucy leaned over to look.

The boy stood near the fire. He was tall and slender with an exorbitant quantity of russet curls crowding his shoulders. His features were good, as Valora had said, but what chiefly distinguished them was an unusual vivacity; his expression had undergone several lightning changes in the few seconds of their examination. Feeling himself observed, the boy looked up. Unabashed, he waved a friendly hand and smiled.

Lucy and Valora smiled back, then descended the broad, shallow stairs and were welcomed into a comfortable hum of warmth and talk. Sir George waved his tankard, splashing Lucy's aggrieved cat, who was nursing her kittens to the side of the hearth.

'Lady Grey! Lucy! New friend for you – Cathal O'Connor. Comes to us from the Dublin Laceys, fresh from Ireland.'

'Ireland!' The word conjured up instant pictures of bloodshed and strife.

'And why not, Miss Lucy? And isn't there only a small little sea between the two of us, and that like a duckpond when I came over?'

She was fascinated at once by his accent, which was more like music than speech and made her feel something like seasickness because it went up and down so much. But she wanted to hear it again at once.

'Is it not very dangerous for you to be in England?' she asked.

'Well, I wouldn't say I'd be welcome everywhere, but so long as I stay close in Tom's shadow and keep as quiet as I can manage, I should come to no harm – though I'm as willing to take up my sword for King Charles in London as I was in Dublin, should it be needed of me.'

Sir George frowned. 'From what my cousin Lacey tells me, you're a damn' sight too willing to take it up, wherever you may be. We'll have no such talk as that while you're under Heron protection, eh Tom?'

'No indeed, sir,' said Tom, looking somewhat grimly at the boy.

Cathal, it appeared, had left Ireland under a cloud. His family, having found it impossible to keep his sword out of his hand or off the necks of Protestants, had determined, knowing of Walter Lacey's English connections, to send him away from the trouble he was courting before it caught up with him and despatched him forever. The fighting was only just beginning in the part of the Pale where he lived and his parents felt they would all live longer if the family firebrand were out of the way. They had bribed him by making him their messenger to the Queen. What they had to say to her had not been revealed to him. He carried a coded letter, which he had already delivered. He had then made himself known to Tom.

He declared himself delighted to be amongst them and looking forward to spending Christmas with them. He had the easiest manner that any of them had ever encountered in man or boy, and generally behaved as if he were in his own house, so that soon it seemed that he was. Lucy and the twins were thrilled and everyone else a little sceptical when, after a little friendly questioning, he revealed himself to be descended from one of the High Kings of Ireland.

'I am named for Cathal of the Red Hand, son of Turlough O'Connor, King of Connaught.' He flashed a disarming smile. 'But we stand on no ceremony nowadays. There is only one King in Ireland now.'

'But could you claim your throne again – if you had a big enough army?' asked Humpty excitedly.

'Sure and I could – but that is a powerful mighty "if",' Cathal replied lightly.

Humpty was silent for once, thunderstruck by the thought that tonight he would share his bed with a rightful Celtic king.

'It is not my own throne I'd be claiming, had I an army in Ireland now,' their guest said softly, 'but the rights of King Charles and his Queen, God bless her. And yet, I believe, though I find it hard to understand,' he added with a wondering tone, half-accusation, in his voice, 'that we are not of the same mind on this most important matter?'

Sir George grunted and coughed. Tom's mouth twisted.

It was Jud who spoke. 'The rebellion must be put down, even though it claims to be in the King's name. This is a Protestant country, Cathal, and the Irish Protestants have a right to our protection.'

His father glowered at him, then smiled sourly. The boy was right for a change. It was a difficult moment. At this very time, any member of Cathal's family might be dying for the opposite point of view.

'I think,' said Sir George with a kindly look for the waiting boy, 'that we had best regard ourselves as one family, rather than the two sides of an argument – else we shall make a sad Christmas of it. You are right. We in this house cannot agree that your rebellion has a just cause. But that is no reason why we should not love you as one of our sons. I want no further discussion of this subject here.' He looked sternly round the circle. 'Let that be understood and we shall do very well together.'

No one there, except perhaps Tom, knew how much of an effort it had cost his father to express so liberal an attitude. A more truthful description of his feelings towards Irish Catholics had been given at St James earlier in the week. 'If we don't soon vote the men and money to put down these insolent bog-trotters, I'll be over there myself with my own militia and stick them like the pest-ridden papist pigs they are – saving your poor mother's unfortunate connections!' Now that one of these unfortunate connections stood in his hall, he had schooled himself accordingly, as he always did. Sir George loved his wife very dearly.

Tom, however, who had fallen into his own harsh reflections, did not appear to have marked his father's stricture. 'For once I am half in sympathy with John Pym,' he said angrily. 'How can Parliament vote to furnish an army when there is this suspicion lying over His Majesty's doings? Christ's blood, after watching him in Scotland I would not vote for it myself!'

There was an awkward silence, broken by Humpty's whistle. Tom never made emotional statements, and that was what this one had been; his bitter expression made that abundantly clear.

'Damme, sir! Mind how you speak. I am surprised at you,' snapped Sir George, glad of another target than Cathal, with whom hospitality forbade him to argue.

Tom groaned. 'If you had seen it, sir. He has lost any goodwill he might have had among the Scots. With Montrose in jail we all thought he would go carefully. But no. He spoke them fair enough, I'll give him that. He scattered douce words and titles like manna from heaven, but this talk of army plots and papist plots had already broken his reputation. And he did nothing to mend it by receiving those army officers so foolish as to attempt the kidnap of Argyll!'

'Argyll! That descendant of the serpent! Even St Patrick could do little against that one, I'm thinking.' Cathal's gentle tone was gone. 'When he banished the snakes from Ireland, sure they took up residence with the clan of Argyll. They call him King Campbell, and king is what he will be in Scotland, if King Charles does not scotch him quickly.'

Tom gave an impatient sigh. 'He is King in all but name already.

We have lost all the concessions we hoped to gain from this visit. The Scots will give King Charles no help that is not sanctioned by those members of his Parliament who will agree to implement their damned Covenant on English soil.'

Cathal made the sign of the cross to ward away such a heinous possibility. 'And the poor Marquis of Montrose?' he asked. 'Did they let the gentleman out of prison yet?'

Montrose was no Catholic; indeed he had been among the first lords to sign the Presbyterian Covenant. But he had also been the loyal instigator of the Cumbernauld Bond, a more political document, signed by those who thought that the Earl of Argyll was becoming an overmighty subject in the style of the Earl of Strafford. During the war with Scotland, Montrose had served his king well. His king had repaid him by letting him languish in jail while he wined and dined the man who had put him there, the man, too, who had put his King in a beggar's suit and had refused him all that he asked. Montrose, for his honesty, was a hero to Cathal O'Connor.

To Tom Heron he was also a personal friend, and his own loyalty to King Charles had been sorely tested by the disgraceful fact of that continued imprisonment. He had returned to London at odds with himself and his duty; London itself being much in the same situation, and Tom's relations with Valora being strained, perhaps, more than ever before, he found himself glad to be diverted from his troubles by the presence of his engaging young visitor.

'Argyll will let him go free,' he said gloomily, 'now that he has made his point and shown his power in Scotland.'

Cathal, hating anyone to be in the dumps, clapped Tom cheerily on the shoulder, causing his siblings to exchange covert grins. No one touched Tom. He did not like to be touched – except presumably by Valora.

'Hasn't King Charles more to vex him that he can rightly manage, God help him? But he'll do the right thing by all of us in the end, you'll see. But first, he will succour his loyal subjects in Ireland. I have absolute faith in it!'

'I have spoken to the four winds, it would seem!' Sir George was offended. 'We'll have no more of this. Be told, damn you!' He was uncomfortably aware of Pym's Militia Bill, which had passed its first reading by 150 votes to 125. His Majesty's reply to that had been to insist that all absentees must return to the House before January 2nd and the second reading. If Pym were to hurry the bill through, he might well win. Sir George did not want to have to discuss with Cathal what would happen to Ireland if he did.

Luckily, Cathal was a well-mannered youth whose parents had impressed upon him the need to tread delicately about his London hosts. 'I'm begging your pardon, Sir George. My tongue runs away with my poor fool of a head. I'd no wish to insult your great kindness to me, divil a one! How shall I make amends?' he added extravagantly. 'Will you make me your lady's slave, or your own ollave?'

'What might an ollave be?' enquired the baronet, relenting so far as to restore his smile.

'It is a kind of well-born servant of a great household whose work it is to sing songs and tell tales and make his master's name famous throughout the land.'

'A sort of minstrel,' said Lucy, intrigued with such an archaic employment. 'I should love that; we'd be the only family in England to have our own troubadour.'

'And I'd begin with a poem for your sweet self, Mistress Lucy – with its sounds as liquid as Lough Neagh beneath the moon. I'd compare you to Nieve of the Golden Hair, the daughter of Mananaan, God of the Sea, who wore a cloak set with red stars and a golden crown on her head, and sat proud and light upon the back of a white horse shod with gold.'

Lucy caught her breath and stared at him, unable to take in the wonder of this picture of herself. 'Oh,' she said, and no more.

It was Valora who covered her unusual confusion, and by now everyone agreed with her words. 'I think the first tale must be of Cathal of the Golden Tongue. It'll make your fortune yet.'

There was laughter at that, and then it was Julia who set the ultimate seal of approval upon the newcomer. Climbing down from her seat beside her mother she walked gravely up to him and presented him with a dog-eared and dirty cloth animal of nondescript appearance which was normally clutched tight against her heart. 'His name,' she confided, with her presently gap-toothed smile, 'is Belzabub. He likes you.'

Cathal bowed solemnly in the direction of Belzabub. 'And isn't that a fine, fighting name? I am glad he likes me for I fear that otherwise he might be very fierce.'

Julia considered. 'He is only cross when he has to go to bed early,' she said, with a diplomatic blink at her mother.

Mary was having none of it. 'If he were a sensible creature he would know that he needs his sleep,' she said firmly, 'and so do you, and that very soon. But you may stay until after supper.'

'Us too?' bargained Humpty, eager for more of Cathal's company. Mary nodded and was rewarded with hugs.

Cathal thought afterwards that he had probably never had to work so hard for his dinner in all his born days. Kit and Humpty sat on either side of him, with Lucy opposite, and the bombardment of questions, he felt, was very likely not dissimilar to the drubbing his compatriots were suffering at home.

'Sir George does not need an ollave,' Lucy told him as he threw his mutton pie down his throat in a merciful interval. 'He makes his own speeches. But you can be mine, if you like. You shall tell me stories of the gods and kings of Ireland, and I will make music for them.'

'Nieve of the Golden Hair,' said Cathal, his eyes making the promise.

As a special pre-Christmas treat, Lucy was going to visit Valora in the chamber in Whitehall Palace where she stayed when she attended the Queen. It was afternoon and a carriage bearing the royal coat of arms had come all the way to Chelsea to fetch her. It was a bitterly cold day and Lucy was muffled up to her eyes in cloak and comforter, clutching a stone hot-water bottle from Margery Kitchen with heartfelt gratitude. Coaches may be as grand as they please but they are not warm.

Whitehall was more like a puzzle than a palace. Every phase of architecture, from the time of Henry VII onward, was represented in the rambling warren of buildings. Lucy was left at the door of the oldest Tudor part. This was not at all imposing; in fact it needed repair rather urgently.

The coachman had told her she would find the Ladies' Chambers upstairs. She was a little early as there had been no street trouble to hold them up. She stood looking about her in the harsh grey light. It felt as though it might snow. She was in a stone quadrangle flanked by buildings of varied age and size. There was a half-hearted patch of grass in the centre. She shivered and decided she may as well go inside and look for Valora.

As she turned to do so she heard her name called from across the square. It was Cathal, who must be here with Tom. He ran towards her, his face lit with excitement.

'I did not expect to see *you*. I thought Tom was at St James's today?'

'He was – but listen you here, Lucy. There is a thing I have to tell you – only you must promise never to tell another soul about it – or your brother will eat me, so he will.'

'I swear on my grandfather's grave,' promised Lucy instantly. 'What is it?'

'Well, it's this. It's all on between Tom and Lord Bulmer – in five minutes – in the fencing gallery! Since you are here, you may as well come along and see the fun!'

'What do you mean? What are they doing?'

He saw her look of fear and took her hand. 'Ah, come now, there is nothing to worry about. It is just a little bout between friends?'

'They are *not* friends. They loathe each other.' She looked at him suspiciously. 'It is a duel, isn't it? You wouldn't be so excited over a friendly match.' The King had issued an edict against duelling and the punishment for disregarding it was severe.

'Who gave the challenge?' Lucy asked, seeing Cathal look sheepish.

'Sir Horatio, of course. He is a gentleman who takes fire for his breakfast. But tell me, don't you find it a grand, romantic gesture, the two of them, fighting it out over the beautiful Lady Grey?'

'No I don't,' snapped Lucy, now thoroughly frightened for Tom, 'and neither would Valora. She will be furious.'

'Ah, nonsense. There's no woman born would not be thrilled at the prospect. Now are you with me, or are you not, for I am going and I am going *now*.' He held out his hand again and she took it, though her brow was as cloudy as her father's could be.

They crossed the quadrangle and dived into a modern section of the palace which smelt strongly of horses and polish, sweat and leather, and must be, therefore, entirely populated by the male sex. As they hurried down endless passages, Lucy wondered seriously if this could be a reality. It seemed impossible that staid, sombre Tom, who always did the right thing, could have so far lost his command of himself as to agree to slight the King's wishes and commit his dignity to the idiotic waste and display of a duel.

'Margery often says men are fools,' she muttered as they pattered over the flags towards a distant drone of voices.

'Don't be saying that until you are an old woman,' counselled Cathal, grinning. 'Men will be many other things to you before you find them fools.' He squeezed her hand.

'I'll be the best judge of that.' She threw him a withering look.

When they reached the fencing gallery, they found quite a crowd of young men there, standing about and smoking the disgusting weed that Raleigh had made so popular. They took no notice of Cathal and Lucy, apart from a few half curious glances, and they were able to make their way to where they would have a good view of the proceedings. The room was a long, wooden-floored rectangle, one-third of which had been roped off for the duellists, and the rest filled with a couple of rows of benches and the eagerly talking crowd. Tom stood with two friends, presumably his seconds, behind the rope on the left; he looked grim and edgy and Lucy determined right away that it would be better if he did not discover her presence.

Cathal, who already thought he knew Tom well enough to agree with her, found her a place in the second row of benches, where she could peer between two stout pairs of shoulders and was unlikely to be noticed.

'Hold hard! What's this?' enquired the gallant to one side of her. 'Not really the place for young ladies, what?'

'I have come to watch my brother fight,' said Lucy with great firmness, settling herself with a permanent air.

'Oh, well, if that is the case—' The gallant subsided, and those who had looked round shrugged their shoulders and minded their own business.

As Cathal, with his usual open friendliness, made himself acquainted with his companion on the left, Lucy allowed herself to relax a little and take her first look at Sir Horatio Bulmer. He was as elderly, portly, lined and veined as she had imagined, sustained on his feet by an afflatus of self-importance that surrounded him like an invisible blown-up bladder. She could not envisage his handling a sword with any degree of precision.

This was where she was much mistaken. Had she been less preoccupied with the novelty of it all, she would have noted that, in the eager betting that was going on all around them, rather as though they were at Newbury than at Whitehall, the odds were mostly in favour of Sir Horatio.

Now the noise declined. The two men, stripped to shirt and breeches faced each other and measured their distance until the seconds were satisfied. Tom looked very thin. The signal was given and the duel had begun.

Lucy's only experience of such a thing was when she had been taken, far too young, to see a performance of *Hamlet, Prince of Denmark*. Although she had gained absolutely no idea what was going on in the play, she had wept buckets when Hamlet and Laertes had fought and died. The memory inspired her with no great confidence in the present. Sir Horatio, she soon saw, was light on his feet and in full command of his weapon.

At first they were only circling and jabbing, making the occasional lunge without contact, but it was evident from the outset that Lord Bulmer was the fresher man, despite his age and weight. Tom was transparent with lack of sleep. He had sat up, arguing in circles with Valora until well after midnight, ignorant of the morning's challenge. He was glad enough of it, however, now that it had come. Both he and Bulmer knew full well that, as Cathal had said, they fought on Valora's account, and not for any imaginary insult to the King, given as the official reason.

Tom just wished he didn't feel so damnably tired; it slowed a man's reactions and that was dangerous. He didn't want to kill Sir Horatio; he was no such fool as that; but he might like to scratch him a little, to make a mark upon that insufferable vanity of his. He would have to look out for himself, though; Bulmer's jealousy had grown strong enough to make *him* do something he might afterwards regret. Whatever the outcome, Valora would hardly marry him if he badly wounded Tom. The thing was, Heron decided, to remain defensive and avoid rousing too much choler in the old man. Accordingly he parried, feinted and disengaged as often as he could, but soon discovered that this was not what Sir Horatio had in mind.

'Fight, you scurvy young coward! Fight! I didn't bring you here to practise your knitting!' This sally won laughter for Bulmer and ruptured the flimsy structure of Tom's pacifism.

'Since you ask for it, you conceited old wineskin!'

Fully awake now, he laid on with all his skill and a new speed, so that then the cheers began to go up for him, in company with shouts of 'Come on, Horatio! Don't lose our money,' from the less sporting spectators. The room became very noisy and everyone, including Lucy, stood up so that they could shout louder.

Suddenly there was a cry of 'first blood!' from Tom's seconds and they saw Sir Horatio grimace at a scarlet line running down his shirt from his left shoulder.

A second held up his hand and there was almost silence. 'Very well, gentlemen; blood has been drawn. Does that satisfy you?'

Bulmer protested and there were immediate roars of 'No! Let them go on. Chance to get even,' from the punters.

'Ah, let them go on, do,' Cathal encouraged, his eyes shining, 'Tom will not take advantage of the poor ould divil.'

There was voluble argument. Tom, naturally, did not wish to continue the attack upon a wounded opponent. Sir Horatio, bristling, declared that it was only a scratch and that he had so far had no satisfaction.

The altercation threatened to last as long as the fight had so far done, and doubtless would have done so, had not a sudden silence dropped, somewhere near the door. It spread quickly and icily until it reached the hot centre of contention. With the sense that there was something unexpected, and probably unpleasant, behind her, Lucy spun round in her chair.

The doorway framed the tall and at this moment decidedly commanding figure of Valora Grey. She wore her violet taffeta and every inch of her expressed outrage. Lucy had never seen her in anger and would not have believed that even she could feel so blasted by it.

Not a sound was heard, other than the irrepressible creaking of boot-leather, as Valora allowed her daunting gaze to travel the faces ranged about the room and come to rest in glacial displeasure upon the principal actors in what suddenly seemed to be a rather shameful pantomime.

'You my lord – Sir Horatio! Pray explain yourself to me, sir. I confess I did not at first believe it when I was told that you were taking part in such an unintelligent escapade, but now I see that truly "when the age is in, the wit is out".' She ignored the half-swallowed laughter at this and swung savagely towards Tom. 'As for you, sir – if your manhood has need of such tawdry games to prove it, you are sorely mistaken in thinking yourself to be a man.'

Tom's eyes widened; hurt passed through them, then fury.

Relentless, Valora continued, her audience, all but three, agog with curiosity and enjoyment of the scandal. 'I am given to understand that I am the chief cause of this undignified and, may I remind you, criminal procedure.' She waited, looking from Tom's white, immobile face to her guardian's red and perspiring one.

Sir Horatio bravely marshalled the few wits not ambushed by the disastrous interruption. 'Valora – my dear. What can I say?'

'That is what I am waiting to hear.' Her voice was thin and dry. No one laughed.

Sir Horatio squared his shoulders and opened his mouth.

'I think,' said Valora tightly, 'that it would be courteous if you would lay down your sword.'

The embarrassed steel clattered to the floor. 'I – beg your pardon – most earnestly,' Horatio beseeched. He looked round for non-existent aid, gulping as if for air. 'I can only offer you my extreme regret that you should have been distressed in this way.' He shook his shoulders and pulled himself up a little, attempting to recapture his lost dignity. 'But I cannot say to you that I regret the provocation of this bout. I challenged Captain Heron in defence of His Majesty's appointment of the Lieutenancy of the Tower, which he saw fit to criticize.'

Pusillanimous toad, thought Lucy, sniffing disdainfully, aloud.

Valora made no acknowledgement of this information. She turned to Tom. 'Captain Heron, do you substantiate this?'

Tom stared coldly into her colder eyes. 'I do.'

'Very well. I would be glad if you would both remain here for a moment. We need not detain the other gentlemen any longer.'

There was a second's stunned appreciation of what was most certainly a marching order, and then the other gentlemen, sheep-faced and with surprising speed, piled out of the gallery with as much enthusiasm as they had come in.

Lucy, though transfixed with interest, did not know whether she should leave with them. She made a move as though to do so; after all, this did seem to be rather private business, for all it had been made so uncomfortably public. Besides, she felt slightly afraid of Valora just now, and extremely so of Tom.

Cathal, however, who had no intention of missing the hooly, gripped her arm to keep her in her place. 'Sit you down again, me darlin' girl. They'll have need of an arbitrator,' he whispered. Lucy did so but then wished that she had not as Tom discovered her presence.

'What in the devil's name are you doing here?' All his anger was turned on her.

She shook her head. 'I was just watching.'

'I brought her, Tom,' Cathal said quickly. 'Didn't we all think simply to enjoy a little swordplay and a wager or so, without the least of an idea of all this contrariness?'

'It is just as well that she *was* here,' Valora said, her voice a little warmer for Lucy's sake, 'otherwise I might not have learned of your abysmally foolish behaviour. I was looking for Lucy when one of your witless friends informed me of it.'

'God damn it, Valora, why can't you mind your woman's business? Were you invited here? Was your comment canvassed?' Tom could hold his spleen no longer. He had never been so angry with her. Love, for the moment, was laid aside.

'I need no canvassing to look after my own reputation.' Valora was equally sour. 'God knows it has come to grief in your hands! So look you here, both of you – it is well known to me, and to others, where your true quarrel lies. You should think it shame to abuse the King's name in such a sordid business – and even greater shame to indulge your childish spite at my expense.'

'I can't for the life of me see how it is at your expense, my dear,' puffed Sir Horatio, whose eyes were glazed with misery.

'Because the whole of Whitehall and St James knows that your quarrel is over the disposition of my person and fortune!' Valora's temper approached white heat. Lucy would not have been surprised if she had picked up one of the fallen swords and driven into the breasts of each of her suitors, in turn. It was at this juncture that Cathal decided to offer his attempt at arbitration, seemingly immune to the sulphur fumes which whirled about his head.

'King Charles may dislike the duel,' he began reasonably, 'but it is an accepted, even a respected fact that in most civilized countries in this contentious world, men will do battle for the honour of a lady's heart and hand. It is the most natural thing in the world, Lady Grey – don't the little birds do it, and the herds and every manner of creature?'

'How many men have you killed, Cathal O'Connor?' was Valora's sardonic counter to this plea.

Cathal looked modest. 'Three.'

'Good God!' A ring of startled faces examined him afresh.

'That has nothing to do with it,' Valora said hastily, not wishing to lose her advantage. 'Kindly do not interfere. I have little to say but I insist that you both hear it.'

She turned to Sir Horatio, her large eyes judging him. 'I find it insupportable that you, who are the legal guardian not only of my fortune and myself, but of my reputation, should suffer my name to become a byword in your quarrel. You have lost your own integrity in this, and have thrown away mine, as far as the world is concerned.'

'But I assure you, I—' Horatio was purple with discomfort.

Now it was Tom's turn. Grim-faced, he stood like a rock and let her angry waves wash over him.

'If I were to come into your keeping – you, who have offered me your love in exchange for mine—' She raised her chin a little and carefully maintained her frigid tone. 'I doubt I should be the better for it. You prove yourself as rash and unthinking as you are selfish and unyielding! One does not dishonour what one truly loves. I thought your instinct would have directed you better.' Only now did the hurt show, in the slight waver of her voice.

'At least,' said Tom wearily, 'I know my own mind and can *tell* what I truly love. I intended you no dishonour, nor do I think you have sustained any. You are acting like an hysterical woman; a creature you always claim to disdain.'

'Small wonder if that were true!' she cried harshly. 'I ask you – both of you – did it ever begin to occur to you how it would be if one of you killed the other?'

'It would not have come to that,' said Tom flatly.

'If you had seen your faces just now, you would have thought it could.'

Lucy applauded inwardly; she had thought so too.

'However – you shall have a solution, and a better one than a bleeding wound. I have made up my mind at last, Tom, and I hope you will like the cut of it. I shall marry neither of you, ever! Sir Horatio, I could not love you as a wife, and so pray excuse me. Tom – you could not love me as a husband; you are all for yourself. I have some little freedom at present. I am not anxious to give it up for a lifetime of dissent.'

'I no longer ask you to,' said Tom cruelly. He saw that she was almost in tears and had reached the end of her anger; but his own had been steadily refuelling. 'You make too much of yourself, my lady; your reputation remains what it was; that of a noisy termagant who happens to have a certain attraction. It is not I who have let the world know your business but your own uncontrolled tongue. Had you left us alone today this affair would have been over and no one the worse for it. It is you who have made it into a scandal.'

Truth allied to unkindness were too much for Valora. Gritting her teeth, she managed not to sob, turned on her fine French heel and left the room. A taste of ashes seemed to remain.

'Oh Tom – how could you?' Lucy accused. 'She was only afraid for you!'

'Get out! Cathal, get her away from here!' There was a subdued groan from Sir Horatio as they obeyed.

Outside, Lucy fled down the corridor in a welter of tears. Cathal easily overtook her and stopped her flight, holding her companionably in his arms while she wiped her eyes on her sleeve. 'There now, take a deep breath or you'll have hiccoughs.'

'I'm sorry. Oh dear! Now they'll never get married.'

'Now clear up; you're heavy weather. They'll surely marry one day – just not today. They love each other dearly but there is a demon of pride in the both of them, burning up their good sense.'

'Christmas will be all spoiled.'

'It will not. I will see to that. Now stop crying and kiss me and see how you like it.'

'What?'

'Kiss me. You *will* like it, I assure you. I do.'

Astonished, she found herself moving to touch his lips; she had meant to go quite the other way. He kissed her softly and lightly and did not insist; he didn't want to frighten her. 'There now, doesn't that take your mind off other people's troubles?'

She laughed shyly. 'You are a rogue, Cathal.' But she did like it; he was right. She looked at him thoughtfully. 'Tell me, did you really kill three men?'

'I did. But we will not speak of that just now,' he said firmly.

She conceded his right, but sensing the beginning of a new power over him, she ordered imperiously, 'Then tell me instead, about Nieve of the Golden Hair.'

Cathal looked about them at the drab, draughty and slightly dirty passageway. 'This is no place for such a tale,' he said fastidiously. 'I will tell you when we are in some beautiful place together, and you will remember it all of your life.'

Christmas, although not spoiled precisely, was not the light-hearted occasion it had been in former years. Everyone was more or less in a bad mood, either over their own or someone else's troubles. Valora had packed her bags and gone home to Spindle-sham so that she should not have her made-up mind unmade again by contact with Tom. She had refused to see him before she left. He had swallowed some pride and sent her a jewel. She had sent it back. Tom, therefore, went about pale and taut and bit off your head if you spoke to him. This caused particular distress to his mother, who had become very fond of Valora and had thought to hear wedding bells by the spring. She ached for her firstborn's obvious misery, but could not for the life of her understand how it had come about. Her instinct was that it was all Tom's own fault, so that her sympathy was charged with irritation. On the morning after the duel she viciously rooted out every dead annual left in the garden.

Even Sir George, whose mind now lived at Westminster, wherever else his body might be, was out of temper with his paragon. The news of the duel had seeped out as such things always do, and Tom had to suffer parental displeasure in a manner not displayed since his childhood. 'If you had to pick a quarrel, God's boot-tops, why couldn't you pick it with one of Pym's nasty company instead of lighting on a man who's as straight as a pike and near the King's heart? I never thought you a fool, boy!'

'It was not I who brought the challenge,' Tom said coolly.

Sir George glared at him. 'Never mind all that. What concerns me is your critical attitude to His Majesty – at a time when the lousy mob is howling about his gates and he hardly knows which way to turn—'

'He might discover the way to turn,' offered Tom bitingly, 'if he were to allow his right hand to know what his left was doing.'

'By God, sir, I'll not have this insolence, even from you. Look to your loyalty, Tom, or by heaven you'll have me to deal with, never mind Horatio Bulmer, curse him!'

'My loyalty is unaffected by my ability to see the King's faults. He is a man, not a God, and shows himself to be a very fallible one. Surely, sir, you yourself can see—'

'I'll hear none of your carping. I want to see you do your duty and to hear no more of your opinions.'

Tom shrugged and went off to St James to do that duty. His way was much impeded by gangs of apprentices enjoying their Christmas Eve holiday in most unchristian roarings about the walls of the royal residence. In order to get through them he used elbows, boots and a large vocabulary of ungentlemanly epithets; it somewhat relieved his angry tension.

Lucy, though cast down by Valora's defection and the general unseasonable temper of her family, allowed herself to be somewhat cheered by the efforts of Cathal, who now devoted himself to her entertainment. He forbade her to talk any more about Tom and Valora since it could make no difference to their situation; they must simply wait until the next turn in their story should be revealed. He was confident that there would be a next part for he now saw them as lovers on a grand literary scale and knew that this was only the end of a chapter.

Lucy also worried a little about Jud, of whom she saw almost nothing, despite the raising of the ban on his presence at Chelsea. She was somewhat hurt by this, but Jud seemed in such excellent spirits when they did meet that she could not really complain.

Cathal took her all over London at a breathtaking pace; he wanted to see everything and do everything and neither the cold, the rain nor the frost prevented him. They explored the streets and alleys from Bridewell to the Tower and back to Guildhall on the north bank of the Thames, and the exciting and odiferous maze of ill-repute of Southwark on the south bank; they went to the bear-baiting, which was cruel, and the theatre, which was enjoyable; they teased the monkeys and birds for sale on London Bridge and shot the rapids beneath it – an event which they kept carefully to themselves, although Mary Heron questioned them abstractedly as to why they had come home so wet on a day when it had not rained.

On Christmas morning, after helping to stuff the goose because to do so brought good luck, they went skating on a frozen pond they had found. They were both confident performers and took great pleasure in showing off their expertise, both to each other and to the world in general. Cathal thought Lucy an exquisite sight as she spun and streamed and turned, glowing in her green gown, her body given over to the gods who delighted to keep her on her feet.

They soon devised a kind of dance together, a constant separation and reunion, full of dipping and swaying and breathless moments when he would swing her up into the crackling air and whirl her round and down and up again so that the whole world turned for her and only his bright, knowing face was dependable.

'Oh, stop, stop! I must breathe; my side hurts,' she begged at last, and he pulled her in close to him so that she slid into his arms.

He looked gravely into her flushed and happy face. 'You were light as a lark up there in the white sky, and as lovely as ever was its song. You are a beautiful thing, Lucy and you turn my heart to fire and water both.'

She examined him closely, panting a little still. She found no sign of humour in him. 'No one has spoken to me like that before. It is like a poem.'

He stroked her cheek, his fingers cold and gentle. 'It is yourself that is the poetry; I am just the poor poet who will catch it and put it down in dead words with nothing like your living sparkle.'

It was lovely to be talked of this way, but it was also disturbing. 'I think that you live in your poems and your stories and now you want to make up one about us,' she said repressively.

'And whyever not? Wouldn't we make the grand tale – the descendant of Turlough O'Connor and the golden-haired daughter of an English baronet. A Protestant. Born to be enemies but linked in love and ready to suffer the torments of all the fates for it!'

He was humorous now, but not completely. He saw that she was becoming unsure of his true mood, and, since he was only half sure of it himself, he solved the problem by kissing her again. This time the kiss was harder and more demanding and he did not stop until he had warmed her lips into a trembling participation and felt her arms encircle him more tightly.

He stopped and felt her cheeks and nose. 'There – there is nothing like it for chasing away Jack Frost!' While she was still staring at him like a startled fawn, he swung her out onto the ice again and they resumed their circling of the pond. When they had finished he kissed her again, but quickly and softly this time. 'A merry Christmas to you, Lucy.'

'And to you, Cathal. I am so very glad you came to us.'

'May it never bring you sorrow,' he said.

She smiled at him, thinking it a strange reply, but did not question it. 'We should go home now,' she said.

The word 'sorrow' seemed to lay upon her heart. Perhaps it was because there seemed to be so much of it in the air. But not, surely, for her and Cathal? Perhaps, she thought wisely, it might be better if they did not try to make up too grand a tale around themselves. But how difficult that would be, now that he – that they – had begun to weave the tale. She looked forward to being alone soon, so that she could think calmly about those kisses and the wonderful words he could pluck from the air like cherries from a tree. She would not have that precious time to hug to herself quite yet, but she was more than prepared to wait. First they would celebrate the feast of Christmas in fine style around the long table in the 'little great hall'. They were both hungry after their exertions. Hand in hand they hurried home.

The house smelt deliciously of roasting goose when they opened the door. They were met by the twins who had worked themselves up into a high state of excitement in honour of the day.

'We've taught Henry Morgan to say "God bless Christmas",' said Humpty, who had the parrot sitting on his left shoulder with its claws firmly dug into his best velvet suit. It appeared to be eating the lace edge of his collar. 'Come on!' he encouraged it.

'Hell's bells and buckets of blood!' said Henry Morgan.

'He'll say it later; he's in a bad mood,' Kit explained.

'And why might that be?' Cathal enquired, helping Lucy off with her cloak.

'Because father called him a filthy imp of Satan when he fouled Mother's cushion. I told her it was good for the garden, but she said he never did it in the garden. We said we'd collect it if she liked – but she didn't like, did she Hump?'

'No – but they haven't said we can't keep him. They can't really give away a present from Will Staunton.'

Cathal had to know who that gentleman was.

'You'd like him,' said Lucy. 'He seems very arrogant and carries himself as if he is important, but if one is alone with him he behaves like one of the family – almost.'

'He's a pirate,' said Humpty unequivocally. 'That's why I called the perroquet Henry Morgan – as a compliment.'

Lucy sighed. 'He's a privateer.'

'It's all one to me,' Humpty grinned.

Their father's special occasion roar invited them to their dinner. Lucy clapped her hands in approval as she entered the hall. Mary Heron had been busy while they were out. Decorating the house at Christmas time was something that she always liked to do for herself. Yesterday she had sent out John Coachman, who had little enough to do when they were in London, to comb the nearby countryside for more holly, ivy and anything else that was green or had pretty berries. They had all been tied up in garlands with scarlet and gold ribbons and hung upon the walls and the backs of doors, care being taken to keep them away from the candle-holders which stretched gilded hands out from the panelling at intervals. Today there was a prodigal amount of light; they would not count the cost of the candles. The grey illumination from the windows did not signify against that mellow celebration. Margery Kitchen had even brought the best candelabra from Heron, along with the silver, to grace the table.

The family assembled, combed and burnished, trying not to look too greedy while Sir George took the brassbound Bible out of its handsome carved box and laid it on the sloping lid to read the story of the Saviour's birth. It was a long story, and much as they loved it, they wished it were shorter.

At last it was done and they were bidden to sit down. They were a very small party this year. At Heron they would have had up to a dozen visitors; here there was only Cathal, though several of Sir George's friends, including Will Staunton, had promised to call on them later. They were nine at table, though they had allowed the servants to bring their table into the hall, to add to the cheer. By the sound of it, Margery and John were already cheerful enough. Both were addicted to quantities of wine and there were more than adequate supplies of that about just now.

Lucy saw Tom's lips straighten as he sat down opposite her at Sir George's left hand. He lifted Julia onto the chair next to him, where Valora should be. Next to Julia was Kit, then Jud, on his mother's right, as far away from her husband as she could place him. Humpty was on Mary's left, then Cathal and Lucy. For a moment there was a silence, as often happens when people expect something of an occasion, then everyone began to talk at once in their usual way.

The meal was splendid. Margery had surpassed herself. The

goose was cooked to perfection, the meat tender and succulent and the skin crisp and brown. There were also pigeons, partridges, a rabbit fricassee, a veal pie and anchovies and larks on little spits for *bonnes bouches*. There were parsnip fritters and carrots and blue cabbage and a dish of cold beetroot. Afterwards came all manner of creamy concoctions with wine or brandy in them and preserved fruits and cheese. There were grapes, kept fresh by leaving a piece of the vine-wood stuck into a huge apple to be nourished with its juice. And of course, there were plenty of Lucy's favourite comfits; a new one that appealed to her most was green ginger, flavoured with orange and dipped in syrup.

Talk languished at first, tending to consist in the main of everyone encouraging everyone else to have some more of this or that. Even Sir George, who could eat a great deal, very fast, and talk as well if he had to, confined himself to a few punctuating belches. Tom ate silently and sparingly, though Lucy kindly kept offering him specially nice bits, thinking he must be missing Valora. Cathal, she noticed, dealt very gracefully with his food, as befitted a true King of Connaught. Jud got his head right down and ignored everything but his meat until he began to feel satisfied. Observing this, Mary asked him gently if he got enough to eat at his master's house.

'Eh? Oh, yes, Mother. Plenty. It's just that I've been doing a deal of running about lately. You know how it is,' he added vaguely, 'Messages to here and there. Makes a fellow hungry. We eat very well, but I'll always miss Margery's pastry.'

'You should come home more often,' said Mary hopefully.

'I'll try. I really will. But this printing work occupies all my free time—'

'And what, exactly, d'you print, if I might make so bold?' his father enquired, his brows wavering.

Jud shrugged lightly. He did not want to spoil the meal, nor yet his second chance to inherit his share of the patrimony. 'Whatever I'm asked. Pamphlets. Religious texts—'

'So well as you have nothing to do with these scurvy broadsheets that the disloyal faction are putting about.'

Jud smiled and shook his head. Guilt must be his penance for the lie. He was fond of his father, despite their disagreements and it was Christmas.

'A printing press must be a mightily interesting machine. I would like very much to see one at work, if you ever have the time,' Cathal said to Jud with his nicest smile.

Jud, who knew when he'd been rescued, offered to show him

at any time he liked, preferably at evening. For the first time, he began to consider the character of this affable young papist rebel who sat so cosily at home at their table. He must possess positively ambassadorial tact and diplomacy for Sir George to have accepted his presence, and waived his politics, with such apparent ease. Jud decided he liked the look of him; he would take time to get to know him better.

They were well into the fruits and cheeses and Lucy into the comfits when the baronet, with appropriate solemnity, produced his very best claret, brought from Bordeaux by way of the *Gallant Lady*, charged all the glasses and stood to propose a loyal toast. 'Here's health unto His Majesty, God bless him and save him – and confusion to his enemies, the Devil damn them to perdition!'

Everyone rose and drank, Kit assisting Julia whose chair was too high. When they sat down again, Sir George found that he had already drunk a little more than he had thought. A wave of depression lapped over him as he thought of the sovereign whose health they had just drunk. 'I wonder how His Majesty is enjoying his dinner,' he said sadly. 'It must be the first time in history that a King of England has had to eat his Christmas goose to the tune of the vile mob dancing about his doors. I went by the palace this morning and there must have been a thousand of them raving round the walls, shrieking against the bishops and the Lords and that blasted nuisance, Lunsford—'

'So you do not approve of Colonel Lunsford either?' Tom drove in swiftly. He had been piqued at the dressing-down he had received.

Sir George glowered at him. 'He is not the man I'd have chosen for the job, since you ask. But I defend to the death His Majesty's right to make the appointment. And so should you.'

'Let's not have that quarrel again,' said Tom impatiently. 'If only the King would give them *something*,' he mused, 'We might avert this disaster that faces us. He will not dismiss Lunsford and his reply to the Remonstrance was so much windy words—'

'What right have they to ask anything of him? He is the King.' The familiar purple was colouring his father's cheeks.

Tom was on a tight rein and had slept little in the past weeks. 'Cannot you understand that unless these riots are stopped and Pym and his friends are pacified, he may well cease to be King?'

Mary Heron gasped. Everyone studied first Sir George's face and then their plates. Tom had said a tremendous thing. They half expected him to be struck down for it then and there.

'My God, sir—' The baronet was rising from his seat.

Tom saw that he had gone too far and put out a placating hand. 'Wait. Wait. It is not my wish; nor are they my words, but what is spoken in the streets; streets filled with discontented people who have been encouraged to accuse their King – and who *will* have their answer.'

'Tom is right, sir,' Jud interposed, 'you know it; if the riots aren't stopped by some concession from the King, he will set Lunsford's troops on the mob, and the mob will fight back, and both sides will lay claim on the Trained Bands for help—'

'It will be like a little war, all in London,' said Humpty brightly.

'Humphrey. Be silent. You know nothing of this.' Mary spoke breathlessly, strongly disturbed. She was no fool and she made her husband keep her abreast of events. What Humpty had said was no less than the truth.

'And how long, do you think,' asked Cathal seriously, 'would such a little war *remain* in London?' And what, he wondered privately, would then become of poor bleeding Ireland?

They were all quiet now. No one knew what to say after that. The feast was broken and all their merriment was drained away. It was Mary who did her best to salve the wound, her gentle voice pleading with them all. 'For God's sake can we not have an end to these discussions at this time? We are here to remember the birth of Jesus. We do him a discourtesy by bringing these sorrows to this table. Let us ask for his blessing and his peace to fall upon all of us, and upon the King and his ministers, and his poor misguided people – and then let us have no more of this talk; for I tell you, talk in this house will not mend matters, and I will not have my household at war with itself.' She rose and said a brief prayer for a blessing, and then sent them all into the parlour, bidding them to crack nuts and not each other's heads.

They did as they were bid, the men a little shamefaced even as they exchanged glances that suggested they were merely humouring a foolish woman on Christmas day.

'Shall we play cards, or tell fortunes?' was Cathal's remedy against further conversation.

'Oh, fortunes! Can you really do it?' asked Kit excitedly.

'No – but you will never be able to tell the difference,' grinned Cathal. 'The Irish always tell you what you want to hear.'

The younger members of the family gathered in a group on the floor, a little way back from the fire. There were the dogs to lean on, for a comfortable back, and you could see the cards better, laid out on the rug.

Sir George, tired after so much claret and emotion, sank into his favourite chair and soon entertained them with a concert of snores. Tom turned a chair towards the window and pretended to read a book, while Jud, uncertain where he belonged, hovered for a moment until Cathal looked up and made a space for him on the rug.

The self-appointed gipsy was very generous with his fortunes. To Humpty and Kit he gave an extraordinarily bloodthirsty life on the Spanish Main, terminating in riches in retirement on a Caribbean island. Jud was to build his own merchant empire and own his own publishing establishment, and marry an heiress into the bargain. Julia was to marry a prince and eat from a gold plate, while Lady Heron, who came in softly to demand her share, was to become the most beautiful elderly woman in England and people would not know whether they had travelled so far to view her wonderful looks or her superlative roses. Cathal had purposely saved Lucy's turn until last and he was as disappointed as she was when John Coachman, who took over Tibbett's duties in Town, announced rather thickly that Master Will Staunton had called.

Sir George, woken by Tom's shaking his shoulder, snorted and grunted for a minute, then shook his head like a wet dog and looked ready for anything.

Will came in like a lion, as usual, with the breath of winter behind him and his arms full of boxes and parcels. He looked like some extreme form of Yuletide decoration, in a white fur cloak which he removed to reveal a green suit covered in red rosettes, with a broad golden sash and gold lace boot-tops. He wore earrings that were piratical enough to satisfy the twins and Lucy caught the whiff of scent. She hoped it had not rubbed off some portion of Lady Hartley, whom she was relieved to see he had not brought with him.

He took advantage of the day to kiss Mary Heron soundly, while thrusting several packages into her arms. She blushed and thanked him and was glad she had Cathal to present to him; his attentions always made her head swim and she liked to have something to take her mind off them.

'Cathal, I'm glad to make your acquaintance. Jud has mentioned you. I hope this is to your liking.' He tossed a packet to be caught.

'Why, save your kind heart! A gift from a stranger is welcome indeed.'

As Mary discovered a Venetian lace collar and two kinds of scent, Will walked about raining gifts into their laps, except for the baronet's, which was more claret, and Jud's, which was money. Even baby Edward, staggering about in a corner in his walking-rail, was remembered with a rattle in the shape of a horse.

A whistle from Cathal revealed a small but deadly Turkish dagger, its hilt smothered in showy turquoises. He worshipped it at once. 'It is extraordinarily generous of you, sir.'

'Not at all. It is what I would have liked at your age.'

Lucy wondered idly just how old Will could be; he made himself sound a hundred when he spoke that way, but Tom was only twenty-three and Will could not be very much older.

Her own gift was a feather-light shawl, woven in fine green wool. 'My favourite colour. Oh, Will!'

'I knew it. It is not a fashionable garment, but it will keep you warm when you sit out under trees in the dusk to read.' His smile reminded her of the night when she had lost her fear of him.

'It is a tissue of moonlight,' said Cathal softly, wrapping the shawl around her. 'A green girl in a green pool. If you wear this out in the dusk, sure no one will believe you are real at all.'

Will saw how Lucy glowed at him for his words. He felt a little shock of recognition; the girl had discovered something that was new to her since he had last seen her. She had found, or was beginning to find, how it was between a man and a woman. Well, the boy seemed engaging enough, and certainly silver-tongued for his age – what was he, sixteen? He supposed he must wish him well. He would have liked to arrange his gift upon her shoulders himself, but all he said was, 'It becomes you beautifully, my dear,' then he moved on, to give himself the pleasure of watching the twins shredding the expensive silk wrapping off the Italian breastplates he had brought them, while Julia crooned over a small figure dressed like Queen Henrietta Maria; none of them were to know that this had come to him from a county acquaintance who had got it from a witch-finder. The pinpricks were all beneath the silk of the bodice, where Julia, it was to be hoped, would not find them, or if she did, would make nothing of them.

The evening became merry again after Will's arrival. He too must have his fortune told, and a very splendid one it was too, bursting with riches and adventures and the love of gallant ladies.

'S'death, is that all?' Will feigned disappointment. 'I confess I had hoped, at the least, for some *change* in my dreary round!'

'Ungrateful!' said Lucy, teasing him with her eyes.

It is your handsome young rebel who has given you the

confidence to look at me like that, said Will to himself. She saw him frown and laughed at him outright.

'To them that hath, shall be given. Cathal takes his fortunes from the holy Bible; you must take it with good grace.'

'Must I indeed?' He grinned at her, wondering just what it was that he must learn to take with good grace. He knew that he was touched in some way by her happiness tonight. He supposed that it was simply that it was always sad to see a child become a woman, in some way. He must be getting old. 'Tell me,' he asked on an impulse, 'have you mastered your guitar yet?'

'Not mastered it; but I can play a little. Shall I show you?' She fetched the instrument and the night turned towards music. Will sang with her, alone at first, and they made themselves as happy as their audience.

Cathal was the first to compliment them. 'It is like the two highest among the angels,' he declared, 'except, of course, that I suppose they would be of no mortal sex.'

'Unsex me, would you?' demanded Will. 'I'd rather do without your praise in that case.'

Cathal smiled. Will was the most richly vital and animal man he had ever met. 'If I join you in the music will you allow that I meant well?' he asked.

Thereupon he left them and returned with a small pipe, made plainly in dark wood, with which he proceeded to drag their listening hearts from their bodies. The notes were wild and sorrowing, piercing yet fluid; they came from his native woods and hills and had the desolation of Ireland's history in them. Lacy felt tears stab the back of her eyes. This was another side to Cathal. She thought she might love him more for this than for his swift laughter and his easy poetry.

Her face was transparent and Will ached for her newness to it all. He passed his hand over her hair as he came by her to a seat at last. Her smile for him was as bright as ever through the tears.

Mary wanted them all to sing 'As Joseph was a-walking' after that, and they did, even Jud joining in with his deep, comical drone. He could sing well enough at the inn, when he and Robin were among their friends, but he never could hold a serious tune without sounding like a Puritan at a wake.

Mary privately blessed Will Staunton for saving her Christmas and allowing her to look round the fireside and see more or less what she would have wished to see; the family united in music and pleasure. If only Will could put a similar spell upon tomorrow.

*

On December 27th, when Sir George made his way through the heaving press of humanity that besieged the House of Commons, he found that the King had been persuaded to dismiss the wretched Lunsford. He had also issued a proclamation against Unlawful Assembly, but none of his subjects took any notice of that; few of them, indeed, were informed of either resort.

Any hopes for a *rapprochement* between His Majesty and the disaffected Members were speedily disintegrated by John Pym, who had been so busy during the last two days that he had not noticed it was Christmas. With grim satisfaction he presented a validated report from Ireland giving evidence that the Queen, not the King, had indeed lent her authority to the Rebellion. The House fell into turmoil.

Sir George privately cursed the Queen for her foolhardiness and Cathal O'Connor's parents for supporting it.

With malice aforethought, Pym followed his revelation by reading aloud the contents of a letter from the Irish Lords of the Pale, of whom Cathal's father was one. It asked for official toleration of the Roman Catholic religion in their country.

Naturally, it provoked an explosion of contemptuous mirth. Pym stepped down, well pleased with his morning's work. Sir George went into hasty conference with the King's friends. It was about then that they noticed for the first time, as their own rumblings died down, a most infernal din going on outside in Westminster Hall.

Had he been able to spare the time, the leader of the Commons might have enjoyed the proceedings in that vast anteroom almost as much as those he was engaged upon. Certainly he would have recognized and approved their cause, as well as a number of the participants.

The citizens had brought their quarrel onto the ground where, most would allow, it ought rightly to be disputed. Led on by several apprentices and two youthful distributors of broadsheets, they had come looking for trouble. Much to their pleasure they had found it, in the unequivocal guise of Colonel Lunsford and a score or so of his brother officers, who were pursuing their usual dispiriting occupation of lobbying for their arrears of pay and new commands in Ireland.

'Damme, boys, what have we here?' cried Jud Heron enthusiastically, dashing into the Hall at the head of an ebullient crowd of holiday-takers.

'Double damme, if it isn't Butcher Lunsford and his bold cavaliers!' This newly fashionable epithet was insult of the highest degree, having the connotation of the universally loathed Spanish cavalryman.

'Tell 'im to sling 'is butcher's 'ook!' cried a crop-haired fellow in a leather apron. Those at the back still stolidly bellowed 'No bishops!' as they had done all morning.

Lunsford, already humiliated by his dismissal, was half drunk and wholly enraged. 'You filthy mess of plague-gotten bastards! What do you here? Get out, the lot of you – or we'll show you the way with the flat of our swords!' He was a bulky, muscular creature, hirsute and built like a bull, his fellow captains likewise; it was no empty threat.

'We've come to sell you a broadsheet,' grinned Jud, holding one out.

'The work of Master Lilburne – you'll find it improving,' added Robin cheekily. 'Gawd knows there's room for improvement!'

'Why you turd-tongued young pipsqueak, I'll have your guts for breakfast!'

'We've as much right here as you!' complained a voice from the back. 'If you can cry "More pay!" in this place, than we may cry "Less bishops!"'

There was a growl of approval, whereupon one Captain Hyde, as empurpled as his leader, clapped his hand to his dagger and bellowed, 'I'll cut the throats of any round-headed dogs that bawl against the bishops!'

'Ho, ho, will you so?' demanded the brave voice at the back.

'I will that, you son of a poxy doxy! Come on then! Who says "No bishops"?' The captain's wattles shook, scarlet, as he turkey-cocked up and down, his hand advertising itself as itching upon his hilt.

There was a brief explosion of laughter, then a concerted shriek of '*We* say no bishops!' and the fight was on.

Hyde and Lunsford were the first to show steel, followed by half a dozen more. The citizens, having no steel to show, looked intelligently about them and lighted upon the several loose bricks and tiles from walls and floors much in need of repair. These they cast at their aggressors, retreating meanwhile at a dignified pace. They did not wish to become the Butcher's meat.

Jud and Robin exchanged rash comprehending glances and offered to engage Hyde and Lunsford in back-to-back bravado, using their rolled broadsheets as cudgels. The challenge was derisively accepted, and as soon regretted, as these comic drama weapons were systematically shredded by a few expert passes with the butchering tools.

Robin was the first to squeak as the cold sword slithered across his wrist; he put the offended member lovingly inside his doublet and ran for the door, Hyde pursuing him with guardroom oaths and great sweeps of his sword. Robin didn't care; he could afford a slice off his bacon, as long as the rest of him survived.

For Jud it was not so simple. His broadsheets were scattered in ribbons like the aftermath of a fair, and he leaped in and out of them in one man's morris to avoid the skilful scything with which Lunsford was now amusing himself while driving his victim slowly backwards to the wall.

'Just,' jerked Jud as he danced across the blade, 'what I'd expect,' as he jumped hastily back again, 'of one whose name,' as he levitated a good two feet, 'makes a midden of the mouth that spits it out!'

This was the ultimate insult. 'I'll teach you to foul my name, you pig's miscarriage!' he cried, making a genuine effort to slice off Jud's legs at the calf. Jud, who was no longer enjoying himself, muttered a prayer as he flew sideways to save them. He cursed Rob and the rest, who were by now a mere turbulence in the air in the vicinity of the Court of Requests.

'Blessed St Jude, lend me your aid!' he pleaded, deeming his case nothing short of hopeless. St Jude, or rather a small company of the King's gentlemen, conjoining to discuss the news from Ireland, did lend him, happily for that future, the requested aid.

Chief amongst them, indeed, was his brother Tom who, after a single startled, disbelieving blink, launched himself across the great chamber as though imitating the action of the tiger. His sword was out and had dashed the astonished Lunsford's to the floor before he had completed the trajectory.

'Tom! It's good to see you!' His endangered legs had by now turned to jelly and he leaned against the wall, grining inanely at his brother.

Tom grimaced in disgust. 'I can't say the same,' he said savagely. 'You bloody young fool! What d'you think you were doing? And you, sir,' he turned on Lunsford, 'a rare example of soldierly courage! One of His Majesty's officers attacks an unarmed boy.'

'Be dammed to you, Captain Heron! I had provocation enough, as you shall hear!'

'I don't wish to hear. The boy is my brother. I will not have him damaged for your amusement.'

Lunsford's eye lit red. 'A pretty sort of brother for "one of His Majesty's officers",' he mimicked. 'A foul-mouthed, mischief-minded little traitor. He was belting out "No bishops!" with the worst of them. Look there if you want evidence.' He pointed at the floor. 'Put *that* ignominious jig-saw together and you'll find the traitorous claptrap of Master John Lilburne!'

Tom's look shrivelled Jud. 'Is this true?'

'What if it is? I earn good money by it.'

Tom slapped his face. Jud stood, wooden. 'Come with me, you graceless young mischief-maker. We'll hear what Father has to say about this. Colonel Lunsford – I make no apology. The boy was unarmed. I assure you however that you may safely leave the correction of his ideas to his family.'

'You mean – of his loyalties,' jeered Lunsford.

'You will hardly question the loyalty of Sir George Heron—' began Tom, angry again.

Lunsford knew better than that. The sorry scene was ended.

For Jud there followed an even sorrier one when he was brought face to face with his father. The baronet was at white heat. He beat Jud as though trying to transform him to a fine paste, and then drew him through the painful sieve of his bitter recriminations. At the end of it all Jud was given to understand that his brother was deeply ashamed of him and that his father did not wish to see him, ever, again.

His mother pleaded and Lucy wept, but to no avail.

Will Staunton, when required to act as jailor, kept his own council as to his opinions, but suggested that a sea voyage might be what was needed to calm the boy down and give him time for philosophical thought. 'The *Lady* sails for the Italian ports in mid-January. Jud can go along as one of my factors. You would be surprised how much he has learned, despite his wildness. And then, when he comes home, and has done well for me, as I expect, perhaps then Sir George—'

'I think not.' Tom was tight-lipped. 'My father is much hurt by Jud's behaviour.'

Will sighed. 'I think it a pity. There will shortly be other hurts to consider, if I read the signs correctly.'

'That has no bearing on this matter.'

He had the last word for Will was content to let him. 'Poor young bugger,' he mused. 'Still – he wanted to go to sea!'

Within the Palace of St James, as the twelve days of Christmas wore on with tense and febrile gaiety, the riotous entertainment outside the walls crashed towards its augmented crescendo as thousands more, each day, joined in the anti-clerical chorus. The

King, disliking their music, called out the Trained Bands and a strong percussion of clubs and stones was introduced. In the House of Commons, Pym allowed himself his little grim smile as the apprentices set to, once more, against Lunsford's men and the chamber caught the echoes of the repeated opposed refrains of 'Roundhead!' and 'Cavalier!'

The riots would have to be stopped. Of course they would. And Pym was quite secure that, by now, there was only one way to stop them: the bishops would have to go.

On December 30th Archbishop Williams of York lodged a protest at the forcible exclusion of his colleagues from the Lords by sundry citizens. He phrased it unadvisedly, implying that their absence meant that Parliament was no Parliament, and that any actions it might have taken in this absence were, therefore, invalid.

Pym's smile broadened and became more grim. Within half an hour he had secured the impeachment of the fourteen bishops who had signed the protest, and the eager citizens were treated to the sight of the venerable churchmen being tipped out into the frost and dark of a bitter evening, on their way to immediate imprisonment.

The apprentices rang all the city bells in celebration, and on top of cheerful bonfires they offered a hearty warmth to ragged episcopal images that their originals, coughing from phlegmatic lungs and hugging their skinny ribs to stop themselves shivering, might well envy.

Surely now the King would take some strong action? He had been given enough rope. Once more, he commanded the Trained Bands to be ready to make a stand against the mean and unruly people who disturbed the peace. Pym, in answer, sent to ask the King if these same Bands might be put to guard Parliament against the increasing violence of Lunsford and his cavaliers. He was refused.

The rumpus continued. As usual, the only casualties were the meanest and most unruly, whose heads were broken as carelessly as rotten eggs. Sir George had himself escorted to the House by John Coachman and several paid bargemen. He wore his sword.

By far the most insistent refrain to assault the King's ear was the bass threat of impeachment to the Queen. His next action, therefore, was to put himself firmly on the side of the (Protestant) angels by roundly denouncing the Irish Rebels as traitors. Pym could hardly counter *that* with any accusation of the Queen, who was legally regarded as one with her husband in the issue of any royal proclamation.

As though to underline his adversary's inability to move, King Charles now took the step, booted in insincerity and spurred with irony, of offering Pym the office of Chancellor. Naturally, Pym refused, though he appreciated the gesture. The post went to the moderate, Nicholas Culpepper, while another of the King's friends, Viscount Falkland, became Secretary of State. The King was lining up his troops.

But Pym's smile remained broad and grim. In the long game of chess that they were playing he had no doubt that King Pym would win. The King had lost his bishops; it remained to be seen what he would do with his knights.

On January 3rd, Sir George came home in a state of high jubilation that he had not manifested for months. 'The King has accused Pym and his juggling junto of treason! We had it from the Lords today. God be praised, this should be the end of all our troubles.'

Tom, who had been deep in his Scots committee work, had come home late and knew nothing of it. 'Have they been arrested?'

'Not yet. The Commons claimed breach of privilege. Neither Commons or Lords will give them up to arrest. Lord Mandeville is one of the five named.'

'And the rest? Pym, Hampden, Holles?'

'Hazelrigg and Strode. Would there could be more, but those five are the head of the serpent. We'll tie the rest in knots when they've gone.'

Tom considered. 'It's a surprise, I confess. And it *is* a breach of privilege to accuse a Member of treason.'

'Poppycock. They are traitors, every one.'

Tom avoided temptation. 'What are the charges, exactly?'

'Subversion of the law, alienating the affections of the King's subjects, terrorizing Parliament by raising riots . . .'

'I wonder what His Majesty intends to use for evidence.'

'I don't like your tone, Tom; I should have thought the rabid state of the city was evidence enough. The King is in such fear for his person that he has called up the gentlemen of the Inns of Court, as well as Lunsford's crew and the TBs, to protect him. There are muskets and clubs all over town.'

'I do not think,' was Tom's grave opinion, 'that this move of the King's is liable to lessen hostilities; it is more likely to provoke people into taking sides once and for all. It could even lead to open warfare.'

'Nonsense. It will prevent it. Why else does His Majesty act so?'

'According to you, he has not yet acted,' Tom worried. 'The delay could be crucial. He should have arrested them at once, not waited for them to cry "Breach of privilege!" '

'His Majesty wishes all to be seen to be legal and correct,' was Sir George's hope. 'He is publishing his charges openly; there is nothing hugger-mugger about this.'

'From what I've seen, it will get him little sympathy in London. No, to my mind, if he wishes this move to succeed, he should have acted swiftly and *used* his troops to secure the arrest.' The argument continued into the night.

In the House, next day, Sir George was to discover which of them was right.

The atmosphere was like that in a field hospital, while men wait to hear if their General still lives. Pym alone, for reasons known only to himself, appeared as spry as ever, though his sour stomach evidently troubled him somewhat. It was notable that Lord Mandeville had demoted himself to the rank of Commoner for the day. There was an attempt to prevent honourable members from huddling together in groups to prophesy the turn of events, and to get on with the morning's business. It was not successful. All that was accomplished was the sending of messages to Mayor Gurney and to the Inns of Court countermanding the King's assumption of their support as a matter of form. The King's friends bit their nails as the time trod on in leaden boots and no arrest was made.

'Curse my breeches if I can see why John Pym sits there like a duck on the nest and *waits* for the King's guard!' puzzled Sir George, who by now was sharing the leader's dyspepsia.

His remark had been addressed to a King's man, but it was overheard by the Member for Cambridge, who was stretching his legs behind their bench. 'He waits,' began Cromwell in the manner of one who explains to a backward child, 'because the King will not make the attempt if the duck does not sit; and, more importantly, because we wish it to be clearly seen by this nation how its anointed King offers violence to his chosen Members of Parliament.'

'It is rather certain members of the Parliament who offer violence to their anointed King,' raged Sir George, but he found himself without an audience. Oliver Cromwell was continuing on his constitutional path.

At noon they adjourned for dinner. Sir George began by gobbling his food nervously but soon lost the desire to eat. Then there was a stir in the dining hall, as the Earl of Essex, a stout Puritan of noticeably military bearing, strode in to lean at Pym's ear. Soon the whisper came round; the King would make the attempt in the afternoon.

They reassembled at half-past one in a state of breathless excitement that broke into brief hysteria now and then as someone lost his nerve. The rumour was that it was all arranged for Pym and his four companions to hide out at various addresses in the city. They would not go, however, until they heard that the King's Guard was on its way to the House.

It was three o'clock, and the chamber ready to combust without the aid of Master Fawkes' machinery, when the message came: the King was coming in person to make the arrest, with an armed guard of between eighty and 100 men.

The King's friends, greatly outnumbered, could do nothing but look on in horror as Pym, with his usual cool formality, begged leave of the Speaker for himself and his four fellows. Sir George's heart lifted a little as William Strode made some demur. Apparently he wished to confront the King rather than demean their cause by running away.

His friends had heard enough of his argument and the baronet despaired again as they dragged Pym out by his cloak. A barge was waiting at the watergate to take them to safety.

Sir George put his head in his hands and groaned. He wished he could spare his sovereign the humiliation to follow. They all waited in silence until they heard the sounds that told them the King had completed his journey from Whitehall. They remained in their places and maintained the silence with as much dignity as they could muster, correct behaviour being their bare weapon of defence in the face of invasion.

They need not have feared. When the door of the chamber was at last thrown open, a single, slight, black-clad figure entered it. The King was very small and at this moment looked very lonely as he stood upon the threshold to accustom his eyes to the interior light. Those who were near to him observed that his eyes were dull and his skin seemed as thin as gauze, a faint flush giving the illusion of a man who had slept last night. Behind him was his nephew, the Elector Palatine, the only man to accompany him into the room.

Unless anyone should still be ignorant enough to think this loneliness anything but an image of the singleness of monarchy, that hot-headed lord, Roxburgh, leaned back upon the open door so that the Members could have a view of the soldiers outside. As soldiers will, these amused themselves by cocking their pistols and taking playful aim at the Members. Even Sir George was heard to grumble that there could scarce be need for that.

The King, always punctillious, removed his hat as he came amongst them. He walked slowly towards the Speaker's chair, and as he passed the little group of loyalists that contained Sir George, he nodded to them and gravely raised his hand. The baronet blessed him for this recognition at such a time.

'Mr Speaker,' said King Charles, 'I must for a time make bold with your chair.' His high-pitched, slightly Scots-accented voice was courteous but not cordial, as precise as his appearance, not a curl displaced, not a hair of his moustache touching the line of his lip, his collar and cuffs as pure as though he were to say mass in them.

He took the chair and looked about. Coldly and reasonably he told them why he was there. 'You sent us a message,' he said with more emotion, 'concerning your Privilege. No King of England has ever been more careful of your privilege than I have been. However, in cases of treason, no man has privilege.' He looked about again, finding several faces hostile. 'Is Mr Pym here?'

You could cut the silence.

Impatiently, the King asked the Speaker, 'Is Mr Pym in the chamber?'

Speaker Lenthall, perhaps more from a sudden weakness in the legs than from access of loyalty, fell to his knees. 'Sire,' he said unsteadily, 'it is not my part either to see or to speak but as the House shall direct me.'

The King drew himself up, his eyes narrowing. ' 'Tis no matter,' he snapped. 'I think my eyes are as good as another's.' The quiet became oppressive as those eyes bored their way along the benches for what seemed a very long time.

At last he acknowledged his defeat. 'I perceive that all my birds have flown,' he said tightly, 'but I expect that they will be sent to me as soon as they return. I intend no force, but will proceed against them in a fair and legal manner.' He did not look about him again as he descended the chair and left the chamber.

Outside, the voices were gathering already, with their new cry 'Privilege of Parliament!' Others, but very few, responded with 'God save the King!'

Sir George Heron, certain of what he had seen, but as yet confused as to what it might mean, took his confusion home to his wife. As he sat in his barge and was rowed against the current towards Chelsea, he began, unhappily, to work it out.

On Twelfth Night Lucy and Cathal were walking along the riverbank some way from the house. It was cold but not yet quite dark. The sun was going down in subdued russet sulks, wreathed in grape-coloured rags of cloud. They walked hand in hand, but they did not talk because each of them was preoccupied with a separate problem.

Lucy was worrying about Jud. She could not understand why her father had taken such an intractable stance. Surely a man can be a bully, even if he is King Charles' bully? And if Jud had got into bad company, perhaps they should blame Master Pym, who had seemed to be responsible for at least a part of what her brother was doing. But Sir George had not suffered her to speak up for him, under pain of a similar displeasure. 'If only we didn't all have to fight,' she said despondently, more to herself than to Cathal.

'You have the gift of second sight, lovely, for that is just what I am thinking. See, here is a comfortable sort of tree; will we sit beneath it for a while? There are things I have to tell you.'

The tree, a stripped willow, grew close to the water's edge. They sat down and Cathal wrapped both of them in his cloak so that Lucy should be doubly warm. She turned towards him with such a serious attention that he couldn't tell her, not yet.

Holding each other as carefully as glass, they kissed. They did this rather soberly at first, each tremulously aware of a depth of feeling that was almost too sweeping. He stroked her hair as he loved to do, learning the shape of her head.

'You feel so – familiar. Like a part of my home, or of myself. How warm your head is; so round and small, no bigger than a spaniel's. To think of it, throbbing with all that thought and life!'

A gust of exhilaration caught him and he hugged her suddenly, so hard that she thought her ribs might crack. 'You can't imagine how *alive* you make me feel, Lucy, how *real* you are to me.'

'Real?'

'Yes. Because I can stand here and touch this fragile little skull and wind this bright hair about my fingers and *know* – as I think that one is rarely blessed to know – that I am fully present in what I do, that I *feel* with every ounce of my being, and am *aware* of every ounce of yours.'

Lucy did not have to tell him that she shared his knowledge. They had come so close during the brief time they had been together that they almost seemed to share the same skin. The world seemed both to have stopped and to have expanded into an infinity of gladness, and they were the only people in it.

'I feel very *new*,' she said shyly, watching her pink fingertips move over his brown face and outline his lips, so that she would be able to draw them when he was no longer there.

'You *are* new, and also unique, and so am I, and so is tonight,' Cathal said with complete satisfaction.

'Your fingers feel so nice; I should like you to stroke me all over like a cat.'

Lucy laughed and moved her hand to the open neck of his shirt.

'There are hairs on your chest.'

'I'm going to be a very hairy man.'

'Like Esau.'

'I hope not; if I must be Biblical, I'd rather be – let's see – like King David.'

'He had dozens of concubines,' said Lucy severely.

'Not when he was my age. He was still slaying Goliath.' He guided her hand inside his shirt and held it over his heart. 'There. You are the very first to make it beat like that.'

'That makes me feel sad. If I am only the first, that means there will be others to follow me.'

He frowned. 'Don't think ahead. We can't, for too many reasons. Let's think only of tonight, otherwise we shall not live it properly.'

A small shadow was formed by his words. It hovered above them and they pushed it away, to hang in the empty branches above them. Cathal began to kiss her again, a sense of protectiveness rising in him, and with it the desire to know more about her body.

He was not ignorant of girls' bodies. There had been several obliging servant girls at home. But this was Lucy and she was very different. He wanted to know her because he loved her.

She made no complaint when he unfastened her bodice, though he heard her catch her breath in surprise and perhaps a little fear. She wanted him to touch her; she was sure of that. At least, her body was sure. It seemed to have developed imperatives of its own that raced ahead of the prohibitions of her mind. So while her head was a jumble of her mother's warnings and her father's whip, her hands were helping Cathal.

He gazed at her breasts with the wonder of a boy who sees two moons in the sky. He touched them very gently. 'Beautiful,' he murmured. 'You are beautiful. I knew you would be.' He kissed one rosy tip.

'More beautiful than Nieve of the Golden Hair?'

'Far more, though she too was an enchantress.'

She pulled his head down and kissed him with a new passion that had seemed to rise from the pit of her stomach and took her by storm. She soon found herself fighting for breath as he returned and doubled her wonderful ardour. She pulled back, gasping. 'There must be a way to kiss and breathe as well.'

They tried again. Cathal took it more slowly this time. This did not help. He found his desire rising now in a way that was already frustratingly familiar to him. He tried to control it, to take it with him rather than be dragged by it to the usual unseemly finish. This was the first time passion had its true object for him. Servant girls were only experiments, though tremendous fun, of course. But he was truly falling in love with Lucy. It was the first time and it was very important. He opened his eyes as they kissed, and found her own, dreamily green, swimming into them. He broke off and held her away from him.

'You are too much for me.'

She smiled, accepting the tribute and leaned back in his encircling arms. Her breasts peeped, round-eyed, out of their covering. She had forgotten their nakedness.

Cathal had a sudden sense of her complete innocence, which was also an awareness that he was losing his own. He should not be doing this to her; it was cruel in the circumstances. He buried his face in her breasts.

She stroked his hair, aware of a change. Proximity did its work and his tristesse was banished by the glorious adulthood of kissing a girl's breasts.

Lucy shivered.

'Don't you like that?'

'Yes. But I'm not sure that I should.'

He smiled as he might at Julia. 'I hope you are not going to turn Puritan against me.'

'No. But my father would *kill* me if he knew.' Her mind was catching up on her truant body.

Cathal reluctantly covered her up. 'I shall not allow him to do that,' he assured her proprietorially. 'And anyway, it isn't as if I had stolen away your virginity, and made you unmarriageable – though I should very much like to,' he added boldly.

'I am not sure that *I* should like it,' Lucy said doubtfully, no longer convinced that she meant what she said. For whereas, on one hand, the mysterious act to which he referred had to do with making babies and being married and doing one's duty, on the other, it was becoming clear, it had just as much to do with the singingly pleasurable sensations that Cathal had drawn from her body like notes from a softly swept lute. She would be less afraid of it after today.

She had not known that such wonderful sensations existed. Her mother had not told her. She supposed this was because one was meant to wait until one was married to experience them, and must not be told how marvellous they were in case one should seek them out prematurely. Well, she had made her discovery and did not regret it, but thought she had better not go any further. She did not, she thought suddenly, want to place herself in the same class as Lady Eliza Hartley. The memory annoyed her; it was out of place.

'What will we do, Cathal?' she asked with swift urgency, blotting it out. 'Will you speak to my father?'

But rather than the joyful agreement she expected, she saw him close his eyes and groan. 'If only I might,' he began slowly, wondering how, after this, he could possibly sound anything but treacherous to her. 'The thing is – I meant to tell sooner, but I couldn't bring the words to my lips – I have been thinking that I will have to go home. Very soon.'

'But surely—' If he needed punishment her look of waking pain gave him all he deserved.

'It is not that I want to leave; never think that. If I had the choice, I would like to spend my life here with you, all my days, to know you and love you better day by day – for I do love you, Lucy, you must believe that. I think you do.'

Her great green eyes could have swallowed him then as easily as could the river. She said nothing, only waited.

Hating himself, he tried to tell her. 'You know that King Charles has declared the likes of my family and myself to be traitors; that this is not so, you also know. I find it hard to believe that he would throw us to the dogs of war and leave us to shift for ourselves, knowing us to be loyal – and yet, not only has he done that, but he will eventually send his army against us, as your father has said. If you were me, my linnet, what would you do? Would you hide yourself away in a land that calls you traitor, bringing danger to your friends – who, in truth, should be no friends to you – or would you go home to your family and your people and fight for your own piece of land and your own blessed faith?'

'You have no choice, have you?' she asked bravely. She was weeping without noticing it. 'It all seems such a mad muddle; I can't really understand it fully. But I can see that it is dangerous for you to stay.'

'It is not that; I do not care for my own danger; it would be worth it to me to stay with you, and to try, perhaps to see King Charles and tell him how it is with us at home—'

'Would he listen? Would he even speak with you?'

'Perhaps not, now. And, now it would go against my pride to try.'

He straightened and took on a look of conscious pride. 'I am an Irishman, and a Catholic, before I am King Charles' subject. And so is my father. I must go home. He will need my sword.'

Lucy gave a long, hopeless sigh. He was right. He made it all seem clear enough. 'I wonder,' she said bitterly, 'how many men you will have killed by the next time we meet?'

He strained her closer to him, his cheek in her hair. 'Never think of that, *mo chride*; only be sure that one day we *will* meet again, and that we will never let the wars come between us. I will write to you – there are ways for me to reach you – and I will tell Tom what to do to get your letters to me.'

'Oh, Cathal! Don't. You make it all sound so final, as if it had happened already. I cannot bear to think of you at war; suppose you were killed . . . or horribly wounded . . .' her voice began to rise towards panic; she was frightening herself with her own words.

He turned and gripped her arms, steadying her. 'It will not only be myself who will see the war, Lucy. There will be a civil war fought here in England before ever English troops are sent to Ireland in any number.'

'It makes no sense,' Lucy despaired again. 'How can you have a war between two lots of Englishmen?'

'It made sense during the wars of York and Lancaster, or between Steven and Matilda.'

'They were barbarians then.'

'You were right. We are all barbarians; we use swords where we should use words and will prey upon our brothers as if they were strangers, just to prove ourselves in the right.' He smiled at her, trying to lighten the load with which he had so abruptly burdened her. 'And yet, we *are* in the right, Lucy – and must fight for it, if that is what it comes to. The King of England cannot give over his crown to John Pym's Parliament for the asking, even should he be so weak a vessel as to wish it. And King Charles is no weak vessel; he has been harsh with Ireland; he will be equally harsh with his enemies in his own land.'

'And my father will have to fight, and Tom, and even Jud.'

'They would think scorn to do otherwise.'

'And that foul Nehemiah will fight for the Parliament renegades and set Heron by its ears.'

'Stop frowning; you look like an angry fairy. Let's have done with talking of war; we can do nothing to change what must come. But we can please ourselves, just for a day or two . . .'

The panic returned. 'When must you—?'

But he shook his head and gathered her to him, cutting off her questions with his mouth on hers. He had never kissed her with such seriousness before and his lips trembled, transmitting the change in him better than words. Pity and sorrow welled up in Lucy, for him, for herself and for the unknown future. She clung to him in a new desperation. Before, they had taken time to test each other and these delicate new feelings that fed upon daily increase; now, there was no more time and the delicacy fled before their urgent need to crowd the future into this moment.

Sensing her abandonment of hesitation, Cathal groaned and grated his mouth and his body against hers. Threads of totally new and wild sensation coursed through her causing a pleasure that she wanted and yet feared. It was as though they were thundering along in a coach from which the horses had been cut free.

He touched her breast and response flared in her. She pulled back her head and gasped. Then she shook her head violently several times.

'I can't do it, oh I can't! I cannot take in both love and death in a single moment.'

He lifted her hand and kissed it very slowly, to give her time to be calmer. 'Forgive me, sweetheart; I was carried away by the drama of our situation.' His wryness brought her to earth. 'And not by my astonishing likeness to Nieve of the Golden Hair? I am disappointed.'

It was good that they could smile again. They kissed once more, but without desperation, and Lucy shrugged down so that she could rest her head in the curve of his shoulder. 'Shall you tell me her story now, for this is a beautiful place and it may be a long time before we are together in another.'

'I will,' he said gravely, 'for I think you will find it appropriate to ourselves at this time. Now listen well, and remember.

'It is the story of Nieve and of Oisin, who was as brave as he was fair, the son of the great warrior Finn Mac Cool. Now Finn and Oisin were hunting one day when there came a maiden riding up to them on her white horse, wrapped in her cloak set with red stars, and her gold crown on her golden hair. Finn greeted her first, and asked for her name and her business.

' "I am Nieve, daughter of Mananaan, the God of the Sea, and I have come from my father's kingdom, for love of your son, Oisin. For his fame, and the sound of the songs that he makes, have reached even to the palaces of the immortals." She turned her brilliant blue gaze upon Oisin and he was drowned in the sea of it.

' "Will you come with me, to that fair land where the leaves are green all the year round? You will never grow old, or weaken in your strength and you will never die. And I shall be your wife and love you into eternity."

'Oisin came forward and laid his hand upon her hand and his eyes never left hers until he leaped into the saddle behind her. Far behind him, in a dream as they rode, his father's voice cried out to him not to go, for they would never meet again.

'The horse reached the sea and galloped over the waves, through mist and strange, shifting shapes, until they came to a fair green coast. Hundreds of people came down to the shore to greet them and they were all young and lovely and blithe. They were wed at once and lived joyously in a palace of bright marble studded with precious stones. Their time was spent in a dream of love and music and they did not mark the passing of the years.

'But there came a day when suddenly, in the midst of the golden dream, Oisin called to mind the days of his youth. The memory waned, but it returned again and again until it became a gnawing in his heart.

'He said to Nieve, "I am sick with longing for the hills of Ireland and to see my father's face. Let me leave you, for only a little while, and I shall come back to you a whole man again."

'Nieve was silent. At last she said, "Go if you must, but I fear that I will not see you again. And you will not find your father, nor Ireland, as they were when you left them."

'Oisin laughed. "I have been here too short a time for such change."

' "You do not understand me," said Nieve. "Only remember

this; do not dismount from your white horse – or you will not come back to me."

'He promised, then he kissed her and departed. His heart sang in his breast as the white horse sped towards Ireland. But when he reached the shore he saw no sign of the life that had been there; and when he sought his father's folk he could not find them. Gone were the sights and sounds that he knew and vain it was to search for them.

'He came to where his father's stronghold had stood, and beheld only a desolation of stones and heather. He wondered what enemy could have been strong enough to encompass such a momentous downfall, and sought one among the people to tell him.

' "Where is Finn Mac Cool?" he asked. "For I have come a long way to find him."

'The man seemed surprised. He laughed, not comfortably.

' "You must surely know he is long dead? He was a great hero, but never the same after his son, the poet Oisin, was spirited away by an enchantress."

'The truth was very terrible to Oisin. He spurred the white horse, riding as if he would escape from what had been. He rode all over Ireland, and came to a place where some men were trying to raise a great stone from the ground. Pitying their difficulty, he bent from his saddle to lend them aid. But as he bent, the strain was too much for the saddle-girth; it broke and he fell to the ground.

'No sooner did his feet touch the soil of Ireland than he became an old, old man, white-haired, weak and purblind. Horrified, the men asked him who he was. When he told them they shook their heads. "Finn Mac Cool died 300 years ago," they said. "How can you be his son?" '

There was only the sound of the river when he had done.

At last Lucy whispered, pleading, 'And he never saw Nieve again? And he was old until he died?'

Cathal nodded. 'But I do not tell you to make you weep.'

'How could I not? Is this what you see for us? Such a fatal parting, and our loving scarcely begun?'

'The parting is certain; but that is not all you must see in the story. You must see a man whose love of his roots and his country was as strong as an enchantment. Oisin would have had both if he could; as I would. But that is not possible. Oh, do not look at me as if I were tearing your heart from your body to bear it with me. I cannot be strong, and a man for my father, if you look at me like that.' He shook her a little. 'Only be glad that we have a little of the old magic—'

She smiled then, proud that he thought so and tried to match his spirit. 'The magic is as certain as the parting – but I cannot see my father as a sea god; he loves his land too well.'

'You may be sure, too,' Cathal flashed his old satisfied grin, 'that I shall not be fool enough to slip down from my white horse, not though the King himself should ask me.'

She laughed because she knew he wanted her to.

'That's my brave girl. Never fear; one day we shall sit here together and tell tales of how cunningly we each outwitted our enemies.'

He saw that this did not comfort her. 'Have faith, Lucy. I have lucky stars. My horoscope is filled with good things. Venus and Mars have linked our fates together, yours and mine, and nothing can sever them.'

She nodded, still with glistening eyes. She did not want to think that he could be wrong. She reached up for him and they tried to hold back the hours with their kisses. Like Oisin, they lost the tracks of time.

These, tonight, were their first real kisses as adults and neither ever forgot them; both would always be grateful for their intrinsic innocence and sweetness, their courage in the face of such immediate loss.

The very next day the breaking up of the family began. On January 14th Cathal would take ship for Ireland; on the 12th most of the family would go home to Heron, leaving Sir George to the bitterness of the divided House of Commons and Tom to an unhappy attendance at Windsor Castle, where the King would take his family for safety. Lucy had extracted a promise from her father that she would at least be able to say goodbye to Jud, who was to sail for Italy on the 10th, Sir George having refused all notion of rescinding his sentence.

Mary accompanied Lucy, the twins and Cathal down to the wharf. The crowds were still dense, but markedly more cheerful. The graceful *Lady* was dressed for departure with all her brave flags aloft and every inch of wood a mirror for her snowy sails. It was no time of the year to be sailing and her crew were layered in wool and good buff leather as they worked, while Will paced his quarterdeck with his usual fashionable excess in a long coat of Russian sables, the gift of an admiring female relative of the Tzar, upon one of his more successful expeditions.

He was delighted to see the Herons and at once consigned the twins to the care of his two best swimmers, with orders to show them everything and keep them out of as much as possible.

Jud appeared equally delighted but unusually subdued. He felt an infernal fool. Emotional farewells did not sit well with his present plans, which were known only to himself and Rob Whittaker, and certainly did not include a visit to Genoa and Livorno. However, he braced himself for the task and suffered his mother's tears, the twins' stomach punches and Lucy's stubborn brightness as patiently as he could.

'I am only sorry,' he told the sympathetic Cathal, 'that I shall not, after all, have the pleasure of showing you our printing press; I would have enjoyed it greatly, and so would you, I think.' They clasped hands, each wishing that they could have time to discover the other's friendship.

'We'll meet again,' said Cathal, and Jud was surprised to realize that he was not mouthing mere courtesy.

'I hope so,' he replied, 'Only I can't think where it will be. In distant Cathay if my father has his will.'

Lucy had wandered over to the rail, leaving the two young men to their talk, and was staring pensively into the water, unaware of Will Staunton's interested gaze. He was wondering if she were really as pretty as he was beginning to think her. There was also a luminous quality about her today that she had not previously displayed; as though her flesh were worn thin by an intensity of light or heat within. She was very quiet, no doubt distressed by all these imminent partings.

He came and stood by her at the rail. 'Don't be so downcast; the *Lady* will take good care of Jud,' he encouraged kindly.

Her gaze seemed to focus slowly upon him, as though it had travelled a long way. 'Oh, I know,' she said, almost casually. 'I have no fears for Jud, Master Will.'

'Just Will, surely, by now, don't you think? Then why so sad?'

She knew he could keep a secret, and she wanted to tell someone; someone not too near home. 'It is Cathal,' she said simply. 'He goes home to fight, and may be killed.' The tone of her voice told him the rest.

'Ah, so that is the way of it; I had thought so. It is a very hard thing for you to face.'

He was surprised how much he was touched by her sorrow. 'I wish there were some spell I could cast,' he said slowly, 'that would put all back as it was – but we both know that this is not possible. You will have to conjure up courage instead, Lucy, but I think you are capable of that.'

'I suppose I shall have to be,' said Lucy testily. He was no help; she didn't know why she had thought he might be. She pushed herself away from the rail and eyed him stonily. 'I'm going for a walk round the deck,' she told him. It was quite obvious that she did not want his company.

Not offended, Will applied himself instead to entertaining Mary Heron who was far more flatteringly receptive to his courtesy. As it was hardly good manners, in present circumstances, to praise her remarkable blue eyes, he praised her children instead, Jud especially, which he was able to do with a clear conscience.

'I wish that you were to sail also, Will; I would feel far more secure of her safe return.'

'Lady Heron, I assure you that Captain Bellow handles the *Lady* with the experience of twenty years and the instinct of a born sailor. His grandfather sailed with Drake and his father sails still, though he is seventy, with the Dutch fleet. When I sail with him, he is still captain; he would sign on under no other understanding.'

'Forgive me; of course you are right. It is only that I am foolishly afraid of the sea and the dreadful toll it can take of sailors' lives.' She lightened her voice, not wishing to burden him with her grief.

'And what will you do while you wait for her to come home? Shall you stay in the city? I know you have much business to attend to, but I hope you will visit us at Heron very often. We shall be lonely there without the menfolk – but if you would like simply to rest and hunt and live an easy life for a time, you would be most welcome.'

Like her daughter, Mary blushed easily and she did so now. It was Sir George himself who had bidden her make the invitation, so there could be nothing improper in it, but Will was the sort of man who, without the least attempt to do so, made one feel that it must be.

He was on the point of accepting when a fearful commotion broke out down-river. Everyone made for the rails and sailors were sent to find out what the trouble was. The cacophony increased, resolving itself as it came nearer into the separate noises of yelling populace, thudding drums and shrieking trumpets.

'Oh Jehovah! Has the war started?' cried Lucy, dismayed.

Will yelled in tune with the citizens, clapping her on the back.

'Bless you, no – that's the Trained Bands if I'm not mistaken. They are marching up the Strand by the sound of it, though I can't tell you why.'

'Look ye here, sir – here be *why!*' an exuberant sailor cried. They followed him to the sterncastle from where they obtained an excellent view of the cause of this apparent rehearsal of the Last Trump.

Up the river towards them came a decorated barge, ecstatically convoyed by a cheering regatta of other craft. Every boat was packed with jubilant citizens; several were lurching wildly under their elation. The swift strokes of the leading bargemen soon brought them abreast of the *Lady* and it could be seen that it carried five figures standing proud and upright in the mid-section. As they drew alongside, two of them raised their arms in salute.

'Devil take me if it isn't Pym and Hampden – and there's Holles – and it must be Strode and Hazelrigg with them! They are going back to Westminster to take their seats, by God, and the Trained Bands are pacing them down the Strand!'

'God save us, sir – this is a great day for England!' The informative sailor could not contain his glee.

'So now then,' he exulted to his companions on the wharf, 'when those good men be back in Parliament – where are the King and his cavaliers?'

Will, who had been smiling broadly as he recognized his friends in the barge, now ceased to smile. 'Don't be premature in your crowing, my fine cockerel. This is a victory, aye. It is the first. And it is also blessedly bloodless. The next may not be so blessed.'

'No, sir. Your pardon, sir,' the sailor parroted dutifully. He was a staunch adherent of John Lilburne and thought Pym akin to John the Baptist, as the precursor of a kind of salvation for himself and his like that he did not understand but sensed to be imminent.

Lucy, in an agony of worry, glared at him hatefully. There were no more such open declarations heard aboard the *Lady*, but Will Staunton, even had he the desire to do so, could not have controlled the ecstasy taking place on the riverbank and along the moving shoal of cheering folk that was the Strand. And though Lucy at last clapped her hands over her ears in furious desperation, she could not cut out the derisive cry that bounded repeatedly up into the cold, clear air – 'Where are the King and his cavaliers?'

Part Two

King and Parliament now engaged in a struggle for the control of armed forces. The King held out his right hand towards Westminster in a mime of misunderstood friendship, and his left in a mendicant scoop towards Scotland, Ireland, Holland, wherever he thought he had friends. His inability to see who *were* his friends increased daily. He courted Argyll, who backed away, and ignored Montrose, now free and influential again. He intrigued against his own government in Ireland; and even in Holland, rumour had him invading England at the head of the Irish Papists.

This was especially embarrassing to his Queen who had recently wrapped up the Crown Jewels and taken them to Holland to pawn as the first step in a fund-raising tour. The court of Orange was solidly Protestant, and its crown-prince was married to Charles' young daughter, Mary; his uncle, King Christian of Denmark also ruled a Protestant nation. Both might well like to help their co-religionist in his hour of peril, but neither would stir a stump to aid an army of papists.

Travelling with the Queen, and vastly relieved to be out of England, was Valora Grey, restored to equanimity by the absence of would-be husbands. She went about The Hague, bright, brittle and exuding sensual charm, crunching up hearts for her breakfast as if she had never taken part in a previous scene, up on the windy white clifftop at Dover, that rivalled the leave-taking in Cathal's romance.

There, while England's King and Queen had wept openly in each other's arms, she and Tom Heron had each stood alone and devoured the other's face with a fierce and burning dryness of eye that caused the very air about them to crackle.

There had been one long, wretched, impassioned and accusing embrace that left them both weak and furious – and then she had gone without a word.

There being no alternative, other than the kind of slow self-destruction that is the result of self-contempt, Tom made a conscious effort to replace love with war in the forefront of his mind. He renewed his acquaintance with his old commander, Prince Rupert, who had placed his formidable energy and military talent at his uncle's disposal. The Prince was everything that Tom admired in a man, an officer of integrity, sympathetic and intelligent company, and though unshakeably loyal, disinclined to play the courtier. His troops had idolized him. With such men as he would attract to the cause, His Majesty would be well served. Tom began to look forward to the coming conflict when he was offered the leadership of a troop of Rupert's own cavalry, soon to start their training.

He thought of Valora only at night. Even then he could not subdue her wayward image to his will. If he envisaged her as gentle and loving, she would suddenly break away from him, taunting and amused. If he conjured their most sensual, most animal moments, he would find her weeping on his breast like a lost child. Thus, even in his waking dreams, the only time he could be wholly hers, her singular spirit of independence drove him to distraction, and, eventually, to feverish and unsatisfied sleep.

They had agreed, each as though making a tremendous concession, to write; but it was a long time before either could put pen to paper.

At Heron they waited with the rest of England, while King and Parliament shifted about each other as though slowly recalling the steps of an old dance. John Pym, tiring first, passed his Militia Bill in the form of a military ordinance, thus indicating that Parliament had taken over the defence of the realm.

After that the mismatched dancers dropped hands forever. The King moved the court and the judiciary to York. Parliament cheered. Let him go to Strafford's county; perhaps Yorkshiremen, when asked for their loyalty, might remember how fragile was Charles' faith to Strafford.

During the six months' build-up to war, while both sides counted their assets and rattled their swords, the village of Heron behaved much like the rest of their countrymen. Their opposing factions, if they happened to meet, discharged their duty by throwing stones or calling names, only occasionally fighting, and rarely with weapons, while most sensible people minded their own business and hoped it would all blow over.

When it did not blow over and they were summoned with their neighbours to the village green to hear Sir George read out the King's Commission of Array – the call to battle – they heaved great sighs of relief or dismay and crowded the insufficient space with alert and willing faces. At last something was happening!

The baronet sat on his horse in the middle of the Green, ready to declaim the contents of an impressive parchment dangling with seals. Behind him, also in the saddle, were half a dozen of his lieutenants, among them Sir Joseph Stratton and one of his Catholic nephews. These two excited mumbled insults and signs against the Devil in the crowd; the Irish rumour was doing its work.

Dominic, sitting his horse as soldierly as Ignatius Loyola, a pistol at his belt, listened with a mixture of guilt and sympathy as the curses flew about their heads. He had Lucy up before him on his saddle-bow, while the twins shared one of the stolid coach-horses who could be trusted not to bolt, no matter what the provocation.

The villagers surged around this central group, for the most part good-humoured and eager to listen. Many of them had brought their children and there was an air almost of holiday.

Sir George cleared his throat, spat and commenced. He called upon all well-affected and able-bodied men to bring any arms, armour or horse they might possess and to sign on for His Majesty's forces with the Recruiting Officer, whom they would find established in a tent on the football meadow during the next week or two. There were loud cheers, chiefly at the centre.

So as to waste no enthusiasm the Recruiting Officer opened his list there and then and was soon doing a brisk trade; there was an accompaniment of proud male boasting and sour female recrimination as wives wondered how they were supposed to manage when the provider of the household should march off with a shilling in his pocket and a silly grin on his face.

The blacksmith's tiny, sharp wife clouted him soundly for being the first to sign. 'Can't wait, can ye, ye girt daft ha'p'orth? I only hope as you'll still be so keen when you be stuck at the wrong end of some bugger's pike!'

The Puritan element, who had hung well back so far in the proceedings, kept up a warm barracking and promised those who enlisted that they'd keep them their favourite spots in the graveyard.

At the edge of the green, Martha had set up a table and was doing excellent business with her ointments and cures, particularly those for swordcuts or diarrhoea. She sold them more cheaply than usual, feeling it unchristian to take advantage of men who might shortly be suffering these discomforts. The village women, with no such scruples, bought them up as fast as they could and stored them away in their kitchen hutches, delighted with the bargain.

When the rush was over, Lucy wriggled down from Dominic's saddle and went across to join her friend. She picked up one of the jars of ointment that was left and sniffed at it. It was labelled 'Cuts. Superficial' and smelled of cloves.

'I hate to see these. It makes it all seem more real; far more than all these men telling each other how splendid it will be to fight for God and the King.'

Martha, who was not a romantic, agreed. 'It is hard to know what to expect, but I do not think we shall enjoy it, as some of these overgrown infants seem to imagine. But tell me, Lucy – I saw the carrier's cart in Highgate yesterday – have you any news from – either of your brothers?' She longed to speak Tom's name but denied herself even so small a part of what was not hers.

'We should not expect to hear from Jud quite yet, though I believe he is in Venice,' replied Lucy. 'But Tom writes from York that fewer men than they had hoped have turned out for the King. Many follow Sir Thomas Fairfax and his son, who are strong for the Parliament. Tom is fretting to be away from the court and join up with Prince Rupert who is recruiting in Holland.'

But Lucy had much more interesting news. 'Do you like my gloves?' she asked abruptly. They were pale primrose satin and lace, knotted with yellow rosebuds. She wore them tucked into her sash.

'They are exquisite,' admired Martha, 'but why don't you put them on?'

'Because I don't want to wear them out. Cathal sent them to me.' She flushed delicately.

'How very kind,' said Martha diplomatically. Lucy had told her, as soon as she had come home, how she had lost her heart to the heir of Oisin, and the gentle girl ached for the sudden sadness that had come in its wake. She hoped that the situation would resolve itself as kindly as possible. Lucy was at the right age for longing and dreaming; but it was also an age when one could suffer dreadfully. She did not want to see Lucy hurt by her first love, but she thought that, considering Cathal's heritage, it was as well that they had been separated by the tides of war rather than by Sir George's irate arm. Forbearing as the baronet might have been with the boy, there was no manner in which he would ever consider him as a son-in-law. Lucy would know this herself, had she thought so far.

'He writes that he is well and happy, and doing "warm work among the heather" to the detriment of the Protestant settlers.' Lucy bit her lip. Cathal did not seek to spare her the truth about the direction in which his allegiance would take him. 'It is so strange, and so terrible – if I were in Ireland, it would be his duty to murder me. How can God permit such a thing?'

'He does not. He gave us free will to commit our own murders,' said Martha with a bitterness born of anger that Lucy should have to make such sad realizations so early in her life.

They exchanged helpless looks, since they could not criticize God. Dominic was leading his horse towards them now, taking a rare chance to speak to Martha. He had avoided her lately, for her own protection, but could hardly be faulted for addressing her on such a public occasion, no matter whose prying eyes were upon them.

Martha looked so very pleased to see him that Lucy excused herself, first making Martha promise to visit her soon at Heron, for she was allowed to go nowhere alone now that the countryside was so disturbed. It galled her and she relished today's small freedom.

She was standing watching a group of children skipping over a long rope in the Lowgate, when the game was rudely scattered by a party of horsemen led by Nehemiah Owerby. He had not been seen about for some time and the consensus was that this was as likely to mean trouble as not. Some of the children indignantly shouted 'Roundheads!' and Nehemiah caught one boy a clip with his whip-end as a reward. Another lad piped 'Cavalier!' just for the fun of it. The ensuing scuffle was no longer Lucy's idea of entertainment.

Scenting other interest, she walked swiftly in the wake of the horsemen. The riders had pulled up at the edge of the crowd on the green and now Owerby stood in his saddle and called for silence.

As always, his presence commanded respect and the noise subsided. Even the man who was in the act of signing his name looked up to hear what he would say, and was sharply recalled to his duty by a poke in the belly from Sir George, who bellowed, 'What do you here, sir? Are you come to lay your sword at the King's command like the rest of us?'

This was appreciated. Nehemiah smiled with the others. 'Like the rest of us, I am the King's loyal subject,' he agreed.

'Could've fooled me,' growled the baronet, suspicious.

'And it is upon His Majesty's account that I come here today—' he raised his voice, '—to beg *every* loyal subject to consider what it is they do, if they set their name to that paper.' He paused, allowing the break to become portentous. The man who was still signing dropped his pen.

'Be damned to you, Owerby. This is not your business. Take yourself off!' Sir George ordered.

The enlistments were sluggish enough without this mischievous presence. People seemed to have no sense of loyalty unless he threatened their tenure.

'The King himself would not question my right to speak in his interest in a public place.' A rumble concurred with Nehemiah. Sir George scowled but had to let him continue.

'Now my friends, you may think the best thing you can do for His Majesty is to fight with the army he seeks to command . . .' They bleated further agreement. 'But I say to you that this is not so!' He was using his pulpit voice now. There was no escaping its self-confident resonance. 'The officers of that army will not be men to whom you should give your duty. They do not know it; the King himself does not know it for they have his trust – but they are men who give, or are guided by, evil counsel, and only harm the King. If a man shall see his friend persuaded by another to leap from a high cliff, shall he not earnestly seek to *dissuade* him from such sinful folly? Indeed would he not seize him by his garments and drag him from the edge? How much more eagerly would he do that if his friend is also his King under God?'

He had them now, as he had nearly half of them on Sundays, nodding wisely and looking virtuous; all except the small knot about Sir George, who wore expressions of weary disgust.

'You will ask – what may I, a humble man, do to prevent my King from such bitter self-destruction? And you would have the right of it; you can do nothing – in your own right. But there are those who will do it in your place. You have the Parliament to stand for you in what you would do – that brave Parliament who are *your* representatives and have your good and your rights safe at heart – as they have the King's good and the King's rights.'

This was easy. They could follow it, or they thought they could. It made good sense.

'I tell you that in that Parliament are the only body of men in this Kingdom who will drag back His Majesty from the evil brink he faces now; from the perils of a papist invasion—' There were hisses in Stratton's direction, '—from the influence of lords and bishops whose interest is only their own worldly power – men such as Strafford and Laud. Do not think that because Black Tom is dead and the Archbishop in the Tower that there are none who will rise to take their place! And if we give over the army to the King's evil councillors – and he is so misguided as to loose it against his faithful subjects – then we shall be lost, and the King will be lost and we shall have the Pope preaching at Paul's Cross, and Parliament – if there *be* any Parliament – may be arrested and flung into jail whenever it is thought they speak out of turn.'

They were simple men and women and this was all that was needed to make them throw their caps in the air and cry 'God bless the Parliament!' and 'God bless His Majesty!'

Sir George ground his teeth. 'God's curse on their damned stupidity!' he groaned.

'Never mind, sir,' Joseph Stratton laid a calming hand on his shoulder. 'It's all one in the end. No matter how many speeches he may make – or you may make – each man will follow his own best interest in the end. Your tenants may be blessing the Parliament now – but they are still your tenants, and must fight for the King when you bid them.'

'Aye, I should hope so,' sighed the baronet. 'If only we didn't have to have all this altercation. I'm sick to my stomach of windy words and useless argument.'

'Oh, I think it has its uses,' mused Sir Joe, but he would not be drawn on that. Best not to suggest to his old friend that *some* of his tenants might be beginning to think for themselves.

But Nehemiah had not finished. 'God bless Parliament, you cry! But what have you to say to the Member of Parliament who cares nothing for the sacred duty of those he represents – who is one of those who would push the King towards that very cliff edge? What have you to say to Sir George Heron, who orders you to sign away your lives in the King's army, to serve alongside those very devilish Irish who have slaughtered thousands of your kinsmen?'

There was a smothered roar at this but many people looked apprehensively at Sir George, who shook his head and rose unwillingly to his feet before the Recruiting Officer's table. He had had enough of this.

'I have no interest in replying to personal slander,' he began, in his Westminster boom. 'But I can assure you that this foolish rumour of an Irish army is nought but a scurrilous falsehood put about by the King's enemies. It serves well enough to convince the halt of mind. As for Parliament,' he grunted with distaste, '*I* am the Parliament, as far as any of *you* may be concerned – and I scorn these lawless traitors who have traduced its name! The King is the King, look you, when all is said and done – and neither the rebels in Parliament nor Nehemiah Owerby can un-King him with their talk of evil council and papist bugbears.'

They said nothing. He sounded so *right*. They were used to his being right. Even Owerby's group had to agree with him. That was the trouble with argument, with words; they were so slippery.

'And now,' said Sir George in a businesslike way, 'I'll have an end to this, if you please. There is work to be done. I want William Blacksmith and a dozen of the strongest, over here to me.'

They stopped looking sheepish and looked curious instead, pushing the village stalwarts to the front.

Nehemiah appeared satisfied for the moment. He did not attempt to regain attention but sat his horse quietly, looking affably about him. Then his wandering eye fell on Martha and Dominic. He slid from his horse and made for Martha's now empty table.

Deep in talk, they did not notice him until he observed pleasantly that it was an excellent day, as far as the weather went.

Dominic looked up as if affected by a sudden stench, then grinned. ' 'Deed, sir and it is. Colossal good huntin' weather.' The grin was consciously reminiscent.

Nehemiah did not appear offended. 'Ah, very soon now we shall discover who are the hunters and who the hunted.' His eye strayed to Martha who was studying the table top. 'Mistress Knyvett, I expect to be very busy about these parts in the next weeks. I would count it a great favour if, before I am given over entirely to the Lord's work, you would grant me a brief interview at your home – at some time convenient to us both.'

His speech was quiet, not urgent, but as always it seemed to place a great weight on her spirit. 'I have told you,' she said colourlessly, 'I do not wish it.'

'That is not charitable, Martha. You'll see little enough of me when hostilities begin.'

'That is excellent news!' Dominic was on his feet. 'Curse my britches, sir, will you never leave off your persecution of the lady? Do her words blow straight through that inflated noddle of yours like the wind through an empty house – if you distress her further, you'll have me to deal with!'

At this Martha suddenly sat up and brought down her fist upon the table, her face vivid with resentment. 'So now, Master Lacey, it is *you* who think fit to interfere in my business? You, who are even more a stranger to me than Master Owerby! Sweet Jesu! It had always seemed to me that by taking no husband I should avoid that galling yoke with which men seek to control the life of a woman – but here are two men, neither of them in any way related or committed to me – who dictate to me without hesitation how I may spend my time! Well, gentlemen, I will not have it, indeed I will not! And since you are both like to stand here all day giving your orders out, I will save myself the trouble of listening to them by bidding you both a cold good day!' She rose from her chair, her lips set in a fine line of disapproval, and passed between the two of them like a queen.

Silent now, neither dared to follow her as she marched off towards her cottage. Instinctively, neither would speak of her to the other. Nehemiah stared thoughtfully at Dominic for a moment, as though about to introduce some new subject, then, evidently thinking better of it, inclined his head gravely and strode away.

Dominic chuckled, watching him go. Martha had been very convincing. He only hoped she *had* been acting for his benefit, otherwise he could expect a roasting when next they met.

It was then that his cousin's secretary, spindle-legged Ninian ffoulkes, approached him, looking both pleased and amused. 'I don't know what all that to-do was about, Master Nick, but Sir George will hand you a parcel of gratitude. Your little set-to with Nehemiah has lent him just the time he needed to get his stout fellows down to St Mary's. He plans to commandeer the arsenal in the roof. The Puritan is bound to be hot on his trail as soon as he gets wind of it, but with luck he'll be too late.'

And so it proved. By the time Nehemiah realized that the ancient but by no means useless hoard was being pillaged, Sir George's bully-boys were emerging from the church with their arms full of pikes and guns that had not seen a threatening daylight since the sighting of the Armada. The weapons though old, were not rusty, for the baronet's troop of the county militia had polished and carried them, at least as far as from the church to the Golden Ram, at every monthly drill session. As the men blinked, thus heavily laden, out into the churchyard, they found Nehemiah and his smirking henchmen surrounding the doorway in a suggestive ring.

The massive Tibbett was the first to act. Slinging his booty back into the porch, he clubbed his sword and made for the first man he saw, put him to sleep with one blow and passed on to the next, whose weapon was only half out of its scabbard.

The rest did not need Sir George's bellow of encouragement, nor Nehemiah's 'Lay on, in the name of the Lord!' to go at it with a will. The struggle was long, energetic and extremely noisy. They used their swords, clubbed for the most part, as no one had got used to the idea that they might, one day, attempt to *kill* each other. Those without swords battered away with pikes and pistols from the church hoard. Sam Hudson, hesitating too long as he searched for the pike he had carved his initials into during training sessions, was felled by Ninian ffoulkes, who then thought himself no end of a fellow, being bookish and normally apprehensive of violence. He had little time in which to congratulate himself, however, for Sam's mate, Straightways Sawyer (he was bottom-sawyer, Sam was top) cried feelingly, 'An eye for an eye, thou tricksy scrivener!' and swept him off his feet from behind with a well-aimed pike, with which he now prodded him painfully in the ribs while relieving him of the sword he had newly acquired and anyway, was holding all-a-cock. 'Stick to thy quill. Thou'll have less to regret.'

The tumult attracted quite a large audience, who although they cheered each side from time to time, with scrupulous fairness, made no attempt to join in. They simply watched until the contestants ran out of breath and began to move away, carrying what arms they had won.

At the end of the day, when the count was made, it was found that the Heron party had salvaged just *over* half, which they naturally accounted a victory. As they were counting, over a well-earned jug of ale, Nehemiah was riding hard on his way to Gloucester. He was going to place an order with the city's best-known armourer, a man who was hot for the Parliament. He did not know whether he would ever recoup the money thus invested, but he did not propose to enter the conflict ill-prepared. He knew, even if the bulk of his neighbours did not, that when the war began in earnest, village play-acting would no longer serve.

Martha had no desire to prosecute either side of a war. She was loyal to the King, though it was the King's law that had let them burn her mother to death. She thought the Parliament were very likely justified in some of their grievances and she wished that both sides would argue it out between them up in London and not come bothering honest folk with their Trained Bands and their battle talk.

She was far more deeply interested in the problem of Dominic. He was having increasing difficulty in finding safe places where he might say mass. As the prospect of war loomed, his widely scattered flock, often hounded by their frightened neighbours and fearful for their lives, felt an urgent need for the comforts of their faith. Martha thought of the poor Strattons, living in this constant fear among their empty rooms – Sir Joseph thought it pointless to refurnish; it would only hold out a further challenge to their enemies – and she came to a determined decision.

Dominic should hold his services under her roof. Few people ever called on her. Most, though they liked her well enough, did think her a witch, however white, and such are best given a wide road by ordinary folk. If by chance they *should* be interrupted, she would see that they were well prepared for it. It took a long and exhausting time to persuade Dominic of the virtues of her plan, but in the end her argument defeated him and he agreed, though not without a great deal of soul-searching.

He held his services for single families at a time. They must always bring a pretended 'patient' among them and it must always take place after dark, when no one was abroad who did not have to be.

He used a simplified form of the mass, for the sake of brevity and Martha was amazed, as she became familiar with its ritual cadences, how little, in all but one essential factor, were the differences between the Roman and Anglican modes. It seemed foolish to the point of incredibility that the entire foundation of society had been rocked by the Reformation and its insistence that a morsel of bread and a sip of wine *cannot*, in holy truth, be transubstantiated into the body and blood of Christ. What did it matter? God would judge men, when he came to do so, upon how they had lived, not upon a theological argument. If Dominic had told her, when she said this to him, that she was talking like a Puritan, she would not have believed him.

One night towards the end of July, mass was said before a family of yeoman farmers named Weston: two brothers, their wives and their older children – one young man and two apprehensive girls. They knelt in two rows in Martha's living room while she sat, as was her habit, at the end of the low bench table serving as the altar, with her dried leaves and powders spread in front of her. She occupied herself by grinding herbs with a pestle and mortar. They had worked through about a score of such services by now and had put away the fear of the booted tread and the knock upon the door.

When, tonight, it came, they were each one hypnotized by the unlikelihood of it. They trembled. Then Dominic clapped his hands and quietly reminded them 'You all know what to do – just as we have practised.'

He restored to Martha her best cup and plate that he had blessed for use in the mass and she filled them with herbs. All had taken communion so that the sacred bread was no longer in evidence. He removed the few necessary sacred vestments he had worn and bundled them beneath the bedding of a faintly protesting Sir Topaz, who had grown into a champion sleeper and would stir for nothing short of an earthquake from his rush basket beside the grate.

While Martha opened the door and found Nehemiah glowering on the step, her guests disposed themselves about the room and put on the expressions of those who are engaged in a medical consultation. Dominic lounged by the fire.

'Master Owerby. I told you not to come here.' She made no attempt to be courteous. 'And just now it is particularly inconvenient. I have visitors. They have come a good distance to ask my help. It is late and I would not keep them longer than necessary.'

Nehemiah ignored this. 'Let me in, Martha,' he said neutrally, 'for I know that you have a priest in your house and that he is saying his abominable mass.'

Martha's only apparent reaction was impatience. 'Do not be so foolish! Who has told you such a tale?'

'Someone who was very sure he spoke the truth.'

She clicked her tongue. 'Aye, through the bottom of a flagon! God's wounds, man, surely your own common sense tells you I am the last one to take such a risk – and for a religion for which I care nothing!'

'Perhaps you care more for the priest,' Nehemiah suggested, his tone still as neutral as though he were not dragging at the reins of his control like a man on the brink of that very chasm he had called up to impress the villagers.

'The priest?' Martha repeated with contempt. 'What priest? I have said there is no priest here.'

'Don't lie to me, Martha. It is less than you owe yourself.'

'And do not you *preach* to me, Nehemiah! Go on your way. No one here is your concern. Have they not told you – I am a witch, not a Catholic?'

'Are you so?' he smiled. 'Well, I will remember that you told me so. But for now – I will come in.' He put his hand on the door. 'I am not alone.' He thumbed over his shoulder. There were shadows in the road. 'They are members of the militia – but you will not want them trampling your floor unless they must.'

She shrugged. She had delayed him long enough. A longer wait would only make the Westons nervous. Ungraciously, she motioned him in.

He stood in the doorway, filling it, and looked about the room. He recognized everyone there. He was sure now. 'In God's name, good evening,' he began mildly. 'A small congregation, Father Lacey, but doubtless encouraging.'

The Westons gave wonderful imitations of perplexity, while Dominic brought out his inane laugh. 'Piss take it, I know you don't care for me, sir – but don't you think this is takin' a joke too far?'

'Do you deny, then, that you are here for the purpose of saying the Roman mass before these people?'

'My purposes are none of your affair! Goddamned, piggish insolence!'

Nehemiah sighed and turned to the older Mistress Weston, a worn-looking woman in shabby clothes. 'You mistress, what brings you here?' he snapped.

Mrs Weston, who had borne fifteen children, eight of them dead, who had suffered disillusion, disease and near-starvation in turn, kept her frail being anchored to this earth only with the iron strength of her Catholic faith. She raised clear eyes to her inquisitor. 'I suffer with my lungs,' she told him, her breathing, a little laboured, giving credence. 'Mistress Martha is able to help me a little. And now I have a fear that my daughter may have taken the sickness from me, so I have brought her here.' The girl's cheek was flushed with fear, but it would serve for fever.

Nehemiah looked openly sceptical. 'And you, sir?' he addressed her brother-in-law.

'I have been troubled with the stone, sir, though I don't know what it matters to you. You'll hardly have me up before the bench for seeking a cure for it!'

'I see. And the reason for your travelling in such numbers? It seems to me that one of you might have collected the simples from Mistress Knyvett, without making a family outing of it.'

The farmer looked at him as though he had not met his like before and did not wish to again. 'I think you overstep your duty, Master Owerby. Mistress Martha has powers of healing beyond the blending of herbs, as everyone knows. We wished to consult her in person. We travel together for safety, as any fool could fathom – and because we do not, as a rule, get much in the way of "family outings". Do you grudge us that small pleasure, sir?'

Nehemiah made a gesture of impatience. He returned to

Dominic. 'Do you still maintain that you are not here to say mass, Father Lacey, when everyone here is a papist?'

Dominic looked embarrassed. 'I do wish you would *not* keep calling me "Father Lacey".' He waved his effete wrist. 'It feels so very – out of character!'

Nehemiah was unimpressed. 'I heard of a priest, once, who gave excellent service as a lady's maid before they – unfrocked him.' His hand dove into his pocket. 'Perhaps if I were to show you *this*, it would remind you who you are and whom you serve.'

It was a small, black book, a Roman missal, in which the Ordinary of the Mass is printed. 'It was found in your chamber at Heron Hall. Do you deny that it is yours?'

Dominic sighed irritably and kicked at the fire. So little Lucy had been right. 'What is it to be, then – Bibles at two paces?' he drawled. 'Why should you suppose that it is mine? There are a hundred books at Heron. And I should very much like to know why you feel so free to investigate my chamber. As Master Weston has said, you overstep yourself, my friend.'

Nehemiah was not interested in his complaint. 'Is the book yours or is it not?' he growled.

'Does it say it is?' Dominic asked innocently.

Following his hint, Nehemiah opened the book and looked at its flyleaf. 'Father S. Ward S.J. 1637.' At first he was taken aback, then he remembered. 'Father Ward was executed recently, was he not?'

Dominic shrugged. 'It is a common enough name.' He met Nehemiah's eyes. 'And no, it is not my book,' he added quietly.

It was true. He had taken it from Father Ward's coat after the execution. They had not let him hold it as he died.

Martha, who had sat tranquilly putting her cures and spices into little boxes and bottles throughout the questioning, now stood and shook out her skirts in a determined manner. 'Well now – it seems you can find no proof of your accusations, Master Owerby, and have harassed these poor folk in vain. I have an excellent draught here for those who suffer from delusions. You may take it with you, for I order you to leave my house!' She thrust a little bottle at him.

It was the wrong move, for it made him angry at last. 'Enough of your play-acting, Martha. It is not I who must leave. I have matters to discuss with you. You may give your guests their leave – for the moment.'

'Don't fret, Martha,' said Mrs Weston hastily, seeing the girl's face whiten with rage. 'We have stayed longer than we meant.'

She brought out her purse and counted out three small coins. 'There – that's what we settled, is it not?'

'Thank you kindly, Mistress Weston.' Martha handed her several little parcels, including a soothing syrup for the cough. The mother, she knew, would not succumb to it for many years yet. The girl, alas, would be dead before the year was out. She wondered wearily why she could not have these devastating 'seeings' about such as Nehemiah. Perhaps it was because she always had them about those for whom she could do some measure of good – and she could wish him none.

The Westons left them, ignoring Owerby and giving Dominic the neutral goodnight one gives to near-strangers.

'Those men outside?' worried Martha, hating him.

Nehemiah quieted her with a wave of his hand. 'They will not molest them. They have no such orders.'

He came and stood before the fire and looked back and forth from her to Dominic. Martha felt the tension in her too much to bear. 'Why do you not *go*?' she cried. 'The sight of you is horrible to me!'

That hurt him but he kept his voice steady. 'I will leave when I have spoken with you alone.'

Dominic uncoiled his legs and changed the angle of his sprawl. He yawned, 'Listen to me, you damned, insolent fellow – she does not want you here. Is not that enough for you?'

Their eyes clashed and their bodies strained to do the same. Nehemiah lost patience. 'Put it like this,' he said brutally. 'There are a dozen men outside who will see you safely in hell if you hinder my way any longer.'

'Christ's blood! Have you no shame?' said Martha furiously. 'I had never thought you such a *little* man, to come persecuting innocent folk like this.'

Nehemiah looked at Dominic. 'He is no innocent,' he said flatly.

'You are a fool, Owerby,' Dominic said cheerfully. He got up. 'Martha, I am loathe to leave you in such company and I will stay if you bid me.'

'What – to have them beat you half to death for the pleasure of it? No, Master Lacey, I bid you go, and that at once.'

They both knew there was nothing else for it. She went with him to the door, so that she could satisfy herself that he had mounted his horse and ridden away unharmed. Then, unwillingly, she came back to Nehemiah.

'It is only a matter of time,' he told her, almost kindly, 'I shall soon have proof of his priesthood.'

'How can you,' she persisted, 'even begin to think that such a – very *worldly* man – could be a priest?'

'Perhaps *he* has overstepped himself – on the matter of worldliness.' He was tired of this. He saw that she would not give in, and her determination to shield the priest strengthened his will to take *her*.

They were both standing before the fire. She bent to prod it into a brief blaze, then straightened and passed her hand across her brow in fatigue, pushing back her hair and rubbing at her forehead as if it ached.

She was nearly a foot below him as he looked down at her. How fragile she was, how delicate. How easily he might crush her if he wished. She would come to pieces in his hands. He put out one of his hands to her. 'Martha—'

'What is it?' she said, depressed by him. 'What do you want?'

He watched his hand waver, then come down with excruciating gentleness upon her shoulder.

She flinched and pulled away. 'You know I have no defence.'

He knew. And now, even less so, because of the priest. It was God's wish that she should make *him*, Nehemiah, her defence. He had never dared to touch her before, but now he wanted to. He felt that she had devalued herself by having to do with the priest. She had *made* herself touchable. The jealousy that had ached in him since he had first seen her with Dominic, that had agonized him while the priest was in this room, was mingled and transmuted into this other ache, of physical longing for her, making it stronger and impossibly painful. God did not, surely, wish him to suffer this way for long. He had sent him this pain so that she too might feel it and know that her duty was to assuage it.

She did feel it. It threatened her so that she could hardly breathe. She began to talk, to cover her animal fear. 'How can you go on with this infamous cruelty of persecution?' she asked, her voice too emotional. 'You must know what will happen, even to harmless, good-living people like the Westons, if you continue to set such an example. I have heard you say yourself that the burnings are a cruel way—' she broke off, entreating him, hating to speak of burning.

He recalled his words. It had been just before they had thrown him down the steps of Heron Hall. 'I spoke those words to a woman, a very frivolous and misguided woman. I did not wish to distress her. A priest is quite a different matter. Their execution is cruel, yes, but it is also necessary.'

She knew better than to argue with him. She had done so too many times before. She wanted to sink away, down into her chair and wait for him to go. She stepped backwards, but he caught her by her arm.

'Martha, your soul is in more peril now than I had ever hoped to see it.' He was urgent, his voice and his thoughts thickened by the effect of touching her skin. He was bewildered. He had always known that he wanted her, but not that there was such a hunger in him as this.

He had been undermined and often ambushed by his own flesh since he had first grown to manhood. He had sinned often and repented as often and had thought never to come to grace because of it. But God had enriched him beyond the compass of his own narrow imagination. He had taken his spotted soul and his sullied body into His keeping and made him His soldier. Grace had knocked him down and beaten him and stood him up again and fought with him until he too had learned how to fight. That had been when he was nineteen and he had walked about the world in wonder, ever since, in the sure knowledge that he was one of the Lord's elect. He strove to deserve it. He sinned less often with the years. He felt the strength in him go out to strengthen others. He became a leader among his neighbours. The fact of his manhood continued to undermine him. He would frequently take what women offered him. He was an attractive man – his own despised virility saw to that – and they did not often have to be persuaded. If they did, he would repent all the more vigorously. He knew that what he should do was to take a wife, a godly woman who would sanctify his appetites in the bearing of his children.

But Martha was not a godly woman. And yet she was the one towards whom he had been moved. God wished him to have Martha. He had been chosen to bring her to the grace that was his own.

'Please – do not touch me, Nehemiah,' he heard her say. 'I do not like your touch. I am not your dog, to be fondled when you please.'

He scarcely heard her. He drew his hand down the astonishing softness of her arm. He took her hand. He saw her breasts move and longed, more than he had longed for anything other than his Saviour, to touch them.

'Do not be afraid,' he said tenderly, 'I have only your good in my heart. I cannot allow you to continue with the life you are leading. We must marry. At once. I may soon be called away to fight. But first you must—'

'Are you mad? What are you thinking of? Oh, I have told you and told you until I am near desperate with telling you. *I will not wed you. Never!* Now, please, go. Leave me alone. I can't stand up under this any more.'

She was so near to weeping that it turned over his heart and his loins so that he could not keep back from her. It was as though her worn-out refusal were acceptance. They showed him again her defencelessness and her fear, and these were things, he had always half-known, that above all other things made his senses quite drunk.

He pulled her to him and began to kiss her as though she were water to his blistering thirst. He felt her pulling away. Her strength was so little.

A wave of tenderness and lust lifted him up. He moved her hands and held them lightly behind her back, so that he could go on kissing her. The sweetness was so close to pain. He undid her buttons and uncovered her breasts.

She wrenched away her head and screamed.

'Martha! I beg you—'

She shook uncontrollably but her eyes were dry. They told him he might die of his thirst and she would rejoice. 'Oh, you man of God,' she keened, 'is this your way to grace?' She wished impotently that there was some threat she could utter, some retribution in her power to promise. But there was nothing. Nothing. She felt, not now for the first time, how bitter it was to be a woman. She had neither physical strength, social influence nor even the law to stand for her. She may as well have been born a domestic animal–his dog, as she had said. There was a hammering on the door. The shadows were becoming bored with waiting.

'I ask your pardon,' Nehemiah said to her, his eyes soft with extenuation. 'It was not how I had meant to be with you. You must understand, I love you. It is simply that. I will go now. I am sorry.' He bowed his head. He really was sorry. He did not know what it was in her, or in him, that made him act this way. 'We must be married, and soon, my dear. You will come to see that.'

She groaned as he left.

When she had barred the door behind him, she picked up Sir Topaz and settled him on her knee for comfort. She was shaken. She had not expected this. She had always been above him, safe from him in her own imperviousness. Now she was no longer safe.

That night she prayed with all her strength, which was not, after all, so very much, that Nehemiah would receive a commission which would take him far from Heron. The thought of war was very terrible, but if it would release her from the sick weight of apprehension that had been laid upon her tonight, she could almost be selfish enough to welcome it.

Now, as she lay nerveless in her chair, swallowing the bile that filled her throat with fear, she began to experience that unwarned *distancing* of her spirit that told her there would be a 'seeing'. She did not want it. She was far too weary. But the choice had never been hers. She lay in her chair and endured it.

It gradually became clear, though she would never be able to describe what she meant by the word 'clear' – that for the first time in all the years, it was for herself that she saw. Trying to resist the forces, she brushed Topaz's fur until he scratched and bit her, but still the choice was not hers. She closed her eyes, exhausted.

In a ringing void, black wings flapped and hovered over her. There was heat and stench and hideous noise. She felt Nehemiah's presence close around her like a cloak of stifling darkness. He had the mastery and she could do nothing. She knew with certainty that, whatever this anguish would be, she would not suffer it only on her own account. Others would be with her, those whom she loved.

The noise increased, a shouting, ragged and excited. There was something very bad here, something worse than – it touched her so closely that she felt her soul sink, and then it had passed her by, not, in the end, her cup, though deeply her affliction.

She could not see – no, it was that she stubbornly *would* not bear, not now, what it was. This was, after all, too dure a test for her spirit. She did not break under it, but she forced herself to bend, curving away towards the light, away from such unclean knowledge as was offered her.

No, she would not see it. She would attend it. It would come. She thought it must be quite soon. In the measurement of fear a year is soon.

But it was all undeserved, all such cruelty, all monstrous inhumanity. Was there no way in which it might be taken from them? A voice went up. 'No! No! No! Please God, please God, please!' And then she found herself seated upright, gripping the arms of her chair, sweat-soaked and shouting in an empty room.

*

Nehemiah drilled his new militia, ignorant of his new importance in Martha's life. It would be more truthful to say that he drilled *half* the militia, for Sir George took care of the other half, just as he always had. Both expended much time and energy in continuing recruitment. In general, the better-off yeomen and their labourers, who were Puritans, joined Owerby, while the gentry and peasantry followed the baronet. They were also apt to steal each other's troops as a cat will steal another's kittens. There was still a good deal of bribery, cajolery and threat, and the countryside took on the air of a newly awoken wasps' nest, so busy were they all about the war.

The question was, what should they do next? Should they go on as they were until King or Parliament sent them their marching orders? Or should they set out to join the King or Parliament? The drawback to this was that, whichever company was the first to march off, the other would take a mean advantage and overrun the place when they had gone. So both must stay, especially as neither yet knew where they should go.

This being so, they wondered, should they make some sort of a fist, just to show willing, of fighting each other? But this would only cause depredation and inconvenience among their own homes, and anyway the women would not have it.

They decided they would not fight. They would defend their territory against any intruder of the opposite faction – they must learn to call them 'the enemy' – who might march through Heron, but they could not bring themselves cold-bloodedly to opt to split each other's sinews. They would only be sorry afterwards. And so they continued to argue and brawl and steal horses and pewter, and enjoy drunken fistfights and clubbing each other into brain soup.

'Has the war begun yet?' they asked each other, but nobody was able to tell them.

In quite another part of the wood, the King would perhaps have admitted that it *had* started; and that, so far, he was not doing very well. Having long lost London, he had proceeded next to lose his control of the Royal Navy, once his particular pride. His Admiral of the Fleet, Northumberland, unsure of his loyalties, had retired pleading sickness, first ensuring as his successor that Draconian sea dog, the Earl of Warwick, who could be relied on to secure the seas for Parliament. Warwick's cousin Essex, the popular veteran of the Dutch wars was now Parliament's General-in-Chief, and assisted him by supervising the occupation of the principal ports (Hull, Portsmouth, Bristol) and the royal dock-yards and magazines. Thus Charles was cut off from his source of supply in Europe, his indefatigable, foraging Queen, and had to fall back on the resources of his not altogether enthusiastic loyal subjects.

Towards the end of August he raised the Royal Standard at Nottingham, signifying that the war had officially begun. Loyalists did not rush to the recruiting tents, being occupied with their soggy harvests. It had been a wet month. It was also windy; the Standard, after a week, blew down, and teeth were gnashed at the bad augury.

There were not enough men, and there was no money and few arms. It was all very depressing. The King fell into a peat-brown melancholy. If it had not been for the ebullience and purposefulness of Prince Rupert, his newly created Lieutenant General of Horse, he might genuinely have *meant* his last, hypocritical offer of peace to Parliament. This was made on the advice of Edward Hyde, the great lawyer who had now come over fully to his side, and who really did wish to prevent the conflict, if at all possible. Charles did not object, as the offer was sure to be rejected and he would then have the advantage of looking morally superior. Tom Heron, who copied out for him the letter he sent to Parliament congratulated himself, as he saw through the subterfuge, that he now knew how the King's mind worked.

This did not mean that he understood it. What he did understand was that they were to see some action at last, and like Rupert he thanked God for it. In battle he had always found an exhilaration and a release from himself that he could get in no other way. At present he needed that release as the bow needs to loose the arrow.

They had been hearing of various skirmishes, all over the country, as men ceased to behave as though they were taking part in that old dance, with its back and forth motion, and began to remember how to fight. Houses, castles, towns were occupied, contested, abandoned as both sides tried to discover where the strategic positions were.

It was clear that the King's aim must be to win back his capital. On September 9th the Earl of Essex, the present master of that capital, left it with an army rumoured to be 15,000 strong. *His* intention was to 'rescue His Majesty's person out of the hands of those desperate persons who were then about him, and bring him home again to his loving Parliament'.

At the approach of such superior forces, Charles retreated to the Welsh Marches. Here, the marcher lords had remembered his championship of their claims against the Merchant Adventurers Company when it had sought to monopolize the wool trade. They had raised 5,000 infantry who waited for the King at Shrewsbury. On the way to this happy assignation, Tom had his first taste of blood, and England a foretaste of Prince Rupert's mettle.

It was a day of sudden September sun. A party of Rupert's half-trained cavalry, on reconnaissance outside Worcester, were taking their midday rest, their heads on their saddles, in a field beside the River Teme, when a scout raced in to report a section of Essex's horse crossing the river a half-mile behind them, with the evident intention of cutting off their return to the road north.

'It looks as though they outnumber us by three or four to one,' he finished doubtfully. Rupert clapped him on the back and gave the instant order to re-form ranks, while he swiftly considered the approaches to the open field where they were deployed. 'Nevertheless, we might offer them a small surprise,' he decided. 'They can only come at us down that lane yonder. We'll have the dragoons pepper them over the hedges; that'll slow them down while we make ready for them.'

The delay was brief, but it was enough. Parliament's raw recruits, the straw still behind their ears and apprehensive as to how to go about 'taking' an enemy party, were indeed very surprised – first to find their heads subjected to a fusillade from both sides of the innocent-looking hedges, and then, when they had run that gamut, to find that what awaited them was not the drowsy doze of snoozers they had seen from the bridge, but the cavalry drawn up in full array and – oh blessed Jesus – *charging* at them!

Many of them died with a puzzled frown as they were beaten back onto their comrades by the terrible hooves. Others turned and fled without waiting for the order to 'wheel about', galloping over their own fallen men and horses in haste to leave the field to the bold and brutal cavaliers.

'It could scarcely be dignified by the name of battle,' wrote Tom at last to Valora, 'for we lost but five troopers in all and though every officer was wounded, none was hurt badly except Prince Rupert's brother, Prince Maurice, who must rest his head for a while. I had a scratch across my back from a sabre, but it is well enough now and does not pain me.

'What pleases me greatly and encourages us here, is how this little exercise has already made a hero of Rupert. Yesterday he was unknown and all but unwanted here, being so young, so impatient in his nature, and a foreigner. Today he is the King's

"Prince Paladin", a nonpareil. Every officer wishes to serve with him and every man under him.

'Digby is, of course, eaten up with jealousy, and has to comfort himself with being made Governor of damp Nottingham while Rupert will have the Garter and everyone's praises. Old Edward Hyde's nose is disjointed forever now, for, whatever it may have lacked in dignity or force, Powick Bridge *was* our first battle, and Hyde can no longer hope to prevent the next, which may come as soon as it likes for our strength grows daily. It is a real pleasure to see the Prince drill his recruits on the meadow; how elegant and tight-knit a body he has made of our hard-riding squires whose only previous thought was for the hunt. At least they are all gentlemen who ride and march with us – I could almost pity my Lord Essex, who must make what he can out of plough-boys and pot-men who can hardly comprehend an order, let alone obey it! How can we *not* win over them and bring His Majesty safe home again?'

In a pretty sitting-room in The Hague, Valora wrinkled her nose over her letter. It made her sick for home and for Tom too. Even their quarrels would have been as welcome to her as the comfort of her shoes in the morning, if only they could be back together. Her vaunted independence was wearing thin; the thought of him in danger made it a tawdry pose. She pressed his letter against her cheek, trying to get the scent of his skin from it. He had not written to her of love; they had agreed that this was how it should be. They were to continue as friends and try to put the past behind them. Then, if, after the fighting was over, they still felt the way they had always felt, from the first hour that they had met, well, then they would reconsider.

But that day was a long way off and Valora, for the first time in her sheltered and privileged life, was lonely and afraid that they may already have tempted the gods too far in their contemptuous treatment of the gift of love.

Autumn 1642

By mid-October the King's army had reached a strength of 8,000 cavalry and 5,000 infantry and were now the better for the services of Thomas Bushell, an engineer and mine-owner who, apart from accoutring three regiments at his own cost, with cannon and shot, undertook to produce silver coinage for the army's pay, much of it from melted plate that was being sent in daily by loyalists across the country.

The Earl of Ruthven had also joined them, gouty, crusty, deaf as his walking stick; but he had learned his soldiering with Gustavus Adolphus and was far more welcome to Rupert than the nominal Commander-in-Chief, the sixty-year-old Earl of Lindsey, who had seen no active service for twenty years and who had been given his command largely in thanks for the number of infantry he had brought them. In fact, only the infantry recognized his command, for Rupert had secured his uncle's promise that *no one* should give him or his cavalry orders except the King himself.

This manner of organizing an army was, naturally, derided by the Parliamentarians, who though for the most part ignorant of warfare, were at least united in their ignorance under a single supreme commander. Indeed, they gained a sense of security from the rotund, pipe-smoking figure of Essex. His unconquered stammer was at least as gentlemanly as the King's and they knew him to have suffered nobly in the lists of life when, his wife having run off with the favourite of old King James, that monarch had forced him to divorce her on the grounds of Essex's imagined impotence. The Royalists laughed at him and called him the Great Cuckold, but his own men sympathized with his misfortune and took him for their own, despite his disconcerting custom of dragging everywhere with him, in case of sudden necessity, his coffin, complete with effigy, a fine hearse and six black horses. He had even been known to sleep in it. Many a Royalist trooper, without a tent to shelter him, might have envied him the amenity.

As it was, the search for billets took up a good deal of their time on the march they now made towards London. It was one of these searches that provoked, before either side was prepared for it, the first real battle in this unlikely war.

They were about to settle for the night, under roofs, in barns, beneath hedges or simply rolled in their cloaks. Digby had reconnoitred with 400 horse and had found no trace of the enemy. Again it was Rupert who blundered into them, seeking beds for the night in the village of Wormleighton, just as they were themselves. Taken prisoner, the Parliament men soon revealed their commander's whereabouts.

Essex had quartered his army in and around Kineton, to the west on the Warwick road. The King, some miles away at Edgecote, though unaware of it, had stationed himself *between* Essex and the disputed road to London.

Rupert thought quickly. Though they had not sought it, this was perhaps their best chance to choose their own battleground; for they *must* turn and fight, or be pursued towards London until Essex caught them up.

He wrote as much in a swift message to the King, then roused his exhausted troops and set off on a harshly paced march through the dark to join him. They were to rendezvous at a point between the enemy and the London road, overlooking the village of Radway in the Vale of Red Horse, up on the clear line of the scarp of Edgehill. From these heights, when dawn came, they would be almost as well-placed to view the movements of the enemy as God himself.

They reached the hillside, worn out, in the early morning. It was still dark and very cold. Few of the men had taken much food or sleep in the last two days. Despite this, they were keen to fight, able to summon the will and the strength from the need of the moment, encouraged by the light in Rupert's eye and their desire to justify his pride in their progress.

The trouble was that they would have to wait for the infantry. Those who had spent the night nearby were already coming in, but others were scattered, perhaps several hours' march away. Delay was inevitable but it was bad for the men. They began to think of food and sleep and to brood on the fact that many of them must die today. How would it be to die? Would it be painful? Would they shame themselves before their comrades? They tried not to be cowards, but the waiting killed their courage. It also gave their commanders time to quarrel. Rupert, looking down on the main body of Essex's army, spread out a mile away across the plain, knew that they still lacked the two regiments commanded by John Hampden.

Accordingly, he suggested that his cavalry should launch a surprise attack at dawn. They were over 3,000 strong, enough, given the advantage of utter surprise, to demoralize the whole

Parliamentary army at one glorious stroke. His riders would welcome it.

But cautious old Lindsey would not have it. Nor would the King. It was too risky a business with so few men and that few so tired and hungry. Besides, if they were to attack now, they would lose their advantageous position without assurance of success. And anyway, the scarp slope was too steep to admit a cavalry charge. So here they all sat, glowering at each other, up on the chilly ridge, while the soldiers sat with them and chewed on their own nerve-ends, watching as the sun came up and struck the first light from Parliament's armour.

The next altercation concerned the deployment of the troops. Rupert insisted that the pikemen and the musketeers should be interspersed with each other, as he had been taught by the modern-minded Gustavus of Sweden. Lindsey, however, was content with the old-fashioned Dutch method whereby the musketeers were regarded as subsidiary to the pikemen and were bunched behind them, thus losing much of the possible volume of their fire and giving less protection to the pikes.

Lindsey was irate at what he considered to be Rupert's unwarranted interference with the infantry, while Rupert was incensed by the Commander's inability to understand that one cannot put together a battle in pieces like a jigsaw, but must plan it as a whole picture. Ruthven supported Rupert. So, after some hesitation, did the King.

Lindsey, infuriated by this disregard of his command, threw down his baton in a rage, before the interested troops, and bawled that if he was not fit to be a general, he would die a colonel at the head of his own regiment. He stalked away, leaving an embarrassed silence which no one filled by calling him back.

The Sergeant-major General, Sir Jacob Astley, was appointed in his place as commander of the foot. Though over sixty, he was regarded by the troops as a competent and courageous officer.

What was more, he had once been Rupert's tutor and the Prince both liked and respected him. 'Now, we shall see some progress,' he remarked to Tom, satisfied. He displayed his satisfaction by making a great fuss of a shaggy white dog, the size of a small lion, that went everywhere with him. He was a hunting poodle; his name was Boy. 'Now we'll show them our paces, eh Boy?'

'No doubt of it, sir, but first may I offer you some breakfast?' There would still be a long time to wait.

'Food? Are you a magician?'

Tom found the uninvited image of Martha Knyvett in his mind and dismissed it indignantly. 'Not I, but Josh, my valet, has just caught a rabbit.'

'That precious person! You astonish me.' Rupert chuckled. 'He is always dashing at me with his combs and his potions and a great fluttering of lashes. I'd never have expected to find him a hunter.'

'He surprised himself. He still won't tell me how he caught it, but he has had it cooked in a mustard sauce and it smells good.'

'Lead me to it.'

They moved to where Josh Pye, his effete little person improbably neat, hovered over a makeshift table with an excellent view of the enemy at reveille. There was not only rabbit but eggs and milk.

'I visited an old dame in Radway,' Josh explained modestly. 'I promised her immunity to Your Highness's – depredations.' He eyed Rupert's luxury of chestnut curls with an artist's longing as he served him. The Prince was very untidy. His own valet must be a man of no professional honour. And with such delightful material – Josh allowed himself the pleasure of running his eye closely over their young leader's good points. It was not that he did not take a tremendous pride in serving Tom, who was a perfectionist in every way and afforded him every opportunity – except that for hero-worship, which it was not in his nature to accept and which he would not permit. Rupert, though, was every man's hero, and probably every woman's too, but that was of no interest to Josh who did not care for women; messy creatures.

There was no doubt that the Prince cut a splendid figure. Even lounging on an ammunition box with his long legs asprawl under the table, his pose was naturally graceful as his warm and thoughtful eyes consulted the rabbit, his classic nose twitching enjoyably above full lips whose well-defined marksman's bow seemed permanently amused, and, to his enemies at least, wholly supercilious. Beside Tom Heron's stiff set of right angles he seemed relaxed to the point of coming apart. He let his body do as it liked in a way that Tom, who had every muscle under house arrest, envied without knowing it. He liked being with Rupert, and if it had not occurred to him explicitly to admire his extraordinary good looks, he appreciated his freedom of manner and the breadth of a mind that fastened as eagerly onto the latest development in science or art as upon the narrower exigencies of warfare.

'I forgot to tell you.' The Prince waved his knife vaguely

backwards. 'I met your father earlier. He's over there with Wilmot somewhere. He had just ridden in, and brought sixty men with him.'

'Good Lord, I'd no idea. Will he join us, d'you know?'

Rupert grinned. 'No. I think he'd prefer to serve with Wilmot. They were very thick when I left them.'

'Well, he must do as he pleases.'

'Very thick. They were singing drunk.'

Tom groaned. 'Drunk, before dawn!'

'Good luck to them – as long as they are able to tell friend from foe later on.'

'I'd better go and see him.'

'No, leave it, will you, Tom? I promised His Majesty I'd attend him to complete the ordering of the field. It's time I went, and I'd like you with me. Moral support – in case Ruthven doesn't hear the royal summons.' He rose and swung his scarlet cavalry cloak around his six-foot-four length of healthy male beauty in a gesture that had Josh almost swooning, and they strode off to the King's tent, their path strewn with the smiles and greetings attracted by Rupert's facility for drawing every eye.

King Charles was at the top of his form. He was surrounded by his principal officers. The Princes Charles and James were with him, their obvious excitement causing sympathetic smiles among the wardogs and a crease of worry between the brows of the King's doctor, William Harvey, into whose care they had been consigned for the duration of the battle.

'My cousin Rupert is here!' exclaimed young Charles as they entered. 'Now we can plan the attack. How is it to be?'

Rupert answered him with a faintly repressive smile. The boy had canvassed his support ever since learning that he had commanded a company at the Siege of Breda, at the age of thirteen.

The King, too, greeted them warmly and they settled down to complete the ordering that Lindsey's outburst had interrupted.

It is a simple, even an automatic process, for experienced men to draw up a battle array, but there is no experience that can shorten the drawn-out, dragging, nerve-ragging time between that drawing-up and the battle itself. All through the morning both armies made ready, each watching the other with heightening interest, each man fancying he could pick out the hand that held his death, a mile away on the other side. It was well after noon before the two forces were more or less in position and must begin to feel that in their own hands lay the possibility – no, the dire necessity – of dealing death. Not to a friend, if they should chance to meet. Not that. It was too much to expect of any man. But to an Englishman, none-the-less, and the King's subject like oneself. It did not bear thinking about. Best to put such thoughts away. The Royalists drowned them in cheerful talk, and the Parliament men in full-throated hymns.

At about three o'clock they were ready. Both on the hillside and in the valley they followed the usual pattern; wide bands of infantry were flanked on each side by cavalry. On the Royalist side, Rupert, with his four regiments of horse and the King's Lifeguards took the right wing; Wilmot with five regiments was on the left; the infantry in the centre under Jacob Astley, with the Royal Standard, carried by Sir Edward Verney, flaunting above the red coats of His Majesty's Footguard.

When all the others had gone out, the King, following his ancestral privilege, made a brief speech of encouragement to the men who were the guardians of his immediate future.

'Your King is both your cause, your quarrel, and your captain,' he declared, touching Tom as deeply with the fine poetic balance of his words as with their meaning. 'Come life or death your King will bear you company – and ever keep this field, this place and this day's service in his grateful remembrance.'

His Majesty then moved on and did not hear, though Tom did, the emotional voice which proclaimed behind his tent.

> *'And Crispin Crispian shall ne'er go by*
> *From this day to the ending of the world,*
> *But we in it shall be remembered—'*

A hiccup followed. From long habit Tom picked up the lines as he made his way towards the voice:

> *'We few, we happy few, we band of brothers;*
> *For he today that sheds his blood with me*
> *Shall be my brother—'*

'Well met, Father! I had heard you were here.'

His back was thumped. Sir George, rubicund with wine and tears, beamed at him. He was sitting on a sagging wooden box, having his beard trimmed by Tibbett, who loomed over him in a buff coat with two pistols in his belt, and grinned at Tom.

'Good to see you, my boy!' For a moment the shadow of Jud Heron hung in the air, summoned by Shakespeare and the oddities of civil strife. Neither mentioned him.

'Did you leave all well at home?'

'Aye, pretty well, now that crapulous young toad, Owerby, has taken off to join Essex – not that my lord has cause to be grateful for the parcel of piss-witted Puritans he brings him – useless bastards. Not like my stout fellows. I've given the foot-sloggers to Astley. He'll soon lick 'em into shape.'

Tom nodded. His father did not seem so very drunk now. Doubtless, even at his age, and after his years of campaigning with Gustavus, the thought of battle was a sobering one. 'How is my mother?'

'She is well, though a touch in the dumps at my leaving. I think she had hopes I'd given up Westminster to become a lazy, lumpish landowner all year long. But here – I'd almost forgot. I have letters for you.'

He pulled a bundle out of his pocket. There was a long one from Lady Heron, a short one from Lucy and a blotched and soggy one from Kit. Another small packet, sealed until it resembled a scarlet candle, bore Valora's writing.

He tore it open, hardly listening to his father's opinions on commanders and methods of attack. There was a short note which he thrust into his pocket, and a small chamois pouch. He took out its contents and there was her candid and critical gaze challenging him from the frame of a locket. It was very small; it would hang round his neck as simply as the stone that seemed to have lodged itself in his chest. He ripped the note out of his pocket after all.

'I wished to go with you into battle. Master Honthorst has made it possible. I have no doubt but that we shall both emerge unscathed.' Her arrogance removed the stone and took his breath. He laughed. It was so like her.

So was the miniature. Honthorst's work was impeccable. He showed it to his father.

'Damned fine woman. Don't know why you don't marry her!' said Sir George. His mind was still on Wilmot's arrangements for his riders.

'I've done now, sir,' Tibbett pronounced. It was time to go to their places.

'God be with you, Master Tom,' the monolith offered, stuffing the baronet's razor into his pocket and holding out his hand.

'And with you, Tibbett, and with you.' He wrung the hand warmly, then moved to kiss his father's cheek.

Sir George cleared his throat. 'We'll meet, later, Tom,' he said.

'Of course.' He saluted them and went off to let Josh bully him into a similar object of beauty, before buckling him into his half-armour.

The King, likewise, had now put on a fine black velvet cloak, thrown back to reveal its ermine lining and the blue ribbon of the Garter across his gleaming breastplate, and was riding conspicuously up and down the ranks accompanied by his Gentlemen Pensioners. It was now shortly before three.

Rupert, too, reviewed his lines and gave his instructions to his cavalry. They were short both of arms and experience and must therefore achieve the greatest possible impact right away. As Rupert saw it, everything depended on their first charge. He had moved them downhill to the height from which they would gain the best start. He ordered them to keep as close a formation as they could and not to fire until they saw the whites of the enemy's eyes. Then he rode swiftly through the ranks with his red cloak flying and Boy barking at his stirrup, throwing words of encouragement and comradeship like a shower of gold on all sides.

'They'll follow him to hell, if he should wish,' commented Will Legge, Tom's fellow captain and another of Rupert's chosen friends.

'Aye – but most of them don't yet know just how close to hell it will be,' Tom replied.

The other grinned. 'It's a cold day. We need a warming!'

Meanwhile, before his infantry, that excellent and humanitarian soldier Sir Jacob Astley, having addressed them in calm and simple terms, offered up a bare and practical prayer, 'O Lord, thou knowest how busy I must be this day. If I forget thee, do not thou forget me.'

Just after three, Essex opened fire with his cannon, hoping to cause early confusion in the Royalist lines. It was the King himself who put the touch to the charge that set his own guns thundering in reply. The battle had begun.

Rupert did not waste a second. Stirrup to stirrup they began at the trot, increasing to the canter as they swept down the slope and across the plain, reaching the gallop just before the enemy lines. Here Sir James Ramsey's cavalry was waiting for them on slightly rising ground, expecting them to stop, fire their pistols, then wheel to reload.

Tom, his heart beating, his blood singing up into his head, crowed like a cockerel in exhilaration with the pounding hooves and shaking earth about him and beneath him. The old drum and thunder, this was what he'd needed!

Ramsey's Horse were a study in stupefaction as they took in, too late, that this charge was *not* going to stop, or fire twice, or do anything other than crash right in amongst them against all the rules, their rapiers whirling like the wheels of Boudicca's chariots! A further shock hit them as the troop commanded by Sir Faithfull Fortescue tore off their orange-tawny Parliament scarves and wheeled about to join Rupert.

On came the murderous charge, barely slowed by the marshy ground or the bombardment of the rattled musketeers, loosed too soon in the half hope of holding back the sweep of harvesting horsemen. As often as not, they hit their own men, for Rupert had sliced in at a slant, across their front, not only cutting down the cavalry but carving into the foot as well. There was no withstanding this automated scything machine. Ramsey's men did the only two things they could do; they held firm and were cut to pieces or they turned tail and fled.

Tom, his sword already blooded, he hardly knew how, ploughed on behind Rupert, swinging his way through the defenceless musketeers. He saw the whites of their eyes all right, bulging in fear beneath the brutal battery of hooves. He struck down one, two, three; he lost count. Now they were beating them into their own reserves, drawn up at the rear. Their commander Denzil Holles made a brave attempt to rally them, but few responded, and with clear ground ahead of them Rupert's men pursued them as ferociously and with as loud view-hallooing as they had once pursued the fox.

The reserve cavalry, who should have remained to cover the infantry, caught the scent and pelted after them. The chase led all the way back to Kineton, went belling through the village and a mile down the road to where a surprised John Hampden, still marching up his two delayed regiments, made his first contribution by swiftly placing a battery across the road. Those who escaped his spoil-sport net raced on until the fox was done.

One of the few to resist the call of the hunting horn, Tom had harried his own troop back into some sort of order. Seeing the magnificently mounted Gentlemen Pensioners, intent on giving the lie to their nickname of 'the King's Show Troop', hammering past with the rest, he determined to win through to protect the King in their place.

From the helpful height and concealment of an ancient oak on the fringe of a small wood on the Parliamentary right, an observer approved Tom's movements through a powerful telescope. Jud would be glad to hear that his brother, among so many lace-edged dunderheads, had shown good sense and resource as well as idiot courage. It was a pity he fought on the wrong side of the quarrel. Robin Whittaker scribbled as much, in the shorthand he had almost mastered, then re-applied his glass eye to sort out the rest of the field.

On the slope of Edgehill the King's infantry were hard-pressed, their whole centre left, incredibly, undefended on one side. Sir William Balfour, with a party of Parliament's horse, was moving up under cover of the thick hedges on their left to take advantage of this howling error. For when Wilmot had led the charge on that side, his experience had been complementary to Rupert's on the right; that is, the shock of his impetus had broken Fielding's cavalry and driven them from the field. His riders had streamed after them in pursuit of glory and plunder, leaving the way free for the wily Balfour, who had hung back and evaded Wilmot's charge, to close upon the now naked infantry.

Robin watched with keen enjoyment, which he had to remind himself to dampen to impartial interest, as Balfour brought up the only disciplined body of cavalry left on the field and loosed it upon the King's centre. In no time he had silenced the Royalist's guns and thus given new heart to Essex's infantry, one brigade of whom, demoralized by the rout of the cavalry, had fled without firing a shot. The rest pulled themselves together and closed with Sir Jacob Astley's men in the roughest fighting yet seen. It was all the push of pikes and plunge and suck of knives; the hand-to-hand butchery, with terrified faces whitening above spurting arteries and despairing hands clutching at slithering bowels, that is reserved for the poor bleeding infantry while the gentlemen go riding after their sport. Robin shivered a great deal, glad to be a non-combatant. No rough-and-tumble had ever been like this.

Had Rupert been still on the field, the battle, perhaps even the war, might have been over in half an hour. As it was, Parliament did more than hold their own. Robin recovered with them and gave a whoop when he saw the Royal Standard taken. He could not, at that distance, make out the fact that Sir Edward Verney, who had carried it, had been felled with it, nor that they had to cut off his hand, with the King's picture on its signet ring, to capture the flag. He did see the Earl of Lindsey, mortally wounded, carried as a prisoner from the field to fulfil his own bitter dawn prophecy. There was even a moment when he thought the King was about to be taken – that, too, would have ended the war, in half a minute.

At any rate, what he saw justified Robin in settling down to recount, for his readers, a Parliament victory. He must hurry if he was to despatch his description before sunset. Jud would print the news-sheet early in the morning, and if they could be among the first with such glorious news they would be well on the way to achieving their latest ambition, which was to earn an independent living by the production, modest at first, of their own broadsheet, one which would give people the facts of the war, or of Westminster, or of what was said in the streets of London, *as they happened*, or as soon as possible afterwards.

He would make sure a copy of this sheet went to Will Staunton. It was time his ex-master knew on what side of his bread the butter lay. Rob was fond of Silken Will, had been almost sorry to leave his fine mansion, with its warm beds and its three meals a day; certainly he regretted having to do it so suddenly and secretly. He owed him a great deal. Therefore he would always do his best to keep him informed. He could hardly do better than that.

His escape route from the battlefield was necessarily long and circuitous; he didn't wish to be asked his business by either side. His

point of farewell was up on the scarp of Edgehill, at a diplomatic distance from the Royalist posts.

From up here the battle resembled the antics of enlivened lead soldiers and witheld its reality from him – except for the sound. Its noise seemed to Rob like that of a very large and faraway kitchen, where thousands of cooks scolded thousands of yelling potboys and everyone clashed the pots and pans as though to clatter them to atoms. It was chaos; it was senseless; he was glad to turn his back on it.

As the evening and the fighting wore on, time was caught for some men in the blink of an eye before dying, while for others it seemed as measureless as the rest of their lives. Rupert's and Wilmot's horse began to return in scattered groups, many fortified with food from Essex's wagons. The sight of them was a mighty relief to the flagging and ravenous infantry, by now desperate for aid.

Meanwhile on the centre of the field, a Captain Smith had made a buccaneering dash into Parliament's flank and had rescued the captured Standard. There were cheers and spirits rose.

But the light was fading quickly now, and the last energies of the exhausted struggle drained away with it. Little by little Parliament's infantry fell back, turning to retreat at last into the engulfing darkness.

As Essex drew back, Rupert tried to muster the strength for another cavalry charge, to make their victory decisive, but his men were too far spent, too badly wounded, or just too hungry, and their horses were blown and foaming with sweat.

He gave in and they struck camp on the field. Less than a mile away Essex did the same. Neither was willing to yield it to the other.

At last, now, thank God who had preserved them, they were able to eat! They had what they had taken in plunder as well as what had been kept back from them to sharpen their appetites for blood. They built fires on which they cooked the food and warmed their ale or wine. Afterwards they sat around the blaze and sang songs to comfort themselves for the fact that it had, after all, been easy, in the hot necessity of a sword-split second, to slaughter another Englishman.

When the fires had died into mere glowing constellations, counterparts of the cold stars, and those who had fought had fallen, as suddenly as apples, into the deep sleep of exhaustion, Tom's over-excited mind allowed him no such relief. Like those whose sad work begins when the battle ends, his eyes searched the wastes of the plain. He sensed the groans and the silence. Folded in two cloaks, he sat feeding a small section of the bonfire they had lit before Prince Rupert's tent, helpless before the ambush of enemy thoughts he had avoided during the fight. He envied the prostrate shape of Boy, stretched out in front of him like a vast woolly bolster, his loud, even breathing joining the consort of snores from the unconscious troopers nearby. Boy usually slept at the foot of his master's pallet, but tonight Rupert too was awake and prowling the field, leaving the dog to the rest they both had earned.

Tom experimentally stretched his back. It was painful. He had been wounded in the fleshy part of his left hip, where a glancing rapier cut had caught him. The old sabre gash seemed to have opened up as well. Neither wound was serious, but they would stiffen unless he rested them properly. He did not want this to happen in case there should be further action in the next few days. At least he had now completely stopped bleeding. Harvey had said this was because of the cold, and that many of the wounded, some still lying, uncounted, out on the field, would owe their lives to the night's rude frost. If they could survive the cold itself, the freezing helped their blood to congeal more quickly. The doctor was preoccupied with the behaviour of blood, particularly with its performance *inside* the body, which in present circumstances some might have thought wasteful.

And just what had they gained by it – this prescribed and

looked-for letting of blood from England's uneasy body? The rumour from the chaplains, who even at this ungodly hour were still sending in wounded and ministering to the dying, was that perhaps two men out of every ten had died on that confused and mismanaged field. Could their equivocal 'victory' possibly have been worth such a cost?

He shifted again and there was a sharp twinge from his hip. He took a nip from his flask of brandy. He recalled the man who had given him the blow. It had been in that last mêlée with Balfour's Horse. He had leaned toward Tom from a good black nag, a little round man, with a merry face pulled into an aberrant grimace of concentration which had relaxed into distress for a second as he felt his blade strike home. His soft heart had saved Tom and procured his own death, for in that same second Tom had spitted him on his sword and had not looked again at his face.

But now he found himself forced to remember that it had been a pleasant face, a witness of good nature, and his clothes and armour had bespoken him a gentleman. Had they met, some weeks ago, in a tavern, or at the house of a mutual friend, they would have enjoyed a talk together over their wine. Doubtless they would have argued the toss over the troubles of King and Parliament – but neither would have credited the other had he suggested it might come to this . . . Tom tried to take some comfort from the fact that he had not known the man, but that pleasant face kept telling him that to all intents and purposes he had known him well enough, and now, it seemed, too well.

And then there were the others he had killed. How many? Five or six. He was not sure. They had all been infantrymen. He could not recall their faces. And every one, all six, or seven – had been born, like himself, on English soil.

He felt strange and heavy. If he had been a child he would have wept. He had not felt like this when he had shed blood so many times across the Channel.

There was a movement behind him and a hand on his shoulder rescued him from remorse. It was the Prince.

'A little touch of Rupert in the night,' he misquoted, on his father's behalf. Sir George, in fact, was in Wilmot's tent, baptizing victory and drowning a musketball in the thigh.

'Eh?' said Rupert.

'It should be Harry. And of course, that was *before* the battle.'

'My dear Tom, what are you talking about? What Harry?'

'If you are to be an English hero, you would do well to study Will Shakespeare; he always makes them behave beautifully. I'm talking of Henry V. On the night before Agincourt, the King wandered about the camp in disguise, listening to the talk of the soldiers.'

Rupert gave a very German snort. 'He'd have been better advised to take his sleep. As for me, I prefer daylight and plain speaking.'

Tom grinned, 'Well, you set 'em up right enough today. I've never seen cavalry charge with such a will!'

Rupert looked thoughtful. 'Yes, but it was the devil's own work to get them back again. There's plenty of will, but they have no idea, yet, of the discipline.' He sighed into a yawn.

'I'm twenty-three now; it's taken me ten years to learn what I know about warfare from the best of teachers, the Prince of Orange, and chiefly Gustavus, God rest him. And now I have to try to thrust it all through the solid heads of these country gentlemen in less time than it takes to hone a pike.'

'Give yourself some credit,' suggested Tom gently, 'I think we can count today our victory.'

'Can we, though?' Rupert wondered. 'Not until our road to London lies unimpeded. Essex might attack again in the morning. His troops were better rested than ours, and it looks as if our casualties number about equally. It's true we bested him with the cavalry, but his infantry held well in parts; and that Balfour is a man to watch.'

And so, because they could not help it, they dissected the battle, point by point, until sleep surprised them in the middle of an argument about Wilmot's refusal to charge again.

Tom's thought, as he rolled over at last, his head on a blanket, was that it was a pity that his father had not, certainly not, seen another Crispin's day.

In the morning Essex was in full retreat.

Two weeks later, in a back street near the Fleet Ditch, Jud Heron was taking great pains and pleasure in transferring, in the impeccable Dutch type of Christopher van Dyck, his own words to his own press. True, the words were by courtesy of Robin and had to be edited from gutter to King's English – and the press was by courtesy of John Pym and would one day have to be paid for – but these were facts which enhanced rather than qualified his pleasure. Who would have thought that a great Parliamentary leader would have an interest in developing the latent talents of George Heron? On the other hand, it was probably just this ability to make use of the talents of others that had placed John

Pym on his present airy pinnacle. But certainly no one could have thought that Robin, whose entire previous purpose had appeared to be the pursuit of dubious pleasures, would have taken so keen an interest in the fortunes of the warring parties.

'I'd give half my breakfast to *see* the battle they are all aiming for,' he had said longingly, wolfing bread and beef.

Jud had laughed. 'You – you wouldn't pull a soldier off your mother! What have you to do with battles?'

Robin had looked unusually thoughtful. 'They might, in a manner of speaking, be *my* battles,' he said. He knew a lot of men who had marched with Essex. So did his mother. They were just ordinary men, the commoners of London with whom he had rubbed shoulders all his life. If it was their battle, it was as likely to be his.

He didn't bother to explain this to Jud, who was a gentleman and might well fancy the other side. They never argued about the war, being in complete agreement on the most necessary point, which was that neither of them had the least desire to fight. In spite of this, both understood the importance of the struggle, not simply as they learned of its day-to-day confrontations, but at some new level of thought that had begun to flow beneath their conscious minds as the Fleet flows under London, sweeping away old debris with a strong, fresh current.

'I believe I'll go up and see for myself what happens; I'll follow the drum, but not too close,' Rob had decided next.

It was Jud who had seen the use to which they could put his curiosity. It had taken very little time and encouragement to persuade him that he should try to get some record of his experiences back to Jud and into the newsbooks. Accordingly, they had arranged for one of his mother's more enterprising weekday friends, one Gaudy Leake, a man of no fixed income or abode but a prodigious ability for slipping through, under or behind things, to get the despatches back to London.

He had brought the news of Edgehill even faster than Colonel Ramsey's ill-fated cavalry, who had galloped hell-for-leather through the streets bellowing that Essex was defeated and Rupert and his devils close on their heels, 'hacking, hewing and pistolling' everyone they met.

Jud risked death under the Colonel's hooves rather than leave him in such a shameful state of ignorance. Ramsey was indeed surprised to read, in the newly printed sheet that blackened his fingers, that the victory was Parliament's after all – but then, his troop had never looked back since first they had turned and fled from the whites of Rupert's eyes. There was no one behind them; no one at all.

It seemed to Jud, inexperienced though he was in these matters, that, if the King had any intention of regaining his capital, there should have been. From what Rob had written, the defeat was not a crippling one, and the Royalists still held the road to London. Why did they not use it?

Still, it was all to the good. After all, Jud allowed, it was Parliament, more or less, who were paying him. He did not dwell on this fact as it brought uncomfortable instincts to the surface.

He concentrated on the job in hand, which was the reassurance of the Londoners. The majority of them were by now engaged in some form of defence work; digging trenches, building barricades, drilling with Philip Skippon's Trained Bands – and most importantly, raising money. Their enthusiasm for this last was encouraged when Parliament arrested seventy citizens who had refused a contribution.

It was soon clear from Rob's despatches that the King, who had drawn off to Oxford, did not intend to enter his capital under arms, although the Bloody Prince had had to be restrained from hounding down to tear out its throat. He had then tried to come at it by taking Windsor and cutting off the Thames traffic, but could not get the better of its sturdy little garrison under the aggressive John Venn, and had been forced off, hungry and disappointed, to forage and wreak vengeance on the hapless Vale of Aylesbury.

Rupert's reputation was now sufficiently colourful to make Jud wish he might use red ink rather than black. He didn't believe half he read of him in Rob's pawmarked pieces, but he had to admit he was good news as far as his sales were concerned.

He considered the cover of today's book. He had already set up the founts in the goldsmith's fine, incisive Roman lettering, for

> The Certain News of This Present Week
> Brought by Sundry Posts from Several Places
> But Chiefly –

and here he wondered whether to give preponderance to

> The Parliament Magnanimously Enquire after a Treaty or
> My Lord of Essex Home Again: Hail to the Victor!

or to the more exciting

Rupert the Red and His Familiar Spirit – the chilling tale of twin babies, snatched and sacrificed before their parents' terrified eyes to a hideous Devil in the shape of a Great White Dog, which had Drunk the Blood and then Consumed the Pitiful Remains of the infants

The scarified parents had just sufficiently recovered from their appalling ordeal to be able to recount it to Rob and to accept the sum which he pressed upon them in return. Robin had soon discovered that information which is paid for tends to be the most newsworthy, and had established a self-propelling system whereby he lightened the pockets of the dull majority to line those of the scandalous few. Jud, reserving any doubts in the interest of their joint future, admired his resource. All the same, he would be glad to be able to tell Rob, on his imminent return, of Pym's amazing generosity.

He decided that Essex must take the prime place. Parliament had voted him £5,000 for his conduct of the war; Jud could treat him no less munificently. Privately, Rob's late writings had made him doubt my lord had earned his money; Parliament appeared less victorious with each successive item; in fact, by now Jud supposed Edgehill to have been more or less of a drawn battle. However, this was certainly *not* what he was being paid to print.

He started to select the founts, but was interrupted by a thunderous knocking at the door.

'See who that is. *Don't* let them in,' he instructed Endymion Whittaker, a skinny, snot-nosed urchin whom Rob had left as some sort of help-cum-hostage against his return. His mother had seen the resplendent courtier Endymion Porter go by on the day before his birth, and had fancied some of his good fortune might cling to his name. The two did by now have something in common, but whereas Porter pulled strings and begged monopolies from the King, his namesake simply cut purse-strings and monopolized anything that was not nailed down. Jud had already whipped him twenty-six strokes for stealing and selling a complete alphabet of founts.

Nor was this Endymion's lucky morning, for when he opened the outer door an inch, both it and himself were flung rudely aside by an apparent tornado of rich textiles and richer vocabulary. William Staunton had run his errant apprentice to earth.

'Oh the devil!' muttered Jud.

'No. But the effect could well be similar before I've done.'

The merchant was not jocular. Indeed it was clear that he was very angry. He looked about him, taking in all that was necessary. His gaze swept over the letters set out on the press and across the sheets beside it, close-written in Robin's tortuous script.

'Goddammit, it was I taught the ungrateful little gallows-bait to write!' he exploded.

Jud said nothing.

Will roamed the room, insofar as its narrowness permitted. His magnificence diminished the place even further, showing up its dirt floors and the meanness of its crumbling lathe-and-plaster walls. Only the gleaming new press stood up to him. 'Well, then, you little Judas, let's have it! How did you come to settle in this fine establishment?'

'How did you find me, sir?' Jud countered. Pym had insisted on the strictest secrecy. Jud was his concealed weapon.

'Your volume of Edge Hill was sent to me. Your work is very easily recognized. You use too many adjectives and your sentences continue far too long. You are also prone to an irony that is not required of an impartial observer. I recall that I had to check a similar levity in some of your letters to my company's debtors – in whose number you now rank, by the way.'

Jud ignored that for the time being. 'I had no idea I was such a detectable stylist,' he said with a jauntiness he did not feel.

'Be sure I intend you no compliment,' said Will coldly.

'I still don't know how you found your way here,' Jud insisted. It was important.

'I made enquiries.' This was an unsatisfactory answer.

'I did not come here to answer your impudent questions, Heron, but to hear your explanations,' Staunton continued. 'First, you'll oblige me by telling me why you did not sail, as arranged, on the *Gallant Lady*.'

Jud searched his face for an iota of sympathy and did not find it. He sighed. 'Because I was to sail, not freely and joyfully as I had always dreamed, but as a punishment for an act for which I can feel no guilt.' He met Will's eye unflinchingly, knowing instinctively that Lunsford was not a man for whom the merchant could have any respect. That eye remained icy, however, and the explanation, it told him, was so far insufficient.

'I would willingly have gone, sir,' he said sincerely, 'if it were not under such duress – and if –' he hesitated. The plain truth sounded too bare to pass without ridicule. 'And if there were not so much to keep me in London at this time.'

Will raised a sardonic brow. 'But not, it seems, the gainful employment for which your indentures were signed?'

Jud had no reply. Unless Staunton wished it otherwise, the law bound him in his apprenticeship for seven years. His defection was, if Staunton desired, punishable by a prison sentence.

'I was offered other work,' he muttered. He did not mean to sound so ungrateful, only to point out that he was earning an honest living. The next second he was reeling from a stinging blow to the head.

'You treacherous young pup!' Will blazed. 'How dare you?'

Jud shook his ringing head. His nose bled. He staunched it on some rag and pulled his wits together. He could not bear the words 'Judas', 'treacherous' – that was not it at all.

'I'm no traitor, sir, believe me,' he said forthrightly. 'If I had thought you would have taken me back, I'd have come to you – but I didn't think so. I thought you'd be too angry and would turn me over to my father. I didn't want that. And even if you *had* agreed to keep me – what were *you* then to have said to my father?' He spread his hands hopelessly.

Will grunted. 'Let me get this quite clear. It was all for my sake, was it, that you forfeited the money that your father and I had invested in your future?'

Jud resented his tinder-dry tone. 'I didn't say that. You twist the truth. It is simple enough, God knows.' He was beginning to lose his chastened feeling. He raised his head and his voice.

'I was right not to go. I was right not to come to you – though I wish I might have done, nonetheless – and I am right to take the employment offered me.' He thumbed at the press.

Will made no comment upon all this rectitude. His eyes narrowed. 'I suppose you realize that this is an illegal press? Or do you possess a licence for it?' This was not likely as the number of presses in the city was restricted by the Licensing Act to twenty-three, closely regarded by the Royal Censor and the Stationers' Company.

Jud had an answer prepared for this one, however. He shrugged. 'The King has removed the presses of his own printers, Messrs Robert Barker and John Bill, to York and to Shrewsbury. If His Majesty may ignore his Licensing Act, then so may others. Besides, their removal leaves a space in London. We fill it.'

Will almost smiled. He knew whose reasoning this was. As a matter of fact, he had already discussed Jud's predicament with John Pym – who had, after imposing certain conditions, agreed to give him this unsalubrious address.

'Anyway, the King's licence counts for little just now,' Jud added. 'I see no reason why any man should not set up a press and print what he likes, so long as he can afford it.'

Will looked thoughtful. He agreed absolutely with this, but agreement was not his present purpose. 'And will *you* print what you like,' he enquired blandly, 'or only what your master requires of you?'

Jud, to his annoyance, felt himself blushing. 'It is our aim to publish weekly "corantos", something after the style of Nathaniel Butter who was so popular; he and his partner have recently ceased to print them. There is a need for news. We are not the only ones to think so.'

'Healthy competition is an excellent thing in business,' said Will automatically.

Jud relaxed a little. Perhaps, after all, they would be able to talk.

But Will was not going to let him down so lightly. 'You said "we",' he mentioned in his silkiest tone. 'Do I understand you to refer to Robin Whittaker, whose foul scrabble you have here?'

There was no point in denial.

'Then he too is derelict in his duty to my company.' He sniffed. 'You are nicely placed for Bridewell here; can you tell me of any reason why I should not have the two of you conveyed there as soon as may be possible?'

Jud took a chance. 'Because our debts would be paid – by our new master.'

Will snorted. 'You think so? Do you imagine John Pym could not find a hundred like you, or a thousand like Rob Whittaker?'

Jud's face clouded. 'He has promised us his protection,' he said stoutly. 'I do not think you could make him break his promise.' But he was no longer sure. Obviously it was Pym who must have told Will where to find him.

Will saw his uncertainty. But what Jud did not know was that although Pym had indeed revealed their hiding place, he had done so only after Will had sworn that the information should go no further. He had agreed that Jud owed Will an explanation.

In fact, by now, Will's chief interest in Jud was his own curiosity. Naturally, he had been very annoyed by the desertion of his two most promising youngsters, but nothing more than that. He understood, who better, their desire for novelty and adventure. At fourteen, Will had run away to sea, and here was Jud at nineteen running away *from* it. Both had been impelled by the need to take his own life into his own hands. Will, therefore, was generous enough to forgive in Jud the restless quality he knew in himself. He was not foolish enough to let Jud see this. If he and John Pym were the only responsible citizens who knew Jud Heron's whereabouts, that meant that they stood *in loco parentis*, and this was a position Will took seriously because he was fond of Jud's family. He left the boy to stew in his uncertainty as far as Pym's promises were concerned and tacked in another direction.

'If you have no loyalty to myself and the goodwill I showed you, surely, at the least, you have some sense of responsibility towards your father; and think how it would distress your mother to know what you have done.'

'But they *don't* know. There is no way they could know,' Jud said reasonably. 'They think me safe at sea, or rather, my mother thinks me far from safe. She has always feared the sea. Indeed she would be delighted if she knew I was high and dry here.' He gloomed, 'I suppose you will tell my father now and there will be hell to pay.'

'Do you think I should *not* tell him?' Will enquired mildly.

'I cannot say what you *should* do. I only wish you *would* not.'

'And how long, do you suppose, would this deception be expected to continue – supposing I did not tell him – when the *Lady* returns?

Jud wondered whether he should start to hope, or whether Will was only amusing himself. 'I don't know,' he said honestly. 'I hadn't got so far as to think of that. Of course I wouldn't want to go on like this forever – I'm attached to my family. I miss them, especially Lucy. But I suppose it would have to be until the war is finished. Master Pym does not want these premises discovered, nor my work. He says that in an uncertain situation it is better to keep some certainties to yourself.'

Will smiled wryly. 'I am sure he is right.' He began to wander about again, picking up papers that were piled on shelves, making Jud nervous. '"Ferocious Atrocities in Ireland"; "the Fearful Experiences of A Lady of Quality", hot from Liverpool. Your correspondents travel broadly.'

'That isn't ours. It was sent from Master Pym.'

'Of course.' A little anti-Catholic spice to the permanently simmering sauce. 'And this one?' He had picked up 'A true Description and Explanation of Parliament's Ordinance to secure Masters and their Apprentices After the Hostilities'. 'An excellent aid to Parliament's recruitment, I don't doubt.'

'That is our own. I thought the lads should know their rights. I got it out before Master Pym asked me to.'

If Will was impressed he did not show it. He had already lost about a third of his apprentices to Essex or the Trained Bands and was not pleased with the prospect of losing more on account of Jud's kind assurances of their future security. Indeed he had once thought that Robin had run off to join the army. He was heartened to find that he had shown even greater enterprise.

'You think forward for others, but have not the sense to do so on your own behalf. Where will you find yourself, I wonder, at the end of this quarrel? What will your father and your brother think of having John Pym's mouthpiece in the family?'

'They will think me a traitor. They already do,' said Jud directly.

'And what do you think?'

Jud tried to shrug it off, but he was keenly aware of dilemma. 'I have always disagreed with my family, about many things.'

'So you have chosen your side then, Jud?'

Jud was not yet sure if this were true. And either way, it was his own personal affair. How would Silken Will like it if *he* were to . . . 'It seems I *have* chosen,' he agreed suddenly. 'And what of you, sir? How have you chosen?'

His insolence was guided as much by a natural need to retaliate when under pressure as by a lively curiosity as to how his privateering mentor could expect to steer through the perilous passage ahead of him. It mattered to no one outside his family whom Jud Heron chose to serve, but William Staunton, nephew of great Warwick and partner of Pym on the one hand, close friend to the Court and King on the other – there were many who would care where *his* loyalties lay.

Will regarded him lazily, his good humour oddly restored by the question, which Jud might have felt had earned him another clout. He chuckled. 'You picture me trapped between Scylla and Charybdis, eh?' he apprehended, scanning the main points of an article on Parliament's supposed desire for a treaty. It described the Houses as willing to cease hostilities if the King would return to Westminster and give over all 'delinquents' to their justice. Will knew that this did not represent any wish whatsoever, on Pym's part, for the war to end. He knew that no one in his right mind could expect the King to treat on such a basis. What it did demonstrate was Pym's strength over that of the moderate party, who might have used better persuasion had they been allowed. Jud had phrased his work well, however, and readers might well think it was the true offer of a loyal Parliament to its misguided but beloved monarch, rather than the gauntlet flung down yet again, in a manner that Charles would recognize more easily than his bewildered and easily influenced subjects.

Jud could not think of a polite way to answer Will, so he simply waited.

Will smiled, grimly, but it was a smile. 'Do not, if you were considering any such sentiment, fear for me among these monsters. There is more than one attitude one may take to them – as this paper clearly shows.'

It was also clear that he would say no more on the subject. Jud wondered what on earth he meant. He must read the article again when Will had left. His curiosity still burned.

'They say you have lately given money to Parliament,' he hazarded. It was no secret that he had given large sums to the Queen before she had left. Did he hope to serve two masters?

'Who are they who say so?' Will demanded.

'Well, to tell the truth, it was Robin.'

'It usually pays to tell the truth. How is it that Rob Whittaker claims to know the private dispositions of my income?'

Oh Lord, that had torn it! Rob had in fact been 'taking a look around' the Cheapside mansion before going truant. He had simply been following a natural instinct for sniffing out other people's business, in case he might one day make it his own. What he had discovered, apart from various interesting receipts for pieces of jewellery, with notes of their destination, was that a considerable sum had gone straight into John Pym's coffers, rather than as was more usual into those of the New Providence Company.

'You may tell Rob Whittaker,' Will said, looking very steadily into Jud's face so that he should not forget, 'that if any such word is bruited about the streets and stews, or if I hear the faintest whisper in any chamber, be it bed, board or boudoir – then I shall separate his thoughtless head from his foolish body and throw the useless pieces into the Thames.' He did not raise his voice as he made this promise, but Jud was struck with the sincerity of his tone.

'I'll be sure to tell him,' he said dismally. He did not think he would ask Will any more questions.

'That is good. I rely on you to do so. I shall leave now. We may meet again. I don't know when. I shall be seeing various members of your family from time to time. I will keep you informed of their welfare at intervals.'

Jud's heart lurched. 'Then – you aren't going to give me away?'

The sardonic brow went up again. 'No. I do not think I shall. Now, kindly desire your inky-fingered familiar to open the door.'

This was done and there were no further words between them after a curt farewell from Will and a muted one from Jud.

He stood in the doorway and looked after the tall, vigorous figure in its brilliant tissues, stepping delicately along the bricks and planks that kept him out of the mud as though he trod decks, tossing a coin to the crippled boy who unhooked the heavy chains that barred the end of the undistinguished alley, constituting its entire defence against Armageddon. Jud sighed. He admired Will so much that it caused him pain. He hated to feel that he had let him down. Somehow his great adventure had lost its necessary element of heroism; Will had taken it away with him and it would not come back. He only hoped that Will himself would come back, or at least that he would see him again. He daydreamed that one day, somehow, he would be in a position to help him in some way, so that it would all come right and Will would think well of him again. He already longed for the restoration of that wonderfully easy friendship which he had never, until today, quite realized that Will had bestowed on him.

He felt very much alone. He sighed again, deeply, and then straightened up, cursing himself. There was plenty of work he had to do. He turned back into the tallow-lit murk of the printing shop.

As his eyes adjusted to it, the corner of his vision was momentarily caught by the flash of something bright. He peered at Endymion who was virtuously feeding paper to press. His small face was cherubic.

'What have you got there?'

'Nothing.'

'Give it to me.'

'It isn't anything, honest.'

'Hand it over, or I'll wallop you.'

'It's for my Mum; it's her birthday.'

'She's had a dozen birthdays this year. Give it here!'

His expression as outraged as if it were Jud who was stealing from him, Endymion passed over his booty. It was a tiny, gold pocket pomander, carved and jewelled with fine precision, one perfect sphere inside another. It smelled of incense. Jud whistled. It was obviously very valuable. Absently, he cuffed Endymion. 'You little fool, he could have your right hand for that!'

'If he can get it! It'd go well with our Rob's head he's so keen to slice,' said Endymion cheerfully.

Jud let it pass. There was little point in punishing the brat. His body was so slight that one was simply a bully if one touched him, while his mind enjoyed a natural immunity to any contagion of morality. Besides, Jud was not altogether displeased with him. The theft meant that he would certainly have to meet with Will again. The pomander was too rare an object for him to trust anyone other than himself to return it to its owner.

In the next few weeks, however, Jud's new master kept him too busy to think of his old one. His brief from Pym was simply to make much of Parliament's successes, little of their losses – and less than dust of the King and his cavaliers. If he ever found himself in doubt he was to apply for advice to Richard Overton. He did this a good deal at first for he valued the printer's integrity and experience. After a time he found he could manage his machine very well and wield words more incisively every day.

There was a great deal to be written. First there was the truce. Then there was the breaking of the truce, of which each side accused the other. They disputed this further about the unlucky town of Brentford, which the Demon Prince's blackhearted brigades put to the sack, in a manner, wrote Jud, 'reminiscent of the worst excesses of the German Wars'. He encountered some difficulty in describing this particular piece of action, for though it was undeniable that half of the Parliamentary defenders of the town, captained by Denzil Holles, stood up sturdily to the Teutonic Terror, it was equally true that the other half, under Lord Brooke, fled ignominiously before him. Happily, their honour could be saved on paper by the admirable behaviour of one fire-eating young captain, who had snatched the colours from his retreating colleagues, passionately exhorting them to turn and fight. It is such scenes as this, reflected Jud, that make great reputations and inspire great paintings. The name of the young captain, to his infinite satisfaction, was John Lilburne, turned from words to deeds by necessity.

The next piece of news was that Freeborn John had been captured soon after his brave stand and was now back in jail, to be arraigned for High Treason. 'Will they murder our Prisoners of War in the King's name?' demanded Jud editorially. 'Then has Justice cast down her Scales and Anarchy has taken them up for a Plaything!'

He rather liked the sound of that. It had a ring to it. It paid to sound lofty. People believed you more easily if you took the line that they could not possibly do otherwise. He found that such attitudes, though quite alien to his own daily existence, came quite naturally to him when he was writing. He enjoyed his work very much.

By the time the King had approached London once more, and had thought better of it at the sight of the city's Trained Bands drawn up on Turnham Green and had marched off back towards Oxford, Robin had returned, rich with experience and stolen coin. He admired Pym's generosity and the wondrous press as extravagantly as Jud could wish and agreed to take over most of the typesetting so that Jud could be free for the composition. They would also begin to employ other news-seekers, to feed him with facts.

'Tell you what, though, my old scribbler, London's mighty doleful since I left – the theatres and the beargarden closed, and the shops and alehouses all sick and sorry over the high prices. Can't a Puritan be good without flaying himself towards it? If this is how it's to go on, I'd as soon have the court back, and that's the truth!'

'They'll be back, never fear. We're going to *beat* them back.'

'We?' Robin's voice became more pointed.

'Just a manner of speaking.'

'Then you've mended your manners,' Robin smirked. 'Hey! What'll we do tonight? I've so much to tell you, it'll take a whole barrel of ale to keep my throat open. Shall we visit the Dirty Duck and see how your curly-haired doxy is keeping?'

'She's *not* my doxy. I haven't time for all that nowadays – and you are about to find out why. We go nowhere tonight. We sit right here and we put our heads together to see if we can spice up a piece that will make King Pym's latest ordinance even barely palatable to our citizens' delicate stomachs. We may well be up all night,' he added gloomily.

'Why, what's in it?' Rob picked his nose, regretting the alehouse.

'There's to be a General Assessment of all men of substance for a compulsory loan towards the expenses of the war – the only guarantee of its return being something hopefully termed "The public faith".'

Rob snorted. 'A forced loan? It's no better than the old Ship Money! The whole nation groaned for eleven years while the King taxed us without asking Parliament, and now Parliament proposes to tax us just the same. It's a rum go.'

'I told you it was a difficult job,' Jud frowned. 'Pym can't help himself; he must have money to pay for this war. How else is he to get it? Look, I know we can't make it popular, but we can try to raise some sort of a spirit of solidarity in this – you know – "if we all give all that we can of ourselves and our resources God will reward the righteousness of the cause". And we can point out that Parliament doesn't have any crown jewels to sell abroad.'

'That reminds me.' Rob was grubbing in his pocket. He produced a crumpled paper.

'This should give us some help on that. It's a copy of a letter that was intercepted yesterday, from somebody or other with the Queen in Holland to one of His Majesty's henchmen here. It gives approximate numbers of the men and money they expect to send to the King from France, Holland and Denmark.'

'Splendid! Just what we need to concentrate people's mind on the *real* threats to their security. Who wrote it?'

'No idea. Had no time to read it. I had it from Master Overton only this morning when I delivered a letter from his cousin in Reading. He said the original had been a foolish, scented object and likely they thought no one would bother to check its contents.'

Jud unfolded the paper and glanced casually at the head and foot of the page. 'Oh Hades!'

He closed his eyes for a second. When he opened them again the names were still the same. 'Dearest Tom,' wrote Valora Grey, 'every moment in this tedious place is stretching me out until I feel that my bones and flesh and sinews must soon be spread out, very thin, from here to where you are . . .'

'What's wrong?' asked Robin. 'You look like a bull that's been stunned by the slaughterer.'

Wordless, Jud passed the letter back to him. Rob scanned it, grasped the implications and groaned. 'Oh no. I'm sorry, Jud.'

'What kind of a creature,' wondered Jud when he had regained control of his tongue, 'does this make *me*?'

'I don't know,' said Robin, seriously for him, 'but if you have any doubts about the path we have taken, *now* is the time to turn back.'

Spring 1643

It was four months before Will Staunton was able to keep his promise to assure Jud's family of his welfare. He rode into Heron on a mad March morning, blown in on a frisky wind and a mount that had caught its mood. Tossing his reins over one of Mary's sacrosanct urns of pelargoniums, he was up the steps and into the hall almost before Tibbett, grimacing horribly, could open the door.

'Tibbett, you would never make a courtier, thank God,' he told the giant, who changed into his welcoming face and agreed accommodatingly. 'Where is her ladyship?'

'In the gardens, sir.'

'Of course. And Miss Lucy?'

'At her lessons. In the library. Shall I—?'

'Thank you, no, I'll announce myself. You might have someone see to my horse.'

In the library Lucy and her brothers were labouring under Mr Davies and a tome of sermons. These were in English, for a change, but were numbingly boring, so that when the door snapped open upon the tall, travel-stained figure, the twins scrambled up and threw themselves upon him while Lucy, though more restrained, was not far behind.

'Will! How marvellous!' she cried and was soundly hugged for her welcome.

'There will be no more book work today, Mr Davies,' the visitor lordly informed the tutor. Davies, though he did not care for Mr Staunton, was not up to challenging such assured authority.

Lucy, catching sight of her mother conveniently passing a window, raced over to bellow out of it, 'Will's here!' Then, demure again, she conducted her guest politely to the small parlour, sending Kit to command refreshments from Margery Kitchen.

Her mother joined them, her hands full of pruned branches and early blooms. Her dress was earthy and there were smuts on her face.

Will swept her into his arms. 'You look beautiful. Oh how comfortable it is to be in an uncivilized household again!'

'Am I to take that as a compliment?' Mary wondered. She

271

straightened her gown and poked at her hair, destroyed by his embrace, then sat beside him on the softest settle and glowed at him.

'Believe me, it is. I have just come from court.'

'Not from London? But you have news of your ship? We have heard nothing—'

To be kind he answered as briefly and truthfully as he could. 'The *Gallant Lady* is safe home – and Jud is well and happy.'

'Thank God. Oh thank God!' Mary cried into her grass-stained handkerchief.

Seeing her relief he added, 'I have a letter from him in my baggage.' He had dragged thus much filial duty from the boy when he had appeared on his doorstep, half-arrogant, half-ashamed, to return the errant pomander. The contents of the letter, he knew, gave no hint as to Jud's new employment. He had suggested heavily that Lady Heron might have trouble enough to occupy her.

'So you've come from Oxford?' asked Lucy then, over brightly. 'Is Father well? Was Tom there?' For if he were, there might be a letter for her from Cathal.

'No, Tom is harrowing the south with Prince Rupert. They were threatening Bristol the last I heard. Did you know your brother was a major now?'

'Yes. They promoted him after Edge Hill,' Mary answered proudly. '*Did* you meet my husband at court?'

'Briefly. He serves with Wilmot still and is not often at HQ.' He did not add that he could wish Sir George a better commander. Harry Wilmot was a sly self-seeker, headstrong and often foolish.

'Did he tell you how they sacked Marlborough before Christmas?' Humpty was turkeycock proud and seething with envy. 'My father and Digby and Wilmot?'

'He did indeed.' Many times and with the aid of many flagons. 'It was a shrewd move, striking right into the heart of the Puritan wool towns, but a bad blow to trade as far as your own cloth is concerned, I'd think. Unless Sir George can argue for redress this year's profits will help to line the King's war chest.'

Mary frowned and shook her head. 'It seems as if we shall have precious little cloth this year,' she said grimly. 'Most of the able-bodied men on the acreage have trailed their pikes behind Sir George; some of them, Satan toast them, with Nehemiah Owerby. The shepherds remain, thank God, and the shearers and the cattlemen and the lowest of the labourers who will not leave what poor homes they have and want no part in this great, wicked quarrel. And the women are here to spin and weave the wool, and to work the fulling mill if they must – but think how we are situated here, lying between Oxford and Puritan Bristol, and between Puritan Gloucester and the Thames and the road to London. This has all become Parliament country during these last months . . .' Her voice shook despite herself. 'It is not only that we can *do* nothing but wait and hope we are not overrun – but we cannot prevent them from stealing our sheep and cattle. Our flocks are scattered and the few packmen we *have* furnished have been unhorsed and pillaged either as they brought the wool to the cottars or as they tried for London with the finished cloth.'

'Our own clothiers are all pissing Puritans and would not give us a fair price,' added Humpty belligerently. 'God's boots! Sitting here like butts on the green, *we* may as well turn Puritan and make an end of it!'

'You are not to say "God's boots",' said Mary automatically.

'I'm sorry to hear of your trouble,' Will said. 'Has there been more? Have you been harassed by troops at all?'

'No, not greatly,' Lucy answered him. 'Nehemiah is back, that is all. We all heaved a sigh of relief when he went off to join Essex and were correspondingly dismayed when he reappeared after Edge Hill without a scratch. He breathes fire and brimstone about us in the village, but he doesn't *do* anything, except a lot of riding about with his frozen-faced followers, looking very busy and secretive.'

'But his presence makes you nervous. I'm not surprised. Yet I wonder that he stays when there is so much to occupy him elsewhere. I gather that Parliament's Major-General for Gloucestershire, Sir William Waller, has strengthened their defence of Bristol, and tossed the King's garrison out of Malmesbury – a little too close for comfort.'

Mary shuddered. 'We were lucky. We heard men marching, up on the Oxford Road, but we were not touched. I don't know why.'

'Waller is a decent man, and a god-fearing one like so many of his fellows. His mind would be on moving his troops, not on tormenting women and children. Has anyone taken your horses yet?'

'No. The best of them are game with Sir George. Nehemiah knows that. But we have had the most tremendous fun burying every plate and cup that is fit to put on the table. I do so detest eating out of pewter. It has a taste like old blood.' Mary added ruefully. 'And if you have brought me gold, as my husband wrote you might, we had better bury that, too. I hope you are handy with a spade.'

'A very sexton I assure you. I have brought what part of his profits Sir George could save from His Majesty's outstretched hand – the King's nose for money is like a pig's for truffles – but it won't bring him so far as Heron. And you will be safe from Waller's men now. He has gone off across the Severn to reap the harvest of his victory over Lord Herbert's Welsh contingent, singing psalms and thanking the Lord.'

'Don't. I don't want to hear of their victories.' She bit her lip. 'It has almost seemed, lately,' she said steadily, beckoning Kit and tucking in his shirt to give her hands something to do, 'as if God *were* on their side. The King has lost so much ground, Yorkshire to those terrible Fairfaxes, Cheshire to Brereton; now even Lancashire is Puritan, despite its numerous papists.'

'What is lost can be regained,' comforted Will with a gambler's optimism. 'The King does well in Cornwall – and there was Rupert's capture of Cirencester. It was because of *that* victory that I enquired after your horses. I hear the Prince has been "sweeping the commons" for cavalry mounts; friend or foe, it's all the same to him.'

'Well, let us hope that Tom is near enough his elbow to prevent him, though he'll get little good here if he does come.'

Just then they heard someone come through the hall, whistling, and Dominic appeared, his boots the muddy witnesses of hard riding. He beamed when he saw Will. 'God bless you, my friend. I'm glad to see you,' he declared happily and there was mutual back and shoulder clapping.

'And I you. Are you still at the old, dangerous game?'

Mary raised her eyes to heaven. 'He is never in the house. Where he goes he will not say. He stays out all night very often and forbids us even to notice.'

'What else can you expect from a reprobate like me?' demanded Cousin Nick, looking pleased with himself. He *was* pleased with himself. Today he had said two masses, twenty-five miles apart, and had also met a young priest from France whom he had been able to connect with the underground network of Rome, so that he might find hiding places while he carried out his work.

'Be sure your sins will find you out,' drawled Will. He brooded at Dominic, wishing the lad would take a warning once in a way. In the present climate, if he were to be found out and captured, he would certainly die. Will did not believe in martyrdom, considering it a waste of life and talents and moral blackmail on the part of any institution that encouraged it.

'I hear you,' said Dominic gently, 'but how about your own sins? How have you been passing the war?'

'Yes indeed,' augmented Lucy, curious. 'What *have* you been doing, Will? We haven't seen you for – my goodness – over a year, not since last Christmas in London.'

'As long as that?' He looked at her. She was taller now, he saw, though still as slender and her breasts nestled like doves in the warm grey velvet of her dress.

'So much has changed since then,' Mary deplored, and to chase away the worried look that kept returning between her smiles he launched into the tale of some, at least, of his exploits in the past year.

'Well – you will not admire me for it, I fear, but chiefly I have been minding my own business, both as a merchant and as master of my Norfolk acres.'

'But surely Parliament holds East Anglia,' said Dominic, 'under Manchester and his Association of the Eastern Counties?'

'So it does, but I have not so far been discommoded. Lord Manchester is, as you will know, Warwick's son-in-law and will hardly offer violence to a member of the family, however far removed.'

Lucy, noting the urbane and casual tone in which he claimed these gorgons for his own, remembered too his friendship with John Pym, the architect of all their present evil, and colour swept her cheeks. 'But you come from court, you said, from the King. Does His Majesty receive a man whose Norfolk estate is "not discommoded" by his enemies?'

Will grinned, enjoying her attempt not to sound accusing. 'Indeed he does. King Charles is most graciously pleased with me at present. I went to Oxford at his express invitation, to accept his thanks, and a small, a very small, reward.'

He had their rapt attention. It was Kit who breathed, 'What for?'

'I captained one of my ships as part of the convoy, under the Dutch Admiral, Tromp, which brought home Her Majesty the Queen with her shiploads of arms and money for the cause.'

'Hell's bells and buckets of blood!' cried Humpty in fine imitation of his parrot.

Quelling him, Mary asked concernedly, 'Did you happen to meet Valora Grey at all? I believe she is still with the Queen.'

'I did. She is well and sends you her most loving duty. She will stay in York with her mistress. It is too dangerous for them to attempt to cross the country to the King. There is the fear of kidnap – and then, it is perhaps wiser if the consort and the monarch run their risks separate- ly—'

'Tom knows she has returned – Valora?' Mary was not concerned with her Queen at this moment.

Will nodded. 'But he does not speak of her easily. He has a high pride, your eldest son.'

'He's a fool if he lets her go again,' said Mary grimly. 'I had hoped this separation would teach them their proper value to each other.'

'Perhaps it has. Tom is too deep for me to fathom.'

Humpty, who had been quelled long enough, seized advantage of the small silence. 'Did you meet any of the Earl of Warwick's ships at sea?'

'Happily, no—'

'What if you had – and you his nephew?'

'Third cousin, in fact. What indeed? But this embarrassment did not take place.'

'I expect you would have weaseled out of it, if it had,' said Kit sweetly, while Lucy, more acidly, agreed with him.

'Where did the Queen land?' asked Humpty, frowning.

'In Bridlington. Yorkshire.'

'Then how did *you* get to Oxford, through all that Parliament territory, if she could not?' He was eager for tales of masked rides at midnight.

'I didn't. I sailed the *Frances Rich* back to Tilbury – and yes, I did meet a couple of Parliament vessels. The first I persuaded that she should offer no hurt to my Uncle Warwick's third cousin if she wished to keep her keel in the water – do not look so disappointed, Humpty – the other I fought.'

The twins took in their breath like nectar.

'It was a brief engagement. We were well matched for size, but my guns were better and my crew bored and ready for a brawl. We boarded her and fought our way clear round her decks, then tied up her sailors in neat bundles and transferred half my own crew to bring her home. She also lies at Tilbury, with new sails, a new coat of paint, and a new name.'

'What name?'

'Ah, well there I had no choice. My cousin was with me when it came to painting on the name, so of course she had to be the *Lady Elizabeth*.'

'I suppose they're usually named after women,' said Humpty kindly, 'but *Sea Dog* would've been better.'

Lucy sniffed and said nothing. She had forgotten, until now, the existence of such a person. She ignored the reminder. 'So then you went to Oxford,' she said briskly. 'Was it a hard journey, with so many soldiers about?'

'No.' He sighed. 'You see I had a safe conduct from Pym, as well as the King's letter. I travelled with the party of the Parliamentary Peace Commission. It was most enlightening. Though I must confess,' he added impudently, 'I did experience a certain amount of apprehension from the knowledge that I had the Queen's private letter to His Majesty sewn into my best French collar.'

'You're the King's spy!' crowed Kit.

'Or John Pym's!' declared Lucy, looking as though she kept the scales of justice in the nearest cupboard and might fetch them out at any moment.

Mary clicked her tongue at her daughter. Will Staunton, she was sure, was by no means the only man in England whose interests were in conflict at this time. She asked quietly, 'Was the Peace Commission able to achieve anything? I know it was not the first to be sent, but the others have not been successful. I fear it will be a long business.'

Lucy's stern face required Will to be honest. 'No such commission could succeed at the moment,' he said without regret, 'since neither the King nor John Pym wish it to be so.'

'I don't understand you. Surely His Majesty wishes for peace?' Mary looked incredulous.

'No – or rather, not yet. As I have seen it, matters are thus – the King has no intention of giving in to any demands that Parliament might make of him in a peace treaty. He would put all back as it was before the conflict. Pym knows this, but he is under pressure from a broad faction, especially in the Lords, who are strong for peace at any price – as indeed, perhaps, is most of the population, if you were to ask them. To quiet this peace party then, John sends up his commission to Oxford and terms are discussed, terms which are neither sincerely offered by Parliament nor sincerely entertained by King Charles. But those who require it have been shown the attempt to gain peace and are content—'

'—While all the time they are miserably cheated by both their King and their Parliament, if one is to believe you,' cried Lucy, outraged.

'Perhaps,' he admitted, 'but if they are intelligent they will see that you cannot have a peace treaty at a time of stalemate – for naturally, neither side will agree to terms. The trouble is that no one is winning this war as yet; but both sides think that they *can* win it. So I'm afraid that, whatever the people or the peace party may desire, it will simply go on and on – until someone does win it.'

Their despondent faces saddened him for a moment. 'I know,' he said softly. 'There is very little honour in it, for those whose unenviable task it is to lead us through this chaos – but there is honour enough for each man privately, in his own cause.'

Then, as he saw a question trembling on Lucy's lips, he clapped his hands and cried, 'No more of the war for God's sake! I have eaten, drunk and slept it for a month. I'll give you a far more agreeable subject. I also met your daughter Jane in Oxford.'

Mary pulled herself together. 'I am so glad. She will have made you very welcome, I know. She is well? Not that she ever ails.'

'Very well. To dine at her table was one of the most exquisite experiences of my life. Her gift is nothing short of genius. Was it yourself who taught her?' He did not remark that he had found Jane full of her younger sister's praises, to a degree he might have found odd had not Sir George occupied the same city.

'Not at all. I am no cook. I leave all to Margery. Jane's genius is her own entirely. Dear Jane, I do miss her. We all do. But she loves her James and is happy. Tell me, is Oxford much changed by the presence of the court?'

Will set himself to disperse a small storm cloud that persisted in Lucy's part of the room. He sat back and took an expansive breath. 'I take it you all know Oxford, that mellow city of towers and spires in thought and stone? Picture then the green lawns studded with gay cavaliers, stiff with fighting metal over a competitive preen of different uniforms, each designed according to the whim of a commander. Having duly surrounded themselves with trenches, earthworks and fortifications enough for the siege of Troy, they proceed thenceforth to ignore the existence of the war. War is boring; war is plebian; war is not in good taste. They mention it as little as possible, drifting through their scented days in a continual pageant of myth and fantasy, vying with each other in elegant attempts to amuse His Majesty. There is constant music; quartets lurk under every stairway; ladies are serenaded with guitars; every gallery is stuffed with a consort of viols. There are daily *divertissements* involving the gods and heroes of Ancient Greece, and sprightly dancing nightly in the halls of academe. An inordinate amount of festive eating depletes the local parks and the fowlers offer sparrows in despair of better birds. The nobility of both sexes rest from the pressures of these exacting activities while having themselves immortalized on canvas by young Mr Dobson, lately dubbed the King's "Sergeant Painter", who does his best to carry the boots of the giant Van Dyke – shall I go on, or have you got the general feeling of things?'

'I think so,' said Mary, laughing. 'A rather wearing Mount Olympus.'

'You make it sound amusing, and I'm sure it is,' said Lucy shortly, 'but while some men play fools' games in Oxford, in other places better men are dying for the King.'

'And he does not forget it, believe me,' said Will repentantly. 'For every lily-wristed courtier there are a dozen with Prince Rupert, becoming part of a war machine that may well wrest the victory for His Majesty. Yet do not grudge the courtiers their attempt to make him feel that he still has a home and a kingdom.'

'Oh I don't; I don't. You shouldn't twist things so.'

He saw that she did not know what to think of him and determined to win back into her good graces.

In the evening, after they had eaten, he persuaded her to sing with him again and found that, as his instinct had predicted, this was the very swiftest way to make her stop glowering. Afterwards, he asked her to walk with him in the garden, claiming that he needed to clear his head. They had all drunk more than usual that night. Heron had visitors so rarely these days and Will was always a festive event in himself. It was cold, but Lucy too felt as though her head could do with clearing. They wandered towards the sunken garden so that she could show him the improvements by moonlight.

'You see – we now have a seat. No need any longer to lean upon the urn. If you do, the ivy will reach out and strangle you; beware, it is the one thing that grows without mercy.'

Will sat down obediently upon the wooden seat, curving his arm around one raised knee, presenting a picture of effortless elegance suitable, Lucy thought, to the court he had mocked. Sitting primly next to him she pointed out new felicities among the plant life, begging his indulgence for the waning light and the winter mood of the shrubs. Will commented politely when necessary and privately admired the effect of the moonlight upon her hair.

'The Quickenberry has become very robust,' he noted. 'Your mother will be delighted.'

Lucy laughed. 'It should grow ferociously; it is fertilized with rubies and diamonds.'

He raised one brow.

'We buried my mother's jewellery there, all but her wedding ring and the necklace she is wearing now. She keeps that in one of the dog's dishes most of the time.'

'How sensible; even if he happens to swallow it, one may hope to retrieve it. Are there any further hidden hoards of Heron?'

'Certainly. There are the guns and swords and pikes Father left in case we had to defend the house – only I don't suppose we could drum up enough defenders. Let's hope it doesn't happen.'

He thought of Eliza Hartley with her beautifully tailored household guard of ex-mercenaries, and of his mother at Stanton with her sturdy, well-trained troop of yeomen; he'd seen to that himself. 'But surely Sir George left sufficient men to guard the house?'

'He did. But they must also do their work about the demesne. You can't expect the enemy to come calling exactly on rent day when they might all be together, can you?'

Will hoped her father had known what he was doing. But then, the baronet had not expected – none of them had expected – the war to continue so long or to become so widespread.

Lucy now abruptly introduced one of the subjects she had been saving for such privacy. 'When you were in Oxford, was there any news from Ireland?' She looked straight ahead, shy now that she had asked.

'Nothing of specific interest. Hostilities there are conducted more in the style of border raids than of organized warfare, so that there are no battles and news is hard to come by. But it is your friend of whom you are thinking, of course,' he relented. 'You'll not hear from him so often?'

She had already accepted that there was no letter. Talking about Cathal was the next best thing. 'I hear rarely. Cathal is "on the moors" as he puts it, fighting in your border style I suppose. It is difficult to get letters to England, unless they go with some great lord. The last one came at Christmas when Father and Tom came home for two days. Cathal sent me this—' She didn't know why she wanted to show him the ring. She pulled it, on its green ribbon, up from the front of her dress and held it out to him.

Will moved closer and took the ring in his hand. It was heavy gold, carved in the shape of some fierce Celtic animal swallowing its own tail. He smiled, then took her hand and slipped it onto her finger. 'You should wear it. It is very striking.'

She was angry for a moment because it was his hand and not Cathal's that had guided her love-token. She did not want to wear it. It was not for all to see. It was a personal link between herself and Cathal. Also she had the sense that to wear it would tempt fate in daring to claim reality for a bond that was still only the stuff of legend.

He had been gone for more than a year now. It had been the longest year of her life and she did not expect to see him again in the bearable future. It seemed, to her loving and lonely heart which he had awakened only to leave at once, that he had, despite his promise, stepped down from the white horse onto the beloved, bloodstained soil of Ireland.

There was just one, thin hope. She took off the ring and let it fall back between her breasts. 'Cathal's father is a member of the new Parliament that the Irish Catholic Confederacy have set up at Kilkenny, in opposition to the Protestant Parliament in Dublin. They are loyal to King Charles as they have always been. Cathal says that since His Majesty has ordered the Dublin Parliament to make peace with the Confederates, it is likely that when this happens the Confederate troops will be free to fight for the King in England. It sounds like the answer to several prayers,' she added hopefully, looking up at him.

'Unless you are John Pym, or the Duke of Ormonde, the King's Irish Protestant Governor, who pray for quite different things,' Will said dryly. 'I wouldn't place your hopes in that quarter, Lucy. In fact I'd place your fears there. Even in the unlikely event of peace in Ireland, I don't think you would find a possible reunion with your young friend in the uniform of a Catholic Confederate quite worth the turmoil that will overtake this country if the King invites them over here. Think, Lucy, think!'

'I have thought,' she snapped, 'and I don't suppose it would be much worse than it is now. Fighting is fighting, wherever it is – and at least Cathal would be *here*, and he could fight with Father, and perhaps I could—'

'Perhaps you could persuade him out of the army and into your lap? I don't think so. From what I saw of him, I'd say Cathal O'Connor is as much in love with battle as he is with you, and that he is faithful to Ireland before he is faithful to the King.'

Her eyes blazed at him, full of hurt. 'What do *you* know about him? You've hardly met him. You know nothing about him!'

He was penitent at once though he had spoken the casual words quite consciously; for some graceless, and as yet unanalysed reason, he had wanted to show her that her dream was too fragile to stand the daylight. He had not been kind. 'I'm sorry. I spoke too bluntly. Lucy, don't cry.'

'It doesn't matter. You can't spoil it.'

'Indeed I'm sure I can't. It does matter, though. I'd no wish to make you unhappy.'

'Then why say such things?'

'I don't know. Perhaps because I feel that a small hurt now might save you a bigger one later.'

'Why should *you* care?'

'No reason. I do care, that is all.' He offered to put his arm around her, for comfort and to keep out the cold, for she was shivering a little. She shook her head.

He decided to continue. 'I will tell you why you must not hope for such things to happen. If Irish troops come here, our people will fear them as though they came from hell itself, and that fear could lead to fighting of an appalling ferocity. You were right to remind me that men are dying daily in this war while peace is daily receding – but believe me you are not right when you say that "fighting is fighting wherever it is". Compared to what has already happened in Ireland – and what *could* happen here – we are managing this war like gentlemen.'

'We?' she stung, still hurt and willing to hurt in return.

'Ah, bitchery. That's better!'

He gave her his best buccaneer grin and she was tempted to return it for she was angry, she knew, within the bounds of friendship. She did not want to repudiate that friendship. Heron was a cold place with so many away from it, surrounded as it was with enemies. Will was one of the few who could warm it in an instant. She valued that as much as her mother did.

'I don't understand you all the same,' she said thoughtfully, her voice now at its normal pace and pitch. 'Everyone I know, and most people I don't know, seem to choose their side in the war without even thinking – only you seem somehow able to float above it all, without coming to rest on either side. But you will have to, one day, won't you, surely? Or not?'

'I comprehend your puzzlement,' he said gravely, 'for it is equalled only by my own. I should in truth be delighted it might continue to float, in your charming analogy, until both sides have beaten each other into insensility. However, my good sense tells me that this, however desirable, will not, in the long run, be possible. Unless one is an accredited idiot – or an astrologer – one makes more enemies by keeping out of a quarrel than by joining in.'

'So you must choose. Or have you already chosen?'

His smile looked suddenly tired. 'Perhaps I have. But I shall leave you in delicious uncertainty. Goddammit Lucy, you are exactly like your wretched brother! He wanted *me* to shout out loud for King or Parliament, even while busy persuading himself that *he* was airily floating!'

'Jud?' She caught his sleeve urgently. 'His letter was full of tales about Genoa and Livorno and Pisa, but he said nothing about coming to Heron.'

Trust the young devil to enjoy himself with a geography book, thought Will, chuckling. He had no choice but to back him up. 'I don't think he'll come home just yet. Presumably his father's prohibition still stands? He'd be too proud to chance a rebuff.'

'But he knows Father isn't here, and Mother would never turn him away. Besides, surely Father won't keep all that up, now that the war has gone on so long. If Jud were to speak to him—'

Will sighed and captured the hand that tugged absently at his sleeve. 'As to Sir George, I don't know. But as far as Jud is concerned, matters are not so simple as you think. He did not wish any of you to know, not just yet, but curse it, you will only worry at it until you tie both of us in knots. The truth is that Jud did not sail on the *Lady*. He never left England.'

'What? Never saw Genoa and Pisa and—?'

'No. You would have to know sooner or later, and I have neither the heart nor the fiendish cunning to deceive you. I imagine your brother will forgive me – but only if you promise to assist him in continuing to deceive your lady mother. He does not want her worried – do you hear?'

Lucy nodded, large-eyed, and sat very quietly while he told her the chequered tale of Jud's recent career. When he had finished she kept silent, still holding his hand, very hard, and quite unaware of it. 'So – Jud is for the Parliament,' she said at last. 'In a way, I am not surprised. We might have seen it coming, had we thought. And you – you are perhaps more to blame than anyone, for it was you who took him into your house and introduced him to John Pym and the King's enemies.'

'They are not his enemies. They wish only to be his physicians,' Will said tersely. 'And if I had known that to pull that pickpocketing little jackanapes off your prostrate body was going to lead to such a Machiavellian involvement with your family, I swear I'd have left him where he was!'

'I wish you had!' raged Lucy with swift unreason. 'Then our family would not be all broken up and miserable.'

'And there would have been no war, I suppose, and no Valora Grey, no Nehemiah Owerby. My dear Lucy, it is time you grew up a little. It is *ideas* you must put in prison if you want to stop young men like Jud discovering who they are and what they think, not poor Will Staunton, nor even John Pym.'

The hint of asperity in his tone had redeemed her good sense at once. 'I am sorry. It is just that I miss Jud so, and Father – and even Tom. He has been so good about Cathal's letters.'

He put out a hand and stroked her hair. 'I know. I know. Life has changed a great deal and it is not easy for any of you. And now I have made you the keeper of your brother's secret. Perhaps that was not fair of me?'

'No. I would rather know. I shall be able to help Jud with Father later.'

'Well, I hope so. Meanwhile I think it is time we went indoors and practised, if necessary, telling lies to your mother.'

'Very well – but,' she hesitated, 'you don't *really* wish you had never met us all?'

Her eyes were so very green, frozen to emeralds by the moon. He wished that she were older as he looked into them. Then he realized that, of course, she was. 'I have no regrets,' he said gravely, 'and I shall prove it to you.' He drew her to her feet and pulled her close and little upward, holding her so that she stood on her toes, then tipped back her head into the helmet of his hand and gave her a kiss of such deliberate and expert masculinity that when at last he let her go, she could think of absolutely nothing to say.

She stared at him enormously for a while and said at last, with faint severity, 'And what was *that* for?'

This was not a reaction to which Will was accustomed. He released her stiffening body and laughed like a schoolboy.

'I don't know what you find so funny.'

'Myself, not you, I swear. Don't be offended, for Christ's sake.'

She looked at him coldly. 'You told me just now that I should grow up; perhaps you should consider taking your own advice.' She turned away with exquisite dignity and walked, not too quickly, towards the house. Once inside she adhered so dutifully to her mother's side for the rest of the evening that Mary wondered if she were sickening for something.

When Will rode off next morning, on some unnamed and unpostponable errand, he found Lucy's farewell most correct, if a little formal. She met his eyes once only, and then looked down furiously because he seemed to be laughing at her again. But when he wheeled on the crest of the hill and looked back, she was waving with the rest of them.

Alone, she wondered again why he had kissed her like that. It had been a bewildering experience and such a very *definite* one. If he had kissed her gently, to comfort her, she could have understood it; but a kiss like that – she had enough kisses to her credit now to know passion when she encountered it. That had been a passionate kiss, a man's kiss.

In the end she put it down to Will's probable insolent certainty that every female he met was in love with him, or should be. Then she tucked it firmly to the bottom of her mind and set herself to write to Cathal. Very likely he would not receive her letter, but it was better to try to believe that he would, and that one was not pouring out one's heart and soul in ink for nothing. She mentioned Will's visit for the sake of his unattractive opinions on the question of the Irish troops, but did not feel it necessary to refer to the kiss. She remembered Cathal's kisses instead, with an ache of longing that was worse than the toothache.

'You taught me so well how to miss you, in our brief time together, that I could wish you had not taught me at all. I have no patience, any longer, with the unnatural war. I want so much to be with you that I feel it like a little flame of pain, deep and low inside me, especially at night when I lie and look into the dark and see you, just as you were with me. I can call back everything about you, no matter how small – the way you wrinkle your nose when you are pleased – the way your voice curls round at the end of a sentence – the sense of your arms about me—' She saw that there were broad drops of water on the paper before her and shook her head impatiently. She turned to less moving concerns.

'In the last letter I had from you (at Christmas), you told me you had been fighting but you did not say how and where and in what manner of conflict, and if you have been hurt at all. You make it all sound very bold and brave, and fill it with the colours of all your favourite tales. Please, I would rather have the plain truth.

'Speaking of tales, I have a new book of Celtic legends. Dominic got it for me. It is called *The Red Book of Hergest*, and is about the ancient Welsh heroes, though most of the stories are very similar to the Irish. They have no Niave of the Golden Hair, but there is a very fine poet-god called Gwydion, to whom I think I shall pray occasionally. He is the sun god, like Apollo, and his sister, Arianrhod, is the moon goddess. I will try to send you the book, later, when the countryside is a little quieter. I still have yours which I treasure dearly. I read a good deal now, as well as studying and playing my music. The time passes so slowly when all one may do, being a mere peaceable female, is to sit, and wait, interminably – for news, which comes seldom, always late and ever to be feared lest it should be evil – and then lately there is always with us, as it must be with you – the constant apprehension of the horsemen on the hill—'

When those horsemen, so long apprehended, came at last to Heron, the set face of their leader was so familiar that Mary Heron, visited by irony, called out to him from her herbaceous border, 'Well, Nehemiah, have you burst your way through locked gates just to pass the time of day, or is this a muscular attempt to convert us all?'

Ambushed, Owerby abruptly pulled up his mount while the men behind him, self-consciously exhibiting equally familiar faces above neat uniforms in restrained russet, did their best not to run into each other. Some of them bared their heads out of habit as Mary clambered out from among the tall lilies, wiping her hands on her apron. Dominic, who had been helping her, followed after, his eyes alight, apparently, with the possibility of entertainment, though he must have seen clearly from Nehemiah's sepulchral look that entertainment was not the order of the day.

Their enemy leaned from the saddle, thrusting a rolled paper towards Mary. 'Do me the favour to read this.'

She took it silently. Already she half-knew what it must be. They had heard, through Margery's village gossip, that Nehemiah was now a member of one of Parliament's new County Committees. These were to be responsible for the government of the areas where Parliament held sway and for financing its army. The means by which they would manage the latter were both criminal and obvious.

Mary read the paper through and handed it without speaking to Dominic. Her face did not alter its expression of tolerant contempt, but she paled and stood very still. She waited for Nehemiah to speak.

'As you have observed, that is an order for the sequestration of the manor and demesne of Heronscourt, together with all of its rents and profits, which must henceforth be paid weekly to the Committee of Sequestration. You will, of course, be allotted the required amounts for your own living purposes. You will do well enough. It would be no profit to Parliament if the estate were to decline under our husbandry. And as a Justice of the Peace I can assure you that you will suffer no other depradation.'

Still Mary said nothing. She was concentrating entirely upon his words and upon her own determination not to tremble.

Nehemiah shrugged and went on. 'Your stewards will be required to give a monthly account of every aspect of their administration. Should this not prove satisfactory, the Committee will replace them with men of its own. Your movable goods which may be valuable, together with any arms, monies, or good horses in your possession, I am empowered to remove. We are present today for that purpose, as well as to serve notice of the Committee's intentions—'

'—But this is monstrous!' blazed Dominic, making a swift, unconsidered movement towards Nehemiah, causing the dun horse to shy. Its rider had it under immediate control.

'Not so,' he replied, looking at Dominic with a kind of pitying satisfaction that made his blood race. 'It is most fitting that Sir George Heron should pay his debt to the Parliament he has betrayed. And as for what he will lose by it, why, had this not been Parliament territory, then sooner or later the King would have had as much from him. Wars must be paid for, Sir Priest, though I cannot expect one of your cloth to concern himself with such worldly practicalities.'

Their gazes met and clashed, Dominic breathing hard, his fist crushing the paper he held. Mary, sensing the danger he was to himself, took the unspeakable order from him and tossed it back to Nehemiah.

'Very well,' she said with perfect steadiness, 'since we can hardly contend with, how many is it? – thirty or so armed men, you had better come in and do your – duty.' She made the word an excretion. 'I shall accompany you myself upon every inch of your errand, and I do not expect,' she added, raising her voice, 'that your men will comport themselves with anything other than complete courtesy towards myself and my household.'

Nehemiah smiled. 'I would not expect, Lady Heron, that either you or any member of your household would give us reason to do otherwise.'

But there he was wrong. Dominic, warned, now had himself in as rigid a control as had Mary, though both still suffered considerably from shock. That shock had yet to communicate itself to the other members of the household.

In the great kitchen, the alert Margery, hearing the percussion of hooves and naturally curious, peered from a hall oriel to see her mistress and young master Dominic walking sombrely ahead of a troop of uniformed riders proceeding at a funereal pace. On recognizing Nehemiah she deduced that dinner would not be required for the visitors. She could see that something was very much amiss. Racing stoutly back towards the pantry she called for Tibbett who was giving a somewhat contemptuous rubbing to the pewter. 'Come quick as winks, and bring that devil of a gun with you! I do fear that nasty Ne'miah has taken poor madam prisoner!'

'Don't talk so daft, woman,' said Tibbett grandly, but he put down the jug he was polishing and marched heavily towards the main door, behind which his precious carbine was housed. He took it off its hooks and stood listening with his ear to the door. 'Plenty of them,' he admitted as the hoofbeats jumbled on the terrace.

The clatter of pattens behind him announced Lucy, trailing Julia with Belzabub squeezed against her chest. 'What is it? Why are they here?'

'I don't know, miss.' Margery kept her fears to herself.

Lucy ran to the nearest window. 'Mother is bringing Nehemiah up the steps – you'd better hide the carbine, Tibbett. I don't think Mother would want you to use it now, and we might need it later. We don't want Ne'miah to steal it for his filthy troop.'

Tibbett saw sense in this and melted away, leaving a quavering Margery to open the door.

Lucy saw that her mother's face was colourless. 'What is it?' she asked urgently again, ignoring Owerby who had entered giving quiet orders to several men.

Mary moved past her. 'Where are the boys?' she asked.

'In the stables I think, waiting for Calliope to drop her foal. *Please*, tell me what's wrong!'

'Heron is to be sequestered.' Mary's voice was tired.

Lucy could not believe it. 'Oh no. It *can't* be. We can't *let* them!'

'I'm afraid we must. I don't want any discussion, please, Lucy. Hysteria will not help us. I want you to find your brothers and bring them to me. I want them where I can see them. Take Julia.'

Lucy could see, despite her own hammering rib cage, that her mother could not keep up this astonishing imitation of calm if she herself were to give way to her instinct and rave at heaven and Nehemiah. Mary wanted to get rid of her. Lucy accepted this and, still without so much as a glance at Nehemiah, she pulled Julia after her and departed in the direction of the stables.

The little girl trotted her fastest, troubled by the prevalence of a mood she did not understand. 'Why are we being requested?' she demanded worriedly.

'Sequestered,' said Lucy grimly. 'It means that Nehemiah is going to take away everything we own, and all our money too.'

'Lord have mercy on us!' said Julia, clutching Belzabub more firmly.

'Amen to that!' said Lucy savagely. 'But I don't think He's listening, just at present.'

In the stable no foal had appeared as yet, which was just as well since its first impressions would have been of a world gone mad as Humpty and his twin heard Lucy's news. The mare, accustomed to turbulence, stood quietly in her stall, whickering softly and rolling her eyes while the boys went berserk among the hay bales and the harness, wildly flinging anything that could be flung and raging like small, white-hot crucibles in a bubble and froth of inventive and foul-mouthed invective.

'We should have *killed* him that day we painted the horse! We should have poisoned his goddam' well and put a mantrap in his shitten bed!'

'That loathesome, slimy, miscarried spawn of an anthropopha-gus—'

Lucy let them rant. There was nothing else they could do. Her legs suddenly felt weak, so she sat down in the strong, hot-smelling straw of an empty stall, trying to realize clearly what this terrible event would mean to them all.

The task was as far beyond her at that moment as was the morning that had just passed. She felt herself to be in a kind of limbo, a place and time without feeling or thought. She sat and stared into space, hardly hearing her brothers' noise.

Then Humpty cried, 'They won't get any decent horses, anyway!' and the numbness left her, routed by the small triumph in his voice. It was true; they had loaned the workhorses to the poor, stripped Strattons so that they could do their ploughing, and only Calliope and the lesser of their riding horses were left. Sir George had taken the carriage pairs away with him, together with every reasonable piece of horseflesh on the demesne. There would be no silver either, to satisfy the predators, and the gold Will had brought, thank God, was also safe in the shrubbery. But one did not make a home out of valuable items, as had been so clear when they had sacked Stratton Hall, and they had not hidden the carpets, the hangings, the portraits nor, of course, any of the fine new furniture, all of them things which could be sold to enrich Parliament's coffers. All depended, she supposed, upon Nehemiah's whim, which was why, despite what must have been a powerful impulse to the contrary, her mother was treating that monster as if he were human. And it could only make their situation worse if the rest of them did not do the same.

At this point in her deliberation she realized that the stable had become very quiet. 'Julia! Where are Kit and Humpty?' she demanded on a wave of premonitory alarm.

'Gone,' said Julia unhelpfully, and, grumbling, found herself dragged once more like an overfull basket at Lucy's heels as they made, at inelegant speed, for the house.

'Ne'miah won't get Belzabub,' she panted, to reassure her sister, 'I hided him in Calliope's manger.'

Inside the house they heard an orderly tramp of feet as they passed through the hall, and saw, as Lucy had expected, a neat stack of paintings against the panelling and a thick swathe of tapestry hanging over a table, waiting to be carried away.

'They mustn't have Great-grandfather Heron,' Lucy wailed, seeing the raw clean patch above the fireplace. There was no one in the room except themselves but neither was there anywhere she might conceal the old privateer. She gazed hopelessly about at the denuded walls. They had left Sir George senior – presumably his expression was too smugly self-appreciative even for Puritan stomachs. She knelt before the pictures and detached Thomas the Pirate from the stack, her eyes racing stupidly from walls to windows. Then, as though the old reprobate had dropped it into her begging brain like a pilfered orient pearl, she knew exactly where his hiding place must be.

'Stay by the door and tell me if anyone is coming,' she directed Julia and, moving as quickly as she had ever done in her life, she picked up Great-grandfather and carried him over to the chimney. Then she tore off her petticoat and wrapped it around her arms and hands. 'Thank God the chimney was cleaned so recently,' she muttered. 'He'll not come to much harm.'

She was just climbing back into her sooty garment when Margery, heralded by Julia's squeak, came through the dining-room door. 'Holy Jesu, what next?' she demanded. 'Don't you know better than to go parading your underthings when there are soldiers about?'

Lucy was about to explain herself when a hideous shrieking broke out above their heads, mixed in sex and fearsomely voluble. Without speaking the three of them ran for the stairs, knocking several surprised troopers sideways on the way. The row had diminished by the time they reached the gallery from where it issued, the shrieks having descended to groans.

As Lucy entered, with Margery, Julia and half a dozen stalwarts behind her, her eyes were drawn at once to the open doorway of the twins' bedroom, directly off the gallery, whose threshold was strewn with the semi-recumbent bodies of Nehemiah's two closest lieutenants, Sam Hudson and Straightways Sawyer. It was they who were responsible for most of the noise, as was betokened by the bloody decoration of their uniforms. Lucy did not need her mother's accusing glance to tell her who was responsible for the blood. She hurried forward.

'I'm sorry,' she wailed. 'I didn't see them leave.'

'You'd have seen them hang if these two hooligans had got anything worse than a hedgehog's prickle,' hissed Mary, her fine composure dissolved like a warm jelly. Dominic, at her elbow, steadied her with his hand.

Kit and Humpty stood before Nehemiah next to their bed. They wore their Venetian breastplates and in their hands, pointing dismally downwards, were the two small, dripping swords which normally enhanced the chamber wall. When they had left the stables they had easily managed to avoid the tidy party which was methodically visiting and stripping each room in the house and had lain hidden in their own chamber until its turn came. When the door had opened they had hurled themselves upon the two hapless turnips who were the first to enter. They were only sorry that it had not been Nehemiah. Now, their unrepentant gazes were locked with his while Sam's and Straightways' blood despoiled the floorboards.

'Give me your swords,' said Nehemiah very quietly. He revealed nothing of anger.

'Do as you are told!' Mary's voice cracked behind them.

Kit passed over his sword, Humpty hesitating only a second longer. Nehemiah thrust them impatiently at a hovering minion. 'Your mother is very exact in her estimation of what would have happened to you had either of these men been fatally injured,' he observed, his voice unnaturally low and chillingly bleak. 'As it is, you have inflicted pain and inconvenience.' He looked sharply from one blank, unflinching face to its image. 'You will therefore be awarded similar treatment. Sergeant Bottler, take these boys outside and flog them a dozen times each. And lay on! It is a lesson I don't want them to forget.'

'God rot you, man, they've had such lessons enough before now.' Dominic's effete syllables dropped like loose stitches amid the tension. 'Now I've a notion you dislike *me* as much as any man you've met. Why not spare the lads and lay the rod on *my* back,' he suggested, tempting and insolent, a faint, vacuous smile calculated to goad the Puritan to take him up.

Nehemiah answered with his own mirthless rictus. 'Thank you no, Father Dominic. Although I do, as you hazard, dislike you most thoroughly, I also dislike the notion of justice perverted. Justice, though she demands that you should suffer, does not do so today. She requires rather that these youths should take their punishment.'

'Mr Owerby, I beg of you—' Mary had jettisoned her pride. 'They are very young. Please do not—'

'Old enough to wield a sword, as they have always been old enough for any mischief to hand,' grated Nehemiah. 'You only demean yourself in pleading for them.'

He swung out of the chamber and through the gallery, his small prisoners marching sturdily behind, having shaken off all guiding hands. He turned at the stairhead as Mary and Lucy moved to follow them. 'Please to remain where you are. This is no business for women.'

'Nor for a Christian gentleman either,' said Mary in a last effort to catch his conscience.

'The Lord had made himself quite clear on such a point,' replied Nehemiah mildly. 'You have been so misguided as to spare the rod. I shall return your sons to you in a better case for heaven.'

Julia burst into terrified, hiccupping tears. She spoke for all of them, as, during the next fifteen minutes, they were subject to one of the more overtly unpleasant tricks on the part of time. It stretched, endlessly elastic, as they crowded, family and servants, into the windows which overlooked the broad courtyard at the back of the house.

There, while the ornamental fountain played its delicate music, they watched in shamed impotence as four soldiers stripped Kit and Humpty of their shirts and bound their arms around two of the pillars which supported the arcade of the old priory cloister. Then they listened while at the heart of the numb, dull silence the harsh whistle of the lash came down again and again, cross-hatching the narrow backs with an interweaving lace of blood and weals.

At first neither boy cried out, though both of them shook under the force and the nausea that follows such blows. For three lashes they kept silent. On the fourth Kit gave a bitten-off gasp. On the fifth both let out brief cries. At the sixth some unspoken pact strengthened them to silence again. The blood ran in rivulets down onto their breeches. It was now that their punishers began to cross the weals they had already raised, and now, therefore, that the boys could no longer hold back their agonized cries.

'My God, I cannot stand this,' muttered Mary with tears streaming down her face and breast. She ran down to the doorway, with some hapless notion of preventing the last blows, but her way was barred by a pair of serious-faced guards who gently forbade her to pass. By the time she had regained the window, all the blows had fallen and the boys hung limply from their pillars, less than half-conscious.

They were carried into the cloister guest chamber and Mary was permitted to wash and salve their wounds. She did so through a haze of tears and heartsickness, though she was able, by a continuous effort of will, to steady her hands. She knew that she would remember this moment above all else, above even the knowledge that now her husband and elder son conducted their lives upon battlefields, as the time which brought home to her the true evil that sits at the heart of war. For the first time in her life she wanted another human being dead. Had she not been certain of what it would inevitably mean to Heron, she would herself have been glad to sink the dagger into Nehemiah's dark, unloving heart.

For the rest of that dreadful visitation they seemed to be blanketed in a deep, merciful fog that separated them from any further pain as the troopers went about their careful, ordered business of tearing the insides out of the house. Cries and commands penetrated the fog occasionally, demanding, listing and confirming.

'The rents will be collected on Fridays at ten.'

'I will require a list of the amounts of timber, grain and animal fodder you have stored.'

'You will please direct me to the brewhouse. How much ale have you there?'

'What is the estimated weekly yield of your game preserves? Your stewpond? How many deer are in the park?'

'What are the numbers of your pigs, ducks, chickens, geese?'

'Where may I find your shepherds? Your cattlemen? How many horses have you left, and of what quality? How much land have you under crops? What trees are in your orchards?'

And out of the same numbing, isolating miasma, Mary heard herself and Tibbett and Rollins give their terse, unwilling replies.

Sometimes, if they thought it would go unchecked, the men told less than the truth. Nehemiah seemed to accept all that he was told, nodding curtly at each answer while his ancient, Balfour, wrote it all down in a thick ledger.

So, slowly, they listened to the plan for the ending of their world as they had known it, and cooperated with it, and dumbly watched it begin to take place.

There was no search for the plate, or for jewels or other trivia. Even Nehemiah had irritably to admit that he could hardly dig over every inch of the estate for the sake of a few portable treasures. The greater treasure was already in his keeping.

It was many hours before they had done with the sound of voices numbering and of feet trampling and staggering under heavy loads, but at last, long after night had fallen, it was over. The voices and the steps receded and the horsemen rode away. Only then did the mist lift itself from the minds of those who remained and they began to understand what had happened to them.

Humpty, lying painfully upon his stomach beside his brother in the cool priory cell, was the only one still to be able to sound a note of derision. 'They bled like slit-gulleted swine, didn't they, Mother?' he said with a pride which, under the circumstances, was forgiven him.

Shortly after the beginning of the changes in the quality and dignity of life at Heron, Lucy was surprised and pleased, when she came in from her daily ride, to find Martha waiting for her in the small parlour. It was an inconsiderately hopeful spring morning when all the land looked fresh and young and the sun shone as if Nehemiah had never been born.

Martha, Lucy realized after they had kissed and held each other a little longer than usual, was not alone. Sitting bolt upright in a rush basket at her feet, his yellow eye full of mortal offence, was Sir Topaz.

'Why have you brought him?' she asked, stroking his dense black fur and watching the angry flare of his long-haired tail.

Martha did not really want to tell her, but had been unable to think of any sufficiently credible lie. 'I think he would be safer if he could stay here with you.' She smiled as though this were perfectly normal.

Lucy knew that it was not. 'Safer? Why? What do you mean?'

'Oh, I am probably making a pother about nothing. It is just that some of the villagers have been a little boisterous lately and I wouldn't want him to come to any harm.'

'Martha! What do you mean by boisterous? What have they done?' She knew that Martha would diminish any danger to herself.

Martha sighed. She found the situation oddly embarrassing, even with Lucy. 'It is being put about among the more credulous of them that the Black Mass has been celebrated in my house. They are beginning to call me a witch to my face – oh, just a few of them, old and silly most of them, or born mischief-makers – but I would hate to think what could happen to a witch's cat if those lackwits should catch hold of him. So, my dear Lucy, if you would not mind, I would feel so much happier if I knew he was with you.'

'Oh, Martha, of course I'll have him.' Lucy hugged her friend again, a fierce surge of desire to protect her almost choking her words.

'But listen to me – and believe me. *You* must come to Heron, too. If a mere cat is not safe, how secure is a suspected witch? You must come today, right away. I will go home with you, now, to fetch up anything you need.'

Martha shook her head. 'No. I can't do that. It would not be wise. It would only assure those who say these things that I am indeed a witch, and that I have flown to Dominic, who is the devil's black priest and the author of my wickedness. I am well able to look after myself, believe me. And most people are still my friends and speak slightingly of those who accuse me. And in addition,' she added wryly, 'do I not have the most powerful protection of all? Nehemiah will be my rod and staff, no matter how much I despise and refuse him. You may be quite sure no one will harm me while he is here to speak for me, though God knows I wish him gone from the face of the earth to account to the Maker of whom he is so certain for what he has done here at Heron.' Her silver-birch body quivered with a rage she scarcely knew how to express. 'And tell me,' she said more calmly, 'how your brothers do? I hear they bore their torture nobly. Even the wretched Sam Hudson has said that they carried themselves like the bravest of men.'

'I'll tell them that. They'll be mightily pleased. Their wounds are healing better than we expected, though they'll bear the scars for the rest of their days, most likely. The pain is much less though, and it is only stiffness that really troubles them. Our chief worry is their constant talk of revenge.'

'I hope they may have it. I should like Nehemiah to know cruelty.' Lucy squeezed her hand.

It was then that Dominic wandered in, looking for a mislaid whip. His face lit up like Christmas when he saw Martha. 'My dear! But this is wonderful! I have been so worried about you. Did you get my message through Mrs Weston?'

'Yes. And I thank you.' She rose and took his hand. 'But you must not take such risks.'

He grinned ruefully. 'It is a question as to which of us is the most danger to the reputation of the other, is it not?'

'My only regret,' she said quickly, 'is that I can no longer continue to help you in your work.'

'Why, Martha,' he replied gently, 'we shall make a Catholic of you yet.'

'It was not for the sake of your faith that I helped you, but because of the obvious strength and comfort you bring to those who practise it. You know that.'

'I do know it, and I bless you for it. But what about yourself, Martha?' Her cheerfulness had not concealed her tension from him. He felt the taint of fear in her and was filled with compassion. 'If only I might bring strength and comfort to you, who are my friend. I am a poor priest if I cannot.'

She smiled at him, her grey eyes unfathomable. 'You do,' she said briefly. 'Come and walk with me in the gardens, if Lucy permits it. Since we already have the pleasure of each other's dangerous company, we may as well get the best out of it. You shall show me all the penances you have performed among the flowerbeds, and we will talk.'

Though Dominic had an appointment among the hills that morning he did not hesitate. He tucked her hand into his arm, saying, 'By all means. I only hope we shall not encounter any of Mr Owerby's myrmidons; they are apt to appear in unlikely places.'

Lucy, listening to them, had suffered a moment of misery when she wondered if Martha were right, and that it would lessen the safety of both of them if she were to come to Heron; then she decided that since the danger existed anyway, in a greater or lesser degree, they would all be able to bear it better if everyone were together. And she couldn't bear to think of Martha at the mercy of the village boors and boobies.

'Wait a moment, Dominic,' she ordered firmly. 'You must make Martha tell you why she is here – *everything*, mind – and then you must make her promise to live with us here until the world is sane again.'

'What *is* this, Martha? Has something happened?'

'No,' said Lucy, 'but something may, if she doesn't do as I say. I think, don't you, that she is as much Heron's responsibility as any of us?'

Dominic needed no such reminder. They went out, he looking troubled and Martha rather cross.

Sir Topaz had left his basket and was now curled on the most comfortable chair that Nehemiah had left them, a mediocre affair in splitting plush. 'It's all very well for you, you spoiled beast,' Lucy addressed him, frowning. His reply was a deep-throated rumble.

Leaving him to his sleep, Lucy went to present herself to Mr Davies for her solitary tutorial. The twins were, with difficulty, still confined to their room and were excused from their books. Meanwhile it had been agreed with her mother that the tutor should supervise Lucy through Thomas Tusser's *Household Book*, a monstrous manual that held the key to every domestic skill. It represented no great strain on her intellect and she was aware that she was of an age when, in normal times, she might soon be expected to have the running of her own household, so she was by no means averse to its homely strictures. When she entered the library Mr Davies was standing at the window overlooking the sunken garden. She went to stand beside him, bidding him a polite 'good day'.

He turned, rather unwillingly, she thought, and before they both moved back to the table where they worked, she caught a glimpse of two figures, very close, walking slowly into the shadow of the pines behind the sheltered and secret domain of the Quickenberry tree.

Gloucester, Summer 1643

Spring had come early that year, fresh, bright and blooming as a Botticelli canvas – the perfect weather for warfare. Military activity was brisk throughout the country, the map being gradually redrawn in general favour of the King in northern and western areas and of Parliament in the south and east. Among the most notable exploits was the fall of Reading to Essex, bringing him dangerously near to Oxford, and Prince Rupert's assault on the Cathedral Close at Lichfield, remarkable for the use of the first explosive mine to be employed in England and for the startling and bloody efficacy of this novelty.

The King, Tom Heron wrote home, chided his nephew for the cruelty of the device, while those who wished to draw comparisons about cruelty noted that His Majesty, though he blew up no enemies, exploded instead all notions of royal humanitarianism by his ill-treatment of his Oxford prisoners, who were given little food, less water, no warmth, no bedding and no surgeons to tend their wounds unless they consented to re-enlist in the Royalist ranks.

Rupert rebuffed all criticism by fighting a battle in an Oxford-shire cornfield which routed Essex completely and confounded his hope of a blockade on the King. It was in this engagement that Parliament sustained an even greater loss in the death of John Hampden.

Lucy, reading of this in a Parliamentary newsheet left at Heron after a Friday rent-taking, learned that he had taken a ball in the shoulder and that the wound had mortified, it taking him six days to die. She found herself weeping as she remembered the fatherly kindness he had shown her aboard the *Gallant Lady*. Enemy or not, he had been a man of high integrity and his great good sense would be missed – by Royalists as much as his own kind, for it was they who would suffer most as the good sense died and left more room for extremists among the Puritans. It might have cheered her had she known that the Earl of Essex himself, bedevilled by disease and desertion among his troops and hag-ridden by Rupert's cavalry, was at that moment on his knees demanding of his Lord and God just how He expected His battalions to win if He took unto Himself the greatest and godliest among them.

But the Lord, it seemed, had not finished chastening his lambs, for in the same month of June the hitherto victorious Fairfaxes, father and son, lost their iron grip on the West Riding to the Marquis of Newcastle and had to withdraw their troops to the shelter of the fenlands, under the energetic command of the rugged Member for Cambridge, Oliver Cromwell, who had equipped and trained his own excellent troop of cavalry and had risen to the rank of colonel by reason of their impressive showing under his leadership. More and more, he was taking the responsibility for the Eastern Association out of Manchester's overladen hands.

The Fairfaxes' defection cleared the roads for Queen Henrietta Maria to rejoin her husband after their sixteen months of separation. She brought him 3,000 infantry, thirty companies of horse and six fine cannon.

Among her train, Valora Grey, battering over the shattered roads in a vehicle drawn by bone-shuddering demons, clamped her hands to the edge of her seat and fastened her mind onto the approaching possibility of seeing Tom Heron again. She did not know how she would greet him, whether they would meet as lovers or as friends. His few letters had been more guarded than hers; affectionate, yes, but containing none of the pent-up flood of molten need she was certain he must have found liquescent between the lines of her own. She knew that he had every right to his pride, that her behaviour had merited his reserve, but she intended to break it down in any way she could, to abase herself before him if necessary to obliterate the sting of the angry condemnation of him that she so much regretted.

As they reached Stratford, racked from skull to crossbones, she descended hopefully on learning that Prince Rupert and a chosen number of his troop had ridden out to meet them. She was disappointed to learn that Tom was not among them, but her mood was lifted by the novelty of waiting on the Queen at New Place, the home of Shakespeare's granddaughter, Judith; it brought her a fraction closer to Tom to be so forcibly reminded of his father.

When at last they entered Oxford, they were greeted with the news of a splendid Royalist victory at Roundaway Down near Devizes. Parliamentary forces, under Sir William Waller, had menaced the spent and wounded troops who were limping under fire into the little town after the previous day's engagement on the slopes of Lansdowne Ridge, some fifteen miles west, which they had also won.

Seeing that they were likely to be trapped, Prince Maurice and two brother officers had brilliantly evaded Essex's vigilance and made a wild, successful dash into Oxford for help. They had come back with 1,800 horse under Wilmot and the cut-throat Sir John Byron, Sir George and Tom Heron amongst them.

By the time they arrived, Tom told Valora later, their companions were almost done-for, having fought, already battle-weary, for two days and two nights. Their ammunition was exhausted and they were melting the lead gutters to make bullets and unstringing bedropes for match-cord.

Their rescuers threw themselves furiously upon Waller before he had time to draw up his forces and won themselves a runaway victory. They accounted for 1,400 of Parliament's men that day, either to death or to the jailor, and brought back thirty-six of their standards and all of their cannon, ammunition and baggage. All this was accomplished by a hard-riding force, less than half the number of the enemy. Parliament's army in the west, like the Fairfaxes in the north, had reached the nadir of their fortunes.

Oxford ran mad that night, and as the bells swung and the fireworks flared, the courtiers caroused and the musicians made pandemonium, Valora at last came face to face with Tom. They were in a long hall in Christ Church. At one end of it the King and Queen, with Rupert and Wilmot and the other local commanders were being mobbed by the court. Tom stood a little apart, drinking quietly and steadily, now and then exchanging a few words with a friend who passed. Wilmot had clapped him on the back and called him a 'good lad', and Rupert had grinned and waved his glass from the middle of his frenzied throng of fashionable admirers.

He felt, rather than saw her come in, through a narrow door behind and a little to the right of him. He did not turn. And then here she was in front of him, in a deep crimson gown with her black hair clouding her shoulders and her eyes and her garnets shooting crystalline fires.

'Tom.'

'Valora.'

'Are you glad to see me?'

'I am delighted.' He forced his voice to hold steady as all those nightly images fled before the breathtaking reality of their original. 'How was your journey?'

'Appalling beyond belief. How was your battle?'

'Victorious beyond expectation. You are thinner.'

'I have done a great deal of walking. A mendicant trudge through the courts of Europe, my begging bowl in my hand.'

'You appear to have the knack of it. Our cause has profited remarkably, it appears, from your peregrinations.'

' "The cause; it is my soul, the cause." God forbid otherwise – but I am very, very glad to be home. Especially since it seems our fortunes sit high in a manner beyond the merely financial.'

'For the moment. The fortunes of war are notoriously fickle. If we can build upon our present position we may win through.'

All the time that they spoke their eyes were held, unblinking, in the shared, hypnotic fascination of each other's presence. They had hardly noticed what they said, only that they spoke in a low, challenging tone that for some reason made them feel secure.

'What other news have you?' she asked, taking wine from a passing servant so that her hands should be too occupied to find their way to his face. She longed to touch the long plane of his cheek below its high, stark bone.

He frowned. 'None good. Heron is sequestered and that damnable bastard, Nehemiah Owerby, is in charge of it.'

This brought her sharply out of her langour. 'May God help them and keep them,' she said gently. 'Tell me how it was.'

He told her rapidly all that he and Sir George had heard from Heron. 'My father and I thought, at first, that he should take back his troop and attempt to defend the demesne. We would never have left it so ill-prepared had we guessed that things would come to this pass so quickly. But Wilmot was loathe to let him go; he pointed out, rightly I suppose, that if every man went off to defend his own acres, the war would go on forever. We must fight together if we are to win.'

'But surely – couldn't you take leave until you had beaten off Owerby?'

He shook his dark head. She saw suddenly how tired he was. 'No. What would be the use? The whole county is more or less in Parliament hands. If we garrisoned Heron, we might well have to defend it to the death. It is better, we have decided, to accept sequestration for the moment, and put all our energies into winning the war; then we may recover what we have lost. They say that Nehemiah is a fair enough landlord, according to his lights,' he added grudgingly. 'They do not want for necessities and are left to come and go as they please. But I will never forgive him my brothers' whipping,' he finished in a clenched whisper, his fingers working round his glass so that some of the wine spilled on his white shirt.

Valora stared at the bright stain, trying not to see it as an ill omen, then blotted it firmly with her handkerchief. The chance gesture provided them at last with the physical contact they needed and he stopped her hand against his breast, caught beneath his own.

'Ah, so you are truly pleased to see me,' she murmured, smiling.

'Indeed yes, how could you doubt it – but I would like, I believe,' he said very carefully, so that his breathing should not quicken foo fast, 'to express my pleasure in a more private situation.'

'Very well. By all means let us leave this contesseration of apes and peacocks. Where shall we seek our privacy?'

His dark eyes reflected a pinpoint of red from his wineglass. 'Where is your room?' he asked deliberately.

She thought of telling him that the room was not hers alone, but she knew that the ladies with whom she shared it would not wish to occupy it until well after midnight. She thought of claiming that the Queen needed her, but he had only to glance at Henrietta Maria, vivid and glowing as she flirted with her husband, to know that she did not. 'I will show you the way,' she said.

They had made love only twice during the two years they had known one another, once near the beginning when they could not help themselves, and once later, when he had first asked her to marry him. It was too dangerous an occupation for an unmarried noblewoman – and yet, despite their conditioned ability to deny themselves, both had felt from time to desirous, frustrated time, that the fatal appearance of a Heron bastard might be the sole solution to their conflict.

She could not, she knew, refuse him tonight. Nor did she wish to. When they reached her room, he pressed her back against the closed door, leaning his whole, famished body into hers, his lips feasting and drinking, his hands remembering their way to her breasts. They flared to his touch and she pushed down his head to assuage their need. Their clothes were a desperate insult to passion and as he roughly began to pull up her skirts she reached blindly, hanging upon his lips, for the opening of his breeches, wanting him in her hands. So often the victim of discipline, he was just able to drag himself back.

'No, not like this,' he whispered unevenly. 'We have waited so long, love. Surely we can wait until we reach the bed.'

They laughed at themselves and then he picked her up and carried her, dishevelled as a gipsy, across the room. He put her on her back upon the bed and entered her almost at once. For both of them the need was urgent enough to make nothing of all the graces they would normally have shown each other. Their bodies enlaced like those of a drowning man and his saviour. Unable to tell the seeker from the found, they were swept into the gale of their passion careless of any landfall, carried through surging straits and dizzy whirlpools, balancing on great breakers, cradled in still pools, letting the winds take them and the waters enfold them, buffeting, rolling and caressing them until at last they had done with them and let them be quiet and lie together, spent upon the shore. If they had died in that moment they would have known just enough of their existence to know that they were completely happy.

They continued to be happy, although they hardly saw each other after that first, overwhelming reunion. Tom was in the field again almost at once and Valora was left to wonder dreamily whether she were pregnant and to count, as they poured in during the succeeding days, the bright drops in the bloody stream of Royalist victories.

The invincible Rupert had harried the unhappy Waller out of the West and sent him down the Thames Valley, tail between legs, to complain to Essex that he had been abandoned in his need. Rupert had then besieged, stormed and taken Bristol, as he had always aimed to do. His losses were heavy but the gain was more considerable – a port to rival London from which they might recoup their trade and consolidate the slow advances they were also making at sea, supported by the loyal governors of the Channel Islands and a variety of international pirates.

After Bristol, the remaining towns in the south-west dropped like ninepins to Rupert. Valora danced all night in honour of the fact, casually collecting a new cavalier love-lock for every victory. She even kissed one of them one night, in an excess of euphoria, then cast him down with quite unconscious brutality by telling him that it was because she had heard from Tom that he was well and not wounded and that he loved her.

In London, while Oxford danced, John Pym clutched at his agonized bowels and worried deeply. In addition to the dismaying series of defeats, Parliament now had to contend with an outbreak of faction fighting on behalf of her generals as Waller and Essex accused each other of criminal incompetence and unfitness to command.

There was also the hampering drag of Lord Holland's anti-war group, who wished, with the naivety of babes or Black Africans, to give back control of the army to the King; what was worse, they had all but persuaded the mortified Essex that the time had come to cut their losses and seriously sue for peace.

Pym, thrusting away his increasing sickness into a mental compartment marked 'later', took a deep breath, looked about him again, considered, and saw what was needed – a remoralized Essex and a reassured army. What's more, they should be inspired and supported by that much feared bugbear of the Royalists, an Alliance with the Scots Covenanters. The time was more than ripe.

He could not go to Edinburgh himself; he was too ill and too badly needed at Westminster. In his place he sent Harry Vane, thus conveniently ridding the Commons of one of Essex's most clamourous critics.

On the very day that young Harry left London, the need for his errand was stressed yet again by the surrender of Parliament's garrison at Gainsborough to the Marquis of Newcastle. This loss threatened their eastern front so gravely that Colonel Cromwell, trying hopelessly to defend it without any infantry, bombarded his commanders with furious demands for relief, his exasperation crying out from the page: 'Is this the way to save a kingdom? Haste what you can! The enemy will be in our bowels else!' John Pym, had he read it, might have been detached enough to find in it a personal irony.

In the King's camp it was clear that Parliament's weakness begged to be exploited. Should they, then, chance all in a bid for the capital? They could expect support from Kent where there had been a recent rising in their favour. Or might it be wiser to consolidate their present position by taking Gloucester, the enemy's last bastion in the West?

The military opinion was that they had not the enormous strength needed to take London, and to fail would be disastrous. Gloucester, the Puritan centre of the Cotswold wool trade, blocked the Severn waterway to them from Royalist Shrewsbury and Worcester down to the estuary at Bristol, and also interrupted the route between the King's main forces and the Forest of Dean, in whose protective depths the Royal engineer, Sir Thomas Bushell, produced his hephaestian prodigies of arms. Therefore, let it be Gloucester.

But they never took Gloucester. With one of those lightning changes of sensitivity and pace that confound the expectation of the most experienced critics of war, Parliament fought back.

There was no reason to expect it; every sign was against it. The King's astrologer swore it was impossible. Yet it happened. While the citizens of Gloucester under their twenty-three-year old governor, Colonel Edward Massey, steeled themselves to withstand the attentions of their twenty-three-year old besieger, Prince Rupert, who was busily undermining their walls, their co-religionists in London were suddenly seized with the notion of coming to their aid. This grew into a passion for their succour that had all the zealous enthusiasm of a crusade. Defeat was forgotten, despair dismissed. Their regiments must be mustered; the Trained Bands must be marshalled; they must have new horses, new uniforms and new money – and good old Essex must be their leader and trail his coffin into a New Jerusalem of godly deeds and glorious victories.

Their fervour was intensified both by the warm certainty of help from Scotland and by an infamous piece of news from Ireland: the Marquis of Ormonde, the King's Lord Lieutenant, had overthrown the Protestant opposition in the Dublin Council and the way lay clear, therefore, for Charles' unholy alliance with the murderous hell-hounds of the Pope's army. These must, and should be, with God's help, overcome. But first, Gloucester.

By the time that Essex' army came up like bad weather on the brow of Prestbury Hill, the siege of Gloucester had already lasted a month. It had been a notably unsuccessful month. The King had forbidden Rupert to take the city by storm and rain had put paid to his alternative plan, the mines. There had been nothing to do but wait and waste their ammunition in fruitless bombardment while the mines were relaid in fair weather and Essex marched daily nearer.

In the end they had been forced to abandon the siege and draw off to engage Essex. They had so far been lucky as to beat him back to his road for London at Newbury where, in the heavy damp of early morning, they chose their battle ground, a sloping common due southwest of the town. The two sides were more or less matched as to numbers, the Royalists having the advantage of cavalry and artillery and rather less foot. What they did not have was anything approaching enough ammunition; supplies expected from Oxford had not arrived.

Tom Heron's troop, waiting on the hillside with Rupert, the collars of their scarlet cloaks turned up against the chilling rain, watched narrowly as Essex began to advance infantry across the level ground between the common and the town. The land was criss-crossed by hedged lanes and fenced kitchen gardens. Tom gave it a doubtful shake of the head before turning to scrutinize the menace to their flank presented by John Hampden's old regiment who had already managed to take and hold some high ground known as Biggs Hill. From there, it was obvious, they hoped to account for as much as they could of Rupert's horse. Tom caught sight of his father discoursing cheerfully with a brother officer, over to the right with Wilmot. No doubt he was giving him the benefit of one of old Will's battle scenes, as was his custom on such occasions. Tom raised his arm affectionately but Sir George did not see him.

Tom had fought in countless engagements by now and if he had lost some of that inspired exhilaration that had urged him on at Edgehill, there had also been a diminution, enough at least to allow him to sleep at night, in the dismay and agony of conscience that had accompanied the slaughter of his own countrymen. He would never get used to it, but he was a soldier and he would do it as long as he must.

He could see that they were going to have a sticky time of it unless their ammunition arrived very shortly. The cavalry might well hold its own against Essex's horse; that was to be expected. It was the infantry who were the problem. If they had to fight too long across that enclosed and overgrown terrain, the musketeers would run out of shot and then they would be at the mercy of the enemy, for the pikemen could not protect them on such unmanoeuvrable ground. Rupert's plan was to come to their rescue should it be necessary, in a series of outflanking sweeps which would catch the enemy in the rear, releasing the pressure on the musketeers; but this would draw them perilously near to the enclosed ground, a murderous trap for cavalry.

Tom gritted his teeth and prayed they would get the ammunition through. As they day progressed, however, he, like everyone else, abandoned prayer as the hapless musketeers, after putting up an admirable resistance despite their depleting stocks, watched hope run out with their shot. Battery after battery fell back before the relentless fire that they could no longer return. Their losses were worse than any they had yet known. Tom's eyes seemed filled with the poor devils, crawling, their bones shattered by enemy balls, or clutching at guts wrenched out by the pull of a pike, desperate to escape from his own horse's hooves as he charged down yet another accursed hedge-muffled alley in the blind maze of lanes which he had been unable to avoid.

It was a filthy business. He hated it. All their skill went for nothing in nightmare sorties where he would lead a small party in to attack the rear or the flank of the London trained infantry, hoping to inflict the maximum damage in the first furious onslaught, and then, because of their own small numbers, dictated by the inimical terrain, they would find themselves unable to draw off and must fight with a ferocious and literally cut-throat dedication, hand sawing at hand and horse jammed against horse, until some less hard-pressed group of their comrades could come to their rescue. There was simply no space for them to charge, so that they became simple swordsmen, even their pistols useless for lack of bullets.

The carnage was unparalleled. Tom's men were going down all round him. It was on his fourth dogged attempt at this self-destructive form of human salvage that he at last received his own incapacitating wound. He already had several scratches, some deeper cuts and a musket had nearly removed half the back of his cloak, but what eventually blotted him from the field was a simple clump on the head from a healthily swung, old-fashioned mace. This was the property of one of William Waller's more adventurous dragoons who had liberated it from Winchester Town Hall and civic duties and had since found it a most efficacious weapon and well worth the trouble of carrying it.

Tom was in a field tent when he came round. It was dark. There was a lump on his head that felt like a small cannon ball. He groaned and Josh Pye was at his side, his face serious. 'How is it, Mr Tom?'

He struggled to sit up. 'My head somewhat resembles the inside of the Tower of Babel. Otherwise I seem still to possess all the requisite bits and pieces. How many men did we lose?'

'Thirty, sir, I'm afraid.' Josh looked down. It was a grim total. They had started with 100 that morning. 'But, sir –' the valet hesitated.

It occurred to Tom that Josh was completely without trace of the normal light irony with which he treated the world. Accustomed, when his wounds were not serious to a sarcastic disquisition upon the ruin of his looks and clothes, he began to wonder if he had sustained some lethal hurt of which he was ridiculously unaware.

'What is it, man?' he demanded, impatient.

Josh tried for words but was winded. He tried again. 'I hardly know how to tell you, Major. It's your father, sir—'

'What, dead? Let it not be so, for the love of God!'

'No – but not expected to live. He has taken a ball through his lung.'

Tom was already on his feet. 'Where is he? Can you take me to him?'

Josh threw him a cloak as they left the tent. 'It is some way. He was over towards Biggs Hill. Their cavalry took a beating there.'

'Hurry, man, hurry!' Oh my God, Father, he thought as Josh talked steadily on about the battle, trying to shorten that forced walk through the dim-lit tents, among the wounded and dying, moving aside for the carts that were still coming in from the darkened lanes, hearing the groans that came from them and damming up pity, sacrificing every ounce of energy and emotion to their hurry, as though he might buy time with sheer determination.

They had taken Sir George to Wilmot's tent and Dr Harvey himself was attending him. He looked up as Tom came in and right away shook his head. 'He is very low, I'm afraid. There is nothing to be done. I've made him as comfortable as I can. I have given him laudanum. Do not tire him more than you can help; he may leave us at any minute.

Tom nodded, his throat constricting, and leaned over his father. He lay propped on Wilmot's lace-edged pillows, his eyes closed and circled with a greyish aura which seemed to seep outward into the rest of his face, vanquishing the ruddy cheeks and ebullient nose, even dismissing the bush fire of his beard that now lay combed and neat upon his chest like a pet spaniel. This in itself was enough to tell Tom that all was amiss with him, for he was accustomed to let it sprout like furze about his face, its wilderness disturbed only by the passage of wine and food or particularly vigorous conversation.

Tom listened to his harsh breathing for a moment, then put his hand gently on the arm that lay like a piece of wood upon the sheet. 'Father. It's Tom. Can you hear me?'

The baronet's eyelids fluttered and he tried to smile. His lips were colourless. 'My boy.' He had so hoped that he would come, would not be too late. 'Glad you're not hurt.' He gasped and fought for breath.

'Don't talk,' said Tom, then, hideously, could himself think of nothing to say. 'Are you in much pain?' he managed, stupidly.

A movement of the hand dismissed the idiocy, all the effort saved for the voice which came thinly from far off, through rivers of blood and phlegm.

'Tom – you must – set right – this business at Heron –' God's bollocks, how he detested this weakness. He could have spoken for an hour or more on the glories of his unsurpassable Heron, to read its eulogy as they would read his over his grave, but there was no wind in his pipe and that was that. Anyway, as to Heron, Tom knew – Tom knew—

'Of course, sir,' his son said, 'but you – you mustn't leave us,' Tom wanted to cry, but the futility of it closed his lips. His father would not thank him either, if he said anything that might shake his determination to make a good end. 'Heron shall be my faithful trust and care,' he promised, laying his hand over Sir George's pale, mottled one.

Again came that almost illusory smile. It deepened. 'Tell Mary –' he began. The lovely, self-possessed girl he had courted smiled at him in a rose-coloured gown, discoursing gravely on plague in the shrubbery. So long ago. '– That I have never loved another. That she is my dearest heart.' He knew he should begin to speak in a past tense, but could not. He would not imagine her, or Heron, without him.

Tom was nodding and gripping that blanched hand that lay so quietly upon the coverlet and still belonged to him, though he could no longer feel it. He sent it a message. To his surprise it obeyed him and returned, very faintly, the boy's grasp.

'Say to the children that they are to be their mother's prop and stay, and to obey her in all things. They are also to obey yourself as they would their father. Say to them that I love them all, and tell Lucy – my sweet, wayward bird – that she is to be happy.'

Tom smiled wryly, even then. Lucy elected for happiness, the others for duty. 'I will tell them.'

Sir George sought his eyes, questioning. 'It would be well for her,' he said, aware of the responsibility he delegated, 'if she were to marry Will Staunton. I love the rogue and should like to bind him to us—'

'I will do my best, Father,' said Tom. Then he thought to ask. 'Is there anyone you wish to see, anything you wish to be done?'

There was a small movement of that dreadfully quiet hand. 'No. I have seen the bishop, and my affairs are all in order at home. Though I don't know, what with this blasted sequestering – but you'll see to it, Tom, if it can be done, eh? You're a good lad. I have been proud of you.' Yes, a good lad, but he had himself on too tight a rein; he needed a woman to let it out for him a little. Mistress Valora – she'd look after him – 'You should marry Valora Grey, my boy. You will, won't you? I truly wish it, Catholic or not.'

Tears scalded Tom's eyeballs and he bit down upon his tongue to dam them with pain.

'It is my dearest wish.' Sir George squeezed his hand again, trying not to have inappropriate thoughts about the exquisite Lady Grey. He felt a little tired now. There was something else he wanted to say, someone else he must mention – ah yes, Jud, his black sheep, the image of his great-grandfather; a mind of his own and as fearless of any man's opinion. He had treated him harshly, but he could take it well enough. He would have come to no harm on Will Staunton's ship. Such a pity not to have seen him again, to have told him – he closed his eyes, fading into sleep, his words for Jud still forming in his mind. In his dream they were spoken and Tom had them safe in his memory.

Tom watched as he rested, seeing how the familiar face was already indelibly marked by death. It had simply never occurred to him, he realized now, that his father would ever die. Even eight years of shared battle had failed to teach him the small truth that one's father and oneself are as vulnerable as the rest of that legion of corpses that have passed one's way in the field. Sir George had been such a splendidly healthy man, a vital energy beaming out of him at all times like an enveloping, incandescent cloak, so that wherever he was there was life and commotion and keen physical enjoyment. To have those magnificent animal spirits laid so low was surely a travesty of God's purpose. Tom swore. He looked into that unnaturally peaceful face and hated war.

After a time his father reopened his eyes, struggling to the surface of life with another commission for those who would continue to inhabit it. 'Tom, promise me one thing more.' His voice was stronger for this one thing mattered a great deal. 'Promise that you will never desert His Majesty, but will remain faithful to his cause and his heirs and do all in your power to help him to his own—'

'My oath on it. My allegiance will not change,' Tom responded firmly. ' "The mirror of all Christian kings," ' Sir George quoted fondly.

Tom's tears were ambushed by this trace of the beloved bard.

'What, weeping?' The whispering voice was very gentle. 'Never weep for me, my boy. "We owe God a death", eh? I have been well content.' His only regret, he thought, was that he could not have been at home at Heron, now, with all of them gathered around him; but a man may not choose his moment for himself. He was full of simple happiness in the knowledge that he was dying for his King, in the manner of generations of English knights. It was a very proper death.

'I am sorry,' he pursued, panting a little, 'that I shall not see the end of this hateful conflict, and know the King safe home – but we prosper, do we not? And today – what is the outcome? I saw some ill chances before I was struck down.'

Tom had given not a single backward thought to the battle, but he supposed they had been defeated. The losses were so very great. But this was not the news with which to speed a dying soldier. 'We prosper – all over England,' he said steadily.

Sir George looked satisfied. 'We shall prevail. You will see. God will not allow "England that hath made conquest of all others to make a shameful conquest of herself." '

Tom's heart cracked with tenderness. 'Henry VI?' he smiled.

'Richard II! I could always best you.'

'Yes, you could.'

The old man was tiring again, he could see. The grey shadow was annexing new territory minute by minute. A fit of coughing racked him and the handkerchief Tom held to his lips was flushed with blood. Sir George lay back, gasping shallowly, his lips moving soundlessly.

'Don't talk for the moment, Father. Rest for a while.'

'It's no matter, not now. It is only – it will be strange to go home to Heron and not to see it.'

Tom steadied himself. 'Perhaps you may. The Lord may permit all manner of wonderful things.'

'Pray for me. And if I am placed conveniently so to do –' a wisp of humour clung to the grey lips '– be sure that I too shall pray most lustily for you – for all of you.'

'No doubt of it.' Tom hardly trusted his voice.

'The bishop has given me his safe conduct. I only hope I must not cross any of Parliament's lines.'

Tom laughed, freely and wholeheartedly. Sir George grinned back at him, well pleased that they had managed some merriment. 'God damn and blast the Parliament to Hell!' he said with an echo of his old, robust quality, then fell back in a deep paroxysm of coughing. When he had done he closed his eyes and his face cleared, becoming calm and strangely fresh, as though he had gone out into clean air. He lay there in a deep quiet that was unaffected by his rasping breath, his hand beneath that of his son.

Tom could not have marked the moment when he died. There came a time when he knew that it was over, that was all. Still holding his father's hand he dropped to his knees at the bedside. He tried to pray but his sorrow destroyed his thoughts. He knelt for a long time, his mind a turmoil of anguish and memories, his body infinitely weary.

It was from the end of a long tunnel of time and space that he looked up, eventually, at the movement of the curtain over the opening of the tent. It was pulled half back and Prince Rupert came in, his hand on the woolly neck of the dog, Boy. 'I came as soon as they told me.' The tall young man, bone-weary, was dabbled with mud and blood. 'I'm sorry, Tom. May he rest in peace. He was one of the best. We can ill afford his loss.'

Tom mumbled something.

'I did not come alone,' Rupert said. 'Your brother is here.'

He could make no sense of it. 'How did Humphrey –?' Was there some new disaster at Heron? Oh not now, please not now.

It was not Humpty. The stocky, dark-clad figure which moved through the curtains was smeared across the chest with the orange-tawny that distinguished a Parliament man. He came in and, like the Prince, stood looking down at the bed, his face full of shock.

Tom could not believe it. His voice, when he could get it to function, was hollow with loathing. 'What the devil are *you* doing here?'

Jud, very pale, gave him stare for stare. 'I came to bid him farewell. I see I am – too late.' His jaw was shaking. He had an overwhelming desire to weep, even to throw his arms around Tom and clasp him close so that they could weep together.

One glance at his brother's face told him that he could never do that. Tom rose and came round the foot of the bed, his lips working. Rupert moved from his path, amazed at the passion in his face.

'Why do you carry that shameful colour on your breast?'

Jud's mouth was dry. 'I came up country with Essex. The scarf enabled me to move more easily.'

Tom was trying to control himself. 'With Essex?' he snapped, his eyes curdling with hatred. 'What have you to do with Essex?' Then, incongruously, 'Why are you not at sea?'

Jud's precarious balance reeled. Of course, Tom knew nothing of him since the *Gallant Lady* had sailed for Italy. 'It's a long story,' he said, 'but I do not get my living at sea. I am a printer.' His brother gazed at him blankly. 'I publish a newsheet.'

If Tom took in any of it, he gave no sign. 'Why come here?' he asked.

Jud sighed. 'I am here to write down what I see. This was a time of great importance, perhaps a turning point –' He did not have the sense to keep the sheer interest out of his voice.

'It's for Parliament, isn't it?' Tom grated the words through his teeth like bitter peelings. 'You write this filthy rubbish for Parliament?' His whole body shook with violence.

'Hold hard there,' his commander murmured, setting a firm hand on his shoulder. 'The boy only came—'

Tom shook him off. 'Your Highness can know nothing of this,' he said peremptorily and waited, obviously, for the Prince to leave. Rupert regarded him with doubtful affection for a moment, then shrugged and quitted the tent, the huge shaggy animal, tail down, close at his side.

Jud gazed at his brother, his grief as plain as a child's. Tom watched him without speaking until he saw that he was being asked for what he would not give – an admission of grief shared. 'You have not the right to mourn him,' he said viciously. 'He had cast you out for the traitor you are. He died without a word for you.'

It was cruel. Jud stepped involuntarily towards him, his fists curling. It was what Tom wanted. Putting every ounce of his sorrow, his hatred and his incomprehension behind the blow, he felled him to the ground.

Jud rolled over and came straight up at Tom, all his street-fighting instincts roused and raw. Their battle was brief, berserk and eventually bloody as Tom's sword cuts opened and Jud's lip was split open by a savage right hook.

It was all over when Rupert erupted back into the tent. He had gone only far enough to give them their privacy, fearing they would use it in just this manner. 'Christ in heaven, are you barbarians, that you shame yourselves before your father's corpse?' he cried as he dragged them apart with a cuff for each of them to keep the distance. 'My God, I think I have never seen an officer so demean himself, no, not even a Spanish trooper or a heathen Turk! Sir George himself will curse you if he can, be sure of it!' The German conquered the English in his accent as his voice rose and it was clear that he too was beside himself.

Tom, faced with the distress of his battle-worn leader on his account, felt his anger fall away with a suddenness that left him empty. 'You are right, sir, in God's name. I'm sorry. I regret this sincerely.'

Rupert, now so tired that he could hardly stand, swayed and nodded. 'Very well. The matter rests with myself alone. But for God's sake – and your own, Tom – and for the sake of the men you lead – get a hold on yourself, will you?' Shaking his head as though its weight were newly too much for him, the Prince left for the second time.

Jud looked hopefully at Tom. 'Listen, I—'

Tom turned away from him. 'No. I will do you no more violence – but I must ask you to go away from here. You are not wanted.'

'Christ, Tom! You're inhuman,' Jud shouted bitterly. 'You always were. We used to call you "The Icicle", when we were small, did you know? Very well then,' as he got no reply, 'God damn you to hell!' When Tom, after a long, blank space, turned round again, he was alone once more with the unjudging, unsuffering presence of his father.

While the only George Heron now to bear that name, outcast, angry and injured, trailed back to London in the wake of the triumphant Essex, he had time to ask himself some questions. He found himself recalling, over and over again, Robin's advice just before they had published, much disguised, the contents of Lady Grey's letter to Tom – 'If you have any doubts, *now* is the time to draw back.' That time, his answers told him now, was long gone. He had chosen his path and, better educated than when he set out, could produce several well-researched arguments to uphold that choice. He had learned a great deal from the men he now met so frequently, from the precise and brilliant Pym, the passionate Lilburne, calm, certain Richard Overton. Why, then, did he feel so disastrously, so miserably in the wrong?

He had been shocked and horrified when he had learned, during an interview with a Royalist prisoner, of his father's mortal wound. He had hoped against hope to reach him before he died. He had, he knew now, been counting, as another man might count on confession for his salvation, upon Sir George's forgiveness. All he had wanted was to be a part of his family once again – but he began to see, as he rode through the rutted roads behind Parliament's victorious cavalry, that perhaps he had indeed cut himself off forever from all that depth of love and warm security that Heron had always meant to all of them.

And then there was his father himself. That great good-natured giant gone from the earth – it was a blasphemy. Now he would never know, never, whether he would have obtained the absolution and understanding he had so longed for. As he rode, released now from the prohibition imposed by his brother's glacial presence, he cried like a small child lost and far from home, allowing his horse to stumble unchecked in the broken track. He had never in his life known such sadness.

Heron, Autumn 1643

More people came to the funeral than they thought still remained in the county. Anglicans, Puritans, Catholics, they all crowded the stately monastic chapel at Heron to overflowing; those who could not get in stood outside, heads bowed in the October cold. For this one day the differences which inspired them to take each other's lives and goods in the promulgation of the war were diminished to a mere matter which it would be in bad taste to mention; Lucy found it incomprehensible that so much could be accomplished by the death of one man.

Her father, however mixed had been his qualities in the eyes of so many, had been universally respected, and here was ample proof of it as the men of his company, who had brought him home, formed the guard of honour about his coffin, looked upon with sympathetic approval by their sworn enemies. Even Nehemiah Owerby, amazed at his own sense of loss, sent his condolences and allowed all those under his command who wished to do so to attend the funeral.

Beyond the old stones of chapel and cloister, Heron's magnificent trees, flaming in red and gold, counterfeited a funeral pyre fit for a Celtic chieftain. Lucy found their flamboyant presence reassuring as she stood to watch her father's body committed to the earth in the monks' small graveyard. Somewhere over in the glowing depths of the woods was her private place. It waited for her with its comfort as it always did, and it was there, not here before all the world, that she would do her mourning. Just now all her care was for her mother who had taken the shock with brutal impact.

The service had been dignified and austerely beautiful. The chaplain, though no Shakespeare, had delivered a finely pitched eulogy, choosing his words with great care, so that the baronet walked again among the graceful gothic pillars of his chapel in his most benign and beneficent mood.

Now that it was over, the family gravitated towards the small parlour, coming and going about their business but never separated for too long, bound in that cold realization of total loss that comes after the first flood of sorrow and the strange, light-headed euphoria that follows the burial.

They were supported in this black period by the presence of Martha who had taken a dispensation from her self-imposed banishment from Heron. Valora Grey and Will Staunton had also joined them and gave all that friendship could give in the way of continual understated comfort.

'We must have a very great care for your mother,' said Valora to Lucy, who appeared wan and rather too controlled. The best cure for one's own troubles being invariably someone else's, Valora was busy consigning each grieving Heron into the care of another – thus Lucy must tend her mother; the twins, naturally each other and Dominic for good measure; Julia was deputed to comfort the ignorant baby; and Lady Heron must coddle Julia for whom the experience was terrifying because she was at an age when she could begin to understand the concept of death, and found it very fearful.

Valora set herself, knowing Tom's preference for relying on his own resources, to help Lucy, who was at a loss to deal with her mother's complete surrender to grief. 'I think Mary has persuaded herself that she cannot do without her husband. This is very understandable at this moment, but we all know that she is, in fact, an excellent manager, and has kept Heron in your father's absence many times over the years.'

'Yes, but she knew he would always come back. This is different.'

'Lucy, he could have failed to come back at any time – but yes, I agree, it *is* different, now that it has happened. But we must not concede that to your mother. Can you not see? She must come to feel that life goes on. She does not feel that necessity at present.'

Ever since the dreadful day when Tom, now Sir Thomas, had ridden from Newbury to bring them the news, Mary Heron had seemed entirely to relinquish her own hold on life. She no longer directed her household, answering 'Do as you think fit', to all requests for orders; she kept to her room, even at mealtimes; and not once, since they had laid Sir George next to his father and Thomas the Pirate, had she so much as stepped into her beloved gardens.

She was not a self-indulgent woman. There was no hint in her of any desire for fuss or cossetting. She calmly and courteously rebuffed all attempts at comfort. Even Valora's suggestion that her children had need of her strength provoked only an abstracted nod.

Valora, at a loss for the moment, temporarily gave up her

efforts in favour of restoring to life Mary's drooping houseplants. For Lucy, it was as though she had lost both parents at once, so changed did she find her mother, with whom she would like to have spoken of her father, but was not permitted. She was more than grateful to Valora, who would hold her and stroke her hair and whisper loving phrases to her when she needed it, or sensibly discuss the domestic problems if that were what was wanted.

'If you would stay – for as long as you can – I think I shall manage to take Mother's place, until she is herself again,' Lucy said, trying not to put too much pleading in her tone.

'Of course I shall stay,' said Valora serenely. 'Where else should I be,' she added with calculated effect, 'save in the house that is soon to be my home?'

'Valora! Oh, is it true? At last!'

'Tom and I will marry when the mourning period is over.'

This premonition of joy was just what was needed to leaven their sadness. Lucy threw her arms round Valora. 'I am so glad. It is the one thing I have longed for.'

'I too, I am forced at last to admit.' Her smile was a little ashamed.

'But why now? What changed your mind?'

'Fear, I think. Simple fear. The war, though it cannot alter my conscience, has changed my mind. I find I can't continue to stand only for my religion, denying happiness to both Tom and myself, when—'

Lucy met her thought. 'When Tom might be killed at any moment. So it was Father's death that decided you?'

'Partly, I am sure. It is difficult to explain. I fear it is that I am beginning to put man before God in my thinking – or at any rate before my church's view of God's will. It is sinful and selfish and may even be a blasphemy.'

'But you don't care!' cried Lucy triumphantly.

'Oh, I do. I care very much. But that will not prevent me from marrying your brother.' She would not voice the awful thing that she hardly dared to fear – that God would punish her for this presumption in the harshest way possible, with Tom's early death in battle. That was for her to bear alone.

She left Lucy after this conversation, to seek out and confide also in Martha, for whom this would be a particularly exquisite form of torture. Lucy, for her part, went off to give the news to Will Staunton, whom she ran to earth in the library, gracelessly asleep beneath Raleigh's *History of the World*.

'My dear girl! I'm so sorry. I must have taken too much claret last night.'

She forgave him. The reason he had drunk so much was that Tom, drowning his sorrows in spectacular style, had forced a similar pace upon Will and would not be refused. It had been this unedifying event that had decided Valora to propose marriage to him first thing that morning in the cruel, crisp light that blared at him amongst the trumpeting colours of the leaves as they walked in the woods. She had shocked him out of his hangover, and, she hoped, prevented several future ones.

Will greeted the news with pleasure and approval. 'This may perhaps do something, too, to turn your mother from her grief,' he said. 'God knows I respect her sorrow, and indeed I share a great deal of it, for your father and I had become fast friends, but she is in the way of making herself ill at present, and anything that will distract her can only be a blessing.'

'If only she would go back to the garden,' said Lucy despondently. 'I keep reminding her how much Father loved it and her care of it, but she just nods and does not listen.'

Will watched her as she stood at the window before the stupendous blaze of autumn beyond. She was pale and there was much of Tom's tension in her body. It was a hard thing to find oneself in veritable command of a large demesne at fifteen.

As though she read his thought she turned back, her brow creasing. 'She won't speak to the steward either, and will answer none of my questions on household matters. However,' she sighed, 'I daresay I shall do well enough with the help of Thomas Tusser.'

Will grinned. 'I remember my mother's volume of Tusser. It was so valuable to her that she kept it under lock and key in her chamber and used an inferior edition about the house. But listen to me Lucy – you are to take care of yourself as well as of others. I don't like your white face and your skinny ribs. You were made to be warm and golden and remind me of ripe wheatfields. You won't do much good to your mother, nor to Heron either, if you waste yourself to a skeleton.'

Lucy nodded impatiently. 'I know. I am not foolish. It is only temporary. And Margery has begun a campaign to feed us all up like Christmas geese—' He saw her face crumple suddenly and tears began to flow. 'Oh, damnation!' she sobbed scrabbling for a handkerchief.

'I'm afraid you'll have to use your sleeve. I haven't one either.' He left his chair and came to take her in his arms, holding her bright head against his chest. 'There, there. What was it? Christmas?'

The head bobbed vigorously, then she raised it and shakily tried to tell him. 'How shall we bear it? Without him we are not a family any more.' He held her quietly, sharing her saddness, remembering that warm Christmas feast, two years ago, when they had all seemed to Will, the eternal guest, the very epitome of family happiness, gathered round the festive table with Sir George presiding like Jove over the minor deities. And yet, even then, dissent had stood in the shadows and mocked their confidence; and behind dissent a darkěr figure who never mocked.

He held Lucy to him as though she were very precious and wondered what the devil he could say that would alter one iota of what she was suffering now. 'I'm reminded,' he said, feeling his way, 'of when my own father died. I was younger than you – thirteen years old. At first I could not believe him gone; like Sir George, he was such a vital presence in the house. He was a big man, never still. Always laughing, but with a will of steel beneath the ease. We used to fight a good deal in fact, as I tested out my character and began to need to be my own man. But I always had a tremendous respect for him, and loved him too. He was an easy man to love. When he died, I couldn't begin to think how I could take his place with my mother. She could have no more children and he was everything in life to her. Even as a child I could see how much they were each other's world. One does not often see love like that, I think. But gradually, without trying, just living from day to day and learning as best I could how to grow into my responsibilities, I found that, in all *practical* ways I *had* replaced him by the time I was fifteen, like you. It was then that my mother determined to let me go. She wanted me to have a choice, not simply to grow into a hollow replica of my father. She was both wise and brave. She sent me to my Uncle Warwick – and my own fortunes developed from there.'

'You once said you ran away to sea.' Lucy had stopped crying. 'Was it then?'

'Ah, no. Did I tell you that? That was when I was only eleven. It was part of my early rebellion. I was always in love with ships.'

'You told Humpty. I wish you hadn't. They were restless for days afterwards; we had to keep sending Tibbett after them every time they took horse. The twins too have a keen desire to serve under your Uncle Warwick!'

He laughed, pleased to have lightened her mood.

'You think, then,' she said, reverting to her original fear,' that I shall become as efficient as I shall need to be?'

'I am sure that you will, and more swiftly than I ever did. My mother had – still has – remarkable strength and a great deal of pride. She soon put on a brave face after my father's death, but she was very hard to please at first.'

'My mother has always been very insistent that we should all adhere to her standards in every way, but now I believe she does not care enough about the rest of the world to mind what we do. My hardest task will be to make her do so again.'

'Don't take it too much to heart. Thank God, grief can only last its natural span, and that's as variable as clouds, from one person to another.'

'Yes, that must be true; we could not bear it else.'

'As to the running of Heron, Lucy; that will change very little in truth. Though you may feel a leaden yoke of responsibility, in fact you will find it all marches with the seasons and all you will really have to do is to make a few simple decisions that your servants will make easy for you. Tom will be away, true; but so, often, was your father. Dominic and Tibbett and Margery and your steward are here – and all the others on whom you rely – and, should you ever need me, or think that there is the slightest thing that I can do to help you, I shall be here too, just as fast as my horse can bring me. I want you to remember my words, and to promise me you will act upon them.'

Her eyes rewarded him. 'Thank you, Will. You are a good friend to us. I'll remember.'

That reminded him of another duty. 'I hope so. I also wish, since I am so providentially placed for it, to prove a friend to your brother Jud. I know you must all be distressed by this new development with Tom.'

'I am worried, but I don't think Mother even took it in, and the twins are all on Tom's side now, and call Jud a traitor. Dominic is sympathetic of course. He feels Jud is misunderstood. I think now that, whatever Tom believes, he should give up the quarrel. I'm sure that's what Father would have wanted – but he says that Father turned Jud out of the house and has said nothing to alter that, so that is how it will remain. He prefers we will not speak of him,' she finished tightly.

'Then he is a pig-headed numbskull,' said Will. 'Whereas you, my dear, are a miracle of good sense. I'll tell you what! You shall write to Jud, will you, and I'll deliver your letter. It would cheer him. He must be feeling uncommonly low after Tom's virtuous harshness.'

'I had already started a letter. Poor Jud! All he did was to follow his nose and, as always, it led him to trouble. I wish he had stayed at home.'

'I don't think *he* does,' Will mused. 'In general, I'd say he was very pleased with life. He is becoming a skilled printer and quite a good writer too. I think you'd be surprised how good. If John Pym began by making use of his youth and enthusiasm, he now finds he has an instrument he may rely upon.'

Lucy shuddered. 'I hate to think of Jud being any man's instrument, especially Pym's.'

'Don't mistake me. Jud has a mind of his own, but he is rightly grateful to Pym for the chance he gave him. He also admires him greatly. So do I. And I fear, alas, that John will trouble none of you much longer. He is a sick man. The last time I saw him he was dreadfully wasted and his belly caused him obvious torture; though he would give up no time in the House, day or night.'

'I'm sorry for that, indeed I am,' said Lucy quietly. 'But, if he should die, what will Parliament do for a leader?'

Will laughed shortly. 'They don't lack for leaders. They spring up daily in the House like rhetorical mushrooms. You'll recall Harry Vane and St John. Pym's boots would fit either, or so they think. Then there is the "moderate" faction – Essex and his friends – who'd put an end to the war, and the Fairfaxes who raise their voices louder than Essex these days, and that odd corncrake of a fellow with the genius for the military, John's cousin Oliver Cromwell; he's gaining a good hearing among the troops. There is no end,' he added dryly, 'to the possible combinations of leadership among our hard-pressed Parliament – but whether *one* leader will arise, I should not like to hazard at this time.'

'But the war will go on?'

'I'm convinced of that, at least. Especially now that the Scots and the Irish have entered the arena.'

'It could go on,' said Lucy with a sudden wild misery, 'until Tom is killed as well as Father, and Jud, in some London brawl – and, yes, even you, though you pretend to be so safe above it all!'

'Let's not have hysteria; it isn't your forte. And there you are wrong,' he added deliberately, 'you will be glad to know that I have stopped floating, and am about to descend.'

'Don't tell me. I know already,' she said fatalistically. 'On Parliament's side.'

'Yes. Do you mind very much?'

'Of course I mind,' she said irritably. 'It makes you a traitor, like my brother Jud. Tom will mind most of all.'

'He may go to hell if he does. I shall not tell him anyway, not yet. I don't think he can stomach any more unpalatable facts just at present.'

'But I can?' He caught the whiff of irony.

'I didn't think it would distress you greatly. You are still prepared to countenance Jud.'

'He is my brother. You are – I don't know. I think I preferred you floating. It suited you.'

'I'm sorry. I assumed you would care very little.'

'You must think you know me very well.'

'Well enough to expect a sensible reaction.'

'Hm. I suppose that is a compliment.'

'Most women would not think so.'

'Most women are fools.' Then, as though this recalled something to her, 'And how is your cousin, Lady Hartley? I had quite forgot to ask after her.' Her tone told him they would discuss his political allegiance no further.

He grinned, taking up the cudgels. 'She flourishes. Though we are perhaps not the *best* of friends at the moment. After a certain amount of dalliance with Parliament, Eliza has taken it into her head to become the most fanatical of Royalists.'

'How wise; just when we are winning,' said Lucy sweetly. 'Not that it *feels* much like winning,' she complained; 'not to us while we have to turn out our pockets every week for that serpent, Nehemiah! If only the King would win a battle near enough to take this territory, but he seems to manage only to be victorious all round our edges, while we are left to work for Parliament.'

' 'S'teeth, yes. I entirely sympathize with your feelings. But this is the way wars have always been waged. I may sound callous but only think: Heron has not been sacked – no, not by any means – nor burned, nor have any of your women been raped, and no one put to the sword, apart from the twins' conquest. So you see, you have much to be thankful for. There are so many who have suffered far greater depradation, especially the poor devils of Catholics.'

'I know all that. But how will it end? Shall we be paying the Committee forever?'

'I can only guess. I'd say that when the fighting is done at last,

322

whenever that may be, even should Parliament be the winner, there will be a desire to put back the clock in many ways, to have the country tidy again. Perhaps, in this spirit, there may be a restitution of lands.' It was as far as he would go to cheer her, and further, perhaps, than he believed.

Lucy sighed. 'Oh, I shouldn't try to look ahead. It's hard enough to know what to do day by day.'

He took her by the shoulders. 'But you will know. There is a strength in you that has never been tried.'

His smile was so encouraging that she began to believe him. 'I hope you are right. Perhaps God gives us the strength we need sometimes. If only he would also give it to my mother.'

His hands tightened for a moment on her small bones. 'I shall go now and try to persuade her out into the garden,' he said. 'It will be a beginning.'

'Very well. I wish you more success than I have had. She thinks well of you; she may listen to you.' She was suddenly overtaken by gratitude for the uncomplicated warmth of his presence. 'Oh, Will, you are so good to us. There must be a hundred more pleasant ways for you to spend your time. Why do you do it?'

He looked as if the question interested him, head on one side. Then he shrugged and turned to go. 'I have no idea,' he said.

When he entered Mary Heron's chamber, some minutes later, the small sense of success that Lucy had given him was to be destroyed at a single stroke, leaving him dull-witted with surprise. All he said, after the usual courtesies and demands after her health, was that it would give him great pleasure to walk in the gardens in their autumn glory, with a woman of matching beauty on his arm, and would she do him that honour?

But Mary, without grace and with no regard for that beauty, had astonished him by bursting into heaving sobs. Covering her face, she had waved him desperately from the room. He could not know, and was not so self-enamoured as to guess, that the sight of so much vital and cock-sure masculinity spreading its youth and magnetism before her widow's couch would only bring home to her, as nothing else could have done, the leaden fact that her own life as a sensual woman was over; that she would never again know the heat and weight of a man's body over hers. It was not even that she mourned, at this moment, for her husband – but, for the first time, for the empty casket of her own woman's body, as much a coffin to her, living, as the one below the earth outside.

She allowed herself to know, in that bitter minute, that she had wanted Will Staunton. She had not let it trouble her. She had scarcely even admitted it to herself, but had simply rejoiced when he was under her roof and been glad that he had given Sir George his friendship.

But now, as he stood before her in his beauty and his kindness, she could not support it, but raged within her undead sexuality and wished him to the very devil. He left her at once and was unnaturally sombre for the rest of the day.

Despite its necessary sadness Lucy was to look back on that brief time after the funeral, spent with her friends, as the last few hours of pleasant wakefulness before the headlong descent into a nightmare whose evil would spread its stain upon the daylight for years to come.

It was a Friday morning, about a fortnight after Tom and Will had left them, when Nehemiah rode up to Heron with his usual following of a dozen men or so. There was nothing out of the way in this; he frequently came in person to assure himself of their steward's diligence. It was only when he strode into the office before his lieutenants that Lucy, seated in her mother's place behind the broad rent table with Tibbett beside her, saw that they had Martha with them.

'Why, what is this?' Her first thought was that Martha, coming to visit, had unwillingly fallen in with Nehemiah on the road. But the way she stood, straight and still between two troopers, told her that this was not so.

'Mr Owerby has surpassed even his own expectation of dedicated duty,' Martha spoke up with cool, edged contempt. 'He has arrested me. Though as yet I am uncertain whether I am indicted as a witch, an heretic, or a mere provoker of malicious rumour.'

'Be silent,' snapped Nehemiah. He did not look at her. It gave him pain to do so.

'But this is not possible,' breathed Lucy. 'Surely there is some mistake. You cannot seriously mean to arrest *Martha*? You – above all others?'

Nehemiah felt the back of his neck prickle with heat. 'You are not required to speak on this matter, but to do as you are ordered, which is to send for the man known to this household as Dominic Lacey.'

Lucy felt herself stop breathing. So it had come at last. Her heart beat strongly and slowly, to the drumbeats of fear. She tried to control herself. Whatever was about to happen, she must not lose her head. 'I believe my cousin to have ridden out,' she temporized.

'Then we shall wait.'

That would be unbearable. She turned to Tibbett. 'Do you go and seek Mr Dominic. He may not yet have gone.'

The giant left with a venomous glance for Nehemiah.

'Martha, will you not sit down?' she asked. 'Or have you to spend the rest of your days clapped between two gateposts?' She glared at the stupid-faced soldiers.

Nehemiah nodded and one of them placed a chair for Martha before the table. She and Lucy exchanged a minute flicker of fear and then the unspoken determination that neither would reveal any such thing to the oafs who surrounded them.

'How is your lady mother?' Martha enquired busily, as though attending a hen-party, and they spoke of Mary's progress, shutting out the awkward faces.

After about fifteen drawn-out minutes, Tibbett returned with Dominic. It was obvious that he had told him all he could, for the priest confronted Owerby as he might the physical manifestation of a mortal sin. 'Will you never have done with your warring on women?' he demanded, his eyes dense with dislike.

'When *you* have done whoring *with* them,' Nehemiah replied, as coldly as he could.

'Oh for God's sake! Not that old tale again,' sighed Dominic wearily, with a vestige of his limp-wristed ennui.

'No. No, indeed. I have a new tale to tell today,' Nehemiah said with a slow, knowing satisfaction that warned him to be very careful.

'Do tell us,' he said, draping himself over a chair and smiling cheerfully at Martha.

'You will please to stand up. It is not customary to accuse a seated prisoner.'

Accuse. Prisoner. Fear stalked them all now and they did not dare consult each other's faces.

Dominic rose slowly and stood, his arms at his sides, waiting in quiet. He knew very well what it would be, as he had known all these months that, one day, it must be. He had made enough preparation, during his long days of service and nights of prayer, to be able, he trusted, to support it.

'Say on,' he invited Nehemiah.

His enemy looked at him, wondering just what he saw. That Lacey was a priest he had known almost for certain soon after the man Davies had become his spy. That hardly concerned him. The law would take care of that. What Nehemiah had to know, *must* find out, though he had to tear every inch of this contained man's flesh screaming from his bones, was whether Dominic was also whore-master to this fragile, stubborn woman whom, against all sense, he loved. He must strike now, while they sustained the first shock; they would never be more vulnerable.

He looked into Dominic's eyes like a lover. 'Dominic Lacey, it is my duty as magistrate in this honour to inform you that you are accused of being a priest of the Roman faith and a member of the so-called Society of Jesus, and therefore of heresy according to the law of England. Proof positive of your guilt has already been established by the confession of one Pierre Fournier, of the Society's seminary at Douai, whom you aided in his seditious movements about this country.'

Poor Pierre, thought Dominic, poor young man. So young, so very fervent in his faith. They must have tortured him.

'You are also accused,' went on Nehemiah's grating voice, rising to a strange pitch, 'of the filthy and abominable practice of the Black Mass, and of the abuse in that foul ceremony, in blasphemous fornication, of the body of Martha Knyvett.'

'No!' Dominic's utter disgust filled the room. 'Not even you could think that! You *do* not think it, in your heart. Why, man, you *know* her. You know that she is chaste.'

Nehemiah burned, but he did not know. It was to be expected that Dominic would deny it, naturally, at first.

'And as to witchery and Black Masses – this is the foolishness of ignorant tongues. You cannot mean to take it seriously. A man may be a serving priest, or he may think himself a warlock and serve Satan; but I gravely doubt if there are any who consider themselves to be both.'

Nehemiah looked at him mournfully. 'I can think of nothing more serious than the perversion of God's worship, even of so unhallowed a form as the papist mass.'

'Very well.' Dominic smiled at him now, almost with pity. He knew that, in whatever tortured manner was given to him, the man loved Martha. 'I will give you what you want – and let that content you.'

Lucy gave a cry like the solitary note of some small marsh bird. She knew what he would say and was powerless to prevent him.

'As you have so diligently, and no doubt cruelly, discovered, I am an ordained priest and a member of the Society of Jesus, which it is my privilege to serve—'

'One moment. The Heron family were, I take it, a party to this treachery? Sir Thomas, his mother, the late Sir George?'

'If you mean were they aware of my activities as a priest, the answer is that they most certainly were not. You yourselves have found it impossible to track my whereabouts; you cannot think I went to any less trouble to cover myself before those most dear to me. To Heron I have been simply Dominic Lacey, Lady Heron's somewhat effete young cousin. Indeed I believe cousin Mary would much prefer my more sober self to the butterfly to whom she has been exposed,' he added, grinning. He was a good liar, for a priest. He hoped Nehemiah believed him.

'But surely – Lady Heron, at least, must have known you for a priest?' Nehemiah frowned.

'I had not seen Lady Heron for some years. I was a schoolboy when last we met.' He had been newly released from the seminary, it was true. He remembered the day, the sunshine, the joyousness; his first marriage service.

'Then how did you explain your sudden appearance on her doorstep?'

Dominic banished memory. 'As you might expect. I said I had been expelled from home for youthful misconduct and begged her indulgence.'

'Indeed.' Nehemiah did not sound convinced. 'All this may be put to the proof later. At present all that is necessary is for you to sign your confession.'

'I will sign to say that I am a priest. Nothing more.'

'Very well.' Nehemiah sat down and scribbled a swift statement, then pushed it towards Dominic. He sighed slightly as Dominic signed. Lucy and Martha, though they kept faith with silence, felt their heart's blood drain as he signed away his life.

Then there was a dull sound as Martha slumped fainting to the floor. Nehemiah regarded her relaxed body with sadness and inappropriate lust. He wished he might now let her go. He had no desire to see her suffer – but because her suffering was for the priest, he must question her until he had the truth.

He waited until they had sent for wine and revived her. Then when, pale, she sat once more upon her chair and looked anywhere in the room but at him, he began to worry at the shameful matter that most deeply concerned him. 'Mistress Knyvett, you have also been accused. How do you speak?'

Her voice came to him, silvered, across a great gulf of her own construction. 'If you say that I am a witch, I say that I am not. If

327

you say that I have been this man's mistress, or any man's, I say that you lie. I am chaste.'

'Then you will stand trial upon these matters,' he said quietly, 'for you have many accusers and they must be satisfied.'

'But you have no need!' Dominic cried furiously. 'It is not her life you seek, but mine!'

'On the contrary,' said Nehemiah fiercely, 'I do seek her life – the life of her very soul – in her salvation by Christ the Lord. Unless we can be sure whether she is guilty or innocent, how may we proceed to help her?'

'She has sworn.'

'Others have been forsworn at such times. And the law demands her trial if she will not confess.' He sighed, discovering in himself an inordinate weariness. 'And now, Father Lacey, you must prepare yourself to leave with us. You may bring with you such of your belongings as you may think necessary.'

Tibbett, his face creased into folds of compassion, went to perform this small office for the courageous boy he had learned both to love and to admire, papist or not.

'It is my order that no occupant of Heron is to leave the immediate grounds until further notice,' Nehemiah told them finally.

'Where will you take them?' Lucy asked unsteadily, ignoring this.

'To my own house, where they will be safe from what rough justice certain of the populace might see fit to attempt.'

'And may we visit them?' This time she begged.

'I regret – no.'

'But—'

'That is final.' He allowed her one last embrace however and Lucy was vanquished at last by terrible emotions as she held close first Martha, then Dominic, and told them that she loved them.

'Be brave. Hold up your head, little cousin; it is the best thing you can do for us,' whispered Dominic as he hugged her with deep affection. 'I think he will free Martha in the end,' he added quickly, 'so do not despair of her.'

Oh but *you*, what will they do to you, she longed to cry, but would not distress him further. So she nodded and smiled and kissed his cheek, then stood back to let them take him. 'Will I ever see them again,' she wondered blindly as they left.

As if she had spoken aloud, Martha turned on the threshold. 'We shall meet very soon,' she said. There was certainty but no comfort in her voice.

When they had gone Lucy sat for a long time in the empty room. At last she marshalled her thoughts enough to pray, kneeling before the great table as though it were God's altar and putting all her heart and all she knew of goodness into her pleading. Then, having done the only thing there was for her to do, she began to think of how she was to describe these terrible events to the rest of her family and household.

It was Tibbett who helped her in this, appearing quietly when the last hoofbeat had died away. 'If you will speak to your lady mother and Lady Grey, I will find Master Kit and Master Humphrey. Then I will tell the servants what has taken place. I think you will find Lady Grey is with her Ladyship at the moment.'

In the end it was easier than she had expected. The news brought her mother further back to herself than any of their strenuous efforts had done, though to ask her to face such horror seemed near to cruelty. Valora, after once gasping 'Dear God, no!' had instantly become her sterling self and had promised to write at once to Tom. Coping with the children was the saddest part; Julia did not understand what had happened and kept asking for her Uncle Nick, and the boys were once again transformed into small devils, howling all the time that they would *not* stay within bounds and they *would* go and set fire to Nehemiah's house and rescue Dominic and then hold Heron at siege point if necessary. In the end Mary, her own heart riven, tired of their tempest and ordered Tibbett to beat them. He did so, not hard, but firmly enough to master their passion. Without it they became as dumb and sorrowful as Dominic's bewildered, pining dogs.

It was two weeks before they heard any more, and then the news confirmed their worst fears. Dominic was to be hanged and his body burned in the market-place. Nehemiah sent them word by one of his Friday henchmen that he had been successful in a plea for mercy; the other judge on the magisterial bench, the stern Puritan who had taken Sir George's place, had been all for the full penalty due to the law; by Nehemiah's magnanimous grace Dominic would not be drawn and quartered.

They had expected his sentence, but such expectation always leaves room, unkindly, for hope. It took a little time for them to accept the coming death and to begin to hold up their heads for Dominic.

'We must all be present on the day,' Lucy decreed with grim pride. She understood now the sombre respect and loyal love that had inspired her father to take them all to see the Earl of Strafford die.

They decided that Mary, alone, should stay at home with the younger children, knowing that the scene would be too great a strain upon her waking spirit, so hard upon the first bereavement. She demurred and said that she wished to go, but Valora told her firmly that her presence would only distract them from the proper object of their care and concentration, and sensing that this would be true, she agreed to remain at home.

Julia, of course, at eight, was too young for such sights, but there was no gainsaying the twins and no one attempted to dissuade them. They were quite certain that Dominic would wish to see them.

It was Kit and Humpty, in fact, who set an example to Lucy and Valora in getting themselves up in their very best clothes for the occasion. No sad black for Dominic who had laughed with them and joined in their games and told them countless tales of spirit and adventure. They wore scarlet and green, with white plumes in their hats and silk gloves and bright silver buckles. Applauding and catching their mood, Lucy followed suit in her apricot gown and a flaming orange-tawny cloak, while Valora was regal in violet.

There was a brief tussle over the garnets, terminated by Lucy's snatching them and locking them in her strong-box. 'I don't have to say it, do I?' she asked tersely. Valora shook her head, ashamed. She did not have to say it.

When they rode through the busy village in their flaunting colours, with their heads disposed at arrogant angles and bells jingling on their bridles and Tibbett in his Sunday best riding rearguard on his huge horse that no one had dared to take from him, the crowd watched them in slack-jawed amazement. There were sneers of 'Cavaliers!' from those strangers who had come in from the countryside to see a priest burn, but the men and women who had known the Herons from their infancy kept quiet for the most part. There were even civil greetings from many of those who had been at Sir George's funeral.

'I guess they do think he be agoin' to be wedded, not swung,' remarked Sam Strangeways to his new and unsatisfactory brother sawyer, a good Puritan but a useless hand.

'So he be; to the devil,' was the sour reply.

'No, no. They do hang 'em so as to save their souls,' protested Sam.

'Why, how can that be?' grinned Nehemiah's acolyte. 'With him a soul-destroyed papist and a priest?'

'I cannot tell,' confessed Sam, scratching his head. But he knew it to be God's truth, all the same.

The market-place, behind Lowgate, was teeming with folk as though it were Michaelmas. There had not been an execution in those parts for over three years, and nothing so fancy as a priest for much longer.

There was a stone platform abutting on the back of the Market Hall, that haven of rainy days and perishable produce. They had raised the gibbet upon this and men were piling brushwood and logs about its base as Lucy led her small party towards it. At the sight of the white, set face above her April finery and Valora stalking, rigid with pride, beside her, people instinctively made way for them, though their wake rumbled with comment and complaint.

They reached the front and waited, the twins and Tibbett keeping their space well clear, while the half acre filled up with women and children and wounded men, old men and boys, farm labourers, and Nehemiah's soldiers. Lucy could not look at the gibbet but Valora glared at it as if her basilisk gaze might reduce its every splinter to dust. The twins, according to a previous plan, were at this time subjected to a serious discourse from Tibbett upon the inadvisability of any foolish behaviour during the coming ordeal. They watched him flex his knuckles into fists like boulders and were convinced.

'Look,' said Lucy on a rising note. 'They are bringing Dominic.'

There was a ragged outcry among the crowd as a score of infantrymen marched into the square with Dominic in their midst. Though this was a civil matter, Nehemiah, as Justice of the Peace, had wished to give the occasion due ceremony. More of his men mingled with the crowd to ensure a proper show of distaste for Catholicism and respect for the law.

Dominic in his black suit appeared slight between two guards chosen for their imposing height. He climbed onto the platform and stood looking about at the shouting crowd, showing no sign of fear. His hands were not bound and his arms hung loosely relaxed at his sides. He wore black gauntlets, with a froth of lace, not so much as a last affectation as to conceal the fact that there were no longer any nails upon most of his fingers.

Lucy called his name and he saw her at once, his face breaking into a delighted smile. Then it clouded. 'Lucy! How I have longed to see you all! But you should not have come here, any of you.'

The others waved at him mightily. 'It is not fitting—' He seemed distressed.

'Did you think your friends would desert you?' Valora's contralto rang out. 'You surely know us better than that.'

So Dominic smiled again and spread out his arms, signifying both impotence and acceptance. 'Thank you,' he said. 'Thanks be to God for giving you the strength.'

At this Lucy was aware of ugly sounds directed at them by their neighbours, though no one molested them. Then there was a small scuffle to the side of the platform and they saw the crowd give way again as Martha was led towards it. Instant apprehension flooded them all.

'Please God they do not intend – Tibbett, thrust through to those guards and ask them why she is here. Oh, hurry!' cried Lucy. Tibbett moved through the mass with the inevitable impetus of a bullock-cart and was back before they had time for more than one fervent prayer.

'She is here to watch only,' he told them quickly. 'They want to frighten her, I think, and thus induce her to confess.'

It was a cold morning but Lucy realized she had been sweating. Now she felt weak with relief. Of course Nehemiah would not let Martha be put to death; but his was not the only power here today. There was Sir Solomon Shepherd, JP, a Gloucester Puritan known for his enmity to witchcraft. And perhaps Martha's worst enemies were the people among whom Lucy had been born and bred, many of them poor, ignorant and credulous enough to believe that the devil walked abroad in whatever guise he chose. Already several of them had made the sign of the horns at Martha as the soldiers had helped her onto the platform.

She wore her grey dress and her silver fall of hair hung loose to her waist. Ignoring hoarse cries of 'Witch!' and 'Priest's doxy!' she went straight to Dominic and made as if to take his hands. Shaking his head, he threw up his arms and motioned her away, his raw fingers throbbing unmercifully.

'Don't be foolish, Martha. Would you have them burn two of us today?' he asked her gently. 'Now stand back a little, where I can see you. We may talk very well a few yards apart.' He gave her a little push with his palm and she obeyed him unwillingly.

The soldiers who stood on both sides of the platform parted their ranks to the left, and the thin, hollow-faced figure of Sir Solomon Shepherd came forward, accompanied by Nehemiah and various other Puritan worthies. They ranged themselves behind the gibbet, well back from the pyre, and Martha moved forward so as not to be near them. Nehemiah stepped to the fore of the stone stage and held up his hand to silence the twang and jangle before him.

'Good people,' he began commandingly. 'We are gathered here to see justice carried out in God's holy name. Dominic Lacey is a member of that misguided family which heretofore held your lives and livelihoods in check – a family who live *their* lives so far from God's grace as to give shield and shelter to His enemies. I have no need to remind you of their championship of that stubborn misbeliever, Joseph Stratton. And you are fully aware of their opinions concerning the great issue of our time – the struggle for the mind and heart of our good King Charles, may God preserve him—' He hesitated and there was a half-hearted cry of 'God save His Majesty!' Impassive, Nehemiah continued. 'However, the head of this sad house against whom God hath witnessed now lies in his grave, and it is to hoped that his survivors many soon take better counsel.'

Lucy and her brothers gritted their teeth and showed no reaction.

'And yet, my friends, it would be less than Christian charity if we were to arraign this man simply on the grounds that he is a Heron –' This time the hiatus gained him smiles and cries of 'Why not?' – 'although in other parishes it *has* been known for a cavalier to be strung up just for being what he is, we have a kinder justice here.'

He really believes that, Lucy thought, listening to the sincere and dogged tones.

'Dominic Lacey is to lose his life today, not because he is a Royalist, but because he is that anathema to the Lord, a Roman Catholic priest and a member of that evil network of spies and blasphemers known to us as the Jesuits.'

The crowd fulminated, their anger rising like yeast. Most of them had not known this. Now several cried out 'Burn the priest! Burn him alive!'

Nehemiah turned to face Dominic who had stood looking imperturbably into the crowd throughout the shower of insults, smiling once at Lucy when her father was mentioned. He met the grimly portentous gaze without fear.

'Dominic Lacey, you have confessed that you are an ordained priest of the forbidden Roman faith and a member of the Society of Jesus. You have been sentenced to the penalty of death by hanging, your body afterward to be consigned to the flames. We carry out that sentence in the name of God whom you have betrayed, in the hope that He will see fit to put aside even so heinous a sin as yours and grant to you the exquisite grace of His mercy.'

He stopped and the crowd obediently muttered 'Amen!'

'Master Lacey, before the sentence of the court is executed, do you have any last request to make or is there anything you wish to say to anyone here present?

'There is,' said Dominic. He spoke quietly, but he was heard. A man had the right to his last words. 'I have little to leave behind me in this world,' he began, smiling, 'but what little I have I leave to the members of that family whose name you have been so exercised to dishonour.' There was an implosion among the crowd, its mood hard to define. 'Sir George Heron, my good-cousin, is dead and cannot speak for himself, but you have heard him speak often enough and know what language he would employ to repulse the attack of so mean an adversary.'

'Aye – good strong curses, no doubt of it!' cried a wit and though Lucy could hardly credit the sudden swing of their emotions, they laughed with genuine affection.

'It was so indeed,' Dominic smiled with them. 'But Sir George's strong words clothed stronger principles, and none of you knew him for anything other than a man of honour – '

' – He wanted more than his honour; that were half the trouble!' the wit interrupted and there were murmurings about fences and hedges.

'He took no land to which he could not prove a legal claim,' protested Dominic swiftly. 'And besides, your quarrels in that respect are gone with the fences. I knew him as a brave man and a kind one, and his gracious lady as the same. And if his children alone are here today to defend his name from your mischievous tongue, Nehemiah Owerby – well, they have already proved themselves rarely capable of doing so!'

This sly reference to the well-publicized sufferings of Sam Hudson and his colleague made his listeners roar delightedly and the man behind Humpty dug him approvingly in the ribs. Both twins went scarlet with pleasure.

'There is another whom I would mention,' Dominic continued, taking advantage of their good humour, 'and I beg you all to heed my words most carefully. There are some amongst you, not the wisest nor the best, though certainly those with the longest tongues, who, not satisfied with the despatch of a priest, look forward to burning a witch in this parish.'

All eyes swivelled to Martha who remained as still and

outwardly composed as though she stood in her own living room.

'Martha Knyvett came amongst you when she was little more than a child—'

'Aye – a witch's child!' came sharply from the back.

'You sin mortally if you say so, for you cannot know,' replied Dominic with authority, and his assurance was somehow as great to them as Nehemiah's had been. 'All that you know of Martha is that she has great gifts of healing and a deep knowledge of herbs and their uses, beyond the ordinary. She has used these gifts without stint in your service, and has taken small payment over the years.'

This shamed them. It was true. Martha would give away her own food or fuel to anyone in want.

'You have been glad to know her in your troubles, and to make use of her. You have always known her for a sweet-natured woman who prefers to keep close to her own home. And now you turn like mangy curs and say she is a witch! Martha, who never sought harm to any member of God's creation, who sought to bind none to her, even with cords of kindness. Think shame to yourselves for such falseness and weakness! Ask yourselves, each one, who it was who said to you that she is a witch. Was it one whom you would trust with the valuable pearl of your *own* reputation? Or was it one whom fortune spites, who ever turns his tongue against his neighbour? Or perhaps a man who is in another man's pay, so that he owes him for bread, board and opinion? Think very deeply about this, for it is a terrible thing to put a fellow creature's life in danger – and God himself will not forgive you if you err in your judgement of this gentle and innocent woman.'

His tone as he finished was low and humble. Silence lingered after his words and people would not look at each other, but bowed their heads and questioned their inner hearts.

But not all of them. 'Pay no mind to him; she is his whore!' a military voice called strongly. 'Of course he will speak up for her!'

'Enough of this! Be silent, I charge you all!' Nehemiah strode forward, his eyes striking sparks where they rested. Singling out the trooper who had shouted he threw him a glance that demoted him to the lowest camp servant. 'You *shall* hear this man,' he said harshly.

He owed the priest this, at least. For in Dominic, Nehemiah had been forced to admit defeat. He had taken no pleasure in his torture, but it had been done and it had gained him nothing. He had even threatened the same for Martha, but Dominic had shrugged and said it was better they should flay her alive than that he should call her a witch. He fought with the same stubborn strength as Nehemiah's own, and in the end the Puritan was conquered by his own love for Martha, as the priest had known he must be. They had come to understand each other very closely in the past few days.

Now Dominic directed a slight bow of thanks to his captor. 'I think Mr Owerby knows the voice of persecution when he hears it,' he said softly. 'And I know that no good man or woman among you will heed such mischief. I am about to die before your eyes. I take good care what I say, knowing that I am heard by the God I am so soon to meet. Mistress Knyvett is innocent of all the charges against her. This I swear.'

He paused to let this sink in, and then spoke straight to the group about Lucy, his voice filled with tenderness. 'It is time for me to say farewell to you all. You know that I have loved each one of you, and have taken great joy in our kinship. I carry that joy with me to heaven. Keep it also in your own hearts, and keep my memory there until we meet. And, sweet cousins, never weep for me, but only envy my great fortune – that I may die for my Lord and for His blessed faith.'

His merry voice might have described an invitation to a ball. Lucy could not bear its certainty. It was all so wrong, so desperately wrong. Pushing Valora aside, she elbowed her way to the steps and ran up onto the platform. She hardly felt Dominic's protesting hand on her arm as she turned and began passionately to address the crowd.

'You cannot let them do this,' she raged. 'It is dragging justice back to the days of barbarism. Dominic has taken no man's life or property. He has done no one any form of ill. He has only brought comfort to those who freely sought it of him. How does this harm you – or you – or *you*, Nehemiah, or you, Sir Solomon?' She pointed an accusing finger at the cadaverous-faced baronet. 'Will you let this evil war that no one wanted turn you into monsters who consume your own kind?'

Sir Solomon, startled, coughed then frowned intently, at a loss, while Nehemiah made his answer for him. 'All that need concern us, Mistress Heron, is that his actions were against the law. You will please to step down and not to interfere further.'

Her thoughts whirled like snowflakes. 'But if he were to take an oath,' she pleaded, 'never to say the mass again. To stay quietly at Heron—'

'Lucy, my dear,' Dominic now took her arm and squeezed it softly. 'You know I could not agree to that, even if it were permissible. Mr Owerby is correct,' he added with deadly clarity. 'You can do no good by this.' He led her across to the steps.

'God bless you for your courage,' he whispered as she turned and flung her arms about him. 'But try to believe this – for it is true, I swear – this will be so much harder for you than it will be for me.'

She looked at him through her tears and tried to believe it, forcing a smile for his sake. It was so hard to let him go. Behind him she saw Martha's compassionate face and caught her little nod of encouragement. How was it that Martha could summon so much strength? She felt as if everyone was brave and doing what was fit and dignified except her. She separated from Dominic and stumbled back to her place beside Valora, red-faced and miserable, nudged by the murmurs of the crowd.

'You tried; we're proud of you,' whispered Humpty, hugging her shoulders.

It all happened very quickly after that. They brought Dominic to stand before the gibbet. He refused the blindfold and Nehemiah still did not order his hands tied. Then Lucy felt a movement beside her as Valora stepped forward, as serious as a celebrant in her requiem violet, and knelt in front of the crowd where he could see her.

They heard her low, beautiful voice, perfectly controlled, begin to recite the prayer first spoken by Ignatius Loyola, the young Spanish nobleman who had laid down his sword to take up the Word and had founded the army of God on earth, the Society of Jesus:

> *Take, Lord and receive all my liberty,*
> *My memory, my understanding*
> *And my entire will,*
> *All I have and possess.*
> *Thou hast given all to me.*
> *To thee, O Lord, I return it.*
> *All is thine.*
> *Dispose of it according to thy will.*
> *Give me thy love and thy grace*
> *For this is sufficient for me.*

Dominic, his own voice as calm and steady, said the words with her, a smile of sheer, sweet triumph reflecting light upon all of them as he looked on each face that was dear to him as though committing them to memory for a journey, then slowly ascended the mounting block with its thicket of brushwood.

It was a tearless alliance they kept with him now. Valora's voice did not falter as she continued to pray, nor did any of their eyes as he blessed them for the last time, then held up his hand for the hangman to do his work.

Tibbett stepped swiftly in front of Lucy while the derelict body played jerking traitor to the delivered soul. She turned her head into his chest and wept now for the pity and the cruelty of it, and for herself, too, because her life would be the lesser for it. Then, intrusively, as close at hand it seemed almost to echo inside her head, she heard Humpty say, without any emphasis other than that of complete concentration, 'Some day, when I am able for it, and the time is right, I shall kill Nehemiah.'

'And I shall help you,' said Kit swiftly. They had said it before, but before they had always sounded like angry children.

The fire was lit now. The wood had been well dried and the flames leaped up almost at once. They had bound the body to the spine of the gibbet. Soon it would begin to burn.

Valora came back to them, her vigil of prayer over. 'We should go now,' she said resolvedly. 'He has gone from this place. There is no reason for us to remain.' Her eyes were as dry as the kindling. Would she never weep?

'One thing first,' said Lucy quickly, wrenching her mind around. 'Please wait for me. There is something I want to ask Sir Solomon.'

Valora looked surprised. 'If it is Dominic's ashes, it is already—'

'No. It isn't that. I'll not be long.'

'Very well,' Valora called after her. 'We'll fetch the horses and wait for you in front of the market hall.'

Lucy found the magistrate toasting his toes at the fire and chatting as cosily with Nehemiah as though they were at a Guy Fawkes party. 'I wonder you do not think to roast chestnuts,' she said bitterly, unable to help herself.

'Ah Lucy – will you not go home?' asked Nehemiah, wearily forbearing. There were yellow circles of fatigue beneath his eyes.

'First I have a request for Sir Solomon,' she said sternly.

'Then make it, my dear young lady. I will serve you if I can.' Sir Solomon was not an unkind man. 'I was damnably sorry to hear about your father.' They had been acquainted once, before the war, holding each other in mutual respect.

'Thank you.' Lucy began to hope. Despite his austere reputation, she could see that there was a softer side to Sir Solly. 'It is the matter of Mistress Knyvett. She is a very dear friend of my mother. Lady Heron wonders if it might be possible, since we are kept as close as convicts by Mr Owerby's dispositions, for you to release her into our custody. She would be almost as much a prisoner with us as anywhere else, and we would go surety for her oath not to escape.' She looked over to where Martha now sat, as far away as though she were in another country, staring out across the flames. Her face was strangely at peace.

Sir Solly had coughed again and was now frowning. He fetched a draughty sigh and brought his fist down on his bony knee with a blow that seemed likely to have cracked it. 'Young mistress, I'd like to accommodate you, be sure. But a witch now; that is a terrible responsibility; more so to her friends. No, I can't allow it.'

'She is not a witch.'

'That is not proven, and until it is, *if* it is, we must keep Mistress Martha far closer than the hospitality of Heron. I'm sorry, my dear. You'll bear me out, Nehemiah?'

'Yes, indeed,' said Nehemiah coldly, giving no sign of the turmoil that had afflicted him during their exchange. If they had taken her from him, she might well have become lost to him forever. While he had her safe in his house, he could continue the daily visits he made to her. Morning and evening, without exception, he had gone to her to beg her, often on his knees – pride was of no importance to him here – to confess herself to him, so that he might offer her in return, her salvation, pardon and his own unbearable love.

'You won't reconsider?' he heard Lucy beg and longed to close her mouth with his fist.

But Sir Solly ruefully shook his head. 'She is no fit friend for Lady Heron, or for yourself,' he deplored. 'But I will remember that you spoke in her favour.'

'What will happen to her – if – if –' the words stuck in her throat.

'She would burn, and her soul be saved,' the magistrate said sombrely.

'She will not burn,' Nehemiah snapped. Lucy was somewhat reassured by the violence of his tone. But Sir Solly was looking at him in amazement. 'That is – I am already more than half convinced the woman is no witch,' Nehemiah said more temperately. 'This business of a priest in the district has caused a great deal of hysteria.' Sir Solly grunted and continued to reflect.

Lucy, seeing there was nothing she could do, went to take leave of Martha, who still gazed abstractedly out across the square. On hearing what her friend had tried to do, she gave her a quick hug of gratitude. 'You must not worry about me, Lucy. I shall be very well.'

'I think Nehemiah will save you. I pray he will.'

Martha frowned. 'It is Dominic who should have your prayers.'

'Oh Martha!' Lucy did not want to leave her, but, like her cousin before her, Martha took her firmly by the shoulders and gave her a firm shove, so that already she was walking away from the next horror of that bright and hideous convivial morning, as above the vigorous gossip to which the diminishing crowd now felt released, there coiled and spread across the sunshine the sweet sick stench of burning flesh.

The air that blew in through Martha's small barred windows carried the scent of the hills to her. She liked to sit and gaze out, thankful for the sights and sounds of the landscape she knew. Immediately behind the house stood the pinewoods. Their clean, astringent tang delighted her with its strength. She would watch for hours, dreaming, while small birds flew in and out of them, swooping and spiralling up into the clear sky above the frieze of brown and gold hills. She loved to listen to their optimistic chirping and would clap her hands loudly and severely when they were harried by the demonic colony of magpies who were the pines' chief tenants.

Her prison was a pretty room, furnished as though for a beloved daughter, perhaps, with blue and white flowered curtains and counterpane, a table upon which leaves and berries glowed, and a small writing desk piled with books and tracts, evidence of Nehemiah's hopes for her spiritual enlightenment. In fact it had been his mother's room; he had told her so one evening in the course of their long, all but one-sided conversations, and her heart had sunk, knowing why he had brought her here.

A guard stood outside the locked door, night and day, with instructions to inform her jailor if she wished for anything. Martha had never been so long idle in her life. Because she did not, at first, speculate very deeply upon her condition, feeling, fatalistically that this could do nothing to improve it, she had until today almost enjoyed the luxury of having her meals served to her and coals brought in for the small fireplace in the corner.

But this evening she had not eaten and could not have told you whether it was warm or chill. She had known, ever since that night when Nehemiah had interrupted the Westons' mass, what must eventually happen to Dominic. If this terrible gift of hers, this *seeing* into the fates of others, was part of the nature of witchcraft, why then she was a witch; but if this were so her witchery held no powers to prevent the dreadful suffering which came to its subjects, and indeed to herself. All she could do, sometimes, was to persuade a man to put his house in order, to leave his life as neat as when he had first received it.

She had not done this for Dominic; he would have known what she was at. She had confessed her gift to him soon after they had met, a forceful proof of how easily and how much she had learned to trust him. Their friendship had grown firm and strong, with a depth which had surprised them both. They had previously accepted that their lives, hers of necessity, his from choice, must be solitary. They had not expected the grace of a human relationship that, in the two years they had known each other, had become as committed, within its own delicate bounds, as that between man and wife. She had sorrowed over their recent separation, knowing that they had, probably, very little time left to them.

Because of her foreknowledge she had prepared herself as best she could for what would take place. She would have no need to do that office for Dominic; he had been prepared since he first came from France. Alone, then, she had filed her courage to a keen edge. She had held up her head in the market-place and had not yielded to the weakness of tears.

Characteristically, he had dedicated his last moments to her welfare, and had perhaps even saved her, who could tell? Even there, even then, they had made themselves comfortable with one another, and she had kept her vigil with him until only his ashes remained.

Why then, now that it was accomplished and that black book closed, was there this searing agony of mind or soul, this foul uncertainty that mocked at his victory and dragged her, powerless, toward the dark pit of despair? Why did she suddenly feel that there was no God?

The moon climbed up behind the pines. She thought how men had once worshipped that ghostly beauty with as deep a fervour and as harsh a cruelty as they offered now to Christ. Perhaps these ancient men had been right; perhaps the old gods still ruled, had never fled, and the gentle Galilean possessed no power to confound them.

She glared into the pale disc of the moon until it seemed as though she had left the casement and was floating towards it. It *drew* her towards it with a pure, cold, unhurried influence, towards itself, towards emptiness, towards infinity. There was no longer any pain or horror, only the unending void. Willingly, she let herself be drawn.

When Nehemiah found her, she was lying on the floor near the open window, chilled to the bone. He closed the casement and sharply ordered the guard to build up the fire. He hesitated before lifting Martha to lay her on the bed. To hold her body was an unspeakable pleasure to him. He trembled as her breast touched his own. Her beauty took his breath. He felt lightheaded. He called for wine to sober himself. He held her as long as he dared, his hands under her back and beneath her knees. Her head had fallen back and her long hair swept the floor. He longed to kiss the white arch of her neck. He thought of her breasts under her grey gown and there was an ache in his loins that almost made him cry out. She was as insubstantial as clouds, and so cold.

He put her gently on the bed and pulled the coverlet over her, tucking it close. It was goosedown; she would soon be warm. He saw that she had not touched the food they had sent her and gave orders for the soup to be heated again. He sat next to the bed and waited, poring over her face.

She did not appear to be asleep but rather in some deep realm below consciousness, farther removed. Her breathing was slow and regular and her colour, though pale, gave him no cause for alarm. He found that he could not look at her for very long at a time. It was like gazing into the heart of some bright light. He was reading a book of prayers, his lips moving over the words, when Martha opened her eyes and was in hell again.

Sensing the change, he turned to her. 'Martha. Do you feel better?'

'Yes.' The question was meaningless.

'That is good. Will you eat a little now?'

'No. I want nothing.'

'You will weaken yourself to no purpose if you do not eat.'

She made no reply.

'Very well.' He was silent then and she saw that he was praying, as he always did before he began his onslaught upon her. She supposed she would bear it. It all seemed far less important now.

'I have begged you every day to try to save yourself Martha,'

Nehemiah began, his grating voice as soft as he could make it. 'And today, God help you, you have seen the way that lies before you, should you too be sentenced.'

Martha turned her head to the window. Stars, she thought. I will choose one and let my mind fly to it. That one; you; with the faint blue aura as though the moon had passed too close to you.

'On this day, above all others, I exhort you with all my strength to think, to dwell upon how you are placed and what you must do.'

You are lovely, cool and pure in your blue gown, but you cannot shut out his voice. Weary, she relinquished the star. 'Nehemiah?'

'What is it?' He trembled. She rarely spoke his name.

'Do you think you might find it in you to be kind enough – on this day, of all others – to leave me in peace?'

The leaden whisper pulled down his hope. 'You think it unkindness? It is not. I only want to give you your life.'

'My life has less value to me as each day passes. I can only suppose that it has a greater one for you. It should not, for there is nothing in my life for you. Can you not, please, accept the truth of this and leave me to my judges?' She was very tired of arguing with him, but if she made no replies he only talked the more and she did not want to hear him speak of God, or of salvation, and most of all, not of love.

'You are a fool, Martha,' he said with unusual impatience. 'You know that I hold that life in my hands. If I speak for you at your trial, there are none who will condemn you.'

'Then speak for me, if you wish, and let them set me free. Or not. But do not continue your ceaseless attempt to make me buy my freedom with my body!'

Anger rose in him. 'That is *not* what I seek. You dishonour me in saying so.'

'Then why should you insist that we marry? What would you gain from such a contract, other than the use of my body?'

He hated to hear her speak like this. But he could not prevent the salacious images her words brought to his mind. The use of her body. He dwelled on it and prayed not to be mad. He called back righteous anger to banish his lust. 'It shames you to speak so lightly about the vessel God gave you. Have you already put that body to as light a use? *Have* you, Martha? Before God, I must know, and very soon, very soon now, for my patience is at an end. You *must* tell me!'

She caught the tremor in his voice and knew that he spoke the truth. Until today he had held himself in rigid control, grinding his endless question over and over as lifelessly and inevitably as a millwheel. Now that control was threatened.

She was so tired. So tired. If only he would let her sleep. 'I have told you the truth,' she sighed. 'But you wish to hear lies. Why? Why is it more necessary to you to hear me say that I am a witch and that I served Dominic upon a black altar, and served him also in his bed? Do these things secretly delight you, Nehemiah, is it that?' She sat up a little, and stared accusingly into his face. 'Do you wish to know me a whore so that you may use me as one without regret? While I am at your mercy here?'

Nehemiah gave a great gasp as though he were drowning. 'You don't know what you are saying. These are evil thoughts. Most foul. When you say such things I *know* you have not spoken the truth.' He stood over her and took her wrist in his hand, crushing it. 'Even if there is evil in you, God can make all clean. Tell me, Martha, *tell* me – did you lie with the priest?'

'You have hounded him to death. Is that not enough to satisfy you? Or will you do the same to me?'

He let go her wrist and sat down upon the bed. 'Your death would take away all my joy,' he said quietly.

'Do I bring you so much joy, then, while I live? Do you take so much pleasure in these hideous interviews?'

'Hideous? I am sorry you find them so. But you have the power to end the questioning at any time—'

'By giving you a lying answer! Oh God, is there *no* way to make this pig-headed man see reason? Nehemiah, *I am innocent.*' She put all her strength into her eyes, boring into his as though to force the truth through their lenses. 'You must let me go, or you commit a vile sin.'

'I cannot let you go.'

'Because I am bound by law to come to trial? Or because you don't wish to?'

'Both,' he admitted sadly. 'There must be a trial; there are many accusers – though none whom I cannot dismiss quickly enough in their examination. But if you go to trial before I am sure, what is to become of you?'

Martha cast an ironic glance towards heaven. 'I will burn, doubtless. I have long been wondering whether it might not be well enough to exchange a few minutes agony for interminable hours of – I have no word for it – of *this!*'

'Think again,' he said cruelly. 'It may *not* be a few minutes.

Only if the executioner is kind and causes enough smoke to choke you. The people will want to see burning flesh, and hear the screams of the evil-doer. He may wish to accommodate them. They may pay him to do so. I cannot prevent that.' He fought down her eyes with his next barb. 'Remember your mother.'

She plucked at the counterpane. 'What do you know of her?'

'I know that she was a long time dying. My father was at her burning.'

Martha pushed back the terror that flapped its wings about her. 'And you, who say you love me, would watch me burn?'

He could not keep up the pretence. Her fear melted him. He caught her in his arms and buried his face in her hair. 'No. No. I am sorry. You will go free, I give you my word.'

She kept very still. He had not touched her before, not since the night of the mass. She sought for something to distract him. 'Of what,' she asked, turning her head from him, 'am I accused, exactly? What deeds of witchcraft?'

He loosed her regretfully. 'There is first the black mass, of which several accuse you – on the occasion at your cottage, when I was later present and on two other—'

'But you know it was no devil-worship, only the Catholic mass for those poor troubled folk.'

'I believe that. But the Westons will not testify against themselves, and Sam Hudson's cousin Ezekiel will swear that there was a smell of incense and a dead cockerel in the room, its throat slit.'

'Indeed there was. It was Farmer Weston's payment for the syrup I had made to help his wife and daughter ease the cough.'

'And then there is your cat. It is said that he was your familiar and that, demon-like, he has deserted you now that you are in trouble.'

Martha laughed. 'Had he stayed, *he* would have had his throat slit by now. I took him to a place of safety, and can prove it.'

'It will prove nothing save that you are fond of the creature. It is unimportant. There is a girl in the village, quite young, who says you have bewitched her. She vomits pins, nails, thread and such things.'

'Who is it?'

'Jemima Dulce.'

'Her mother begged me for a spell or a potion to cause extreme sickness, unto death. I do not know for whom. I refused her.'

'There are others. Similar. And they also accuse you of eating the flesh of newborn children.'

She almost retched with nausea. 'From whom procured? From the butcher?'

'You took away a stillborn child from Goody Newman.'

'Aye, to the Vicar of St Mary's who gave it burial, poor mite. Ah, Nehemiah, you make me weary with all this. I shall answer them all when the time comes, and they will all be ashamed. They are only the people I have always known, frightened and confused by the war and the changes in their lives. They have built me up into a fearful monster between them, but when they come to the trial and see that I am only Martha, who has cured them and cared for them, they will come to themselves again, I am sure of it. They have already sent their scapegoat into the wilderness. They will find that this was sufficient.'

'There may be something in what you say,' Nehemiah agreed doubtfully, 'but don't underestimate their mood. One scapegoat is not enough, perhaps, to pay for a provider lost, a rent to find, food missing for small mouths. And afterwards, when you are free, how will they look upon you then? With my name to protect you, you would be safe. Otherwise, perhaps not.'

'My position will be the same as it ever was, within a year. I trust to my own good sense to make sure of that.'

'If only you would put your trust in God. And in me.'

'I do. I trust in you to see that justice is done and I am released.'

'I have told you. I can do it only if I know the truth.'

'Oh Jesu! Have we come full circle once more? As regular as the sun or moon are we set on our course.'

'So it seems. You may end it when you will.'

'Then for God's sake let us end it. Send for some physician whom you trust – and let him make a test of my virginity.'

His shock was palpable. She looked at his white, shamed face in dry amusement. 'Is it not a sensible notion? Never think I welcome it – but it would serve your purpose, would it not?' She wondered that she had not thought of it before. Or that he had not. Certainly the other judges would do so.

'A woman must be known only to her husband.' His lips twisted.

'It is somewhat different, I fancy.'

'It would not be fitting.'

No one should touch her, no one! She understood at once. His agony lost her the remnant of patience. 'Oh, then, discover the truth for yourself Nehemiah, and go to the devil! Let us at last have an end to all this.'

She threw back the covers and leaned, panting, on her elbows, challenging him, her skirts rumpled about her bare knees. 'It is such a simple thing – and then, all your doubts, gone forever.' She parted her legs a little, watching him suffer. Perhaps she was becoming mad; and if not yet, then his obsession soon must make her so. This must end it, whatever it cost her. She almost smiled at him. She would not let him know how much her private self was already damaged, even by her own suggestion. She wished that she had not made it, wanting now to deny the perverse instinct that had made her clutch blindly at the one thing that would end his torture and give blessed rest to herself at last.

He hardly knew what she meant him to do. He could only see, in the rumpled figure spreading its legs on the bed like a welcoming whore, a mockery of all his worship, his manhood, and his iron control. 'You go too far,' he muttered, his voice thick in his throat. He brooded over her, feeling his organ rise. She looked up, in fear now at the change in his face.

Her lips were dry. She moistened them with her tongue. Before she could close them his mouth was on hers, his own tongue seeking, hotly, wetly, the one that had invited him. His kissing bruised her mouth as though it were the forced entrance to that soul he had so coveted. Her senses swam under his pressure upon her, and her huge sense of his unslaked thirst for her.

'Too far,' he said again druggedly, lifting his head at last, but only so that he could look at her, look into her, draw her image into himself in this new, provocative guise, spread out across his bed like the justified spoils of war, the feast for which he had so hungered laid down for him to consume. He did not think of God, though Martha, seeing, too late, what she had done, whispered his name just once before Nehemiah tore her clothing from her and sank upon her with a great moan of anguish and pleasure. He wanted to go into her at once but forced himself to try to gentle her first. She was shaking all over and wept ceaselessly without a sound. He stroked her hair and her breasts and her flanks and kissed them all as though each was the holy grail. He parted her thighs further, murmuring 'Sweet Jesus' as he move his lips and hands about his newfound land. He had never known a woman to be so sweet. She did nothing to stop him, knowing that she had in truth gone too far. To make him force her would be a fouler pollution than the one which was taking place.

When he could wait no longer he thrust into her with a great cry of triumph spearheaded with months of wanting and praying.

He hurt her but she made no sound. She tried not to think, not to feel, staring across at the window where the unmoved stars still hung. The bright one, the one she had picked out, had gone. It must have been a planet, she thought, or perhaps it too had fallen.

When Nehemiah moved carefully away from her she was aware first of a tremendous relief that it was over and then of a fierce need to wash herself. She lay and looked at him as he put his clothes to rights, making no attempt to reach for hers.

'Am I innocent of the charge?' she asked. Her eyes were slitted and unreadable as he turned back to her, his face transfigured by a joy that was more terrible to her than had been his lust.

'You are innocent,' he said tenderly. He bent over her again and she pulled back. She need not have feared; it was only to kiss her brow. He bent to retrieve the coverlet, then threw it over her, arranging it gently beneath her arms. He made an ineffectual attempt to tidy her dishevelled hair. 'You are innocent. You are most beautiful – and you are my wife.'

Valora Grey had been forced to leave Heron much against her will, by the news that Parliament were now about to sequester her manor of Spindlesham. If she wished to prevent the wholesale rapine invited by her absence, she had to move swiftly. This she did, speeded by Lucy's assurance that she could now do splendidly without her, though she must return as soon as she could.

Now that she had gone, Lucy felt lonely. Her mother, who had recovered a certain amount, had left her chamber and gone out into the garden the day before yesterday, and except to eat and sleep had not come out of it. Lucy supposed this to be a good sign, though Mary still spoke very little and avoided company when she could.

Under these circumstances, Lucy found herself growing closer to her young brothers. They were growing up very quickly. Not that there was any diminution of their mischief; indeed Lucy thought she could not have sustained her own clear-minded control of affairs without the sudden, healing sparkle of their humour that took her sadness by surprise; but their voices had broken and they grew tall, taller than Lucy already. There was also a new willingness in them to wait, to consider, even to put a rein on their tempers. When they had sworn, in the market-place, that one day they would kill Nehemiah, Lucy had put it to the back of her mind, safe from any immediate cause for concern, that one day they would try. So she was thankful that they had gone off to race about with the new colt, leaving her to attend to some paperwork in the office, when, about three weeks after she had last seen him, Nehemiah was announced with odium by Tibbett.

'Oh no. I *can't*. How can I speak to him? What does he want, Tibbett?'

'He would not say, Mistress Lucy, except that it is important. He asked for my lady, but I told him that would not do.'

'Thank you. Yes. Well then, I will see him, but stay with us, please.'

'I should not think of doing otherwise,' said the giant darkly.

Nehemiah, when he came in, was so changed that Lucy forgot to be afraid of him, or even sickened by him. His clothes were dusty and looked as though they had not been changed for a fortnight. His abundant dark hair lay lifeless on his shoulders, unwashed and uncared-for, while the eyes that could compel a crowd with their glittering sheen of command and sheer good health were dull and opaque, and filled with something very like despair.

'What is wrong?' asked Lucy. She did not invite him to sit.

He did not answer immediately. His gaze was fixed on the small chair that stood before the table. It was the one in which Martha had sat on the day he had made his dual arrest.

'Mr Owerby,' Lucy insisted, 'what brings you here? Please state your business and be gone. You cannot imagine you are welcome. Indeed, it surprises me that you have the indelicacy to come here.'

Nehemiah dragged his lack-lustre gaze from the chair and transferred it to Lucy. 'Yes. I offer my apologies. Were it not that the business is imperative –' His voice died. He did not really seem to be interested in what he was saying. The word 'imperative' might just as well have been its opposite. She had never seen him like this, so wan and sallow and lacking in the virile energy that characterized him. What could have happened? She waited.

'I have bad news for you,' he said dully.

She was taken aback. Sweet Virgin in heaven, what more could there be?

He nodded, as if in accordance. 'It is the Committee for Sequestrations. They require larger accommodation for their headquarters. They wish to use Heron.'

She did not fully understand him. 'But they have already given their orders for Heron—'

He sighed vaguely. 'The family is to evacuate the house by the end of the month of January.'

She had to believe it. She tried not to rage aloud. Christmas, uncelebrated, was just behind them. That gave them a little over four weeks. They *could* not mean it. They *must* not. 'I wish to appeal to the Committee.' Her voice was hysterically high.

'It would be of no use.'

'The fiend-gotten bastards!' came from Tibbett, enraged beyond proper silence. 'Have they not done enough here?'

'I am sorry. I would have prevented it, but it is not in my governance. It is a county decision. If there is anything I can do – your goods are not forfeit – If there is carrying to be arranged—'

'But where are we to go?' asked Lucy in bewilderment, trying to accept that there was no longer ground beneath her feet. 'There is no house fit for us in the village. Do you plan to set us on the road with a hand cart, like a mess of peasants? What have we done, a small parcel of women and children, to be turned out of our home and have our land stolen from us? How have we harmed the blasted Parliament?'

'I don't think . . . I hadn't known—' Nehemiah gave up.

Lucy began to think, despite the shock. It was, in fact, far less of a shock than it should have been, for she was quite unable to imagine, for a single second, any life that did not take place with Heron as its centre. There was some instinct which protected her from that, even at the expense of reality. It would be sorted out. Of course it would, in time. Tom must come back and do something.

Meanwhile, there should be some contingency plan. They could go to the Strattons; they would be very welcome there. Only poor Susannah had barely enough to feed her own household. No, they had better try to get to Jane at Oxford, though goodness knows . . .

'What about the rents? Are they to be taken from us?' She did not know what she would do if they were to be penniless. The Committee left them little enough, it was true, but they could manage on it if they were careful.

'No. The Committee wish to see Sir George – I beg your pardon – Sir Thomas, as soon as may be possible. I believe they will come to some acceptable arrangement. There is no wish to see you starve. And Heron will be well looked after,' he added strangely, almost as though he cared.

'What is that to us, if it is taken from us?' said Lucy bitterly. She had by now grown accustomed to the terrifying sense of impotence that accompanied every event in their lives during these apocalyptic days. In the face of this further insult to their family and their common humanity, there was nothing they could do for the moment except to obey. She understood that even now. But the twins, she thought tiredly, would not understand. She foresaw the things they would do; the pistols at the windows; the swords and the carbine at the door. She wondered if she could summon the effort it would take to dissuade them.

Perhaps because it was just too much, too great a setback for her overburdened mind to consider until she was alone, she found her interest flickering even as Nehemiah's had appeared to be. Out of nowhere the question came to her. 'What about Martha? I had meant to ask you.'

To her astonishment Nehemiah first flushed crimson and then there were undeniable tears glossing his muddy eyes. He swallowed and tried to speak.

'I do not – I fear for her,' he got out. 'Matters are not turning out as – I had hoped.'

'What has happened? Tell me, man!' Tibbett, too, looked as if he might shake him.

'Sir Solomon is convinced of her guilt. He has spoken to most of the witnesses. He is perhaps a more simple man than I thought. He wishes her to confess or die.'

'But she has had no trial.'

'There will be a trial, but—'

'Then you will speak for her, won't you? *Won't you?*'

He hung his head. 'I cannot. They will not allow it – or if they do allow it, my words will be discounted.' He looked at her, a supplicant, from out of his depths, and uncomfortably, against every instinct in her history, Lucy began to pity him.

'Why is this?' she asked steadily.

'Because they say that Martha,' he paused upon the name as though it were already only a sweet memory, 'that she has bewitched me, that I am her victim and cannot, therefore, be her judge. You see, my affections towards her – are better known than I had thought – and apparently certain of my own men have harboured this foul suspicion for some time. I can do nothing, nothing . . .' he dropped his head into his hands. He was shaking.

'How can you bear it and *live?*' Lucy whispered. She was scoured by cruelty. 'It is you who have brought her to this. You would not leave her alone when she begged you. Is this the nature of your love? *You* have destroyed her, no one else.'

She watched the words fly like arrows and strike home. It gave her no satisfaction. Behind, Tibbett was muttering prayers. Nehemiah hung awkwardly before the table. There was nothing further to say. He took the Committee's order from his pocket and put it on the table, then left them as quickly as he could.

'How can you bear it and live?' Lucy's voice repeated as he spurred over the hill and down the driveway. He would bear it because he must, he thought dreadfully, because he knew – oh yes, he knew why it had happened. It was God's appalling punishment for his sin in taking her virginity. Instead of joyfully making her his wife he must now watch her die. He was as convinced of this as was Sir Solly that Martha was a true witch. The knowledge had broken him. He had not gone near Martha since that night when he had thought he might die from the happiness he had known with her. It was upon the next morning that Sir Solomon had told him. He had not known that she had waited in shame and in fear for his coming, and then, when he did not come, in far deeper fear.

When he had gone Lucy still sat at the table, lost in thought. Her face was buried in her arms. Tibbett touched her shoulder. 'Don't weep, Miss Lucy. It does no good to weep.'

She raised dry eyes to his distress. 'I think I have done with weeping. Somehow, Tibbett, we are going to find our way through all of this. There will be a way; there always is for those who are strong enough to survive and I am going to find it. And Martha must be with us too. We must find a way to save Martha. Do you think you can discover where she is? I imagine she is no longer in Nehemiah's house.'

Tibbett, whose large frame was a battleground for pity and pride in his young surrogate mistress, did his best to match her for purpose. 'I can indeed,' he said firmly, and then, with an heraldic quaintness, '*Nil desperandum*, that's what I say.' A pistol in his belt, he stamped off to make his enquiries among Nehemiah's idle infantry. No one had as yet attempted to keep Tibbett within the bounds of Heron's massive stone walls.

Lucy, meanwhile, put off the revelation of the worst to her mother and brothers until she should also have something positive to offer. She spent the next hour writing two very succinct and desperate letters. One was to Tom, commanding him to come home and do what he could, if anything, to prevent his heritage from being given away over their heads. The other was to Will Staunton, who had offered help. Well, now she needed it, and called on it with all her powers of persuasion. He had influence with Pym, with Vane, with the Earl of Warwick; let him use it, then, in Heron's cause, and let them find the thrice-accursed County Committee another home.

When she had finished writing, she was empty of all emotion, having spent a great deal of it upon the paper. She had just enough energy left to write one more letter, to her sister Jane, to tell her that if the worst did happen despite all her efforts, she was to make room in her tiny house for up to a dozen new incumbents.

To send the letters meant the possible loss of three horses and three good men, but they had ridden post before and come to no harm. She must pray that they could do it again.

If she delayed Jane's courier until tomorrow, she would have time tonight to write to Cathal. She had no idea, by now, whether or not he was receiving the letters whose composition brought her such comfort at the end of her busy, bewildering days, but she put her trust in the eternal victory of legend over life and hoped that he did. She wore his ring around her neck and that last hour of the day would always be his, until he came to claim the others for himself.

'It seems,' she told him, her eyes itching with tiredness as she scribbled by the light of her single candle, with Julia's faint snores for company, 'that the shadow on the dial has stopped at the nadir of our existence and will shift no more until the sun itself be altered, for it is sick unto death and can no longer make the motions of our poor fate.' Then, less poetically, 'I miss you, oh I miss you—'

Whether or not the sun was sick, to satisfy Lucy's tragical-poetical fancy, the Quickenberry tree, with or without its aid, was thriving on its diet of diamonds. It was ten feet high now and a lovely spreading shape, leaning a little over the water to admire itself in the smooth surface. Its branches showed their flexible strength now, flaunting the proud rags of autumn riches, dry gold, blood-red and dull purple. Soon it would be bare. Lucy had got into the habit of sitting beside it in the early evening as the light faded. Her mother, strangely, had not gone near it since her return to the garden. Once she had given it so much care and affection, talking to it as though it were one of the wiser members of the family. Now Lucy took her place, grumbling at it for half an hour each day, bringing it all the worries with which she would not burden those she loved.

'I shall have to disturb you shortly, I'm afraid,' she told it a few days after Nehemiah's visit. 'We shall need Mother's jewels when

– if – we have to leave Heron. Though I must confess I can hardly get it into my head that we may really have to go. I think none of us are capable of believing it. Herons *are* Heron, and that is all.

'And yet, I know I must try to accept it, so that I can begin somehow to build again on what we will still have – each other and the King's favour. All our energies must be aimed at getting *back* to Heron. The war can't last forever. The Parliament say we are losing, but that can't last either. We shall win through and the King will give us back all that we have lost. *That* is what we have to believe, if we must go.

'But oh, the number of things I wish I could be sure of before we leave – they say they will keep our steward and that the estate will be run in much the same way as it is now – but they are no part of this land and cannot have the sense of it that we have.

'And then there is the question of whom to take with us to Oxford. Jane can't be expected to house many of us, and even when we take lodgings of our own, they mustn't be too expensive. It all depends how Tom will be situated. If only he were at home more. Who, then? We must have Tibbett, of course, and Margery. I wish Dick Stable had not gone with Tom; he was so reliable. Mother should have her maid, and we must get a governor for Julia and Edward. It was so odd of Davies to run off like that—'

'My dear Lucy, are you gone mad at last, or are you in commune with unseen spirits?'

Lucy jumped. Then she rose and held out her arms. 'Oh Will, you can't *imagine* how glad I am to see you.'

'So it seems. Most pleasant. I came as soon as I could after I had your letter. And only just in time, apparently, since I find you talking to trees.'

'Only this one. Mother does it too. Will, thank you. I am at my wit's end.'

'And you hope I may roll them all up into a nice neat ball again?'

'If only you might. I hope you don't mind my sending to you. I could think of no one else.'

'You put it charmingly.' He bowed, with his remembered grin.

'How else shall I put it?' she asked, her spirits rising to his gentle teasing as she would not have thought possible ten minutes ago. 'You are our only friend among the enemy,' she said simply. 'The only one who might have the power to change their minds.'

'You credit me with altogether too great an influence.' Her face fell.

He had not come all this way to torment her. He said quickly,

'But my relatives, as you know, move in more exalted spheres.' Her heart raced. She waited.

'Warwick has promised that Heron will not go to the County Committee. You may stay in your home.'

She felt her knees wobbling. 'Will! How did you do it?'

'On the usual exercise of manly charm and modest address. My aunt, the Countess, has a weakness for me.'

She found herself laughing then, laughing at such a wild pitch that her lungs hurt. 'Is there any woman alive who hasn't?' She coughed between gusts that rode up and down the scales.

When it became obvious that she was not able to stop, Will stepped forward and thoughtfully slapped her face. 'I'm sorry,' he said as she burst into equally wild and noisy tears, 'but I'm sure you'll find *that*'s what you really want to do. Oh my God, don't just stand there, streaming like Niobe. At least make yourself comfortable while you do it.' He put his arms round her and pulled her head into the curve of his shoulder. He gave her his handkerchief. 'Here. I've got one this time.' He stroked her hair in a comforting, rhythmic sort of way. 'I seem to have done this before,' he said abstractedly.

He was not thinking at all about the words he said, because he found that some quite different ones were racing, shouting, about his brain, telling him something he didn't particularly want to know. You love her, they said, you are in love with Lucy Heron. She has taken your whole hitherto impregnable heart and has worried her ignorant way into your very soul. 'O envious moon,' he muttered. But not yet. This is quite obviously *not* the time for such interesting revelations.

His hand had not interrupted its regular sweeps of her soft hair, lying golden and refulgent upon his sleeve. Her sobbing was quieter, but not much diminished in strength. 'How long, precisely, do you propose to keep this up?' he asked politely. 'Because if it's much longer, I suggest we sit down. I've ridden a deuced long way today and I'm tired.'

It stopped her at once. The sobs shuddered to a breathy halt and she raised a pink-tinged nose to him and snuffled apologies. 'And I told Tibbett I'd done with weeping. Humiliating to find I'm still such a cry-baby.'

'Pray don't apologize; I'm sure this isn't the last time either.' She blew her nose on his handkerchief. 'Do you mind if we go inside. I'm not sure I share your fancy for talking to trees in the December cold.' She laid her hand on his arm as they walked. He found, to his enormous self-ridicule, that the light touch made him weak with desire and warmth and a fierce protectiveness.

'Now that we have tidied Heron nicely away into Uncle Warwick's piratical care,' he said as they approached the dark bulk of the house, its lower windows winking with candles, 'we may turn our attention to Mistress Martha. Has there been any change that you know of, since you wrote?'

His arm was pressed in gratitude. 'No. She is still held in Nathaniel Thatcher's house. He is a dreadful old miser, and a Puritan, naturally, and has ten stout locks on every door and window. They often use his home as a jail. In normal times, of course, they would send prisoners over to Gloucester.'

'But these, thank God, are far from normal times.'

'Thank God?'

'From Martha's point of view. For while I do not think we would stand much chance of spiriting her out of Gloucester jail, I do think we might study how to remove her from Nathaniel Thatcher's cottage.'

'It's quite a large house. Thatcher did well in the old days. He's a sheepmaster now and used to be one of Father's best tenants. But Puritans pay no rents now, roast their damned thieving souls! Saving your allegiance,' she added with a swift smile which all but addled his wits.

'I hold no allegiance to Puritanism; a depressing religion in the best of men, and dangerously bigoted in the worst. No, I am for Parliament because I see in them the only chance of winning through to some sort of sensible government.'

He stopped and turned to face her. He wanted above all things to make himself clear to her on this. 'Believe me, Lucy, I did not choose lightly. Many of my instincts are with the Royalists. Respect for the Crown is as ingrained in me as it is in you; but I have begun to fail – and I regret it deeply – in respect for the man who wears the crown. The King does not keep faith with his word. He makes and breaks agreements, and gives and takes back his support within a labyrinth of intrigue to which he alone holds the clue. When he takes advice it is more often from the foolish than the wise. If he should win the war, he will bring his country back to where she stood in the time of his tyranny. Too much has changed since then. Too many people have seen how it can change.'

'I know you speak treason, but there are things I've heard, from Tom, even from my Father, God rest him, that tell me you are not so far from the truth. Only I love the King, and want him to win. I believe he can learn, like any man, by his mistakes.'

Will held his peace on that. 'Perhaps I am not so much for Parliament,' he mused, seeing it himself in these terms for the first time, 'as for England. It is England I love. I want to see *her* win. I long to know her a great sovereign state again, as she was in Elizabeth's day. Mistress of the seas, pushing at the frontiers of her trade; relatively calm and balanced in her government. Lucy, there is a whole world of opportunity to be taken, for growth, development and great riches, if only we can gain the peace to take advantage of it.'

'You speak as a merchant.'

'That is what I am, but I should speak no differently were I a sheepmaster or a vintner. War is bad for trade, and bad trade makes for a poor existence.'

This made Lucy think of the New Providence Company and its members. 'How is Mr Pym?' she asked, recalling his sickness.

Will shook his head. 'He is gone two days ago. I shall miss him as a friend, and all of us will miss him as a leader. Your brother printed his funeral sermon. I have brought you a copy. Poor John; he fretted so much about what he had left undone; but I think he was pleased with the Scots Alliance. That may turn the fortunes of the war irrevocably. And the money he prized out of the City's pockets will come in useful too,' he grinned. 'But I am very sad for John. He died hard and deserved far better.'

Lucy thought of the bonfire the men had built, out beyond the stableyard, to be lit when John Pym had breathed his last. She was ashamed. She had spoken severely to them, but to no avail. They would light it tonight. 'Jud was fond of him too,' she said sympathetically. 'He wrote to me recently. His letter was full of Pym's cleverness.'

'I'm glad he wrote. He misses you. And anyway, I told him if he did not write to set your heart at rest, I'd tan his hide for him.'

She laughed. 'Thank you. He did seem a little afraid of his reception. Poor fool. As if anything could turn *me* against him.'

That determined loyalty; it was one of the first things he had noticed about her. She had even extended it to the conscienceless scapegrace who had stolen her purse, because he was small and poor and powerless, and Will had threatened to dismiss him. He loved her for her championship of others. He only hoped that it would not one day stand between them in some way.

'If only I could tell Mother about Jud. But I think I had best wait awhile yet. She is still far from herself.'

357

'Then let us go and give her at least one cheerful piece of news.'

'Oh yes! Oh blessed Jesus, how wonderful to think we need not leave Heron!' She ran ahead of him, eyes shining, bursting with the news.

He followed her at a sober pace, warmed by her happiness, but wishing she could be thus happy for a more personal reason. Ah well, there would be a time.

Next morning Tom arrived, having ridden hard from Oxford whence Rupert had grudgingly spared him, and leaving behind a hotbed of jealousy and dispute between the commanders. The Prince was at odds with Wilmot in the field, while at court it was Digby who constantly undermined him with the King. The climate was further depressed by the stream of Parliament's victories in the eastern counties where the Fairfaxes and the bold Oliver Cromwell, now a general, were the disciplined leaders of a well-trained body of men from all walks of life and had put their own quarrelsome and dilatory chiefs to shame.

Another disaster had been the loss of Wrexham, the port at which they had hoped to disembark the Irish Royalist troops. So it was the old Tom, strung like a bow and suffering fools ungladly, who tossed them his package of bad news in one strongly worded paragraph, and a letter into Lucy's lap at the same time.

'From your rebellious acquaintance, Miss! He had the confounded cheek to make the Earl of Antrim his courier, who was on his way to parley with the King. I'll be interested to hear whether he expects to join us shortly. If so, he is like to be taken at Wrexham and put in a cage to amuse the Parliament's ladies. God's teeth, is there nothing to eat in this house?'

There was and he was given it along with their own exchanges at a more pedestrian pace. There was no mention of Dominic. The wound was still too raw to bear probing. One day, Tom would ask, and Lucy would tell him how nobly their cousin had died, but not yet.

By unspoken agreement they gave themselves a holiday from grief and their talk was light and cheerful as they ate, with Mary presiding at her table in something of her old style, wearing the necklace reprieved from the dog's dinner and responding to Will's sallies as if she had quite forgotten the time when his ebullient presence had caused her to feel herself dead and buried with her husband.

Tom was given the news about Heron, but was made to wait until after dinner for the details. 'Why spoil good beef with business?' as Will put it. He had brought the beef himself, from Warwick's kitchen.

Lucy, though she longed to read her letter, saved it until the others were settled in the parlour with the mulled wine, then raced up to her room, her heart pounding with the possibility that Cathal might indeed be in England soon. She had caught Will looking at her strangely as Tom had thrown her the letter and supposed him to be recalling their old discussion on the subject of Irish troops in England. Well, he could be right and they might be all the devils out of hell, all but one; still she would wish for them to come, for the sake of that one. In the light of her chamber window she tore open the packet.

'Lucy, my heart, His Grace of Antrim himself consents to carry this piece of myself to you, since he has had the luck of the Irish recently in escaping from a Scots jail in Ulster. I hope the luck may last him till he reaches Oxford where he goes, I joyfully add, to give His Majesty the glad tidings of the army we have raised and are ready to send him! And myself amongst them, my golden-haired enchantress – now, never say to me that I once descended from my white horse, for I shall set sail from the soil of Ireland as cheerfully as the bird that wings to its mate. I don't know just when it will be, but be sure I will come to you as soon as I may . . .'

There was more but she stopped reading there and threw herself across her bed in a paroxysm of joy. She rolled over and over, kissing her letter and gasping out her delight in wordless cries of love and longing. The whole world was changed in this one glorious day! Heron was to be saved and Cathal would be with her. She lay staring into the future making happy plans for a long time before she read the rest of his letter.

Downstairs, Mary had departed to look for festive table decorations in the shrubbery, a sign of more or less complete recovery, and Tom had, at last, the opportunity for which he had been fretting ever since he had arrived, to get to the bottom of this business about Will Staunton and Heron. He seated his guest before a huge blaze in the small parlour, where they had gathered all the remaining comfortable furniture, and filled one of the six good glasses with Oxford claret. Then he invited the merchant to explain himself.

Will knew that it was not going to be easy. Happily, Mary Heron and Lucy had been so relieved by the superficial fact of their salvation that they had done no embarrassing delving into its foundations. Well, he had enjoyed their relief as much as their gratitude. Now, alas, enjoyment was no longer the order of the day. For he had to explain to Sir Thomas Heron, Bart that he was not, in simple fact, the owner of his inheritance.

'I had to work very quickly, you understand,' he began. 'There remained just over three weeks before the order was carried out.'

Tom nodded, shifting impatiently in his chair. He wanted to hear all of it at once.

'First of all you must comprehend that Parliament is proud of the efficiency of the County Committees and their members do not care for interference, neither from Westminster nor any other source. The Gloucestershire Committees are particularly jealous in this respect.'

'Yes, yes. Go on.'

'It was clear then that very great influence must be brought to bear if I was to have any chance of success. John Pym could have done it . . .' He ignored the acute distaste in the face of his host. 'He would have done it, for me. But he was dying, God rest him.' Tom still wore that look of a well-bred horse sneering down its nose. Would it change at all, in the next few minutes, Will wondered. Best get it over, either way. He took a long draught of his claret for moral courage and plunged on headlong. 'So then I thought of the Earl of Warwick.'

Tom's brows shot up. Distaste appeared to have been routed by surprise.

'I had the devil's own job to find him, but luckily I caught him with one foot on shore, and well, we managed to come to an agreement.'

'What kind of an agreement?' Tom began to sense that it was not, had he ever been so naive as to suppose it, a simple matter of an order from an earl to an underling. Now he waited, every muscle knotted, for unpleasantness to follow.

'A financial agreement, of course. A trade agreement, if you like, between my uncle and myself—' Will took another swallow, then finished quickly, '—which enabled me to purchase Heron from the County Committee.'

His mine went off into utter silence. Tom stared at him as if one of them must be mad and he was not sure which, his face drained of colour.

'It was, I think, the only way,' said Will in the tone of a surgeon to an amputee. 'Even then, it took all Warwick's clout to do it. Apparently one of the Commissioners has had his own eye on Heron for some time, and hoped to buy it himself when peace comes – assuming Parliament wins, of course.'

'Who was that?' asked Tom numbly.

'One Michael Taylor of Gloucester, a well-to-do clothier with an itch to play the landlord.'

'I know of him. He was an old antagonist of my father. Always wanted our wool, but wouldn't pay the price.' Tom shook this unimportant person out of his head and managed to phrase the only question that now held any meaning for him. 'Will, who owns Heron now?'

Staunton met his eyes and found it hard. 'I do,' he said gently.

'Oh dear God.' Tom covered his face with one hand for a moment, then removed it to ask bewilderedly, 'But *why*? In God's name, why?' That was a question, oddly enough, that Will had not once stopped to ask himself, and although now he knew the answer well enough, after his revelation beneath the Quickenberry tree, he was not by any means prepared to disclose it. Happily, there was an obvious and acceptable surrogate. 'Because I owe your father a great deal. A great deal of money, in fact, which I am unable to pay at present.'

'Then how in Hades—'

'As I said, a business arrangement. I borrowed the price of Heron from Warwick.'

'Christ's sweet ravaged body! It must have been a fortune!'

'In return for which I have loaned the old sea dog three of my ships. He'd have had more, if the *Lady*, the *Eliza* and the *Mercury* had not been well out of his grasp on the high seas. As to the fortune, it was rather less than you may imagine; Parliament is in need of gold at present and will exchange even their good sense for it. I'd say we have a fair bargain. I'm to pay no interest and my uncle will restore ten per cent of the capital after the war.'

'And I?' Tom discharged bitterly. 'Where do I come into your fine "arrangement" – now that you have enriched the coffers of Parliament by the sale of my land?'

Will shrugged. 'I thought you might take Heron as a loan, to last, like everything else these days, until after the war; less, of course, the considerable monies coming to you on Sir George's behalf from my voyages. I can't tell you yet what the exact sum will be, but if all goes well, and I am not pirated or sunk, there should be something in the order of ten to fifteen per cent of Parliament's price for Heron. Should you wish to leave the monies invested with me, they will, of course, accrue. If I do as well as I hope to do in my present Venetian venture, there will be less left to pay than you could even hope.'

'How? How can you do well during the war?' Despite his shock Tom was curious. The man was a continual surprise.

Will did not think Tom would really like to know. 'The war extends its influence over a very small section of the globe,' he said tactfully. 'It's a wide world. The *Mercury*, for instance, lies just now in Constantinople. Eastern trade is unaffected by our troubles – and my captains are past masters at bringing home the bottoms.' He did not feel it necessary to remark that the *Eliza* was plying between England and Holland, sporting a full wardrobe of international flags and carrying arms to Parliament. Nor did he say that he had recently ceased to provide a similar service for the King.

Tom's eyes widened, but he decided not to enquire too closely into Will's oriental trade, sensing a network that would take many hours to unravel. 'You had better tell me, Will,' he said more coolly than he felt, 'for precisely how much I am to be your pensioner.'

'They had valued the estate at three thousand pounds a year. I persuaded them to reduce this to two thousand five hundred, pleading the present difficulties in farming and the sale of cloth. The Committee accepted this and demanded ten years' payment in advance. But,' he held up his hand to stem Tom's imminent flood, 'should you wish to invest part of your rents and profits, as your father did, why then the sum would diminish both in itself *and* on account of the profits it would bring in, d'you see?'

Tom blew out a long breath and regarded the keen face opposite with a mingling of defeat and respect. 'Twenty-five thousand livres – to keep Heron. It must be worth ten times as much! And yet – goddamn it, Will, why couldn't you have asked me first?'

'Could *you* have found the money?'

'No.'

'And would you have made the bargain, even if you could, knowing that Parliament stood to gain from it?'

'I would not.'

'Well then, this – though you may dislike it – is as good as you'd get. You lose a little pride maybe – I don't know – it's not a commodity for which I have any use. But you keep Heron.'

'It is not pride I lose by it, but honour.'

'How have you been dishonest?'

'I am dishonest if I accept.'

'Your acceptance,' Will said brutally, 'is not required. The thing is accomplished.'

'That is what I'll find hard to forgive.' He felt an inward stab of irony at his own understatement. He wondered if Will had any idea at all of how deeply he had struck – at manhood, honour, pride too. He pitied the man without pride. His brain raced, seeking a way out of this appallingly unacceptable trap. He could find none. Either he lost Heron or he kept it on Staunton's terms. It had been an insane piece of whimsy on the merchant's part, of course. God alone knew why he should have committed such an irrational act. He might have paid the debt to Sir George as such debts are normally paid. He knew he must say something more now. He must repudiate, and give up Heron for all of them, family and dependants, some fifty souls in all, or he must scrape the bottom of his soul for some trace of – God save the mark – gratitude.

'Don't think I'm not aware,' he began, the words tumbling out stiffly and too quickly.

Will waved an impatient hand. 'Don't. Do me the credit to expect that I should realize a little of what you feel. I would not have done this if I could have thought of any other way. But damn it all, it's none so bad when all's said! A good deal better than having the County Committee trampling all over your mother's fine floorboards, let alone her precious borders. I'm very tired, Tom. Why don't we just leave it for awhile? Relax, and take a glass or two?'

A certain amount of pleading in the tone recalled to Tom that he was still, however strangely translated, his benefactor's host. He filled their glasses, ashamed of his ungraciousness. 'I must just say this,' he said, still awkwardly, but with obvious sincerity. 'I – apologize for – seeming ungrateful. Shock, I daresay, as much as anything.' He got up and went across to the window, to stand looking out over Heron's acres. 'It was such an enormous thing for you to do.'

It came to him, in a rush like the advent of tears, how much this land, this house were a part of him. He could never leave them. 'I am sensible again now, I think,' he said, his spirits rising a little. 'I do thank you, Will, with all my heart.' He raised his glass gravely and drank to his guest. 'But there still remains the question – why?' he murmured, almost to himself. 'I can't believe that the debt to my father and a letter from a panicking schoolgirl could alone inspire such an act of generosity.'

'The debt is a real one and must be paid,' said Will quietly. 'And your sister is no longer a schoolgirl, have you not noticed? Nor did she exhibit any sign of panic.'

'Then what in heaven's name made her write to *you*?' Tom's resolution shook under a thunderous desire to beat Lucy's behind until it was black and blue.

'She knows, as you do not seem to apprehend, how closely I regard the members of your family.' Tom flushed.

'Don't blame Lucy for your embarrassment,' said Will, tired of kindness. 'Blame your own stiff neck.' He defused the remark with his most likeable smile, holding out his glass again. Tom filled it.

He went on filling it, and filling his own, for the remainder of the afternoon. It seemed as good a way out of his discomfort as any he could think of. Conversation, circling less and less determinedly about the disposition of the estate, became first desultory, then disjointed, and eventually failed altogether because neither participant was willing or able to put two words together. They grinned inanely at each other over their glasses and lifted them occasionally in a warm and increasingly companionable silence. Sometimes one of them fed the fire.

After an hour or two, Tom gave a sharp nod of his head and woke up, surprised that he had been asleep. Will was snoring softly opposite, his yellow hair falling in his eyes. He looked very young and very contented. He should be, damn him; he had his fine Spanish boots well planted in his own hearth, if he chose. Tom reprimanded himself severely for this unworthy thought, which he put down to slight inebriation. But devil damn it pink and blue – it *was* an extraordinary thing for a fellow to do! For a family not even his own. Without any real guarantee, in these unpredictable times, of being repaid. Tom could not leave it alone. It nagged him like toothache. Will must be repaid. That was certain. He could not retrieve his honour else, could not hold up his head in the world. He could hardly hold it up now. The demon drink. He shook it about a bit. His eyes hurt. He noticed suddenly that Will had woken up and was peering at him blearily.

'Excellent wine,' Will said, grinning.

'Not bad. The Queen brought it from France.'

'With the arms. And the men.'

'Yes.'

'Excellent.'

'You were with her? Convoy. Weren't you? Fine thing. Fine woman.'

Will began to weave his way through the fumes of the said excellence, thickly circling in his brain, to the realization that there was something he still had not told Tom. 'Not any more,' he enunciated, fairly clearly, considering.

'What? *Damn* fine woman, the Queen!'

'Not that. No more convoys. Stopped floating.'

'Eh?'

'Come down on Parliament's side.'

Tom was suddenly sober. 'You've done *what*?' he cried, sitting upright so abruptly that his head gave a painful thud.

'Was afraid you'd not be best pleased. As I say. I'm more or less a Parliament man these days.' Will was surprised at himself. He had not known he was going to say this. He had simply woken up with the urge to come clean. He would have felt uncomfortable and ridiculous had he chosen to go on pretending.

Tom felt weak. He had been asked to accept too many unacceptable things in one brief span of time. Perhaps in order to escape from this latest outrage, he found himself thinking instead of his young brother, Jud, whom he had barred from the house. Jud, whose crime was to be a traitor to his King and his family. Jud, whom he had sent from their father's deathbed without comfort or kindness. Well, he could hardly order Will Staunton, equally a traitor, equally criminal, from the door he had just paid for! He stared at Will, his head reeling with wine and complexities.

Will nodded. 'I'm sorry. It doesn't help matters, does it? I suppose, if we are to be particular about it, we must officially call ourselves enemies.' His grin was still wide; the paradox evidently gave him pleasure.

Tom threw up his hands and groaned. A sense of humour struggled to be born in him. 'It's all too damned ludicrous! Here am I, and here are you and there is the war. And now you say you are for the enemy. Yet you are webbed into this family as close as ever kissing kin could be. And I'd as soon drink with you as any man I know. Again, in a way it doesn't bear thinking about. You traded with my father for a partner; you took my young idiot of a brother for apprentice; you buy and give me back my inheritance; you are kind to my sister; you are good to the very dogs; my mother dotes on you; my young brothers worship you – you are probably the best friend any generation of this family ever had – but you are our enemy. You just said so. None the less, is there any way, I repeat, that we could be closer? Unless you were to marry Lucy, of course,' he added unseriously. 'That would complete the insanity. Why don't you?' he asked laconically. 'It was what Father wanted. Why not take her, Will, as a security against my debts? Then, if Heron collapses about our ears, you'll still be a wife to the good!'

Will's smile was very careful. He noticed that he was no longer at all drunk. 'I doubt,' he said pleasantly, 'that Sir George would so willingly give her to me now. I was a King's man, more or less, when he knew me.'

'More or less. It's always more or less with you. But you're right, without doubt. He was fond of you, though, Will, and would berate you in sound Shakespearean couplets if he were here with us. But he wouldn't give you Lucy, not now.' He was suddenly quiet.

'What's the matter?'

'I was just thinking – what would Father have said to all this? I'm thankful he is not here to see it.'

'Don't be so sure. Things have changed very quickly. I imagine that if I had made him the offer to do what I've done, he would have accepted it. It might even have amused him, and the business side is sound enough. He was a practical man.'

'You'd have made him an offer, then. It's more than you did for me.'

'In the same circumstances, I'd have done exactly as I have done,' countered Will quickly, not at all sure that he would. Sir George did not suffer from the same species of pride as did his son. On the other hand, perhaps he would not have dared play so high a hand in the baronet's interest.

Perhaps he would not have dared, even for Tom, had Tom's interests once crossed his mind during his mad ride after Richard of Warwick. They had not. He had thought of nothing save Lucy. He knew that now, even as he knew that he could not accept Tom's offer of her hand. It could be made a serious one at any time, that had been implicit; but this was not the time. She did not love him. She still fancied herself in love with the Irish boy. Perhaps, honesty forced him to recognize, she really was in love with him. But Will Staunton had never yet wanted a woman he could not have and did not expect, in the long run, that it would prove that he had found one now. It might be a very long run. Meanwhile, it suited him very well to wait and see. There were plenty of other amusements to keep him content until she should decide to fall in love with him. What he did have to guard against, he thought, as he tried to exude reassurance towards the perplexed and frowning Tom, was allowing her to put him in place of her father. All this weeping on his bosom was very fine, as far as it went, but where the delicate balance of their relations was concerned, it went in the wrong direction. He thought he might at least redress that balance a little before he left her this time.

'I am trying,' said Tom painfully, stuck in a prickly thicket of doubt and prohibition, 'to work out what I should think. But I'm cursed if I can!'

'Keep it up and they'll make you a saint,' said Will easily, thinking that this new drinking companion did in fact have much in common with Sebastian of that ilk; his face wore the permanent expression of one stuck with arrows. He would not like to be Tom.

He was saved from further commiseration by the entrance of Lucy, who, having read her letter and written most of the reply, was feeling loved and happy and solicitous for all the world. 'You look comfortable, both of you,' she said approvingly. 'Well, have you decided what to do, and when you will do it?'

The two men exchanged mystified glances.

'Only you *must* let Kit and Humpty go with you. It means so much to them. I'd really like to come myself,' she added winningly, looking hopefully at Tom.

He examined her as if she were at the end of a perspective glass. 'What,' he demanded helplessly, 'are you talking about?'

'Rescuing Martha, of course,' she replied crossly. 'What else?'

'What indeed?' agreed Will suavely. 'By all means let us discuss the subject.'

Lucy came closer and peered at them suspiciously, sniffing the air. 'I believe you're both drunk!' she said indignantly.

'Don't be uncharitable, Lucy,' said Will. 'We have imbibed, I admit, but we are sensate objects, both fit and willing to talk of Martha, aren't we, Tom?'

'Certainly,' declared Tom in a colourless and mannerly tone. He had every intention and desire to see to Martha's safety, but the thought of her embarrassed him all the same.

'I think this is the most irresponsible thing I ever heard of,' Lucy said contemptuously, looking from one flushed face to the other. 'How *can* you be so selfish and so sottish when Martha lies in that vile old man's house?'

'We can't,' said Will placatingly. 'She is not forgotten, I swear. First we must have a counting of heads. You shall count the ones that swing from your girdle.'

'What?'

'Nothing, Boadicea, nothing at all. Now, let us get down to business. It shall be tonight – do you both agree?'

The result of the discussion which followed, and of the head count, was that after darkness had fallen that night, eight able-bodied men, including the twins, but not Lucy whom Tom had threatened to lock in her room if she were not amenable, stuck pistols in their belts, muffled themselves and their horses' hooves in thick cloth against the wind, cold and prying ears, and set off for the comfortable residence of Nathaniel Thatcher.

When they reached the least frequented gate of the demesne, Kit and Humpty tied up their horses among the trees and ran ahead of the others to act as scouts, spying out the land they knew so well by dark or by day, a hundred committed nuisances acting as their *aides memoires*. The precaution proved itself when they raced back some minutes later to report a party of horse approaching along the only strip of road that they must use themselves. They melted into the trees and became mere shadows of men and horses, while the Parliamentary reality trooped smartly by, oblivious to the odd unmuted equine expression that echoed their passing.

They went more carefully after that, holding to the trees where they could and keeping out of the moonlight when they crossed open country. They met no one else until they stood on the sloping ground behind the Thatcher house.

They stood still in a half-circle, listening. There was no sound other than the ghostly bleating from the hills. The stars were white in a frosty sky and the wind scraped at their exposed faces. They pulled up their hoods and rewound their scarves and waited while the twins, who had demanded the right in vigorous dumbshow, crept down to the house to discover who was about and where everyone was. Until they knew Martha's exact position they would not decide whether she should be taken by storm or by stealth.

It was perhaps fifteen minutes before Kit crawled back up the hillside. 'At first we thought they had her in the barn; it has so many padlocks! But no such luck. She's inside, second window from the left, upper storey. Everything's double locked and barred. It won't be easy. Why don't we wait until dawn and dash in when he wakes up and comes out to piss?'

'And have him recognize every one of us? Talk sense!' said Tom curtly.

They were silent then, each one trying to think of the magic key. Then Will said, 'You said he was a bit of a miser, this Thatcher; do you know if he has money on the premises?'

'God's boots, yes,' said Kit quickly. 'Everyone knows about

Nat Thatcher's black box. It's a damn great sea chest, barrelled in iron and full to the brim with gold, or so they say in the village.'

'Do they?' Will stroked his chin. 'The thing is, do they exaggerate?'

'Not a great deal,' Tom was able to inform him. 'Thatcher lives in constant fear of theft. He's been advised a hundred times to put the money in safekeeping, but he wouldn't listen. Trusts no one. Now he's terrified lest Parliament take it from him; he keeps giving them a taste of it, hoping to dampen their appetites, saying he has no more.'

'Then he'll think only of his gold when he receives mysterious visitors at dead of night. I think we can accomplish our task very delicately, and without the aid of pistols, gentlemen.' His eyes gleamed in the dark. 'Tell me, Tom, has Thatcher ever laid eyes on me, to your knowledge? Would he recognize me?'

'I shouldn't think so, though he might have caught sight of you at the famous football game. Ten to one he'd not remember.'

'Then this is what we'll do.'

Will spoke low and clearly for a few minutes. At one point there was muffled laughter. When he had finished, the party divided into two groups. Tibbett, leading one of them, took all the horses and circled off towards the road at the front of the house, to take cover among the thick trees that bounded it. Will, with Tom and two of Heron's sheepmen, all muffled to the eyes, scrambled down the slope and presented themselves at Nathanial's back door.

Tom hammered violently on the door with the butt of his pistol. Will threw back his head and shouted 'Open in the name of Parliament!' in a voice like the crack of doom.

It was not long before they got results. An uncertain voice quavered, 'Who is it? Who's there? What the devil d'ye want at this time of night?'

A little more hammering and shouting brought the voice to the keyhole in front of them. 'What d'you want?' it repeated in obvious fright.

'Open, in Parliament's name, Nathanial Thatcher, or I shall have to break down this door. I am Colonel Heavy, and I serve with Sir William Waller. I have urgent business with you, sir.'

'Lord God of Hosts!' said the voice dolorously. 'How do I know—'

'You *know* the force of my displeasure in one moment, sir, if you do not open with despatch!'

Will sounded gruff, grim and fifty, and in no mood to be trifled with. Nathanial Thatcher opened his door. It took some time. He muttered as he jangled and clicked his keys and tutted as he dragged at the protesting bolts. He moaned as the four swathed and enigmatic figures strode into his kitchen.

Will glared down at the unfortunate little man in his rumpled nightgown and cap. A woman cowered behind him, similarly attired, grey hair straggling about her neck. 'Your wife?'

'I sh'd think not. My housekeeper.' He sniffed.

'How many more in the house?'

'My two men-servants and two infantrymen that are billeted on me.' The old man commenced to shake as he imagined horrible things.

'Very well. You, madam, will go and bid them all to remain in bed.' The woman fled, glad to be out of it.

'Good. Now sir, have the goodness to escort us to the room where you conduct your business,' the colonel ordered frostily.

'A stroke of genius,' murmured Tom as they followed their trembling host into a room containing table and chairs, a desk and a large black box banded in iron. The colonel frowned hideously at this object, about which Thatcher's rheumy eyes were already darting protectively.

'Open it,' came the stern command.

'But sir, I—'

'It has been brought to my notice,' the colonel continued sonorously, 'that you have been deficient in your loyalty to the Parliament. I am here to assist you to make up for that deficiency. Open the box.'

Nathanial made one bold stand. 'Sir, it is all I have – the profits of a lifetime's work. I am sure the good Parliament does not wish to rob an old man of his savings.'

The colonel looked offended. 'It would seem to me to be t'other way round; it is you, sir, who seek to rob the Parliament of the life-blood it must have if we are to overcome these devilish cavaliers. Open the chest this instant! We shall count the money. While we are doing so I wish the rest of the house to be searched. Kindly hand your keys to my major.'

'I assure you, Colonel Heavy, there is nothing else here to interest you. A few little articles left to me by my dear mother—'

'The keys, if you please.' The colonel sounded impatient.

Nathanial scuttled to his desk. He reached down the neck of his bed gown and hauled up a bunch of keys on a string. With one of these he unlocked a drawer in the desk and took out of it another enormous bunch of great black keys. These he sadly presented to the major, whose visored features appeared to be trembling slightly.

'Excellent. And now we shall sit down and you will offer me a cup of wine, and we shall discuss how much your loyalty is worth.' Nathanial whimpered and gave himself up for lost.

'Very well,' he said. 'There is one thing else. We have a prisoner here. Upstairs. A local girl who is to be tried for a witch.'

The colonel raised blond brows. 'Indeed. It is a brave man who will shelter a witch under his roof. Have you no fear of her evil enchantments?'

Nathanial Thatcher smiled for the first time that night. 'I have known her all her life, sir. She has cured my rheum and aided my sleep often enough, and good cheap, too. I am not one of those who call her witch.'

'A brave man, is he not, Major? Be sure to give the witch a wide berth in your search.' The colonel made a superstitious sign and the major stamped off with the keys, followed by his two silent comrades.

Fully dressed upon the bed, Martha was tossing in the half sleep that seemed to be all that would come to her since her imprisonment. Her mind ranged far and wide in a freedom that she knew in her clearer phases to have much in common with madness. She had the madman's cunning ability to push away all unwanted images so that it was not the most recent, unbearable events that occupied her wanderings, but older, kinder memories. The figure of her mother appeared to her, not as the tortured victim of the executioner, but the gentle, resourceful woman who had turned from her loneliness and helplessness after the death of her husband to the perfecting of a skill that not only fed and clothed her little daughter, but brought comfort to the entire community in which she lived. She had always had a beautiful laugh, and Martha heard it now as though it rang in the room beside her. Warm arms wrapped her round and a soft voice sang to her. She was perfectly aware that it was a dream, but she knew that if she could hold on to it strongly enough, it would stay with her for a while.

When the hammering had begun beneath her, it had not penetrated her trance at first, but gradually the disturbances in the house became more insistent than the thin forms of her vision and the sounds of her childhood receded. She felt herself floating inevitably towards the present. If she could, she might still cheat it, by dropping at last into deep, refreshing sleep. She had almost completed her escape when she was dragged back by the awareness of a source of light, somewhere close to her face. Someone spoke her name.

She moved the weight of her lids and there was candlelight, and another face, hanging over hers. She gasped. For a heartbeat she took it for Nehemiah, child of darkness, come to claim her body once again; but she saw instantly that, far from the form of her waking nightmares, the face that bent above her, filled with concern, the thin features as familiar to her as her own, was that of Tom Heron. It was not possible. She closed her eyes again.

'Martha – are you well? Can you get up, do you think?' His voice was real and urgent and she tried to bring herself back and respond.

'You must hurry. We have come to take you away from here. To Heron.'

Away. Freedom? Could it be true?

'Tom? Is it you?'

'Yes, well, look – you must hurry.' He found her hand and began to help her to sit up. 'That's the way! Have you a cloak? Over there?' He brought it to her and put it round her shoulders.

'Thank you. But Tom—' She stopped, overwhelmed by the amazing gift of being able to speak his name again.

'I'll explain it all later. Now come.'

'Oh yes. Yes!' She tried to stand, but swayed at once, so that he caught and steadied her. 'I'm sorry. I stood up too quickly. Tom,' she repeated in hazy wonder.

'Can you walk? Or shall I carry you? He thought she looked half asleep and half bewildered, like a child awoken too suddenly.

'I can walk. I can't believe you are here—' She breathed deeply as they left the chamber.

He smiled reassurance and put one arm about her to support her, holding the candle high with the other, to light them down the passage. The Heron men guarded their way.

'Quietly now. We are stealing you,' he whispered. He brought her swiftly down the stairs and out through the front door which he had previously unlocked.

Once outside, a few hurried steps brought them into the trees where Tibbett and his party were waiting with the horses. Two figures detached themselves from the gloom and hurled themselves upon Martha, miming exquisite triumph and racing her into present, truth and reality as nothing else could have done. She hugged both boys briefly before Tom swept her up onto his horse.

'There'll be no trouble,' he muttered to Tibbett as he prepared to mount behind her. 'He had only four men in the house. You can follow after us in twos. Take your time and keep a look out, just in case. Are you set, Martha?'

She grasped the pommel of his high-fronted Spanish saddle, pierced with an almost painful happiness as his arms came about her to reach for the reins. They moved off, slowly but easily in the darkness, the mare nosing her path through the trees until they were out on the hillside again, following a wide arc above and well beyond the house.

It came back to her at once how they had used to ride like this before, long ago when he had loved her. She wondered if he too were thinking of that now. But he had no reason to do so, of course. There was Valora. It was not any affection for her that had been the inspiration for this piece of moonlight madness; she knew that. Duty would be the cause – and the traditional care of the Herons for the people within their governance. These, and perhaps Lucy's urging had brought him to her.

Nevertheless, this unexpected journey was one she would store up among her few treasures, another tiny jewel to wink against the darkness that seemed to be moving inexorably over her life. For now the other, abhorred memory overtook her. Her bitter regret for the change in herself was iron in her mouth as she matched it against her unchanged love for Tom.

She did not speak as they rode. Tom began to find the silence uncomfortable. This was chiefly because he did indeed remember times gone by, when they had roamed the hills together, sharing his horse just as they did now. And there were other things too, which it was not suitable that he should remember. Her fragile weight against his shoulder had a familiarity which he recognized with a shock of unexpectedness after so long a time. Unchanged, too, was the scent of her hair – the tang of camomile floating out of that silver veil that seemed to be woven out of the night frost but was warm and alive, as he knew because he had so often buried his face in its silken mass. It had used to drive him to distraction.

He started suddenly to talk, breaking her idyll with determined and cheerful male noise. He told her how the plan for her rescue had come about, and made her smile gravely up at him as he described the exploits of Colonel Heavy. He had almost run out of words when he remembered. 'My dear girl, forgive me! You must think me an unfeeling boor. I have not asked how you fared

373

among your jailers. Did they treat you well? Did they offer you any harm?'

The stars fell about her ears as she listened. The beginning of a belief in her freedom fled her mind, leaving only the inescapable nakedness of the truth.

He sensed that something was badly wrong. She had tensed in his arms and held herself free of him. 'Martha? What is it? You must tell me. Have they hurt you?'

She shook her head violently. 'No. I am not hurt.' She made a further effort. 'I was treated well enough.'

'Then what—?' He was at a loss. The change had been so sudden.

Martha called upon her self-control. It was not his injury, and should by no means be his interest. Dear God, if he should learn . . . She was deeply ashamed before him. He should never know, never. No one should.

She forced herself to put her humiliation away from her, until she should be alone. She relaxed her body again and made herself ask him, in a conversational tone, 'Where are we going?'

'I'm taking you to Heron, of course. I told you.'

She could understand that there was nowhere else she might go. This would be the price she would pay for her body's freedom – to live in his house, and suffer his presence, and know her own defilement.

'You can't go back to your cottage. Surely you see that,' Tom insisted, thinking she was worrying about this.

'No, no. I do see. Of course. I'm sorry.'

'Nothing to be sorry about.' Tom's spirits rose. He hugged her. 'You're going to be free and happy and live at Heron till the world comes to its senses again!' His exultant embrace reverberated through her. She hoped her voice would not betray her.

'But surely they will look for me there,' she queried. Oh, she had no right to take flame from his touch.

'In less than two weeks neither the County Committee nor Nehemiah Owerby himself, nor anyone unwarranted by myself will have the right to set foot on Heron soil – so you will be safer there than you have ever been.'

It gave him pleasure to know himself her protector. Her fragility had always awoken an uncharacteristic gentleness in him. He settled her back against his chest. 'You may as well ride comfortably,' he said casually. Then he began to tell her about Will Staunton's astonishing purchase.

'And he has done all this, just to discharge his debt to Sir George?' she asked in amazement when he had done.

'I don't know. That's the devil of it. The fellow won't *let* me know. He simply portrays himself as a good friend of the family. I suppose that is not really beyond the bounds of belief, Martha. Or is it?'

She thought about it. 'It is not. But I do not think it will prove to have been his only reason for his action.'

When she encountered Will Staunton again he was effervescent with the success of their adventure and falling about with the twins and their dogs like another thirteen year old. He took one look at Martha and yelled for brandy. The next time he yelled it was for Lucy, who was furiously pounding the virginals above their heads, to take her mind off things. Hearing the quarterdeck roar, she stopped and raced down the stairs two at a time. As she came towards them, crying out her welcome, Martha noticed that Will's eyes never left her and that they held an expression of intense satisfaction oddly tinged with regret. She found this most interesting and began to have her own notion of the root of Mr Staunton's uncommon philanthropy. Tom, of course, would never take note of anyone's emotions, since in general he so much disliked his own.

'How did you win home before us?' was his only concern.

'I had no particular reason to dally in the moonlight,' said Will naughtily, unaware how unkindly he was repaying Martha's acumen on his behalf. Tom gave his slight frown.

'And what is more,' Will ran on, exceedingly pleased with himself, 'we wanted no pursuit. I sent your two men off, noisily, on the Gloucester Road, while we hounded back here with our booty.'

'Booty? You mean—?' The frown was gone and Tom's eyes sparkled.

'Nat Thatcher's gold. I couldn't leave it all sitting there, not when I'd told him we'd come expressly to collect it, so we transferred a fair share of it to some handy sacks, and hung 'em at our saddles. We'll go halves, eh, Tom – and a bounty for the men?'

'Do we count as men?' asked Humpty anxiously.

'Certainly. You have proved yourselves such beyond question.'

Humpty executed a rather cramped somersault, in deference to the furniture, and was expertly caught by Kit.

Since Will had relieved the unfortunate miser of £2,000 in good yellow gold, the twins found themselves in credit for £50 each, more than they had ever hoped to see before they came of age. They celebrated their luck by joining in, rather insidiously, the general tendency to get drunk.

For Will and Tom this represented more of a topping-up operation than a new beginning and the others kept them company out of respect for their status as rescuers. The party soon became mellow and reflectively sentimental. They adjourned to the gallery and persuaded Mary to join them as they sang ballads – often badly – and recalled the sad fact that somewhere in the wake of the last desperate months another Christmas had come and gone. Towards the end of the evening Will remarked warmly that he was glad to see them thus cheerful again as he would be going to sea for some months shortly and would like to think of them just as they were tonight.

'Months!' repeated Lucy reproachfully. 'You didn't say so.'

'I am saying so now,' he said airily.

'Where are you going?'

'To warm shores and swaying palms, to the Caribbean, to lend my support to one Captain Jackson, who is carrying out some – privateering – on my uncle's behalf.'

For the twins this was now a ratified code word and they whirled into storms of jealous demand. Tom felt a queer relief; he was not sure he could have kept up a permanent gratitude. For Lucy the evening had suddenly gone very flat and she felt irritable and a bit sick.

'So we shan't see you for – how long?' she asked crossly.

'Several months. I can't be sure.'

'But what about the war – and your mother – and the London business?' she demanded. She disapproved of his calmly walking out of his responsibilities.

'They will certainly be here when I return. They have always been so before. It will not seem long.'

'Oh, I don't care how long it is,' she flung at him. 'It just seems rather inconsiderate of you. But it's none of my business.'

'No. However, I should like to say my farewells to you in a little more privacy, if you are agreeable. Should you object to a brief address to the Quickenberry?'

'If you like,' she said ungraciously, and fetched her cloak.

Martha was the only one who watched them go with any sense of destiny. Mary hoped they would not catch cold and asked them to take a look at a recently transplanted tamarisk on their way.

'It feels as if it is freezing,' grumbled Lucy, shrouding herself like a mummy.

'I won't keep you long.'

They reached the ornamental lake and saw the white face of the moon drowning in its depths. 'I wanted to give you something to remember me by,' he said, his expression hard to define.

'You'd not be easy to forget!'

'Somehow your tone is not quite complimentary.'

'I have never known you to solicit compliments. I thought you certain enough of your inestimable worth.' She softened then. 'But I will lavish you with compliments if that is what you want. Dear Will – you have been Jove in a shower of gold to us, and there is no manner in which I know how to thank you. Come back to Heron as soon as you may – and let us have news of you if it is possible.'

'Why Lucy, what a pretty speech. And it will suffice very well for this year. I do not wish to become spoiled. So you may spare me your thanks for my gift.' He handed her a small box made of gilded Florentine leather. 'Open it.'

Inside was a lady's ring in heavy gold with the bear and ragged staff of Warwick incised upon its shield. It had been his mother's signet, his grandmother's before her, but he did not tell her that.

She raised puzzled eyes to his face. 'It is very handsome. But why do you give it to me?'

'Perhaps just to puzzle you. Where will you wear it, I wonder?' He looked mischievously at the ribbon round her neck.

She frowned. 'I don't know. It looks big.'

'Try it.'

It fitted, though not closely, the middle finger of her left hand.

'Wear it sometimes, then, when you wish to remember that you have a friend.'

She nodded. 'I will.' But she still looked puzzled.

He returned her gaze with a sudden rueful appreciation of just what had happened to him. Will Staunton, pirate, courtier and enthusiastic womanizer had been caught by a skinny chit just more than half his age, with a sprightly tongue and a doubtful temper, while she, wrapped up in some greensick dream of book romance with that damnable sprig from the bogs of Leinster, remained smugly and superlatively unaware of his interest. At this moment he didn't know whether he wanted more to strangle her or to awaken her very rudely to life's more exciting possibilities with an embrace which would destroy her complacency forever. He had, he supposed, brought her shivering out here with some idea of the latter. But now, as he looked into her grave face, and thought of all that had happened to her and about her in recent weeks, then looked closer and saw what she had become, how her strength was growing daily in adversity and her courage increasing to meet every test, he found he could not treat her in so light a fashion with his body as he might with his tongue. So he took her very gently in his arms and kissed her without passion, resting his cheek against hers afterwards, in a moment of simplicity and sweetness that was as new to him as his knowledge of this unlooked-for love.

'Oh Will,' she said, with a yearning in her voice that lifted his heart like the lark for an instant. 'I wish you did not have to go. We need you now, all of us.'.

He made some appropriate, over-courteous reply and they returned to the house, both subdued and neither very happy. When the time came for him to leave, he saw that she had left his ring on her finger.

She saw him go with a new sense of loss. It was nothing like the wave of unsteadying sorrow that had beaten her when Cathal had left her; the knowledge of that had always provided an undertow to their relationship; it was rather as if, when she had turned back to the house after Will had crested the rise, she had found that it had given a great lurch, as though some staunch rock had been prised out of its foundations. It was an idiot's fancy but it taught her how much she had come to rely upon Staunton. She must not do so any longer, for her own sake, despite the proof of his friendship on her finger.

During the next week Tom also left, for Oxford, to visit the King and to consider whether or not he wished to inherit his father's seat in the splinter Parliament that Charles had called in that city. Since Westminster's numbers now stood at two hundred or so in the Commons and fifteen to twenty in the Lords, His Majesty might expect about a hundred Commons and thirty lords to respond. Though he would make some polite show of interest, Tom knew already what his own decision must be. He was a soldier, not a politician. He wished to remain a soldier as long as the war continued.

He had stayed at home until Heron had become the official property of Will Staunton and every last Committee man had been seen off the premises. Will had left behind a testament by which, in the event of his sudden death, the estate should revert to Tom, so all was as secure as parchment and sealing wax could make it.

In the weeks that followed, as no unauthorized person came near them, and the fighting moved away to the Midlands, it seemed that Will's enchantment had succeeded in putting back the clock for them, so smoothly did Heron begin to run again under Lucy's increasingly sure hand. She soon discovered that it was much as Will had suggested, that her work consisted mainly in making decisions based upon the very sound foundations offered her by others. With Tibbett at her right hand and Margery at her left, she gave interviews to the steward and the head gamekeeper, the sheepmen, the cattlemen, the spinsters and weavers, the packmen and the wool merchants, to the dairymen, the stablemen, the kennelmen, to the smith and the woodman. She left the ordering of the baking, brewing, pickling, smoking, sewing, washing, polishing and cleaning to Margery, and the gardens, naturally, to Mary who now cared for them with a renewed dedication that surpassed even her previous fervour.

Martha made an immediate place for herself in the household, seconding both Mary and Margery in their own domains, taking the strain from each in turn and finding herself content in her usefulness. She thought of Tom occasionally, like a child who awards itself a sweet for comfort or good conduct and, sorrowfully and with abiding love, of Dominic whose presence seemed still to hang in the air about the house, as though he had just left each empty room she entered.

She did not think any longer of Nehemiah, except on those few nights when she awoke, sweating, with the sensation of his weight upon her body and her spirit. On those occasions she would rise and take up a book, reading far into the night, banishing the nightmare with the beauty and good sense of poetry or essays.

London, Spring 1644

Beneath the handsome new sign of the Lion of St Mark, the proprietors of this hopeful imprint were engaged in furious argument.

'A joke's a joke, and I'm as game for a laugh as the next man, but this stuff, Rob, it's sheer irresponsible nonsense!'

'You wouldn't have said that a year ago.'

'Well, I do now.'

'What's wrong with it? It's the same kind of drivel that all the others turn out.'

'Exactly! There are a good two dozen newsbooks in the city now, and if we want to *sell* as many as *Britanicus*, or the *Diurnall*, we have to establish our own character. We have to offer something different. And we won't do that by parroting Royalist calumnies about soldiers buggering horses.'

'Don't be so po-faced, Jud. That correspondence between the *Britanicus* and *Aulicus* sells them both 700 copies a week. People want to be entertained and there's nothing they like better than a bit of dirt.'

'Well, at least let's make it *new* dirt,' Jud grumbled, tossing the offending article into the bin.

Robin sighed and shuffled his lapful of paper. Jud was right. There was no point in the *Intelligencer* trying to enter into the flinging of ink and excrement between the Oxford-based *Mercurius Aulicus* and their own greatest rival the *Mercurius Britanicus*. They would simply be marked down as cheap-skate intruders. He envied the *Mercurius* their luck, that was all. Last December a Parliamentarian prisoner had been caught, according to the Royalist *Aulicus*, committing buggery on a mare, and on a Sunday too, when the good Cavaliers, they would have you believe, were every man jack at church. 'Thus,' it righteously declared, 'do we tell the world what Puritans do on a Sunday.'

In London, the *Britanicus*, fired by the insult to religion, retorted that the soldier in question had in fact been trying to steal the horse in order to escape, and it very much doubted if any Cavalier had been to church 'since His Majesty first levied war against his Parliament. Unless,' it added unpleasantly, 'it had been to attend the Mass.' *Aulicus* responded with further provocation and insult, and the flyting had continued since, much to the satisfaction, personal and financial, of both publications. Rob's correspondent had been trying to out-Herod them with an obviously fudged report of pig-buggery in Oxfordshire. Rob had split his sides over the mechanics of it, but Jud, who was getting ambitious these days, seemed to have lost his sense of the absurd.

'There's this that came in about Rupert and one of his officers sharing a man's four daughters after Newark,' he discovered hopefully. 'No. I've something else on Newark. I don't know whether to print it or not. Here – read it. See for yourself. It would be an unusual step to take, but may be just what we need.' Robin looked at the heading. 'A true and Unbiased Account of the Losing of Newark by an Irish Gentleman.'

'*Is* there any such animal?'

'Don't be so brutish. Read it.'

Rob gave the article the intent concentration he had learned to give everything he read. He was soon engrossed. It was a clear and exact account, flourishing with ingenious metaphor, of the event which was presently upon everyone's lips – Prince Rupert's brilliant relief of the siege of Newark in a lightning campaign whose surprise and speed had won the Midlands for the King and earned him the idolatry of his own side and the unwilling admiration of the enemy.

'This fellow, whoever he is, he has a pen like Pandar's tongue – and without the props of buggery, witchery or lechery!'

'Very persuasive. I thought so too. Elegant, amusing and not too heavy a touch. He doesn't waste words on praise of Rupert, just makes it quite clear where Parliament went wrong. Shall we use it, then?'

'Why not?'

'No reason at all – unless you object to the fact that he is one of Rupert's troopers.'

'You're gulling me!'

'No, I assure you. D'you remember me telling you of Cathal O'Connor?'

'That young sprig who was with you that first Christmas?'

'Himself. Well, this is his work. He came over with the first Irish contingent. He writes that he has read all the newsbooks he can get hold of, theirs and ours, and that he has "a powerful desire" to put down his own experiences. So naturally he thought of me. He realizes that the *Intelligencer* is not exactly pro-Royalist, but has noticed that it prefers the frequent approximation of the truth to the usual full diet of scandal – though he offers to provide plenty of that, too, in time. The man's a born storyteller. Shall we give him permanent employment?'

'Mr Vane might not like it.'

'We owe nothing to Harry Vane. He isn't John Pym, God rest him.'

'We still need his patronage; it's worth a lot of copies.'

'Then we'll persuade him that to be the only London book with a regular Royalist correspondent will double our circulation.'

'Especially since he's an Irishman as well as a Cavalier. Most of us think they run about in nothing but tattoos, gnawing on shinbones and slaughtering anything on two legs or four – Mr O'Connor is going to surprise a lot of our readers.'

'Do them good. Now let's hurry up and sort out the rest of these, then we can go for supper.'

'Soon as you like. We mustn't be late. Ma's a chancy sort of cook and she's put on a roast, seeing it's you.'

Skimming through the rest of the articles, they accepted a sober account of the plight of their Scots allies. Then there were Vane's own notes on the composition and purpose of the Committee of the Two Kingdoms to be written up. This was the executive and advisory body set up for the conduct of the war, to which Parliament now delegated its responsibilities. It consisted of the Scots Commissioners as well as several of their own members, among them Vane, St John and Oliver Cromwell, whose victorious generalship in the Eastern Association had made his insistence upon firm religion and Spartan training an example to all thoughtful commanders.

Jud and Robin had become keen Cromwell watchers. They did not find him a sympathetic character; he was too grim, glum and godly. But he had formidable powers of energy and intellect, and though his detractors might snigger at his conviction that he was marked out by God's own hand for victory, Jud and Robin did not, for he seemed well on the way to proving it. They applauded his successes in the field and liked what they learned of his political opinions. The price of the Scots Alliance had been that England should take the Covenant and become Presbyterian. Cromwell had taken it, as had most of his fellow Parliamentarians, but much as one takes evil-tasting medicine, his own conviction being that a man's religion is a matter for his own conscience. They expected to hear more from him on this subject.

'Come on. That'll do for today. Let's go and broach a keg of my mother's Sunday ale and drink to old Noll till he'd clap us in irons for our evil example!'

Mistress Nan Whittaker's establishment was in Leech Lane, off St Olave's Street, just behind the river in Southwark, and Jud now treated it as his second home. It was a drunken disaster of a house, its lower storey teetering back from the street, and the upper one lurching, ramshackle, over it. An empty upper window, covered in black cloth like an eye-patch, completed its air of helpless disorientation. Inside, there were two rooms downstairs and two more upstairs, sparsely furnished with only the barest of necessities and decorated with the changeable and sometimes surprisingly artistic efflorescences of rot and damp. Given its obvious deficiencies, how was it, Jud wondered, that he thought of it only as a warm and comfortable place where he could be entirely at ease and utterly content?

As they entered the kitchen they were engulfed by heat and noise and the smell of roasting meat. It was a small, oblong room, with an oven in the chimney corner. It contained one sizeable table, two long benches, two rickety chairs and a rough, woven cradle near the stove. A colourful assortment of odd, chipped crockery concealed the worst of a worm-eaten and derelict dresser. Several stone jars nudged each other in the corner opposite the chimney; someone else's cat was snoozing on top of one of them. On the earthen floor, Endymion Whittaker and his brother Charlemagne were playing Fox and Geese on squares they had hacked into it. Mrs Whittaker liked to name her children for heroes or queens and Charlie's father had been a French merchant sailor. Robin, her firstborn, had never ceased to thank his stars that the mother of Sherwood's outlaw had not shared this predeliction. Nan herself was better fitted by nature to be a queen than many who held that dignity. The uncertain country girl, with her ready smile and her alluring body, had matured into a complete woman, sure of herself and of her command over men. Her colouring was blackberries and cream and her shape now shared the felicities of an Attic vase. She was kind and content and she adored her children.

'Give you a game for money?' suggested Endymion, grinning gappily at Jud as he entered.

'No thanks. You cleared me out last time. Are those our founts you're playing with?'

'No, it's only Cleo's alphabet. She let us, honest!'

' 'S'right, Jud. I did. Only don't you go and lose any or I'll lather your breeches. I've hardly got enough as it is, now I'm learning such long words.'

Jud was engaged in the process of teaching Robin's sister Cleopatra to read and write. Whatever labour this entailed was more than recompensed by the fact that Cleo was a bewitchingly beautiful girl, her body a wand of willow, her face a pale setting for sapphires between silken curtains of hair as dusky as the Egyptian midnight her namesake had known. She was sixteen and a virgin and Jud loved her to distraction. Robin had threatened to cut off his balls if he laid a finger on her. But Cleo herself bathed him consistently in the great blue pools of her eyes that were swimming with hopes and promises. He greeted her softly, his voice catching his throat as she turned away to bend and look at something in the oven. The shape of her ravished him; the slim back narrowing to the handspan waist and then the miraculous womanly rounding into hips and buttocks; it was pure poetry. He longed to walk over to her and take her by those hips and just hold her, not out of any overwhelming lust, but just to be intimately near her and to pay reverent tribute to the mere existence of such singing curves. Her voice delighted him too. Softer than Rob's and lacking his spiced conversation, its cadences echoed the streets around them just as his did, but somehow made them beautiful. Just now, as she leaned to dandle a snatch of song above the latest occupant of the cradle, it was as if Circe herself called him to her side.

'Has your mother named him yet?' he asked, inspecting the swaddled, ill-smelling bundle.

'No. I thought of Alexander, but she doesn't think it grand enough. She favours Hercules, today at least.'

'Oh Lord! What about Julius? For Caesar?'

'Not bad. Mother! What about Julius – for 'is Majesty, 'ere?'

The smell of burning told them this was not the time to ask. 'You can call 'im 'Ot-Buttered-Toast for all I care – get me another pan, quick! And Charlie – go and fetch Ettamaria an' Podge from down the street, and be sharp about it. Robin, you start carving, there's my good lad.'

In some ways, Jud thought as he set out the least damaged plates with the worn knives beside them on the table, it was like being at home when he was a child; the same warmth and bustle and back-chat. Heron. His home. How much things had changed in these last two years or so, and how very much he wished they had not. Not that he would exchange even his old life at Heron for his work at the press, of course; he wouldn't take an Emperor's ransom for that. But Tom had no right to shut him out. A man needed his family life. It was natural to him. He looked into Cleopatra's melting eyes again and wished it was not entirely ridiculous to think of marrying her.

The last two members of the irregular household were hauled in, quarrelling fiercely, and set down on opposite sides of the table so that they could only glower and recriminate.

'You dropped it right in front of 'is nose, you bloody fool!' complained Henrietta Maria, four feet six of ginger curls and freckles with a very dirty face.

'I couldn't 'elp it. You saw 'ow 'e tripped me. 'E knew 'e'd bin taken. I bet 'e woz a perfessinel 'imself,' defended Podge, properly Tamburlaine, who at ten resembled a senior and overweight cherub.

'My arse! You woz as clumsy as if you 'ad a cloven 'oof! You're lucky I wasted my time leadin' 'im off you – and bugger-all to show for the work!'

'Ettamaria,' said her mother sternly, ' 'ave you been thievin' again?'

The ginger curls bounced. 'No. I just said, did'nt I? We came 'ome empty-'anded. Stupid little shag-'ead.' She kicked her brother under the table.

Nan sniffed. She looked regretful on the whole. 'We'll say no more then,' she allowed diplomatically. She knew perfectly well that all her children stole; she stole herself when the opportunity was too good to miss. But she did not like all this to be obvious in front of Jud, who was a gentleman and couldn't be expected to understand. She was fond of Jud. They all were, especially Cleo; you could see *that* with a glass eye. It was a pity in a way. If it had been any other gentleman there would almost certainly have been something to gain by it – but you couldn't ask for money for Cleo's cherry from a friend of the family, now could you? Well, at least it would start the girl off enjoying it, and that would be all to the good. Nan was quite unaware of Rob's chivalry on his sister's behalf and it would have astounded her to discover it. But Robin had seen enough of the privileged world to know that Cleo's beauty was something rare in any part of society, and he knew her bright nature to be equally praiseworthy. He did not plan for her to throw herself away on the first fellow who got her hot for him. She could have a better life than this, one day, if she played her cards right and listened to him.

This reading and writing now; that was all very good and would help to bring her up a peg or two, and he supposed he didn't mind if she and Jud shared a kiss and a cuddle occasionally, but he had let his friend and partner know, very plainly, that it must stop at that. Jud had Marion down at the 'Ship' if he wanted a tumble, and Cleo had plenty to occupy her with improving her education and keeping up with her work as a seamstress. When they had eaten their beef, greens and gravy and a delicious apple pie, Jud suggested to Cleo that they might take a brief, digestive walk. This won him a nod and a wink from Nan and a keen look of warning from Rob.

'Yes, please. I'd like to very much,' said Cleo herself.

'Don't be long, that's all,' muttered Rob as they left.

'We might drop in at the "Bear",' Jud threw over his shoulder.

A fine spring evening in London, with the Thames gleaming softly at one's side, is one of the pleasures to be shared by the privileged and unprivileged alike. It was quiet on this side of the river now that the beargarden and the theatres were closed and the gaiety and extravagance and sheer economic force of the Court had gone, but the ordinaries were still open for those who had anything to spend in them, and in those which still had coal to feed their fires, the welcome was as warm and the company as cheerful as ever.

They strolled by the waterside for a time, Cleo's hand resting on Jud's arm, so that he swelled with masculine pride and responsibility. He patted the hand in connubial fashion.

'You've made tremendous progress with your writing, in such a short time,' he told her, trying to distract himself from the swing of her walk. 'We shall soon have you writing articles for the newsbook.'

'Get along with you! What'd I write? A girl like me?'

'Oh I don't know. Why shouldn't women have something to read as well as men? We could have a domestic page – all about the prices of things and so on.'

She thought. 'You mean what they *do* cost, and what they ought to cost; things like that?'

He hadn't really considered it, but it wasn't a bad idea. 'Something like that perhaps.' He smiled at her. He hadn't been serious and she knew it.

'I do so envy you and Rob sometimes, having something really worthwhile to do. I wish I'd been born a boy, so I do, so that I might've learned more than just sewing.'

'I'm glad you weren't,' Jud said selfishly.

She sighed for lost opportunities, then, never negative for long, laughed, a clear uncomplicated peal that sent sweet shivers down the length of him. 'It's such an odd thing, when you think of it; you 'n' Rob. Who would've guessed you two would get on so well? Rob's been lucky, knowing you.'

'I've been lucky too, make no mistake. Rob's brain is as good as mine; better, I often think. He's so quick –' he smiled, 'and so *suspicious*; that's a quality I lack, and it comes in more than useful, I can tell you.'

'Yes. Each of you knows about different things, different ways of life. You have different, well – feelings, too—'

'Instincts?'

'Yes. But it doesn't seem to make you disagree as one might think; do you never fall out together?'

'We argue sometimes, of course. Quite viciously on occasion. But we usually manage to compromise. We *need* each other, you see; that's a pretty good discipline in itself. We both know it, and don't often go too far.'

'When did you last – go too far?' Her question was idle but it drained him of pleasure as though she had splintered a cask.

'It was over an article concerning the execution of a Catholic priest in Gloucestershire. I didn't want to print it. Rob made me see that I must.'

'I'm sorry.' She was quick to sense his distress. 'I should not have asked.' She offered no further question and Jud was grateful. In certain respects he would never be a Parliament man.

'*Shall* we warm ourselves by the "Bear's" fire?' she suggested as they came beneath the black bulk of Tower Bridge.

The 'Bear at the Foot of the Bridge' was a large and popular tavern whose foundation was laid in 1310. It was a home from home to the Whittakers. Nan met her gentlemen friends there. Endymion and Charlie acted as frequent temporary potboys, continually sacked for picking pockets and taken on again for their mother's smile. The younger children helped with the washing-up on Saturday nights and even the baby was taken there for an occasional change of air. Jud and Rob often ate their dinner there and Cleo would sometimes join them. They were too late to get a look at a fire, but the rooms were hot with the press of bodies and Jud managed to find them a space on a settle in a dark corner, so small that she must sit almost in his pocket. He ordered spiced wine and leaned back with his arm around her.

'You don't mind? It's easier to sit so.'

She looked at him with the lack of pretence that always surprised him. 'I don't mind. I like to be close to you.' They stared seriously into each other's faces and did not notice when the potboy brought their wine. Jud took the cannekins and handed her one. His mind was racing.

'Cleo, I want—' What could he say? He ought to say nothing.

She laid her hand on his sleeve, with a sad, wise smile that hurt him. 'Don't be troubled, Jud. I know what can and cannot be.' He was her first love and she could not imagine any other.

'But I'm no longer sure that *I* know. I seem always to put myself beyond the pale. Perhaps that is where I belong.'

'You do not belong in St Olave's Street. Nor I at Heronscourt.

That is as it is, and will not change. It could only distress me if you were to make me think so.'

He lifted her hand and kissed it. 'Then I shall simply be your schoolmaster. But you must not mind if I read you love-stories.'

'Oh, I don't know that it need stop at that,' she said, matter-of-factly. She had a great deal of her mother's sureness, already knowing her value as a woman. She stood up, setting down her cup on the bench. 'Come on. Drink up, and we'll take a stroll round St Mary Overy's.' The church had a certain reputation by night that it was pleased to ignore by day.

Jud leaped up and followed her to the door.

They crossed the High Street and plunged into the darkness surrounding the ancient church. A watchman moved ahead of them, lonely in the light of his lamp. They walked entwined, murmuring to each other, feeling their limbs grow heavy with the knowledge that soon they could be as close as they desired. Soon Jud spied a covered porch jutting from one of the outbuildings. He drew her into it and she came into his arms with a passion that was as honest as her lack of female dissembling. They kissed as though no man or woman had ever kissed before, their lips, their tongues, and as they felt their very souls exchanged. They went willingly into the fire and emerged cauterized, chastened and shaking.

He stepped back from her a little, though still holding her. 'Whatever we may have prohibited ourselves,' he said unsteadily, 'it is clear that there is one thing we *will* do, and that instantly, if we don't stop this here and now.'

'But we will not do it here,' was all she said.

'Devil take it, Cleo, do you know what you're saying?'

'Both what I say and what I want to do. Be content with that, and don't upset yourself over what should not or cannot 'appen. Happen.' The small correction made him ache with love and he pressed her to him as though he were trying to combine them into a single body, until Cleo complained that he was breaking her bones and she wouldn't be much good to him as a cripple.

While they were walking back beside the black slither of the Thames with its diamond glitter, he kept telling himself, with all the happy incredulousness of the newborn, that Cleo had insisted that she become his mistress; he told himself so over and over again as she walked like a goddess beside him, her head held proudly upon her long neck, her firm steps leading him unhesitatingly into the future – but he simply could not believe it.

York, July 1644

The room was small and narrow. A single high window slanted a shaft of light across the bed in the mornings. The bells of the great Minster sounded clearly through it. They were tolling for the dead. Tom heard their strong bass note sometimes through the spiralling polyphony of his fever. He tried to hold on to the sonorous monotone through his slipping consciousness, because it told him that he was here in York, that he was alive despite the wound beneath his shoulder where the shot had smashed through muscle and tissue into bone. They had probed him through screaming pain and into unconsciousness, but the hole kept filling up with pus and the possibility was gangrene.

He could wait and hope, they said, or he could lose his arm. He had chosen the former.

He thought it might be improving; he didn't feel so bad when he was awake, which was rarely. But the wry, tireless little doctor whom Rupert had sent, would make no comment. He simply dressed the wound with exemplary care and cleanliness and dosed Tom with opiates that sent his wits winnowing down a tunnel filled with heat, wind and voices into a spinning, rumorous vortex that was half nightmare, half memory.

It always began in the same way; with his father's death. He would hear the words intoned over the coffin and feel the soft blows as the earth was thrown upon it – for by one of the strange shifts that are logical in dreams, it had become his own coffin now, and he was stifling, alive and helpless, shouting and beating upon the wood that lowered over him – but the parson was bellowing the words of the service, the echo of his voice reverberating from the walls about him, its clamour like that of a giant bell, so that no one could hear Tom. Somehow, even in that smothering terror, he knew, in the kernel of his consciousness, that it would end, and that he would suddenly find himself free and on horseback, on a great open plain with limitless sky above him. There were a thousand others like himself, but oddly diminished in size, wheeling and caracoling in front of him, to his design and at his orders. He was training Rupert's cavalry recruits at Shrewsbury, the bold Welsh Marchers and the wild Irish, bending all that ebullient energy and will into a tough, fighting unit that would react as one man. As his commands grew more assured and their obedience more automatic, his toy soldiers began to increase in size, the sound of their voices growing with them, louder, louder – until they were no longer on the green fields of Cheshire but racing through the Chilterns on a never-ending raid, looting, burning, fighting their way through Parliament country. Tom's sword was always wet; it came wet from the scabbard.

Now he was back in Oxford. He was in a ballroom, among lambent lights and languorous women. Valora was in his arms. Valora! He would try to wake then, but that was not permitted. He must go back to his troopers and to the bitter echo of Oxford's quarrels among men who had grown slack and insolent after the summer's raiding, men who threw away their training and their dignity in crude scuffles with the infantry, in horse-thieving, in highway robbery. He must have them ready, for the testing time would come.

Another face swims up, dark curls, proud head, a soft Scottish voice – Montrose. Back in Oxford, then, where the King practises his deep deceits with the enemies of the Covenanters. Montrose will rouse the Scottish Royalists and Argyll will be forced to turn back from his Parliamentary allies in order to engage him. And behind Montrose, another soft voice – the liquid, Catholic promises of the Earl of Antrim: a thousand Irishmen to join Montrose, making twenty, perhaps thirty thousand in all – and the war as good as won!

Surely Tom may awake, on such a rising note? Or is he awake? If he is, his release is not yet. After the sweets of victory, the ashes of defeat; not his, not Rupert's, but the taste is strong in his mouth. It was not a great battle, no vast set-piece in the main theatre of the north, but a modest affair in a small town near Winchester. Alresford. Where Waller outwitted not one but three of the King's generals. The confidence of Newark begins to drain away with the hope of victory in the south.

But the taste is more acrid than the blood of one defeat can account for. Is he awake or asleep, goddamnit? It fills his mouth until he is choking with it. He makes a superhuman effort, trying to rise, but an iron hand is on his chest, holding him down. The taste does not diminish and the voices are there again, loud, declamatory, fierce.

Rupert's is the loudest, despairing that he is only human; he can't be in two places at once. They are at Shrewsbury. The King wants him to rush to his defence at Oxford, now threatened after the loss of Alresford. Rupert knows he should go north to York, where the Marquis of Newcastle is under siege by the combined armies of the Scots and the Eastern Association. But he gallops off and gives his uncle his advice – to sit tight and play the defensive game – listens to the howls of dissent from the Council of War, leaves them still arguing and hares back to begin the march for York.

The countryside is in terror. It is Rupert the Invincible, Rupert the Devil. In Preston the fat burgesses piss themselves and chuck out their pride to invite the arch-fiend to a banquet. 'Banquets are not for soldiers,' says Rupert stuffily, replete with thieved beef.

They take Liverpool. At last the port for Ireland. Young Cathal is with Tom. They spend half a morning finding a sailor who will take a letter to his family. Plucky little beggar. Always smiling, and the very devil of a swordsman. Who would have thought it?

Rupert is shouting again. What now? Oh God, how sickeningly predictable. The despatches are in. The King has taken other advice since his nephew's mad race to his side. He has gone adventuring in Oxfordshire and has lost the whole bloody shoot! Garrisons, towns, even Oxford itself. He is in Worcester now, licking his wounds.

He wants Rupert back. He'll take his advice next time. He sends no *order* to return, but the threat is always there. Rupert puts it away in the compartment he uses to keep himself sane, and concentrates on York.

The melancholy Scots and Puritans sit about its mellow medieval walls like vultures, waiting for their sappers to do their work. Something spectacular is called for. As always, Rupert provides it.

The enemy know they are at Knaresboro', fourteen miles west of the city, so they are expected to march due east and engage at a convenient point. The Scots C-in-C, Leslie Leven, withdraws his troops from the north of the city, crosses the River Ouse by boat-bridge and blocks the road into the town on some level ground near the village of Long Marston.

Rupert, well satisfied, takes them on one of his lightning dashes, six miles to the north, to Boro'bridge, where they cross the river and race for the abandoned north gate of the city. Leven stupefied! York saved! Its citizens are relieved of their troubles and its predators of their store of ammunition, plus 4,000 pairs of boots, over which there is great joy in the heaven of the Royalist camp, Tom among the first to benefit. His old boots were showing their mileage, their uppers ragged and sagging, and the soles unskilfully cobbled by Josh with cowhide.

That foul taste is rising in his chest again. He pushes it down. He knows it now. It is the flavour of defeat.

Tom is quite awake. His mind is perfectly clear. Only his memory insists. The battle will decide the domination of the north, that is plain. Rupert is tense, full of plans, expectant of victory. He believes his own legend; he has little reason to do otherwise. The Marquis of Newcastle has written to him, a flowery extravagance of compliments, making no mention of the knowledge he must have gained during the two months' siege, of the enemy's dispositions. Where is Sir Thomas Fairfax? Where is the redoubtable Cromwell? Would he place himself opposite Rupert in the field, as the latter hoped? The Prince longed to match himself against this man, the only one among the enemy to challenge his known superiority as a leader of cavalry.

'Write to Newcastle to be ready to march with us at four o'clock in the morning. At least we know where Leven is – still milling about at Long Marston, wondering how we managed to get north of him. It's as good a place as any. We'll pay him an early visit!'

'That early?' asks Tom.

'Never too soon. We must meet and defeat them as soon as we can and get back to the King before matters grow worse down south.' There is a gleam of mischief in his eye. 'We'll send a troop or two to feint south as we march west. It worked last time.'

And it very nearly works again. Parliament take the bait and start sending their infantry off southward to bar our road; but then one of their regular patrols runs into our main march west and the ruse is known. If only we could have attacked *then*, while their foot were still streaming off in the wrong direction! We had such an advantage of time and numbers.

Rupert won't do it. He has promised to wait for Newcastle and his 3,000 infantry. The Marquis does not come. We don't know it then, but he has a full scale mutiny on his hands. He rides in at nine o'clock, in pouring rain, at the head of a small party of civilian gentlemen of York.

Tom admires Rupert's control. He remarks once that he could wish the Marquis had arrived earlier, and with his troops, and turns at once to the business of the day.

He presses for an immediate attack. They still have an advantage. Newcastle wants to wait for his infantry, who should be behind him on the road. Against his own judgement, Rupert gives the older man the deference he desires.

All day we wait, reproved by repeated showers of heavy-dropped summer rain. Across the field, on an axis between Long Marston and the neighbouring village of Tockwith, we watch Fairfax arrive, and Cromwell. They begin to draw up their ranks. Leven's infantry trickle back from their nose-lead. By four o'clock they are fully drawn up and singing their goddamned, mournful psalms. If Rupert is suffering from an almost uncontrollable urge to murder Newcastle, he keeps it to himself, which is more than his officers can manage.

Tom is cursing aloud, even now. His brow is damp. He wipes it on a handkerchief. He gazes at the blank white wall ahead of him, seeing nothing but uniforms still, and horses and blood; hearing the screams and the whimpers, the whole savage menagerie over again, but so much worse, this time, than he could have imagined. It made him weak. He didn't want to think about it. He had done his best. They all had. But it had been no good. He couldn't *stop* thinking about it.

It is half-past four by the time the wretched infantry straggles up – Newcastle's Lambs, in their white coats of undyed wool. Wool in the head as well, God rot them!

They complete their dispositions. Cromwell is facing us and the deep ditch will break the force of his charge; we will remain on the defensive. Let Cromwell be the initiator.

Time passes. Cromwell makes no move.

Rupert is getting edgy. The evening is coming. If they are to see any action today, they had best begin it themselves. But no. Newcastle won't hear of it. Nor will Eythin, his second-in-command. They have their way because Eythin is able to remind Rupert of an occasion, back in the distant past of the German war, when 'his forwardness lost us the day'.

Rupert gives in. Both armies are very quiet. Tension departs. The usual crowd of spectators vanish with it.

'We may as well have supper. There'll be no battle today,' says the Prince, sick and tired of it all. So we break ranks – and that is when Cromwell attacks!

Should Rupert have expected it? I don't know. The hour was late, the light uncertain. At any rate, that lack of expectation was our fatal flaw. We never caught up with ourselves that night. And we never caught up with Cromwell either.

It was mad dog Byron who was first off the mark, responding at once to that terrible charge while the rest of us were still catching flies. But Cromwell was already across the ditch and it was Byron's cavalry that sank into the soft ground that should have slowed him up, and masked our own musketeers who could not shoot to check Cromwell for fear of hitting Byron's men.

When Rupert took this in, we raced up from the rear to meet some of the first line already in retreat. Rupert turned them and they followed us back in. There were musketeers everywhere in our path. The same old nightmare; the same old mistakes. We made what we could of it for half an hour, fighting well enough. We even began to make headway. But then in came Leven with his Scots, line upon line of them sweeping over our undefended flank.

The reserves! Where in Christ's name are the reserves? The impact was too strong.

We couldn't hold. We began to break. Then to scatter. Then to turn tail and race from the field towards York. There is nothing so degrading as to be among cavalry in headlong flight. Panic spreads amongst you like wildfire and there is no stopping it.

Rupert tried to keep some of them together. Several of us tried with him, but we may as well have saved our breath in that devil's cauldron. All those months of training gone for nothing. We were running like terrified schoolboys.

And then to be felled by a stray shot, one of ours as like as not! Didn't feel it at the time, not really. Only noticed it when the world went black and I felt myself slump in the saddle. They said a sergeant of foot picked me up and got me to the surgeons' tent. I hope he knows how grateful I am for that. It was a messy business. Painful. Still is.

The rest of the fight was hearsay to me. It was Cromwell's battle, they said. That victorious first charge had given him time to survey the field and judge where he was most needed. He soon spotted his chance. Goring had driven off young Fairfax with a splendid charge and had gone dashing off after him on the road to Hull, hell and Halifax without a backward thought for the rest of us.

Cromwell turned his troops and pounded across the middle of the ground between our reserves and our infantry, taking up Goring's old position. Our infantry, poor devils, were already going down to theirs. Now, surrounded completely, they fell in their hundreds. We had no resistance in us. Goring had gone. Rupert had gone. Our Lancashire foot had thrown down their arms in terror at the savagery of the Fenmen's opposition. All that was left was murder.

It was Newcastle's Lambs who were the victims. Reconciled to their duty, perhaps knowing the responsibility their general should accept for this night's work, they fought stubbornly, proud and unrelenting, now that their hour had come. Wrecked by Cromwell's troopers, they would take no quarter, but were cut down where they stood, without hope, without a moment for a prayer. It would have shamed them to have done otherwise. They say that, after that, Newcastle and Eythin could not face the court. They have left the country.

Cromwell, though! The man is brilliant, no doubt of it, and to our most grievous cost. That was a breath-taking manoeuvre, to take his squadrons through the centre like that, and almost without a scratch.

And such an indomitable, unyielding presence. Tom had seen him, quite closely, just for a few seconds. His eyes were everywhere, his lips set, his arm never ceasing its signals of command. What was it Rupert had called him afterwards? He had spoken almost with affection. Old Ironside, that was it. It suited him.

Dear God, what a night. It had lost them the north. It had lost them 4,000 men. And how does one estimate the loss of pride, of confidence, of belief in the legend? If only they had realized that . . .

'Sir Thomas.' He forced his eyes to focus properly. They showed him an orderly looking at him from the doorway. 'You have a visitor, sir, if you are able for it.'

Who was it? There was an impatient susurration of silk and Valora pushed past the man into the room.

'Is it really you?' He couldn't tell if he spoke aloud.

She stopped and slowly unwound the veil of lace that shawled her hair. He looked so fragile. His skin seemed no protection for his bones. Transparent. She was afraid. She had been afraid ever since Josh had sent to her.

She smiled at him, not yet sure of her tone. It was such a shock to her to see him lie there. So limp. Too ill even to dislike his own disadvantage. 'I asked for leave. The Queen is fully occupied with her new daughter. As I am neither a wet nurse nor very patient with small infants, she was easily persuaded that I was dispensable.'

'Yes.' He was struggling to realize the enormous change that her presence must mean to him. Now he could no longer lie, bodiless, except for the floating notion of pain, upon the swell of a current that carried him along or held him suspended according to its own mysterious impulse. He must become a swimmer again, accept the effort to draw breath, make the movements of life.

She saw that he looked at her, that he knew who she was, but his eyes were drugged and she thought that perhaps he had not spoken for a long time. She motioned the orderly to leave and came over to stand beside the bed.

'I missed you too badly,' she said, choosing this remark rather than any mention of his condition, about which she was not qualified to judge and would not speak idly.

She *was* really here, then. Not still the dream-memory. He fixed his eyes on her. He was almost through to her now. If she could just wait a very little . . .

There was a chair. She began to pull it towards her. 'No.' He *could* speak. Good. 'The bed.'

His voice was weak, but the same; not the one she had dreaded, that far-off whisper, already claimed by the tomb. She knew that Josh had thought he was dying. She sat carefully beside him and took his hand. Bones again. No weight.

He tried his voice again. 'Journey? Dangerous.'

She shrugged. It had not been easy. There had been one or two hair-raising moments. But they were not for now. 'I am here. I love you.'

'Yes. I am glad.'

'You will recover now. Soon.' It was an order and he must obey, because now that she saw him, now she knew him still in her world, she could not bear anything else.

'Of course. Very soon.' Why was it such an effort to talk? His mind was clear enough. It was the physical part of it that was so infernally difficult. He had never been as weak as this before. It was a strange sensation, or rather, the lack of it; as though one were hardly there at all. She seemed so vibrant with life in contrast. He could almost see the blood pulsing in her veins. Even sitting there like that, as still as she could ever be, she seemed full of movement, of overwhelming energy.

'Don't talk any more today.' She had seen him look suddenly more tired. 'We shall take it day by day. I will come in and tell you all the news.' She saw that this recalled his thoughts to the moonlight on the moor. 'Not all of it is ill. The King has won a fine victory over Waller, at a place called Cropedy Bridge, not far from Edge Hill.'

He had heard the name hovering over his delirium. Josh, it must have been. 'And Rupert?' He had no idea where his commander was.

'He has gone west, to Chester I think. York has surrendered,' she added very gently. 'You may stay here until you recover, and then you will join him again.' She did not tell him that Parliament offered him the alternative of remaining in York to join their own ranks.

He did not try to reply and she realized that he did not fret about his position as yet. Was this to the good, or not? She must wait and let the passing days tell her. 'I am going to leave you now, but I will come back tomorrow.'

'You are beautiful. And brave. And I love you,' he managed before sleep came down and shut her out.

The little doctor, whose name was Picard, was not at first disposed to tell her any more than he would tell Tom himself. But he soon observed that he had a more than usually determined questioner and responded, after a time, with the cautious suggestion that there was room for hope. 'I never like to amputate, unless I must, but the risk is as great, truthfully, one way as the other. I will not disguise the fact.'

'But it is more than two weeks since he was wounded. And he has not died,' she said, trying out the word with simulated courage.

'No,' the doctor admitted, 'but there is still fever, and the infection is very stubborn.' He peered at her through odd, square spectacles. 'But since I see you will force me to give an opinion, then I would repeat, there is room for hope.' He smiled dryly.

It was good enough. Greedily she fed on it, building up the strength that would make *him* strong.

When she saw him the next day, he was different. They had given him less of the opiate and his eyes were wide awake and full of pain. There was a curious innocence in them too; they were without his habitual defences, the look of judgement, or of the subtraction of self from circumstances, with which he distanced the world. Just the eyes of a man in pain.

She talked to him about small things, how they were managing at Heron, about her brief spell of duty with the Queen, who had insisted that she be with her for the birth of small Henriette. She did not speak of battles and the whereabouts of generals, but of books and music and gossip. She would not let Tom talk at all.

The next day, after chatting in a similar fashion for a while, she announced that she was going to read to him. Not prayers, or sermons or the Bible, as most would have thought fitting, but plays, essays and poetry, anything that had love or grandeur or laughter in it. She had no intention of preparing his soul for the life hereafter, but of recalling him, mind and body, to the here and now. Especially she read the love poems of John Donne, that great saint and sinner who had loved both Christ and Eros, and each with a whole and subject heart. Her Church, naturally did not approve of him; he had, after all, been the Dean of St Paul's; but Valora had never lived close to the rule and could not think her soul in any danger from the work of such an evident seeker after all that was good and true.

As the days went by, Tom became noticeably stronger, and her fear subsided gradually, though it did not entirely leave her and would not do so until little Picard was content to pronounce him out of danger.

Now the fever had gone and he slept for long, refreshing, dreamless hours. The wound still oozed pus, but less than before and the pain was not so strong.

'If only Martha were here,' said Valora one day, curled in the shaft of sunlight at his feet. '*She* would close up the wound in no time with one of those sweet-smelling unguents of hers. I have always wondered why anything made up by medical men can be relied upon to stink worse than corruption. Martha's potions smell of the gardens from which they come.'

'She would be best to leave off her medicines for a while,' Tom said. His eyes were not innocent now, but inhabited by irony.

'You are always so curt when you speak of Martha,' said Valora lazily. 'I think you are a little afraid of her.'

'Why? Because she has the reputation of a witch?' He was startled.

'No.' She laughed. 'I think that for some reason that I couldn't begin to fathom, you are reproved by her goodness.'

This came too near the mark for Tom. He shifted his position, causing himself discomfort and eliciting her instant sympathy. 'Do be careful. You were bleeding yesterday, remember.'

'It was good, fresh blood. Nothing to worry about.' It was true. He felt much stronger now. He wondered how strong. 'Come here. Closer. Don't sit at the bottom of the bed like a cat.'

He made room for her on his good side and she crawled up to rest on her elbow, leaning on his pillow. He kissed her. It was not the first time. There had been several kisses over the days.

'I don't know if it is your eternal poetry, but I begin to feel dissatisfied with mere kisses. If I am to recover, I shall need a great deal more.'

'How much more?' she enquired, her voice velvet.

'I cannot say. We shall just have to find out.'

She lay acquiescent while he unfastened her dress, then moaned softly when his lips found her breast.

'Come. Beneath the covers.'

'But if I hurt you—'

'Nonsense. I want you close to me. Not a mile of confounded silks and sheets away from me.'

She wanted it too. She undressed and slipped in beside him. They held each other without speaking, kissing as carefully as they could. Both trembled with the effort to be so gentle. Their hands travelled lovingly over known territory and they whispered things they had said many times before, conscious all the time of what they must not do.

In the end, that time, they brought each other to a kind of relief with hands and lips. It was not what they needed but it was very necessary all the same.

It was the next day that she asked him to marry her without delay. 'It is why I came here.'

'You mean – now? Here?'

She was adept at surprise. 'That is what I mean. I don't want to wait any longer. Before we have finished mourning your father, I may well be forced to mourn *you*. We have seen how easily it is possible. We have come very near to it. Please, let us not waste any more of our life together. I want to be with you, not with the Queen, not even at Heron. With you. Marry me, tomorrow, today if you like, and I'll be a leaguer lady like the rest, and go with you wherever your duty takes you.' She finished triumphantly and waited for his reply. 'Is it so hard to agree?' she asked, as he continued to look as though she had hit him on the head.

He laughed then and the rare sound filled her with happiness. She would teach him to do that more often.

'You might at least crow a little, in view of our past heart-searching. Here am I, trailing my banners in the dust for you – religion, pride, propriety, all in rags at your feet – and all you can do is laugh! You do not appear properly to know when to seize your advantage.'

He surveyed her through slit eyes, without speaking. His worse nature reminded him how deeply she had made him suffer during the last two years. If she could do this now, why not before? He would never understand her. He saw her face begin to change as his silence sowed the seeds of uncertainty. He dismissed the past and held out his arms to her.

'If you will ring for Josh,' he said between kisses, 'he will be more than delighted to go out and find the nearest parson.'

'Excellent,' she murmured into his hair.

'He will be an Anglican,' he warned.

'But we may have a priest as well? As soon as one may be found? An Anglican may marry *you*, my love, but assuredly he cannot marry *me*.'

He sighed. This would never end, not for a lifetime. But by God, whether he be English or Popish, it would be worth it!

'Are you sure it is what you want?' he asked her, just once. 'I know many officers do have their wives with them, but it is a hard life for a woman, to be a camp-follower.'

'I am quite certain,' she said firmly. 'I have never cared for soft living. I shall thrive on army life.'

'Then, I will send Josh at once, and my orderly for the priest. Only it might not be quite the thing if the two gentlemen were to meet!' He chuckled. 'If you would not object to a seemly interval between the ceremonies?'

'You are still laughing at me. But no, I have no objection.'

'Then shall we have the Anglican first? He'll be the simplest to find.'

'By all means. I daresay, having lived so long in sin, I can face the prospect a trifle longer with equanimity.' He would never know how much it had hurt her to do so, knowing as she did how much more she had hurt her Lord in so sinning. One day He would ask her for payment.

In the event, the priest appeared almost upon the heels of the parson. It was Cathal O'Connor, who somehow contrived never to be far from Tom, who found him. His name was Father O'Laoghaire and he had come over with the first wave of Irish infantry and was ministering to those of his countrymen who lay wounded in York. He celebrated the nuptial mass, upon the desk at the end of Tom's bed, in a brogue so thick that the new-wed husband declared it might as well have been a recipe for soup for all he could make of it.

'Not at all,' said Lady Heron sweetly, tossing her crown of black curls. 'It was a recipe, I can promise you, for something with a great deal more of a kick in it!'

Heron, September 1644

Lucy was standing with Kit and Tibbett at the foot of one of the smaller oaks in the game park. Humpty, halfway up the tree, was examining the damage done by recent storms. If it proved extensive they would drain the sap and fell the tree for firewood. 'Blasted to Hades and back!' was the cheerful diagnosis.

'Then you can start to strip the bark,' Lucy told Kit. Oak bark was prized by the tanner for its rich dark stain for leather.

'Someone coming! From the house!' Humpty yelled again.

She narrowed her eyes and peered. They did not expect anyone. A tall man in a red cloak, moving quickly. 'Tibbett, you're far-sighted. Can you make him out? If I didn't know better, I'd say it was Will Staunton.' Her voice brightened on the name.

'No, 'tisn't Mr Will. He has more breadth of shoulder and more of a swagger to his walk.'

Lucy was disappointed, but set off towards the approaching figure. There was certainly something familiar about him. Then, swept by a sudden intuition, she broke into a run. 'Oh it can't be! Please, dear Lord, *let* it be. Sweet Jesus, it is!'

In half a minute she was in Cathal's arms. 'I *knew* that you would come. How I've waited! It has been so long!'

'I know. For me too. I am sorry. The Prince would not give me leave until now, and then only after Tom had begged it of him. I have so much to tell you all—'

'Not yet. Just let me look at you—'

'Just let me kiss you!' He held her steady while the world exploded into a million brilliant particles of delight, showering down upon them through the mist of the September morning, making it luminous with their joy.

'You are just the same. You've grown, I think, and there is that little moustache, but your face is just the same. How well I know it; I have thought of you every day. Oh but, Cathal, so *many* days.'

'Eighteen months,' he said sadly. 'How did we bear it?' He kissed her again, lingering this time.

She hung on his lips for a few precious seconds, then regretfully pulled away. 'We mustn't. Tibbett will see and tell Mother.'

'I'm sure Tibbett is the soul of discretion.' He still held her shoulders, unable to let her go completely. 'Can we walk?' he asked, 'I promise to be perfectly proper – as long as we are in sight!'

'Well yes, but come and speak to the boys first. They'd never forgive you if you didn't.'

'So that is Humpty, up aloft like a monkey in the rigging?'

'It is. They fancy themselves as woodmen now. Kit is very accurate with the axe, and to tell the truth they handle the sawpit as well as ever that pair of miserable Puritans did.'

'I admire the self-sufficiency of the Herons. It isn't every family who have set to and fended for themselves as well as yours.'

She tossed her head in faint self-mockery. 'You don't think we'd allow a mere war to distort our scheme of things?'

'Ah, don't be too easy against the war. Wasn't it just that thing that brought me to you, the first time? And doesn't it bring me again to you today?'

She smiled. 'Not enchantment, or the toils of destiny? Only the war?'   'Well, we'll say it made it simple for fate to do its work.'

The boys had seen him now, and were waving frantically, Humpty shinning down the tree at an alarming rate. Kit, a nasty-looking barking tool in his outstretched hand, came to meet him. Cathal adroitly avoided the sharp handshake and clapped the boy on the shoulder instead.

Kit's eyes admired him. 'God's boots, how splendid you look in your cavalry cloak! Do all the Prince's men wear their hair so long?' His own yellow curls were tied back in a workmanlike fashion.

But Humpty was there now, with a more pertinent question. 'How many of the enemy have you killed? Added to those three you slew in Ireland?'

Cathal grinned. 'I haven't counted. I'd not the time. But you seem to be pretty well yourselves, I'd say. You must have doubled your strength since I saw you.'

Humpty looked modest and flexed the fine development of muscle which covered his thin torso. He was obviously the stronger, and promised to have his father's broad build, but Kit was no weakling, either, and was by far the more elegant of the two. 'Have you ever felled a tree?' he challenged now. 'You may take a swipe at this one if you like.'

Cathal hesitated. He longed to be alone with Lucy, but he sensed that his manhood was at stake. 'Give me the axe,' he ordered.

It was not yet a fully grown oak and an accomplished hewer

would fell it with a single stroke. This Cathal proceeded to do, to his own satisfaction and the twins' clamorous commendation. 'We have oaks in the park at home, too,' he admitted, 'and my father believes that a man is better able to command the respect of those beneath him if he can himself perform any task which he might ask of them.'

'Excellent! You are just what we want.' Humpty pulled a grubby list from his belt. 'There is all this timber to be got this month – for the fires, for the carpenter, for the sawpit—'

'Give me leave, just for today?' begged Cathal, holding up his hands. 'I have ridden all night in the dreaming expectation of walking on the green grass with a golden girl, and that is what I intend to do.'

It was Tibbett who rescued them. He considered that Lucy deserved a holiday. She had worked without stint both inside and outside the house ever since her Ladyship's illness and had scarcely slackened when that had run its course. 'I daresay we can manage without you, miss,' he told her, 'if I might just ask one question of Mr O'Connor before you leave us?'

'Ask away, Tibbett.'

'It is only that I wondered how Sir Thomas was. We have had scant news of him since his marriage. The couriers don't get through so often now.' Lucy and her brothers nodded, contrite. In the excitement of seeing Cathal, no one had thought of Tom.

'He is better and better, thank God. He is riding again now, and swears he is fit for battle, but Prince Rupert won't let him go back to his post yet awhile – though he won't give him leave either. He says he has the right to pick his brains, even if there aren't pickings fit for a crow on his body.'

'And tell me, how does Valora like her new life?' asked Lucy.

'Monstrously well. She orders the whole camp like a true captain-general. There isn't a soul in uniform but walks in fear of her.'

Lucy chuckled. The picture was familiar.

'But listen – I'll give you all the news, and their letters too, at dinner. I looked for your mother, to give the packets to her, but she's nowhere to be found.'

'She and Martha have gone to the village to speak to the weavers.'

'Then I have no duty except to you,' Cathal said, well satisfied. He gave the group about the tree a polite but final inclination of his head, clapped Lucy's hand onto his arm and marched her off.

'Every inch a soldier now, that boy,' Tibbett approved as they strolled away.

'I wish it would hurry up and be our turn,' grumbled Kit, still eyeing the scarlet cloak.

'They're taking them younger all the time,' comforted Humpty, wondering if Cathal *would* tell him how many men he had killed.

'In the army,' threatened Tibbett grimly, 'it is considered advisable to concentrate upon the job in hand.' Kit reached for the axe.

Lucy waited until she and Cathal had covered some distance, each happily conscious of the other's nearness, before she asked 'For how long has the war sent you to me?'

He sighed. 'Not long, I'm afraid. Rupert is a hard master. He simply says he needs every moment of every man's time. The only reason he let me come is because he had despatches for Oxford which I might take as well as any. I go back to Chester in two days.'

'Oh, no! I have you again only to lose you at once. That's cruel.'

'Equally cruel to me. And then – I didn't want to tell you this, not yet, but I may as well be done with it – I may have to go back to Ireland quite soon.'

'To Ireland! But you have so recently arrived in England—'

'I know. And I had thought to stay, at least for as long as the war lasts out.'

'Then why—'

'The thing of it is this – I left home without my father's leave. At night and by stealth, without saying where I was bound. I didn't want them all wearing themselves into sticks thinking I'd been spirited away by demons or knifed in the dark and cast into the lough, so I wrote to my father that I had a fine post with the famous Prince Rupert, and your brother to keep an eye on me, and that I wished to stay and serve the King. He wrote back that I was to be on the next boat or he'd be over here himself with his seven-tailed whip.'

'Did you not expect that?'

'I don't know. I think I had persuaded myself he might for once accept an accomplished fact. And perhaps he might have done, if the King's treaty with the Protestants had worked out as it was planned. But the Prots won't stand for it, unless every inch of their misgotten property is restored to them and their infernal religion – pardon me, Lucy – established throughout Ireland. And *we* won't stand for that kind of nonsense and heresy. So the fight goes on, just as before. Most of us never stopped.'

'Then what,' demanded Lucy, irritated, 'is the point of the treaty?'

He shrugged. 'It has got a good few of us over here to fight for His Majesty, myself included.'

'And so what will you do?' she asked then, sadly. 'Will you obey your father, or will you stay in England?' For the second time that day she implored her maker; let him stay!

He stopped walking and faced her. 'I don't know. I thought it would help me to decide if I talked with you.' He looked so perplexed that she felt sorry for him.

'Tell me what you feel; that is what matters.'

He smiled gratefully. 'I am my father's heir. I owe him my duty. That is one fact that I cannot deny. There is another; I cannot justify staying to fight for the King in England if other men are doing it on Irish soil.'

The soil of Ireland again. Down from the white horse to kiss its holy, greedy, blood-soaked turf. Lucy felt that she hated Ireland. 'Why so?' Although she knew the answer really.

'Because my clansmen are not just fighting for King Charles; they are fighting for our faith and our land as well. My duty is there. I know it. I *want* to deny it – but that is only for your sake. I love you, you know that. I love you on the grand scale, and I don't want to be parted from you.'

Some half-recollected words of Will Staunton's swam in her mind. 'But you will always love Ireland more.'

He shook his head, smiling at her tragic air. 'Sit you down here, and listen to me. There is no reason in the world why I should not love both – and have both, and keep both, as long as birds sing.'

'And how are you going to manage that? With more of your magic?'

He picked up her hand, twisting tensely in her lap, and kissed the fingers one by one. 'No, by the banal and thoroughly natural means that has always been employed by both king and tinker, by marriage.'

'Marriage!' She could only repeat it, eyes widening.

'Have you never thought of it?'

'I have dreamed a little,' she admitted, shy now.

'Then let us try to make such dreams come true. They are mine too.'

She kissed him willingly then, careless whether they were out of sight. He longed to lie down with her in the soft, hay-scented grass and kiss and whisper the morning away, but he had not finished what he must say. It had to be said. 'I wish I could ask you to marry me here and now, and demand you of Tom in two days' time, but it can't be as easy as that.'

She said nothing, still bemused by the whole idea.

'You see, my father has other ideas for me. His letter tells me that he has accepted the fact that I can wield a sword or fire a pistol as well as the next man. Since I have so far mastered myself as to merit a place in Rupert's troop, he concedes that I deserve equally well to ride at his own side. Also, he was wounded quite badly some time ago and this has made him take thought for the future of his lands. He wants me at home and he wants me settled. In fact, he wants me married—'

'Then, surely that is good?'

'Not for us. He wants me married to one Orla McDonagh. Orla is a fine girl whom I've known all my life. She is like a sister to me, and that is how I am willing to keep it. But her father and my father have fought together and drunk together all their lives, and I suppose the notion has always been there that I should wed her one day. But that is neither my wish nor my intention. I want to wed no one but you. But it will be hard. The O'Connor is a man who does not know what it is to change his mind, and he has no love for England or the English, and less than love for a Protestant,' he ended gloomily. 'Although he thinks kindly of your family for your mother's sake, he'd have the hide of me if he thought I was anything more to you than a passing guest.'

'Then, either you must disobey your father, or we must not marry. There seems no other alternative,' said Lucy with a practicality she did not feel. She did not know exactly what she felt at all, as yet. It was true that she had told herself stories of living, happy ever after, with Cathal one day, in some land of dreams made flesh that might have been England, Ireland or Ultima Thule for all the likelihood there was of it ever materializing. And now this. It was hard enough to get used to having him sit before her, himself no longer the image of her private hour before sleeping, but the talking, laughing, kissing reality, without having to take in the possibility of a change that would affect the whole of her life, at one and the same time.

'There is waiting,' said Cathal. 'I may refuse Orla, but stay at my father's side. If I make him proud enough, and wait until the point when he can refuse me nothing, he might overlook your religion to please me. I have to have hope,' he pleaded. 'And there is no other I can think of. What do you say?'

'How long do you think it will take to make him sufficiently proud?' She was conscious of a tinge of irony in her tone.

'It's all up to the fighting; if I were to kidnap Ormonde, now, or defend Kilkenny against a monstrous horde—'

'—Or slay a dragon, or sow furrows full of fighting men. I begin to understand your father.'

'He is simple enough to understand. And the devil's own work to turn from his road. But I hope to do it. But here am I ranting on like the fool I am, and I have never this once demanded of your sweet self – do you even *want* to marry me!'

She smiled, wanting to weep suddenly, at his look of comical self-reproach. 'I think so,' she said carefully. 'Only you must give me time to become accustomed to the idea. I love you well enough, only—'

'There is something that worries you, I can see. What is it? Tell me, Lucy.'

'Very well then. Yes, I would marry you as soon as possible – if you were to stay here. It is Ireland that is wrong, or *might* be wrong, perhaps, for me. I know I would not be welcome among your people – and it is not a place I would ever choose to go to.'

At first he seemed surprised, then he became even more contrite. 'I am sorry. I did not think. Of course it will be a very foreign place to you. But never think my clan would not make you welcome. Once the O'Connor had given his consent, all would follow his will.' She smiled but did not believe it; in her experience men did not always behave as their overlords desired.

He moved closer and encircled her with his arm, wanting to make her feel warm and wanted, for Ireland as well as himself. 'It will all be wonderfully well, you will see. You have time, my heart, all the time in the world. I will use it to make magic upon my father, and you will use it to learn to love my country. We will go on as before. I will visit you whenever I can. We will write whenever anyone will carry our letters. And one day, we need set no limit, but one day, we will marry. Do you agree?'

She kissed him by way of sealing the contract, grateful for his wisdom in not pressing her too closely. She was afraid of Ireland. But she did not lack courage and she would try, as he said, to learn to love it. She would not even begin to think, now, of how it would be to leave Heron.

'And now we will not talk of it any more. But it will be our secret and our aim and we will fight for it in our own way as boldly as we all fight for King Charles.'

'Like the Jesuits,' she said, oddly. He raised a brow.

'A secret army. With very small numbers. But they accomplished a great deal.' There were tears in her eyes. 'I suppose it is the thought of marriage that brings him back—'

'Ah, yes, your cousin the priest. I was destroyed with sorrow for him, the poor brave gentleman. But wouldn't he give out the hosannas, up in heaven, now, if he knew you were to marry a Catholic?'

'That is unfair,' she said flatly. 'Dominic knew me as a member of the English church. That is what it is, to hold to a faith – to keep to it, not to change with every wind that blows.'

'Don't be angry.'

'I am not. Only, like Tom, I will not change my faith.'

'Then I will never ask you to.'

'Tell me about your home,' she said then as much to steer them clear of argument as out of curiosity.

'Ah Lucy, the beauty of it is beyond the power of my mind or my tongue. You could not help but love it and be uplifted by it.' He looked cursorily about him, at the sweep of green studded with trees in their changing colours, at the valiant sunlight struggling through the web of mist, at the outlines of the hills, still comfortably asleep beneath counterpanes of cloud. He sighed. 'All this is fine enough in many ways, but it is terrible tame, girl! Where I live, in Leinster, we are close to the ocean. It terrifies us and feeds us, kills us and inspires us; it is our goddess and our grave. And the wild mountains of Wicklow! They do not sit like dogs in wait for their masters as these do, but crowd us and threaten us and demand things of us.'

Lucy shivered. 'There is a wild thing dances in your eye, too, when you speak of them. Oh Cathal, how am I to fit into such a scene. I am a corn dolly, not an elemental spirit.'

He laughed at her estimate of herself and reached to kiss her again. 'We grow corn, too, in Wicklow,' he murmured into her yellow crown.

'And I suppose you sow dragon's teeth to get it,' she complained. 'You seem to do everything the hard way.'

'Not at all. We are far more easy with ourselves than the English. But we do demand a little grandeur from life. If it is not there, we find it very simple to manufacture. There is much to be said for living a legend if you can.'

Eighteen months ago, Lucy would have agreed with him wholeheartedly. Now she was not so sure. But she was very sure that she loved him, and that meant she must go as far as she could to meet him.

Meanwhile, for the next two days, her life was perfect. Such a gift as this must be enjoyed to its limit. The future had no place here. Cathal's presence filled her whole horizon and she asked no more of fate than that nothing should mar their time together.

Nothing did. The only difficulty they encountered was in disguising, particularly from the twins, who were inclined to follow them about, the true depth of their relationship. They were lucky in this, however, for such a connection simply did not occur to Mary Heron, who saw in the tall, charming boy only Tom's messenger and an old friend. It had never, Cathal reported amusedly, occurred to Tom either.

'Can't people *see*?' Lucy wondered with a lover's contempt for the less blessed. 'It is written all over my face!'

'Mine also, I swear, whenever I look at you.'

But no one was reading faces at Heron, and Martha, who had already kept Lucy's secret for so long, would continue to guard it as closely as her own.

London, December 1644

Land still felt a little untrustworthy beneath Will Staunton's new land-lubberly boots. The foul and slippery cobbles of the running kennel above which swung the Lion of St Mark, creaking in as unpleasant a piece of weather as he had met for months, did nothing to aid his equilibrium. He narrowly avoided falling as he handed past him an extremely lovely and very pregnant young woman who was having her own difficulties.

'You're very kind, sir,' she said with a bewitching smile. Her eyes were a truly incredible blue; Will had lately seen every shade from here to the Caribbean. And with that dark hair! He kissed his hand to her departing rotundities, wishing there were time to become better acquainted.

The door of the print shop was open and he found Jud Heron embroiled in the same stink and noise in which he had left him, with the presses clattering like drums in black Africa and every inch of space as clogged with paper as Ailsa Craig with birdlime.

There was also Rob Whittaker, hunched over one of the infernal machines, while Jud himself was deep among the paper. If Will waited to be noticed, he might well wait till dinnertime.

He stepped up behind Jud and touched him on the shoulder. Jud, accustomed to this means of attracting his attention, did not start with surprise until he had turned round. Then he grinned from ear to ear and signalled that Will should follow him into an inner room.

Rob, having sensed that something was afoot, looked up. He waved at Will and gave him a sparrowlike hitch of the head that lost none of that bird's impertinence, while displaying his unimpressive teeth. Will nodded with the utmost politeness in reply, noting that Rob's confidence had increased to intolerable proportions, and also that unfortunately he was mysteriously no longer a suitable candidate for a good clip on the ear. Will was possessed of excellent instincts and these informed him that the boy had somehow grown in stature since last they met, not physically certainly, and by no means morally, he was sure; it must, therefore, be his success in his profession that had added these unseen inches. Will bore no grudges. He changed his polite nod to an appreciative grin and followed Jud.

A doubly stout oak door slammed behind them, cutting down the fierce battery of the presses to a distant artillery. They were in a small, book-lined room furnished with a large, businesslike table piled with more paper, a couple of good leather armchairs and a corner cupboard from which Jud took a decanter and two glasses. They passed several pleasant minutes in the mutual exchange of business news and in drinking each other's health.

'To printing and piracy!' observed Will heartily, draining his glass.

'Piracy and printing!' Jud returned. 'Long may they prosper!'

'I was aware that *you* were prospering,' Will said, 'almost before I could leave my ship. My feet hadn't hit the quayside before someone clapped *this* into my hand. I'd as soon have had a glass of this excellent Madeira just then, I can tell you – where did you get it, by the way – but I found it a most remarkable document.'

He had taken a folded paper from his cuff which he handed to Jud, who gave it the most cursory scrutiny before giving it back. 'I'm glad it impresses you. And I'm sure my satisfaction will be shared by the source of my supply of Madeira.'

'Which is?'

Jud tried to keep a certain amount of smugness out of his smile. 'An old friend of yours – Harry Vane.'

'Ah, so Harry has taken over where poor John Pym left off – in every possible way, if what I hear is true? I thought it might be so.'

'Very much so. The pamphlet is his drafting. I'm his mere editor.'

' "Alas, poor Parliament" – it's a radical demand, Jud. Matters have moved quickly while I've been at sea.' The article in his hand had revealed, by its very existence, the interesting state of Parliament's affairs. 'Alas, poor Parliament, how thou art betrayed,' it declared, and went on in the strongest of language to accuse the Earls of Essex and Manchester of failure to prosecute the war with any conviction and to demand that the leadership be taken over by the one man in whom the people might hopefully place their confidence, Oliver Cromwell.

'I notice you don't put your name to it? You expected trouble?'

Jud grinned. 'There has already been trouble. The Lords have applied the ordinance against unlicensed printing and are chasing their tails trying to find the author. John Lilburne is chief suspect. He was flattered when I told him.'

'But you have your licence, surely?'

'From Parliament, yes. But we don't give our name to everything we print.'

'So your more radical pamphlets remain anonymous while you gentle along your regular readers in a less alarming style?'

'Something like that. But what do you think of Cromwell, eh? You'll have heard about Marston Moor?'

'I've heard about all of it, I think. I was with my Uncle Warwick yesterday. He's none too happy with the new climate.'

'Ah, no, he won't be. When Vane gets his Self-denying Ordinance through, the Lord Admiral will lose his post.'

'I have the impression it is a temporary move; the desired result of a careful campaign against the old-guard Presbyterians rather than a lasting piece of legislation. After all, if Essex and Manchester go, so does Cromwell, unless he wants to resign his seat.'

'You're right. But as long as the earls leave the army now, Parliament can always recall Cromwell to the field later. Warwick too.'

'All this certainly has the twist of Harry Vane's mind to it. Pym would have been proud of him.'

Will couldn't fault the new ordinance. Basically, it prohibited

411

members of either House from holding army commissions. Vane offered it as a means of putting an end to the consistent disruption of military progress by quarrels of a political nature. In effect, as no machinery existed by which a peer could resign his seat, it would remove all peers from the army. What it proved to Will, above all else, was the enormous influence now held by Cromwell, Vane and the independent faction.

'Cromwell has been extraordinarily outspoken in his criticisms, of Manchester in particular. Do you reckon they are deserved?'

'Absolutely. Manchester failed utterly to follow up the advantage after the Moor. It's said he couldn't abide the slaughter, and the sack of York sickened him. It was no time to become squeamish. And he should have won Newbury. Have you heard what he said after that piece of bungling?'

'What?'

'It was as good as an admission that he had no desire to defeat the King. Listen, and then tell me whose side the earl is upon! He said to Cromwell, "If we beat the King ninety-nine times, yet he is King still, but if the King beat us once, or the last time, we shall all be hanged, we shall lose our estates and our posterities be undone." "My Lord, if this be so," replied Cromwell, "why did we take up arms at first?" Logic enough for any man!'

Will nodded. 'So you think Manchester is for peace at any price?'

'And Essex too. After Lostwithiel—'

Will chuckled. 'Poor devil! He seems to have parcelled up Devon and Cornwall and given them back to the King and then been forced to make his own undignified escape in a rowing boat. No room for his precious coffin there!'

'A pity if he's lost it. He'll need it soon, if Cromwell has anything to do with it.'

'Goddamn the old fool! I gather the King is doing far too well in the south.'

'In the north, too. Montrose has done miracles in Scotland. Indeed I wish he were fighting for us. But he has helped in one sense. His victories at Perth and Aberdeen have made the Covenanters look foolish on both sides of the border. As long as their stock is low, we can only profit by it.'

'That "we" comes out loud and strong now, Jud. Am I to suppose you've become an Independent? I've never thought there was much of the Puritan in you.'

Jud shrugged off the teasing. 'There's not. Not a particle. There's not much religion in me at all, to tell the truth; but I've always liked Vane's and St John's way of thinking, and I like Cromwell's way of fighting. I'm with them all the way. You should be delighted with the way things are going. You stand to have all your friends in high places. Not that *that*'s anything new.'

'Oh I *am* delighted,' Will replied, ignoring the barb, 'so delighted, in fact, that I am considering joining them.'

'Eh? You mean *you're* turning Puritan?' Jud had his revenge.

'Not Puritan; politician.'

'I don't believe it!'

'Why not? We are bound to have elections soon, despite Denzil Holles' rabid fear that the populace will return a Parliament of upstarts and sectaries, drunk on John Lilburne's burning prose! The Houses are getting low in numbers. I have influence enough to prove a popular candidate. I don't know that I'm flattered by your incredulity.'

Jud whistled. 'My apologies! I swear I'd no idea—'

'– That I too am concerned with how my country shall be governed? Well, perhaps it has been rather a well-kept secret,' Will allowed. 'But I promise you, I am serious. I shall leave my little ships to my captains while I see if I can learn how to help steer the big one.'

Jud accepted that it was not a joke. 'You'd be capital!' was his reaction. 'You have an excellent mind, wide influence, a tongue like a razor—'

'Why, thank you, Jud. If I should require a reference—'

Jud was embarrassed. 'I'm sorry, sir. I wasn't thinking.'

'God, there's no need for "sir" between us. I was only codding. And I shall rely on you for all kinds of useful information from now on – not to mention the odd cask of Madeira!'

Jud filled his glass gladly, sensing the beginning of a new understanding between them. It was what he had always wanted. What with one thing and another, he felt remarkably cheerful today. 'Lucy will be pleased. She was asking me to be sure to let her know the minute you arrived back in port.'

'How kind,' said Will lazily, noting with distaste an inward leaping at the sound of her name. Callow, very callow. 'You must give me all the news from Heron. I hope they lead a quieter life than previously?'

'Yes, indeed,' said Jud warmly, 'thanks to you. You know, I never understood exactly what it was you managed to do about that sequestration order—'

'Nor is it ordained that you should,' said Will firmly. 'I am glad to hear they have no trouble. They have had their share.' He wanted to hear more about Lucy but did not wish to ask. 'Is everyone well?' he attempted lamely, furious with the unpleasant sensation of being at some ridiculous disadvantage.

Jud told him exhaustively how well everyone was, except Lucy, whom he saved for last, almost, Will thought, as if he knew he would cause the maximum of impatience by so doing. 'As for my sister – her letters are full of a certain young man.'

'Do you tell me?' said Will languidly. 'And is it still the handsome Gaelic storyteller?' Of course it must be.

'Cathal O'Connor. Himself it is. But things have changed. He is no longer in Ireland. He serves with Prince Rupert, under my elder brother.' Tom's name still came stiffly to his lips. 'And, what's more – he writes for us, for the *Intelligencer*,' he finished triumphantly.

Will nodded and exclaimed automatically while the story was told, all the time asking himself what this piece of news must mean to him. He had thought of Lucy far too often during the quieter periods of his recent voyage. The uncomfortable passion was, if anything, even more deeply rooted than before. And this was without either seeing her or hearing from her for nearly a year. It could have been worse, he told himself, as Jud carolled on about Martha and the twins, retailing every piece of news got from Lucy herself; he might have returned to find her married. 'Do you think anything will come of it?' he asked.

'Of what?' Jud, in the middle of describing old Lady Stratton's latest social *faux pas*, was mystified.

'Of Lucy's romance?'

'Eh? Oh, God no, I shouldn't think so. It's all very well for my brother to marry a papist. He's head of the house and may do as he pleases. But it'll not please him to send Lucy to live among those murdering fiends of Irish, I'll lay odds on it.'

Smiling charmingly, Will brooded. He hoped Jud was right. He was ludicrously cast down. He had seen himself, upon his return, riding to Heron, with his Parliamentary seat in one pocket and the tidy new fortune he had acquired in the Caribbean in the other, laying gentle and expert siege to Lucy until she should confess herself outmanned and gracefully surrender. But he could see that he might have to put off the siege; it seemed that the city was too well defended just at present.

'Have you been home at all?' he asked Jud.

The boy shook his head. 'No. And I won't. Not until Tom gets down on those stiff-jointed knees of his and begs me in the dust!'

'Then you'll have a long wait. If it were myself, I'd ignore Tom;

he's hardly ever at Heron anyway. Go back one of these days. I know they must all long to see you. You're no longer a black sheep, you know, whatever Tom may say. You're a very respectable citizen!'

Jud laughed. 'I doubt even my mother would think that, but yes – I'd like to see Heron again. One day. Not now.' It was final. Jud hadn't given a thought to Heron for a very long time. He had other attachments to occupy him now. He wondered if he should mention them to Will. How would he react when he learned that Jud was going to be a father? The first of this generation of Herons to reproduce, by God! Not on the right side of the blanket, it was true, but he'd wager his son would prove to be as fine a specimen as anything Tom could get, finer probably. He hesitated. No, perhaps not today. He was not sure he had quite enough courage today. He still could not help but see in Will a little of the father and mentor.

But he'd have to be fairly swift about it, if he didn't want Cleo to let the world know first, in the most definite manner.

That night as Will lay, temporarily spent, amid the soft hospitality of his cousin Eliza's bed, he reflected that fate had now presented him with rather a thorny problem. Despite the generous and altogether satisfactory manner in which she had greeted him and was continuing to treat him, there was, he sensed, a new and ominous quality of *waiting* about Eliza. The trouble was that Will knew exactly what it was that she was waiting for.

During his recent interview with his disgruntled Uncle Warwick a great many subjects had been discussed, most of them connected with cargoes, money and ships. Naturally, the war had been mentioned. So, of course, had the question of Will's entry into Parliament, with which the earl had professed himself highly delighted. It was bound to be good for trade. There they would be, all the most influential members of the New Providence Company, snug together, cheek by jowl, with Warwick as President keeping a weather eye on them from his soft seat in the Lords.

He would, he had said, continue to exert himself on his nephew's behalf in any way he could. He was mightily pleased with Will's success on the Spanish Main. It wouldn't be Spanish much longer, not if he and Captain William Jackson knew anything about it! In the last couple of years the bold captain had executed a series of lightning raids upon the West Indian strongholds of Spain, which had severely shaken their thieves' hold on that part of their empire. Will, in going out to assist him, had added his own peculiar brand of wild logic and impetuous daring to the expeditions and had made his name as feared as Jackson's own.

The marooned sea dog then, was very well disposed towards the pup still happily shaking himself on the mat. But there was just one little thing that Will might do for him, in return for past and present largesse. Warwick was beginning to worry about Eliza; at least his wife was, which amounted to the same thing, as she would not let him rest until he had done something about it. The girl had remained a widow for far too long. It seemed she was getting flighty. She had taken to bad company; was always seen in the houses of the most exaggerated sort of Royalist and also with that intriguing, meddling hag, Lady Carlisle. Obviously she needed a husband to keep her in her place. One look at the baggage was enough to tell you where that place should be; as tasty an armful still, as the earl had ever seen. When questioned on this delicate matter, Eliza had intimated with the prettiest of blushes that if she *must* give up her celibate state, the man to whom she would most wish to do so was her cousin Will.

Warwick would have been thunderstruck if anyone had told him that this was not entirely his own idea. Elizabeth, having played her fish so skilfully for so long, took an expert's pleasure in landing him so effortlessly.

If only she might have the same luck with the bigger fish. There *should* be no difficulty. She knew that Will could by now be in no doubt as to where his duty lay. And she had done her level best to remind him how much of a pleasure it would also be. Why then this silence? They had been together every night and three afternoons since he had landed; she had no doubts about his complete satisfaction with her person and performance. His fortune was set, his future assured; what was holding him back? She had been patient for so long. She would not spoil all her good work by a hasty word at this important juncture. But, by Satan and all his devils, her patience was wearing monstrous thin!

Will, indeed, could almost *feel* how thin it was, as current after current of alien irritation flowed through the body that normally, by now, would be lying somnolent and glowing beside him, sated with voluptuary pleasures. It was like lying with a tigress who had not quite eaten enough.

He decided that his best means of defence was attack. She was far too proud ever to mention the subject herself. 'Is something troubling you, my orchid?' he enquired silkily, stroking her long, rosy-fleshed flank.

'No. Why should there be?' she replied, moving slightly so that his hand fell upon her musk-scented mound of Venus.

'You are unusually restless. I thought perhaps I had not satisfied you in some way,' he continued innocently, combing the soft hairs with his fingers.

'By no means. But we have a great deal of time to make up,' she said huskily. Neither fire nor sword would drag any question out of her. She would give him no help. Sooner or later, unless he was a complete fool, which he surely was not, he would be forced to sue for her hand as she would have had him do years ago.

As he parted her thighs and felt the ready juices come to his hand, he was surprised by a wave of depression. Damn Warwick for forcing this game on him. He had no more intention of marrying Eliza than he had of providing meat for a tigress. Another woman filled his mind, even at this unscheduled moment, and he detested the notion that he could not simply tell Eliza and get it over with.

But this, he knew, would be very foolish. Warwick's humour was uncertain; if he removed his favour, that seat in the Commons might be gone with the wind. Will wanted that seat. He was tired of suffering other men's decisions. He wanted to be among those who made them and carried them out. He had developed his own view, half instinct, half based on knowledge and experience, of how England's future should run. He couldn't let go of his chance.

Eliza was writhing beneath him, moaning and pressing down on his sternum. Another second and it would be too late. He thrust into her purposefully and began the turbulent voyage all over again. But although he tried to concentrate on the wonderful troughs and billows of his most intemperate ocean, he found swimming beside him the uncomfortable image of Lucy at her most disapproving, her mouth buttoned up like an old maid's bodice and her eyes loosing jade arrows of accusation. For the first time in his long and successful career as a lover of gallant ladies, he failed.

Eliza couldn't believe it. Snatched from the centre of her whirlpool by an unmistakable shrinkage, she applied all her natural talents to resuscitation, thanking her stars that some traveller had left a copy of a Japanese pillow book to one of her friends at court. But although she bit his right ear and worked her tongue gently into it, brought up her left leg and twined it about

417

his waist, and insinuated her middle finger searchingly into his anus, Will's Precious Tower of Ivory remained ignominiously deflated. Lugubriously, he rolled off her.

'Are you ill?' Eliza asked solicitously. 'Was there any sickness on board that you have not mentioned?'

'No. I don't know what's the matter,' he lied. 'I suppose it could be over-use. Or the advent of old age,' he added solemnly.

'What nonsense. You're nowhere near thirty yet. You're probably right,' she sighed, self-congratulatory. 'We *have* been rather busy these last few days.' She snuggled down beside him, content to offer simple affection for the rest of the night. 'I am so glad you are home,' she murmured. 'I had missed you abominably. Life is going to be splendid from now on.'

'Yes, indeed,' he responded mechanically. Then he blew out the candle and lay brooding into the darkness, conscious of how heavily she rested upon his imprisoned arm.

Heron, March 1645

Eliza had sulked when Will had refused to take her with him to Heron. She had justly accused him of churlish behaviour, for he had given her no adequate reason for declining her company, simply stated that he wished to travel alone. She had retorted that she would have thought he'd travelled long enough alone as captain of his beastly ship, then flounced off to dine with an admirer. When she returned, very late, Will had left for Gloucestershire.

He found Heron awash with Strattons. They had come over in a body so that the boys could help with the ploughing. The house was full of noise and laughter and everyone wore a festive air as though a general holiday had been declared. Except for Lucy.

It was difficult to say what was wrong with Lucy. She had seemed pleased enough to see him and had kissed him warmly in greeting. She had said all the right things and was assiduous in assisting her mother to play hostess. She even managed to be delightful to that old harridan, the ancient Lady Stratton, and to keep her temper with silly, pretty Isabella. But to the careful watcher there seemed to be none of her characteristic spontaneity in her voice or her actions. She presented a charming picture of affectionate duty but the essential Lucy simply was not there.

It was some time before Will could arrange to be alone with her. The opportunity occurred when everyone took it into their heads to eat dinner in the fields like peasants. It was a day filled with the promise of spring, biting and exhilarating. They sat in the hedgerow and admired the fine new copper-coloured furrows, eating bread and cheese and cold meats washed down with Margery's cider.

When Lucy had finished handing the food out of the huge woven baskets, Will beckoned her to sit beside him beneath a budding blackthorn. She settled companionably and munched her bread, smiling at him but not, it seemed, inclined to talk.

He tried to entertain her, telling her the parts of his Caribbean experience that he had edited out during last night's table-talk. '– And so there I was, with the Negro on one side, rolling his eyes and jabbing with his cutlass, more afraid than brave, and the Spaniard grinning at me on the other, just waiting to move in – damn it, Lucy, you're not listening!'

'Oh I am, Will, honestly!'

'What did I say?'

'Something about a Negro?' she asked hopefully.

'Never mind the Negro. Suppose you tell me what it is has stolen your tongue and taken the spring from your step. Perhaps I might be able to help?'

She shook her head. 'Dear Will. Not this time, I'm afraid.'

'Then tell me anyway. Just because I care.'

She looked down, then glanced quickly around the semi-circle of enthusiastic eaters. No one was taking any notice of her.

'Very well. It is Cathal,' she said. She wouldn't look at him.

Will was as alert as though she'd cried 'Sail to starboard!' 'What about him?'

'Oh, it is – well, it does not matter really, only he has just become betrothed.' She swallowed a chunk of bread like a stone. 'To a girl named Orla McDonagh,' she continued resolutely, as if the name could make matters more settled, even further beyond her power to alter.

'So then, he has gone back to Ireland?' Will said gently, keeping pity instinctively out of his tone.

'Yes. You were right. Remember?' Lucy declared staunchly.

'I remember. I am sorry to be right.'

Lucy shrugged. 'You are only right in that he had to return home. His father sent to say that he had been seriously wounded, for a second time in a few months, and ordered him to hasten back. In fact he found his father hale enough, it seems,' she grimaced. 'Only very set on keeping Cathal with him. And even more set on this betrothal. It had been planned since they were children. When Cathal spoke of me, his father locked him in one of those horrible thin round towers they have and fed him nothing but bread and water until he promised to accept the betrothal. But he will not marry her,' she added fiercely. 'He has sworn to me that he will not. Only he must, he says, keep his father sweet for the moment, if he is to come into his lands.'

She was startled by a short burst of ironic laughter from Will. 'Forgive me. I was not laughing at you, but at something in my own life.'

'What?' she asked suspiciously, unsure that he spoke the truth.

'I shall not tell you. I do not cut a very fine figure in this particular episode,' he said firmly. 'I shall tell you about the Negro and the Spaniard instead, and how it was that I survived to tell the tale.'

He could not, after all, tell her that he had laughed because his fate appeared at present to run parallel to her precious Cathal's. All one had to do was to substitute the Earl of Warwick for the patriarch O'Connor, and Cousin Eliza for the despised Orla McDonagh. No, on reflection, they did not run parallel, but formed the two sides of a triangle narrowing towards the same apex, upon which point, serenely unaware of this uncomfortable position, Lucy sat. It was worthy of one of Donne's most extreme metaphysical efforts. It was also absolutely damnable.

On the other hand, the present situation made it very unlikely that Lucy would be married, either to Cathal himself or anyone else, in the foreseeable future. That, at least, was a point in Will's favour. Settling gracefully back against the roots of the thorn, he set himself to charm her out of her grief. But although he soon succeeded in making her laugh, he was not destined to reach the end of his tale.

Will had just sliced the belt of the Negro's voluminous breeches when a silence fell upon the rest of the group, leaving his voice stranded on a peak of animation. A party of horse was coming up the lane. The regular trotting indicated that the visitors were military.

It was Kit who raced up the field until he could see through the hedge. They waited tensely until he waved his arms and jumped up and down with an ebullience which declared them to be King's men, then everyone abandoned the picnic and made for the road.

The children ran behind the horses, most of which were unusually splendid specimens, eclipsed only by their riders in the matters of figure and lustre. The adults followed at a dignified pace.

When Lucy reached the house with Will, they found the leader of the dashing troop drinking wine in the best parlour with Mary Heron and two or three of his subordinates. He presented himself with a jingle of spurs as Major Valentine Rowley. He was tall and slender, with shoulders like crosstrees and a waist that any woman might envy. His dark curls appeared to have been glued into position and one of them was fetchingly draped down his left breast, tied up in a lavender ribbon which contrasted delicately with the pale blue coat of the uniform worn by all the troop and designed by himself. They were not in armour, this being a quiet time as regards the fighting, though some of them did carry wonderfully feathered helmets which would look more in place in their portraits than upon their elegant heads. They were, Major Rowley gave them to understand, merely riding about the countryside on routine reconnaissance.

'Getting to know who's who and what's what, y'know. Finding out where we'll get a warm welcome and where we might find one that's a little too warm, if y'take m'meaning.' The major laughed. He did so frequently, upon a rather high-pitched but not unpleasant note which Lucy identified as G.

'Glad t'find you at home,' he addressed Mary respectfully. 'Knew Suh George. Capital officer. Sadly missed. Wanted t'pay m'respects t'your ladyship.' He bowed at an angle of ninety degrees and then repeated the compliment for Lucy at seventy-five.

They spoke of the progress of the King's plans for the coming campaign. He was back at Oxford now and had made Rupert Commander-in-Chief at last, an honour which the major thought long overdue. '*Now* we shall teach 'em a thing or two, mark my words! We'll soon put paid to their New Noddle Army!' laughed the major.

'It would be best not to take that for granted,' said Will mildly, speaking for the first time since he had been introduced. 'Cromwell acquitted himself pretty well with the old model. His Majesty would be well advised to take the new one very seriously.'

Major Rowley sniffed and twizzled the end of a fine, oiled

moustache. 'God damme, sir, we'll take 'em seriously enough. We'll take 'em seriously to hell! Begging your pardon, ladies.'

This seemed to be some kind of challenge to Will's loyalties. Lucy struggled not to laugh, wondering just how the powder-blue trooper would manage to express himself if he were told the full nature of Will's relationship to Heronscourt, not to mention the more recent fact that had taken them all by surprise – that of his impending entry into Parliament.

'I think Old Ironside might have something to say about that,' Will replied innocently. 'I believe he takes his orders from quite another direction.'

'He'll take his orders from the executioner when we catch him and string him up for the traitor he is.'

'Is that how you imagine His Majesty will deal with his opposition, supposing he were to win this war?'

'You're damn' right I do. And there's no supposing. This campaign will be the last. We've got them on the run. They're so busy quarrelling among themselves, they'll have no energy left to spend on us. Cromwell is only one man.'

'So is Rupert,' said Will quietly, tired of the man's idiocy. If this was a fair sample of the Royalist officers, it was a wonder they had done as well as they had.

'Will you take supper with us, Major?' Mary intervened, seeing the cerulean back stiffen. 'We should be proud to entertain every one of you. We can set a good table still, despite the war.'

Again the ninety-degree inclination. 'Well, we'd be delighted, madam, if you're sure you can accommodate twenty hungry men. You'll not have been sequestered then? You have been lucky. Not many houses escaped in these parts.'

Mary flattered him with her wide-eyed and guileless smile. 'We were indeed sequestered for quite some time, but I am happy to say that a family connection made it possible to countermand the order.' It was quite clear that she would say no more and it would have been unmannerly to ask further questions.

Dinner was a cheerful affair. The troopers were all valiant trenchermen, and probably as valiant soldiers when it came to the testing point. The Herons did not grudge them their sumptuary glory, for it soon became obvious from their reminiscences that most of them had seen a good deal of hard action. As for their gorgeous leader, it was allowed to be known, by his admiring lieutenant, who affected the same lavender ribbon in his love-lock, he was in fact somewhat of a hero, having acquitted himself with almost suicidal bravery in every major battle fought so far.

'Just goes to show you can't tell a horse by his colour,' muttered Lucy to Will, next to her at table.

'Did someone speak of horses?' enquired the major's light tenor to the accompaniment of a most engaging smile. 'Only the fact of the matter is, horses are very much to the point, just at the moment. D'you see the trouble is, we're damned short of them. They keep getting killed y'know. Lose more horses than men in the cavalry. Good thing really. But you see where it leaves us?'

'I believe the expression is "sweeping the commons"?' suggested Mary sweetly, offering more wine.

'Eh? Oh, well yes it is, since you mention it. Point of the matter is, well, not to put *too* fine a point on it—'

'That's three points to the major,' whispered Lucy behind her napkin.

'—It did occur to me, that is I've been wondering, well, exactly how *you* stand, at Heron, in the matter of horses?'

'I see,' said Mary noncommittally. She caught the eye of her eldest twin.

The major blushed, looking, if possible, even more handsome. 'God knows I've no desire to inconvenience you, especially after you've shown us such generous hospitality—'

'I quite understand, Major Rowley.' Mary was magnanimous. 'You have your duty to do.' Humpty, followed by his shadow, had left the table. His withering eye dared Isabella to do the same.

The major relaxed. 'It's damned fine of you to say so, madam. If only everyone were so understanding.'

'It is very difficult to manage one's life without horses,' said Mary modestly. 'I am sure you will wish to leave us the few that are absolutely necessary for us to continue to work the land and ride out occasionally.

The truth was that at present the stables were better filled than they had been since first Sir George had ridden away. Not only had the twins augmented their own numbers by unmentionable methods unlawful in peacetime, but the Strattons had all ridden over on passable mounts newly acquired from sympathetic relatives. There must be at least a dozen which could be considered fit for the cavalry and half a dozen more that would do for draught horses.

However, by this date, the visit could by no means be called unexpected. Arrangements had been made for such an eventuality. It had taken some time to persuade Mary of their integrity, but once persuaded she had abandoned all scruples. Now she plied the soldiers with more wine, then with Madeira and port.

Margery was sent to pick out the tastiest cheeses. Lucy offered fruit she had candied herself.

'We must keep them in here as long as we can,' she murmured to Will before moving into Humpty's empty place beside the lieutenant and beginning lightly to flirt with him.

Will perked up and ceased to be mildly bored. He made an opportunity to launch into a description of the dangers overcome during his historic convoy of the Queen back to these shores. This held tremendous appeal for the gallant troopers and they bombarded him with questions for fifteen minutes, after which they drank Her Majesty's health. Then someone brought in Humpty's parrot, which could sing 'When the King comes into his own again' quite creditably. Lucy gave them an encore or two with her guitar, and then old Lady Stratton, reliving her youth in a haze of Madeira, gave a surprisingly lively rendering of 'Cuckolds all Awry'.

'If only she might have given us a duet with the perroquet,' sorrowed Will as they took her off to bed, exhausted by her triumph. 'They are an exact match for range and tone.'

The festivities continued until well after nine. Even Isabella was allowed to shine. Lucy was forced to admit that she lisped her way quite prettily through her poem of love and death and roses. She had grown into a handsome girl, all bold black eyes and gipsy tresses and saw herself as a romantic contrast to Lucy whom she still idolized and dreamed of as a future sister.

As she finished her recitation, Tibbett appeared, to cast a blight on the applause with a gloomy and harassed countenance, sleeves rolled coarsely above the elbow and smelling distinctly of the stable. 'I d'beg pardon, madam, for this interruption, but a most unfortunate thing has happened. I thought it right you should know. It is the horses, my lady. They have taken sick during the evening. I don't know what ails them; it's not a thing I've seen before. I sent for Mistress Martha, up to her room, but she do say there's little she can do for the poor beasts. I did wonder' – he threw open the problem – 'if any of you gentlemen might be able to help, being so close to horses, as you might say.' Tibbett was enjoying himself. He liked acting.

There was a murmur among the men. A few of them looked sceptical.

'Only, I warn you, 'tis a messy business,' the giant deplored, gazing respectfully at the blue coats.

The major and the lieutenant followed him out to the stables. So did Will Staunton, avid with curiosity. There, by the flickering light of the wall lamps, their eyes were met by one of the most disgusting sights they ever hoped to see. Several men, Kit and Humpty among them, were engaged in shifting and bucketing steaming heaps of ordure that dolloped out of the behinds of a couple of dozen horses at an alarming and stultifying rate. The animals, understandably, were shrieking with discomfort. They would not or could not keep still, so that anyone who came near them was liberally spattered with shit.

Will hung well back, with the major pressing himself close and the lieutenant, thankful for the small mercies of inferior rank, not so close behind. The stench was indescribable. It pulsated about them like a living entity. You could almost *see* it permeating the heavy blue silk, not to mention Will's almond green velvet, which he had rather liked. He began to understand why Lucy had stayed behind.

'B-but – what is the matter with them?' gasped poor Valentine from behind his lace handkerchief.

'Can't say, sir,' said Tibbett sadly. 'They started by foaming at their mouths, and then they went on to—'

'Yes. Quite.' The finely built stallion nearest to him, which was being ministered to by Kit who was wiping down its flanks with a wet cloth, chose this moment to release a particularly large and noisome offering, dark green with salient wisps of straw. It sprayed the major's boots as it clattered to the floor and adhered in noxious clots to the fine stuff of his breeches. This was enough. The heroic officer turned tail and beat the swiftest retreat in his regiment.

'What a terrible thing,' he said, shaken, to Will outside. 'My God! Supposing it is infectious. I'd best get my men out of here and myself bathed and changed. You too, Lieutenant.' They stood not upon the order of their going but fled, the sound of equine wind and water speeding them on their way.

Only Will Staunton, by now more than curious, had the stamina to go back into the domain of Augeas. The men and boys were still shifting and bucketing, but the expression on their faces was markedly more cheerful.

'We'll give 'em a good mash for being such fine performers,' Kit declared, grinning at his favourite Calliope. 'There, my beauty, you'll soon be comfortable again. I'm sorry we had to do it, but you'd not like to leave home, now would you?' He looked up at Will, drunk with triumph. 'Not one did they get! Not even the whiff of one!'

'Oh, I think you'll have to allow they got *that*,' Will corrected.

The major had thrown away his handkerchief in the yard and ridden away denuded of his magnificent coat. 'Now, are you going to explain the miracle, or not?'

'No miracle,' Kit snorted. 'The simplest of God's works – humble soap and water; a pinch of pepper. All it took was the grace to see the possibilities,' he added piously.

'What we did,' said Humpty, impatient for the praise that must be forthcoming, 'was to shove the soap and water in both ends, with the pepper for added encouragement at the rear. Then we soaked their coats so they looked as though they were sweating, and well – they did the rest!'

'It was contingency plan number four,' added Kit modestly.

'You must tell me about the others,' Will said, shuddering. 'Later,' he pleaded, as two mouths opened at once. 'Just at the moment I have the most pressing urge to take a bath.'

When he rejoined the ladies for a last celebratory glass before bed an hour later, he remarked to Lucy that she might have warned him what to expect. He had been particularly fond of the almond coat.

She surveyed him reflectively with those eyes of a similar, but deeper and more disturbing green and thought for a moment before she said, 'Yes, indeed, I might have done. But then I suppose that poor Major Rowley must have been just as fond of his beautiful blue one. And he is on *our* side!'

Part Three

Daventry, June 1645

Outside, the sun shone, birds called and the deer ran like water for the King's pleasure across the fine chase of Fawsley Park. Inside a stuffy inn in nearby Daventry, Tom and Valora Heron pursued their own preferred pleasures, their opportunities being as few nowadays as were those of His Majesty to hunt. They had thrown the bedclothes onto the floor and the mattress beneath them resembled the recent sack of Leicester. Perhaps it equally represented a victory, in this case over the exigencies of nature. Valora was six months pregnant.

According to the closet whispers of her matronly friends they should, therefore, have ceased this unseemly and dangerous activity some weeks ago. Happily Valora, who was healthier and more content than she had ever been in her life, developed a deaf ear for all depressing advice and they continued to enjoy one another whenever they found the chance.

For the last half hour they had slept, a refreshment demanded by the exertions of the hour before that. Now Valora awoke first and lay on her side looking at Tom's relaxed face, the swelling which was almost certainly Heron's next heir resting comfortably against his scarred hip.

He had changed so much since they had been married. The rigid, downward lines around his mouth had softened; so had his perpetual frown. His manner, even with others, was far less guarded and he had developed a new willingness to amuse and to be amused. He moved his head upon the pillow and his lips opened slightly. She leaned to kiss them, still as ravished by his delicate, honed, slightly cruel face as she had been when she first saw him standing like a supercilious hawk astray among the jays and cuckoos of St James.

She kissed him more searchingly, using her tongue, letting the weight of her engorged breasts rub against his chest. His mouth was warm and welcoming. He began to bite her lips gently, only half awake. Then his hands cupped her breasts and kneaded them, caressing the large brown nipples with thumb and finger. She pulled herself up until she could hang them above his mouth. She loved him to suck them, even more now that they were growing heavy with the milk.

She was stroking his penis now; it was awake almost before he

429

was, questing about with its single blind eye beneath her palm. She slid down to take it into her mouth, cramming it between her breasts and moving rhythmically until he called out to her to stop or she would waste her work. His voice was fogged with sleep and pleasure but his hands knew their business well enough and soon it was Valora's turn to cry out too much too soon as he opened her thighs and slid his fingers into her warm wet crevice.

'Woman, you're far too demanding,' he slurred easily, stretching and preparing to turn sideways to accommodate her.

'Stay just where you are,' she murmured, pressing him back on the pillow. 'I'm not demanding a thing.'

She threw one long leg over him and moved herself up until she straddled him comfortably, teasing the tip of his penis with a hint of what would come. Then she slowly guided him into her, holding his half-slit, delighted eyes with her own, while he stroked the smooth skin of her thighs and gently squeezed her small round buttocks. She moved above him in a measured erotic half dance, the upper part of her body weaving back and forth, round and about, in answer to the impulse from below. She made soft sounds in her throat, then they became louder and more urgent.

He began to take over then, pulling her down upon him so that he was clothed in her soft flesh, her scent filling his nostrils with herbs and flowers and the sweet tang of woman. They moved together towards the climax with a triumphant sureness. He had long since learned to match himself to her needs. It was no longer a question of simply waiting for her; it was a matter of a perfectly orchestrated fugue. When it ended, it was with a concerted cry of victory that rivalled Rupert in the field.

There were small tears in Valora's eyes as he laid her softly back amongst the pillows. She quietened the kicking contents of her stomach with reassuring hands.

'He's complaining because he couldn't join in,' Tom suggested, kissing the still turbulent mound.

'I'm sure he'll learn soon enough,' she said, smiling. 'We shall have to be careful to choose very ugly milkmaids. Or should we choose very pretty ones, and let him enjoy himself thoroughly, since he will probably do so anyway?'

'Oh, the latter, certainly,' said Tom lazily.

'And you? Did you make your first experiments with milk-maids?'

He grinned and kissed her ear. 'I shall not tell you. I don't want recriminations when we are fat and fifty.'

'We shall never be fat, either of us. That is already obvious. We shall be most elegant at fifty. The whole county will come to Heron, just to see what is *à la mode*. And young Thomas will be the most elegant of all. He will be very tall and straight, with splendid dark hair and a veritable fire in his eyes – and his loins – and he will—'

But Tom was not then to discover what the future Sir Thomas's distinguished career might be for it was cut off by a peremptory knocking on the door. 'Major Tom, sir,' called Josh, who preferred military titles when they were not at Heron. 'I'm sorry, sir, but it's urgent!'

Tom threw a coverlet over his wife and went over to unlock the door. 'Well, what is it? Can't it wait?'

'No, sir. It's the enemy. At last, sir. Fairfax has been spotted, just five miles away!'

Tom groaned but he was alert at once. 'Very well. I'll be down in half an hour. Has the King given the order to withdraw?'

'Not yet, sir, no.'

'Good. Then go and find out what more you can, there's a good chap. I can manage everything here.'

Josh clattered off down the stairs and Tom and Valora swung without thought into the routine that had become second nature to them, whether they were lucky enough to be at an inn, as now, or in a field tent, or even, as they had been known to be, stiff with discomfort after a cold night on the floor of Valora's coach between one billet and the next. Soon they were both dressed, Tom's scarlet uniform impeccable, she clothed for comfort, in her present condition, in a cool cotton gown, blue and white striped, like one of the milkmaids about whom she had just teased him.

With time to spare, he sat down beside her on the bed. 'I don't know what will happen,' he said seriously. 'Rupert may get his way and we may march north still, but I think it more likely, now that Fairfax has come looking for us, that we will fight. If that is the case I want you to take no unnecessary risks. If it seems at all possible, and our position is good, I want you to remain here. If you must move on – if we change our position tonight – then stay close among the other ladies and don't go far from the coach.'

'You have no need to say all this. But you do so every time.'

He took her face tenderly between his hands. 'That is because I worry about you, and about young Thomas, every time.'

'That is foolish. We have always been perfectly safe.'

'I know.' He kissed the tip of her nose. 'I want you to stay that way.'

'We will. I promise.'

'That is good.'

When Josh returned, in somewhat more than half an hour, the news was that the King, hastily recalled from his hunting, had given the order for the army to evacuate Daventry and move to Market Harborough, which should prove a good rallying point for the troops and also the march would give them the chance to choose a favourable battleground.

'Then Rupert has lost. Is there any news of Goring's men, or Gerrard's?'

'Not yet, sir.'

'Surely the King will not fight unless he has sufficient numbers?' said Valora.

'What are Fairfax's numbers? Do we know?'

Josh sniffed. 'Cromwell has not joined him yet. But even without him –' He did not want to alarm his mistress.

Tom sighed. 'I see. Oh well, as usual I don't suppose we shall know anything worth knowing until we are face to face with the enemy. However, I must go and find out what I can – and I must rejoin Rupert. Ten to one he's out scouting for himself. If we do fight, tonight, or tomorrow, which is more likely – I may not see you again until after the battle.'

Valora stood and he brought her to him, holding her carefully and lovingly, kissing the mouth that had started to form into a doubtful line. 'Remember what I have said,' he told her, smiling.

'Remember that I love you,' was her only reply.

He left her then. It was not their custom, upon such occasions, to say goodbyes.

Tom did not manage to track Rupert down until they had reached the small town of Market Harborough that evening. There he found a council of war in progress. The voices were high.

He waited until it was finished to fall in with his leader, who had come out with a face like thunder, much as Tom had expected. Rupert grunted a greeting and they stalked down the road in silence for a time, with the cheerful Boy holding his nasal inquisition of every object as he ran before them.

'Why, in the name of God,' growled the Prince at last through clenched jaws, 'does he make me Commander-in-Chief if the only advice to which he is prepared to listen is that of ignorant and stupid civilians?'

'Digby again?' guessed Tom sympathetically.

Rupert nodded. 'And Ashburnam! I ask you! His Gentleman of the Bedchamber! Fit only to deal with sheets and towels and chamberpots! But the King listens to him. And does not listen to me. Ergo – we shall go into battle tomorrow outnumbered by more than two to one, lacking many experienced men and forced to rely on raw infantry who might turn tail at any moment and run for home. Only one thing cheers me in this sorry decision,' he added, grinning at Tom for the first time, 'and that is that Cromwell is reported on his way. I shall enjoy meeting Old Ironsides again. This time we must show him who is master.'

Some of his royal uncle's optimism was beginning to infect Rupert after all. Or perhaps not. But at any rate his public approach would never be anything less than positive, now that the decision was made. He was first and foremost a fine professional soldier and his duty was no longer to attempt to postpone the confrontation that some people said would be the last great battle of all, but to throw all his force of character and leadership into winning it.

The choice of battleground had been an obvious one. From Market Harborough the terrain sloped upwards in a series of ridges towards the village of Naseby on the highest crest. It was wet country, the watershed between the Avon and the Welland, and the hollows had been turned into bogs by a rainy spring. It was raining now, though only lightly, and there was a frisky northwest wind which made the best of bright banners and waving plumes as the two armies faced each other in the early morning from two opposing ridges divided by a shallow dip. Because of this pattern of dip and crest neither side could yet be sure of the other's numbers, though both were aware that Parliament had the advantage.

Where was Goring? Tom thought irritably as he drew up his troop behind Rupert. At that point the only man who could have answered him was Fairfax, who had intercepted a message from the absent cavalier objecting to Rupert's summons on the grounds that he had his hands full in the southwest. Goring would not come, but his comrades would not cease to hope for his arrival, however late. The spirit of optimism rode high in the King's camp.

They certainly were a splendid sight. The King himself rode at the head of his army, the sunlight creating a legendary figure from this small man as it struck glory from his gilt armour and further burnished his superb Flemish horse. The insouciant young men of his Life Guard surrounded him, each one as dazzling as a mirror in polished armour and sheened silk. The breeze caught the embroidered banners and the sweethearts' scarves and played havoc with carefully combed curls. On the opposing hill blunt Philip Skippon commanded Parliament's infantry in its buff jerkins and its worn cuirasses, with its accents from country lanes and the back streets of London.

As for the cavalry, Rupert's magnificent flyers in their red cloaks found themselves facing, not the anticipated wall of Cromwell's Ironsides, but the angry little Henry Ireton, elevated only that morning to the rank of Commissary General. It was a great disappointment. It was that old skeleton, Sir Marmaduke Langdale, with his controversial Northern Horse, who would have Cromwell to deal with, God help them.

By eleven o'clock both sides had completed their dispositions. Tom knew that Rupert would begin hostilities; he would not risk another Marston Moor. He began to feel the excitement rising in himself; he could scarcely help it; it was all around him in the eager voices and expectant eyes of his troopers. Whatever Rupert might have thought of their chances, the great majority of the men wanted this battle. They wanted to redeem themselves for the year's losses and they wanted their revenge. And they too were troubled by the ghost of Marston Moor. They needed a big, bold, magnificent victory to exorcise it. Would they get it? It was impossible to say. So much depended upon just how greatly they were outnumbered; but that was not the only factor. The right charge, the wrong manoeuvre, luck, God – a battle was as unpredictable as the rest of life.

The cannon sounded. They were off!

Tom just had time to approve the brisk, disciplined manner of old Astley's advance down into the valley. He still favoured the old-fashioned solid formation with the musketeers flanking the pikemen on either side; but they were invaluable men, each one as much a veteran as their gallant sixty-six-year-old commander. Behind them, supporting the King and his Royal Life Guard, came Rupert's own foot regiment, the Bluecoats, the only infantry to bear his name. As they moved off, Rupert gave the signal for the charge.

Tom was in the first line as they thundered down the hill. The exhilaration of it was like a dream of flying. His own voice clamoured in his ears above the drumming hooves. 'For God and Queen Mary!' he roared as the King had commanded, and then, more emotionally, 'For Rupert and Victory!' They were all shouting, and laughing too in the sheer joy of the movement, the moment and the morning. They were hawks at the stoop and their prey lay waiting for them.

They winged down the slope and up again with no loss of impetus and as they breasted the crest they saw them – the long line of Ireton's opposition, far more than they had expected. And on the right they were getting oblique fire from behind a long hedge that ran at right angles to the enemy lines. It didn't stop them; it hardly even pricked them. They swept on up to the crest with undiminished vigour and hurled themselves on Ireton's front line. They tore into them and drove them back, thrusting them towards their own infantry. They fought back and for a brief time there was a chaos of panting, snorting and screaming horses and scything swords. Dust was rising all around them, clouding into nostrils and caking the sweating bodies. Tom, fitter than he had ever been, used his sword as though he were swiving stubble. He no longer saw the faces of the men he killed; they had become numbers to be accounted for.

At first the going was hard, the resistance strong, but soon the immense confusion of cavalry began to rupture outwards in a soft explosion towards the rear. The dragoons in the hedge dared not fire. The two regiments nearest the infantry lost their nerve and broke completely, scattering, turning and flying headlong. Rupert's hawks swooped after them, jubilant harriers, coursing them out of the press and away!

To Valora Heron the battle was only a terrifying din centred around an even more terrifying fear – always the same one – that Tom would, this time, be killed. She was now a part of that other great force that accompanies and sustains any army on the move, its women, its camp-followers. Some of them were officers' wives like herself but for the most part they were a more useful breed; cooks, laundresses, skivvies and whores. They were drawn up, with the kitchen and other supply wagons and the coaches of the ladies and those who were not ladies, in a field at Clipston, a small village between Naseby and Harborough which the quartermasters had designated as out of the danger area.

Valora was trying to cheat the terrible elasticity of time and to concentrate her mind by playing chess with Helena Dowson, a rather quiet and bookish person with whom she had struck up a friendship. Helena's husband was also a cavalry major and she came from East Anglia, Cromwell's country, as she ruefully admitted. The two women had breakfasted together in the early hours, seated on camp chairs and using the steps of Valora's coach as a table. Now it was high noon and they were using them for a chessboard to rest upon.

'We seem to have been here for *weeks*,' complained Valora, arching a stiff back. 'I wonder, should we take a walk down the road and see if we can find anyone with some news?' They did receive news of the battle from time to time, but the lads who had been doing the running appeared less and less often. Either they had been seduced into joining the fight, or they had fallen prey to snipers.

'I shall stay here. I promised John,' said Helena serenely.

Valora made a face. 'I promised too, but it is more than human nature can bear to sit here in stupefied ignorance!'

Helena moved her knight.

'That noise. Has it changed at all, do you think? Or is it just the same? If only one could tell which were the triumphant voices.'

'They probably sound much the same as their victims after all this time,' said Helena practically.

'The baby is kicking again. I'm sure he wants me to walk about.'

'You can walk about here. It's your move.'

'Oh – I can't think. Not for the moment. I don't know how you manage to be so calm.'

'It is only my appearance that is calm. In that respect, I am not good for you. You used to be far more peaceful yourself before I brought what John calls my unnatural stasis into your life.'

Valora laughed and kissed her cheek. 'That was pregnancy, not me. I've never been able to sit still for more than ten minutes.' She made an effort however, and for half an hour they played with controlled interest. Valora lost the game, not without some relief that it had ended. At least, now, she could occupy herself by fetching their dinner from the cooks' tent at the other side of the field.

She chose the right moment to arrive. A very young cornet, with blood streaming proudly down one arm, was regaling the cooks with steaming hot news from the front.

It was not good. As Rupert had completed his victorious charge against Ireton, Cromwell had swung into action, leading his first line against Langdale's unseasoned horse. Mercifully, they did not break, but they did give ground enough to discourage the King's infantry who had to take too much of the charge.

The King himself had tried to put back the heart into them, spurring into the middle of them and trying to lead them forward. But just then someone had caught at his bridle and turned him back out of the obvious danger. Unfortunately the King's new direction was seen as a command and the larger part of the infantry wheeled away to the right, sweeping the King with them. By the time they could be got to stand again they had fallen back disastrously far. They were now without cavalry cover to the left, where Cromwell had pounded Langdale's diminishing force until it had given way at last and fled, galloping north as it had wanted to do all along.

The Ironsides now laid into the infantry, who seeing their hopes draining with their blood, gave up being heroes and surrendered, company after company, on the ignominious proviso that they might keep any booty they might already possess. Their officers fled, some of them joining Rupert's frantic cavalry, who had returned to the field to help the infantry but had found themselves, no longer so swift of wing after their wild chase, forced to face Ireton's reserve, as fresh as stallions on the scent and twice as dangerous. It was a flank attack, glancing and deadly, but it did not slow them down completely and they managed to fight their way through to the King's side of the battle, if only so that they might cover his retreat . . .

It was not a very clear picture, but it was the best the boy could do, put together from what he had heard and what he had seen for himself. When he had finished they bound up his arm and fed him.

Valora walked slowly back to Helena, trying not to spill the contents of the plates she carried. She felt a little sick. She did not want to eat. Neither, when she heard the news, did Helena.

'So – it does not go well for us?'

'No. I think not.'

Neither would speak the word 'defeat'. For one thing, it may not be the case. The sounds were different, lesser perhaps, but the battle was not yet over. There was firing still and the rest of the dull roar, though ragged occasionally, still continued. They had learned to believe nothing until the evidence was unmistakable.

They gave their discarded dinner to several grateful dogs and forced themselves to settle to another game of chess. Between moves, Valora told the beads of her rosary with an absolute and concentrated fervour.

After another sly, slow shift of time – the din was still the same, the rosary half complete – they heard the sound of many horsemen coming from the battlefield. The two women looked at each other.

'They must be in retreat – or perhaps come to order us to move out.'

There was movement on the other side of the field, about the gate. They saw the horses and the swirling red cloaks. Valora half rose, but Helena pushed her down again. 'I'll go,' she said. 'If your Tom is amongst them I'll bring him to you.'

Amazingly, Valora found herself obediently sinking back. She did feel ridiculously faint. It must be the baby. Oh, if only it were Tom. She wouldn't care if it was defeat. Only let him live. There was some kind of outcry at the gate now. More and more of the cavalrymen were sweeping in. She couldn't see Helena.

The riders began to race around the field. They were shouting and waving their swords. Perhaps, then, it was *not* defeat. A man was riding towards her now. It was not Tom, but he might be able to tell her where he was. She rose and went towards him.

Tom, at that precise moment, was ten miles on the road north to Leicester with the King in full retreat. It had been a desperate and desolate flight. Trailing their bruised and beaten wings, the hawks circled their monarch, down from the clouds and worn out by the clay. Tom had never been so tired. Half of it, he knew, was simple depression.

For the last twenty minutes or so, now that some form of organization had taken over the march, he had been trying to find out what had been the arrangements made for the baggage trains and the women's coaches. The answer, when he had completed his questioning, appeared to be – none at all.

Together with several brother officers, he requested permission to turn back and look for them upon the road. Rupert, having no other use for them, gave it. His face was grey.

In less than an hour they had retraced every inch of the road. They met and despatched one small party of Cromwell's men, killing all except for one prisoner whom they interrogated to no avail. They killed him too.

They moved more cautiously as they approached the battlefield, expecting to be ambushed at every tall hedgerow. But they met no one. The sun shone and everywhere was silent.

Another ten minutes took them near Clipston field. They spurred up, in sudden worry and haste. They came to the end of the hedge and reached the gate of the field.

The first thing Tom saw was the wheel of an overturned coach, almost blocking the opening. A woman sagged next to it, her arms caught in the spokes. Major John Dowson, riding next to Tom, slid from his horse with a soft cry. 'Helena!'

She was dead. She had been stabbed through the breast. 'Gentlemen, it is my wife,' the young major said in a wondering tone. He spoke as though he had left her asleep in the garden at home. Someone put an arm around his shoulders. They continued into the field.

Tom felt a terror that filled him with a vicious hatred. He cast round the space, ignoring the fact that it was hideous with corpses. Where was her coach? He saw it at once over on the other side, its blue and silver paint sharp and bright in the sunshine.

He galloped around the edge of the field; the centre was too full of things that his mind refused to acknowledge. He could see now that there was something, someone, lying in front of the vehicle. The blue and white stripes made him cry out aloud.

He was off his horse and bending over her. Her eyes claimed him, filling with steady, thankful tears. They ran into her smiling mouth and down onto the fresh cotton gown and round into the deep, thin gash that striped her neck.

'I prayed you would come.' The blood pulsed out with her words.

'Dear Jesus.' The sword had cut near to the great artery.

'How long have you been here like this?'

'I don't know. It seems – very long.' She was very white. The grass was bloody, but only in a small neat patch beside her head. The soil beneath was extremely porous.

One of the other officers was a surgeon. 'I'll get Withers. He'll—'

She laid her hand on his. 'No. It's not worth it. I'd rather have you stay close for the – time that's left.'

He could not bear it, but he must. He had seen enough of such wounds to know that she was right; she was dying. There was no point in leaving her now. She was very weak already. She must have lain here bleeding for an hour, perhaps two.

'I love you,' he said. It was all there was to say.

'Yes.' But her tears were coming faster now and her face, which had bloomed in welcome, was sad and bitter. 'Young Thomas,' she said. 'We were never punished. It is Young Thomas who must pay. I think he is dead. Do you think so?'

In a waste of rage and pain, he put his hand gently over the soft mound. It was quite still. She would not ask him to listen for the heartbeat.

She wished passionately that he did not have to suffer all this. He had only just learned how to be happy. 'There must *be* a Young Thomas,' she said, her face clear again. 'Later. Though I shall not be his mother, I shall take a deep interest in his well-being, if I am able. No, don't say anything. It is how I want it to be. But I shall not be a good influence on him if I do not now make my peace with God. I must make my confession, Tom. Do you think you can find a priest?'

Even now her wretched religion would steal away their time. But he knew that now, above all times, she must be satisfied. He signalled to one of the men who was still sorting out the dead from the wounded women and told him what was wanted.

'Do you remember the last time we needed a priest in a hurry?' Valora's smile was tender and oddly smug.

He kissed her very carefully. 'I do. We should have sent for *that* one years ago.'

'Ah no. The chase was a fine one, for both of us. I'd not have had it any other way,' she lied. They might have had Young Thomas and a brother or sister by now.

He looked at her dumbly. She should not talk so much, he thought. But then, what difference could it make?

'Was it a terrible defeat, today?' she asked, to give him back his tongue.

'The worst. And this field the worst of it. We – I shall never forgive myself. The orders—'

'Oh, Tom. Looking for guilt? How foolish. It was no fault of any of ours. It was the work of some misguided creatures, beside themselves with blood and battle. I don't know why they killed us; I think they mistook us in some way. Except – I know that the man who wounded me did not care for my rosary.' She hesitated, almost as though to beg his pardon.

He shook his head. The hand that was clasped in his still grasped the beads.

The priest came soon after this, and Tom went to sit impatiently upon the steps of the coach, grudging every moment as the black figure knelt, murmuring, over her.

It was not long, and when the man had gone Valora looked at him so gloriously that it was even worth the minutes lost to them. 'Thank you,' she said simply.

He hated the priest for the finality of his visit, for he saw that now she was composing herself to die. She had waited for forgiveness as stubbornly as she had waited for himself.

'I suppose that now I should leave pious messages for everyone and dispose of my fortune,' she said then, and her ironic note gave him brief joy. 'But that seems a dull occupation, and I had far rather just hear you tell me again how you love me, and I will tell you the same, and in that way we shall pass the time very sweetly together.'

He bent his head on her breast and held her as tightly as he dared. The time did pass very sweetly, but it was not long. He buried her at sunset, where she had died. A warrior's grave. The rosary was still in her hand.

Heron, July

It was Josh Pye who sent home the news of Valora's death. Tom could not do it. The letter was short and stark, written with obvious emotion. The valet promised to keep close to his master, who 'does not seem to care, scarcely even to know, where he goes or what he should do'.

Rigid with shock, Tom remained with Rupert while the Prince did his hopeless best to convince the King that they must join the poor remainder of their cavalry with the still strong army of the west, before Fairfax and Cromwell could sweep down to undo all its good work in the southwestern counties.

The King appeared to have no inkling of the disaster that Naseby had been. He insisted upon delaying on the Welsh Marches to repair the losses to the infantry, setting up a miniature court at Raglan Castle, surrounded by his favourites and living as if he had forgotten he had ever gone to war. There was music, there was ceremony, there was hunting, hawking and good conversation. Charles would hear no mention of defeat and every small success was wildly lauded.

At Naseby he had lost the battle; he had lost the Midlands; he had lost his infantry, his artillery and most of his baggage train. And although he was, perhaps, the last to realize it, he had also lost, and ultimately this time, his reputation. He had been foolish enough to keep it, as an ageing woman might keep her face, all in the same box.

Although this was fated to be a desperate circumstance for the King, it was a most convenient one for Jud Heron. For, when the chest that contained the monarch's entire correspondence with his wife during the last two years fell into the hands of Parliament with the captured baggage train, its contents were found to be so damning in their revelation of his perfidy that they were at once made public.

Jud was one of those to publish the most popular newsheet since the war began. It was called 'The King's Cabinet Opened' and in it an excited readership found ample justification for every rumour they had ever heard regarding their ruler's machinations with European powers and with the devilish Irish Confederates. The paper would do more to damage the Royalist cause than even the Ironsides might do. Parliament would see that it was read by every man in England who could read.

Jud, in a celebratory mood, decided he would circulate it for himself. He packed several thousand copies and set off for Gloucestershire. It was as good an outlet as any, and he had not been home since before the war. He was brimful of confidence just now. Part of this might be ascribed to the fortunes of Parliament and to the continued success of the *Intelligencer*, but a great deal of it was the work of Cleo Whittaker and the healthy, black-haired baby, the image of his mother, whom they had called Edmund.

Jud was proud of himself these days; he could almost feel himself expanding. There was no room in his life for old discords. He wanted to see his home and he wanted to see his family, his *other* family. He could afford the time. He would go and make his peace.

Cleo had looked wistful as he kissed her and little Ned goodbye. 'You will come back?' she had asked, half apologetic. He had laughed at her and called her a great fool for even beginning to think otherwise. He had delayed until he was quite sure that *she* was sure, then he had gone through the goodbyes again and left them at last, grinning all over his face.

His welcome at Heron was everything he could have wished. It was also a great relief, for the nearer he had come to home, the greater had been his apprehension of disapproval, despite the fact that Lucy had written saying she had at last told their mother the truth concerning his present way of life. Tom's condemnation still weighed on him, together with the suggestion that his father had died with his mind still turned against him.

Mary's greeting was all that he had longed for. She had him all to herself at first, for it was a glorious day and the rest of them were all at the haymaking. She happened to be inside the house when Jud arrived, consulting Mr Tradescant's invaluable notes on the subject of puckered and distorted foliage in phlox. She was standing at her desk in the small parlour muttering 'eelworm' in a very nasty tone, when a beaming Margery raced in to announce the return of the prodigal.

Mr Tradescant fluttered to the floor and Jud was enveloped in her arms. 'Oh, I have so longed to see you! Nothing could make me happier.'

'Mother! I too. So you can forgive me, can you, for my unpopular opinions? I wanted to write, but—'

'I know. Heavens, child, how large you have grown.' She thought quickly. She had always had a soft spot for Jud, above all her children, and now he was back; nothing must mar this reunion.

'I won't pretend I like your political preferences. I don't. I am very sorry for them. But we don't forbid Will Staunton the house; how could we? How then, could I forbid it to you? My black sheep,' she smiled, 'we'll not talk about the war or the Parliament. It's my guess we'll find a hundred other things to speak of. Oh, I am so *gladdened* by the sight of you! Whatever you are doing in London, it certainly suits you. You remind me of your father when he was about your age. Come with me; we'll go and find your brothers and sisters presently – but first you must see the gardens; there is much that will be new to you—'

So Jud found himself officially forgiven. He felt himself expanding even further at her compliments to his appearance. How strange that he should be the one to resemble Sir George. If only he could have spoken with him before he died – but these things were best not thought of. He was here and he was happy and everything was well.

He had never had a welcome like it in his life. Only the twins professed to have strong reservations about 'the family traitor', but these did not prevent them from hurling themselves upon him in their old established fashion, a collision from which all three deduced that they had grown heavier, stronger and more capable of bruising since last they met.

Julia took a fit of shyness at the first sight of this broad and personable young man, but recovered at the temptation of the doll he had brought her from London. Belzabub had long since been discarded and Julia at ten was grave and ladylike. She thanked him with a curtsey and followed him with her thoughtful blue eyes for the rest of the day.

Young Edward, now an energetic five-year-old, did not recognize his brother, but was prepared to accept him as soon as he was allowed to mount Jud's large and mettlesome horse. 'I'm Prince Rupert,' he announced, tossing back an imaginary cloak and digging his heels into the chestnut's flanks.

'Hey, there; he'll be off back to London with you if you do that,' cautioned Jud, grinning up at the fearless rider and catching the reins just in time.

'Good!' said Ned, returning the grin. Two teeth were missing from it. Jud swung the boy down and took his hand, which was rarely detached after that. He became Ned's instant slave, bewitched by the sturdy limbs and the non-stop questions.

He wished that he might tell them all that he, too, was the proud father of a young Ned, but had enough sense to realize that they had sustained enough of a shock for the moment, in his return. Besides, if he told his mother, she would be sure to insist that he *did* something about his irregular relationship with Cleo, and that was something he did not wish to discuss. He and Cleo were idyllically happy as they were, and any changes they might want to make would develop in their own good time.

He had, in the end, asked her to wed him. She would not. And there, for the present, was an end of it. True, they were more than crowded at her mother's, but the house next door was soon due to fall empty and something more comfortable could then be arranged. But either way, it was hardly an address of which Mary Heron might be expected to approve.

There was, however, as Mary herself had suggested, plenty to talk about without going into either Jud's private life or his politics. Naturally, Tom's tragedy cast its shadow over them at first. It was too recent to be passed over with the heady speed at which they had all begun to exchange their news, and slowed them at once with the renewed realization that it had actually happened, that Valora, that courageous and gallant spirit, was lost to them and would not come again, that she had died by the sword and her murderer had walked free.

'Merciful God,' said Jud quietly when they had finished telling him, 'how you must hate the Parliament.'

'Yes,' said Mary bluntly, meeting his shamed gaze very straight. 'But the soldiers who could take such a cruel vengeance on the defenceless more than the Parliament – and the war more than the soldiers. It was an act of consummate viciousness, as though all the real evil in this war were drawn together and unleashed in this one hideous climax. I hope that one day our poor country may recover from the blow she has dealt herself in this conflict, but I fear we can never forgive ourselves for Naseby.'

'It is not *you* who must forgive yourselves,' said Jud sadly, 'it was only Parliament's troopers who behaved like that.'

'That is not what I mean,' said Mary. 'I think that we all share the guilt for such an evil deed, as we all share the war. I wonder if you can comprehend that at all? You see, we all are English.'

Jud looked non-plussed. It was Martha, who had kept almost silent as was her custom, who came to his rescue. She understood his sense of guilt as a Parliamentarian, for the terrible thing that had happened to Valora. She shared it herself. She knew it was no more rational in Jud than it was in her own breast. It had been a very long time ago when she had foreseen how Valora's fierce pride in her faith, and the wearing of its outward sign, would bring her to her death. She had even warned her, fruitlessly, knowing that no warning could affect her fate.

'I think it is natural in people who have any goodness in them to feel a share in the responsibility for the actions of those who represent them,' Martha said. 'Those troopers did not act according to the will of good men on the Parliament's side, but they represent them nevertheless – and we may feel the same; there is cruelty on both sides.'

'But why did they have to *kill* them?' Lucy cried, her grief unaltered by all this irrelevant heartsearching. 'Josh says they murdered more than five hundred women after the battle; why didn't they take them prisoner? They have 4,000 *men* still in their hands.'

Jud put out a hand as though to touch and heal her pain. 'It is still not known for certain. Some reports say the cavalrymen slew them because they thought they were witches, all in thrall to Rupert the Devil and able to perform black miracles; you know the old story. It may be true. Many of them were marked on the brow, as witches are when the blood is drawn from their heads to let out the demon in them.'

'Oh God,' Mary burst out, 'are we never to have done with this unclean cowardice?' No one could look at Martha.

'But I've also heard it said that since most of the camp servants and many of the light women were from Wales, come in with the new recruits, and spoke only their own tongue, and defended themselves with long knives as is the custom in the wilds of their barbarous country, the soldiers were mortally afraid of them and killed them out of sheer terror. I have one description that would harrow your blood – a shrieking horde of eldritch hags, coming at the daunted footslogger with bare blades, howling spells and incantations. I don't know what is the truth. They slew them out of poverty of mind, out of ignorance and cowardice, because they were the victors and because their blasted religion tells them they shall not suffer a witch to live. I'm sorry, Martha. This is not a subject that can be tolerable to you.'

Martha said, 'I am alive to listen; that is more than I might have expected, as you must be the first to understand.'

'But Valora was with the *officers'* wives,' pursued Lucy, undeflected. 'Surely they could not mistake *them* for anything other than what they were? I think your Puritans are even more cruel than you know. They did not kill out of fear, but out of hatred. God damn them to everlasting fire, every one!'

It was not easy to go on after that. There was a subdued and heartsore silence for a long time. Jud got up and paced the room, still feeling stupidly guilty for what he couldn't have helped, and detested as much as they. He was sick, too, for his brother, their quarrel forgotten. He wished there was something, anything, he could do or say.

He settled again, sombrely, in one of his old haunts, on the windowseat, his feet pushing at the stones of the embrasure. Lucy played a few lacklustre notes on her guitar. They remained in this discomfort until mercifully, Ned was brought in to say goodnight and to take away their speechlessness to bed with him. The sadness would not leave them, though, and they exchanged the history of their separate war in low, thoughtful cadences, and if they smiled at each other sometimes, they did not laugh at all.

They began to recover the next day, taking new strength from Jud's evident delight in being with them again. He made them repeat every tale he had already heard from Lucy or from Will and even coaxed Martha to tell the story of her fabled rescue by the impressive Colonel Heavy. It cost her an effort to cast aside her sorrow for her friend, and the agony she was privately suffering for Tom, but she sensed Jud's kindness and did not grudge him the forced lightness.

It was not good weather for grief, being brilliantly sunny, with gorgeous azure skies and a spectacular series of sunsets. It was also harvest time and there was work to be done. The Herons took themselves and their history outside, therefore, and soon the sadness was only a part of them, familiar and accepted, no longer the angry wound it had been before.

Jud could not help regaling them with his tuneless singing as he helped with the hay, proud of the fact that he had not lost his facility with a scythe. There was one awkward moment when he found himself roaring 'Confusion to His Majesty' to a stupefied circle of tenants, but he laughed himself back into their good graces before they had properly grasped what it meant.

He felt himself to be a bottomless well of bubbling optimism. He had rarely seen Heron look so well. The land seemed to have suffered very little despite the insufficiency of workers, and in this weather it was the most beautiful and the most blessed place on earth. How marvellous it would be if he could bring Cleo and little Edmund up here. How the boy would thrive in this air. And he would have his small uncle to play with.

They would have to find him another name, though, to prevent confusion. He laughed as he recalled the argument that had ended with his christening. Nan had wanted something outlandish, as usual – what was it? God, yes – Tiberius, to go with poor little Julius Caesar. That one had stuck, worse luck for the innocent scrap, but he and Cleo were having none of that nonsense.

Instead, Jud had again called to mind his father's love of Shakespeare and inspiration had clouted him like a thunderbolt. 'Now, Gods, stand up for bastards!' King Lear, he was almost sure. He could just hear the old man spouting it—

> *Why brand they us with base? With baseness? Bastardy?*
> *Base, base – Edmund the base shall top the legitimate.*
> *I grow, I prosper; now, Gods, stand up for bastards!'*

And they would, too; Jud would see that they did. He was amazed at the strength of the love he felt for the boy. He should not remain illegitimate. Even if Cleo *never* consented to marry him, there were other ways; he had not been at Lincoln's Inn for nothing. He tossed a swathe of sweet-scented grass up high towards the sun, death forgotten in the warmth of life about him.

Lucy, following behind to fork up and turn his swathes for drying, was reminded of someone by the generous gesture. 'Do you see a great deal of Will these days?' she asked. They had spoken briefly last night of his approaching bid for the Commons.

'Not much; he's busy wooing his electors. It'll be a stampede in his favour. He gave me a letter for you, and a book, I think it is.'

'Oh, what book?'

Jud scratched his jaw. 'I don't know, but I'm sure it will be nothing improving. You had best treasure it, for I doubt you'll get many more gifts from Will.'

'Indeed? And why not?' What an odd thing to say.

'Well, he is like to be married soon, and his prospective bride is not, I fancy, over fond of you.' He chuckled.

Lucy stabbed into her next swathe as though it were a nest of adders. 'Cousin Eliza?' she guessed contemptuously. 'I would never have thought it of him.'

'Then you have not used your powers of observation. She always meant to have him. And he to take her, just as likely.'

'The fool!' Lucy would not say any more but went on attacking the grass. She felt hot and miserable. What did Will want to go and get married for? Now they could not be friends any more; horrible Eliza would see to that. And she needed a friend just now. Not that she saw him very often, but the knowledge that he was *there*, just as he had said, had been very comforting in her bad moments. She hated Eliza Hartley.

She didn't want to hear any more about it. 'Tell me the news of Robin,' she said firmly. 'I should so love to meet him again. He must have changed a great deal since I last saw him.'

'No. He's still the same bellicose scruff,' said Jud feelingly. He was not getting on so well with Rob, just at the moment, though things were better than they had been before Edmund was born. Rob had not taken the news of Cleo's pregnancy at all well. In fact he had knocked Jud down. Twice. And afterwards had spoken to him only when their work demanded it. But Cleo would thaw him; trust her for that. They had caught the ghost of a smile on Rob's grim face as he had leaned over the cradle. It was only a matter of time. Meanwhile it was good to be away from his crabby looks.

Lucy was looking rather crabby herself, come to think of it. Surely she was not jealous? What could Will be to her? You never could tell with women. But it was a pity Lucy couldn't take to Lady Hartley; she was a really handsome woman and full of spirit too. And positively weighed down with gold. Will had not actually said he would marry her, but he *had* said most men would think him a fool not to. And so they would.

If the afternoon had lost its splendour for Lucy, it was nothing to what the evening had in store. Everyone had worked hard and there was a general sense that they owed themselves a little pleasure. There was no wish to be boisterous nor even especially gay, but Mary agreed that a little music was permissible and they grouped themselves about the fireside while Lucy played and Martha softly sang the old country ballads they all knew. The firelight seemed to draw them in together and each one was conscious of shared sorrow and shared joy standing quietly among them. They were acutely aware of themselves as a family. Jud sat next to his mother with Ned on his knee. The boy was half asleep, burrowing into Jud's shoulder. The twins were asprawl on the rug and Julia sat holding wool for Margery who was rhythmically winding it into balls.

It was into this complete and peaceful scene that the master of the house came, unannounced, at once to feel himself excluded and knowing, as soon as he saw the company, that he could not be wanted among them. Martha was the first to see him, looking up from the music to catch the wild light from his eye as he looked at his brother. She lifted her hand as if to ward off something. Her small movement alerted Lucy who stopped playing and said gently, 'Good evening, Tom; welcome home.'

Tom did not reply. He did not look at her. He looked at no one but Jud. He stripped off his riding gloves and threw them down on the table. Nobody could mistake the metaphor.

Humpty would have got up and embraced his brother but Kit held him back, pulling at his jacket. 'Leave it, you fool!'

The fire crackled. It seemed very loud. Mary half rose, her arms going out to Tom. He motioned her back with a gesture of one hand, without turning to her at all.

Jud, whose breath had caught in his throat, sighed gustily as he released it. He wondered if there was any way to make the next few minutes any less unpleasant. He doubted it. He put Ned, woozily protesting, beside his mother. 'Well, Tom?' he said curiously, half-question, half-greeting.

His brother looked, he thought pityingly, as though he had just risen from the grave and his only destination must be to return there. 'No, sir,' Tom said with a hideous control. 'It is not well. It is no manner of well. I ask you what you are doing in my house?'

Jud swallowed. Damn it, he would not be put straightway in the wrong. 'I came to see my mother.' His chin lifted. He stood up.

'But I had told you never to come here.' Tom's tone menaced him with its reasonableness.

Julia dropped her ball of wool. Margery let it lie.

'I did not think you and I would meet.'

'You are honest in your words, but not in your behaviour. I repeat, this is my house. You are no longer welcome here.'

'That is untrue.' Mary spoke quietly but determinedly. 'Jud is welcome for my sake. I have lost my husband. I have no desire to lose any of my children, if it may be prevented at all. If this is my home still, as I make no doubt it is, then I too am to have my say in who comes here and who does not.'

She did not want to have to outface him like this. All she wished for was to take him in her arms and let him spend a little of his grief with her. Her heart cried out within her at the beaten look of him. It was obvious that he no longer cared for life. Surely someone must *make* him care. There was only herself. But she would not have this quarrel. It was foolish and it was wicked.

'Then, Mother, it distresses me, but, if he is to remain, then I must take my leave again. I am sorry.' Tom reached for his gloves again, his face like iron.

'Why, Tom? If you could only tell me why.' Jud allowed enough of appeal into his tone to hold his brother back, as he thought. He did not expect the concentrated venom of the answer he got.

'Are you foolish enough to ask *me* that?' The ghost of Valora stood between them as plainly as though everyone saw her. If he really wished for that guilt, it was offered him now. 'Since you are ignorant enough, and calloused enough to need an explanation, I will give it to you. You made yourself an enemy of this house, of your family, of my father and all that he stood for, on the day that you became the enemy of your King. Since that day you have worked constantly and thoroughly to bring us down. Why, this very week you have gone about to encompass His Majesty's shame. Do you think I have not seen your filthy rag?' He pointed to the pouch that was still slung over his shoulder, from which there protruded a copy of 'The King's Cabinet Opened'.

'You descended into a mire of treachery and baseness when you took up this evil employment, but it is not my intention that you should take the reputation of this family down with you. Therefore, I say again – are you listening, Mother – you are not, and you never will be welcome here.'

Jud had nothing to lose. He pitied Tom but he would not stand for insult and untruth. He knew he must keep a hold of his temper. When he spoke he was astounded at his own mildness. 'You called me ignorant a moment back. But it is you who are ignorant. There is no treachery in me. I love my family as I have ever done, and could in no way seek their harm. As for His Majesty, though I am still his subject, and not disloyal, I trust I have the liberty that God gave a man when he gave him his brains – to disagree with him? If any man is a traitor to those who have trusted him, it is the King. Deny it if you will!' The sureness of a just challenge was in him now and he was no longer afraid of Tom. Loathing closed Tom's throat. He could not and would not admit to this most vile of traitors that yes, the King had made mistakes, and mistakes whose nature and magnitude might yet lose him the war. His Majesty would always take bad advice rather than good, and Tom had never felt himself so critical of him as he had lately been; but nothing would drag that out of him in this company.

Oh God, how tired he was. He had slunk home like a beaten dog, only to rest and lick the wound that would not close. He had not bargained for this. It was too much. He must end it or he would break down in shame before them. Oh Valora, Valora.

'I owe you no answers,' he said, as though he had not been listening. 'Make your farewells to my mother, and leave as soon as you can.' He left his gloves where they lay and went out of the room. They heard his heavy step ascend the stairs.

'God save me, I did not expect that.' Jud shook his head in bitter regret. 'I did not think he would be here. I'm sorry, Mother. I had better leave. He will not change. You know him.'

'God's truth, are my children going to fight this war all over again in my parlour?' Mary was angry, though hurt had made her so. 'He *must* change. Is my will to count for nothing with him?' She got up and made for the door. 'Stay here, Jud. I am going to speak to him.'

'No. It will be no use. Let us leave it there, for the present. I value the time we have had together too well to ruin it completely. Let me go, while we still have pleasant memories to last us.'

'Jud is right, Mother,' said Lucy quickly. 'Tom won't change in this. Not now. And then, too—' she searched for words, 'Jud is a whole man, and a happy one. And we are the happier to have seen that. But Tom is in a far different case. I think our love and duty must be mainly towards him now. He needs us more.'

'Child, you have an old head,' said Mary slowly. She resumed her seat. 'You'd best pack up, then, my son.'

'Yes.' He summoned his old grin. 'I have been glad to be among you again. I look forward to the next time. And at least now, I may write to you all, and I shall. God bless you!'

There were no farewells. He left very quickly, so that when Tom came down some time later, he was gone. As he rode away, he forced his thoughts aside from his brother. There was work waiting for him in London. Lilburne was in jail again and they were getting up a petition to have him out of it. And yet, he promised himself, one day, one day he would have the courage and the sense to tell Tom, and the others too, exactly why and how it was that he had chosen the course he had taken. It was such a simple matter really, when you came right down to it; what he had now – and he did not think Tom had it, in his hidebound observance of an undeserved loyalty – was an earned and developing freedom of mind. It was worth all the kings in Christendom.

Martha had taken to spending her afternoons in the Italian garden. No one else seemed to go there nowadays, perhaps because it had become Dominic's especial domain; he had used to exorcize the frustrations of his vocation in the vanquishing of weeds and the pampering of the exotic lilies and heavily scented roses that grew there. Martha felt his presence there more than anywhere else at Heron. She remembered their time together in the garden and was comforted. She would take a book with her but seldom read more than a few pages, allowing herself instead to drift down her memory. Sometimes she found herself talking to him. It did not matter. There were only the statues, in their suave Roman draperies, to see her.

She came there one hot, lucid afternoon when all the family were still faithfully harvesting. Her back was aching and she felt justified in failing to go back to the fields. She carried a book of music with her, a collection of the work of Thomas Tompkins, the gifted organist of St David's Cathedral. It was in fact Will's gift to Lucy, a reminder that their friendship had begun with music; it had left her oddly unappreciative, Martha thought. But she might learn some of the songs so that she and Lucy could sing them together. If she concentrated hard, she might keep her mind away from another subject towards which it was drawn more frequently than she wished.

But as she came down the path, rather overgrown now, to the seat that commanded the 'vista' of the heart of England, she saw that she might not avoid that subject after all. Tom was leaning on the simple balustrade, gazing outward, his shoulders hunched over the parapet.

At first she thought she would go away. Although he was perfectly polite to her when forced to speak, he had not sought her company since his homecoming, and she did not want to impose on him. Then a kinder instinct impelled her forward. She was not the only one to whom he could not speak. He could communicate with no one and did not try to; his family, though they longed to break the awful loneliness to which he thus condemned himself, found every effort blocked by a solid wall of silence of which Tom himself, Martha was sure, was completely unaware. He was, as far as he knew, behaving quite normally. He had always lived somewhat removed from his fellows. Now he was a man inhabiting an iceberg.

She came up behind him. He would hear her tread though he made no movement. She went and stood next to him. 'Do I disturb you?'

'Oh. No. No, of course you don't.' He did not know he was frowning.

She placed her book on the stone between them. 'I have for a long time wished to thank you. You have been kind beyond the ordinary in letting me stay here—'

'Oh come, Martha. There are no thanks needed; you must know it. You are one of us now; perhaps you have always been so.' He sounded impatient, weary, irascible. She ached for him.

'It is not always so facile a business to receive goodwill as it is to give it out. You must allow my pride to speak its thanks.'

'Pride?' he said wryly. 'I was not aware of any pride in you – or at least, not of that kind,' he added quickly.

'Only of that kind,' she said deliberately, 'or else I should not be able to stay here.'

He looked at her, turning his head away from the soft green hills for the first time. 'Indeed. And why not?'

Her smile reserved a certain right. 'I think I will not answer that.'

He shrugged. 'As you will.'

There was silence. She was annoyed with herself for causing the breakdown. She would have to begin again.

She decided on shock treatment. 'Was Valora very fond of this garden? I should think its extravagances suited her own style. That splendid violet climber for example; what is it, do you know?'

She saw his hands whiten on the parapet. 'I have no idea,' he said grimly.

She continued on her chosen course. 'I would have thought you would wish to speak of her, Tom. All the rest of us do; it is only you who will not. Do you not think that strange?'

He glared at her, tormented. 'Talking will not bring her back.'

'No, but it will help to keep her presence amongst us.'

He looked at her as if he hated her. 'Do you think it is absent from me, at any moment?'

'Yes I do. I think that if she were with you in the way that she would wish to be, you would be more at peace.'

This was more than Tom would stand. 'Who the devil told you

to come meddling into my state of mind? I wish you would simply go away, Martha, and take your ill-conceived interference with you.'

She stood her ground and tried not to be hurt. 'I don't want to meddle, but I think it is time someone told you how you are behaving. I respect your grief; we all do. But you are feeding it as though it were the dearest child of your heart. Can you not look about you a little, and not so consistently inward, and think sometimes of the others in your life?' She felt greatly daring and rather ashamed but instinct told her that gentleness would achieve nothing.

'By what right do you speak to me like this?' Tom demanded angrily.

'You have allowed, only a moment ago, that I am a member of your family.'

'My family leave me alone,' he growled.

'Only because they do not know what to do with a man who will not suffer the touch of kindness.'

'Oh, so this is kindness, is it, this unspeakable prosing? If you want to be kind to me, take your leave as I ask. No, damnit, I'll do so myself!'

He swung about and walked quickly away from her, a diminishing figure between the long rows of cypresses. Martha sighed. It was going to be even harder than she had bargained for.

That night Tom got systematically and thoroughly drunk. He drank claret, alone, in his father's old chair in the study, his feet up on the scored old desk and his head resting on the same greasy patch of leather that had supported Sir George on similar occasions. He drank as deeply as he could without vomiting, but it did not help. His father, he recollected, had been a cheerful drinker, often an uproarious one, but Tom, especially now, was wretched at the game. He drank without verve and without appreciation; all he wanted was to get enough of the stuff inside him to numb, by however small a measure, the hollow ache of his loneliness.

It was a terrible thing, he found, to be solitary. He had never considered it before; he had rarely needed anyone, or they him. There were those he had thought of as friends – but that was not the same, they did not matter, were nothing in comparison to what Valora had been to him. 'Valora.' He spoke her name to the empty world and conjured her image before him as he had used to do when they were apart, she in Europe and he half asleep between one battlefield and the next. This was the only sweetness left to him. He indulged himself like this a hundred times a day, remembering her in every phase of their life together, like a man besotted by a portrait gallery. He had learned not to do it just before he slept; it was too painful to turn into her pillow and find it bare.

Now he raised his glass, twirling it mindlessly in his hand, staring before him in concentration. But it was no good. Perhaps because of the wine, it had left him, his wonderful facility. For the first time, he could not see her face. He groaned and tensed, gripping his glass so that the wine spilled onto the floor.

He could not see her face but he knew she was weeping, weeping – they were in Clipston's field and she wept for their unborn child. There had been no life there. There was no life here, or at any rate not for him. He knew himself to be less than a ghost at Heron. 'I should have died with you at Naseby,' he cried to her hovering faceless presence. 'Why could I not have died?'

Martha, who knew where Tom was and what he was doing, who had passed and repassed his door several times in the attempt to steel herself to go in and recommence her effort to recall him to life and responsibility, caught that broken-spirited cry and was instantly filled with the stuff of martyrs. She marched in without knocking and stood in front of the sorry figure, an expression of stern disapproval cloaking the insubstantial garment of pity.

He lifted his head, peering at her with poached eyes. For a split atom of time they widened in wild hope; it was soon tamed. 'Oh, it's you.' He slumped back, regarding her without friendship. 'I thought I had told you to leave me be.'

Martha discounted this. 'I see you have reached the bottom of your wine jug,' she said coldly. 'And did you find oblivion there – or simply an aching head and a sottish tongue?'

'If it proves as sottish as yours is shrewish, we shall make a swinish conversation,' he slurred nastily. 'I suggest, therefore, that we do nothing of the kind and that you remove yourself whither you will be more welcome.'

'You order *me* to go – but it is you who are running away.'

'What the devil do you mean?'

'Oh never fear – I don't accuse the courageous cavalier of cowardice. But you run, nevertheless, and not only from those who wish you well; I think you have also turned your back on yourself.'

'Indeed. I gather you have become apprenticed to a philosopher.

God help us all. And just how have you reached *that* asinine conclusion?'

'You may call me all the asses you please, but it will not alter the truth. You go about clad in your grief as though you were wrapped in the flag of your battalion, ready for the grave. Just now I heard you call out to that very grave. If it is death you seek, there must be nothing easier for a soldier to find; but recollect that to Valora, that would be the most heinous sin of all, the sin against the Holy Spirit, and that her faith teaches that suicides spend eternity in hell.'

Tom became truculent. 'Damn her religion. Damn all religion.'

'Damn it all you like; that does not release you from an obligation to respect what must obviously have been her deepest conviction.'

Tom was embarrassed. Her attack galled him with its accuracy and also because he could not, at this precise moment, claim that he did wish to die. He knew that this was so because he did not seem, despite her odious smugness and unwarranted interference, to want Martha to leave. If he could react with any interest at all to a fellow human being, he was no longer in limbo. Certainly he still desired an end, in a general sort of way, to the intolerable condition that was now his life – but not in particular, not at this present hour. He wondered if his thoughts made sense. Just how drunk could he be? He could think of nothing to say to Martha. 'Pray continue,' he temporized. He waved a laconic hand.

Martha was as surprised at herself as he was; she had not meant to say those things; she had meant only to offer comfort; but Tom's physical state prohibited comfort. A drunken man may easily be reduced to tears and if that should happen he would never forgive her. She lessened her severity, mellowing her tone to reason. 'If you wish to remain with us, then be one of us. Speak to us; help us, make us feel that we exist for you and that you are still capable of taking some care for the living.'

The words stung, and so did what he interpreted as her self-righteous manner. What call had she to say such things and what did she presume to know of the sorrow that she would have him slide like a pack from his back? Anger welled in him. There was another flagon in the cupboard. He got up and fetched it, and also another glass. 'Here – wet your insolent little whistle; it will be all the more piercingly presumptuous.'

Martha, who needed it, accepted the wine. Her legs seemed to be shaking. Tom settled back in his chair with an astonishing feeling of being about to enjoy himself. He swallowed a great deal of the wine.

'So – you want me to care for you, do you?' he drawled brutally. He looked her up and down in the flattery of the candelabra. 'In what manner, I wonder. In the old way perhaps?'

He saw she was ambushed by surprise and smiled, enlarging. 'I used to care for you a good deal, as I remember. But you were a slippery little fish, weren't you? Always coolly elusive at the most inappropriate moments. Do you still say no – or has your carefully guarded virginity gone the way of all flesh?'

Martha said nothing; her spirit sank. She tried not to feel shame.

'Well, has it?' He held out his hand. He wanted to hurt her, to humiliate her. If she wanted to take away his pain she must bear it herself. Understanding this, she took his hand, willing to be his victim.

She was infinitely desirable standing there like a statue of the Virgin, the candlelight making a penumbra of her silver hair. He thought of the days when he had wanted her, when he had been young and gay and full of hope, and she had seemed the incarnation of all beauty. Now he felt old and sad and empty of everything. He wanted to take that beauty, which had never been his, and spoil it as his life was spoiled. In some part of his mind he observed his own hideous childishness with contempt.

'Come here. Closer. And answer me.'

She obeyed, in the half-hope that the contact would restore him to some sort of warmth. He pulled her nearer and passed his hand roughly over her breasts. 'So, my self-appointed guardian angel, *are* you still a virgin, or one of Satan's fallen?'

She tugged at his hand but it only tightened. 'I am not a virgin, no,' she said colourlessly.

'I see.' His heat and anger increased. 'Who was it? Some bucolic swain who tossed you in the hay? Or did you couch with the devil, as they say you did?'

Even as he regretted the words her free hand struck his face with all her strength behind it. Automatically he put his hand to his burning cheek, staring at her as though he had just woken up. 'My God, Martha – what can I say?' He suffered mortification gladly, knowing it a less than fit punishment.

'It doesn't matter.'

'It does,' he said fiercely. 'Forgive me. I think I have been a little out of my mind.'

Their hands were still clasped. Martha did not draw away. She stood looking down, thinking of his question, wanting to answer it. She had to tell him, almost as though he were her confessor. However tenuous their relationship was to be she could not support any lack of honesty in it. 'I do not quite know how—' she began in a low voice.

'No. Please. I had no right to demand that of you. I am ashamed. Say that you forgive me, if you can, and let us forget it.'

Gently now she detached her hand. He would no longer want to touch her. 'No – I want to tell you. It is best. The man was – Nehemiah Owerby.'

Tom moaned, overwhelmed with pity for her. He saw now how it must have been. He could not speak but he stood and opened his arms to her, then held her and stroked her head as she laid it on his shoulder.

'I should have been here. I should have looked after you,' he murmured. Hating himself for the way he had treated her, he was willing to do anything to make amends. She sensed this and his regret was very sweet to her. She did not weep and soon raised her head again and was able to smile at him. There was a moment when each was illumined with the realization that they were no longer condemned to loneliness.

It was easier for everybody after that. Like the sin-eater who carries away other men's sins in return for subsistence, Martha seemed to ease the burden of Tom's bereavement from all of the other Herons. Gradually they ceased to be tongue-tied in his presence and were delighted to find him responding at last to their ordinary kindness. There was still very little life in him and it was an obvious effort for him to take an interest in the estate for Lucy or the garden for his mother, but he managed to smile at them occasionally, to hold short conversations about nothing much and to eat his meals. He had left his iceberg.

Martha was happier than she had been since their early days together. Whereas before he had been unaware of her existence, now he sought her out every day. He did not touch her again, except perhaps to take her arm as they walked through Heron's brilliant autumn, but he accepted her friendship as completely as he had at first rejected it, knowing and being grateful that it was slowly bringing him to a point where he could begin to reconcile himself to the world without Valora.

For a long time he took no notice of the war. Neither did anyone see fit to bother him with it. It was hardly a tale with which to confront an already hopeless man. Cromwell and Fairfax overran the west and the hard-pressed north surrendered. Only

Montrose, happily ignorant of all tragedies, continued his victorious sweep through Scotland. The news came to Heron chiefly from Jane in Oxford and from Jud, who now sent the *Intelligencer* openly to all of them, apologizing for its triumphant tone.

It was not until early October that Tom himself received a letter that blew a new spark from dead fires. It was from his brother officer John Dowson, still faithfully doing his duty attached to Rupert in Oxford. The news was bad. A great quarrel had arisen between the King and his nephew over the latter's handling of the siege of Bristol. Rupert, threatened by the weight of Fairfax, had held out for twenty-one days with a garrison of a mere 1,500 men. There was no relief force, the only bleak hope lying in Goring whose performance was now permanently impaired by alcohol. If Fairfax attacked, it would be to sack the city.

Seeing no sense in pointless slaughter, Rupert surrendered, on very favourable terms from Parliament. The King's reaction, far from gratitude for the number of lives saved, was a tempest of rage and disappointment. He sent a letter to Rupert, in Oxford where he had withdrawn under Fairfax's safe conduct, which forthwith dismissed him in disgrace and ordered him into exile! Meanwhile he was placed under arrest. If Tom had ever had any love for his commander, Dowson pleaded, he should come now to his side.

Tom kept the letter to himself for a day or two, brooding over it while there unfolded inside him that complex series of loyalties and obligations by which he had previously been accustomed to live. He was shaken, he admitted it to himself, by the contents of the letter – the King's desperate ingratitude and blindness – and what must be Rupert's despair and frustration – but the single element that drew him firmly enough from his own private slough of self-pity was the identity of the writer.

'Gentlemen, it is my wife,' John Dowson had said in Clipston's field. He had lost his wife but he had not lost his sense of duty. He had remained with Rupert without the loss of a single day. It had not been, Tom knew, that his mourning was any the less, but rather that his loyalty was very great.

Tom read the letter again and was invigorated by shame. The next day he rode out with Martha for a very long time, and on the day after that he left for Oxford.

Martha was well satisfied. He had kissed her once, upon the lips, before he left, but she set no particular store by this, only treasured the memory of it with those other, older recollections. She would miss him, but she would not suffer as she had when she had seen him every day and he had ignored her existence. Their friendship would be a lasting thing, she knew, and besides, there were other people with claims on her sympathy. Most of all, there was Lucy.

Lucy was not happy. She was short of patience and temper and went about looking like a much older, bitter woman. Mary, who thought that she worked too hard, tried to stop her doing so and got her head bitten off for her trouble.

As was now the custom in the house, Mary applied to Martha for advice. 'Sometimes I think you are the only person who has any influence at all with my children,' she said ruefully. She had felt a want in herself where Tom was concerned; she had paid the price of their earlier lack of understanding in the coin of her own inability to help him in his need. Martha had taken her place, and, after a brief period of resentment, she had been most grateful for this.

Lucy, on the other hand, had always come to her with her problems, great or small, and it cost her a good deal to admit defeat. 'I have tried to discover what ails her; if it is not the work, what can it be? She has no personal sorrows that we do not all share.' Mary sighed. 'I suppose, you know, that it is time she was married; that would be a certain cure; she would have no time to dream and imagine herself unhappy.'

Martha knew that it was not that she did not sympathize with her daughter; it was simply that they had all seen enough of unhappiness. 'She is at a restless age,' she said diplomatically, 'and feels the land as restless about her. And whom could she marry, at this time?' she added practically.

'I know.' Mary shook her head. 'There is Ralph Stratton, but—'

'—But it does not make good sense to confide her to a Catholic who is poor and may well be landless.'

'Poor Joseph. It has been terrible for him; we have been so very lucky. God himself sent Will Staunton to us. If only—'

'I will speak to Lucy, and help her if I can,' said Martha quickly. She did not want to be part of a discussion of Will Staunton's marriage plans. She had her own thoughts upon that subject but they were not for publication, and anyway, if Jud was to be believed, she was wide of the mark.

Her opportunity came when Lucy asked for her company to walk to the village. One of the cottars had been producing substandard cloth and she wished to discover the reason for this. They would also call at the Golden Ram to see if the carrier had left any mail for Heron.

Their business with the cottar, who had been sick and should not have been weaving at all, was soon completed. There were three letters at the inn, one from Oxford in Jane's precise script, one from London, in Jud's abominable scrawl, and one, wrapped in several layers of buckram and sealed as fast as a Pharaoh's tomb, which Lucy recognized with joy as coming from Ireland. They decided that they would go along to Martha's cottage, where they could drink mead and eat fresh lardy cake from the inn, and Lucy could read her letter in peace while Martha attended to her beloved garden.

The little house looked lonely now, and the garden very quiet as it prepared for its winter sleep, but they soon had a fire going in the hearth and there was a feeling that the place welcomed the touch of its mistress. Martha went off to speak reasoningly to the winter-flowering jasmine, which she had transported from Heron earlier in the year, and Lucy, warmed with the mead and the fire and expectancy, took a knife to the string and sealing-wax and released Cathal from its wreck. The paper was crumpled but the writing stood out black and firm, as positive and stylish as its author.

'My dearest love, it is late, very late, and the stars put me in mind of the nights I've held you to my heart. I long to do so again so much that I sometimes find myself hugging my bemused but grateful horse for the sake of filling these empty arms.'

There followed a passionate declaration which Lucy enjoyed all the more for its being in the Irish language. She recognized *mo chride* and *asthore*, as being the kind of endearments she had already heard in that most personal and persuasive voice of his. His news was as usual full of blood and battle and derring-do. He was unable to hide the exhilaration he felt when he had sent an enemy down to the Devil, as he put it, and no longer attempted to do so; if she was going to marry him, she must know him as he was, a fighting Irishman and proud of it.

'The best time we have had lately was the night when we put down the misbegotten brood of the Fitzsimons; they have stolen our cattle and carried off our girls and meddled in our lives, I think, for the last time. We rounded up all our own clan, and the McDonagh brought his men with us and we rode down upon the luckless Fitzsimons even as they were feasting upon our bullocks, in celebration of the fine raid that had taken them off. Well, there was none left to celebrate at the end of that meal, and hard it was to tell the bullocks' blood from that of hosts and guests.

'Young Orla rode beside me that night, and I declare she's as fierce as her father and twice as delicate in her ways; wasn't it she who thought of the way to force Kevin Fitzsimons to tell where his dead mother's treasure was buried – they are terrible untrusting, this whole family – she had them bring in Kevin's young wife and cut the clothes off her, piece by piece, with her little bright dagger, and her with her little bright eyes above it, merry as a maybird. When she had done with the clothes and the girl stood naked and ashamed before us, be damned if the unchivalrous bastard still would not tell!

' "Fine," says young Orla, her eyes brighter than ever with the mischief that was in her, "I'll go on, so, and begin again with the flesh."

'And so she did. She started by taking just a little bit of a sliver from the girl's arm, and her with the pleading in her eyes would have melted a stone saint; still the wretched husband held his peace.

' "Would you ever tell me just how far I have to go before you'll give in," asks Orla, in a very practical tone of voice, "or will I just pare away till I get down to the bone?" She would do it, too, they could all see that. She is a fine girl and no denying it, though she is not you, nor anything like you, my nightingale.

'The Fitzsimons whelp started to cringe soon enough when he saw that there would only be blood upon blood in that sad and sorry chamber. But there'll be no more trouble there, that is the good of it; they had been thorns in our flesh for a century or so too long.'

'My precious lord,' thought Lucy as she read, held prisoner by fascination and horror, 'I said to him once "thy people shall be my people" – but there is no way in which I can become one of these careless savages. Oh Cathal, you had better take your Orla McDonagh and her bright little dagger and her bright little eyes, for I will never shed the blood of your enemies at your side.'

When Martha came in she found Lucy weeping. 'Oh, what is it?' she murmured, her arms about her friend. 'Is he well? Has he been harmed in some battle?'

'Not he!' said Lucy with unexpected venom. 'And if he were I doubt he would feel it. Here, read it!' She thrust the letter at Martha and went outside to recover her temper if she could. She had not even finished reading; she knew there would be a thousand tender things at the end of the letter, but what was the good of them, if there was so much difference between them? How could she go on dreaming and hoping for a future with him if that future was to be spent in hideous, bloodthirsty Ireland, among men who were no better than animals and women who were worse?

She stamped about in the small garden for a while, undoing all Martha's good work with the plants; if speaking to them encouraged them, then her black glowering would surely send them shrinking back into the earth. Then she sat on the step and tapped her foot, trying not to feel angry, trying to understand this love of killing and the dreadful laughter at violence. When Cathal was with her he was not like that; it was his going home that had made him that way, that and his fearful old patriarch of a father. If only there were some way to bring him back to England, then he would grow gentle again and they would be together as they had been before. Why did the Irish have to be such savages anyway? Tom was a soldier, and must have killed numbers of men; her father, too, had been a soldier all his life, and yet none of the family had ever heard either of them describe how it was to have taken a man's life, unless perhaps to the twins, who might one day have to be soldiers themselves. Lucy discovered that she felt very English.

When Martha came to find her she confided these thoughts to her, by now more in distress than anger. Martha, who had never thought there to be any possibility of a marriage between Lucy and Cathal, but had never said so, looked yet again for words which would comfort without promising. 'He is very young still; boys *are* younger, you should know that. He is making a little of a display, as the male bird does for the female, that is all, I think. No doubt he was as horrified as you at Miss Orla's cruelty. But he is very loyal, just as you are, and would not say a word against a friend.'

This had the effect of making Lucy very jealous of Orla McDonagh, a thing which Martha felt she should have foreseen. 'And then there is Silken Will,' Lucy said suddenly, with seeming irrelevance. 'He is going to marry that appalling woman, and we shall probably never see him again.'

'I should not believe that,' said Martha with certainty. 'He too is a staunch friend; he will be back before you know it.'

'I don't care if he comes or not,' said Lucy. Martha began to find her slightly trying.

'If only something pleasant would happen,' Lucy went on. 'Everything has been the same for so long.'

Her mother was right, thought Martha. She was uncommonly restless; and that letter had not eased the situation. 'Perhaps it will,' she said. 'You might attempt to attract such an event by exuding a little pleasantness yourself. I've never known you such a cross-patch.'

Lucy looked surprised but did not reply. She supposed she deserved it. She stretched and grinned. 'I'll do some weeding,' she suggested. 'Mother's sovereign remedy for evil moods.' As she extended her fingers on either side, enjoying the fullness of her stretching, they encountered a hard object on the right. This was the stone which Martha used to leave for Goody Bartlett to place over the buttermilk that she would only bring in the very early morning, being afraid to visit the witch by day, though very glad of her excellent remedy for rheumatics.

'Look, Martha, there's something under here!' Lucy drew out a faded packet, tied and sealed. 'It's a letter. You too!'

Martha took it. She never received letters, She handled it gingerly, sensing something she did not want. She opened it and read the superscription. It was from Nehemiah.

Lucy saw her stiffen and blanch. It was her turn to cry, 'What is it?' and to support Martha's thin shoulders in instant sympathy.

'I'm all right. Would you – leave me alone for a minute?'

'Of course.' She got up and went back into the house, consumed with curiosity. She sat down in Martha's old rocking chair and finished reading her own letter. The tenderness was all there, as much as she could have wished for, but she could not forget that triumphant paragraph in which Orla displayed so scarlet a shape. She would find it hard to answer him, for she must say the things that she felt, even as he had done, and to do so would only serve to draw them apart.

Outside, Martha stared at the paper. Her hands trembled and the words danced involuntarily, like a hanged man. It was a hanged man who was in her mind at this moment, a hanged man and a fire and the heavy figure pressing her down into the soft mattress; they were all present at once and shutting her eyes did not keep them out. She waited until the storm of fear was over, then swallowed hard into her dry throat and began to read what Nehemiah had written. It was not a long letter.

'Dearest Martha, I knew that you would not wish to see me. I did not try to find you, though others soon let me know where you were. I know that the Lord is displeased with me for what I have done to you. I was mistaken as to his will and fell into sin in my ignorance. But my Lord God saw my penitence and I know

now, through His most glorious revelation, that the way is clear back to his bosom.

'Martha, more than ever now, *we must marry*. Only thus can I gain both my salvation and your own. I serve with General Cromwell now and cannot come back to Heron at present, but I trust that you will find this, and will know my heart and rejoice, as I do, in God's holy will. I will come to you as soon as I may, but perhaps not until the war is finished. We shall soon be victorious and then you shall be at my side forever and we will do God's work together. You are my wife in His eyes and I love you most dearly. Yours in Christ, Nehemiah Owerby.'

Martha crumpled the letter and threw it away from her like something poisonous. She had the sense of a trap closing on her. He was incredible; he had seen nothing, learned nothing, could be made aware of nothing that he did not choose. It was as though he were never responsible for Dominic's death, as though he had never heard the long, silent scream of her refusal of him, of his body, of his mind, of his terrible obsessive love that reached out to possess her from the paper. She stared at it where it lay crushed upon the path; it was moving, unfolding as though it were alive and had the power to make her pick it up again and let its words deflower her all over again. That was what her every contact with Nehemiah had been, not only that last and strongest one but every time – a deflowering, a stealing of her bloom, a cutting and carrying into his house, where he would stand her in some corner and look at her and call her his until she died from lack of air to breathe and from the cutting off of everything that she needed to sustain life.

She got up and edged back from the screwed up paper, calling breathlessly for Lucy. 'Come. We'll go home now.'

Lucy caught her urgency and came at once. 'Don't you want your letter?' she asked curiously as Martha locked the door and replaced the flat stone beside the step.

Martha shook her head briefly and hurried off down the path. By now Lucy knew her too well to ask questions.

Winter 1645

Time played knavish tricks that winter. For weeks it would stretch out like pulled toffee, full of anticipation without event, then suddenly it would slip past as swiftly as the swallowed sweetmeat, leaving them all with difficulties of digestion. Everyone was on edge.

Lucy held long midnight harangues with herself about what she should say in her next letter to Cathal, mumbling and irritating Julia who was trying to sleep. Martha, hourly expecting Nehemiah to come riding up to Heron's door, was abnormally silent, even for her, and was provoked to anger for the first time in anyone's experience over something so insignificant as a cat digging up and enjoying her newly planted catmint. The fact that, even if Nehemiah *should* return to the district – and even he had declared it unlikely as yet – he would hardly be so bold as to show his face at Heron, did nothing to lessen her unreasoning fear. She no longer felt safe. Mary fretted about Tom and about the garden, in that order for once; they had heard from him twice since he had left them, but his letters were chilly, stilted things that might as well have been written by a secretary. The twins raged because they were not allowed to take their horses and go and join Prince Rupert. Julia was unhappy because everyone else was, and Ned was having trouble with his teeth.

It was a hard winter; rivers froze; the roads became impassable. The carriers and couriers stopped running for weeks at a time and the family languished without news.

When it did come, it was not what they wanted to hear. Tom's concise bulletin, over a month late, told them that they were losing the war. The King had made his peace with Rupert, on the persuasion of his council of war, but he had not yet regained enough trust in him to give him any further command. The Prince kicked his heels in Oxford, despairing at their losses.

A cry for help had come from Montrose, no longer victorious but on the run in the heather after a crushing defeat at Philiphaugh in the Lowlands, where his Irish infantry had been butchered to a man, 700 of them, *after* they had surrendered to the godly men of the Kirk. The commission to find and aid the gallant marquis had gone not to Rupert, the best hope of success, but to that malicious and meddling fool of a Digby, the very man who had engendered the foul rumours about Rupert; that he had sold Bristol to Parliament for money; that he had sought to make peace in order to sell his uncle to his enemies; and least credible but most infamous, that he had plotted with his brothers to take the throne.

Charles had made Digby Lieutenant General of all the forces north of the Trent, much of it part of Rupert's old command, and the Prince had been forced to sit impotently by, paralysed by the grudge that the King could not yet drop, and wait while the velvet courtier jingled off up into the highlands, allowing his Northern Horse to desert him on the way, discovered Montrose to be without hope as far as he could see, and turned back with alacrity only to find himself facing the Covenanters. At this juncture the rest of his troops bid him adieu, leaving Digby and his few officers to make a run for the Isle of Man, where he enjoyed the lavish hospitality of its governor and wrote amusing accounts of his adventures to His Majesty. Tom did not say whether Charles had laughed.

There was very little to laugh at in the situation of the Royalists at the moment. Their troops were in a parlous state; desertion was now so frequent that the King's own army was reduced to a mere 2,000 men, with an overload of twenty-four senior officers to command them, each exacting his pay from the resentful countryside in gold and goods wherever he moved. This pattern was repeated throughout the armies, all of which were so over-officered that often the more junior of them formed companies of their own, known as 'reformados', whose discontented station turned them, as often as not, into brigands, adding the hatred of the populace to the general demoralization.

If Tom's reports gave cause for disquiet, Heron's London correspondent was cheerful enough. Jud's letters were full of enthusiasm and frequently amusing. He had them all laughing over his rumbustious routing of the poor Presbyterian divine who had entered the sacred premises of The Bear in order to press its offended customers to take the Covenant. 'I took no poxy Covenant, but *he* took a full pot of good piss, upside down over his scurvy pate, then he took to his heels and we took a flagon of ale to salute his confusion!'

There was a more sober paragraph in this jolly epistle, however, in which its author begged them to read and consider a crumpled enclosure which accompanied it. This was a pamphlet in the sturdy Dutch type of St Mark's press which carried the stirring title 'England's Birthright' and was written by John Lilburne.

'I hope Jud is sending us no proselytizing for the Parliament,' said Mary, frowning, when Lucy proposed to read it aloud.

'He knows better than that, Mother. He says that since so much of Heron's substance comes from sheep – or would do, if we had more than half a dozen left – we might find this of interest.' The pamphlet proved to be a vivid protest against Parliament's permitting the monopoly of all purchase, sale and export of cloth in the City of London to be held by the ancient and powerful Company of Merchant Adventurers.

'Doesn't Will Staunton belong to that?' asked Martha, listening with her head bent over her sewing.

'Among other things, I think so. But listen; Lilburne says that Parliament have done nothing to stop this monopoly because the Company have subsidized their war chests. He says such a thing is no longer legal; it was one of the ills for which they had castigated His Majesty; and in a time of want and difficulty such as this, it is the cause of unnecessary suffering to sheep farmers, clothiers and small merchants all over England. It is true; you have to admit he is right. Think how much we would save, in normal times, if we could use the port of London as well as Bristol.'

'That's as may be,' said Mary, purse-mouthed, 'but isn't this man, Lilburne, the agitator who is always in and out of prison for stirring up some trouble or other among the London commoners?'

'He's the man who stands up to the Presbyterians and tells them no Church minister owns *his* conscience – and the man whom, Jud says, first made him begin to think, really think, for himself.'

'Bad cess to him for that,' Mary said acidly. 'If he had not come to thinking so much, he might have stayed at home.'

But Lucy did not hear. She was deep in Freeborn John's further scorching attacks; on the censorship of the press; on those very Presbyters; on the widespread corruption of the law which made it useless to poorer citizens; on the inability of any of those citizens below the rank of alderman to have a say in the election of their Lord Mayor.

'I should think not, indeed,' said Mary roundly when Lucy revealed this last. 'What should we come to if the common folk were allowed to dictate who should come to office?'

'I don't know. And I don't pretend to understand all that is suggested in this document, but I think Mr Lilburne would be only too ready to give you a serious answer to your question.'

'Do you say so?' Mary stared hard at her daughter. 'Then I can only hope that he is soon put back into prison again, for the last time!'

'I'm not so sure,' said Lucy thoughtfully. 'Jud obviously thinks this paper is important – for all of us, not just for his side of things. Perhaps we should not dismiss it too easily.'

Mary rose and shook out her skirts in the way she had when she wished to disassociate herself with something. 'Well, you may puzzle over this seditious squalling as long as you like, so be you do not catch its infection. I have better work to do.' She departed, grandly, for the garden where there was no question of the uncommon weed of democracy raising its impudent head.

'What is your opinion, Martha?' Lucy turned to the girl beside her. 'Do you think people have a right to question such things?'

'I do,' said Martha softly, 'but I think they will have to fight for that right, for it will never be freely admitted by those who have power over them.'

'But surely it is right that some men should have the power and others, less fitted, should not? Some must govern and the rest be governed, in small things as in great? It is the way of the world.'

'It may be; there may be no better way; but what your Mr Lilburne would say to us, I think, is that we should perhaps consider who should *choose* who is to have power.'

'That is foolish. The King holds the power under God, and Parliament under the King when it is in its right mind.'

'Very well. But we are still left with the question of who is to choose the mayor.'

'Yes. Well I suppose if *everyone* was able to vote, there would be less chance of a corrupt election.' She remembered with a new discomfort Sir George's 'arrangements' to get into Parliament. 'Do you know – I believe Jud *is* trying to convert us,' she said suddenly. 'He's just as bad as his wretched Presbyterian!'

'Ah no,' said Martha on a note of mischief. 'I would say he is only wanting us to begin to think for ourselves.'

'I have done *that* ever since I was born!'

'Have you? So long,' marvelled Martha.

When Lucy settled at last to putting her thoughts on paper for Cathal, she was herself surprised to find that she spent almost as much ink upon the intriguing statements of 'England's Birthright' as she did upon her own pacifist attitudes to Irish warfare. It was quite a change from legends and poetry, but she felt like a change.

Besides, he had been a little too eager to sing the praises of his supposedly despised betrothed for Lucy to want to send him poetry. If he missed it, he could work out the reason for himself.

She gave in at the very end, unable to prevent herself from crying that she missed him, that the world was grey and full of labour without him. 'I love you, I do, only what is to come of it?' she finished on a note that, after the carrier had left, she found to be shamingly pathetic.

The other letter she had to write, in this season that was all letters and no happenings, as she put it to herself lugubriously, was of course to Will Staunton. He had remained a faithful correspondent, sending her news, views, and, if not poetry, a regular supply of new music. Although very busy 'feathering my bench' in Parliament, he seemed to find the whole thing rather a bore, complaining that Honourable Members seemed to spend more of their time arguing about religion than about the affairs of the realm. The growing contention between the Presbyterians and their Scots allies on one side, and the new Independents with their strong support of high-ranking Army officers on the other, was in danger of coming to some sort of testing point.

Outside the House, Will confessed himself more deeply interested in the robust sense of its own identity that characterized the New Model Army. Far from falling into demoralization in its idle state, it seemed to thrive as a unit upon inactivity, shooting up to health and strength on a diet of discussion and debate. Its soldiers kept their wits as bright as they kept their armour. Sermons, lectures, pamphlets moved among them like fresh winds. They were Independents – like Lucy they thought for themselves – and, like John Lilburne, their champion and mouthpiece, not all their thoughts were about religion.

Lucy, reading, had a sense, as she had with Jud's letters, of something beginning to happen in England of which she was not a part, and could not understand without far more information, but something that was new and had excitement in it. It was not for her, but she wanted to know more. Her letters to London were filled with questions. The replies did not come often enough, nor did they tell her enough.

'Wait,' said Will. 'The event will show you what you want to know.' But what would *be* the event?

When Will came at Christmas she would force him to tell her everything that was happening in London, and she would write it all down and think about it. That at least was something they could all look forward to; to have Will with them at Christmas would be a great treat. His spirit of enjoyment was equal to any occasion and he would make a true feast out of it, they could be sure. And the best part of it was that he had not mentioned anything about Cousin Eliza coming with him, so he was almost certainly coming alone.

In fact he had *never* mentioned her, not once in any of his letters. Lucy had found this strange. She thought he might tell her about his engagement; it would be natural to do so. But perhaps everything was not yet fully arranged between them. Engagements in great houses like Warwick's tended towards lengthy wrangling about money and property and settlements. Poor Will. She hoped beastly Eliza was not going to cost anything. She wasn't worth a groat.

It was with Will in mind that Lucy rode fat Beatrice into the village one afternoon, with Humpty for company. The family had thought of giving him a saddle for his Christmas gift.

Conveniently, Adam Wrenshaw, who was the best saddler in the shire, had left Sir George's old troop after Naseby, dragging one shattered leg but perfectly able to carry on his trade. He welcomed them into the pungent depths of his hide-hung workshop that always reminded Lucy of the tents of the Tartar in the voyages of Marco Polo. Adam was glad to see them and even more glad of the work. Few could afford the luxury of a new saddle nowadays. Lucy proposed a scheme whereby he was to be paid partly in precious silver and partly in Heron's farm produce.

'That'll suit powerful well, Mistress Lucy,' the saddler smiled. He was fond of her and would not for the world reveal that he took in more eggs, butter, milk and meat than he knew what to do with and was setting up as a seller of dairy produce on his own account.

'This must be a particularly splendid piece of work,' Lucy warned, 'the gentleman likes to cut a stylish figure.'

'Who'll that be, then – Sir Thomas?'

Lucy told him. His face broke into a weathered smile. 'I remember Master Staunton from the day we had that famous victory at football. A very elegant gentleman, and a goer, I'll say that for him. But I reckon I can come up to him, you trust me. Something in the Spanish style, I'm thinking, with a bit of brass about it.'

'As long as it is flamboyant enough. But not vulgar; well, not *very*.'

Adam's travels had broadened his appreciation of such minutiae and he caught her drift exactly. 'It'll be fit for a true cavalier!'

Lucy sniffed.

'Hallo – here's the fellow as'll give me a hand with the brass!' They turned and were amazed to find the large figure of John Blacksmith filling the doorway. There was something awkward in his stance.

'Why John!' cried Humpty. 'We didn't know you were back. When did you come home? Are you wounded?'

The big man looked wretched. 'No, not wounded, Master Humphrey,' he said quietly, nodding in Lucy's direction.

'Then what brings you back? Are you on leave, you lucky fellow?'

John shook his head, his face flaming. 'You might as well hear it from me as from another. There was no wound, not lately anyways, and no leave – save what I've took myself.' He drew himself up and waited, as if for sentence.

Humpty stared, incredulous. 'You mean you've – *deserted?*'

'Call it what you like.'

Lucy looked down, sorry for his shame.

'I call it criminal, that's what I call it!' said Humpty passionately. 'At a time when the King needs every man he can get if he is to rally at all and meet Cromwell and Fairfax this spring. How could you do it, John? I'd never have thought it of you, of all people.'

'No more would I, not when we began; I was the King's man, life and limb, until I came to see no purpose in it. We were with Goring, you see, down in the west. He was a good enough commander at the outset, not brilliant like Prince Rupert, but a brave man, who loved a joke. He loved his bottle too. Even your father – beggin' your pardon – used to tell him it'd be his death one day. It will, too. We were a disaster in the west; you must have heard of our disgrace; the loss of Langport, the way we failed Rupert at Bristol. We just seemed to – fall apart.' He lifted hands like hams in uncomprehending despair. 'The officers didn't care, or too few of them to make any difference. And when Goring left us and fled to France, well – ' He finished there, incapable of explaining to them what he couldn't expain to himself.

'But could you not join the King, go to Oxford, even now?' demanded Humpty. 'Surely you don't wish to desert *him?*'

John looked at him wearily. 'I reckon I've had enough of it,' he said. 'I'll do more good here, to my way of thinking. I'm not the only one.'

It was true. The village was filling up again with gaunt and crippled men, many of whom had been on the run for many weeks as they made their way home from the army, from the place where they had been wounded and left behind, or even from the opposing army; some had simply joined the enemy after a battle rather than become prisoners. From John, they learned at first hand what it was like to slink from one isolated farmhouse to another, avoiding towns and their unknown garrisons, often turned away by angry and fearful tenants who had too many of their own mouths to feed; tired, hungry and ignorant of the fate of the home that was the only surviving goal.

Lucy suddenly recalled the blacksmith's little sparrow of a wife, belabouring him with her tongue for being the first, and proud, to be recruited. So long ago, that sunny day. They had all treated it as a holiday. She felt a rush of sympathy for the thin man with his great frame and his look of defeat. 'It's best to forget all that now, John,' she said gently. 'We are all glad to have you home. Now tell me, can you shoe Beatrice for me. She's in dire need; the boy who shoes our horses is always out in the pastures these days.'

A smile of relief relaxed John's burnt-out features. 'I'd be glad to. Bring her along now if you like.' He looked at Humpty, as if to seek the same acquittal, but the boy was sunk in thought and hardly noticed when he left with Lucy.

'I'm glad to have the chance for a word with you alone, mistress,' John said when they stood outside the horseshoe-shaped door of the forge. 'Only, I was taken prisoner, for a time, after Naseby, and I had the bad fortune to meet up with Nehemiah Owerby. 'Twas he sought me out, by the truth of it. He wanted me, if so be as I might happen to escape, as he said, to deliver a letter for him; I did so happen, as you might guess, though I can't for the life of me fathom what could be so important to old Ne'miah as to let me get away for! Howsomever, the letter was for Martha Knyvett, and not knowing then that she was up at Heron, I left it by her door. I hope I did right? 'Tis there no longer; I did look.'

He saw that Lucy was looking very thoughtful. 'You did right, John.'

'Only I couldn't think what he did want with 'er. And all the less when I found out what had been going on here, the witchery an' that.'

'Don't worry, John. Martha has her letter.'

He looked down, scratching his head. 'I'm desperate sorry about Master Nick, mistress, desperate. The village does seem to have run mad while I were away.'

'I sometimes think the whole land has gone mad,' Lucy agreed. 'Thank you for caring about my cousin Dominic.'

Beatrice was shoed then, and conversation replaced by the uneven iron song of the anvil. When he had finished and Lucy had paid him and stepped into the saddle, he asked, almost shyly as she nudged the plump flanks, 'D'you think the good days will ever come again, miss?'

'We had best believe it,' said Lucy gravely. 'If we do not, we are defeated for certain.'

At Heron that night, Humpty would not let alone the vexed question of deserters. It was useless for Lucy to insist that much of it was because the network of command had broken down.

'What do you know? You have only letters to inform you; Tom hasn't deserted, has he, or Paul Stratton, or most of Father's men? I think they should be forced to go back – or hanged.'

After this, as everyone had known must follow as night the day, came the customary wrangle with an increasingly harassed Mary as to why the twins should not go to Oxford and throw their lives and swords at the feet of the King, or Prince Rupert for preference; he was bound to hold command again soon. 'By God, if I am to have this insolence every other week, I shall simply clap the two of you into your chamber and leave you there, with bread, water and the Bible for company! I will say this to you for the last time; you are too young; I have too great a need of you here; this is no time for inexperienced boys to join the army. You would be more trouble than use to any officer who might be so unlucky as to command you. Now, we will have peace. Choose. Kit? Humphrey? Which is it to be? Do I lock you up or do you lock your mouths?'

The boys shot crestfallen glances at each other but were silent. They had thought that, this time, she might have relented. They were no longer too young; there were plenty of sixteen-year-olds in both armies; they knew how to fight, after a fashion, and could trust their own ingenuity to get them through, whatever the odds. They held their peace however. There was no point in subjecting themselves to a dreary incarceration; they could see that Mary meant what she said. They went back to their various tasks with no further murmur. They would try again after Christmas.

Christmas, as it turned out, was no great excitement after all. Three days before the feast, on the eve of Will Staunton's looked-for arrival, there came a personal courier from him, bearing a most depressing letter. It told them that Will was desolated not to be able to join them after all; his cousin, Lady Hartley, was seriously ill of a fever to the lungs and her physician feared for her life.

'She has been as close to me as a sister all my life and I would not leave her now; she wishes me to stay at her side and it is my own wish to please her. She is very ill. I beg that you all will pray for her.'

Poor Eliza. Lucy felt her dislike evaporate as she thought of that vibrant, if sometimes viperish lady laid low. A sickbed would not be to her liking; it was not her setting. If she was as sick as seemed likely, however, perhaps she would not even care. They were all sad for her and Mary asked the vicar of St Mary's, who had been turned out of his living but still carried his cloth, to offer up a mass for her in the chapel.

They kept Christmas very quietly and Lucy spent most of her holiday writing to Will, trying to cheer him with inconsequential items of news, such as the terrible Humpty's attack upon the unfortunate Isabella, who came languishing after him once too often and was sorely punished for it.

It seemed that she had offered him a Christmas kiss. They were in the stables at the time, alone in Calliope's stall where Humpty was ministering to the wound made by a warble fly. Half to teach her a lesson and more than half to continue with the experiments he was beginning to make among the young girls of the neighbourhood, the ungallant lad had thrown her down in the straw and given her a far more earthy embrace than the romantic one she had had in mind. Having kissed her till her lips were swollen, he had made free with her blossoming young person with both hands and had finished by riffling her petticoat and hanging it, flagwise, out of a front chamber window.

'I'd have had her stockings if I could, only they wouldn't come off!' had declared the unrepentant Humpty when Lucy taxed him with the crime after pacifying an outraged and tearful Isabella.

'Better not let Mother find out,' was all she would say to her. 'She'd tell *your* mother, for sure. I'd be quiet if I were you.' Stunned, Isabella had gone off to find Martha, in whom the spirit of sisterhood was surely not so decayed as it appeared in Lucy.

'Isabella is quite pretty these days,' Lucy wrote, to be fair, 'and is in general less of a fool than she used to be. She has begun to play the recorder very pleasantly. It would make you laugh to see us, so serious together, over our music. I'm afraid that, this time,

Humpty really did go too far. I'm sorry for Bella now, though I never thought to be. She still idolizes the barbarian.'

She chewed her pen over what to say about Lady Hartley. She supposed this was not the time to mention the marriage; anyhow, she was not supposed to know about it. 'I have prayed, as you asked, for your Cousin Eliza, as all of us have done. We offered a service for her here and the vicar preached upon Christ the Healer in a very hopeful manner. Please to let us have news of how she does. I know this must be a sad and trying time for you. I can't imagine you without your gaiety. I hope God soon sends you reason to restore it.'

God did. Eliza Hartley recovered, very slowly, and having sustained a greater shock than she had ever hoped to know. The experience left her weak and uncharacteristically dependent. She hated to see Will leave her house. She also discovered that her feebleness awakened a great gentleness in him. She took care of her looks and ate as well as she could bear to, keeping her character in this new low key.

He had still not mentioned marriage. Warwick, who had forgotten all about it by now, suddenly remembered and sent to ask her what Will's intentions might be. She had replied that time was ripening and could not be hurried. But perhaps, now, she had found a way.

Lucy, unaware of her progress, soon forgot Eliza Hartley. They knew she was well again and Will had said that he would visit them as soon as he could steal the time. Meanwhile there was a new setback to assimilate.

It was on the day that Dickon Stable reappeared, in much the same case as John Blacksmith, with the honourable addition of a nasty gash, not properly healed, in his upper back. He had come back to his old place, never thinking to do otherwise. He found himself welcome on all sides – except one. As soon as they heard his story, a sequel to the smith's, the twins began to treat him very coolly. He was hurt by this at first, having so many memories of them as children, claiming his time and his experience, sharing his own deep love of the animals he cared for. He understood better when Lucy explained their fever to go to the war.

'I'll talk to them if you like,' he offered shyly, 'tell them what it is really like; then maybe they'll not be so hot for to go.'

No one ever discovered quite what it was that Dickon said to them. He himself could remember nothing that could possibly explain what happened next. But whatever it was, it had quite the opposite effect from the one he was seeking, for that night, leaving their beds tidy and a folded note placed neatly between the pillows, they were gone from Heron. They took their swords with them and a couple of muskets, food and ale from the kitchen, and rugs from their beds.

'Dear Mother and All,' read the note in Kit's careful hand, 'I hope you will forgive us (eventually) but we could stay at home no longer when we are needed elsewhere. We are sure that Father would have wished us to do our duty, as he did, and as Tom is doing. I am sure no harm will come to us. We are very quick on our feet and can give most men a run for their money. We will send news as soon as there is any to send. Do not think too hard of us; we feel Heron can make do without us now that so many are coming back. Pray for us. We leave you our best love and respect, dear Mother. Your loving children and most affectionate brothers, Humphrey and Christopher.'

Spring 1646

It might have seemed to Charles Stewart, had he known of it, or to Kit and Humpty Heron, had they thought of it, that from the time his two self-appointed St Georges raced to his salvation, his fortunes plummeted with those of the dragon rather than rising with those of the maiden.

In Oxford the King was cut off from all his chief sources of security. His wife was in France. His eldest son had already taken refuge in the Scilly Isles. His advisors were dispersed or fled. There was no army to command, no generals with whom to confer. Charles might do as he pleased.

Thus isolated, he cast his lines, with the desperation of a man who has no other prospect of a meal. By now his best hope was in Ireland. However, the likelihood of the crossing of a Confederate army had been procrastinated by the Papal Legate who used his great influence to prevent the Confederates from signing either Governor Ormonde's open treaty or Charles's more liberal secret one, insisting they hold out for the full restoration of Church and property and the appointment of an Irish Lord Lieutenant.

By the time the intelligent Lord Muskerry had persuaded them that, whatever was signed or not signed, the King must have his troops and have them *now*, the Royalists had lost Chester, the only port left from which they might have received them. After Chester they lost Hereford and the rest of the Welsh Marches.

Down in the west, the King's generals quarrelled bitterly among themselves, while their armies fell deeper and deeper into disorder, a circumstance of which Fairfax took full advantage. Upon his storming of Dartmouth a miraculous draught of fishes was taken in the bay, and with it a royal ship carrying letters from the Queen to her husband. These gave Parliament interesting details of His Majesty's own fishing successes, including an attempt to raise troops from France, and the more dangerous intrigue between the Scots Commissioners and the French Envoy, Montreuil. In this the latter urged the Covenanters to make a separate peace with Charles and the English Presbyterians; Charles must then abandon the embarrassing Montrose with his Catholic followers and encourage his subjects to take the Covenant – a strange position for a Catholic monarchy to take, but indicative that it appeared by now to be the sole means by which they might restore their relative to a measure of dignity and security.

Parliament, in the Independent person of Harry Vane, took note of these casts, which provoked all the more thought in consideration of the fact that the King had also dangled his fast putrefying bait before the House in the form of a private treaty with the Independent faction. Westminster had also received information on the 'secret' treaty with the Confederates.

The tangled web was wrapping itself ungratefully about the form of its weaver. Time pulled it tighter as the last Royalist strongholds gave way: Belvoir, Cardiff, Pendennis. The finishing knot was tied at Stow-on-the-Wold, where that indefatigable old trooper, Sir Jacob Astley, lost what was probably the last force of disciplined men in the King's service, in a bold attempt to cross enemy country and bring them to Oxford.

What was Charles to do? He could not stay in Oxford, waiting to be taken. Where must he go? He could not flee the country without seeming to surrender his throne. He could not go to London; he had taught Parliament too well how to distrust him for them now to receive him as a free man; they would make no treaty that he could accept. He could not reach Montrose, now fighting gamely on again; nor could his Irish friends reach him.

There remained only the Covenanters, whose army was encamped before a despairing Royalist garrison at Newark in the Midlands. Sir David Leslie had written that he would be glad to receive him. Wanting, if he could, to draw together these disparate supporters, Charles wrote three letters to this effect; to the Confederates, promising to ratify openly his secret treaty in return for immediate troops, who must land where they could; to Montrose, begging him to come to terms at last with the Covenanters whom he fought; and to Ormonde, with the information that he was about to join the Covenanting army who, he trusted, would support Montrose in the face of his enemies of their faith in Scotland.

It made good sense to Charles. He knew that the Covenanters had no love for the English Presbyterians who had bought them with fair promises and had redeemed none of them; the Scots army at Newark was ill-housed and unpaid, and while the Covenanters were assured of the friendship of the Assembly of Divines and their London co-religionists, they would get no purchase at Westminster under Independent rule; whatever peace was proposed, it would be without consultation with the ally who had helped to achieve it.

In the last resort, it was Fairfax who provided Charles with impetus. He marched towards Oxford, rounding up demoralized cavaliers like cattle as he came. Charles, swinging wildly in his web, made a last appeal to his oppressors. He wrote to General Ireton offering to disband his remaining troops if an assurance should come from Fairfax *and* from Parliament that he would keep his life and his throne.

Ireton, somewhat confounded by the letter, sent it to his old comrade Cromwell, now in the Commons; old Ironside would have no such hugger-muggery attributed to Independents and read out the message to the House as yet another example of Charles's duplicity.

Charles, repressing a sudden instinct to disguise himself and attempt to escape by ship to join Montrose, dropped his lines at last and made for Newark. Within a week he found himself marched up to Newcastle-upon-Tyne. Canny Leslie did not intend to share his prize. Behind him his last bastions continued to fall one by one; Ludlow, Caernarvon, Anglesey, Woodstock, and his pro-capital, Oxford.

With the news of Oxford's surrender the Herons were thrown into a torment of rage and hope. Tom had written that his regiment would vacate the city on June 24th, but he did not know whether he would simply be moved to some Parliamentary prison, be released on parole or simply be set free. Negotiations were still under way between the governor and Fairfax.

He had added heavily that there was still no news of his brothers though he had done all in his power, and so had Rupert, to discover their whereabouts. It was certain, however, that they had joined no official regiment; they could only conjecture that they had perhaps met up with one of the private companies that still proliferated despite the obvious termination of hostilities. They would continue with their enquiries and meanwhile, the family was to try not to distress themselves too much as the boys would surely manage to get a message through to them before long.

'They left us in February; it's nearly the end of June! If they were in some sort of trouble, perhaps even – they would have got word to us by now; I am sure of it. Kit, at least, would know how we would worry.' Mary, having run the gamut from white fury and castigation to nail-biting uneasiness, was beginning to give way to despair. She blamed herself for failing to forsee the twins' defection and to lock them up as she had promised.

Lucy, who had argued in vain that they could not lock them up for the rest of their lives and their lust for adventure was sure to have had the better of any efforts to dampen it, looked at her mother thoughtfully, wondering if this was the moment to introduce a plan which she had been nurturing for a time. 'Listen to me,' she said gently. 'We shall discover nothing sitting here, either about the boys or about Tom's next step, unless we want to wait for his further news, which may not reach us until next Christmas, the way things are moving at present. I have something to propose, and I beg you will give it proper consideration before you shout me down.'

'I should not dream of anything so discourteous,' said Mary, trying to smile. 'What have you in mind, Lucy?'

'It is something I have discussed with Martha. You know that she will not leave the house since she heard that Nehemiah might return; well, it occurred to me that it might be best if she were to leave us for a while, go somewhere where she could feel herself more secure. I thought of Oxford – oh I know it is in Parliament's hands, but Jane thinks that will alter very little of people's lives. After all, she and James have decided to remain rather than come back to Heron. I know she will welcome Martha. And the other point is that I will go with her—'

'Lucy, no! I won't have it!'

'For perhaps I may find a means towards the boys that neither Tom nor Jane has discovered—'

'—That is hardly likely—'

'—And I shall be able to seek out Tom – discover his fate at once—'

"He is under arrest!"

'They will march out in good military order. I shall find him then.'

'In 2,000 others? Don't be a fool!'

'They will not move quickly. It will be a solemn occasion.' Lucy hesitated, having more to say.

'There is something else I wish to discuss with Tom. It is the matter of Will Staunton's interest in Heron.'

'What business is that of yours, pray?'

'I want to know whether Tom would be "able to compound".'

Parliament, anxious for a settled country in so far as this was possible, had offered a cruel carrot to the King's remaining supporters by permitting them to compound for their estates, that is to purchase both peace and pardon with a single payment based on the value of their lands. Exceptional terms had been offered to those who agreed to do this before April 1st. Before then, Lucy had written to Tom to ask whether any such thing was possible for Heron, but he had not replied. The realization that neither she nor her mother knew anything of the business between Tom and Will had made her uneasy. What if Tom were to die? Had he left any provision for such a case? Someone should know, and since she had been the one to run Heron almost single-handed during the last few years, she had a right to be that someone, woman or not.

Mary, confounded by her own ignorance, could only repeat that it was none of Lucy's business.

'But you'll let me go, Mother, for my own peace of mind?'

'And what of *my* peace of mind, left here with only Ned and Julia for company? And you and Martha running wild across the country, with God knows what monstrous ruffians abroad on the roads—'

'We'll go on horseback and we'll take half a dozen men. We're not fools. And I'll send back to you at every opportunity.'

The argument lasted for most of that night, but in the end

Mary gave way, saying wearily that she did not want Lucy also slinking off leaving a note on her pillow.

'Really, Mother; as if I would!'

'You would,' said Mary grimly. Lucy lowered her lashes, under which glinted the truth. It was only when the two young women had left that Mary asked herself upon just what feeble excuse for an errand she had let them go.

Oxford, 24 June 1646

They watched with a tense and absolute concentration as the long column wound out of the city gates and down the road to where they stood. They had stationed themselves well before sunrise and now the June heat was taking the stiffness out of the bones that had rested very little in the over-full inn last night. The guard had refused them entry into Oxford itself, even when Lucy had told judicious lies about living with her sister Jane. This was something they had not forseen and Martha, particularly, was disturbed by it.

The traffic seemed endless. Since dawn there had been a drawn-out procession of coaches and carts filled with courtiers and their ladies, administrators, cooks, lackeys, the whole panoply of the extinct court, rumbling sadly over the rutted road amid a last brave flutter of feathers and lace. Some of the common people followed them, their rickety wagons overflowing with pots and pans, chairs and children and the roadside ragged with the barking of their dogs. Those who were too poor to own carts followed on foot with all their worldly goods tied up in a blanket or shawl, their offspring skipping happily at their heels, their journey only just begun, its ending in the hands of God.

There had been a lull for the past hour or so, with only a few hasty late leavers clattering past on horseback. Lucy and Martha had sat back on the grass, taking their ease while they could. Now there came the sound of drums, the steady, encouraging tattoo that is beaten for men on the march, its friendly percussion unfaltering in defeat. The King's infantry were coming.

Their passage did not take long; there was scarcely a regiment of them left; but they bore themselves bravely, smiling at those who stood to cheer them on their way, proud of the uniform they had tried to refurbish for the occasion. Not long after them rolled a small cloud of dust wrapped round a great deal of noise; there was the sound of trumpets, of men singing, and the uneven clatter of horses at the walk.

'They're coming; skin your eyes, everyone, for God's sake! We must not miss him!' Lucy raced down to the verge and held aloft the banner with the heron on it that she had brought to catch Tom's eye, should that be necessary; it might well be, as one rider in a red cloak looks much like the next.

But Rupert's flyers were going slowly, perhaps for the first time in their hectic career, and it was easy to pick out the proud faces. The Prince himself rode at their head, pelted with flowers and lavished with smiles and tears from both sides in acknowledgement of his prowess, his courage, and not least, on this sentimental occasion, his youthful beauty.

'He is so young,' Martha breathed as he passed them, warming them briefly with his smiling brown eyes.

'They are all young. Even Tom is young, when you think of it. Oh Martha, look! There, behind the red-haired one; isn't that him?'

It was Tom. She waved her banner madly for he was looking to neither side, riding with his hands clenched on the reins, looking inward with an impassive face, seemingly immune to the furore around him. 'Give us a smile, love!' cried a plump woman at his stirrup, but he passed her by without seeing her.

'Oh damnation, he'll not look!' Grimacing, Lucy dropped her banner and plunged in among the horses. Martha, fearful that she might be injured, went after her, leaving their Heron escort exchanging doubtful glances on the verge.

'Tom! Tom Heron! Oh, listen, you fool!'

'Eh? What –? *Lucy!* What the devil are *you* doing here?'

'I must talk to you? Can you rein in?' She trotted at his flank, hoping she sounded sufficiently urgent. Tom, always a stickler for protocol, was quite capable of brushing her off and riding on.

'Is there something wrong at home?' His eyes clouded. He looked tired.

'In a way. Please. Just a few minutes.'

'Very well.' He leaned towards a fellow officer and muttered a few hasty words. They were almost the last to leave; he would easily catch them up. He edged towards the roadside and dismounted, much to the interest of the eager crowd, who flattered Lucy with sympathetic eyes, obviously suspecting romance.

'Why, Martha!' He had noticed her at last. 'You here too?' She smiled, firmly keeping her heart out of her eyes.

'Now then,' he said when they had led his horse some way into the nearest field, 'just what is all this about? Please be concise. I haven't much time.'

'What is to happen to you?' Martha asked.

'I am free to go.' His voice was flat, unpromising.

Lucy relaxed. 'How wonderful; then we need not have made our journey. You will come home with us!'

His face closed. 'No. I shall not come home just yet. The Prince is ordered abroad. I go with him. There is still work to be done for His Majesty, and for Prince Charles who may join us soon.'

Lucy stared at him. 'I don't believe it! Why? The war is over. You should come back to Heron; you know you should!'

'I think I can do without you to tell me what I should do. I go with Rupert and that is an end of it. Now, what did you wish to say?'

Lucy fought down the anger and disappointment that threatened to overcome her and met his impatience as coolly as she could. 'I want you to tell me whether it is possible you might compound for Heron.'

He was utterly taken aback. 'What in the name of—'

'It seemed to me that, with the war finished, and Parliament's offer none so bad – the Strattons are going to try to do it – and then we should be free of our obligation to Will –' She stopped abruptly, silenced by the ice in his gaze.

Tom considered a moment before he spoke, very clearly as if to an idiot. 'I cannot conceive how you came to imagine this was any business of yours, but as you have no notion of the nature of the transaction between Staunton and myself, perhaps you had better learn of it. The simple matter is, my dear Lucy, that to all present purposes it is Will Staunton who rents the manor and demesne of Heron, and not myself.' He went on, ignoring her horrified gasp. 'That situation will revert in good time; that is not yet.'

Lucy caught hold of her cartwheeling thoughts. 'Then perhaps Will can compound? And you repay him?'

Tom did not answer her. 'Martha!' he snapped over her shoulder. 'I am surprised that you were foolish enough to join in this junket; since you are here, perhaps you will use your influence to persuade my sister to mind her own business!'

'I do not think *that* to be any business of *mine*,' the girl replied softly, coming forward. She looked pityingly at his eroded face. He had emerged from his iceberg, yes, and was very much alive now, every raw nerve of him, she could see; but the glitter in his eyes was that of near collapse rather than of any interest in life. He obviously did not sleep much and he had to fight to prevent his speech from slurring. 'But I *have* some business here; something in which I must ask your help if you will give it.'

Lucy, surprised, could not think how Tom *could* help her, in his present position. He would hardly possess any influence with Parliament's gatekeepers. Martha had cut across her own attempt, and she did not thank her for that, but there was an urgency in her voice which kept Lucy quiet all the same.

'If there is anything I may do –' said Tom mechanically.

Martha told him swiftly why she was here. She mentioned Nehemiah's name just once and Lucy was amazed to see Tom's pale face flush. 'So you see, I do not wish to go back, and cannot go forward. I thought – I would like to ask – are any of your officers taking their wives or – any other ladies with them, when they go abroad?'

Lucy did not breathe. This was astonishing.

'I – well, yes, I believe so. But, Martha –' he waited. He must have known what she would say, but he did not prevent her.

She looked at him very levelly, still with that odd, pitying smile. 'Take me,' she said. 'I ask nothing of you except your protection and such shelter as we may find. There is much that I can do to be of use in any community. And you will have a friend. You would not regret it and I should be eternally grateful. And perhaps, when you eventually return, I may be able to do so as well.'

'Martha!' Lucy could contain herself no longer. 'When did you *think* of such a thing?'

'Just now,' said Martha calmly. 'It seemed the only solution.'

Lucy looked at her brother. His air of normal human puzzlement made her want to laugh. 'Come. Walk a little way with me. I want to talk to you while Tom makes up his mind.'

Tom shrugged. He appeared to be examining Martha for the first time and finding her a very rare specimen indeed.

'I think you must be mad,' said Lucy when they had stopped beneath the shade of a convenient oak, 'but I *can* see that it would be good for Tom. He does need a friend, though I doubt if he knows how to treat one; but you, my dear, what can you have to gain from it? It is such a wrench; you have never left Heron before this.'

'No. But I should like to see something of the world. And then, it is really very simple. I want to go with him because I love him.' Silence. 'You didn't know? I thought by now you must have guessed.'

Lucy dumbly shook her head. 'No. I never did. For how long?'

'Oh, since we were both sixteen. He loved me also, once. Long before Valora. I am glad he has had that. She has taught him things that I was too young to know, or too shy to confide. He will recover, in France or Holland, or wherever we go, because of what she has given him.'

'And what you can keep alive in him,' added Lucy, beginning to see. 'You must forgive my surprise; it was foolish. Oh Martha, if only he would marry *you* – not yet, but later – it would be a great thing for him. A second chance. Will he see it, do you think?'

'I had not thought so far. I dare not. Let us take it as it is given for the moment, dear Lucy.'

'You *know* that he will take you, don't you?' was Lucy's sudden instinct.

'Yes I do.'

While she had stood there, watching Lucy plead with him, she had had a swift picture in her mind, nothing so strong as a 'seeing', just a warm certainty such as anyone might have, she thought now happily, Tom and she had been walking in a strange town where the roads were not roads but narrow rivers, teeming with colourful craft. She did not know where it was, but they would go there.

'Try to bring him back to us, won't you?' was Lucy's plea.

'Of course,' said Martha, surprised. 'It is a great reason for my going.'

When they rejoined Tom it was as she had said. He would take her. Lucy went back to speak to the men who had ridden with them while he talked with her alone.

'I can offer you nothing,' he said honestly. 'There is nothing left in me worth the offering except what I bring to the King's cause, God help His Majesty. But you may have my protection as long as you will accept it; it is little enough in return,' he smiled kindly, 'for friendship.' He knew that she loved him; she sensed it. But they would not speak of it.

Tom knew he was insane to agree, but there was a strange feeling that he was not given any choice. Besides, he was fond of her, in so far as he was fond of anyone nowadays, and the necessity to care for her well-being would prevent the worst excesses of the loneliness and self-pity to which he too often gave way. He would take her, but she could never hope to replace Valora and he would show her that she was not to think it. In time.

When Lucy came back he was brisk with her. 'I have written to Mother. One of my own men is my courier. Most of Father's troop, a good two-thirds of them, are alive and will return; they are not worth Parliament's keep as prisoners. So you see, I am not needed. You will manage as you have done before. As for compounding, be sure I will think of it, but not now—'

'Will Staunton is to marry Eliza Hartley,' interrupted Lucy baldly, 'I'm sure he won't want the responsibility of Heron after that.'

Tom frowned. 'I see no reason why his marriage should interfere with his business. But I confess myself surprised. I had not thought the wind lay in *that* direction.' He grinned. 'Perhaps you should step in and throw your cap at him, while he is still free; that way Heron would be snug forever.'

Lucy was furious. 'Don't be such a graceless wantwit. I don't understand you, Tom. How can you take Heron so lightly?'

He sighed. 'I don't, booby. It is just that, for now, things are best left as they are. Any spare money I have, I must use to help the King; it is what Father wanted. And what I want myself. All this may look like defeat, but whatever you may think, the war is *not* over. Not yet.'

Lucy groaned.

'Leave it, Lucy. Let us talk of something else. You'll not have heard from those damnable twins, I suppose?'

'No. We hoped *you* might have done.'

He shook his head. 'I have been badly placed; under parole not to leave the city. We've tried to trace them as well as we could, but without success. They could be anywhere by now.' He saw how deeply she was worried on their account. 'Cheer up! Can you imagine them failing to survive? God help their commander, whoever he is!'

'Are there so many left?'

'I hardly know. They tell me Lichfield is still ours, and Worcester, and a few others. But we have armed companies all over the country.'

'I know. We have had to put a guard on our horses night and day,' said Lucy drily.

Tom wished to leave now, and made that clear. 'What will you do, Martha,' he asked, awkward now that the die was cast. 'Will you collect your belongings and join me further on the road?'

'What I have is here; our escort has my bundle. I'll fetch it.'

She slipped away, leaving Lucy to say goodbye. 'Look after her, Tom. She is worth – oh, fortunes!'

'I know it,' he answered gravely, 'and I will. Though isn't it Martha that has lately looked after all of us?'

'And write, as often as you can. Mother will worry else.'

He nodded. He realized with a swift stab that he loved this independent-minded young woman more than he had known. He pulled her to him and kissed her, hugging her tightly. 'Good-bye, Lucy. Heron is in your hands still.'

'Mine and Will Staunton's,' she said grudgingly, smiling after.

'I can't think of a better combination!' He laughed. She forgave him.

'Here I am,' said Martha, returning with her neat bundle. 'I'm afraid I don't have very much, but enough to last, I daresay. I have a little money, too. I never seemed to use very much—'

'You will have no need of that,' said Tom brusquely. 'Now, which is your horse?'

'Take mine; she's the best mount. You'll need her,' Lucy said.

Practical, Martha accepted the tall chestnut mare, tossing her bundle onto the pommel. Then she stood and looked wide-eyed at Lucy, who gazed back, each of them newly aware of the enormity of what she was doing.

'Oh go, please. I *can't* say goodbye!' cried Lucy, feeling her eyes pricking abominably. She felt the light pressure of Martha's arms about her for an instant, and a warmth against her cheek, then the jingle as both travellers took their saddles.

'Only think of what I shall *see*,' called Martha as they turned towards the road. 'I shall describe it all; you will be horribly jealous! You'll see!'

There was a ring of happiness in her voice that lifted Lucy's heart and, for the moment, took away the pain of losing her. After they had gone there was nothing for it but to go back home. She did not dare think what Mary would say.

They rode as quickly as they could upon the crowded roads, and had gone some twenty miles before one of the men reminded her rather desperately that they had not eaten that day.

'We'll stop at the next inn,' Lucy promised, still deep in her imaginary explanation of how she had come to let Martha, an unmarried girl who possessed little more than the clothes she was wearing, ride off in the company of Sir Thomas Heron, in the dubious role of her 'protector', to an unknown destination somewhere beyond seas.

The next inn looked unsavoury. It was ringing with raucous noise and a dozen or so gentlemen of brigandish appearance, in quantities of grubby lace, were sitting outside adding to it. 'When the King comes into his Own again,' they roared, lifting their tankards and cheerily bidding in the travellers.

'I think we'll go on to the next one,' said Lucy firmly.

The men behind her moaned and tightened their sagging belts.

'Pity about that! Damned pretty woman, don't you know,' deplored one of the down-at-heel cavaliers to the companion who joined him at that moment with two foaming jugs.

'What's that?' asked the other, swinging a leg over the bench. He was a sturdily built young man whose clothes were in slightly better order than those of his friends.

'Dashed attractive woman nearly came in. Golden hair; body like an equestrian Venus, if there is such a thing. Lovely! Pity. You'd have fancied her, I tell you, young Heron.'

'Oh I don't know,' said Humpty unregretfully, 'I rather like them dark, for myself. Did she have a friend?'

'No friend. Drink up, then, my boy! To beauty in female form, whatever the colour!'

Humpty drained his pot and refilled them both. Then they drank to the King again, and to Prince Rupert and anyone else they could think of. They were very happy.

Such happiness, as always, was doomed to be brief. At the bottom of the pot they found the surrender of Oxford and the fact that the King was a virtual prisoner of the depressing Scots. Humpty was seated with his head on the table, enjoying the heat of the sun on the back of his head and the far-off sound of his companions' carousal, when his brother's voice buzzed in his ear.

'Come on, soldier. We're moving on soon. You'd better be on form or the Captain'll thrash you with his tongue.'

Humpty dragged up his head. It was heavier than it should be. ' 'S'true,' he said. 'Had one lashing this week; don't wan' 'nother. Good 'ole Kit; never let me down.'

'Here. I've brought a bowl. Wash your face.'

Humpty did as he was told, this being the easiest thing to do. He thought he might be going to have the mother and father of headaches. 'Where're we off to next?' he asked carefully, mopping his cheeks.

'Dunno. The Captain's going to talk to us now.'

No sooner had he spoken than a hush settled along the table and all eyes were turned to the doorway of the inn through which its comely and hospitable owner, Mistress Dulcie Dewhurst of the ample person and soft feather bed, ushered a very formidable presence in scarlet and black. Known to his faithful followers only as 'Captain Attila', he was a foot taller than the doorway and nearly as broad. His garments were newly pressed and his lace shone in the sunshine. The scarlet plumes danced in his wide-brimmed hat and little red lights did likewise in his hard black eyes. His hand fingered his sword.

'Satan's poxed arse, you make me ashamed! Look at yourselves, you fusty, drivel-lipped, froth-swilling, fart-headed bastards! What kind of a company is this to serve the King? Hey?' He drew the sword and waved it threateningly at Humpty who was sitting bolt upright, supported by Kit, gazing owlishly at his leader.

'If you can't learn to hold your ale as well as you can hold your prick to piss it out again, you can get back home to your mother's tit, for you're no use to me!'

'Sir!' responded Humpty brightly. He could tell the Captain liked him. He was always the one to be told off.

Captain Attila growled and replaced his sword. 'All of you – get inside and wash yourselves and put your clothes to rights and try to look like part of a regiment instead of a parcel of Warwick's scurvy sailors on a port picnic!'

'If you please, sir?' hazarded Humpty, having straightened his collar.

'What now, in the name of Beelzebub?'

'May we know our next assignment?'

There was further growling. 'You may, if you think you can remember if for more than half an hour. We ride toward Worcester where we may be of use to the besieged garrison there. We'll travel mostly by night, availing ourselves of what we may chance upon as we go. There is also the estate of one Sir James Lydyard to be investigated; I've heard he's compounded for a tidy sum, back in April. He should have some to spare for the King, and for us, by now.'

A cheer went up, Humpty among the loudest. Kit did not join in. Although he would not go so far as to tell himself he wished to be somewhere else, he had developed reservations about their present situation.

They had met Captain Attila and his hand-picked troop of 'reformados' in just such an inn as this one, nearer to the apparently sealed city of Oxford. They had soon been persuaded that the best thing they could now do for the King was to join the bold captain in his work. These rabid raiders were a painstaking parody of Rupert's fine companies. From the ashes of the cavaliers had risen that bird of dark plumage, the gentleman robber, who menaced the highways, the villages, the houses great and small, taking what he found in the King's name, his honour in his pocket under his handkerchief until more convenient times should require him to take it out and dust it off.

Certainly Captain Attila intended half their spoils to go to the King; Kit did not doubt him there; he had already managed to send gold to His Majesty in Oxford. Their dashing harassment of Parliament's long marches from the west country had been honourable and well worthwhile, also. But Kit disliked the feel of the burglaries by night, the frightened women in isolated homes, the taking of what little people still had. Humpty seemed to find it all much the same as their earlier pranks at Heron, but it was possible that Humpty was wrong. They had found the adventure they had looked for, and the exhilaration was often glorious. But it was not everything. He had not known how to explain their actions in the letter he sent home.

London, Autumn 1646

Lucy was in London. She had vegetated at Heron until she could not endure herself, mechanically going about her stewardship, keeping her thoughts to herself and watching her mother's dead hope of hearing from the twins twitch into life with every strange letter.

The weather was foul. The harvest had failed. They were poorer. She was bored, stale and restless. She missed Martha and the boys. She was far from reassured about Heron's financial status and had written twice to Will asking him to tell her exactly what was his arrangement with Tom and whether he thought there was any possibility that he might compound. She had received no reply, only his usual affectionate letter, full of his own news and outrageous comment, indicating that he had never had hers.

She announced, therefore, that she would go to London and deal with the matter herself. Mary viewed this further travelling with horror; the plague had been very bad this year, so she made her promise to stay away for only a week. This would give her just two days in the capital. 'I cannot understand your obsession with compounding,' she told her determined daughter. 'Why cannot you leave such things to Tom?'

'Because he cares nothing for them, not in his present state. We might *give* Heron away to the Parliament for all he would do to prevent it. *Someone* has to care; it may as well be me. God knows I've worked hard enough for these lands.'

Mary was the first to admit this. She could see, too, that Lucy needed a little excitement in her life. She forced herself not to think of her safety on the road; she had come back unscathed from Oxford, after all, although with such news as had taken her mother's breath away. It was such a different generation; they were different women, taking their fortunes in their hands as boldly as though they were men. It was not what Mary could approve, but she admired them for it, all the same. If Martha could continue to give her inestimable help to her son, who did not know how to ask for help, then she was content. She converted any qualms she might have in the interests of propriety into enthusiastic prayer for their welfare.

Last night Lucy had arrived in Southwark. She had left her escort at The Bear and gone on foot through the filthy streets humming with convivial night traffic, to knock on the door of Jud's ramshackle dwelling. Even the house, she thought, looked surprised that it had not fallen down long ago.

She was welcomed, if that was the proper term, by a small girl with ginger curls and a dirty apron who wiped her freckled nose with her hand and said 'Yus?' very fiercely.

'You must be Henrietta Maria,' smiled Lucy. Jud had described his landlady's family in fine physical detail, though he had been less precise as to social status. She persuaded the suspicious cherub to let her in and found herself pitched abruptly into a small room full of heat and noise and people. She stood still and tried to take it in, her eyes ranging the faces.

'By thunder, if it isn't Lucy!'

And there was Jud, seated like a king at the head of the ancient table, with an astonishingly beautiful dark-haired girl on his knee, her expression of utter blissfulness just changing to one of question.

'Lucy? You mean this is your sister?' She rose swiftly and came over to the door, taking Lucy's hand and giving her a shy kiss. 'I am so happy. You can't know how I've longed to meet you. I have heard Jud speak of you so often; you are quite his favourite person.'

Cleo privately congratulated herself. Not an H dropped, not a single nasal vowel, and the blazingly attractive visitor, although understandably a little overwhelmed, looked as if she were the sort to make a quick recovery. 'I'm Cleo,' she said simply, drawing Lucy over to her brother.

As Jud stood and embraced her, grinning from ear to ear, she became aware of a tugging at her skirt. She looked down to see a chubby toddler winding himself about her legs. 'Julius?' she began, her voice already fading with uncertainty.

The child looked up at her with fascinated interest, then slowly crinkled Jud's eyes up at the corners and gave her Jud's unmistakable smile. She stared at him in stunned amazement for a second, then scooped him into her arms, hugging him strongly. 'Oh, Jud!' she accused, between laughter and tears. 'And you did not *tell* us! What a coward!'

'I was waiting for the proper time,' protested a sheepish Jud.

'He's right, you know,' added Cleo quietly. 'Your poor mother has had enough to trouble her. We can wait.'

Cleo's obvious serenity and happiness touched Lucy deeply. 'He's the most splendid boy,' she said to her, trying to put the welcome of a whole family into her smile. 'You must both be very proud of him.'

It had all been easy after that. The rest of the children had clamoured for attention in their turn and had variously enchanted and amused their guest with their anecdotes, many of a decidedly doubtful nature and all couched in the unequivocal accents of the area, which Lucy found exhilarating as well as quaint. They all seemed to have demonic energy. She loved them instantly.

Then Nan had come home and shrieked with delight at finding another Heron in her house. Lucy saw at once from where Cleo's sureness was derived; Mistress Whittaker was not a lady, but she was a woman who knew how to raise a happy household. She ceased to question Jud's choice of his London home and was as eager as Cleo to go next door to where the couple's own little house was beginning to take shape. It was no palace still, but it was light and pleasant with its new white plaster and good oak floors. Jud had offered to do the same for Nan's establishment, but she had refused, saying she couldn't abide the turmoil. He hoped to persuade her at a later date.

After an evening during which Lucy tried to extract from a bemused Jud the answers to every one of her questions about the various modes of thought and feeling in the city and in Parliament, she was vanquished at last by her own need for sleep. They made up a bed for her in the new house, a warm nest of new material brought to them by Will, with which Cleo had not as yet had time to work. There, worn out with travel, surprise and contentment, she had slept without moving until she was woken by a firm nudge from Ettamaria, who had brought her hot milk and honey to begin her day.

'Jud says as 'ow yore goin' t' see Silken Will,' the child admired. 'I seen 'im lots; ee's gorjus! Ee looks like King 'Erod in the Myst'ry Play at Chrissmus.'

Later, as she stood before the elegant threshold of Will's sumptuous Strand mansion, Lucy found the regal comparison less unflattering than she had first thought it. The house reared and flourished above and beyond her in what she considered an excess of grandeur. It was built in dark rose brick and had a look of Hampton Court about it. She supposed it was all very well in its way but it wasn't a patch on Heron.

A major-domo in black livery and silver lace ushered her through a lofty, tiled hall into a small withdrawing room into which the entirety of Nan's cottage would have fitted snugly. She sat down upon a cane chair of oriental aspect and tapped her feet. The room was filled with interesting objects of similar origins to the chair, but she eyed them quickly and coolly. She had not come here to admire worldly goods. She waited. It seemed that she waited quite a long time.

A door opened deeper in the house, letting out a gust of music and laughter. It closed again and she recognized Will's firm tread upon a wooden floor. She felt nervous; it was foolish.

'My dearest girl! This is the most marvellous surprise.' He plucked her out of the chair, swung her round and kissed her. He smelled of spices and wore suitably Herodian violet and white. 'This is the best thing in the world! How long can you stay?'

'I'm staying with Jud, thank you.' She extricated herself, breathless.

'But you *must* let me entertain you. Think of all the hospitality I have to repay; besides, Mary would never forgive me.'

'I don't know about that. Heron is yours after all.' Her mouth snapped shut in shock at herself. She had not meant to be so clumsy or so precipitate. 'I'm sorry—' she began.

His brows descended from shelter in his hair. 'I see. So Tom has told you; judging from your curmudgeonly expression, you don't like it.'

She tried to look more pleasant. 'It was rather a shock.'

'I understand that. But there is nothing to disturb you. I most certainly do not regard Heron as mine in any way at all.'

'But it *is* yours.'

'It's still Parliament's in law; I don't think you comprehend the arrangements we have made.'

'Then enlighten me; Tom did not feel he had the time,' she said bitingly.

He saw that she was strung very taut about this; the only way to release her was to tell her what she wanted to know. He did so very rapidly and very clearly. '– And so you see, in a few years it will all be Tom's again.'

'Why not now?' demanded Lucy, aware of her lack of all diplomacy. 'Perhaps there may be some way in which you could compound.' She leaned back, letting her breath sigh out at last. It was over. She had said it. The rest was up to Will.

He was quiet for a moment, watching her thoughtfully. 'This matters a great deal to you, doesn't it?'

'Yes, it does.'

'Far more, evidently, than it does to Tom himself.'

'I know. He has said it; this is not my business.'

'I do not say any such thing. I will make enquiries; if that is what you want, and I will write to Tom, should it prove a reasonable proposition to compound. I think there is a great deal of sense in the notion. There. Are you happier now?'

She was speechless, floored by this unexpected agreement. 'Well, yes, but I didn't – yes. Thank you. I can think of nothing to say.'

'Don't let that distress you; it makes a welcome change.' He held out his hand, smiling to take the sting from the taunt. 'Why don't you come and meet my guests? You know some of them. They'll be gone soon and then we can talk again, but meanwhile the music is very fine.'

He wondered that she could not see how his heart was leaping and plunging in him like a stallion driven crazy by the spring. Just to walk in like that, looking as breathtaking as the *Lady* under full canvas, as forthright and impatient as ever, and calmly tell him what he should do with upwards of 50,000 livres – it made him want to sweep her into his arms, then into his bed, and into the nearest church after that. All he said was, 'Or if you don't feel sociable, perhaps you would like a little refreshment here?'

Lucy hesitated. She did not feel particularly sociable, and she did rather want to discover the truth about Will's supposed betrothal. If they stayed here cosily together, it was more than likely that he would tell her about it. 'I'd prefer that, if your guests won't think you rude; I'm a little tired. London is rich fare after Heron.'

He regarded her sympathetically. 'It takes time to recover from the discovery that one is a morganatic aunt.'

She smiled. 'Ned is a fine child. And a true Heron,' she added, so that he would know that she approved of the boy's existence, if not the manner of it.

Will nodded. 'The Whittakers have looked after Jud like one of their own. He could have done far worse than Cleo; and far worse by her.'

Wine came and he poured it for her. 'Now, tell me – what is the latest news of Cathal O'Connor?' He asked as casually as a sated lion might paw at a carcass.

She shrugged. 'I hear nothing. Parliament patrols the seas and I suppose no one has crossed to whom he could give letters. Jud no longer hears from him either.'

'So you have no notion of his married state?' he hazarded, watching her expression keenly. It had hurt her, as he had feared. So then, that torch still burned as brightly as ever. God damn it.

'No, none,' she said, meeting his look with a tilt of the chin, 'But I do not imagine it to have changed.'

He had the idea that she was waiting for him to make some further comment. Her look was definitely interrogative. He cast around for something to satisfy her.

Now he will tell me, she thought; it follows so obviously . . .

'I'm sure he will be as faithful as the times and his temperament allow him to be,' was all he could manage, 'but do not expect too much of him; he is very young, and has the whole of his heritage to fight if he would fight for you.'

'I'm well aware of that,' she snapped. He wondered what he had said to annoy her. She did not usually object to the truth.

'Matters will change in Ireland,' he said, on a purposely hopeful note. 'Parliament will put an end to their internal strife, and to the King's hopes of them. Perhaps when peace comes, Cathal will be able to return to England.' He could not say 'to you'. It stuck in his throat. Grudgingly, he double-damned the absent rebel;

there was nothing like unsatisfied longing to keep a woman tantalized. He knew that well enough; it had been one of his own most successful ploys in the past. Now, he thought ruefully, all his scattered chickens had come home to roost on one perch.

'I suppose by "peace" you mean that Parliament will send an army into Ireland to annihilate the Confederates,' Lucy said incisively.

'Let's say that we must re-establish our government there,' said Will evasively. 'But not yet. We voted last month against Holles's motion to send over six regiments.'

'Only because your Independent generals don't wish to send their troops away from where they can make their presence felt here in England,' she retorted. 'And even if they did, they'd have a mutiny on their hands, like as not; you still have not paid the soldiers. I also doubt if many of them *want* to fight in Ireland. They have barely concluded hostilities at home.'

He grinned appreciatively. 'I should have known you'd be almost as well informed as I am myself. Perhaps you should give up your husbandry of Heron and join me at Westminster.'

Lucy shuddered. 'Thank you, no. I am *too* well informed for that. Tell me,' she asked thoughtfully, 'have you also become enamoured of the sectaries? Jud can hear no ill of Cromwell, or your friend Vane.'

'I know them to be the men who will, in the end, satisfy more of the country than any others. I like their open-mindedness and their enthusiasm for change and experiment.'

'But do you vote with them in the House?'

'More often than not. My dear Lucy, *must* we have such a dry discussion? I have more than enough of politicking these days; I don't want to think about it in my own house, in my own time.'

'It's very well for you,' she grumbled, 'but I am starving for the crumbs from your parliamentary table. We hear so little now.'

'You have my letters?'

'Some of them. I doubt we get them all.' She repeated the dates.

He expressed annoyance. 'And I thought my couriers infallible.'

'The question we most asked you, and I ask again is, what will happen to His Majesty? Will the Scots help him against the army?'

'Or will *he* help the army against the Scots? Who knows? He may think it worth his while to throw in his lot with Cromwell, Vane and the Independents to avoid forcing the Covenant on every free man in England; he *is* God's annointed leader of the

Anglican Church. If he treats with the Scots and the Presbyterians, as careful Denzil Holles would have him do, how will we ever be rid of the wretched Scots? Their army would have to stay in England to "make its presence felt" as you put it, in opposition to Cromwell and company. From His Majesty's point of view, he will get back his throne and most of his power from Holles's lot – but he'd be lucky to keep the bare throne if the Independents have their way. There are other considerations; if the King wants Scots to help he must abandon Montrose and your Irish Confederates. Above all he must stop his ceaseless intriguing between them. And with France, and with the Queen, and with the Vatican and God knows who else! He must be seen to be single-minded, for just long enough for someone to trust him! In other words – he must admit that he is defeated!'

'That is too sad,' said Lucy. 'I think he is brave *not* to admit it.'

'Yes, he has courage, I don't deny it; but that is not, alas, the quality most needed now. He needs to be able to read the minds of those with whom he must come to terms; I don't think he can do this. The present position is stalemate; the Scots will not keep him forever without a promise of the Covenant; if they do not get that promise from His Majesty they will make what capital they can by handing him over to Parliament.'

'There is too much to juggle; it makes the mind quite tipsy! I think I understand less now than I did before. If only war were as simple a matter as it was in our old games of Romans and Gauls.'

'Never mind! Let's see if I can't take your mind off such dreary matters. I have a thing for you I think you might like; it was meant for your Christmas gift, but is something I did not care to try to send.' He excused himself and went off to fetch his gift, leaving Lucy to examine her feelings.

She was immensely pleased to be with him again; her heavy mood had quite lifted now; she could never be cheerless in his company. She began to hope that perhaps he was not to marry his cousin; after all, he had said nothing. What he had said about Ireland was also hopeful, she supposed, although there would certainly be more bloodshed before there was peace; if only that blood should be none of Cathal's. She wondered if perhaps Will might not be able to help her with the problem of the letters; surely Westminster had a long spoon which even an Independent might borrow?

Will returned and threw a small box into her lap. It was in the shape of a tiny sea chest, bound and studded in gold.

'How lovely! It will serve to remind me that you are a pirate as well as a stuffy MP.'

He was glad of the saucy sparkle in her eyes. 'Well, open it!'

'You are always giving me presents.'

'You do not always wear them.'

'The ring? It's too heavy for every day. But I do wear it, especially when I am feeling lonely, or sad. It cheers me up.'

'I am delighted to hear it. Perhaps you will wear this one when you are less doleful.'

She opened the box, still smiling at his teasing. Inside, couched upon billows of sea-green silk lay a brooch that was a tiny relief of the *Gallant Lady*; her hull and masts were gold, her sails white enamel and her pennons and guns flaunted rubies, emeralds and sapphires. She was unmistakable and exquisite.

Lucy said nothing but flew to kiss him. He caught her hungrily and took full measure of her gratitude.

'It's the loveliest thing I've ever seen,' she said, catching her breath, pretending not to have noticed the lustiness of his kiss. He obviously enjoyed it, and certainly he deserved it, for such a beautiful gift. She enjoyed it herself; it was a long time since she had been soundly kissed.

'It is a promise that you *shall* sail in her one day – when she comes back to port,' Will said, a little unsteadily. For a moment he wondered if she should lose his head and beg her to marry him, and take a chance on the luck of the moment to keep the Irish aspirant at bay. But no – there was no sense in losing all for the sake of a little speed. They had a lifetime ahead of them; he could wait. Or at least, he must.

'I shall love that,' she said demurely. 'If you think I am quite grown up enough now.'

He recalled the conversation he had once had with a tow-headed elf who was just commencing that elusive process. 'I think so,' he said quite seriously. 'I think you are grown up enough for anything you care to mention.'

She did not care to mention anything. She blushed. Will was just speculating as to whether his present was good for a second embrace when they were interrupted by the entrance of the one person in the world who was least welcome to both at this particular juncture.

'Will, Mr St John is leaving. Perhaps you –? Why, Mistress Heron? It *is* Lucy Heron? This *is* a surprise!' Eliza Hartley was thinner and it suited her. She wore pale lavender and grey and gave an impression of extreme fragility which astonished Lucy almost as much as her own fresh and sensuous beauty dismayed Eliza. The two women stared at each other, amazed and unmannerly, until Will's discreet cough reminded them of their social duties.

'Well, you have certainly *blossomed*,' said Eliza sweetly, sweeping Lucy's glowing peach and green damask with delicately deprecating lashes. 'And are you just up from the country?'

'No, from Southwark. I stay with my brother.' Lucy wondered if her ladyship could summon a sneer deep enough for the Surrey side of the river.

She was disconcerted to hear her say, 'That will be your brother George? So many people think highly of his *Intelligencer*. It is quite one of the best newssheets we have.'

'And to think he was once a mere clerk in a shipping office,' marvelled Will. He saw Eliza's eye fall on the box still open in Lucy's hand. He did not suppose she would care for its contents; there was no similar replica of the *Lady Elizabeth*. 'See what I have given Lucy,' he said with brazen optimism. 'Is it not an excellent likeness?'

Lucy handed over the brooch. Eliza's long lashes came down like shutters. Her cool voice was level as she said, 'Perfectly lovely, Will. Is it your birthday, Mistress Lucy?'

'No. Christmas. One has to fetch one's presents in these troubled times.'

'Ah yes. I had forgot. I am so sorry that my illness put you all out; I should so have enjoyed the season at Heron.' She turned to Will, an intimate warmth replacing the dutiful politeness in her tone. 'My dear, I really think Mr St John wishes to speak to you before he leaves. Shall I—?'

'No. I'll go to him. I shall not be long. Excuse me, Lucy.'

He went off whistling. Eliza, hearing the spirited shanty, became even more alert. He did that only when he was especially pleased with life. She disliked the probability that the Heron chit's presence might be responsible for such pleasure. She had always found his involvement with the family tiresome. They were good company for Gloucestershire; that was as much as might be said of them. Naturally this commendation did not include Lucy.

They regarded each other wryly, neither inclined to polite pretence. Lucy frostily accepted more wine, as frigidly offered. They sipped.

Eliza gazed vaguely out of the window while Lucy read the gilded titles of the books in the tall rattan cases. Most were by famous travellers or adventurous seamen – Raleigh, Diaz, Columbus. Eliza was brooding over the brooch. She knew how deep was Will's affection for the *Gallant Lady*; she was the pride of his fleet. This, then, was no casual gift. Eliza scented danger to her dearest interests. She could not imagine how this might have come about. Perhaps she was mistaken; most likely. But in case she were not—

Lucy now began to be plagued again by her demon of curiosity. Was there a betrothal or was there not? It had seemed most unlikely while she had been alone in Will's company but Eliza's demeanour made her less certain. She seemed very much at home here. She was evidently acting as Will's hostess, and her manner with him had been markedly affectionate. Then why not simply ask Eliza? Whatever quirk of pride or obstinacy had prevented her from asking Will himself was absent where Eliza was concerned. She didn't give a fig what Eliza thought of her. If Jud's idea were true – and *he* still thought it so – then granted, Eliza would become insufferable; she would also certainly mention Lucy's query to Will who would think her odd not to have put it to him. But if it were not true, there would be nothing lost except Eliza's face, which was no sad prospect.

Their musing and sipping done, both ladies eyed each other like the opponents of a cockfight and opened their mouths at the same time.

'Do you stay long in Lon—?'

'I believe I have to wish you—'

'I beg your pardon,' said Lucy next, with respect for Eliza's greater age.

'I merely enquired whether you planned to stay long in London.'

'No. I shall leave in two days.'

Eliza relaxed. There had been nothing planned with Will; there was not time now. It was probable that she was worrying without cause. In this spirit she observed with an air of some patronage, 'It was kind of dear Will to recall your childish pleasure in the *Lady*. He does not, perhaps, realize you are now a little old for such toys.'

Cat, thought Lucy. 'I do not recollect ever to have been given toys studded with diamonds. I assure you, the little ship is most welcome.'

Eliza's smile was like crushed glass.

Lucy returned it innocently, crossed her fingers and decided, as she so often did, to be hung for a sheep. 'I understand that I may soon be making you and Will a gift in my turn. I offer you my felicitations. Have you decided yet when the wedding is to be?'

Eliza concentrated all her talents upon making a bored and faintly irritated mask of her face. She was thinking very quickly. She had no idea who had given the creature this information, but it certainly had not been Will, since it was not, however dearly she might wish otherwise, the truth. The mistake might, however, be of use to her; for if there *should* be the suggestion of a fancy between Silken Will and this sunburned haystack, then it would serve as an excellent pretext for ridding the girl, at any rate, of all hope in his direction. She would deal with Will's hopes when the baggage was safely packed off back to Loamshire.

'If Will did not mention a date,' she said, just a little regretfully, as though *she* might have been glad to do so, 'then it is because he does not yet wish the news to be made public. There are still several matters to be arranged; it can be a protracted business.'

So it was true. Lucy felt suddenly tired, her mischief all depleted. 'I am sorry. I did not know it was not public property. It was my brother who told me, not Will.'

'And you did not speak of it to him?'

'No,' said Lucy dispiritedly. 'I should have waited until you were both present again—'

'No,' said Eliza quickly. 'You would do Will a favour if you were not to talk of it at present. It is not his favourite subject. You see, my uncle Warwick has taken it upon himself to be my guardian and he has Will sloughed in a quicksand of ink and paper, legality and mortality, until the poor man is like to run mad. Leave your congratulations until all is clear and the way straightforward.' It sounded convincing; enough for Miss Peaches and Cream anyway.

'Naturally I shall say nothing to anyone,' said Lucy stiffly. She felt foolish. There was no satisfaction in learning what she had not wished to know.

Eliza watched her with amusement, noting the sudden fall in humour. 'Tell me,' she said with swift cruelty, 'are you glad we shall marry?'

'No, I am not,' Lucy replied with simple and enjoyable truth. 'I do not think you are worth half of him.'

'What a good thing that your opinion is of no consequence.'

'Then why ask for it?'

'Oh, an intuition, that is all. It tells me that perhaps you still suffer that schoolgirl passion you had for Will.'

'You should not read romances,' said Lucy severely. 'They make the mind soggy and the emotions shallow.'

She was spared Eliza's retort by Will's return, not a moment too soon, he could tell from their straight backs and frozen faces. 'I see Medusa has passed in my absence,' he observed chattily. 'Eliza my dear, Lord Playfair is begging for your company. I do not think you should deny him any longer.'

'Then I shall not.' Eliza rose, her smile most affable. 'Goodbye, Mistress Lucy; I do not suppose we shall meet again.'

Lucy did not reply. She stared out at Will's beautiful garden and forced herself not to cry out to him to abjure this marriage.

Will closed the door behind Eliza and wished Lord Playfair joy of her. It was a flirtation of some months' standing and he had encouraged it as best he could without being detected. He had also used it as a means of fending off Warwick, saying he had suspicions that his cousin's affections were beginning to turn in a new direction. If only it were true. But Eliza sought his bed whether he asked her or not, and had showed signs of becoming tiresomely domestic lately. There was still marriage written in her eyes, and he had to tread carefully with her. God knows he did not wish to hurt her; she had been his mistress for more years than she would care to admit, and he was not going to turn her off abruptly or unkindly, though he was no more in love with her than he was with his deerhound bitch.

But now as he looked at Lucy he longed to throw off all kindness to any woman but her. 'You look like the wrath of God,' he told her pleasantly. 'Has Eliza been tormenting you? You should not mind her. She has so little to sharpen her teeth upon in London.'

She suspected sarcasm and glared at him. 'Why should I mind her? I have plenty of teeth of my own; far more, I should think.'

He showed his own in appreciation. 'Pray pen them up and let us do something quiet and enjoyable together. I am at your disposal. Shall we begin with some music? We could go upstairs to the gallery?'

Lucy shook her head. 'No thank you. Not today. I think I will go home very soon.'

He was puzzled. 'What is wrong, Lucy? Did Eliza really say something to upset you?'

'No. Nothing at all!' Lucy almost shouted. She felt as though she were stifling. She wanted to be by herself.

'Then sit down and don't make an ass of yourself! I haven't seen you for the devil knows how long, and all you can do is to throw a fit of the vapours. It's not like you.'

His annoyance calmed her. She sat down as she was told. But it was no use. Her brightness was muted and nothing he could do would revive it. He fed her. He read to her from Hakluyt's *Voyages*. He fetched his lute and sang to her – the beautiful love lyrics of Sir Thomas Wyatt. But she only looked at him reproachfully with her green eyes and would not be pleasured.

'I think I really must go now, Will,' she said in a small voice when he had exhausted his wits upon her. 'I hope you will visit us soon,' she added primly.

'But what about tomorrow? We could visit Hyde Park, feed the ducks, drive about the town looking for mischief—'

His look was very appealing and she longed to agree, but somehow everything was different now. He should not really be making such suggestions. He was no longer free to dispose of his time with her. He ought not to feel that he was. 'Tomorrow I shall be with Jud,' she said finally.

He raised his hands wide in defeat. 'Let me know,' he said, 'when you have recovered your *joie de vivre*. You are a confounded nuisance without it!'

Heron, Winter 1646

Kit and Humpty returned to Heron, blown in on a furious gale that mocked all hopes of a mild New Year. They brought with them their dozen comrades-in-arms, all wearing their hats and behaving like gentlemen, under the firm pressure of their eye-catching captain.

The twins had just persuaded them that it would not be a sporting thing to sack the already destitute Stratton Hall, even if its inhabitants *were* misbegotten papists. Opinion had it, therefore, that since the boys had balked them of their prey and were about to leave them into the bargain, they owed them at least a dinner.

Mary Heron welcomed her sons, and commissioned the dinner with the aplomb of one whose children regularly disappear for several months and who is accustomed to entertain brigands at her table. Her manner was quiet, dignified and quite as firm as Captain Attila's. She saw that their only chance was to bore the visitors to death and gave instructions accordingly. Lucy was not to be seen. There was no music, not much in the way of food, and an appalling number of prayers were said at every conceivable opportunity.

'We'll keep you in knowledge of our whereabouts, lads,' the captain told them sadly as he marshalled his company. 'I'm thinking you'll soon be looking for us, for it's like a Greek tragedy in this house!'

'I don't want to hear about it,' was all that Mary would say when her discomforted sons confronted her.

'I thought you'd like him; there's something in him puts me in mind of Father,' said Humpty desolately.

Mary slapped his face very hard. She did not tell them how much they had been mourned and missed, and would not listen when Kit said that he *had* written, twice. She put them to work in the gardens, hacking out dead wood, and it was some time before they ceased to feel that she intended them to feel some sort of comparison in it.

They made up for their mother's chilly welcome by revealing their exploits, chapter by chapter, as a bedtime story for young Ned. Lucy and Julia were also permitted to attend, and the boys began to feel their lost virtue creeping back as their listeners' eyes grew steadily rounder each night.

The matter of their share of the company's spoils was, they decided after discussion, a purely private concern. They chose a suitable spot in the woods and buried it; a useful sum in gold, jewels and some church plate that none of their comrades wanted.

They enjoyed themselves hugely for the first couple of weeks; but the first high colour was beginning to fade from their masterly representation of that popular theme, the prodigal's return, when there was another homecoming that conferred upon their own choice of moment the ordination of all the gods.

Nehemiah Owerby was now, by some Parliamentary alchemy, the outright owner of his land and property. His father had become a man of some substance by hard work and good luck; Nehemiah had improved upon it by more of both, especially since he had ceased to pay rent to Heron. His father's only brother, a clothier in Gloucester, had conveniently died, leaving him his house near the cathedral and the sort of small fortune that only an abstemious bachelor is foolish enough to accumulate. Thus comfortably equipped, Nehemiah was in a position to concentrate upon God's work. Since the death of his old adversary, Sir George, he had known how he would do so. He had come back to Heron to become Member of Parliament for the honour. He had also come back for Martha. Something broke within him when he found her gone without trace.

Each separate member of the Heron family, when they were given the news of his arrival, felt a shock of cessation, as though their lives had gone on without them for the moment. The space thus created was for Dominic. It was difficult to reconcile the memory of his gentleness and humanity with the emotions aroused in them now.

'Kill. Kill. At once,' was all that Humpty could think. It was no longer a child's dream of revenge without knowledge. He had killed three Parliamentary soldiers. His mood marched grimly about the house, affecting everyone. They all would wish to see Nehemiah dead, there was no doubt of that. Even Ned knew him as some sort of family ogre.

They left it to Kit to find the middle path, since Humpty would listen to no one else, and Mary and Lucy were too uncertain of their own grip on justice and mercy to be able to speak of them. Kit perfectly sensed his responsibility and took his time, feeling his way while his brother commanded himself from a white-hot rage into a silver-cool one which he now knew to be of greater use to him.

'The damnable point of it is,' said Kit at last, as they mended a fence together where poachers had broken it, 'that if we simply kill him in cold blood, we shall not be considered the instruments of justice, but only murderers. It is untrue and unfair, but it is what will happen. We should be executed. I'm against that.'

He was very clear. Humpty knew when Kit's mind was made up. He did not argue but he thought about it for the next few hours. There was a gradual perception, within the household, of the lifting of thunder.

'The principle of evil does not go away because one wicked man dies,' said Kit later. 'It is continuous and we must continuously fight it.'

'You're right,' said Humpty, relaxed now.

'Not me.' Kit smiled. 'Dominic.'

'Then let us take up our swords and fight the good fight! Metaphorically speaking, of course!'

Lucy was taken into their confidence as they considered methods. At first they wondered whether one of them might not also stand in the forthcoming election.

'Too young – and anyway, suppose you were to win!' Lucy alarmed.

The wearisome spectre of Westminster frightened off that idea. But if they could not become active political opponents, they might do what they could to hamper Nehemiah's campaign.

'Only there must be no more yellow horses,' Lucy warned.

'We are older than that now,' said Kit briefly.

They proved that they were. What followed was an organized campaign to destroy the dignity and efficacy of the candidate's own.

No Royalist was standing for election as, naturally, no Royalist wished to join his enemies in Parliament. Most of Heron's Royalist soldiers had returned to their homes and work, however, and they showed a proper ambition for Nehemiah's confusion when canvassed by the twins. If they could not be represented at Westminster they could at least make their feelings about the man who *claimed* to represent them unequivocally plain.

There were perhaps forty of them, most a little battered but by no means unserviceable. They wore the faded green uniforms in which they had marched away so hopefully behind Sir George, and their sobered hearts were lifted again by the sight of his sons in their steel and velvet and feathers.

'Chips off the old block,' the old foot-soldiers said proudly, and 'Damned fine young fellows!' swore the re-mounted cavaliers.

At first Nehemiah hardly knew what hit him. He advertised that he would speak to the villagers and whoever else might be interested on the Village Green at six o'clock on Saturday. Over two hundred turned up, pleased with the prospect of having an MP again; also among them were those who would rather not. Sitting his horse upon the spot where Sir George had once read out the first fatal call to arms, Nehemiah released all the power of his old pulpit oratory, strengthened by the martial habit of command. There was no doubt in his mind that the electors would return him. His only opponent, put up for the look of the thing by the County Committee, was one Love-the-Lord Crump, a quiet individual with a provoking stutter and a desperate fear of horses.

After twenty minutes' lecture on the virtues of the Independents and the indubitable will of God in this matter, in a voice that would have ground stone, the crowd were in no doubt either. Just as Nehemiah was about to close the meeting with a sermon which he had specially prepared and which lasted another twenty minutes, a hand shot up near the front of the throng.

'Speak!' ordered Captain Owerby.

'I would like to ask, sir,' rumbled John Coachman, recently returned with a highwayman's patch over one eye, 'whether you

507

think it right that the King's loyal subjects should send into his Parliament a man who has fought against His Majesty, and led others to fight against him?'

Nehemiah awarded him a glare of recognition. 'If you say that I, and your Parliament, are *not* the King's loyal subjects, then you lie and I shall have you taken in charge for defamation,' he said vigorously. The row of buff-jerkined stalwarts behind the nearest oak tree confirmed his ability to do so.

'Then why did you fight against him, and not for him?' asked John with an excess of bovine puzzlement. The crowd, who were mostly Puritan, groaned, though with good humour.

'We fought to take His Majesty out of the hands of those who gave him ill advice and place him where he would be better counselled,' Nehemiah said with dangerous patience.

'With the Scots, do you mean?' John riposted. There was laughter. No one was happy about the Scots.

'Do not boil your inconsiderable brains about matters you cannot comprehend,' Nehemiah advised, not unpleasantly. 'Be sure that Parliament will do its duty with regard to King Charles—'

'God bless him!' rang a bright voice.

'And restore him!' cried another.

The people murmured, looking about to see who had shouted. Upon the edge of the green, it was now observed, stood what seemed to be a very large number of men in green. They were recognized at once as the old baronet's company. In front of them was a stocky figure in a vulgar amount of lace, also wearing a very long sword. Beside him was a more elegant person, similarly accoutred. Across the crowd, which was not really very far, Nehemiah met the hardened blue gaze of the young man who was now perhaps his greatest living enemy.

'If it is your intention to cause havoc here,' he began, signalling to his escort, 'believe me I—'

'Not at all; never a thought in the world!' said Humpty ingratiatingly. 'Saturday night. Village Green. Thought you would know. The dancing?'

'Dancing.' The word fell like an angel from grace.

'Why yes. It is to begin right away. *Right* away, if you please. The ground is – booked – as it were.'

From behind the green men there suddenly ran out a gaily clad band of local musicians, their instruments already tuning up. There were quite a lot of them and they made a very fair amount of noise, far too much, certainly, for Nehemiah to be heard any further. But Nehemiah had not been one of Cromwell's russet-coated captains without learning when he was beaten on tactics. He converted his instinctive revulsion into the outward appearance of semi-approval and retired behind the oak with his followers. His audience, immensely pleased with the prospect of dancing, which they had not done since before the war, willingly went without the sermon, of which they had endured more than plenty, and set themselves to be festive.

Nobody could find anybody who knew how the occasion had come about, but suddenly there was ale in tuns at the roadside, and hot pies to go with it. The cavaliers began the dancing with three sets of Morris, performed to rousing Royalist tunes. Everyone was encouraged to sing along and did so, simply because they knew the words. Nehemiah watched unfathomably as Humphrey Heron organized the first evening of his candidature into a celebration for the King, and wished he had the boy stripped between two pillars again.

This, then, was what organization did for Kit and Humpty. On every public occasion when Nehemiah appeared, there also appeared the men in green. There was never the faintest possible suggestion of violence or hindrance, not even of heckling, except in the form of innocent question after question of Parliament's attitudes to the King.

As the campaign went on, the questions became more irritating. It was in this that Lucy came to their aid, having been unable, so far, to accompany the twins because she did not think she could bear the sight of Nehemiah, wrongly and hideously alive while Dominic slept in the shade of the chapel wall, and Martha fled the shadow of his name.

'How if the King will not take the advice you give him?'

'What will the Parliament do about Ireland?'

'How is the Parliament to advise His Majesty when they cannot agree among themselves?'

'Will there be restitution for theft and hardship by cause of war?'

'How shall we elect you to speak for us, if you do not share our faith?'

When she had thus set an example, none too arduous to follow, there were many to take it up. Nehemiah, who had expected simply to address a few meetings and go on his way, secure in his support, found that he was asked to explain his opinions to men who, he knew for fact, had nourished no such thing as an opinion in their own owlish noddles, except as to the relative qualities of ale or cheese – not, that was, before they went to war.

But men who have been to war, especially a war where the enemy is a set of principles rather than a foreign enemy, have lived in a different world from the one to which they return. They have lived under a different set of rules, and have learned to value a man for the metal of which he is made rather than the riches he owns. They have seen their social superiors in fear and extremity and known them guilty of cowardice or stupidity which has cost lives. They have discovered their own worth and new abilities. They have come back with more confidence than they carried away. The confidence enables them to put questions to such as Nehemiah Owerby which previously they would scarcely have known how to formulate.

By the end of the campaign both they, and perhaps Nehemiah himself, had gained a deeper knowledge of what it meant to be an Independent. They had heard the read-out opinions of Cromwell and Vane and the sectarian preachers, Hugh Peter and William Dell, and perhaps one or two of them, not many more certainly, had just about begun to think for themselves in the way that these men adjured them to do.

As for Lucy, who had got her questions as much out of Jud's letters as out of her own head, she began to find that the latter was becoming greatly confused. Jud would have been delighted. Theoretically, he should have also have been delighted when Nehemiah, having answered sufficient questions satisfactorily to a necessary number of his electors, was returned to Westminster. Nobody, of course, had expected otherwise.

Their own campaign had been most enjoyable to Kit and Humpty, if in a more stately style than that of their earlier escapades. They had kept up the level of entertainment to a high standard. There had been more dancing; there had been a collection for the King, which Nehemiah was asked to present to the Parliament. There had been a mock battle with mops and pails instead of swords and bucklers. There had even been a mock election speech by Humpty, who had quoted Shakespeare and his father in equal amounts and had been gratified by the applause.

When, just before he was due to leave the district and take up his new and onerous duties, Nehemiah's house was stormed by a dozen ruffianly 'reformados', led by a terrifying Hercules in scarlet and black, the twins professed themselves as stupefied as anyone else. The Puritan's losses were dismal: chiefly gold, some plate, a very few jewels, his mother's; and what caused him the greatest sorrow, the destruction of his books – sermons, pamphlets and a particularly fine Bible. Outdoors the desecration was less usual. His horses were taken, naturally, and even one of his dogs which must have caught a sporting fancy, but the odd thing was what happened to his sheep, scores of which had been rounded up and had their heads shaven to the shoulder. Round the neck of the biggest ram was a placard which read 'Follow a Roundhead and thou wilt make mutton!'

The unlikely fact of Nehemiah's having been away and his house unguarded was much commented upon in the village. His saintly cohort had, in fact, been attending the last of his election meetings, and, knowing the twins would be sure to be there, he had not thought a guard to be necessary.

It was Isabella who, bearing no grudges for past betrayals, said appraisingly to Humpty, 'I do believe that while you were away you learned – probably painfully – to think before you act.'

'My dear Isabella,' Humpty showed his teeth, 'I have even learned, on chosen occasions, not to act at all – unless I am sure the game is worth the candle.'

Lucy, present at this exchange, noted that they were not necessarily speaking of the offence to Nehemiah's property. She had lately observed a new delicacy in Humpty's tormenting of Isabella. His teasing was as outrageous as ever, but it was now as likely to take verbal form as a physical one, and was not so much a matter of spiders down the bosom as of suggestive glances in that direction. What was also becoming clear, and was the source of surprised amusement to his family, was that whereas he had once loathed and despised Isabella, Humpty now actually *liked* the girl. As for Isabella, aware of and profoundly grateful for her growing beauty, she enriched it by the conscious development of a great deal of patience and the kind of enigmatic smile that she understood to drive men mad.

Lucy watched their intricate sparring with something approaching envy. She felt herself to be in an odd, uncomfortable, unfixed condition; she was full of waiting, but had nothing for which to wait. Her letters from Cathal no longer quickened her heartbeat in joy so much as in dread that she must soon read that he too was lost to her forever. She did not question herself nor think it strange that she should phrase it thus – 'he too' – nor call it unreasonable in herself to feel that Will Staunton, by his choice of a wife, had dealt *her* some kind of blow, whose wound she would neither look for nor try to staunch. It was as though she willed herself to be hurt.

Will had written recently, only to say that although he had sent 'a blistering letter' to Tom, blazing his responsibilities to Heron, he had heard nothing in reply. From Martha, Lucy learned that Tom had shoved Will's letter into a drawer and would not suffer her to mention it. Otherwise, his state of mind was gradually improving, Martha thought, and he seemed, she wrote modestly, to find her presence more agreeable than not.

As they wandered through the courts of Europe in the restless wake of Rupert, she was making a collection of the herbs which were new to her. 'I am putting together a little book of drawings and descriptions of the plants, with their healing properties and instructions for their use. I hope some day it may perhaps be useful to others than myself.' Lucy was impressed. Martha Knyvett's *Herbal*. Why not? Jud might be persuaded to publish it.

She missed Martha badly and was grateful to the twins for returning to provide her with companionship. They made efforts towards resuming their lessons together, feeling that their education had suffered during the war. 'You may as well be self-taught as not taught at all,' Mary agreed with them. 'I don't suppose we shall find a tutor in present times. I wonder whatever became of Mr Davies?'

Ralph Stratton came back from the brief imprisonment that had ended his equally brief military career, having persuaded Parliament that he was not worth a tinker's ransom, let alone a knight's. He and Isabella took to riding over most afternoons to join the young Herons in the library where they would read and discuss together, setting easier work for Julia and Ned to puzzle over while they tackled wise Greeks and Romans on the arts of love, war and peace, and noble Englishmen on the advancement of learning and character.

To help them with the younger ones they used the elementary textbook of Richard Mulcaster, quondam headmaster of both the Merchant Taylors' and St Paul's grammar schools, who had taken pride of place with Sir George in the education of his children for his patriotic declaration, 'I love Rome, but London better. I love Italy, but England more. I know the Latin, but worship the English.'

For themselves, they followed his humanist path, led by Bacon, More and Roger Ascham, who had taught England's greatest queen and was therefore considered good enough for Herons.

There were no sermons and not much Bible-reading either; they left these to Mary who would read to them on Sundays after supper, in her warm, fascinated voice that made heroes of the gloomiest prophets and made the tales of Samson or Moses as thrilling as those of Odysseus.

While they thus passed the winter in trying to repair the broken rhythms of their lives, the Scots sold King Charles to Parliament in return for their army's pay and retired across the border to the accompaniment of English jeers. The King was brought to Holdenby House in Hampshire, a pleasant, easily fortified residence where he read and dreamed and still fished a little in the waters he had troubled. His only discomfort was the knowledge, twice tested, that any movement on his part to leave this habitation was considered by his hosts to be an attempt at escape.

No one had quite known whether he had been the prisoner of the Scots; now everyone knew very well what his situation was.

Saffron Walden; March 1647

In a field which had once been a golden blaze of crocus, and was now a trample of mud and mutilated petals obscured by the persons and paraphernalia of several thousand soldiers of the New Model Army, Robin Whittaker stood on a pile of ammunition boxes and addressed as many of them as could hear him.

Back in January, Parliament had voted, by the slender lead of the Presbyterian faction, to disband the army and re-recruit for service in Ireland. For various reasons, this was not to the soldiers' liking. Rob, his voice pitched high and clear, the vowels rolling round like marbles in his native gutters, rehearsed some of these reasons. 'You have fought this war for the Parliament. You have *won* this war for the Parliament! And how does Parliament repay you now? The answer is that it does not! The infantryman's pay is eighteen weeks overdue; the cavalry's a desperate forty-three! True, they offer you a beggarly six weeks if you will take it and disband. Or you may re-enlist against the Irish rebels. But where is their provision for the widows and children of your fallen comrades? Friends, the very beasts will look to the abandoned young of their kind! Where is their guarantee of indemnity for those actions you may have committed under orders which are held to be illegal in peacetime? Would you go back to your home and your family only to find yourself hauled before the next quarter sessions for the theft of some vengeful neighbour's hoard? And even should you, out of very need, knowing not what else you might do, take up weary arms again for godforsaken Ireland, Parliament will not allow you should go with the liberty of conscience for which you have fought, as much as for any other cause, in the past great conflict, but insists you serve only under officers who have taken the Covenant!'

There was a deep-throated roar of disapproval from the rank and file, Independent to a man.

'Soldiers, is *this* what you fought for? To be thus disregarded and held in contempt by those who should most hold your interests dear? Even were it not a matter for gratitude, and for fair treatment, and for common humanity, I say let the Parliament recall to whom it is accountable! For it is nothing except as the agent of your wishes, and was set up so to be since the time of the Saxon kings, and guaranteed to us by the Great Charter under King John.'

There were cries of 'God save Freeborn John!' as the prime author of these sentiments was now cooling his heels and boiling his ink in the Tower.

'We are not disloyal. We want only what is our due. Our demands are set down in the petition that is passing amongst you. Our good officers, Colonels Pride, Okey Robert Lilburne and others, uphold us in a petition of their own.' Cheers for the colonels.

'You may ask me, and I would expect it, where are the names of Fairfax, and of Cromwell, our greatest commanders, in all this? They sit with Parliament and cannot be here, but do they also *stand* with Parliament? If so, that would be a treachery of the worst kind, for they have had our hearts as well as our strong right arms. You do right to murmur, for it is Oliver Ironside himself who will give us over to those who hold out towards us – not an open hand – but a closed fist! Soldiers, Cromwell has sold us to the Parliament for the sake of his own good name with them. He has put his hand on his heart and sworn before God that we will disband!'

The murmurs grew to a satisfactory loud buzz and Rob stepped down, content that he had sown seeds enough to reap contention.

He found his way barred by a dozen would-be questioners, but behind them he could see Jud, his face clouded, and with him the tall figure of Will Staunton in a dull grey cloak that was presumably intended to conceal his position and character from this martial company.

'Jove, Rob, did you *have* to do that?' Jud was dispirited. 'I don't see that any good can come of trying to take away their hero. What will they do for another?'

'Even heroes are accountable, more so than other men; God, man, they have a right to know what he is doing behind their backs!'

'And are you so sure you *know* what he is doing?' Will spoke quietly.

'His action speaks for itself. He has deserted them.'

'That is one way to look at it. There are others.'

'Such as—?'

'Have you considered that Cromwell might be sure, in his own mind, that they *will* be offered redress, after Parliament has made its protest on behalf of its own privilege?'

'Is *that* what you call their refusal of all the army's requests?' Robin's laughter was unpleasant.

'It may be. They are rattled. It is not an acceptable thing to them to have the army threatening their threshold.'

'We are well beyond the twenty-five-mile limit here.'

'But will you *stay* beyond it, if Parliament refuses the petitions?'

'That remains to be seen.'

'And planned for, I make no doubt. You Levellers do no good here. Why can't you leave all to the Agitators? They were elected by the men to speak for them, and will do so in good faith; they are all Independent officers. I see no need for Lilburne's hysteria. Even in the Tower, the man's influence stretches too far for peaceful solutions to get their proper purchase.'

'Even in the Tower, he knows all and is ready for all,' retorted Robin. 'As for Cromwell, he is a man of some power who sees further power within his compass, if he can get it; and he can get it if he keeps in with Holles and his crew.'

'Don't be bloody ridiculous!' Will snorted. 'If you'd ever set foot in the House and *heard* Cromwell go at Holles, you'd know how foolishly you think and speak. I ask you now, on behalf of the good outcome of this delicate situation – do no more of this powder-box oratory. You don't know the harm you may do.'

'Yes, Rob, give it a rest, will you? Cromwell may well be down here tomorrow with Parliament's consent in his hand. Think how sick you'd look then.'

'I should look entirely delighted, but I do not predict it,' Rob said dryly. 'I wish I could oblige you, but I fear not.' He gave them both the stunted parody of a bow and strode back into the knot of soldiers who waited to speak to him.

'You seem to be raising trouble, over there on the *Intelligencer*,' Will said neutrally as he and Jud turned out of the press and towards a less inhabited part of the field.

'I know. It worries me. It's Lilburne. I used to go along with him, almost all the way. I think he is right to demand franchise for the common man, and basic human rights for all – but this meddling with the army can only serve to cause dissension among them at a time when they need to show a united front to Holles and co. I've even heard talk among the Levellers of deposing the King.'

'So *you* have not lost faith in Cromwell?'

'I see no reason, as yet. Though I don't quite see what he is up to, to tell the truth. I won't admit it to Rob, but it does *look* as though he simply spoke for the army without consulting its sworn spokesmen. What do you think? You're in the House. You hear him.'

'Not often. He hasn't been at Westminster much this year. He's been ill. Some sort of abscess in the head.'

'Don't tell Rob; he'll think it proof of idiocy!'

'I heard him the other day. He did promise they would disband. Perhaps he simply feels that it isn't up to the common soldier to raise his voice in the matter. He is their leader, if they will only let him lead.'

'But he is no longer that, surely. He can hardly lead the army from his seat in the Commons.'

'That, as our hot-headed young friend put it, remains to be seen.'

'I for one, should like to see it,' Jud affirmed, grinning.

'He will have a fine wild dog to lead,' said Will grimly. 'The howling animal that scratched at the walls of St James' back in '41 will not now be satisfied not to be heard, not after he has worried off his master's attackers.'

'And so, you are still for Cromwell? And how will your fair betrothed like that?' Jud enquired, more to turn the subject than out of any real interest. 'They say she can't abide him.'

'Do they so?' asked Will with some freshness. 'And do they also trouble to say, they who know, who the fortunate lady is?'

'What? Why your cousin, Lady Hartley, of course. Stop codding, Will.'

'I assure you, I am not.' Will's eyes suddenly put Jud in mind of a waiting cat.

'Well, I am sorry.' He was mortally uncomfortable. 'I had thought—'

'That I was soon to marry – evidently. I am not.' He waited still.

'But it was you yourself who said—' Jud shook his head.

'That I would be a fool to refuse her – if I am not mistaken?'

'Yes. I—'

'Oh God. And you took that for a statement of intent.'

'One thing,' said Jud cheerily, hoping to lift the sudden heaviness in the air a little, 'Lucy will be well pleased that you are not to wed. She seemed quite put out when I told her of it!'

Will visibly relaxed, but did not appear any the less feline. 'So you told her that, did you?' he asked, his voice almost extinct. 'Then you can damn' well tell her different, and as soon as you like!'

'Why, what does it matter what Lucy thinks? It's none of her concern whom you marry – nor of mine neither. I make my apology for that.'

By now Will had himself in hand. He gave Jud his most charming smile. 'It may be accepted at some time in the future – if a certain event comes to pass. If not, I very much fear for your manhood, if not for your contemptible, unnecessary, interfering life! Don't you understand, you bird-witted, loose-tongued, wool-gathering idiot? Lucy is the only woman I wish to marry!'

'The devil she is!' Jud stood like a man in the stocks, waiting for the refuse he cannot avoid. 'I had absolutely no idea!'

'That is only too obvious. Oh, don't look like that! You haven't been struck by lightning. There's no damage done that can't be put right.' He thumped Jud's back, rather hard.

'But why didn't you *say* something? I was off on the wrong track; but you can see how it was. Does *she* know? Lucy?'

Will's smile was rueful. 'I don't think she has the least idea in the world. Her head is filled with the Gaelic poetry of your early roving reporter, Cathal O'Connor.'

'Ach, he's only a boy; she'll forget him. She has nothing else to think about, stuck up there at Heron. Once you tell her—'

'She will fall instantly under my mature and masculine sway. You think. Perhaps. Perhaps not.'

Jud was fascinated in as great a measure as he was amazed. He had never known Silken Will to be at a loss in anything, and to think that his sister Lucy should be the cause of his present look of almost defenceless uncertainty caused him to marvel deeply at the unpredictability of man.

Will, watching his changing expression, said ironically, 'There are more things in heaven and earth, dear boy, than that which is obvious to the slender-witted. I do hope you did not publish my presumed nuptials in your weekly ragbook? I imagine Eliza too will be after your balls if you did. And I wouldn't lay odds on your chances of escaping her vengeance. She is not so kind as I am.'

'Look, Will, I am more sorry than I can ever say – and of course I did nothing so ludicrous.'

'Excellent. Then I take you would approve of a match between Lucy and myself?'

'Approve! It would be the best thing in the world!'

'Then let us hope your senior agrees with you. I shall write to Tom, requesting his permission to pay court to her – at once. Perhaps, this time, he may do me the courtesy to reply!'

'He were better – or I shall go over to Holland myself and bring back an answer. It would be,' he added self-consciously, 'the least I could do to atone.'

'I may take you up on it – if I have to wait too long.' Will smiled, deciding that Jud had been embarrassed enough. 'Meanwhile, on the matter of Oliver's speech to the House – you'll be interested to know that one person saw fit to challenge his good faith, though in private, rather than from the bench – your old adversary Nehemiah Owerby. It seems that your father has made a Leveller out of him!'

Jud was sombre. 'I wish he had made a dead man out of him, years ago. I am glad that *I* do not attend Parliament; I could not bear to see that man in my father's place. I cannot bear to *think* of it.'

'Then why do you not challenge him for it?'

'Me?'

'Why not? You are intelligent and well-informed, as much and more than many an ex-officer who has crept in since the war ended, under the flag of Independent.'

'Not me,' said Jud firmly. 'You said it once, too. But I mean it; for now, for always. I know my work. It is with the press.'

Heron, Spring 1647

Will delayed in London long enough to satisfy his curiosity a little further in the matter of the struggles between Parliament and the army. He went so far as to take Cromwell's part in an acrimonious debate during which a contemptuous Holles described the men who had won the war as 'enemies of the State' for their insolence in addressing their petition to the House. Will listened with an inward 'View Halloo!" to the Presbyterian vote to send the army into Ireland without either Fairfax or Cromwell. He rode out to Saffron Walden once more to record the resultant convention, under the presidency of Fairfax himself, of 200 army officers who were determined *not* to go without them. It was deadlock. Holles must face it. The army would not be moved.

By the end of April, with the threat of mutiny breathed hourly down their shrinking necks, Parliament grudgingly voted six weeks arrears to those who would not sign on for Ireland. Will could have told them that it was too late. The Agitators were now an organized representative body, perfectly fit to arbitrate with Parliament. The men, they said firmly, would have all or nothing.

The Commons, in despair, at last sent them the only man to whom, despite the suspicions of the Levellers amongst them, they wished to listen. Cromwell, with three of his colleagues, was begged to attempt the restoration of order and obedience in the ranks of his New Model Army.

On the day that Oliver went down to Saffron Walden, Will received a letter from The Hague. It seemed that he might leave matters to themselves for a few days and he therefore had his valet pack his most appealing garments, went out to purchase an enormous *cabochon* emerald that he had seen, to take fire from another matched pair that he knew, and took horse for Heron.

It was the kind of May day that is all very well if one is in tune with it to the absolute degree; otherwise it maddened with its bombardment of birdsong from every bush, its screeching greens and bellowing blossom, its bright, hopeful sunlight that thrust its way between the eyeball and the lid like an unwanted dowager on a charity mission. Will had drunk a great deal last night, possibly to give himself encouragement, perhaps even courage. It was not a light thing that he was about to do; perhaps the heaviest task he had ever undertaken. He was going to take on, if he could get it, the full burden of life's responsibilities. He didn't know if he was up to it. Ships, money, men, women, influence, even politics – he was able enough for all of these – but a wife, children, serious domesticity; even for love, could he do it?

At Oxford he nearly turned round and went back. It was evening however, and he thought he might as well eat a good dinner and take a good night's sleep before he did so. The next morning he continued on his way to Heron. The birds, the bushes and the sunshine had each receded into their proper station and he began to feel more like a hopeful lover on his way to propose marriage.

Even his doubts were proper. In Lucy he had found, to his own astonishment, and not a little offence, the only woman to whom he had ever seriously wished to make such a proposal. That she was also possibly the only woman to whom he would pay court knowing her to have bestowed her heart elsewhere posed a problem whose solution he had, as yet, made no effort to discover. He was accustomed, in general, to rely on the moment and his wits to assist him, and he intended to rely on them now.

It was a ludicrous situation and he felt unreasonably angry with Lucy because of it; a man likes to marry with dignity and certainty, and the fact of her probable indifference to his courtship made him feel like a green boy again, wondering how to assail his first well-defended virginity. Come to think of it, he did not even know whether Lucy was still virgin. She had been close enough to that young sprig of shamrock, but just how close?

He didn't care to think of that. He concentrated upon speed, as though an hour more or less would make a difference to the entirety of their future lives. He arrived before noon and received his usual ecstatic welcome, all the more fervent with surprise.

'You don't bring your handsome cousin?' asked Mary delicately. 'I thought perhaps—'

'No. She is in London, gadding, but sends her kindest regards.'

Then there were the twins to greet, and the little girl, and the baby and half the damn' servants and the wretched dogs and cats – where, in heaven's name, was Lucy? His impatience boiled in him while he smiled and teased and complimented and disclaimed, and showed every inch of his pestiferous horse to the criminally insistent Ned.

'Then where is Lucy?' he asked at last, since no one would put him out of his misery.

'She is out in the sunken garden, reading I believe; she is out of sorts today. Your coming will cheer her, I know.'

Out of sorts; that scarcely boded well. But he must see her; at once. He must know if it were true that she had so utterly confounded him with loving her, or if it were simply some passing infatuation, a foolish dream that would pass in the serious light of day. He more than half hoped for this. He liked his life very well as it was.

The sunken garden was all tender buds and leaves, rose, carmine and blood-red with some metallic green. It was a suitable place for beginnings. The Quickenberry was in flagrant flower, deep creamy clusters with powdered gold hearts, lifted as if to sing to the sun. Lucy sat beneath it on a cushion. She was not reading but writing a letter. There were tears in her eyes.

However swiftly he might have ridden, Will thought with some irony, the ubiquitous Mr O'Connor was here before him. He cursed him and went forward to see her smile. 'Ah, the rainbow!' he approved as it appeared to order.

'Oh, Will! Where did you spring from? I was just—'

'Watering your letter. I'm sure it will grow the faster. I did not, however, come all this way to see you cry. I've seen it before and was not impressed. Please tell me, if you wish to, why you are doing it, and then finish with it.'

She wiped her eyes on her pen wiper and hastily folded the paper. 'There – now you have undoubtedly smudged it.'

'It doesn't matter. I want to rewrite it anyway. Sit down. It is *so* nice to see you. Are you alone, or is—'

'My handsome cousin with me? No, she is not.'

Lucy did not allow herself to betray pleasure. But the thought of Eliza had recalled their last meeting and she felt a little guilty. Her behaviour on that occasion had not, she knew, been very adult. She would not apologize, because she thought she had been right to be angry with Will; they were his friends; he ought to have told them of his intended marriage. Perhaps he would tell them now. She would be extra nice to him, to show that he was forgiven, since he had taken the trouble to visit them again.

'It is kind of you to tear yourself away from Westminster for our sake. Is there any further news of His Majesty?'

'No,' he said curtly. He had no intention of making conversation. He wanted to know what had made her weep. 'I have something I must say to you, Lucy,' he said seriously – for it *was* serious, he had no more doubt of that, now that he had seen her. He felt sick with love of her. 'But it is not a noon-time thing; I prefer to keep it for the dusk. Will you come here again, at eight o'clock? We have so often talked here.'

'You are very mysterious. But I will come.' She supposed he wanted to tell her then about abominable Eliza; certainly *she* was best viewed in the dusk, perhaps thought of, too.

'Good. Now tell me why you are bedewing your lap and looking wan.'

'Cathal is wounded,' she said steadily, looking across the garden. 'Not too badly. But his father has said,' she stopped and took breath, 'that he must stay at home now and fight no more. He is to settle down. And be married.'

'To Mistress Orla of the long knife, I presume?'

'To her, yes.'

Will sighed. The sight of her despondency filled him with pity, as if she had been his heartsick child rather than the only fulfilment of his growing desire. He touched her hair. On the heels of pity came irony. He had certainly chosen his moment! How would she find it, he wondered, to lose a lover and gain a suitor all in one day? He thought perhaps that he should not speak yet, but rejected this; he had waited long enough, and Lucy was already in a state of heightened emotion in which she might find it easier than otherwise to accept further stress. He knelt beside her, making his voice and his movements very gentle. 'It distresses me that you suffer. But I think you have known for some time that it must come to this.'

'No!' she said fiercely. 'I did not think he would give in so easily. I am still not certain – he says that if he is well enough, he will run away from his father's house and come to me.'

'Lucy.' He was weighted with pity. 'And what then? Will he take kindly to exile, however sweet?'

He had touched the wound that hurt the most of all. 'It would be a beginning. But oh, I can't see whether it will happen. I think I know, in my own heart, that it will not.' She looked up at him with the air of one who has discovered her own bravery and is surprised by it.

He thought that was enough progress for the present. She had made her beginning, though it was not the one of which she had spoken, nor that of which she had dreamed.

'I don't know what to say to him,' she said then, very low. 'I have written that he should resist, if that is still what he wishes – but he is so far away and has gone through so much; he may not feel as he used to do. And then, she, Orla, has been with him through the fighting and the telling of tales. She may be more to him than he will say to me.'

Better and better, thought Will, cursing himself for a callous hound. 'I cannot presume to advise you, my dearest girl, but I think your own fine instinct will lead you in the right direction. Now, love, dry your eyes and we will walk about and admire your mother's latest works. I must say, although I think your Quickenberry very attractive, it *is* the only thing in this sunken paradise to put forth green leaves, why so?'

'When my mother first saw it, at John Tradescant's house in Lambeth, it was autumn and the leaves were dark red; she never thought to ask if they were green when they budded. I like it here because it *is* different. It is so determinedly itself, an upstart among all these sophisticated shrubs. I like its insolence.'

'That is what Jud says about Freeborn John,' Will mused, 'with his upstart theories about every man being his own politician as well as his own priest. I must say, I do not think he will find such radical notions to get so deep a purchase in the soil of England as does your mother's tree.'

John Lilburne occupied them for a good half hour, and then it was Cromwell and the army's discontent. They avoided the subject of Ireland, where a despairing Ormonde had resigned his Lieutenancy to Parliament, unable any longer to juggle with Pope and Protestant. Ireland was Parliament's problem now, as well as Lucy's.

As always when they were together at Heron, Lucy marvelled at how easy was Will's company. Conversation flowed between them in a constantly renewed stream of knowledge, opinion and rhetoric, even as the music flowed, later, with its own statement of progress. She was glad of his presence, especially today. Perhaps this visit was proof that he might not be lost to her, despite Eliza. If he could have known these thoughts, Will would have felt considerably less trepidation than he did when eight o'clock came and he prepared to lay down his defences before her. He did not have a great deal of the futile sort of pride, but this would cost him dearly, whatever the outcome.

The garden lay under the warm, heavy shawl of the night air, its colours transmuted to a mystery of gules and grey. The rowan seemed more fragile, its flowers poised, dramatically white against the coming of the moon, as if for flight or even, stranger, speech.

Will had come out a few minutes before Lucy who was still at her music when he had left the house. He threw himself onto the stone seat and contemplated the weird beauty before him. Were these the last few moments of his personal freedom, or the last precious seconds of hope for his love? If it were the latter, it would at least be something deep that he could share with her. They would always be friends; he knew that. And that, of course, would be the most damnable thing of all, to find himself condemned to watch her life forever as her friend and not to let her see him bleed. He could curse the stars. She was coming. Soft you now—

'Will? I hardly saw you there. One can scarce make you out in your ruby and black.'

'Sombre colours for sombre deeds. Will you sit down? And now will you promise to sit quite still and listen to me, and try not to speak until I have done?'

She flounced a little. 'Oh, very well. But it seems hardly – very well!' So much ceremony for undeserving Eliza.

He stood. He needed to pace. 'Please don't think, when you hear what I have to say, that I am not burningly conscious of this morning's tears and respectful of their cause. I wish from the bottom of my heart that you might have been spared them.' He saw her white face, puzzled, as he turned to her, urgent with sincerity.

'I know I have chosen what may seem to you an irrelevant time – but I did not know of your present sorrow, and by Christ if I do not speak out now, and unburden myself of what I have come here to say, I think I will sink under the weight of it and not easily rise! Lucy – I think, truly I think that you cannot get Cathal O'Connor for your husband. And yet one day you must have a husband, unless you are to wither on your golden branch and all your beauty go to waste.'

She stared at him, denial in her eyes. He came to her and sat and took her hand. 'I don't ask that it be tomorrow, Lucy. But I do ask, my dear love, that it be me. Take me for your husband, for I love you as well as a man ever loved a woman.'

Her cry was almost of pain. She looked at him still and did not speak. He watched her eyes change, slowly, slowly; the pool responding to the dropping of the stone. Then she whispered, 'I don't believe it.'

He smiled on the rack of his tension. 'Surprise I will accept. Disbelief is a little discourteous, don't you think?'

It could not be one of his amusements; she could tell it was not. His whole body was in suspense, like a string that is plucked but not released. 'Then let us call it surprise,' she said almost inaudibly.

She raised her head, searching his face. Yes, it was true. 'You must give me a little time. My ears are far ahead of my understanding. I mean no discourtesy.'

He made a brief gesture of impatience. 'I know. I know.' Then, 'How much time – do you think you will need? I should like an answer. But I see that it cannot be immediate.'

She laughed. 'No.'

'I wish you would not look at me as though I had been transformed into some fabulous monster.'

'I am very sorry.' Her tongue, at least, began to revive somewhat. 'But, to me you see, you cannot be the man you were this morning. I will not call you a monster,' she finished softly.

'Then will you call me husband?' he said with swift mischief.

Lucy stood up; now it was she who needed to walk about. 'Great Heavens, I don't know what you expect of me! How can you set a mine beneath my life, then calmly sit and watch it explode, and give me no clue as to how to mend the sticky pieces?'

'A charming metaphor for the gift of my heart and fortune and the invitation to my bed!'

She thought she blushed. She had not yet considered *that*.

Watching her, he grinned satirically. 'Or did you imagine that by marriage I mean to set you on a pedestal in the garden and worship you occasionally?'

'I have not had the leisure to imagine *anything*,' she said quite sharply. 'But since you ask, no, I don't think that to be quite your style.'

He recalled that she had a very good idea of his style. Lucy remembered it, too. 'I thought,' she said bluntly, 'that you were to marry Eliza Hartley. Were you, perhaps, considering two *wives*, like a Turkish pasha?'

'I gather you have completely recovered from any small shock you may have sustained from my importunate proposal. No. Interesting though the idea may be, I was thinking of just the one. Of you. Jud has told me of your misapprehension about myself and Eliza. He sends his apologies, as he damn' well should!'

'But your cousin—' Lucy did not finish her sentence. 'I suppose we all took it for granted,' she said dolefully. Poor Eliza. What a chance she had taken. It seemed that she had lost. 'Do you not think you *ought* to marry her?' she found herself asking next. He deserved some discussion on this point; besides, it would give her more time to think. Not that it was easy, with Will standing there alternately grinning and frowning and confusing her.

'Why? Because she has been my mistress since she was sixteen?' he asked brutally. 'It was her choice as much as mine. I never promised marriage – no matter what she has told you,' he added shrewdly. A spark of joy lit him; he knew now why she had acted so strangely when she had visited him in London.

Whatever else she did or did not feel about him, Lucy had been jealous of Eliza. For once, Eliza had been right. That was enough for now. He would build upon it. He must not harry the ghost of Cathal O'Connor off the boards, but let him play his scene till the end. There was plenty of time for the hero.

But Lucy was now thinking to some purpose. Now that this improbable and still barely credible truth was beginning to settle in her, she felt herself to be an untidy battleground of emotions. She could formulate no idea, as yet, of what she felt about Will's offer of marriage; she hardly knew, any more, what she felt about *him*, so very unfamiliar did he appear to her in his new guise. This morning she had wept because she had been deeply hurt. But she had also been fiercely angry with Cathal. She had long since sensed the weakness in him that would lead him to take the facile course, to please those nearest at hand to be pleased.

However repeatedly he swore to her eternal love and iron fidelity, she knew that eventually he would marry Orla McDonagh, and that her own part of it was to release him with as good a grace as she could counterfeit. The more often he swore, the better she knew it. She was bitterly humiliated by her knowledge and her anger. She wanted to wound Cathal as she had been wounded. Perhaps she had wanted this for a long time; he had not been honest with her in these last months. Letters could lie so easily.

Worst of all was her inability to control her sheer aching lack of him. Her physical longing for him was an empty place in her belly; he veered from distrust to trust in an hour; she was confused, very unhappy, and comfort was too soft a way for her now.

It was a wayward and incomprehensible instinct that made her say to Will now, a little awkwardly, her lifted face a challenge, 'I can't, you must see, think coherently about marriage; let us leave that for now. But if you will again offer me the invitation to your bed, I will accept it. I would like you to make love to me. Now!'

'My dear girl!' Who now was stricken by shock?

'Well, what do you say? Will you take me, or do we sit and

think about it for an aeon or so?' She spoke quickly, pushing back the enormity of her suggestion.

'Gently, my bird. I'd not dream of refusing you.' His voice a purr. He did not know what was going on in her unpredictable and probably devious little mind, and he did not care. She was offering him a better chance to win her than she knew. She could keep her reasons. 'If you are still of the same mind in a few hours time,' he said silkily, 'you know where I sleep tonight.'

She nodded. He left her then, to save any late maiden blushes. He wondered again, more pertinently, if she *were* a maiden. Her forwardness suggested not, but he would not lay odds either way. Lucy was not like other women.

Anyhow, he would very soon know; and it did not trouble him at all. If she had known that particular happiness with her faithless Cathal, then he was glad of it for her sake. For his own sake, as he strolled away from her, he whistled like a bird.

Just before midnight, Lucy sat before her looking-glass and examined herself critically. She was pale, but that did not matter. She had put on a nightgown of fine white lawn. She hoped she did not look too much like a virgin sacrifice. Perhaps not, as the stuff was nearly transparent and was embroidered with little red apples, and would almost certainly put Will in mind of Eve and her fall.

She looked hard at her face, her hair, skin. She wanted to appear as beautiful as she could, and above all, she didn't want to think about what she was going to do. She forced her wavering mind towards the mirror. Should she put tiny plaits into her hair? Was her perfume too strong, or not strong enough? Were her feet clean?

'Lucy?' came a querulous murmur from the bed. 'What are you doing? Why don't you come to bed?'

'Go to sleep!' she told Julia sharply.

'Your candles are keeping me awake,' the child grumbled, but she turned over and humped into her pillow.

Lucy decided on the plaits and braided them carefully. She had to undo the first one because it was crooked and so a proof of nervousness. When she was ready she took Cathal's letter from her drawer and unfolded it. She read it calmly, once through. Then she folded it again and placed it back in the drawer with all the others.

Will was in the best guest chamber over the great hall. She trod quietly along the gallery and tapped softly on his door before entering.

He was sitting in a wide chair before the fire which was still vigorous. He wore an azure gown edged with sables. He looked, as was his aim, so relaxed, indeed so lazy, that Lucy lost some of her anxiety right away.

'Come here. Let me make you comfortable. The fire is so good. I have spiced and heated some wine; it is a delicious recipe from North America.' He offered her the cup, kneeling at her feet. 'How beautiful you are.' He touched her cheek and felt her tremble.

She drank gratefully. She took her time. When she had drained the cup she would not know what to do next.

He knew that to postpone matters would only increase her nervousness. He let her drink as much as was good for her and then took the cup from her and set it on the hearth. Still kneeling beside her, he took her hands and asked her to look at him. 'What I say now may make you angry. It shouldn't. I have only your interests at heart, or I would say nothing and would simply do as you have asked.'

She did look at him then, startled. She wished he would *not* talk; she would rather he kissed her; then she might stop this ridiculous shaking.

'God knows there is nothing, nothing in the whole wide world I would rather do than make love to you, Lucy, but I am not about to do so.'

'What?' To her horror her voice was an indignant squeak.

'So you may relax, and enjoy your wine, and my company, if you will.'

'You've changed your mind,' she accused, telling herself that this flood of warmth that was seeping into her was not relief but offence.

'I'm not even sure that I could answer that honestly. I want you, very much; and the prospect of taking you was a little too much to hold out as a test of character and endurance, even to a saint. And I am no saint, as you have observed. However, I have had time enough to consider the consequences of taking you at your word. First, and least, it would seem a churlish manner in which to repay the friendship and hospitality I have had in this house – from your father, God rest him, your mother, Tom, all of them. Had you thought of the distress such a thing would cause? To take your virginity – for I deduce from your demeanour that you still have it – under your father's roof!'

'Of course I still have it; what did you think?' Her tone was deep in umbrage.

He raised a single brow in that irritating way of his. 'So much offence? And yet you were eager to be rid of it only moments ago.'

'Sometimes I dislike you very much.'

'Ah. Yes, well, that was to be feared. We'll leave that aside for the present. Another point I would like to make is that, much as you may dislike me now, it is a thousand gold guineas to an old infantry boot that you would loathe and abhor the very sound of my name, in a week or two, if I were to deflower you now just to salve your pique at the loss of Mr O'Connor!'

'It is not pique! Oh, you are horrible! I wish I had never thought of it.'

'That is progress. Excellent.'

Lucy rose, doing her best to look dignified. 'No. Don't leave yet. There is one more thing—' He too was on his feet, his hand detaining her. She looked at him mutinously, a child again, and he was overwhelmed by the mixed desire to spank her thoroughly and to kiss her and make her his friend again.

'I wonder if you have at all considered *my* feelings in this,' he said as though it were a matter of no real consequence.

She had not, other than to assume that he would be a willing party to her suggestion.

'I have said that I love you. I would not, therefore, wish to harm you, and in this you ask me to aid you in doing harm to yourself. I cannot do that. I don't deny that I have committed the act of love many times and with many women; some I have loved; others not. Never have I asked any of them to be my wife.' He hesitated, watching her arrogant look turn to shame.

He came close to her and took her right hand in his. 'Lucy, I wanted to do you honour, not mischief. If the time should come when I take you to my bed, I want there to be love between us – or, if you find love not yet possible, at least respect.'

She met his eyes gravely, all trace of childishness erased from her. 'I am sorry. You make me ashamed. I did not think. I only wanted—' She stopped. What exactly had she wanted? She shook her head, unable now to tell him.

'To prove yourself a woman, and desirable, even if Cathal O'Connor is so brutish as to wed another in your place.' He spoke gently.

'Perhaps. I don't know. But it was something to do with you, with us, as well. You tried to give me something I could not take.

I think I just wanted to have *something* to give you in return. I do know that you honour me by asking me to be your wife. I *am* honoured by it. And now I feel that all I have done is to insult you. I would not for my soul have done that.' She stood helplessly, beginning to understand him but not knowing what to say for the best.

He pulled her to him and hugged her simply. 'Don't look so woebegone! You are forgiven. You will always be forgiven. You acted with your heart and not your head, but that's no bad thing. Here, take some more wine and don't stand there as though you expected execution.' She did as she was told, her mind a turmoil of embarrassment.

'There now, that's better. Now, kiss me once, to show that we may still be the friends we were.' His kiss was for the hurt child, not the woman, and something in her perversely wished it otherwise.

He let her go. 'There now – go along to your chamber and tomorrow we shall forget tonight and simply be as we were together – except that I have asked you for your hand, and ask you now to do *me* the honour of considering it very seriously. You may write to me when you have done so to your own final satisfaction.'

'I am surprised that you still want me, after this,' she said flatly.

'Don't be foolish. I shall always want you. In this one thing you will find me very consistent. Now, go. In the morning we will ride out together and pass a pleasant day, arguing about quite different matters. You need mention my offer to no one unless you wish to; never, should you decide against me. But you should know, I think, that Tom is willing for the match.'

She nodded, grateful for his casualness. 'I think,' she said solemnly, turning back before she left the room, 'that you are probably the very best friend I will ever have.'

His eyes blazed at her. 'Then see what a superb beginning we have made! You fill me with hope!' But his tone was light for her sake.

She stood in the doorway and gazed at him, splendid in his azure robe, and was newly astonished. This physical paragon, this adept and original mind, this repository of men's goodwill and wishes, this altogether incomparable man had declared his love for her; not for sumptuous Eliza, not for any high-born daughter of one of Warwick's friends, not for the toast of the royal court or the London soirées, but for Lucy Heron, an insignificant person of no particular address.

She grinned at him and shook her head in a sudden flash of recovery. 'I still do not believe it,' she said. 'Incredible, I insist.' She slipped round the door and he heard her pattering back along the gallery to her own cold bed.

Lucy kept her secret for most of the summer. Martha was the only one with whom she would have shared it, and she did not want to put it in a letter. Every morning when she woke up she thought wonderingly, 'Silken Will wants to marry me!' Sometimes it dismayed her; sometimes she found herself chuckling at the astounding idea of it. Either was a good deal better than her previous sick struggles against the dawn consciousness of Cathal's desertion.

For he had left her, just as surely as if he had told her so in all those beautifully worded letters that had sworn the opposite. She missed him as though he had been as much a part of her life in daily reality as he was in her steadfast mind. Perhaps she had been foolish to go on believing that it was the same for him, but she did not think so. She had only to remember. His words, his kisses, his quicksilver homing to her whenever they were apart for more than a minute. They had made their legend come alive and obey them, so successfully that they had thought they could go on writing their own story. But reality is stronger than legend. It feeds upon it, taking its strength for its own. Cathal's head and heart might be filled with his romance, but his reality was his father's wishes.

What, then, was Lucy's to be? Her own father would have rejoiced in Will's offer. Were Sir George alive today she would not be given the choice that Will himself was kind enough to give her. And Tom, of course, would feel the same. Oh, he would beat his brains as to whether it was an act of treachery to give her to a Parliament man, but he would come to some convenient arrangement with himself about that. Perhaps there would soon be a letter from him, ordering her to accept Will. He might simply take it for granted that she would do so, since she knew he had given his consent. That was nothing less than his right as her legal guardian. She became apprehensive every time the carrier was seen.

But it was not the carrier who justified her expectation. It was Tom himself.

They came home one day as casually as though they had ridden over to Stratton Hall for a night or two. Martha was blooming in a manner they had never seen before and was dressed, cap-a-pie in the latest London fashion. Tom himself seemed to be suffering from some sort of mild permanent embarrassment.

'You may as well know right away, Mother,' he blurted after the ecstatic greetings and unanswered questions. 'Martha and I were married in Paris. She is Lady Heron now.'

'I say!' said Humpty and whistled swoopingly, expressing sufficient shock for the entire household.

Martha stood looking at Mary, waiting for her judgement. Tom fiddled with the fastening of his coat. Mary looked from one to the other, her face giving nothing away, while everyone held their breath.

She sighed. Some enraged ancestor arose in her, crying that her son, a baronet, not long a grieving widower, had married, hastily and underhand, a commoner whose mother was burned as a witch, who had narrowly escaped the same fate and could come to it yet. She recalled Valora's cool, authoritative aristocracy and was filled with misgiving for the brave, pale face lifted for her word. And yet it had been Valora, with her fine carelessness for the lesser proprieties, who had been responsible for the growing acceptance of Martha as a part of the family. But to take her place! Surely the thing was impossible.

But then, impossible or not, the thing was done; they were married and were waiting for her blessing. She pushed down the carping, archaic voices of sieges of Herons and legions of Laceys and came forward to kiss Martha's brow. 'My dearest child, I never would have credited him with so much good sense! Welcome home, Lady Heron.'

Martha smiled and read her victory in her eyes and was thankful for it for Tom's sake. 'It will be a little strange, at first,' she said calmly, 'but if you will help me, I am sure all will be well.'

Lucy came next to be hugged. 'This is wonderful! I am so happy for you. Tom, you wretch, you are the luckiest man in the kingdom.' His smile was repressive of such public transports, but only a little.

The twins were staring at him as though they found in him a novel specimen for their latest collection of nature's more eccentric works. 'Would you ever think it?' whispered Kit under cover of the dispersal of the welcoming party. '*Him* – married twice! Makes you think!'

Humpty shuddered elegantly. 'Rather him than me!'

'Why, don't you like Martha? She's all right. She won't bother to fight him like Valora did. They'll rub along well.' Kit was developing a certain psychological insight.

'Dash it, yes. Martha's fine. But marriage! I'd rather be hung!'
Kit thought it was a good thing Isabella couldn't hear him. She
had been looking quite pleased with herself lately.

'Speaking of marriages,' Tom said to Lucy as they assembled
in the parlour to hear how the world ran beyond the bounds of
Gloucestershire, 'you and I must very soon talk together on the
subject.' She nodded swiftly. At least he was not going to bring
it up in public.

She had a momentary doubt of this when he turned first to her
again when they had all taken their seats. 'Well, Lucy, you'll be
glad to know you have got your way,' he began cheerfully, looking
round to catch the interest of the circle.

'How is that?'

Tom laughed, startling them all. 'It is confounded hard to
believe, but Will Staunton has not only managed to compound
for Heron, but he got compensation from Parliament for taking
too much for it in the first place! The average amount paid to
compound is two or three times the annual value of the estate;
they took ten from Will originally, so he has made them give him
back five! Strike me dead if I know how he does it; he must have
the most persuasive tongue since the serpent!'

And yet, he did not use such persuasion to me, Lucy thought.

'So now I owe him very little, when all is computed – and Heron
is ours again.' A roar went up that Sir George must have relished
could he hear it.

But Tom had not finished. 'You were right to ask it, Lucy, and
I was a thoughtless lackwit to treat you as I did. I hope you'll
forgive me, now that I am more myself again.' That he could say
so, to all of them, said more for Martha's healing powers than all
her hundreds of agues cured.

After that, they wanted to hear how the two had spent their
time on the Continent. Although there had been some private
happiness in it, in general it was a tale of frustration and endless
waiting about in presence chambers, as Tom tried to enlist the
support of Europe's monarchs for their beleaguered brother of
England. Martha had stayed in their modest lodgings at The
Hague while Tom had gone begging in Denmark without success,
and they had left Holland with Rupert when he joined Queen
Henrietta Maria's court at Saint-Germain. They had found the
Queen haggard and ill and in constant conflict with Prince
Charles, now sixteen and very conscious of his young manhood.
His mother treated him like an obstreperous child. The atmo-
sphere was hardly improved by the advent of Rupert, since Her

Majesty's chief friends and advisors were the nine-lived Digby and Lord Henry Jermyn, another cast much in the same mould.

It was partly the quarrelling that had decided Tom to come home for a time. But only partly; he had returned, between Martha's gentle prompting and Will's coldly uncompromising letters, to some sense of his responsibility to his father's memory and his father's house. He had come out of the long sleep of his sorrow and found much in himself to make him ashamed. He wanted to begin to erase the results of his neglect.

He was daily amazed at the fact of his second marriage. He had never intended it and was hardly sure how it had come about. He was aware that Martha had given and given of herself without reserve, and that, as yet, he had been able to give her little in return except the shelter of his name and the doubtful offering of his increasing physical need for her. He had always wanted her body.

He was beginning to recognize himself as a man of deep sensuality. He had never suspected it before Valora, and had been certain, when she died, that his lust had died with her. He was surprised, and at first even disgusted, to find himself unable to live in Martha's constant company without taking her. She had come to him willingly and joyously and he had at first felt himself to be little better than a satyr, satisfying his body at the expense of both their spirits. But Martha, to his wonder, seemed to thrive on the situation. If she was troubled by conscience, she never let him know of it. He began to envy her this clear, unguarded passion of hers and to dislike himself more and more for his own muddied and unworthy motives.

One morning he woke up and decided to marry her. He had no idea what had prompted him, indeed, he suspected that perhaps there was more of the witch in her than even she was aware of. After that, to his immense relief, he was a great deal lighter in mind and heart. He could not yet say with honesty that he loved her as he had loved Valora. Nor did he wish to. But there was more than lust and more than mere liking in his feeling for her. In that, they had made a better beginning than many another mismatched couple.

Upon enquiry, Tom found the family already in receipt of the terrible news from London. Cromwell had left Parliament and had thrown in his lot with the army. They had captured the imprisoned King and had advanced on the capital, calling for the expulsion of Holles and his friends from the Commons, followed by a dissolution and new elections. The death of the Earl of Essex, in addition, had deprived the Presbyterians of their most popular figurehead and England of a moderate man who loved the King.

'We could stay in London no longer,' Tom regretted in disgust. 'It is a madhouse. The apprentices are on the streets just as they were in '41, mobbing for Parliament or against Parliament as the damned stupid mood takes them! The New Model has camped at Putney, more than 20,000 strong. Holles and his crew have fled the House and are trying to raise the militia. His Majesty is locked up in his own palace of Hampton Court and Fairfax and Cromwell rule England, for all the evidence to the contrary. All Independent MPs have joined the Army at Putney and the whole rat-trap are engaged in turning out their notion of law and order. I tell you, the country is in a greater turmoil now than it was when King Charles was still at St James'. God help us all if His Majesty should be restored to us on Oliver Cromwell's terms.'

'What other terms are open to him, if he is their prisoner?' asked Lucy, who had received glowing reports of Cromwell's Constitution from Jud, and more cautious approval from Will. The King was well treated and Old Ironside was engaged in enthusiastic negotiations towards a settlement that would permit of his release; too enthusiastic, it was thought, for the approval of the men under his command, who now referred to himself and Fairfax as the 'Grandees' and were mortified when their lady wives were received by the King in his luxurious prison.

'He still has hopes of the Scots, who will most likely come to the rescue of the Covenant and His Majesty with it. That is what we shall work towards, among other things. We take great heart from the quarrels of his enemies. There is now real hope of help from Louis of France. The Irish Catholics will always be loyal, and we are all still eager to fight who have fought for him already.'

Lucy bit her lip. There was something old and tired about these endlessly repeated hopes and loyalties. Instead of responding she asked abruptly, knowing the reply she would get but determined to speak the name aloud, 'Did you see anything of Jud while you were in London? He does very well these days.'

Tom froze at once into his old hauteur. 'No indeed, why should you think so?' he asked arctically, looking down his nose at her. He continued to posit the King's hopes and fears as if the question had never been asked.

Lucy, preparing another broadside, caught a warning look from Martha. Regretfully she abandoned her course, glowering at her brother. Tom, she thought wearily, no matter how many, men or women, sacrificed themselves for him, would never change. His total selfishness was as much a part of him as his irritability and his damned uncomfortable tension.

It was in a mutinous mood that she met him later that evening for the discussion he had promised her. He had bidden her into Sir George's study as if, she thought resentfully, she were a child to be punished.

He stood looking at her with his brooding stare. He surprised her. 'You look well, Lucy. Very well. You have grown even more handsome.'

She thanked him warily.

'I can see why Staunton finds you so attractive, though he tells me,' he said, smiling, 'that it is chiefly your nature that appeals to him.' She had no reply to that.

Tom took an awkward turn about the room. He looked out of the window in an uninterested way, then came back to her. 'Look her, Lucy, what do *you* think of this marriage?'

'Does that genuinely concern you?'

'It does. As it should. I need hardly say that I would be happy to see you wed to Staunton, not simply because we as a family owe him more than wealth can ever repay, but because he is a fine man and a man whom Father would have wished for you. I say this most confidently, despite Will's political stance. Indeed I think, were Father alive, he would have taken pleasure in debating, across the Commons, with his own son-in-law.' They both smiled at the thought.

'But what I want most to say to you is this – you must make up your own mind about this. You have deserved at least that of me. I know how much you have done here at Heron, and I'm deuced grateful. I won't press you into this, or any other marriage if you do not wish it. Take Will only if you want him.'

'I'm glad to hear that, of course,' Lucy murmured, relief and amazement tumbling in her stomach. 'I hadn't hoped for so much freedom. Will it inconvenience you if I take a little further time to consider? I have thought a great deal about it, naturally, but I am not yet arrived at a conclusion.'

'That is as you wish. But don't leave the poor fellow to languish too long. I believe he loves you truly.'

'I will not. I promise.' She could not imagine Will *languishing*.

'And I thank you for your generosity. Without such freedom I think it would be even more difficult to assess my own feelings.

If you had ordered me to marry, I should have done so, if I had done so at all, with an unwilling spirit.'

Tom looked at her with open affection. 'Don't you think I know that? We are all stubborn and self-willed, we Herons, and you most of all.' She grinned acknowledgment. They were closer in that moment than they had ever come before.

And now she would be able to confide in Martha as she had used to do. Martha, who was married herself now, and would be even better qualified to help her to unravel her tangle of emotions and motives than she had been during the first precious, hesitant days of Cathal. She looked forward to talking to her about it. It would, she was sure, do her enormous good.

But Martha when approached, would, to Lucy's consternation, say nothing. Like her husband she left every consideration up to Lucy. 'Now don't frown and feel hurt. I am simply being sensible. How can I tell you anything that will help you? You know in your own mind what kind of man you think Will Staunton to be. My opinion of him, be it golden and bejewelled, can never alter your own by so much as a pin. What you should do is spend some time by yourself – as long as you need, as often as you need – and just allow your decision to grow in you naturally, as plants search towards the light.'

So, with these wise words in her mind, Lucy came one early autumn afternoon to her old private place in the middle of the wood. She had gone there rarely in the past few years, preferring the instant solace of the Quickenberry. Perhaps, she thought now, she had been saving the solemn, cathedral peace of the place for such a serious contemplation as this must be.

The trees welcomed her, giving her back her childhood. She had spent so many days, in all the seasons, under their interwoven roof, aloft in their ancient branches, lying on her back on the soft carpet beneath. She had dreamed and planned and been herself here, read and wept and prayed. It had always been her refuge.

England had been a forest once and it was here that her roots went down deepest, among the bold oaks and the slender birches, the stately beeches and the sturdy sycamores. Nothing changed here.

Lucy walked slowly, her head full of Will Staunton. When she passed near the place where she had found him with Eliza she was pleased to find that her only reaction was laughter. 'I have committed the act of love many times and with many women – but never have I asked one to be my wife.' She recalled his face when he had been committing the specific act to which she was a fascinated witness; he had been like a cheerful boy on a hobby horse, all smiles because he was doing exactly as he pleased.

But it was no use to her now to remember that facet of him. It was the whole, adult man who asked for her mind and body and hoped, with a humility she had not expected in him, for her heart. He deserved better than her, she knew. At least, to be fair to herself, she was a step higher than Eliza, in honesty if not in beauty.

She was ashamed of herself for the frivolous notion. She had come here to make up her mind and she must do it. The thing to do was to ask herself the questions that Martha would not. That way she might separate the tangle of emotion and duty and find some clear strand to follow. Very well then, did she *love* Will? No, she loved Cathal O'Connor. Did she not love him at all, in any way? Well yes; it had not felt right to deny that completely. She did have a very great affection for him. Nothing more than that? What was this affection like? Did it compare, say, to the feeling she had for Jud, or for Ralph Stratton? No. It was different. How different? It is very hard to find words for it. He is Silken Will. He is different from anyone else.

She sat down on a fallen branch. She was not doing very well. At the back of her mind, something nudged her vaunted honesty. When you saw him, here in the wood, with Eliza Hartley, you were jealous, were you not? She was right? Yes, I suppose so; but so long ago, I was a child. And later, when you found her on the *Gallant Lady*? I did not want her there, no. And when you heard they were to marry, what did you feel then? The questioning part of her began to crow; she wondered if this other, severe self were truly her friend. When I thought they were to marry, I – yes, Goddammit, all right, I was jealous. Jealous as a cat. So what now? Nothing. Only, don't you find that interesting; since you feel that Will is no more to you than a friend? He *is* more. I didn't say— What? Oh, God's wounds, I don't know. Leave me alone!

She left her log and ran off through the trees, breathless with laughter and failure. If only Will could have heard her idiotic dialogue with herself, how he would have roared! Sometime, she would tell him about it.

And *that* was the half-careless thought that began to turn her mind; it was born of the instinct that said she would always be able to share even her most ridiculous notions with Will and know that, although he might laugh, he would always treat them kindly, and that when she was more serious, then so would he be. She had spoken the truth when she had said he was the best friend that she had. And she liked him, now that there were no barriers between them, better than anyone she had ever known outside the family. And if she could not have Cathal – she thrust back the wave of weak self-pity that had no place in this inquisition – then, since he wanted her, knowing of her misplaced love, why not take her friend? Would it be fair to Will, even given his knowledge? He seemed to think so. And beyond all this, did she really want to be married? She had certainly become used to the idea of marriage with Cathal – although never, *never* to that of Ireland – and it was beyond doubt that she needed a change in her life. She was tired of following the calendar through the fields of Heron. Nothing happening; nothing changing. She would welcome some event in her days. Since simply to be in Will's unpredictable company constituted an event in itself, she might expect a stimulating time if they married.

And what, she asked herself delicately, about that invitation that she had lately sought so crudely? How did she feel about occupying Silken Will's bed? Her body, weary of the mind's monopoly of honesty, here put in its bid. You remember his kisses? You liked them a lot better than you wished to know. You will not like them any the less now. Kisses, yes, but were they enough to take her further, far enough? She stopped walking suddenly. She was losing her bearings. She had not intended to come so far. It was time to go back. You have not arrived at a decision. Not today. I need longer. I will put it out of my mind for a little longer. But I shall know very soon now.

She was a little shaken by what she had already discovered. Since she had walked so far, she would circle back through the village and collect Martha, who had gone down to her beloved cottage again, to pick herbs and tidy what was already tidy. She could pick some camomile to rinse her hair. To Mary's chagrin, her daughter-in-law had always been able to raise it better than she could at Heron.

Martha was on her knees in the flowerbed, planting the jonquils to which she feared she showed an undue favouritism, when a shadow fell across her work. She turned, trowel in hand, ready to welcome Tom or Lucy or one of her old neighbours.

When she saw who it was that stood between her and the sun, her fingers, clutching the trowel, became nerveless so that she nearly dropped it, then tightened upon it as though it were a weapon of which she might soon have need.

'I was drawn here. By memory. That is all. I had no hope to

find you. It is a cup filled for me by the Lord.' His voice came to her as though out of a sepulchre, hushed and rusted with the history between them, and with a dreadful joy at his good fortune.

'I wish that you would not come here, Nehemiah.' Her words in her own ears were too small, too inefficient. He terrified her. When had she ever been able to persuade him of anything, save only once? 'I do not think you ought to come.'

'Don't say that, Martha. It is not worthy in you. I praise and thank God that he has directed me to you. I had looked for you, but they told me you live at Heronscourt now.'

'Yes.' Had they told him no more than that? Perhaps they, too, were afraid of him.

'I do not stay in the district long. I have been here only half a day. There are some matters of business to put in order at my house. Then I go back to London in two days. Will you come with me? Will you be my wife at last, and make the angels sing for one right action between sinners?'

So she was not to be spared. 'I am sorry someone has not told you.' she said unsteadily, forcing herself to meet the soft, lugubrious eyes, warm with hope. 'I am married now. To Sir Thomas Heron.' She bowed her head as though as axe might fall.

'What blasphemy is this?'

She thought he was about to hit her, for he took a step forward and stood above her, his hand raised in judgement. 'No blasphemy. We were married by a minister of the English Church.'

There was nothing else to say. Even this seemed too much to give him. She did not want even the edges of his knowledge to touch her life, even the least personal of words to pass between them. At that moment, so protective did she feel of what she had built out of the ruin of her self, that were he a blind man she would not have read to him a verse of the Bible.

Nothing must make her capable of summoning back the hours she had spent as his prisoner; she could not and would not allow them to penetrate her consciousness. She had developed a new control over the workings of her mind since her marriage. There were no more 'seeings'. Free from that terrible visitant, she would accept no others.

'Please leave my house,' she said, far more strongly.

He did not look as though he were capable of movement. He stood like the angel of death on an old tombstone and looked and looked at her. She turned her head away. If she ceased to acknowledge his presence perhaps he would go.

Minutes, she thought, elapsed. The whole of his nature pressed in upon her, stifling her. She turned back, an entreaty forming on her lips.

His face was ribboned with tears; the warm brown eyes welled silently like those of a foal she had once tended, with its leg broken. She could do nothing for it and it had been shot. Christ in heaven! She choked with a sudden access of rage. Was she so perverted, or he so presumptuous as to suppose she might pity him? That he brought her his tears and came dragging his wretched, monstrous, mistaken passion to her feet again? Had he no conception of the evil thing he had become? Not see, feel, sense through every pore of his body the repulsion he caused in her?

'It *is* blasphemy,' he whispered at last. 'You know it in your heart. You are my wife. In the eyes of God you are mine, even though you are married to another.' His voice broke. 'Blessed Jesus, married to Tom Heron! How could that come to pass? I can scarcely comprehend it, though I must believe it, since you tell me. Oh, Martha, what have you done? Why have you perjured your living soul? Why did you not wait and pray and purify yourself, as I have done? The Lord has forgiven us our sin together – but He will not suffer this unclean coupling!'

He reached down and pulled her to her feet. He held her by the arms, shaking her in his urgency, hurting her with his rigid grip. She gasped, knowing she was about to break. She wanted to scream, to rip herself apart with screaming, but who would hear? And if they did, did she want anyone, anyone at all, to see her at the mercy of this moment?

She quietened, inside herself, and stood limply between his hands. She would vomit soon if he did not let go of her flesh. As she pulled back from him she heard a step on the path. It was Lucy, oh thanks be to God, it was Lucy.

She all but fainted with relief as his hands dropped from her and could almost have laughed as she heard Lucy cry out, 'What are *you* doing here?' in a voice filled with loathing. Nehemiah turned wearily, only half recognizing another presence.

'Murderer!' Lucy said, without knowing that she would say it. He still looked only at Martha, scarcely appearing to hear her.

Martha moved towards Lucy. 'Martha – ?' he appealed, his arms held out to her.

With a movement that, for her, was very violent, Martha turned her back upon him. Nehemiah sighed heavily, then brushed past Lucy and went, sightless and suffering, out of the garden.

That evening Lucy let bedlam loose at home. Although Martha had begged her not to tell Tom of Nehemiah's visit, even going so far as to hint at a reason beyond those already known to the family, she enjoyed no success. Lucy had firmly ignored her. It was, she said, her duty to tell her brother that his wife was being harried by her previous tormentor.

'A few bleak words, scarcely a harrying,' Martha had suggested tiredly.

'How dare he? How dare he speak to you? To any of us?' Lucy shook with passion.

'It is because you have not seen him since . . . I thought you had accepted Nehemiah's existence again, after his election.'

'I shall never accept it,' Lucy said bitterly.

She still adhered, as did the twins, to their early vow towards the Puritan's destruction. They no longer spoke of it; but it was there, all the same. To her dark satisfaction, Tom, when she told him, proved to be of exactly the same mind. This surprised her at first. She had not expected such committed hatred in Tom. But it was all to the good.

Musing upon her guardian's developing character, she went to find the boys and report this cheerful turn of events to them. As expected, they were delighted, and nothing would do but that they should abandon the foil practice in which they were engaged and seek out Tom to congratulate him in person.

They found him in the hall, already booted and spurred, his pistols in his belt. Martha was standing in front of the door, her face an unrecognizable mask of cold anger. She spoke to her husband with a disdain they had never heard from her and she did not care that they listened. 'I have said and said until I am worn with speaking! It is over. All over long ago. No action you could take now can undo what is past and prayed for. You cannot bring Dominic back to life. You cannot alter what was done to me. If you kill him, you too become a murderer. And I will live with no murderer, I make it plain. Tom, if you leave this house for that purpose, you leave me. I shall not be here when you return.' She left the hall without a glance for any of them and they heard her go quickly upstairs.

'Never fear,' said Humpty, bright-eyed, when she was well out of earshot. 'we don't have to speak of it until the time comes – but it will come. We *shall* kill him, one day . . .'

One day, one day; it was their constant refrain. Lucy felt cheated. It should have been today. She sensed that, although she did not know exactly why it should have been.

Tom leaned, defeated, against the door, Tibbett's carbine digging uncomfortably into his back. 'I wish you joy of the attempt,' he said unhappily. Then he pushed himself upright as though he were tired to death and slowly followed his wife upstairs.

Lucy shrugged dispiritedly at the twins and went off to relieve her feelings at the keyboard. She thought about Will, and how excellently they made music together. It made her feel better. She would write to him in a few days.

At the end of the summer Will received Lucy's letter. It contained exhaustive paragraphs of news, entertainment and gossip and covered seven closely written pages before finishing laconically, 'We celebrated old Lady Stratton's eighty-sixth birthday last week. It cannot be expected that she will enjoy many more such occasions. It seems, therefore, but common humanity to please her in small matters while we may. So by all means let us marry, my dear Will, as soon as may be convenient to you. I should hate to think of the redoubtable beldame missing the wedding, for if you remember, the marriage was *her* fancy in the first place. Let us earnestly hope her judgement is at least as strong as her language.'

Lucy had felt light-hearted and mischievous when she wrote this, a great burden having floated off her mind when she had come to her decision. It was not until Will replied, in matchingly casual mood, telling her that he had also written to her mother and suggesting mid-December as the wedding date, that she began to appreciate the reality of what she had done.

She moved about the house slowly and aimlessly for the next hour, feeling as though she were wrapped in layers of unwoven flax, numbed to the world. She needed other people's reactions to restore her to normally sensitive existence. She would have thought she should be used to the idea of her marriage by now, but it appeared otherwise. She was glad when her mother, having read her own letter, sought her out and released her from her limbo.

'My dearest child!' Mary's smile was a benediction as she clasped Lucy and kissed her. 'It is what your father had set his heart upon, and I rejoice that his wishes, as well as my own and your brother's should be so happily realized.' She kissed her daughter again to indicate the end of the more formal part of the proceedings, then settled herself upon Lucy's bed for a feminine tête-à-tête.

'The wedding comes post-haste upon the asking, but nothing's the worse for that. What need to wait when you have known each other for so many years? Although the gardens, of course,' she added wistfully, 'would have looked so well for a spring ceremony. However, I daresay we shall manage something by way of decoration. You will marry from Heron, I suppose, and not London?'

'Of course! Great heavens, I don't want to leave before I must!'

'Excellent. This has made me so happy, Lucy. Especially since Tom has acted so oddly in marrying twice away from home. It was hardly his fault, of course, but . . .' Her voice trailed, discouraged. The heir of Heron owed his tenants a wedding feast.

Lucy now thought guiltily of Jud. She had dreamed of asking him to bring Cleo and little Edmund up for the wedding, had visions of Tom clasping them all to his bosom, everything forgiven, in the universal joy of the occasion. The rational part of her simply sniggered at such naivety. And in any case, even supposing such a fairy tale were to come true, how could she face her mother, who had already weathered a witch in the family, with the prospect of a couple who had brought forth a child out of wedlock? The law's penalty for such an offence was to be whipped through the town, naked to the waist, then set in the stocks for all to view the shame of it. Although rarely exacted in loose-living London, it was only six months since such a punishment had taken place in a village near Abingdon, at the insistence of the Puritan parson. An unhappy young mother had been forced to exhibit her milk-swollen breasts to the greedy eyes of her neighbours while her unfortunate lover sat beside her, hands and legs as fast as her own, while the men licked their lips and the women shouted filthy insults.

It was not that this could happen at Heron, but it would be in the minds of many, should Jud's domestic arrangements become public. Mary, who had gone into a private study of how she would make the best use of the December garden in the chapel, came out of it to remark more dreamily than she had intended, 'There are many women who will envy you such a man as Will Staunton.' She tried strenuously not to be one of them.

Lucy thought at once of Eliza Hartley. She frowned. 'I only hope that he will not be – ' she searched for words – 'too *much* for me, if you know what I mean. I am young still, in some ways.'

'Not if you keep your wits about you. You have your own strength, plenty of it, young though you are. Never doubt it. But tell me, Lucy, all this appears so very sudden. Indeed I thought it forgotten long ago. How long have you known of Will's thoughts towards you?'

'Only since his last visit. But I do not think it *was* a sudden thing with Will. Had I been wiser, and less – preoccupied – there were, I believe, signs for me to read.'

Mary wisely did not enquire into her daughter's 'preoccupation'. She had long suspected Lucy's affections to have been sadly misplaced. The young Irishman could have charmed the birds from the trees, she would be the first to admit it, but no match could ever have come from it. Lucy must have known this. Or, if she had wished to deceive herself a little, that was now all in the past and, since Mary had not seen fit to intrude upon her then, she would not mention it at any other time.

'He'll be hard to hold, your Will,' she said thoughtfully. 'You will soon grow *wiser*, in learning to cope with him.'

'He seems to hold me in deep affection,' said Lucy rather primly.

'Well, that is all to the good. And I know you are fond of him. You are lucky, child. It is not every couple who begin in such high regard for each other.'

For a second Lucy longed to fall at Mary's knee and cry out that she loved Cathal and that this was all wrong; she had not intended to go so far. But she recovered instantly from the moment of panic, recognizing it for what it was. 'I have wanted to ask you,' she said shyly, shifting attention from herself to her mother, 'how you felt when you first met Sir George. Did you feel affection for each other? Was the match to your liking?'

Mary laughed softly, her face informed by memory. 'How did I feel? I was terrified! I was fifteen, green and half asleep. He was more than twice my age, with more than ten times my vitality, and as handsome as the Duke of Buckingham. He was my father's companion and I never could imagine that he would be mine. I expected him to think me a poor thing, but if he did he never showed it. He soon taught me not to fear him, and affection – well, it came soon enough. I have been happy in my marriage. And blessed in my children.'

Lucy kissed her, quickly, while the smile still warmed her lips, but what memory has begun, it must finish, and tears followed. 'God damn the war,' said Mary bleakly, wiping them away.

'Come along,' suggested Lucy gently. 'Let us go and give our news to the rest of Heron. It is my opinion that they will all approve.'

And so they all did. For the next few days Lucy went about

with compliments falling around her ears like a soft shower of sweetmeats. She was hugged and squeezed and thumped until she felt like the battered pillow of an insomniac. She began to think she must have made a very wise decision indeed.

Time passed and there were no sudden fears or floods of regret. She used her time to try to think constructively about her new life. She tried not to think how much she would miss Heron when she had to live in London. There would be plenty of novelty and excitement to occupy her. She would be the mistress of that grand mansion in the Strand and it would be her challenge and her pleasure to make good work of that.

Then there was Will's mother to consider. He had described her as a formidable woman, and Lucy hoped that she herself would not appear too insubstantial in character when presented as her good-daughter. In order to prepare her way in this relationship, she wrote to Mistress Staunton, sketching herself and her family and pronouncing herself happy to become Will's wife. She finished with a cordial invitation to Heron.

Her reply came swiftly. Mistress Staunton would not visit before the wedding, but would certainly travel for that occasion. She wished her good-daughter every possible joy in the future and advised her that Will could only be governed by totally invisible reins. 'He is often impulsive, but he is not, thank God, a fool. Neither, I learn from your perceptive letter, are you; this is perhaps the most favourable augury one might expect in a foolish world. God bless you, my dear. I look forward to our meeting.'

Lucy was encouraged by this letter. She knew that Will attributed a great deal of his own strength to this coolly outspoken woman and had felt that same strength to be offered to her if she would take it.

She began, imperceptibly to herself, to look forward to her wedding. As soon as the date was confirmed for December 15th, she wrote to Jud. 'I would dearly love you to bring Cleo and the baby with you. It is hard to believe that anyone would try the spirit of so cheerful an event by disputing their right to be present. However, in such delicate matters I hold *festina lente* to be a good maxim. I will be able to do far more to bring our family back to healthy wholeness when I am living in London. I know you will come for my sake, though you must come alone. Do not consider Tom; his own weddings have both been so irregular as to keep him very quiet upon the conduct of mine.'

This was not strictly true. When she told him that Jud would be present, Tom had exhibited his usual explosive reaction. 'My dear Lucy! I am surprised at your want of tact. And of duty! I have said I do not want him in the house. I have not changed.'

'And *I'm* amazed at such mutton-headed stubbornness! You have your own happiness. I should have thought you could afford to be less selfish. The war is well over. Why should you deny your brother his rights in his own family when the rest of us would not?'

'He forfeited those rights long ago.'

'Oh stuff! How can you say so, with any sort of logic, when you are so glad to give me away to one of Cromwell's persuasion?'

'Will never worked against his King. He joined the Parliament because he honestly – if misguidedly – considered their victory the only road to lasting peace.'

'You dissemble nicely to suit your own convenience. Will and Jud are of the same party and there's no denying it!' She softened her voice. 'Only talk with him, that is all I ask. You may well find that what you can accept in your friend you can also be kind enough to accept in your brother!'

'Damn your insolence, Lucy! I'm sick of your preaching. I have spoken for the last time on this. If you are determined to go your own way, then you must suffer the consequences!' He stamped away from her, very much on his dignity.

Lucy cursed after him. She might as well save her breath. Tom would never change. She wondered at that moment just what it could be that Martha found to love in him. Ah well, if he and Jud came to daggers drawn over her nuptial roast beef, so much the worse; it would be an added entertainment for the guests. Meanwhile there were a thousand better things to occupy her mind and time. Together with every other woman in the household she threw herself into an orgy of planning and preparation of which she set out to enjoy every minute.

Her wedding would be the greatest occasion the county had seen since before the war. Everyone would be invited, gentle and simple, bar the most Puritanical of Independents. The food and drink must be enough in quantity to serve a small army, and in quality to please the most particular of potentates.

Everything would be done as her father would have seen it done. She wanted his generous spirit to be remembered by each one present. They would dig up the family jewels and plate, and damn the expense! The only element over which they would have no control, in braving deep December, was the weather. Mary so far forgot herself as to ask Martha if she didn't know just a small, harmless spell to fit the occasion. Martha suggested demurely that they should pray.

The concerted prayers of the entire household and most of the village had no success during the week before the wedding. Guests arrived by the coachload throughout blustering days of storms and sulking sunshine, soon filling the house to overflowing with their servants, dogs, gifts and wedding finery. Most of the servants had to seek beds out in the barns and store houses.

'Thanks be to God', cried Mary as they juggled with square inches, social precedence and ruffled tempers, 'that we are *not* to be honoured by His Grace of Warwick!' The noble earl had been somewhat confounded by the marriage and had complained bitterly to Will of being bombarded by the great cannon of Eliza Hartley's tongue. He had, however, sent a splendid dinner service for fifty, gilded and stamped with the bear and ragged staff of his own crest. Eliza, though naturally invited, did not accept.

Squadrons of Herons, Laceys, Riches and Stauntons did. Beds were borrowed, or even brought by their owners; the inn was commandeered and so was Stratton Hall; several gentle families found themselves playing peasant in the village cottages. Martha's held several maiden Lacey aunts. There were children and dogs everywhere and cooking was almost a twenty-four-hour occupation.

First to arrive had been Lucy's sister Jane and her husband James Drew from Oxford. They had come in a hired coach packed with Jane's delicious preserves and pastries and heaped with James's precious books which he would not leave to the curiosity of the County Committee, who were apt to disapprove of some of the jollier Roman authors. Jane was as serene and practical as ever, her neat and homely person reminding Lucy of a contented female robin; round, compact and busy-eyed, she added her invaluable contribution to what was by now becoming rather an hysterical campaign, little by soothing little, until, quite unremarked by any of them, she had become its very efficient Commander-in-Chief.

Both she and James (when his head was not in a book) treated the family as though they had met only last week rather than having been parted, by the war and a mere fifty miles of countryside, for over six years. They had not seen the strapping amalgam of mischief and determination that was Ned since he was a babe-in-arms, nor Julia since she was in leading reins. Lucy and the twins were pronounced to be exactly the same as when last seen, though the one masqueraded under a well-tailored garment of maturity and the others disguised their grace- less natures with charm and muscle.

Jane said nothing about Tom, though her greeting of Martha was warm. She had been the only one to get on well with him, when she was at home, and now she sought him out again, fitting into her old habits as a bird rounds out last year's nest.

'Try to get him to see reason about Jud,' Lucy pleaded with her. 'I have begged him, and Martha has begged him, but he will not listen to either of us. He always used to say you had more sense than all the rest of us put together. Perhaps he will still think so and your advice will be the last card to topple this ridiculous edifice that he has built up against poor Jud.'

'I don't think I would be of any assistance to you, Lucy. I am sorry.'

'Oh? Why is that?'

Jane regarded her gravely. 'It seems to me that Tom is the only one who *does* see reason in that direction. You forget, Lucy, I have lived in Oxford all this time. We are apt to be a little *unreasonable*, if you would see it so, in our absolute loyalty to the King who shared his days and his sorrows with us.'

'Oh God, I'm not going to have the argument all over again. I haven't the time!' Lucy told her sister, and fled to her room where she found Alice Jouncey waiting with a mouthful of pins, as was her custom upon all great occasions, to torture her into her wedding gown. Margery Kitchen was with her and they were engaged in serious discussion.

'I don't see why you 'ad to *tell* 'im. You could as easy 'ave said as you weren't willin',' Margery was saying perplexedly.

It was plain that they were speaking of Alice's second child, due in some six weeks' time. It was certainly not of John Coachman's getting *this* time, though the livid bruise that decorated her cheek, equally certainly, *was*. Having married Alice against any inclination to be married at all, for the sake of their son, John had counted it very ungrateful in her to present him with a bastard while he was at war.

'It didn't seem *honest*,' said Alice, after some thought.

Margery grunted. 'But to say what you *did* say – that didn't seem like you was right bright in the head!'

'What *did* you say, Alice?' asked Lucy with natural curiosity. 'You certainly seem to have paid dearly for it, poor lass.'

Alice sighed and patted her troublesome lump. 'Well – *'ee* said who was it, and *I* said it was a soldier, see? Then *'ee* said, kind of quiet like, which side was the soldier a-fightin' for? And I said, I dunno rightly, John. I never asked 'im! That's when he started hitting me, mistress. Ee takes a swipe or two every time 'ee does 'ave a drink nowadays.'

Lucy, smiling, lined John Coachman up alongside Tom and Jane with the intractables of this world, and promised to speak to him. 'We can't have you all purple and green at the wedding, now can we?'

'I only hopes as 'ow Master Will don't beat you, when you've been married a bit,' said Alice generously, slipping the silk and lace over Lucy's shoulders.

'I only hope I never give him cause,' said Lucy lightly. You will always be forgiven, he had said.

The dress was a cloudy dream of pale gold, the merest glance of the sun upon white. It was as simple as fashion allowed without entering the Puritan camp, and it permitted its wearer rather than itself to be the main focus of attention. Will had given her the material. It had come, he said, from Damascus and had been paid for in rubies. She hoped she would do it justice.

A marriage, however, is not simply concerned with the pleasure of the guests and the beauty of the bride. There were also matters of business to attend to. One of these had led to further quarrelling with Tom.

When Sir George had died he had left Heron to Tom under what was known as a Strict Settlement. By this means, his own interest in the estate, like his father's before him, was merely that of a tenant for life. A great proportion of the revenues was reserved for the payment of inheritances. The first of these had been Mary's widow's jointure, a considerable sum, comparable as was customary, with the large dowry she had originally brought to her husband. Now he was called upon to obtain Lucy's dowry. This must be an amount reflecting the status of both families and must be produced from the lands which had been 'settled' in her name. Since this settlement had taken place at her birth, and the revenues severely eroded by the exigencies of war, Will had engaged to accept the sum in installments. Tom had hoped to mortgage Spindlesham, which he had inherited from Valora, to cover this embarrassment, but he was stuck fast in a slough of legal contention with Sir Horatio Bulmer over this and had not been able to extricate himself in time.

However, Will was naturally disposed to oblige him and the arrangement was signed and sealed before Sir Cloudesley Willows, who had been invited, as Sir George's old friend, to supervise the marriage contract, or 'spousals'. This was the formal exchange, before witnesses, of an oral promise between Will and Lucy. If not followed by immediate consummation, this contract could be broken if necessary, which explained the somewhat strained expression of the bride-to-be as she fought to retain her composure while her newly betrothed whispered certain suggestions in her ear.

'Speak up! Hearing not what it was!' roared Sir Cloudesley.

'Just making sure of her,' shouted Will, with his mongrel's grin.

'Oh, aye, get her to bed as soon as you may,' nodded the ancient representative of the judicature. Tom coughed reprovingly.

It was then that Lucy asked her awkward question. As they moved out of the library where they had conducted their business, she laid a hand on Tom's sleeve. 'Have you thought, Sir Thomas, now that Mother is settled and so am I, what your duty might be in another direction? Your brother Jud is well over twenty – and not a sign of his portion has come to him. He will not ask for it, I know. But I have spoken to Mother and she agrees that it must be mentioned. I know it will be hard to find the money, but it is his by right and—'

'For God's sake hold your interfering tongue!' Tom's face was white with anger as, confronted yet again with the distasteful mention of his cadet, he stormed away from them all.

'I do believe you have chosen the wrong moment,' said Will tactfully.

'There is no right moment with Tom. You just have to attack when he shows his face,' Lucy said without compunction.

'I sincerely hope, my goddess of justice and wrath, that you and I never find cause to fall out. Perhaps I should be advised, like Sir Cloudesley, to cultivate a politic deafness.'

'I should obtain a speaking-trumpet,' Lucy threatened.

He kissed her fingers and conceded defeat. He was treating her very carefully during these last few days. His manner was light, amusing, a little less personal than usual, but no less amicable. He neither startled her with a sudden attempt at courtship nor retired to a distance suitable to the drawn-out legalities of the period. He made her so comfortable with him that she all but forgot that it was he whom she was to marry.

The morning of the wedding witnessed a kinder answer to prayers. Although tinglingly cold, it was bright and clear beneath a sky of duck-egg blue, with no wind to speak of. Everyone wrapped their silks and satins in fur-lined velvet and relied for effect upon extravagant decoration of their hats. To Lucy, shivering slightly in her ruby-bought splendour as she walked beside Tom to the altar, the chapel resembled the indoor garden of some legendary giant, nodding with huge flower-heads, plumes and rosettes for stamens arising out of monstrous trumpeting petals of buckram and felt. Three hundred of them had pressed into a space created for the seventy members of the original Cistercian community and as many more waited outside the open doors.

The ceremony itself passed very quickly for Lucy. All that she could remember of it afterwards was the ringing and purposeful tone of Will's vows and the intimate gleam that had flashed towards her when he had uttered the words 'With my body I thee worship'. She tried to match him with her own bright voice, holding up her head and declaiming proudly the words which had bound men and women to each other before Christ since He himself had first taught them to honour marriage as a holy vow. She must have been successful for she heard someone afterwards approving of the pitch and certainty of their performance.

The sermon was long and allowed for a little restful daydreaming before the rout began. The parson from St Mary's was strong for the protection of religion by the family and its adherence to morning and evening household prayers. Lucy wondered if Will had introduced this custom to his house in London. She doubted it. If not, she would do so herself; it would be an excellent earnest of her serious intentions as its chatelaine.

It began to snow as they left the chapel. Will swung her up against his chest and raced through the roaringly appreciative crowd and into the house, dropping her next to the first convenient fire. 'Alone! For at least half a second!' he cried. 'Kiss me, Mistress Staunton and set the seal on all that parsonical prosing!'

He held her very correctly, touching only her back and shoulders but his kiss was perhaps the deepest she had ever known. It had nothing to do with sensuality and it left her shaken with a new tenderness towards him.

The guests caught up with them then, and from that moment all was bombast, bawdy and bedlam as they set out to enjoy themselves. For the next hour Lucy's face was plastered with kisses until it felt wet, raw and stiff. She smiled and talked and said her thanks for gifts until she didn't know which muscles were the most abused, facial, vocal or simply her legs, for she had been standing since dawn. She was delighted when noon came and she might sit next to Will at the head of the table and command the feast.

'What a splendid appetite,' commented Will as she did justice to her first meal that day. 'Young brides are reputed to be too anxious about what is to follow to let a morsel pass their lips.'

'Then they must frequently disappoint their anticipatory bride-grooms by fainting clean away from lack of nourishment,' said Lucy, seizing a partridge and a chicken pasty.

After the food there was a time set aside for rest and recreation. Lucy took several sweetmeats to her chamber and lay on her bed in her shift, eating them and reading cosily. She did not allow herself to become anxious in the manner of Will's reputed young brides, but concentrated studiously upon her book, which was a demanding pamphlet which Jud had sent her. It was written by one John Milton, who had a stirring turn of phrase and an acerbic and inventive mind. It dealt with the freedom of the press and carried the resounding title of 'Areopagitica'. Lucy was so impressed by it that she was determined to give its name to the next new foal.

Her mother had given strict instructions that she was not to be disturbed, as this would be her only period of relaxation during the day, but one by one her friends would put their heads around her door, whisper a few words of good will and go away again. Mistress Regina Staunton was one of these.

Will's mother was a tall, straight woman with the kind of presence that turns every head in a room. She was handsome in as bold a fashion as her son, though her colouring was darker and her eyes gave less away. She carried herself like a queen and other people automatically leaped to serve her. When she entered the room, Lucy got up immediately and offered her the best chair.

'No need. I shall not stay. I have promised your mother to keep her company. She is hiding in the Italian garden from the parson and the judge, I believe. She says they are two men who never stop talking and never say anything she wants to hear.'

Lucy grinned. 'Are you at all interested in gardens?' she asked.

Regina considered. 'I know what I want mine to look like, and I know how to ensure that my gardeners carry out my wishes.'

'Ah – then you may be as well off with the parson or the judge,' Lucy regretted. 'If my Mother is outside, she will not be able to think of anything except what is before her eyes.'

'Then, since I wish to speak of you and of my son, I shall have to make coy analogies with the growth of trees and the develop-ment of marriages; I daresay it will serve my turn.' She came closer and touched Lucy's cheek. 'You and I will have many years to make each other's acquaintance. I have already decided that you were one of Will's better ideas. So I shall spend my time here in getting to know your mother. She will be a little lonely when you have left Heron, and I should like, being in similar circumstances, to show her the advantages of the state.'

Before she left, she placed a small packet upon the bed. 'It belonged to Queen Elizabeth. I like strong women. It will suit you admirably.'

When she had gone, Lucy unwrapped a tiny golden Tudor rose whose heart was an emerald. It hung from a chain which she fastened about her neck. The rose nestled nicely between her breasts. She would keep it on. Her gown for the evening's festivities was her favourite green velvet looped over a gold lace underskirt.

Was she, she wondered, as she dressed and admired the pendant in her mirror, becoming a strong woman? She did not think of herself in that way, but certainly, it would be a very good thing if she were. She admired such women herself. The Empress Helena, the Anchoress Julian, Eleanor of Aquitaine, Elizabeth herself; all those brave and holy women who had made their mark on the history of their time. She could well imagine Regina Staunton to have been one of them, had she been born in the right circumstances. Valora too; there had been the possibility of greatness in Valora. To be born a woman meant that one did not expect to contend in matters of greatness, or of great judgement, or of martial or political importance. From time to time she had wondered why that was, why so few names that were known to her, famous and glorious, were those of women. It became obvious when superior women were left to their own devices, by some trick of fate – women such as Valora, Martha, and now Regina – that they possessed the same capabilities of running their own lives and estates as men did. Was she one of these? Would she have to wait until she was widowed and orphaned in order to find out?

The consideration made her restless. She would talk to Will about it. He spoke of certain women with as much respect as he showed towards men – not that, in his case, it was ever very much. Will was a law unto himself. She liked that. It made her feel as though she were setting out upon an adventure.

When Alice came to dress her hair she had her sweep it up into a severe Roman coronet, with just a few tendrils about her cheeks that were not long enough to go up. It made her look more adult and commanding.

'You have been granted a halo, I see,' was her husband's

remark. 'Oh dear, I hope this does not mean you have forsaken the world of the flesh forever.'

'It means that I am now a responsible young matron who takes her future very seriously,' she said piously.

Will groaned. 'Then you have cheated me,' he declared. 'I thought I was getting a flighty piece with headful of sheep's wool, within and without!'

'I can be flighty enough when the occasion demands. I shall prove it now by dancing with every man who asks me for the next hour.'

'You may, so long as I am the first.'

Her partners were a varied selection. She danced with both parson and judge, with Sir Jo and Ralph Stratton, with Captain Bellow of the *Gallant Lady* who had ridden up with Will, with every county dignitary and title in the room, and, with far more pleasure, with Dickon Stable, with Tibbett and with Ninian Ffoulkes. If any looked askance at her, she let them. These were the people with whom she had shared her life, who had made up its trusted fabric.

She finished by ordering a fierce country jig and dancing it with John Coachman. 'There,' she told him when they had both staggered to a panting halt beside a window. 'Now you'll have less breath left in you for beating Alice about the head!'

John, beetroot with embarrassment, mumbled something incoherent.

'No indeed you *won't* do it again,' nodded Lucy. 'I have your promise!'

After the dancing had winded them all, people began to wander off into separate rooms for cards, for drinking or for music. In the large parlour a group had begun some energetic but not very melodic singing. Lucy could hear them from the hall where she was trying to hold several conversations at once.

The song celebrated a certain portion of a particular gentleman's anatomy. It had come up from London with some of Tom's friends.

You shall have a King, but whom?
Was ever King served so?
To make room for Oliver, O fine Oliver, O brave, O rare
  Oliver O
Dainty Oliver, O gallant Oliver O

Now Oliver must be he

Now Oliver must be he
For Oliver's nose
Is the Lancaster rose
And then comes his sovereignty

Twenty roistering Royalists howled it from well-oiled throats with Kit and Humpty accompanying them on a pair of drums they had brought back from their marauding days, and Tom giving an unprecedented imitation of good comradeship by tootling on Lucy's old wooden flute. It was then that Martha, counting him occupied for the next half hour, went in search of his younger brother.

She found Jud amusing himself in a less rumbustious fashion with a keg of brandy, a pipe of tobacco and Paul Stratton, with whom he was happily recalling childhood exploits. They were sharing the same embrasure in the small dining room, undisturbed by anyone except the servants who came and went from the kitchen. Paul made himself scarce when he realized that the witch Lady Heron required Jud's company all to herself.

Martha curled in the embrasure in his place. 'I wanted to tell for myself how happy I am to see you in this house again,' she said a little shyly. She was not yet accustomed to thinking of herself as the lady of the manor, and would never be so while Mary lived. 'And I wanted you to be so good, if you will, as to carry my warmest greetings to your – to Cleo, and to kiss your little boy for me. I hope I shall meet them soon for myself.'

Jud kissed her hand, grateful for her gentleness. 'It is kind in you to say this, but I know you cannot speak for your husband. Tom would not echo your greetings. He wants me out of the house as soon as courtesy allows.' He sighed. 'At least this crush has enabled us to avoid each other very efficiently.'

Martha smiled. 'No, I don't speak for Tom. But he knows he is alone in his feelings towards you. He knows he hurts his mother and all of us by his insistence on them. I do not think he will wish to stand alone forever.'

'He has Jane on his side,' said Jud with a rueful grin. 'She has given me several pieces of her tongue to take home. She was ever the same when we were children. It's a pity she has none of her own to chastise and set right.'

'They'll come one day, please God.' She smiled more privately, thinking that it was just possible that she had a small secret of her own inside her. She could not be sure yet; she had missed her courses only once, but she hoped. Fatherhood would be a very good thing for Tom. Perhaps it would set his feet on this earth as nothing in his life had yet been able to do.

Jud, already the proudest of fathers, needed no further reminder of the fact to set him recounting little Ned's virtues. He and his four-year-old Uncle Julius were learning to read and write and figure together and Jud planned to send them both one day to one of the free schools that Richard Overton was now campaigning for. 'An education for every child, however poor his parentage; that will be something worth working for. Though I must endeavour to prevent my son from swearing quite so colourfully if he is to present himself in public; he has learned such words from his gang of aunts and uncles as even Humpty's wretched parrot would envy!'

Martha laughed, and Jud laughed with her, happy that they were so easy together. But laughter is easy to kill and there are some who have the slaughterer's gift above others.

Tom, passing through to find Margery, who was forgetting their appetites in the satisfaction of her own for strong ale, was stopped dead in his tracks at the sight of his wife laughing at his brother's joke. He himself had never made her laugh, or so he felt, seeing them there so cosy together. 'Martha!' he snapped, more harshly than he had meant.

She swung round, her ease all gone. 'Why, Tom,' she said gently.

'I don't like to find you in such company. Kindly be gone.'

For a moment she thought of defying him, but she could not improve matters that way. This foolish and wasteful quarrel was between the two of them. Let them work it out for themselves. Without speaking she left the room.

'Your wife is a fine woman. You should not speak to her so coarsely.'

'Be damned to your impudent tongue. It's no business of yours. When d'you leave Heron? I trust, soon?'

Jud lounged. He had been enjoying his visit. He resented Tom's spoiling his pleasure. But then Tom had always done that. 'Oh, I don't know. I might stay for a week or so. I had forgotten how many old friends I had here,' he drawled. He had no intention of staying but he knew Tom would find the suggestion insufferable.

'You will not. You will leave tomorrow. My house is no haven for traitors and sellers of lies and scandal.'

'I print no lies!' Jud bridled in defence of his beloved *Intelligencer*. Tom gave a brief crow of laughter like a rude schoolboy.

'Nor do I set them to music and bellow them like a brainsick bull,' Jud added, thumbing towards the parlour whence the strains of *Brave Oliver* were liquidly issuing once again.

'There's no lie there,' said Tom contemptuously. 'It's no secret what the Nose Almighty will do if he succeeds in bringing His Majesty to trial. Someone must rule England. Whom else would his Godliness think fit?'

'That is foul calumny,' began Jud angrily. Tom had called him a liar. Tom had forbidden him his home. Tom was a bloody nuisance and it was time he taught him a lesson. 'You've given me the lie once too often,' he said, placing his hand unequivocally upon his sword. 'I think it is time we disputed our differences in the manner agreed between gentlemen.'

Tom bit his lip. He had wanted to be the one to make the challenge. 'Delighted,' he rasped. 'I'll send my seconds to you.'

Both relaxed a certain amount at the prospect of spilling each other's blood. 'Swords?' Jud said.

Tom nodded.

It was in this state of perfect agreement that Will discovered them. Martha had sent him to attempt to reconcile the brothers. It was not a task he fancied at the moment, but he was fond of Martha and touched by her unhappy face.

'Oh ye Gods, has it come to that already?' he announced himself in tones of deep ennui. 'And here I am, wrenched from my new-wedded bride, to mediate between the devil and the deep blue sea; I'm hanged if I know which of you is which.' He scratched an ear, looking puzzled.

'I wish you'd reserve your humour for those who ask for it,' Tom said, irritated.

'I intended no humour,' said Will quite coldly. 'It's just that I find it hard to comprehend how you can keep up this quarrel, Tom.'

'It was Jud who gave the challenge,' said Tom ironically.

'I presume there was provocation enough. Nonetheless, I'd be grateful, as a new member of this interesting family, to discover precisely why it is that you want to kill each other.' It had not occurred to either brother that this was what, in fact, he wanted. Will knew this. The shock should be salutary. He sat down on the abandoned windowseat and looked from one to the other, as expectantly as a dog about to go hunting.

'Goddamnit, I – ' Tom began furiously.

'Tom imagines I am a would-be regicide,' said Jud laconically.

'I don't *imagine* you'd depose the King,' Tom said fiercely. 'I have read your mind on that.'

'I'm flattered. Have I not taught you, then, that your King has proved himself unworthy of your trust? If he is set back on his throne he will have the Scots about our ears in no time. He *must* be deposed.'

'But not killed,' Will said quickly.

Jud shrugged. 'He might abdicate in favour of one of his sons. York, for preference; Prince Charles is too much his father's man.'

'Very neat,' sneered Tom. 'I suppose you will deny, then, that His Majesty's so surprisingly clumsy escape was engineered by Cromwell to take away his credit and put him under sterner duress?'

'Some people believe that. I have seen no proof of it.'

'Whatever one believes,' said Will soberly, 'it was that circumstance that changed Oliver's mind towards bringing the King to trial. I, for one, am sorry for it. What we need now is a return to sensible civil government, the restoration of law and order. This is no time to drag the monarchy through the dust.'

'So you're against Cromwell over this?' asked Jud.

'I am. So is Harry Vane and every other honest man in the House. I'll have nothing to do with it; nor will any respectable jurist in England. The thing is simply not legal.'

'Then we must make a law to suit the necessity,' said Jud grimly.

Tom longed simply to knock him down and be done with it, but he observed instead, with what he imagined to be patience, 'That is commonly known as anarchy; is that what you want?'

'No, it isn't. Have you read, by any chance, in my newssheet, about a document called *The Agreement of the People?*'

'I have. That is what I mean by anarchy.'

Will, too, gave a dispirited groan. 'Jud, if you are going to take up seriously with the Levellers, you'll find yourself issuing the *Intelligencer* from jail, as your friend Lilburne issues his pamphlets. This *Agreement of the People* is dangerously radical. It can only split Parliament as it has split the army during their interminable debates. Cromwell will *discuss* it as long as you like; but he won't give in to it. He holds no more brief for the government of the common man than I do, or Tom does, or the King does for that matter!'

'I don't say they should govern, I say they should have the vote.'

'You forget. They are in the majority.'

'That is what I remember. You are a cynic.'

'Self-protective, that is all. I do not consider the cobbler and the knife-grinder to be capable of running the country. And nor does Oliver Cromwell.'

'You may be right; it's too soon to tell; too soon even to know what will be for the best. As long as Oliver brings the King to trial.'

'Then he will be a common criminal—'

'All *I* know,' interrupted Tom with surpassing unpleasantness, 'is that you and your precious Cromwell will hang equally high when the Scots have put the King back where he belongs. You too, Will, if you don't start to be more careful how you choose your friends!'

'Speaking of friends,' said Will, abandoning a hopeless argument. 'Does either one of you wish me to be his second in this culling of Herons you have decided upon? Or perhaps I would do for both? That way we should have less of a public to-do. I should rather like my wedding to remain a cause for celebration. Of course, if one of you should die, we should have the marriage baked meats furnishing forth the funeral feast, a reversal I'm sure your father would have appreciated; almost as much as he would have depreciated your ridiculous duel.'

'Father would just as soon have seen Tom give me a hiding as not,' said Jud bitterly.

'I don't believe that. He was very fond of you beneath his bluster; it was your ideas he couldn't abide.'

'He thought him a traitor, as I do,' said Tom in a final tone. 'As to the duel—'

'Do you *really* want to kill each other?' mused Will lazily. 'Just imagine, if either of you *have* any imagination, how your mother and the rest will feel if one of you lies dead in that field tomorrow. Ask yourself whether you should visit your quarrel on them in such a way, when you have already caused them deep sorrow by it. Ask yourself what your respective ladies will feel—' Tom could not check a curious glance at Jud. '—and even, if you will have the courtesy, what Lucy and I might feel about such a termination of our festivities.' He folded his arms and looked from one to the other.

Jud felt his resolution going soggy. Will was right; this was not the time. And anyway, he didn't want to kill Tom, not really. It was just that this thing between them had to come to a head, somehow. But it could wait. He cleared his throat.

Tom looked even more furious, if possible. As a gentleman he could hardly refuse Will's disguised request. And yet, here had been the chance he had longed for, to give that wretched young numbskull the hiding of his life. As for actually killing him – well, it would be no great loss to the world. Of course there was no question of Jud's killing *him;* Tom was one of the best swordsmen in Europe by now.

There was a hiccup in the doorway and Margery tottered through, carrying four jugs of afternoon punch. 'Oh, isn't that a rare sight,' she observed with a wide, ale-flavoured grin. 'Mr Jud and Mr Tom, a-talking again after all this time. My, I'm right glad to see that!' She staggered off, chuckling and dripping punch.

Tom turned savagely on his brother. 'Be out of this house by dawn tomorrow. Our business will keep.' Jud made no indication that he had heard him. Tom had left without waiting for an answer.

Will looked at him dispiritedly. 'I should like to see this quarrel healed,' he said seriously. 'It would mean a great deal to Lucy, and to your mother.'

Jud sighed.' The thing is – we can't alter what is in our minds. That is where the quarrel is.'

'But both of you are at odds with me, and yet we have no quarrel.'

'Ah, but you are not of our blood. We can forgive *you.*'

'I'm the next best thing now,' grumbled Will.

'And I'm glad of it.'

'So is Tom. At least you agree on *my* good points, if nothing else. There you show your only claim to commonsense.' He went off to look for Martha. He wished he could tell her his task of reconciliation had been successful.

That night Lucy was brought to her bedchamber by a shrieking, giggling regiment of relatives and friends who undressed her, and put her into a new white silk nightgown and a pair of lace gloves. Then they carried her, wriggling, to her bed and sat her in it. Her mother plumped up the pillows. Isabella pulled down the neck of her nightgown and tied its ribbons just above her nipples. Martha leaned over and touched cool perfume behind her ears and across her chest. Julia placed a nosegay upon the bedside table and she and Isabella pelted the bed with flower petals, which must have been hard to find at this season. A flagon of fine wine was left to hand. At last they closed the curtains and left her to herself.

She was cold. She would prefer to go and curl up in a chair near the fire, but she supposed it was customary to sit here like a stuffed puppet and wait for Will to come and approve his bargain. Goodness knew when that would be – the last time she had seen him he had been leading the singing that was still going on in the parlour. She had thought he looked rather drunk, but he had seemed to recall all the words.

She pondered on trying another few pages of *Areopagitica* but somehow didn't feel she would be able to concentrate. It was definitely chilly. She drew up the ribbon of her gown and tied it much higher up.

When Will came in, not long after, she was wrapped in her fur bedcover and rolled into a ball in the chair right next to the fire. She was drinking the wine and trying to stay awake.

'How very wise.' Will built up the fire and poured himself some wine. 'No, don't uncoil; you'll lose valuable heat. I hope there are dozens of bricks in that bed?'

'Oh yes. Margery made sure of that.' She looked at him. He didn't seem to be in any particular hurry to relieve her of her gloves. He wore his azure chamber gown edged with sables and seemed very relaxed and not, after all, at all drunk.

Her cup was empty. He refilled it. She would drink it slowly. When she had drained it she would have nothing to occupy her hands.

Will saw that if he delayed too long it would only increase her apprehension. He let her drink a little for courage, then very gently took the cup from her and set it in the hearth. He drew her out of the chair and brought her to him, fur rug and all. 'You mustn't shake like this. I will do nothing to displease you.'

He began to kiss her. Even her lips trembled a little; he found it exciting. He licked them teasingly, to make her laugh. 'We have kissed before. This is no new thing.' He smiled frankly, reminding her of friendship.

He kissed her slowly and expertly, without passion, until she was used to the touch, to the shape of his mouth on hers. He murmured to her between kisses, saying that she was glorious and that he loved her.

She hardly heard him, aware only of his lips as they caressed and courted hers. His kisses made her want other things. She felt lighter and more free as the fur fell to the ground. She was no longer cold. She pressed against him and his tongue tentatively explored her mouth. She liked that. She recognized responses that she had felt before. Then, they had been forced to break away from each other, gasping and unsatisfied. Cathal – no, it was not fair to think of him. She did not even *want* to think of him.

She did not know that Will had untied her ribbon and that her breasts were naked in his hands until she felt them flare with a sudden and exquisite prick of pain. She caught her breath and he smiled at her with such kindness that she answered it with joy. He bent his head and gave her body such full and overwhelming attention that she began to long for what she had feared. She clung to him and began shyly to make her own first enquiries, stroking his broad chest where the golden hair curled, kissing his nipples – if it was so pleasant to her, surely it must be the same for him? She lifted her head and began to kiss him again while their hands discovered more and more.

At last he raised his head and cradled hers in one hand. 'There is beauty in many things, but perhaps most of all in this,' he told her softly. 'There is also comfort, kindness, pleasure, and, very occasionally, sadness. We shall experience all those things together, but this time only the beauty, for that is what you bring to me, and I will bring you a grateful heart forever after.' She thought that she would not believe, in after days, that he could speak this way, but she was by now too far gone in need of what he also wanted to marvel for more than a moment.

He took her nightgown from her. 'If the gloves are to fulfil their duty as a symbol, I suppose we must leave them on,' he said.

'No, please. They are very delicate, but I think you will prefer my bare hands.'

He peeled them off and kissed each separate hand. She smiled victoriously as he laid her on the bed.

There was a glint of azure as his face closed over her and then it was extinguished by the closing of her own eyes so that all senses were sacrificed to one beneath the pressure of his body. He was hard and firm and heavy, though his movements were as light as those of the cat to which she had always likened him. His skin was cool and smooth and new beneath her fingers. She began to teach herself his body as he learned hers. His delight in her allowed her to abandon any shyness very soon. She felt the great breadth of his back and chest, the scars of old swordfights, the hard muscle tissue formed by years before the mast and on horseback. She traced the strength and curve of his thighs, drew back, and then touched again what seemed the massive pillar of his erection. She wanted to complain that it was impossible he should push all that into her little space, no matter how moist and welcoming it had become. She did not speak, however, being certain that if there were good bed manners, to do so would not be acceptable. There was a great wonder in all this pleasure and warmth and wanting, and only a little fear, after all. The fear had all gone by the time she parted her thighs for him, and an unlimited enormity of bliss came in its place. She cried out with delight and discovery and did not once think again of Cathal O'Connor. It was much to her credit, and even more a tribute to the skill of her lover.

London, 1648

Staunton House stood on the north side of the Strand, opposite the gigantic sprawl of the Savoy Palace, once the magnificent home of John of Gaunt, now reduced to a hotch-potch of lodgings and offices connected with the departed court and therefore half empty. Will's ancestor had got his land from the Earl of Bedford whose family still owned a great deal of that part of the city. There were noble houses all along the Strand; on the river side, Burghley, Somerset, Arundel, Essex; on the city side Bedford and Exeter. Further along, the street discreetly glinted with the work, the fortunes and the strongboxes of London's richest goldsmiths. It was a heady neighbourhood and Lucy had to put a good deal of effort into not feeling like a country bumpkin.

She had soon mastered the house itself. Built in 1485 and used at one stage as a convent hospital, there was enough tranquillity in its wide, high-roofed spaces to allow her to feel at home. On the street its vaulted entrance was guarded by two crenellated towers so that to come in was rather like crossing an ancient bridge. Inside, the house was ranged tidily round a broad courtyard, with the coach-house and stables on the right and the kitchens and outhouses on the left, while the central section was dominated by the fine, tall windows and the graceful steps upon which Lucy had previously stood and disparaged what was now her new residence.

The true splendours of the building were reserved for the garden side, which, like famous Hardwick Hall, had the distinction of being more glass than wall. There was a great amount of light in most of the rooms, flattering their pleasing proportions and Will's astonishing collection of exotic furnishings.

For the first week Lucy had simply wandered about, touching things and staring. Her husband's taste, not unexpectedly, ran towards the barbaric and bizarre. His private rooms might have been the tents of Tamerlane, being full of savage colour and sinister objects.

'What is this?' she had asked, doubtfully surveying a gilded and spiky instrument with an unpleasant tube snaking out of it. It must be either an implement of torture or something nastily uncomfortable from a doctor's bag.

'It is a narghile. From Turkey.' It sounded like the former. 'It is for smoking various soothing substances.'

'God's boots!' One lived and learned.

Life with Will proved to be very much a learning process. As a good wife should, she set herself first to discover any tastes, habits and interests of his that she did not already know, but he soon told her cheerfully not to bother about such matters; the servant had all his wishes well in hand and would soon learn hers. She must use her time, especially the time that he must be away from her, to familiarize herself with her surroundings, with the city, the men and the movements that would be her background. She should visit Jud and listen to Rob Whittaker, though not necessarily with any sympathy. He would bring her to John Milton, the poet and pamphleteer, so that she could ask *him* all her questions about the *Areopagitica*; she should go to Nicholas Culpepper and see what fate was written in her stars.

'But I don't know whether I believe in astrology. My mother's horoscope was read once, and it was a pack of nonsense from start to finish!'

'Excellent. Then you will enjoy it all the more from lack of any apprehension. Besides, the man's a superlative herbalist.'

She was to hear music, go to the plays that persisted despite the Parliament's ban, to meet amusing and intelligent men, such as Harry Vane and Oliver St John, and seek in their houses, if she could find them, equally amusing and intelligent women. She was to take her maid and a manservant or two and explore the district on foot, the only way to see it, and make it as much her territory as the woods and fields of Heron. She had laughed at that, thinking that city streets and clattering crowds could never give one that sense of belonging, of being part of a beloved landscape, that was so much of her security at Heron. But she had been astonished to find how much she came to care for the small part of London that she could encompass in a morning's walk.

In the easy company of pretty, sharp-witted Cissie, her new maid, followed by two stalwart male guardians, she began to get to know the area, firstly from one end of the gilded, palatial Strand, where it became Fleet Street to the other at Westminster, then taking in a wider sweep, back through Bedford's vast domain, up St Martin's Lane where the fine new houses were turning the fields into gardens, along Long Acre's fashionable thoroughfare, and back down teeming Drury Lane, the widest and most hectic road in the district. Walking thus far they had enclosed some forty acres, and afterwards they would penetrate the heart of them and sit to drink spiced wine and eat fresh muffins beneath the colonnades of Inigo Jones' new piazza at Covent Garden. Here they could contemplate his fine Italian hand in the portico of St Paul's church, of which my Lord Bedford had demanded that it should be not much better than a barn and Mr Jones had replied that it should be the handsomest barn in Europe. Lucy, who cared for older styles of architecture, thought that a perfectly sufficient description.

The muffins were even lighter than Margery's and oozed with plum jam. It was during one of Lucy's idle moments in the piazza that she saw Eliza Hartley for the first time since her wedding. Her Ladyship was in the company of another woman and several young men, all dressed to close a Puritan's eyes in shame. They laughed and flirted their fans and chattered and generally made a lot of noise. It was while they ambled back and forth, allowing the fortunate populace to admire them, that they passed Lucy, complete with muffin, feeding bits of it to an Italian juggler's monkey who was tumbling about with his master outside the church. Eliza and Lucy were looking interestedly at each other's similar marten-fur tippets when their offended eyes travelled upwards, met and clashed. Eliza wafted her fan across her face and walked on.

'She'll soon come round,' said Will easily, when Lucy reported this.

'I don't know that I want her to,' said his wife, sniffing. 'Especially if she has an entire duplicate of my new wardrobe.'

Will sighed. 'I got a dozen of them in Genoa. They had come from Siberia and were a bargain. Goddammit, Warwick's wife wears one too! *She* does not live round the corner.' Will sighed again. Eliza lived in Whitehall, but no matter. Since this was probably the nearest they came to a quarrel during those first days of their marriage, it might be assumed that they were more than ordinarily happy.

Lucy was also more than ordinarily tired. Not only was she walking, riding and driving all over London during the daytime, while Will fought strenuously on behalf of the King at Westminster, but they were making love even more strenuously every night, and at any other hour when the opportunity arose. No one had told her to expect this to become her favourite occupation in the world and she was lost in surprise and wreathed in pleasure at the discovery that it was just that.

'Do you suppose I am one of nature's whores?' she enquired, worried.

'Without doubt. Like Helen, like Thäis, like Aphrodite herself,' he assured her, delighted.

Even her mother had only told her that 'the act of marriage' was chiefly for the procreation of children; she had not intimated the amazing, blazing joy of it. Lucy hoped that she had known it. It was difficult to imagine one's parents – but her father had been a great one for enjoyment, of every kind. She was reasonably sure it had all been well between them. Probably Mary had not wanted to prepare her for a pleasure which she could not absolutely guarantee; after all, it would hardly be the same with, say, Ralph Stratton, or Nehemiah Owerby. She cringed in horror at the last. When another name tried to creep into her mind, she slammed its doors fast shut. She found her relationship with Will very satisfactory. She had gained a lover and she still had her valued friend.

Her only complaint was that she did not see enough of him. For this she was uncertain whether to blame the King, who caused constant debate in the Commons because he was suspected of having made a treaty with the Scots and would not make one with Parliament, or Oliver Cromwell, whose side of the debate was opposed to Will's. It seemed that now neither the extremist Independents among the Army Agitators nor the would-be monarchist Cromwell himself could believe that there would be any lasting peace while the King lived. If they brought him to his trial, they would bring him to his death. It was an end that Will could not entertain, and while Cromwell's days of fast and prayer brought him steadily nearer to the knowledge of God's will in the matter, Staunton's days of fierce argument took him further from hope.

In the city the predictable pendulum of human sympathy had swung back in Charles Stewart's direction. While the Independents called him 'that man of blood' and blamed all the evils of the past war upon him, together with the design for further conflict, his old supporters gained new voice and new followers, among Presbyterians who expected great things of the Scots Alliance, and among moderate men of all persuasions who resented the government of the County Committees continuing into peacetime, and who were alarmed by the growth and power of the Army. No one wanted martial law forever. No one wanted an army forever. As Lucy went about the city she saw more and more frequently displayed the badges and mottoes that demanded the King's return.

Jud was disgusted by these signs of softening and sentimentality and gave away with the *Intelligencer* a badge of his own which depicted a foolish face thrust out from under a yoke which carried the words 'My Cod and my King'. Lucy quarrelled with him over its tastelessness and those who wore it were prosecuted for blasphemy, proving that Puritans had no sense of humour.

On every corner there was the rumour that the Scots were coming to rescue the King by force; the extraordinary length of their necessary march did not lessen its repetition.

Would there be an invasion? Would it be war all over again? Lucy knew that Tom, for one, expected it. Martha wrote that he was away from home for days at a time, rousing the countryside in the King's name. 'He is hot for another war, or rather, he will not admit to defeat in the last one. I see little of him these days, and look to see even less if he is not disappointed. He puts so much of himself into this cause that I do not dare to contemplate how it will be with him if they should fight again and should lose again. May God preserve them and bring the King safe home. I am lonely for Tom, but I think he does not feel the same because he has too much to occupy him. Your brothers go with him on many of his expeditions, and on others of their own. I pray that the Scots do not come, for we shall be a household of anxious women again—'

But the Cavaliers did not wait for the Scots.

At the end of March, close to the anniversary of the King's Accession, which was loudly celebrated by loyalists everywhere, Col. John Poyer, the Governor of Pembroke Castle, refused to resign his post to his replacement, declared for the King and set about raising the whole of South Wales in revolt.

Lucy knew what would be in Martha's next letter before she opened it. 'He has gone, then?' asked Will sympathetically, seeing her expression.

Silently she passed it over to Will.

'So Tom is gone again.'

'Yes. Kit and Humpty with him. They have ridden to Wales.'

'Do you want to go home, to your mother?'

'No. She has Martha; and your mother is still with her. My place is with you.'

He nuzzled her hair. 'I am glad.'

She sighed. 'I do not know what to hope for. How many will rise for the King, do you think?'

He shook his head. 'I can't say. Much will depend on the Scots. The country wants no more of war. Most will remain neutral and let the New Model fight it out with the Scots.'

'It is very discouraging. I do not wish our son to be born during a time of war. He will grow up with a martial disposition.'

'Lucy! Dearest girl, do you mean it?'

She smiled smugly. 'Yes. I am certain. In November, I think.'

'That is all I needed,' he said beatifically, 'to make me the happiest man in England.'

'You said that when we married. Your standards have risen.'

'The possibilities for happiness have risen. My splendid, golden girl! He is bound to be argumentative, but not necessarily warlike. Suppose he were a girl?'

'He is not,' said Lucy firmly. 'You must have an heir first. Besides,' she added, somewhat shamefaced, 'Mr Culpepper has assured me he is male.'

He laughed at her but she did not mind on this occasion. 'I hope that Martha's will also be a boy. I can't wait to see the new master of Heron. I'm afraid I shall envy him a little. I always envied Tom. All that time, when I was Heron's steward in all but name, I thought of myself as its mistress. I was happy.' She spoke in tones of discovery.

He hugged her, understanding. 'You have this house, and you will have Staunton St Paul one day. Isn't that enough?'

'More than enough.' She kissed him. 'But Heron is . . .'

'. . . part of you. I remember. I only hope it will not be in danger, if the war starts up again.'

But he could not reassure her. No one knew what would happen. The great thing was to remain tranquil, Lucy told herself. Nothing could matter more than the health of the new life she carried. She made noble efforts to feel calm and untroubled while the world went mad around her.

After the Welsh had set the fuse alight, a series of explosions followed, small and isolated but potentially lethal. Kent went up, then Surrey and Essex. In the north, the Cavaliers took Berwick and Carlisle. The road was open for the Scots. There were none to stand against them, or to put down the Royalists, except the New Model. The rest of Parliament's army had long since disbanded.

Will crowed as Fairfax and Cromwell left Westminster to take the field again. 'Now we shall have Holles and the other Presbyterians back again. At least there will be an element of balance in our debates.'

'If the Scots don't hurry up the balance will be all on Parliament's side in the hostilities,' worried Lucy.

'Well, that *would* be more personally convenient for me, my sweet Cavalier – but one sees that your sympathies must be perplexed.'

'Not at all. I just want to see His Majesty safe home, as you do.'

'Nevertheless, as things stand now, it will be better for us if it is Parliament who bring him home.'

'But has Parliament any power that the army does not give to it?'

'It is in the interests of recouping that power that I spend my days and half my nights racing round the city using my tongue as a blunt instrument!'

'If only Jud could agree with you; he could do so much good with the *Intelligencer*. But he seems to feel that Cromwell can do no wrong.'

'While his disaffected partner feels he will do no right, and calls him traitor because he'll not hang the King out of hand.'

Lucy's smile was slight. 'That's Lilburne again. He has never trusted Cromwell to go far enough.'

Will frowned. 'I think, like me, he distrusts the misuse of the Parliament by the army. Although in most ways I couldn't have less to say to the Levellers, in this we must agree.'

'Rob has left the *Intelligencer*, Jud says, and is working exclusively for Richard Overton now. Cleo is furious with him. They hardly speak any more. Can you imagine it, living cheek by jowl in those tiny houses?'

'They can always keep the urchins posted in the street, to warn each one how to avoid the other's exits and entrances.'

'It isn't amusing, Will. I detest these family squabbles.'

He looked at her affectionately. There were absolutely no other ladies of his acquaintance who would welcome Cleopatra Whittaker as a sister and her bastard as nephew. In fact Lucy now spent a considerable part of her time on the wrong side of the river. She had engaged herself upon the primary education of the 'urchins' who were still too young to do anything but steal, and was surprised to find that they did at least as well as her brother Ned and rather better than poor Julia had ever done. From Cleo she herself learned useful and reassuring things about childbirth; her Ned had nearly been born at the press when she had mistaken her pains for the backache which had plagued her for some months. He had, she said, 'slipped out like an eel from a pail'. Lucy hoped for a similar experience.

It seemed that tranquillity was, despite the fighting, no difficult thing to achieve. She was well, had suffered very little sickness and carried the child high and small. Consequently she ignored fussy little Doctor Bland's instructions to rest with her feet up and went about as much as ever, swathed in elegant cloaks, and sometimes also fashionably masked. She did her best to follow her mother's advice to 'keep doing, otherwise both you and the child will grow too fat for comfort.'

All in all, she had never been so serene and content in her whole life. The single thorn that menaced her bright bubble of well-being was that there had been no word from any of her brothers. Lack of news was something to which they were all inured, however, and she did not worry unduly.

At the end of May, when Fairfax as Commander-in-Chief had dispatched all his Hectors where they were most needed, London was alarmed by the threat from a direction in which it was least expected. For some time there had been unrest in the navy. Sailors are notoriously conservative and there had been several mutinous outbreaks in favour of the King. These had been put down but the feeling that had fired them remained. Seeing the strength of the loyalists on the Kentish shore, the whole of the fleet in the Downs revolted, landed and captured the key ports. Warwick was immediately reappointed as Lord Admiral, but even his vast popularity could not win back the entire navy and he lost about a quarter of it to what now became known as the Revolted Fleet. Neither his reputation nor his temper were enhanced by the mad fact that his brother, Lord Holland, long suspected of cavalier instincts, justified all suspicion by becoming the King's Commander-in-Chief.

Will and Lucy were to suffer personally for the temper. Will had received an urgent message at the Commons. It was from Eliza who wished to see him at once.

He reached her elegant house near the palace in time for

supper. Eliza greeted him as though they had met yesterday, upon the same intimate terms as they had been since childhood. She kissed him lingeringly, pushing her superb breasts against his chest and leaning her thigh along his. She smelled appetizingly of musk and roses and she was wearing a soft flesh-coloured chamber gown that Will had given her.

'You look well, my dear,' he grinned appreciatively. 'I'm glad you have decided that good health suits you better than ill.' She gave her throaty laugh and commanded the supper. There were a good number of oysters to begin with.

'What's this?' His eyebrow raked. 'An attempt at seduction?'

'Eat them. They are good for you. My invitation would hardly have been so indecently pressing if I had seduction in mind. It is business that concerns me, Will.' She gave him wine. The gown floated, revealing classic limbs.

'Business?' he enquired lazily. Really, when one had not seen Eliza for a while, it was astonishing how one forgot how very attractive she was. She exuded sex as a drunkard exudes alcohol. She reeked of it. He wondered if some lucky fellow had just had her, and if so, who it had been. Her nipples were dark beneath the gauzy stuff. He shifted in his chair. Dammit, he was standing up for her already. 'What business?' he repeated, scarcely curious.

'Yours and mine. The *Lady Elizabeth*,' she said succinctly. 'Warwick has seized her and impounded her cargo. He says you may have the ship back, when he has finished with her, but you forfeit the cargo.'

Will sat as though lightning had struck. 'He sent me this interesting intelligence by word of mouth. His courier also brought a letter for you.' She rose and strolled to her bureau. She gave him the package.

He exhaled gustily. 'The old devil! The wicked old sea wolf!'

'Why don't you open it? I'm sure the avuncular advice is to the point.'

She sat and watched him as he read it. It was brief. It took care of his erection quite swiftly. 'My dear boy, as you must know we need every bottom we can lay hands on; so, since I have had the good fortune to lay hands on the *Lady Elizabeth*, I intend to borrow her for a time, being quite certain your loyalty would bid me do so. As to the matter of her cargo; if you recall a bargain you made with me some time ago, you will also realize that your marriage has broken that bargain. I'm not one to hold a grudge. The little Heron is a pretty sail, I've heard. But one must pay for one's breakages, Will. My price is your cargo; some 3,000 livres all told, by my reckoning. I know you'll not grudge it either. God speed till we meet. Your affectionate uncle, Warwick.'

'Is all explained to your satisfaction?' Eliza asked sardonically.

'You know what he says, do you not?' He looked at her with grim respect.

She smiled. 'Not precisely. I might guess.' She uncrossed her legs, releasing another warm cloud of animal scents. She got up and reached for his wine glass.

He held it out of her reach. 'Do you think you are worth it?' he asked, eyes slitted. 'Three thousand livres, just for displeasing you?'

'My dear cousin!' She mimed amazement. 'How could you think you had displeased me?'

'Warwick seems to think I have.'

'Oh no. On the contrary,' she murmured, her eyes reminiscently wide, 'you have always known exactly how to please me. Very deeply.' Her breasts pouted at him, mocking.

He was furious. He could not afford to lose that cargo and his noble relative already commanded several of his ships. It was becoming both expensive and inconvenient to be his 'dear boy'.

'And you forget. We are both injured in this. I had put a considerable sum into that particular voyage myself.'

He *had* forgotten. She was right. All the same, she was a calculating piece, and he knew she had not forgiven him for his marriage, however lightly she might pretend to take it. 'Well then,' he said, removing his coat and waistcoat, 'we had better start trying to regain our money's worth, had we not?'

Her low, delighted laugh brought him to her and he buried his face in her throat. She protested faintly, 'You are using your teeth, you cur!'

'I shall use them further and to better advantage,' he growled, stripping off the gown and tossing it into a corner. 'Get on your back, you bitch!' he ordered her.

He entered her on the carpet. The coupling was short, and for Eliza unusually sharp. But she did not complain when he turned her over and began again from behind.

'Great heavens where have you been?' demanded Lucy who had come out to greet him in the quadrangle. 'You smell like—' In that split-second she realized exactly what it was that he smelled like. '—Like an apothecary's shop that has been invaded by numerous tom cats,' she finished sweetly. 'What do they get up to in the House these days?'

'I had an accident with a container of scent,' he said truthfully. He had by no means intended to begin again with Eliza; and now he intended that the evening's lapse should be the only one. 'I'll go and bathe,' he offered, smiling. 'I'm quite unapproachable as I am. I stink as if I'd been to a brothel!'

Lucy made no reply. She did not know whether she should be suspicious. They had not made love for a few days. Her stomach was troubling her just at present. But surely he was capable of refraining for two or three days. Had she married a satyr?

She thought not. But she thought too that she recognized that scent. Tears scalded the back of her eyes as she watched Will stride off to his prized bath room. 'I could kill you!' she told his broad back.

Her anger disposed of the potential tears. She would not weep. She would not even say anything to Will. But she would not forget. And if it went on – she didn't know. But she would not put up with it.

That night she offered herself with a newly savage abandon which excited him as much as it surprised him. In the morning, when he found the neat marks of her teeth in his shoulder, he thought it a nice whimsy on the part of fate that she should repay Eliza's debt.

While the New Model set off steadfastly to sing the Cavaliers to death with suck of sword and blow of psalm, the House of Commons continued to hum with its own disharmony as it disputed, in two parts, the manner in which England should henceforth be governed. The Presbyterian majority, with a greater distaste for army rule and the Agreement of the People than they had ever had for the King's misdeeds, resumed the negotiations with Charles that had been broken off by Cromwell's motion at the New Year, led by the returned and determined Holles. The remaining Independents called them traitors; to the men who had fought for them once and were doing so again, and to the Parliament which had successfully stood against the royal tyrant who did not hesitate to plunge his country into another bloodbath in order to continue with his tyranny.

Will, representing the former persuasion, put forth one morning the obvious argument that the King's present show of amenability towards a private treaty might well be trusted, considering that unhappy gentleman's delicate position; the Scots Perseus had not arrived and the New Model dragon was breathing most convincing fire.

Suddenly the speaker found himself facing an incensed and white-faced Nehemiah Owerby, who did not wait for him to finish. Owerby had been absent from Westminster for a time and intended to make up for it. He fixed Will with an impassioned glare and raised his right hand as though he were about to create the universe.

' "The words of his mouth were smoother than butter," he rasped, "but war was in his heart; his words were softer than oil, yet were they drawn swords." Gentlemen, we have long learned, to our bitter cost, to put no trust in this man of iniquity!'

'What, me?' asked Will innocently. If he were to take Nehemiah seriously, in any guise, he might, like Lucy's brothers, be tempted to strike him dead.

Nehemiah disregarded him. 'There will be no peace in our land while Charles Stewart lives, to lie to his people. Better that he should die now, than that any man else should lay down his life in his unjust and ungodly cause.'

The Independents applauded and the rest shouted them down.

'It is your glorious army who will bring you peace. For it is said "Let the saints be joyful in glory; let them sing aloud upon their bed. Let the high praises of God be in their mouth, and a two-edged sword in their hand; to execute vengeance upon the heathen" ' – he looked threateningly at Will – 'and punishments upon the people; to bind their King with chains and their nobles with fetters of iron—'

'Hold your blasted tongue, sir,' cried Harry Vane, who was related to several noblemen, as indeed was a good part of the House.

The speaker rapped with his gavel and order was restored. Will continued his moderate and well-reasoned speech, though uncomfortably conscious of Nehemiah's hot, moist and fanatical stare.

'I think he may well be mad, or pretty near it,' he said to Lucy later. 'I have never seen a man less like himself. He is usually over-controlled, if anything, and an excellent speaker in his way, though I could wish he had not swallowed the Bible whole, intent upon its complete regurgitation on the floor of the House!'

'I wish he were not *in* the House, not in London at all.' Lucy shuddered. 'I don't like to think of him so near.'

'Better here than at Heron, worrying the life out of Martha.'

'True, love. I hadn't thought of that. But what will they do if he returns to Heron for good? How will they bear his existence, so very close, and on *our* land?'

'If we restore King Charles, Tom will get the land back.'
'I pray for it daily. Oh Will, if only the Scots would *hurry*!'
'Not until we have our treaty,' amended Will.
'But then there would be no need for them.'
'You have the right of it.'

But Parliament did not get its treaty. Charles had already signed one with the Scots. Like most of the King's transactions, it was intended for future disposal. Neither would the Scots send an army into England until after months of internal argument as to whether the King must take the Covenant. By this time Fairfax had absorbed most of the resistance in the southeast, while Cromwell had taken care of Wales.

It had only been a matter of time. The Cavaliers, however loyal, were disparate and disorganized, lacking the leadership they had once known, while the New Model was as strongly disciplined and as ably led as ever.

The Royalists were on the defensive. There was less now to defend, as Parliament had blown breaches in the walls of most of the fortified towns or castles as a precaution against this very event. Only Colchester kept Fairfax at bay for any length of time, while the bold Poyer held off Cromwell and retribution for seven weeks, fast inside the most formidable fortress in Wales, Pembroke, crouching on its wooded rock above the mud flats, dominated by the great cylindrical keep. With him, among the broad, draughty rooms with their arrow-slit walls, was Colonel Laugharne, another of Parliament's former commanders, who had already withdrawn in defeat from St Fagans. With *him*, circling his airy, shared quarters above the gatehouse until its six deep windows began to spin around him, the lack of action festering in him more foully than any wound, was Major Sir Thomas Heron.

Upon those occasions when he could be quiet enough, or weary enough, just to stand still and look out across the battlements upon the only side which did not fall down immediately into the harbour of Milford Haven, he could see, due southeast of the town, Cromwell's camp on the hills of Underdown.

He could not see that Old Ironside possessed no siege guns that would make an impression upon the castle's twenty-foot walls, but this was easily conjectured from the harmless pit-pattering of what guns he did have. There was a respite from boredom, though not from hunger, when the besiegers attempted outright assault. Their ladders proved as little useful to the height of the walls as their shot had been to their depth; they clattered down amid cackling from the battlements. It was during a better provided effort to take them by storm that Cromwell's reserves failed him at a crucial moment, enabling Laugharne to take advantage of the fray within the city to leave the castle unseen with his men and attack a large party of the enemy from the rear. For men reputed to be starving they did well, killing thirty of them. It occurred to Tom, as he easily accounted for two of them, that if he hadn't been so hungry and so enervated by the longeurs of the siege, his arm would not have been powered by half the anger and frustration that drove his sword into their breasts.

It was as they were mopping their brows and tying up wounds from this satisfying operation that they were disturbed by a group of horsemen. They stiffened, holding swords and pistols at the ready.

' 'S'wounds, gentlemen! I hope you know a friend when you see him!' The leading rider cantered towards them, his own sword waving cheerfully, red-tipped, from the froth of lace that denied him membership of the New Model. He sported fearful oiled moustachios and was dressed in showy scarlet and black.

Before he could introduce himself, a figure rode out from behind him, also waving its sword. 'S'death! Tom! So here you are!' It was Humpty.

Once they were quit of Heron the brothers had chosen different ways. While Tom had at once reported to Laugharne, who was rousing Wales at a gallop at the time, the twins had claimed duties in another direction, with Captain Attila.

'Good to see you, boys,' said Tom as Kit came up to them.

'Where are you bound now?' Humpty asked, taking a hasty look round for New Models. 'Why don't you join us, now that you're out of it?' He waved the sword at the thick-skinned monster on its rampart of grey limestone.

Tom shook his head. 'We're going back. You don't desert a siege.'

'I suppose not,' said Kit, regretfully. 'Well, perhaps we could come in with you? How does that strike you?'

'You'd simply be more mouths to feed, among men who are already feeling the pinch.'

Humpty nodded. 'Come to think of it, your belt *is* damned tight. Well, at least we can give you what we have with us. It's not much, just a bit of bread and cheese and cold meat. And wine of course.'

577

'I have not had meat or cheese for over a week; my horse has fared better. He has eaten several good breakfasts of thatch!'

Attila's men rallied round with dispatch, and Tom's saddlebags were soon bulging. 'It's the least we can do, don't ye know, to repay your lady mother's excellent hospitality,' said the gallant captain, who still puzzled over the coolness of that lady's welcome.

It was obvious from the relaxed and almost playful demeanour of the captain's band that what was to Tom a gruelling and dreary campaign with dwindling hope of any success, was to them a pleasant and worthwhile pastime. It was not the first occasion he had found to envy his young brothers their ability always to be where the amusement was. Still, he was cheered by the prospect of a decent supper for himself and his comrades in that infernal gatehouse. 'One thing, before we part – can you get news home, at all?'

Humpty hung his head. They had simply been too busy to think of it. 'I'm sure we can.'

'Then let our mother know how it is with all of us, and tell Martha—' he paused awkwardly, 'tell her she is not to worry.' He might, he reflected after they had gone, have sent a more loving message. He wondered if he would still be incarcerated here when his child was born. For a moment he had a wild instinct to race after his brothers and beg a horse to take him home.

Once back inside the castle, he found that several men had deserted. With his brother officers he exerted what energy he had in preventing mutiny among those who remained. The mood was black. The high optimism with which they had begun had a correspondingly long way to fall. Daily they peered out to sea, hoping for relief from the Royalist fleet. There was an explosion of rejoicing when at last a sail appeared. It was a brief display, for they were Parliament's ships, and the supplies they brought were for Cromwell.

And yet they held out for another month, their purpose hardened by the very hopelessness of their condition. If the troops were increasingly rebellious, their officers were ever more resolute. In the end it was treachery that broke them.

Although they lacked food and supplies they had not lacked for water, for the castle contained its own natural source in the cave, deep down in its vaults, called 'Wogan's Cavern'. This led to a watergate on the southern side and also along a conduit to a hillside north of the town, debouching near the house of a man named Edmunds. In hope of a reward, Edmunds revealed the whereabouts of the conduit to Cromwell, who severed the pipe and the castle's lifeline. He did a similar service for Edmunds, whose only reward was a hanging. Surrender was now inevitable.

As Tom rode out behind Poyer and Laugharne to cast themselves on the mercy of Parliament, he expected the quality of that mercy to be very finely strained. It was known that the men of the New Model, saints or not, severely had resented the necessity forced upon them to fight their old battles over again. As for the leaders, Fairfax and Cromwell in particular regretted their enforced absence from Westminster, where the Presbyterian mice were indulging in some constructive play.

In their previous victory Parliament had shown a certain measure of kindness to their enemies. This time they could not hope for it. The tenor of the day was set when Poyer, Laugharne and their colleague Powell all returned from Cromwell's tribunal with long, sardonic faces. They were all three destined for the Tower and were to expect execution. Tom had no reason to expect anything better. His rank, his convictions and his record were all against him.

He wished quite desperately, as he entered the chamber where he would receive his sentence, that he had sent to tell Martha that he loved her. At this moment, it was true. Lately, his dreams had all been of Valora, but that was not his fault. He put it down to the light-headedness of hunger and the slight fever he had suffered after a pike had caught him in the ribs as he had raced to get back into the castle on the day he had met the twins.

The room was long and bare. The general was seated behind a table at the far end. A secretary took notes behind him, while several officers stood to one side in murmured conversation. They fell silent as the cavaliers entered.

Tom looked at Cromwell. He had seen him sometimes at Westminster when he had been there on the King's business or to see his father. He had thought nothing of him then; another ruddy-complexioned country squire with a blunt delivery and little interest in the world's opinion. He had only come to especial notice when he had so ably defended that wretched rabble-rouser Lilburne against his imprisonment for pamphleteering for the sectaries. As the irascible Warwick had put it to someone, 'He aggravated this imprisonment unto the height that one would have believed the very government itself had been in danger from it!' Prophetic words, Uncle Warwick. You should have had them engraved upon Lucy's dinner service.

Poor John Hampden had also prophesied. He had said Cromwell would be one of the greatest men in England. Well, here he was, the great man, sitting behind his table, about to dispose of the future of Sir Thomas Heron. How would that greatness manifest itself?

Tom heard his name read out, among others. Cromwell shuffled papers. A major leaned over his shoulder, pointing to aid him. There was no air of ceremony in the room. He kept no consequence. He was a man with a job to do.

He did not appear to have changed physically. The same high colouring; the much serenaded nose a little redder than the cheeks. The warts, of course. The long, leonine features. The simple soldierly clothes. The eyes, when he raised them to his prisoners, were surprisingly fine. He looked at each man in turn, recognition coming and going in the grey-green, rather melancholy eyes. Tom saw that he was known.

'Gentlemen,' began the authoritative voice in the nasal sharps of East Anglia, 'it is not my aim to be prodigal of blood. For "what doth the Lord require of thee but to do justly and to love mercy and to walk humbly with thy God?" There has been blood enough shed on both sides. This does not mean that evil-doers shall go unpunished. Those who have led their brothers into darkness shall suffer for it. I speak particularly of those who have been apostatized, who have wilfully turned their backs upon the light. I judge their iniquity double because they have sinned in the face of their true knowledge of divine providence.'

A faint breath of relief warmed the room as they realized that it was chiefly the turncoats against whom his vengeance was directed. The general leaned back in his chair and shifted his leg. Tom saw that he held it stretched out as though he suffered from gout. He looked tired. He would be more so before long. The news had reached them that the Scots were crossing the border at last. Cromwell would have the devil's own march ahead of him if he was to be in time to greet them.

'There is also a great burden of guilt upon those who have stirred up a quiet-living countryside to further acts of war, who have seduced a simple and ignorant people to their own destruction. This too must bear its punishment. I order you, therefore, to carry your misguided convictions beyond seas, so that your fellow Englishmen shall be in no danger from them, and shall be drawn instead into godly ways. Gentlemen, you will each leave England for a period of not less than two years.'

It was not bad. Two years was not bad. But it was bad enough. They would not, Tom knew, be permitted to go home before their exile. There would be a ship in Milford Haven that would take them to Holland or France.

An almost frightening lassitude came over him. He could hardly move his limbs when the order was given to quit the court. There was a weariness of spirit that was even more paralyzing. It had not been worth it. That was all.

He stared at Cromwell once more as the general moved past them on his own way out. He walked quickly, as though to another pressing appointment, but he limped slightly. Yes, there was something different about him after all, Tom thought ironically. Something that he himself did not even heed as it hung in the air about him. It was a strange thing to see, and Tom would not forget it, the sight of man totally indifferent to his own tremendous power.

Not far off the hour when Oliver Cromwell extended the gift of his life to her husband, Martha Heron gave birth to his son. As Tom bit his lip in anger at the fate that could separate him again from all that he belonged to, she bit down upon her bedsheet in tremulous fear and delight at what her body was accomplishing. The labour, though painful, was not long, and Margery, assisted by Mary and Alice, proved a most skilful midwife. When it was over and they told her that she had a boy and that he was healthy and well formed, she gave a great cry of joy. 'Young Thomas,' she said, with an air of having paid a debt. 'Young Thomas is here at last.' She smiled at them all and then fell abruptly asleep. She too dreamed, untormentedly, of Valora Grey.

Kit and Humpty stank. They had not changed any of their clothes for longer than they could remember. They were in rags and their hair was as full of lice as their bodies of fleas. They were altogether noisesome objects.

Naturally, this did not detract from the welcome they received, though it added a sharper sauce to Mary's scolding. Even the scolding had to be a mild one, however, as Kit was wounded and too weak for displeasure, and it had been Humpty who, single-handed, had hoicked him onto his horse and kept him there for the unconscionable number of miles between the north Lancashire town of Preston and his bed at Heron.

After the fall of Pembroke, Captain Attila and his company had decided to 'follow the fun' as he put it. The Scots army was over the border and Cromwell posting to meet them. They would steal fresh horses and go as well, though by a different route.

Being so small a number, they should be able to find the Scots long before Cromwell.

'It all looked so hopeful, don't you see?' Humpty said, his eye alight. 'They came down between the coast and the Yorkshire hills. If they could have reached the Midlands without hindrance, Royalists would have flocked to them from all over those shires. If that had happened, Old Ironside wouldn't have had a chance!'

'But it did not happen,' Mary deduced.

Humpty's sigh was gusty with regret. 'God blast him, he came down on us from the Pennines like an accursed avalanche! Our company had joined their march a few days back. They had seen no Parliament troops. *We* had seen no Parliament troops. But there they were. It was more like a massacre than a battle,' he went on disgustedly. 'They say there were 18,000 of the Scots, all told, counting Langdale's men and others like ourselves. They should have been enough to see Cromwell off; he had mustered less than 9,000.'

'Then what went wrong?' asked Martha, rocking young Thomas abstractedly.

'The Scots had sent raw troops, mere boys mostly – no, far younger than us, Mother, I swear – and they had little food, very few horses, not half enough for the wagons, and *no* guns! We kept running, fighting when we could make a stand, and Cromwell kept up with us. In three days he'd captured the whole of our infantry and scattered the poor damned horse to the four winds. It was pure bloody murder, I tell you!'

'Then let us thank the blessed Lord that your brother was not one of those murdered,' said Mary with asperity.

'Yes,' Humpty agreed, his face wiped clean of anger. 'He came very near to it.' He could not imagine what he would do without Kit.

'Thanks to you,' came a quiet voice from the bed near which they sat.

'Do you mean to say—' began Mary, rising, about to let loose all the fury and strain of their careless absence upon them both.

Kit smiled. 'No. I mean thanks to Humpty I *wasn't* murdered. I'd not have lived if he'd let a camp surgeon get at me.' He had taken a musket ball in the hip in one of Cromwell's flying sorties. Humpty had dragged him into a thicket and sat the battle out with him. Kit had soon passed out from the pain. His brother had seen such wounds before. They were harmless if they were kept clean and mended properly. If not, they would go to gangrene and it would be all up with the patient. His father had suffered

582

wounds like this; so had Tom. He began to recall his conversations with them, pondering what was best to do. That rout on the road was no use to him; there would be no physicians among the soldiers. They were all at the camp hospital, and by now, if he was not mistaken, that would be in Cromwell's hands.

He examined Kit's wound. He could see the ball, a small grey point which appeared when he slightly opened the edges of the torn flesh. If it stayed in, the wound would close around it. If not, it might still mortify, but it had a better chance to heal healthily. He said a short prayer and unsheathed his knife, glad that he had always kept it clean and sharp.

His surgery had succeeded as well as many a professional's and here they were. He gave his mother his ultimate charming smile and turned to Isabella, who was never far from his side these days. 'I daresay most men can do most things,' he said carelessly, 'if only they can drum up the courage.'

'There are still certain things of which even the most courageous are afraid,' said Isabella sweetly.

'Which are?' Surely she was going to let him be a hero, just for a day.

'Oh, the things that women seem to take in their stride – such as birth, or cooking, or marriage.'

Humpty gave her a suspicious look. 'There is only one thing women may take in their stride,' he suggested unpardonably, 'and that may well lead to your first; but I'll be damned if any sensible man will let it lead to the last!'

'Humphrey, you are coarse,' reproved Mary.

'Yes, Mother.'

He left them, grinning, and went to look for Captain Morgan. He'd get a great deal more sense out of him than from a pack of women. He hoped they'd looked after him while he and Kit were away. Captain Morgan, snoozing on his favourite shelf in the library, opened an eye at Humpty's step.

'There you are, you old reprobate. What have you got to say to me, huh?'

The parrot cocked his head and thought about it. 'Soldier, soldier, won't you marry me?' he enquired coyly.

London, November 1648

When Will came home that night he deduced that he had left one madhouse for another. Behind him the Commons was in an uproar. The war was over. The victors had come home and were demanding their spoils. Their leaders, short of temper with ingratitude, and having to face the unpalatable fact that the desperate King was now negotiating with Parliament, had flung their challenge to the House in a bitter Remonstrance which called for an end to these relations and the immediate trial of the King. Will had carried home this piece of news to Lucy and with it the sense that his days at Westminster were numbered.

He had opened his door on a bedlam of mobile and vocal female activity. Every woman in the house was running across the hall or up and down the stairs, all of them with their arms full of enough linen, jugs and basins to equip a fair-sized inn. As they ran they shouted and cackled and sang snatches of song. The menservants all seemed to have made themselves scarce. Will didn't blame them.

He grabbed one of the skirling girls as she flashed him with a tray of candied apricots. It was Cissie, usually a composed sort of creature. 'What is this infernal racket about?' he demanded.

Cissie stuck an apricot into his mouth. 'Don't you worry your head a mite. 'Tis all going very well, and will be done directly. Why don't you go out and – take the air for a while?'

'What! Do you order me out of my own house, you minx? Answer my question or it'll be you that takes the air, fast between my fists and your moonstruck head!'

Cissie laughed, fearing no such thing. She relaxed her attitude of flight and looked him tenderly in the eye. 'It is simply that madam is at her lying-in, sir. You will have your son directly, please God.'

All was made clear. Will struck himself on the forehead for not having the wit to work it out for himself. He grinned at Cissie, slapped her behind companionably and took another sweet.

She slapped his hand. 'You mind those! They're for mistress.' Even in what he assumed must be near extremity, Lucy's passion did not desert her. He seized the tray and leaped up the stairs as purposefully as any of the women.

584

He heard his wife long before he saw her. Lucy was shrieking; not in pain, by no means, but in energetic wrath. 'I tell you I will *not* lie on my back like an overturned turtle! This is *my* child and *my* body, and by God it's my house, and if you mislike it, you may go your ways as soon as you please! I'll do well enough with Margery. Better, I dare swear.'

'But it is not fitting nor decent—'

'Decent!' Lucy howled. 'What in the name of Satan and all his devils has it to do with decency? Well, you may clap your decent hands over your Puritanical eyes, God blast you, for I am about to rise and walk about the room, and when the baby appears the first thing *he* will see will be a fine Turkish towel on a fine Turkish carpet!' Will heard the pathetic groans of little Dr Bland as he reached the threshold of the bedchamber.

'My good sir,' cried the poor man, his distressed features pink and shuddering like a salmon jelly, 'I appeal to you—'

'You don't, particularly,' smiled Will, 'and you seem to have utterly estranged my lady wife. What is the trouble?'

But Lucy could speak for herself. 'I can't get this dimwit to understand that I will deliver this infant as I please, and not as it pleases him! Pray tell him to go away.' The doctor looked even more mortified.

' 'Tis well enough without him, Mr Will,' Margery added her straw. She had been in residence for two weeks in anticipation of the birth and had already wreaked havoc among his kitchen and household staff. But since Martha had recommended her so highly as a midwife, nothing would have it but that she must attend Lucy in that capacity.

He kissed the top of Lucy's head. Her hair was damp and hung about her shoulders in uncombed curls. 'You must of course do, my full-bellied brigantine, exactly as you wish.'

She looked smugly at the physician. Vanquished, he retired, muttering sadly about responsibility and consequences.

'How do you feel?' asked Will, smoothing back her hair.

'Very well, just at this moment, but I shall have another pain shortly and then I shall want to scream and I'd rather you were not here to listen.'

'So would I,' agreed Will hastily. This was women's business. 'Let me know when the pain is beginning.'

'Now!' cried Lucy, with an unlovely grimace. 'Get you gone! Out!' Will captured one more apricot and obeyed.

Downstairs he looked for his mother. He had been surprised not to find her in the bedchamber, gloating with the others. She was, in fact, in Will's small study which looked out across the lawns and the small lake fed by the river, to the shrubbery and the ancient walls that separated them from Bedford land.

As he had hoped, he found her to be a haven of tranquillity in the midst of the tempest. 'Regina! Thank God you are not fussing with the rest!'

'I never fuss. You should know that by now.'

'And have always been thankful for it.'

'Is Lucy fussing? I would not have thought it likely.'

'In a fashion. She will stop now that she has her own way.' He described the defeat of the doctor.

'As long as your child does not land on its head! Although, I suppose it would have very little significance if he did; all our family have had strong enough heads.'

'I hope you are being complimentary. Do you object to taking your supper here with me, or do you feel you should be up on deck, swabbing or whatever it is they do?'

Regina gave her slightly superior smile. 'I feel no need whatever. Lucy knows that should she want me, I will go to her, but I honestly think she would have no one but Margery and Cissie, by choice.'

'Then that is whom she will have.' Will settled comfortably, content that he was doing his duty in so far as it went, rang to command the supper and prepared to spend a slightly distracted evening playing cards with Regina. He enjoyed her company as much as any other woman's, save Lucy, and more than that of many men. He appreciated her autocratic beauty as much as the individuality of her mind. She was a fine scholar, among her other accomplishments, and had taught him to love the discovery of knowledge as much as she did herself. Her comprehension of a situation was very quick, as she proved when he described to her the day's commotion in Parliament.

She looked thoughtful, setting delicate teeth into a breast of chicken. 'And do you judge it the better part to take your own departure, gracefully, or remain to be pitched out on your face?'

'I think it best to remain. I talked of it with Harry Vane after the Remonstrance was read. If such as we leave the House, who then will protest against it? There's no doubt that the army *will* use force to remove all opposition to the trial. The only question is how long have we got?'

His answer was a sound like a witches' sabbath from upstairs. Regina smiled widely and followed him sedately as he rushed from the room, his napkin in one hand and a drumstick in the other.

The next time she saw him he still held the napkin, and seated on it, in the crook of his arm, in the splendid nakedness of a Raphael Nativity, was a strapping infant of the male sex. 'Isn't he tremendous?' beamed the happy father. 'A forty-gunner if ever I saw one.'

His son let out an ear-splitting yawl. 'I think he is showing a bias towards dry land,' suggested Lucy, holding out her arms to them both.

When Will had done kissing her, she was combed and scented and sat up to receive visitors and be congratulated. 'But don't 'ee want to sleep now, my poppet?' wondered the equally proud Margery. 'New-made mothers usually do.'

'That is because they have wrestled upon their backs like landed fish and have no more strength left in them,' said Lucy triumphantly. 'I feel marvellous and I want everyone to come and tell me that I *am* marvellous!'

'What are you going to call him, Madam?' Cissie asked when they had all obeyed her.

Lucy looked at Will. 'I would like him to be young William but—'

'But *I* feel it would be politic, and probably later very useful, to have him named after the Earl of Warwick,' he said firmly.

'Him!' said Lucy disparagingly. 'He did not even wish you to wed me. He wanted you married to your precious cousin Eliza!'

'Nonetheless, he is a powerful friend, when he is feeling friendly. He will hardly refuse to be the boy's godfather. And there are worse names than Robert.'

'Not many,' said Lucy sulkily. After all, *she* had produced the prodigy; she had the right to name him. But Will was right, of course. Little Robert would need all the powerful friends he could get, in whatever sort of a world these Puritans would build for him. 'Look, his eyes are green,' she said softly. 'He looks like a changeling.'

'That's what I thought about you, when I first saw you,' grinned Will. 'But this one is a sight too large for a fairy's child.' The baby waved an uncoordinated fist and hit his mother in the eye.

At sixteen days of age, Robert Rich Heron Staunton provided an unwilling majority of his parental household with a formidable wakening alarm. His wet-nurse had been found to be stone deaf and Lucy was considering the uncustomary step of feeding him herself if the wretched woman could not discover some method of precluding the raucous dawn chorus.

When Will found himself, as a result of his son's efforts, making his way to Westminster at eight o'clock in the dark of a particularly inhospitable morning, he was cheered, if puzzled, to fall in with his good-brother, notebook in hand, bent in the same direction. 'What brings you here?' he asked, after the usual informalities.

'Can't you guess?'

'You've heard something. It's to be today, then?'

'It is.'

'I don't know how you fellows always manage to know everything before it happens,' grumbled Will.

'Because those who make things happen are always anxious not to be misrepresented in the press.'

They arrived outside the Commons. They were not alone. 'No one,' said Will dryly as he surveyed the considerable number of troops stationed before the building, 'could misrepresent *those* gentlemen.'

'They do appear to nurture a certain firmness of purpose.'

They were stolid Independent infantrymen, their honest work-aday faces carefully blank above trunks that seemed to have taken root behind the slender threat of their pikes. In front of the door itself an officer in an orange-tawny sash thumbed down a list in his hand, detaining the Honourable Members who attempted to pass into the chamber. 'Who is that fellow?' asked Will, frowning.

'A Colonel Pride. He goes up in the world. In civilian life, they say, he was a brewer's drayman, and now he puts down the mighty from their seats!'

'Does he, by God! And whom does he think to put in their place – the brewer's geldings?' Will's hand went automatically to his sword as another Member turned away, tight-lipped, and strode off toward Westminster Hall.

'He is merely carrying out his orders.' Jud was unmoved.

'Whose orders? Cromwell's?'

'Cromwell is not yet in London. He was delayed before Pontefract. The city held out longer than he bargained for. No – the order was likely to have come from Ireton.'

'The Remonstrance came from Ireton, too,' mused Will sourly. 'He is a busy man these days.' The fierce little general was not one of his favourites, being too extreme in his partisanship of the radical element among the troops.

'But whose will the power be, when all this is over?' Jud asked sceptically. 'Not Ireton's, I'll be bound! Our Oliver is playing a cautious game. He has not let his hand be seen in any of it.'

'Except to send Fairfax his forces' petition for justice against the instigators of the second war, meaning the King.'

'Nearly every regiment did the same. It was not especially Cromwell's doing.' Jud gave a sudden spurt of sympathetic laughter. 'Poor Fairfax! He hardly knows which way to turn. The greater part of his army is for killing the King, while he, its lord general and chief spokesman, wants no part of it.'

'Then why is he not *here* – preventing *this*?' demanded Will with contempt.

Jud shrugged. 'Because in all probability it would only lead to further bloodshed. He'd be setting his troops against each other.'

'Yet he marched on London. He authorized the Remonstrance.'

'If he had not, they would have done without him. And what, in the event, has come of the Remonstrance? Parliament shelved it!'

'*This* has come of it. And God knows what will follow.'

'I can tell you one other thing that has,' Jud volunteered. 'Fairfax has moved the King into closer confinement. At Hurst Castle, on the mainland opposite the Isle of Wight. His communications are to be severly curtailed. There will be no more intriguing with the Scots or Irish or his cousin Louis.'

'Then His Majesty is wholly in the power of the army.'

'Indeed.'

Will sighed. 'Then I think he will not live long.'

'No. How can they let him live?' Jud asked reasonably. 'We offered him mercy and he abused our faith and brought down the Scots on our heads. Hang it, Will, he deserves to die!'

Will controlled the instinct to hit him. 'I'm heartily sorry to hear you say so,' he said coldly. 'And now, I think I must leave you. You'll call on Lucy?'

'Of course.' Jud looked softened. 'I would have come when Cleo did; but I've been up to my eyes just lately—'

'Quite.'

Will left him with swift determined strides. He was shaking with anger but he knew he must not break with Jud over this. If he did so, the chances of mending the rift in Lucy's family would be postponed indefinitely. The devil of it was that everything Jud had said about the King was undeniably true. He was as recalcitrant now as he had ever been back in '41. In all these six years of war between Englishmen, he had learned nothing. Nothing. But that did not mean his subjects had the right to take his life, nor even to bring him to trial. Whatever the number of his faults, he was still the King. Despondently, Will walked up to the door of the House and went through the motions of trying to enter it.

As he had expected, his name was on the list and he was turned away. As he had previously agreed with Harry Vane and others of a like mind, he recorded his protest at the use of force to keep Members from their seats.

He stood and watched as several of his colleagues tried to get in by using force of their own. One by one they were overcome and carried off to a nearby tavern, requisitioned as a temporary jail. There they might cool their boiling blood. Appropriately for such a heated occasion, the place went by the popular appellation of 'Hell'.

He supposed they showed spirit, of an impulsive kind. But for himself, now that matters stood where they were, he could see little point for a realist in contesting the proven strength of the army. In a very short time, he was shown to be absolutely right.

It took just three weeks for the arrogant remnant of the Commons, perhaps eighty men in all, to vote to bring their King to justice. In case anyone should doubt their authority to do so, they also passed resolutions declaring themselves the supreme power in the nation, all their acts to have the force of law.

For his first Christmas gift, Lucy gave little Robert a teething bone carved into a likeness of Cromwell's face, with particularly salient warts. 'Chew him to pieces, as soon as you are able,' she bade the boy, who lay cradled in blissful ignorance as she set off with Will to Westminster Hall to attend the trial that, even now, she could hardly believe would actually take place.

There was a black frost that day and the air was like steel. Both Stauntons were well wrapped against the inevitable cold of the hall, and Lucy's mask even had a brief velvet nose-piece, since a red nose is no hint at beauty. She thought, as they joined the crowd who converged upon the vaulted cathedral-like north entrance, that this great cavern of a building had seen its share of the sorrows of kings; Edward II had come here to abdicate, Richard II to be deposed. Men had been tried here in many generations; the Scots pretender, William Wallace, the saintly Thomas More, the arch-plotter, Guy Fawkes, and during those ill-fated days just before Will Staunton's gilded figure had strode into her life so that it should be changed forever after, the Earl of Strafford himself, whose last moments, and last words she would always remember, and never more poignantly than now.

With a lump in her throat formed of anger, misery and a despairing pity that spanned the seven years between the man whom Parliament had forced the King to kill and the man whom Parliament would begin to kill today, she quoted them to Will. 'He asked all of us who heard him to consider well whether the beginning of the happiness of a nation could ever be written in letters of blood. That is what the great majority of the people of England would say to these would-be murderers today! It is they who are the criminals! It is they who should be brought to trial!

'Gently. Such sentiments will get you refused at the door. That would be a pity, after the difficulty I had in acquiring the tickets.'

She held her peace until they had entered the hall. Its vast belly was better filled today than perhaps ever in its history. It was astonishing how the great space, some 300 feet long and perhaps seventy across, had contracted into a tiered oblong of eyes and noise, all concentrated upon a small booth, resembling nothing so much as a horse's loose-box, set near the south end beneath the double row of graceful gothic windows and containing a single, empty, crimson-clad chair.

Their seats were high up on the scaffolding erected to form the galleries. The view was excellent. Lucy had to keep reminding herself that they were not in a theatre, so dramatic was the speaking presence of that empty chair. 'You must tell me who everyone is,' she murmured to Will, who was occupied in bowing towards various acquaintances, many of them masked, but none the less recognizable.

One of the women was Eliza. She was wearing black and her face was painted to seem otherwise. Her smile for Will was far too intimate to please Lucy, but this was not the occasion to voice any complaint. She contented herself with a few smiles and polite inclinations of her own, and in making herself known to her nearest neighbour, who she was surprised to learn was Lady Fairfax.

Anne Fairfax was a pleasant and attractive woman, young, with dark intelligent eyes which shrewdly roamed the hall. She lost no time in declaring herself for the King, unless Lucy should feel ill at ease beside the wife of the enemy's senior soldier.

'Indeed no,' Lucy responded warmly. 'You do not make me feel half so uncomfortable as the sight of those poor tattered banners.' She indicated the rank of worn and shredded Royalist flags that hung on permanent display up among the angels that decorated the two-foot thick hammer beams that supported the mighty roof. They were all regimental colours captured in the great battles – Marston, Naseby, Preston. 'It is not pleasant to see them thus in their shame, especially if one has sewn them, as I have, intending them for glory.' She was thinking of the perfect heron she had fashioned for her father, a piercing streak of white flight against a sky-blue background. It had been lost at Newbury. At least it was not here among the other wretched trophies. Lady Fairfax pressed her hand, generous with her sympathy.

At that moment there was a louder hubbub from below, and then the trumpets sounded as the judges came in to take their places. The long rows of pikemen, who guarded the cordoned-off areas where the public sat, now banged their weapons peremptorily on the floor. The talking died down.

Lucy knew that the Attorney General and the Chief Justices had refused to serve the court, among them St John, now Chief Justice of the Common Pleas. Nor would the greatest lawyers of the day, John Selden and Bulstrode Whitelocke. In the end the High Court had been set up under the Presidency of John Bradshaw, a mere sheriff's court judge from Cheshire, whose chief suitability for the post was simply that he would agree to undertake it. It was he who was making his entrance now, walking portentously among his guard, in a fine scarlet robe of office and a high-crowned beaver hat.

'I see the glint of armour beneath that berry-red velvet,' said Will, close to Lucy's ear.' And I hear that the beaver is lined with steel. Uneasy lies the head that would strike off the head that wears the crown.' She would not smile. There was no humour in her today.

Bradshaw was followed by the Prosecutor, a man named John Cook. Will had never heard of him and did not know anyone who had. These two took their places in the centre of the three rows of judges, who faced the waiting cubicle with its velvet chair across a table draped in an oriental carpet. Nearby, also in the front rank, Lucy suddenly recognized the original of Robert's chewing-ring. She had not seen him before. He did not appear as frightful as she had expected; a severe man certainly, but neither an ogre nor the giant among men his legend was building.

The sight of him recalled Jud to her mind. She looked back among the packed rows of benches behind the accused's box to see if she could find him. She did not see him, but he would be there; so would Robin. They had not invited Jud to sit with them because neither she nor Will wished to associate themselves with a would-be regicide. They had not quarrelled, not precisely, but they were on awkward terms, although Lucy still had a firm friend in Cleo, who was sorry for the King, now that he had come to this pass.

The uneven clamour of the crowd now became full of shushings and smothered exclamations; there was a shuffling of feet and chairs. The guard stood to attention. The King was coming.

Lucy leaned forward, her breath caught and stopped in her breast. Below her, every head turned expectantly towards the door. She felt the sharp searing of tears as His Majesty entered the hall. She had forgotten how small he was.

His diminutive stature seemed to point his comfortless isolation as he made his way towards the confinement of the foolish wooden box. He was dressed with his customary plain elegance in a suit of stark black, relieved by the blue ribbon of the Garter and the glittering medallion of St George. He carried a narrow silver-topped cane. He walked with unhurried dignity to the crimson chair, stood still for a little time before it and surveyed the court with a stern and serious look. He did not remove his hat, signifying his lack of respect for the court. Behind him the people breathed again and the pikemen shifted and stamped.

The first task was to call the roll of the judges. Of the 135 men whose names were listed, only sixty-eight answered. When they came to the name of Fairfax, Lucy sensed her neighbour stiffen as the silence stretched. 'He has more wit than to be here!' came the sudden cry beside her, and there were several tight smiles as Lady Fairfax was recognized by those near to her.

John Cook, as Solicitor to the Commonwealth, read the charges against the King. They called him tyrant, traitor, murderer, an implacable enemy of his country. He had first levied war against Parliament, and was the complete author of the second war. At one point in the rigmarole the King attempted to interrupt, reaching with his cane to touch Cook on the arm. As he tapped him, the silver knob flew off and rolled to his feet. The King and the public waited for someone to pick it up. Since no one did so, Charles bent to retrieve it himself.

Lucy burned with embarrassment to see him stoop; he had been accustomed all his life to being served on bended knee. 'What *little* men are these,' she whispered fiercely to Will.

Bradshaw was now calling on the King to answer the charges, on behalf of the Commons assembled in Parliament and the good people of England. Again there was a movement beside Lucy and Anne Fairfax cried out boldly, 'It is a lie! Not half, not one quarter of the people! Oliver Cromwell is a traitor!'

The vast space hummed and stirred as necks craned upwards.

The colonel in charge of the guard, his face red with fury, levelled his pistol at the masked discouragement in the gallery but the only sound that followed was the hiss of a thousand indrawn breaths. 'We had better get her out of it,' muttered Will, getting to his feet. The friends on her other side evidently concurred and Lady Fairfax was hustled down and out before she could earn herself the court's first sentence.

'If only her husband were as brave,' whispered Lucy when Will returned, 'he would make a stand to save His Majesty.'

'If you are eager for a third conflict, then that is the way to think,' said Will brusquely, tired of the argument and dispirited by its uselessness.

As the trial progressed he became even more dispirited. It was a fiasco. Charles' first question showed it up for what it was. 'By what authority have I been brought to the bar? I see no Lords here who would make it a Parliament. Since I am not convinced that you constitute a lawful authority, I will not answer you. It would betray my trust.'

Bradshaw, flustered by the cool, unhesitating voice, spoke more harshly, perhaps, than he had meant. 'You are brought here by the authority of the people of England, by whom you were elected King.'

Even Lucy could make out the sardonic flight of the royal brow. 'My crown came to me by inheritance, not by election.'

Further put out, Bradshaw continued to press the charges, but he tried in vain to compel the King to answer them. All he would do was steadfastly to insist that this self-styled court had no authority to try him, or indeed the lowest of his subjects, under the existing laws of England.

It dragged on. The two voices, one high, the other harsh, fluttered about each other like battling birds, giving no ground and accomplishing nothing except to weary the opponent. When it was over for the day Lucy was in agony over the hopelessness of it all.

'You need come no more. They will have to continue, perhaps for several days, even longer. You have seen how it will be. Why not stay at home with Robert? You'd be in better company.'

'No. It is my right and my duty to attend. Besides, I want to. The King should have his friends about him. God knows there is a whole division of his enemies!'

The sad piece of flummery mouldered on for a further three days. Lady Fairfax did not appear again. Perhaps the Lord General had persuaded her of the futility of it.

On the second day the King asked if he might address the court on the subject of his reasons for refusing to answer the charges. He was refused.

Charles insisted. 'I do require that I may give my reasons why I do not answer, and give me time for that.'

'It is not,' replied Bradshaw insolently, 'for prisoners to require!'

'Prisoners!' For the first time the King raised his voice. 'Sir, I am not an ordinary prisoner.' There was a silence while all present were forced to record the truth of this remark.

Bradshaw again demanded an answer to the charges. Again he was refused. Brought to a halt by the repeated, unwavering refusal, the President was forced to bid the clerk of the court simply to record the default. Still the King had not been allowed to give his reasons.

'Why will they not let him speak?' demanded Lucy, today more angered than distressed. 'It is his right, more than anyone's.'

'He may speak only in answer to the charges.'

Lucy gave a tut of contempt. 'You talk,' she said, 'as if it were a properly constituted court of law, instead of an army charade.'

'It may not have the right,' said Will brutally, 'but you cannot deny that it has the power.'

'Only because you are all such hang-back, mouse-minded cowards! If every man in London, even, who misliked this mummery, should band together and march on the hall, you could topple those play-actors in twenty minutes!'

Will, who had entertained something of the sort himself, for a mad half-hour, shook his head and would not be drawn. He would not go with Lucy to the court on the third day, however, and when pressed, he admitted he was going to visit Fairfax. He added, as she threw herself upon him in delighted approval, that he didn't suppose it would do any good.

When she arrived at Westminster, Lucy found to her surprise that the court was not open to the public that day. She spent it at home, playing with Robert and waiting with frantic impatience for Will to return.

When he came home, quite late in the evening, his expression warned her to kill her hope. 'He can do nothing. He won't risk war. The Scots were there too, a couple of Estates members, canvassing Fairfax's support against Cromwell. They had already seen Cromwell himself; when they told him they held the trial to be unlawful he quoted their own law against them. Apparently there is some century-old doctrine that allows the killing of a tyrant. Cromwell also seems to have some wild idea that the power of a King is founded on some sort of *contract* with his subjects – a contract which His Majesty has broken, for which he may be deposed and punished. The notion is not new. Kings have been deposed before – what I chiefly sense in this is Oliver's sincere and serious desire to make an act of law and justice out of what began as an act of force.'

'He cannot.'

'No. But it will not matter. He will do as he pleases.'

'Then there is nothing we can do for the King?'

Will took her hand and kissed it, having no other comfort for her. 'He has asked that his friends should pray for him.' Lucy did pray, long into the night.

The next day they both resumed their places in the gallery. The proceedings now took on the character of an old mystery play, intended to uplift but degenerated by the performance of groundlings. Despite the King's refusal to countenance the charges, the prosecution now produced a sorry cast of witnesses. Lucy was impelled to laugh, weep, and stand up and shout, all at once and every other minute, as the shameful procession of moral scarecrows fluttered their ragged depositions, intended to prove that His Majesty had gone to war upon his innocent people. Some said that they had seen him set up his standard at Derby; some that they had seen him on the battlefield with his sword drawn. Others testified to his ill-treatment of prisoners or to his plundering of hapless civilians. There was evidence that he had, during his months of captivity, plotted with divers different men towards a resumption of the war. Most of the things they said were true.

'But,' said Lucy, none too quietly, while the judges were considering what they had caused to be heard, 'whether they are true or false, the only truth that holds any weight is that of who holds the power. As you told me yesterday. He who holds it, does as he pleases. If the King did as he pleased when he was able, can they take his life for doing then as they do now?'

'He would take theirs, if he could,' was Will's unhelpful response.

And yet, it seemed, it was the King himself who would give her the last and best word on that bitter subject. He must have long given up hope, if he ever had any, by the time the bombastic Bradshaw had bludgeoned the floor long enough to feel he could allow the poor accused his crust of dry words. His voice was warm and strong, and hearing its certain tones Lucy felt a great well of affection press up within her that she had never known to be part of her. She loved him and felt for him as she had loved and felt for Thomas Strafford when she was a child. Perhaps neither had been a just man; she did not know; but she had known the nobility in Strafford as she knew it now in Charles Stewart. She wept for it, as she listened to his words, and she was triumphantly proud of it.

The King dwelled, as always, upon the complete illegality of these proceedings. But now he presented himself not only as an innocent man in unlawful hands, but as the champion of the law, the Parliament and the people. '– It is not my case alone; it is the freedom and the liberty of the people of England; and do you pretend what you will, *I* stand more for their liberties! For if power without law may make laws, may alter the fundamental laws of the kingdom, I do not know what subject there is in England that can be sure of his life, or anything that he calls his own.'

Not for the first time, there fell that silence that speaks loudly that it has heard the truth. It was not a silence liked by the court. There was a tremendous clearing of judgemental throats, a banging of chairs, and, when they had caught onto it, a pounding of pikemen's boots and butts.

Lucy wanted to hear no more after that. She and Will left the hall and did not return to it. The sentence, when it came, was what he had prepared her to expect. The King would be put to death by the severing of his head from his body.

The execution was at Whitehall. Pressed close beneath a sky as bleak as bones, the King's Englishmen convened to see him die. They were told it was their sovereign's will that this should happen, but most did not understand it, and few could be said to desire it.

Among that few, standing with Rob Whittaker in the shadow of the scaffold that had risen before the shuttered windows of Inigo Jones's great Banqueting Hall, was Jud Heron. They were engaged in one of their periodical truces, but quarrelling had come to be a habit with them and they were arguing now, impeded now and then by the demands of one or other of the Whittaker children. Endymion, Charlemagne, Ettamaria and Podge were all with them, their fretful hands sewn up into white mittens unless they insinuated themselves into more hazard than the family could well sustain on one day.

Rob was waving his hands. 'I tell you, unless we stand firm for our reforms, we shall simply find ourselves under an army junta instead of a royal despot or a Parliament clique. We must push forward the "Agreement" with all our strength; march, publicize, find out our sympathizers all over the country! If we don't seize the moment now, it'll be all over with us in a few months.'

'I don't see why,' said Jud, 'and I wish you wouldn't speak as though I were a christened member of the Leveller congregation. I'm not.'

'To the devil with that. You're thinking with your arse, as ever. You don't *want* to see the truth. You'd rather keep the image of your precious Cromwell unsullied.'

'It is *you* who won't accept, prickwit, that I *can* stomach a military junta; what we need right now is strong government; law and order and no uncertainty. Cromwell will give us that. What have you to complain of? He was in the middle of negotiations with your Leveller brothers when the question of the trial came up. They'll be resumed. Why can't you have patience?'

'Because I know that what he will do is to cut off our balls and let us go hang ourselves!' Rob's eyes narrowed in his foxy mask, bearded now, giving him a strong resemblance to Machiavelli. 'The trouble with you, Jud, is the same as with Cromwell; you can't forget that you are gentlemen. And no matter what democratic principles you may claim in your high-flown moments – in your hearts and, more importantly, deep down in your comfortable guts – you want to see the country ruled by gentlemen.'

'I want it ruled by those who are fit to rule! I don't care whether they be gentlemen or tallow-chandlers! And neither does Cromwell.' One of the New Model colonels was a tallow-chandler.

'We shall see,' said Robin gloomily.

In another part of the crowd, flanked and protected from jostling by numbers of their servants, stood Lucy and her husband. With them were Kit and Humpty who had ridden down to carry out their last duty to the King on behalf of the inhabitants of Heron.

As Lucy watched Humpty sucking lustily on an orange, its sweet astringency brought a sudden smart of memory. A small girl seated on her father's shoulders, looking out across just such a crowded waste of faces as this; and feeling, as its inseparable babble beat about her, that the world had contracted into an alien arena of bloodthirst and cruelty, where very soon she herself, also condemned, must perish.

It had been a terrifying moment but it had not lasted. Some child had waved to her from another pair of shoulders and she had been herself again. Even so, she had not been able to remain among that vengeful multitude. She leaned close to Will and put her hand in his.

He had been watching her face. He squeezed the hand. 'Let me know when you wish to go and vomit into the river,' he offered, 'and I will take you there.'

Her smile acknowledged his understanding. 'And yet, it is not the same, here, today,' she said. 'Nothing like the same. Oh, we are the same crowd, give or take a few – as vast certainly – and many of these, perhaps, may be the same soldiers who guard and prevent us. But on that day they stood and bayed for blood. Today see how they wait with heads downcast, and many of them pray.'

'Poor Strafford. I imagine that His Majesty may think of him now,' said Will. 'The wheel has come full circle.'

She registered the quotation. Lear. 'My father would have said the same,' she said tenderly. If she turned around, would she find that great oak of a man behind her shoulder, crying out Shakespeare's words to Shakespeare's children here assembled?

'I've heard His Majesty has spent a deal of his time reading your precious Will during his captivity.'

'You are my precious Will. There is little comfort for kings in Shakespeare.'

'No, but much instruction.' They looked at each other in silence. The King had not taken the instruction.

Just then there was a scuffle at Lucy's side and a small white hand plucked at her waist. 'Why it's Ettamaria! What are you doing here, child? I am surprised your mother let you come.'

The thin shoulders shrugged. 'She's 'ere 'erself, somewhere. 'Er Frenchie turned up and 'ee brought 'er. 'Ee give 'er a box of marchpane. Did'n give *us* any!' She wrinkled her freckled nose in disdain for Gallic parsimony.

Lucy nudged Kit, who felt in his pocket and produced a sticky amalgam of Margery's apricots, wrapped in paper. 'First, Etta, let's get those gloves off you, or they'll spoil.'

Lucy was the only one to forbear laughter when they were discovered to be a fixture. She placed a sweet carefully on Henrietta Maria's thrust-out tongue, passed them round but did not join in as they all chewed lingeringly. Her appetite had left her during the trial and had not yet returned.

Etta, swallowing the last morsel, suddenly became conscious of the occasion and addressed herself with grave self-importance to a woman standing next to them. 'My name is the same as the Queen's!'

'God bless her and bring her his comfort and mercy, poor lady,' the woman said pityingly. 'She'll be a widow before the clock strikes.'

Fate, it seemed, was willing to accept this timetable, for there was a sudden rush of movement through the crowd like the wind that freshens the corn before a storm. All eyes were drawn behind the scaffold to the first-floor window that had been unblocked and now stood open. Once again, and only once, the King was coming.

There was a fleeting space while all the world seemed empty of content and then the slight, black-clad figure stepped out into a silence as heavy as snow. He had only one friend with him, he who had once counted half the world his friend; it was his chaplain, Bishop Juxon, who had been at his side since the sentence had fallen. The only other players in this last masque, staged with such poverty upon oaken beams, were the two colonels who stood guard, and with them the only men who needed an actor's disguise that day – the executioner and his assistant, masked, bearded and bewigged lest any among the audience should wish to revenge the purgation of pity and terror that they would surely show them.

The silence weighed as they looked their last on the slender, significant protagonist. Today he could wear no hat and it could be seen that his hair was silver and his beard steel-grey. An old man, though he was only as old as the century. Old, tired, dishonoured and defeated, still as he stood there mute beneath the darkening sky, every inch a King.

They were not to let him speak, Lucy knew. They feared the effect of any appeal upon the great beating heart that was this crowd. Even if they should relent, there were too many rows of soldiers placed about the scaffold for anyone else to come near enough to hear.

She was surprised, therefore, to see him take a folded paper from his pocket and address himself to his companions on the scaffold. It was a short speech lasting only a matter of minutes. They would be able to read, later, what he had said. But now there could be no putting off the moment for which they had all been driven here.

Lucy looked for Ettamaria, with some idea of protecting her from the sight, but the child had slipped away into the throng. In sadness and duty, she fixed her own eyes upon the grim platform.

There seemed an agonizing slowness in every motion as the King first knelt in prayer, and then, having commended his soul to God, bent his head and laid it on the block. There was an endless interval before he flung his outstretched hands and pointed the way for his severed spirit.

'Behold the head of a traitor!' came the executioner's cry.

As he held aloft the bleeding head, there came from the throat of the crowd a deep and universal groan, as though their spirits too went with him, with an awful tearing of dissolution from the body. Lucy, shaking and blinded, felt Will's arms come round her and hold the world still for her.

Part Four

It was as though a great sickness had descended on the house. The servants moved quietly about their business with their eyes downcast. No one sang. When Robert crowed in his cradle, Lucy found herself shushing him without thinking.

'Poor baby. You are the only one who is innocent here,' she told him. She knew it was unreasonable, as Will would quickly tell her, but for her a sense of the guilt of a whole country was as pervasive and as foul as corruption. Even Will himself, now back at Westminster under Cromwell's amended oath of loyalty to the Commons and held fascinated by the prospect of watching him try to turn his vision of a godly state into reality, was quiet in his step and given to long periods of solitary thought.

When at last she ventured out into the streets again, it was into the same dark pool of quiet. People passed each other without a good day and if their eyes met, they parted again with a shifty swiftness as though caught out in collusion.

Lucy decided to keep to her house and gardens and address herself to her son, her books, her music and her letters. Letter-writing had always been one of her chief pleasures; now her pen became a knife turned and turned again in her own wound. 'We have killed the King. England has killed her King,' she wrote, and could find no comfort to smother the bitterness of the description that followed.

The worst task was to write to Tom, perhaps the only one of them, now that they could be counted, who had been the King's man, heart, soul and doubts, without wavering, until the end and after. He was in Brussels now, with Montrose, whom he had found in The Hague, and from whom, when at last it seemed that their cause was dead and done, he had taken new fire. He had known the King must die. 'Long live the King!' he had written last, 'Long live His Majesty King Charles II!' Even before the father was dead, Tom had taken up the weight of another crown. He had asked Martha to add the name Stewart to young Thomas's titles. Montrose was gathering men and would soon be under arms in Scotland. They would crown the young Prince there and his loyal subjects would flock to him. Soon they would march on England and place him on the throne.

Lucy could only guess at the despairing sense of loss and futility that Tom had been forced to conquer before he could take up the cause, the sword, the leaping hope once again. She loved him for his loyalty and she deeply pitied him.

For herself, she no longer harboured such hopes. Like Will, like Oliver Cromwell, she would be content with a return to quiet streets and an ordered society. She would make plans that were small in scale, human and selfish and, above all, possible. She would have Martha stay with her, and young Thomas. She would be close to Jud again. She would make Will happy. She would continue the education of the small Whittakers. She would read everything that John Milton had published. One day, she knew, she would wake up to find that she liked herself again.

But however pleasant this inward-looking and self-preserving scheme of things might have proved, Lucy found that she was not to be left to pursue it. Her first intimation of this was when one day Will found her reading the *Eikon Basilike*, the account of the dead King's sufferings that was being read throughout the country. 'What, are you still wrapped up in the fate of that one misguided man?' he asked.

His lack of sympathy surprised her. 'I thought we shared an opinion of that fate.'

'It is over. It is finished.'

'One life is over. That does not alter what it has stood for, and what, for many, his son will one day stand for.'

Will sighed briefly. He seemed irritable. 'The past. That is what it stands for. It does not do to concern oneself too much with the past, especially when the future is, to say the least of it, open to question.'

'What do you mean? Whose future?'

'Ours, for one. Robert's. I inherited two fine properties and an extraordinarily flourishing business from my father. I hope to be able to pass on the same to him; more, if possible. Such hopes take hard work to make them transpire. Harder than ever now.' His frown had deepened.

'What is the matter?' she asked gently.

He grimaced. 'Nothing. Not yet. But times are getting harder. The war cost a great deal of money. Merchant trade is now a matter of moving across the map of ocean between the monsters of the deep – Rupert and his pirate fleet, the Dutch, the Spanish. I've just heard that the *Regina* has been taken, off Portugal. And Cromwell wants me to lend him a couple of thousand towards the conquest of Ireland!'

'Shall you lend it?'

'Only an idealist or a fool would lend money to a government which is almost as unpopular on its own ground as it is with the rest of Europe. Wear your fur tippet, my dear, you and Eliza both, for it's the last you'll see for a while. The Tzar has kicked every English merchant out of Russia.'

'I'm sorry about the *Regina*. So will your mother be. But surely, we are none so badly off? Six ships came in with full cargoes.'

'And six more are at the mercy of the monsters. Aye, I suppose we'll make do. But I must give more time to trade. This session is going to be a series of scraps with the blasted Levellers anyway. I doubt I'll put in much time on it. Oliver will see them off, as soon as need be; he must, before their voice becomes too strong to shout down.'

'I thought we had finished with strife, for the moment,' sighed Lucy wearily.

'Dear child,' he grinned, 'we have just got our second wind. There'll be all sorts of skirmishing. You'll see!'

Not only did Lucy see, but in the event, and quite without any intention of doing so, she took part herself in a very definite 'skirmish'. She had called on Cleo, thinking to spend a pleasant afternoon with her, doing nothing in particular and talking a good deal.

Cleo, however, had other ideas. 'Oh I *am* ever s'sorry, Lucy; but I'm goin' out. I must go. It's important.'

A supressed excitement in her voice made Lucy ask, 'What is it, that's so important? Have you got work to do?'

Despite Jud's relative affluence, Cleo still kept up her work as a seamstress, being unaccustomed to trust in the future. 'No. I'm goin' over to Westminster, since you ask.' She seemed faintly embarrassed.

'Well, I have the coach. I'll take you. What brings you there?'

'Oh. I dunno about the coach. Leastways, not all the way. I do reckon the road'll be blocked.'

'Why? Cleo, what *is* this about?'

Cleo laughed. 'Perhaps you should come with me, after all. It might amuse you, or you might get more out of it than amusement. I'll not tell you. I'll leave you to find out for yourself. But 'tis to do with Freeborn John and the others.'

Lucy groaned. Parliament had put the Leveller leaders in jail. Lilburne had spurned Cromwell's somewhat half-hearted attempts to come to terms with their increasingly radical aims, and had fomented his followers into a fine froth of activity. Last month a group of them had dug up St George's Hill in Surrey and planted it with beans, as a demonstration of their theory that all the land of England belonged to each and all of her people. Fairfax had soon dealt with this piece of exaggeration but the time was approaching when he would have to face the far more serious opposition of the Levellers' support in the army. Meanwhile Lilburne and his lieutenants were back in their old home. Lucy did not particularly relish the prospect of watching yet another public proof of their popularity; they were apt to be noisy, unruly and often violent. But if that was what Cleo found so important . . .

They plunged into a discussion of the charms and advancements of their respective sons as they were settled inside the coach and this occupied them until they turned to cross Westminster Bridge. Here the coachman stopped and descended. 'I don't think I'd better take 'er over, madam. There seems to be somewhat of a crowd gathering.'

'*Must* we?' murmured Lucy, but she followed Cleo down from the vehicle, glad at least of spring weather and no mud.

The crowd was quite sizable and was moving briskly towards the Commons. The coachman and his boy walked behind them as they came up to make part of it. Both he and Lucy were struck at the same instant with a surprising fact. 'Oh Lord save us,' ejaculated Will's immaculate driver. 'Every live one of 'em's a woman!'

And so they were. Hundreds of them, streaming towards St Stephen's Chapel where the Commons met. (The Lords no longer met anywhere; they had been dismissed without a whimper at the beginning of the session.) They were laughing and talking together with a busy air as though they went to market. Some, further to the front, were singing a catchy little ditty. Lucy caught the last words of the chorus.

> We will not be wives
> And tie up our lives
> To villainous slaver–ee–ee!

'God's boots!' she whispered.

'Come on!' Cleo seized her firmly by the hand and pulled her into the mainstream. There were several greetings as they matched their step to that of the crowd, as though from neighbour to neighbour, meeting at church or in the square. From their dress Lucy saw they were not poor women, on the whole, nor well-to-do, but perhaps mostly of lower middle sort, the wives of the small traders and craftsmen, providers and shopkeepers who supported the teeming life of the City. They wore their best and they walked with a free swing that suggested they thought well of themselves.

A large woman in scarlet to match her face cast Lucy a look of virtuous displeasure. 'Go on, sisters under the skin!' nudged a smaller one next to her, smiling in a knowing fashion.

Cleo gurgled. 'They think you're a whore, because you're dressed so fine,' she whispered impishly.

Lucy, now bent on enjoying herself, hitched up her green silk skirts to show her rose and white striped petticoat and walked with more of a swagger. When they reached the space outside the House, however, a serious mood took over. The great mass of women attained an unnatural hush and the only movement now was at the front.

'They are taking in the petition,' observed Cleo.

'What petition?'

'First, they want lower prices and fairer taxes; and then they want the Levellers set free, for they are the men who will get us these things, if any can.'

'I didn't know you thought this way. Jud is so much against the Levellers these days.'

Cleo shrugged. 'Jud isn't *me*, now is 'ee, Lucy love?'

Lucy's respect for her unlawful good-sister increased yet again. 'Is that what all these women think?'

Cleo laughed. 'It is what *all* women think, isn't it?'

'Perhaps. Yes, I think it is. But I would not expect to profit by it.'

'Wait. We'll see.'

They waited. The Commons, it seemed, would give them an answer. Several men had appeared in the doorway of the Chapel.

'Safety in numbers! Poor shrimps!' cackled one of Lucy's new sisters. The reply was read out and quickly passed back through the throng, in a tone which presaged displeasure.

The woman in scarlet, who had good lungs from berating her husband, roared that the scurvy Commons gave them to know that were petitioning about matters above their heads, and that Parliament had given an answer to their husbands. A great shriek went up at that and the scarlet woman had to beat the air for a further hearing. '—To our husbands, who, if you please, are our legal representatives.' Another skirling engulfed her. When it died down she cast her last flaming piece of fuel. 'They bid us all go home and look after our own business and meddle with our housewifery!'

After that there was pandemonium. The group of gentleman, looking wan and beleaguered, backed off as though threatened by rabid dogs. 'Come back here and give us a proper answer,' commanded a voice at the front. 'For we're not satisfied with the one you gave our husbands!' A shout of agreement supported her.

One of the Honourable Members, stronger than his friends, wavered and came back, holding out his hands for quiet. Surprisingly, he got it. 'My good ladies—'

'Get on with it—'

'It is not a seemly thing when women claim to wear the breeches in a household—'

'If that's all you've got to say, stand down!' There were whistles and catcalls.

The speaker went on doggedly, 'It can never be a good world when women meddle in state matters. Your husbands are very much to blame if they can find no fitter employment for you than to harry those who have your best interests at heart.'

'John Lilburne has our interests at heart. Give us Freeborn John and the rest of you may go hang yourselves!' But the little group had run through its meagre store of courage. In another second it had retreated behind the stout door and barred it thankfully. A voice from behind it stated that they were best to disperse within one quarter of an hour, or the military would arrive to remove the best part of them to the Bridewell.

'We'll get back to the coach,' decided Cleo. 'No point in being locked up.'

Lucy could not have agreed more. Their speed as they raced back over the bridge was a credit to their nurture. 'I've never seen anything like that in my life!' Lucy said breathlessly when they had flung themselves onto the soft seats.

'Nor will again, if men have their way,' said Cleo. 'It's as well, though, I'm thinkin', to let them know, once in a while, that they *don't* have it all their own way – not even Old Ironside 'iself!'

'I wonder what Will will say, then I tell him about it,' said Lucy. 'He always says he likes women to think for themselves.'

'I know what Jud will say,' gloomed Cleo, ''ee'll say too much readin' is addlin' my few wits. But the *Intelligencer* isn't the holy gospel, even if Jud does publish it!'

'Well, Rob will be proud of you,' comforted Lucy.

' 'Ee'll be a lot prouder of *you*; just wait till I tell 'im!'

'Well, it was hardly my own idea,' wriggled Lucy. 'I mean – although I *do* understand why you support the Levellers, I think that what they want will never happen, not on this earth; it's the poor man's idea of heaven, not a practical programme for government.'

Cleo smiled. 'If you don't ask for more'n you want, you don't get nothin' – anything. That's what Mother always taught us. Not that you'd know,' she sighed, thinking of her small siblings, 'that she taught us to *ask*.'

When they returned to the two adjoining cottages where Jud and Cleo lived next door to the Whittaker tribe they found Jud already at home. He and Lucy were on easy terms again by now and she kissed him affectionately as he rose from his usual wooden chair beside the hearth. His likeness to Sir George was increasing with the years, but their father would never have been content to live so simple a life. The cottage was small, bare and furnished only with the most basic necessities. If each separate article was of a better condition than its neighbour in Nan Whittaker's house, it was nevertheless the same article. Whatever Jud's sins might be, neither greed nor covetousness was among them.

'What have you two been doing?' he asked, his hand reaching out for Cleo. 'There's a guilty look about you.'

'I don't believe it!' said Cleo, dismayed. They told him where they had been.

To Lucy's discomfort he neither smiled nor teased them. 'Promise me that this shall be the last jaunt of its kind,' he said seriously. 'The end of the Levellers is at hand, and I don't want either of you there when it comes. Anyway, Lucy, I'm surprised at *you*!' he added as an afterthought.

'So am I,' she agreed. The episode gave her much to think about. There had been a solidarity about that cheerful, purposeful crowd of women that she had not seen so unadulterated in a similar throng of men. Sisters? Yes, perhaps. More than she had ever thought, at any rate. There was an old saying. The hand that rocks the cradle – well, they would not rule the world, not yet, no more than would the Levellers, but there was a power there that, should it ever be needed, should it ever be *directed*, was very considerable.

Shortly after this, Jud was proved correct in his prediction for the Levellers. Their leaders were not released, the war-damaged economy of daily living did not recover and the sense of injustice and discontent fed on their own increase.

The army's Agitators and the City's Rob Whittakers had done their work well. There was mutiny in the great camp at Salisbury. The Levellers, numbering nearly a thousand strong, marched across the downs into Oxfordshire, where they expected reinforcements. The slow men of the shires were not to be persuaded, however, and the fine fleet-footedness turned into dull talk. Cromwell and Fairfax, now dogging the march, talked to even greater purpose, and Old Ironside's appeals won the day. The few that fought for their views were soon put down. One captain was cut down where he stood, and three prisoners were shot. It was the end of the Levellers.

In the City, John Lilburne, though acquitted among uproarious applause by a jury that loved the man and honoured his purpose, knew that purpose irretrievably lost. There were none, now, who doubted the whole and single power of the army.

None in England, that is. In Ireland, for instance, it was a different story. The King's death, that had made Englishmen unable to meet each other's eyes, had brought the quarrelsome Irish together for once. Ormonde, having resigned his Lord Lieutenancy to Parliament, had now been accepted as the Commander-in-Chief of the Confederate forces, in the name of the nineteen-year-old King Charles II. The Protestants had been ousted from almost every stronghold save Dublin and Belfast, and now a great Irish Army was encamped before Dublin. The time had come to teach them a lesson they would never forget.

It was Cromwell who would be their teacher, Cromwell and the New Model Army, who were now simply the Army. Jud Heron, on hearing this, decided that the only thing he wanted in the world was to go with them.

'But *why*?' wailed Cleo, horrified. She had read Jud's own reports upon the behaviour of the monstrous Irish. 'You are not a soldier!'

'I shan't go as a soldier, but as an observer, to write down what I see, as I have done before. I have always come back, now haven't I?' he cajoled.

He did not want to leave her, but he did want to go. He had been feeling restless lately. First there had been the business of the King, which had unsettled him as it had everyone else. Then there had been the Levellers and their crazy notions of equality. That had unsettled him also; he didn't know why. Perhaps it was because Rob was in such a sorry case over it all. He had taken it badly, all his bitterness turning inward. Jud didn't think he'd seen Rob smile since the day before the great march that had come to so little.

As for the *Intelligencer*, he was tired of editing politics for the common taste. There was no fun in the press nowadays, anyway; the saints up at Westminster had put a muzzle on it. He needed a change, to get away, look at something different. The Irish conquest would be just the thing. All first-hand reporting, good, solid, taxing stuff, a challenge to his eye and his hand. And if there was a bit of blood and thunder in it, why he had played the family man for long enough, and well enough, to deserve a little excitement, damned if he hadn't! Cleo, it seemed, either would not or could not understand these perfectly good explanations, so in the end he just had to tell her that he was going and that was an end of it; she would have to put up with it.

Cleo, in an attempt at wiliness, asked Lucy to intervene.

'Dearest, there would be no point in the world. Jud has acted out of character for so long that I am almost relieved to see him sneak back into it. If I were you, Cleo, I'd not try to hold him. The best way to bring him back is to let him go.'

'But he could be *killed*!' Lucy did not seem to have considered that.

She had, in fact. 'Best not to think of that,' was all she would say.

Cleo knew she was right. There was no shifting Jud once he had made up his mind. Sorrowfully, she let him go.

His first experience of sailing was by no means what he had expected and longed for throughout a youth of romantic notions of Drake and Raleigh. The Irish Sea chopped and snapped at their keels as though fully aware of their punitive intentions. Jud was sick; it did, however, give him some slight consolation to discover, when at last they reached Dublin, that Cromwell, although ballasted by the onerous titles of Lord Lieutenant and Commander-in-Chief, had been even sicker.

They were part of an armada of over 100 vessels, fresh from the careful command of the disgruntled Warwick, who had lost his admiralty on account of his brother Holland's late execution as part of the 'example' made of leading Royalists. This campaign, it was clear, was to be another 'example'.

In Dublin Castle, Jud stood shakily on his land legs and scribbled in his notebook while Oliver addressed the good Protestant citizens, his sanguine face still tinged with green. 'I doubt not, by God's divine providence, to restore you all to your just liberty and property; and that all of you whose heart's affection is real for the carrying on of the great work against the barbarous and bloodthirsty Irish, and the rest of their adherents and confederates, and for the propagation of the Gospel of Christ, the establishing of truth and peace and restoring this bleeding nation to its former happiness and tranquillity, will find favour and protection from the Parliament of England and receive such endowments and gratitudes as shall be answerable to your merits.'

Ireland should be restored to the English, to whom it belonged by right of ancient conquest, and her savage native hordes thoroughly dissuaded from any idea that either they or their heretical religion had any rights at all to crawl on the face of the earth. Jud found a way of putting it that was somewhere between Oliver's speech and his own translation, signed it, sealed it, and sent it off on the next boat home.

His next report, which he hoped would contain something more lively, would come from the more northerly city of Drogheda, the gateway to Ulster, where the Confederates and their Anglo-Irish allies still held sway.

He had managed to purchase an excellent horse in Dublin and the thirty-mile ride up the coast, some distance ahead of the army, was very pleasant. It was the end of a fine August and the air was warm and heavy. On his right the flat land stretched idle fingers into a prodigally blue sea, on the left the rich pastoral grass was soaked through with green. He remembered that Cathal O'Connor had once said that Irish grass was 'like the eyes of the first naiad'. For once he had not exaggerated. Indeed, he had in no way exaggerated the gentle beauty of his homeland. It was strange to meander along this peaceful road, all but alone, and then to look back and see the army, in their fine new coats of Venetian red, seeping, like the blood they had come to let, along the route.

He met no one coming from the north, except a single hasty rider in gartered rough breeches and a frieze cloak, who swerved into the fields to avoid him when he saw him for a stranger. An enormous wolfhound loped by his side, nearly four feet tall, running as effortlessly as the horse galloped. Jud recalled that there were wolves still in Ireland; hunting them had been Cathal's favourite sport. However, he expected to see none so near to the sea. He did spy several hawks; he thought one of them might have been an osprey.

Drogheda, when he reached it, was a pleasant surprise. It stood among flowering cornfields at the mouth of the Boyne, its imposing twenty-foot height of surrounding wall enclosing it upon both sides of the river. Inside the wall was Ormonde's one-legged captain, the English Catholic Sir Arthur Aston, who had fought for King Charles at Edge Hill. With the 2,000 men at his disposal, he hoped to prevent Cromwell's march to the north for as long as possible. He would not come out and face the Ironsides in the field, but felt himself as secure as may be behind his granite walls, having published the opinion that 'he who could take Drogheda could take hell!'

Knowing that Aston would try to sit out the siege until hunger and dysentery should do his work for him, Cromwell would want a swift storm of the city. With this in mind, Jud made a survey of its geography from the map he had procured in Dublin Castle. The town was shaped roughly like a leg of mutton, with the fat thigh to the north of the river, which curved to hold it in its arms and the thinner shank to the south. It was obvious that it was this southern section that would present the greatest obstacle to the attackers. Snug in its southeastern corner, protected by the great wall itself and, outside of it, by a long, broad and very precipitous ditch marked as 'the Dale', stood the Church of St Mary, crowned with a tall steeple which would serve defenders both as a lookout and a firing point. Also, the southernmost gate in the wall, called 'Duleek', guarded the road to a useful-looking piece of high ground marked as 'Mill Mount'. The whole shank section could well be held for a punishing amount of time.

Jud was correct in his assumptions. When the army was assembling, Cromwell, who had no doubt had the benefit of the same map, installed his eleven siege guns and twelve field pieces on a hillside south of the town, where their threat could be understood quite clearly from the church steeple. However, it was given out that he wished, if possible, to prevail by peaceful means. Accordingly, he raised a white flag and issued to Sir Arthur the summons to surrender.

Jud, copying down the form of words used, noted that Oliver had 'brought the army belonging to the Parliament of England before this place, to reduce it to obedience, to the end effusion of blood may be prevented. If this be refused,' he warned, Pilate-like, 'you will have no cause to blame me.'

Aston, presumably prepared to take the blame upon his own uneven shoulders, sent his refusal. As Jud felt bound to point out to the interested readers of the *Intelligencer*, the weight of that blame might well be grave; Sir Arthur's 2,000 men and several hundred disgruntled citizens were faced with 8,000 English foot and 4,000 horse, supported by a very generous amount of artillery and a staunch naval blockade in the harbour. No supplies or reinforcements could reach the city, and when their food and ammunition eventually ran out and the town was taken by storm, they could expect to receive no quarter.

Jud began to feel pity for Drogheda. It looked to be a handsome little town; it even had an English look about it, with its spires and the safe, smug air of those walls.

The white flag was now replaced by a blood red one. This signalled the opening of the cannonade. The whole of the army stood still among the corn they had trampled and held its breath as the great guns began to thunder the Almighty's disapproval of all hopeless sieges.

On the hillside beside them, recognizable at this distance only by his stance of complete authority, Cromwell also watched. At first there seemed to be little effect. The great balls fell against the stone and exploded harmlessly a few feet away. But quite soon the formidable wall began to crumble a little, with odd blocks of masonry falling with the shot. And then there was a sudden dramatic fissure; for a moment Jud thought he almost saw light through it, but it came together again and was just a crack. It was a good big crack, though, and would repay further work.

They concentrated now upon St Mary's steeple, the highest point of the enemy defence. When they had reduced it to a smoking ruin, together with the nearest guard tower on the wall, they considered they had done enough for today. They had made a good beginning.

After supper, which he had shared with a company of cavalry who seemed to have adopted him, Jud wrote down the afternoon's events with as much panache and praise of gallantry as he could muster for men who simply stood behind a gun and blasted stone, flesh, bone and mortar to smithereens.

It rained that night. The ground beneath his tent was wet. He was not comfortable. He thought of the women and children inside those walls, counting on their security; women like Cleo, children like Ned. How terrified they must be. Eventually he slept.

He awoke to the intrusive energy of trumpets and the thought that being with the army was like being a member of a beehive, all organized noise and industry and hurrying importance. He did as the trumpets told him and got dressed to join his new friends at breakfast. He found them good company and was glad to discover himself so easily tolerated among them. They had even given him a red coat so that he could follow them into the fighting without being mistaken for one of the enemy.

'Lord, how it does become you, sir,' admired Trooper Jukes, offering him cold ham and fresh bread procured from willing natives who would get fat on the proceeds, if they survived the shock sustained from the fact that they were paid at all.

'It does indeed,' agreed Captain Hurst. 'It seems, my young friend, that the Good Lord is telling you that he wants you to go in the ranks of the righteous.' The captain was grinning, but his intention, Jud knew, was serious.

'But surely, sir, the coat must already belong to someone?' he protested, disliking the fervent glint in Hurst's eye.

'Oh aye. Ralph Tandy.'

'Well then, won't Trooper Tandy be wanting it back?'

'Not he. He has no need of it. He is clothed in the garments of celestial light.'

'Oh. I see.'

'At Preston, it was. God rest him.'

'I'm sorry.'

'No need of sorrow. Trooper Tandy was a godly man.'

So are they all, all godly men, Jud ruefully misquoted to himself. There were times when he wished they were not. He would have enjoyed a song other than a psalm, for instance, and then there were the endless sermons. There would be one now. A sermon had never aided Jud's digestion and he was pretty certain that this one wouldn't, but it was the Lord General's idea of the best way to start the day and there was no escaping it.

His words were not those of the peaceful Galilean. 'Let God arise, let his enemies be scattered! Let them also that hate him flee before him. As smoke is driven away, so drive them away. As wax melteth before the fire, so let the wicked perish at the presence of God. Soldiers, you are enjoined to go against them with your swords smoking in your hands! To drive the barbarian from the sight of the Lord. Cursed is he that shall be negligent in God's work! Cursed is he who holds back his sword from unclean blood. If there is a weapon in their hands, smite them down! For their existence is an abomination unto the Lord!'

Jud listened, fascinated for a while, and then found that he was no longer listening, for it was the same message of blood repeated again and again, whether in the words of the Bible or in the man's own scripture-drunk seethings. He looked at the faces of his companions. Their eyes shone. They looked proud and clear, and also innocent, as though they were children exhorted to do well at their lessons and determined to do it.

He was finishing now. There was a faint smile and a text especially for the cavalry. 'Some trust in chariots – and some in horses – but we will remember the name of the Lord our God!'

Now they could begin God's work. The task was to breach the walls, and the first assault was behind St Mary's. When they had widened the crack, the foot would make the gap broad enough for the horse to enter; if at the same time they could hold the lower part of the church against the enemy, long enough for a good number of the horse to pass, the town would soon be theirs. The church was in an excellent strategic position and its environs should still be defensible, once taken.

But it was no easy task. They were under a continuous bombardment from the walls and breastworks, and there was the added harassment of an unexpected, whining, deadly hail of arrows from the short Irish bows that were still the chief weapons of moorland warfare. Their own cannon fire was measured and insistent. The split in the great wall shuddered and stood firm time after time, but eventually it must open, and it did.

It was five o'clock before they saw it suddenly gape like a roasted chestnut, spewing a half-cooked rubble of stones and men from out of its blackened maw. There was an outlandish second of recognition while the men outside stared at those inside. What Jud saw was an indistinguishable mass of panic as men fought for the control of terrified horses. Perhaps all he really saw was the white roll of an eye as a demented creature reared in the opening, but he heard the hideous screaming and the black dust seared his throat and watered his eyes. Then he was running with the foot as they poured towards the crack.

It took them some time to get in, for it was foot on the outside against foot and horse on the inside. The gap was still not wide enough for the English horse. Jud hung back as well as he could, but in the end he had to hack his way in like the rest. He thanked his father for his early training, and his street fighting for his later guile, as Aston's men tried to run him through his red coat. He hardly knew what he was doing, he had to do it so fast. He thrust and swiped at a succession of ferocious adversaries with mouths gaping red and white in black faces, some of whom were shot down as they stood, some of whom he killed; some seemed simply to fade from his sword-end as though they had been dreams.

Once, as he found himself fighting with his back to the church wall, he was aware of the far-off glow of the corn through the breach. Another time he caught sight of Cromwell himself planted firmly in the crack, dealing furiously with an unhorsed colonel of cavalry. His face was grim and set and he urged the infantry to their work of devastation with a murderous anger. He had not expected to be held back for so long and now he was in the grip of rage at the waiting.

When at last the enemy were driven back enough, the gap was wide enough, and Colonel Ewer had brought up his fresh cavalry, the desperate mask became a human face again, but Jud was troubled by its changes. He had thought Oliver to be the very epitome of self-control.

The real assault began now. Men and horses came pouring through the wall like a ruddy river through a broken dam. The church and its convent grounds soon became theirs and, as the flood increased to seven or eight thousand of them, the whole lower part of the town was at their mercy. They sang their psalms as they dispensed it.

For the first time, Jud could stop his own hack and thrust and take stock. He had not meant to fight. He realized how foolish he had been to think he could have avoided it. He was not sorry for the men he had killed. The Irish *were* barbarians, the greater part of them, and no Englishman could forget the atrocities of '41, even if they had known Cathal O'Connor. These tribesmen must be put down if the country was to be secure again, under English rule. But he had intended only to be an observer, to *make* himself impartial, to try to see both sides if he could. Perhaps he had asked too much of himself. For he could not regret their deaths.

Now he let himself be borne on the tide. It carried him towards the stout hillock of Mill Mount, topped by its crouching fortification. Apparently Sir Arthur and any of his men who had life or energy left in them had taken refuge there and hoped to hold it. It was a brave move, but it was hopeless, and the old campaigner must know it.

Shrieking like schoolboys, the Parliament men clambered up the steep sides of the mound, Jud with them. He was laughing; he didn't know why. There was less pressure suddenly.

Before they had reached the top, an officer ran out of the doorway waving a white flag.

'Will you accept a surrender, sirs?' he called. 'There are many wounded amongst us.'

The climbers stopped. They looked towards their own officers, who staggered towards each other and went into a huddle.

'I reckon they should 'ave quarter,' observed Jud's nearest neighbour in a Lincolnshire slur. 'They do be English, for the most part.'

It was then that the group of officers split open and they saw Cromwell ride fiercely into their midst. His face was fire-red and his whole body shook with passion.

He scarcely listened to what was said.

'No quarter!' he roared. 'Put every one of them to the sword!' And he spurred off towards the north of the town.

Jud was shaken. 'I didn't know he could be like that.'

The infantryman shook his head gravely. 'Not often,' he agreed, 'but he do take a turn for it, now and again. 'Tis best to keep out of his way till it be over.'

'If you can,' said Jud.

Cromwell might have gone, but his spirit had remained with them. Before Jud's horrified eyes, the laughing schoolboys of a moment ago became imbued with a bloodlust that turned his stomach. Their swords smoking in their hands in a manner that would have brought joy to their chaplain's heart, they hounded each man, wounded or whole, to his death in that stark round tower. An especial fate was reserved for Sir Arthur Aston.

The veteran of Poland, of Lithuania, of the wars of Gustavus Adolphus, Sergeant-Major-General of the Army of Charles of England, Governor of Reading and of Oxford, Commander of the dragoons at Edge Hill, and lastly Governor of Drogheda, which he would not give over to its enemies; they dragged him out into the cooling sunlight of the hillside, where an officer took his sword. Thinking he would be courteously treated he gave it willingly.

Grinning, the officer tapped Aston's wooden leg with his boot. 'I'll lay odds you keep your fortune in there,' he said slowly. 'I know I would, if I were you.'

The men about them laughed.

'Well then, we'd best see it, hadn't we?' the officer continued. The hint was enough. One of the soldiers stepped smartly behind Sir Arthur and tripped him to the ground. Another slashed at the straps that held his leg secure. He held it up and shook it. Nothing.

'Gentlemen, surely—' The old Baronet had hardly taken in what was happening. Propping himself on his elbow he gazed up in a puzzled fashion at these uncouth modern recruits.

Jud heard himself cry out 'No!' as the officer raised the disappointing leg and brought it down upon the skull of its owner. They heard a crack like a tree falling, and then another, and another as the old man was bludgeoned to his bloody and undignified death. Then they left him and raced away downhill, still bellowing out the name of God and calling snatches of psalms.

Sickened, Jud leaned against the tower. When he could, he went to Aston's body and did his best to make it look decent. He straightened the body and wrapped his scarf around the fractured head. The blood came through, but it was better than nothing. The leg he kicked away down the hill as though it were a poisonous thing. He could imagine how it would be now, down there in the town. He did not want to see any more. He had witnessed enough of God's work for one day.

Suddenly very tired, he wandered through the doorway, stepping over corpses, into the tower. There were many more bodies inside. There were steps to an upper chamber. With some idea that perhaps there would be less of death up there, he ascended, slowly.

'Come no further, or you're a dead man,' a voice said when he had nearly reached the top. He could not see anyone; they were keeping well back from the hole in the floor that was the entrance.

'You have nothing to fear from me,' said Jud wearily. 'I have had my fill of blood.'

'Jesus, Mary and Joseph!' surprisingly ejaculated the voice. 'Will you say that again. Or anything!'

'What?' There was something about—

'Will you tell me your name, then, since your tongue is evidently pierced with thorns.'

'Yes, by God, and I'll tell you yours!' Jud had leaped up the remaining stairs in an instant and stood, breathing hard, his face split asunder in an incredulous grin as he stared at the semi-recumbent figure of Cathal O'Connor.

'I was just thinking of you; well, lately,' he said idiotically.

'I regret I can't return the compliment, but I must say, if I have to see an Englishman in that particular uniform, I'd as soon it were yourself as another.'

'But what are you doing here? I thought Wicklow was your country?'

'It is. But my Father thought I needed hardening, so he sent me to Sir Arthur to learn to be a proper English soldier.'

'I see you have taken your lesson well,' Jud grimaced, counting the bodies of five Parliamentarians gone to account to their Supreme General.

'Ah, these. Yes. Well I was in a rather good position. Just

chopped them off as they came up the stairs. As I would have done to you, had you not unlocked your teeth at last.'

'Are you wounded?' Cathal was nursing an arm.

'A scratch. But I'm not keen for more. If I read the signs correctly, there is going to be a sacrifice made of this city to your odd Commander and his odder God. I've no wish to be part of it. I'll live to fight again, if I can.'

Jud slid to the floor opposite him.

'We'll have to think of something. Quickly. There are 12,000 of us. One of them won't miss you, eventually, however fast you run.' Even as he spoke he had the answer. He was wearing it. He looked at the selection of English infantrymen. 'That one,' he decided. 'He's about your size. His coat, take it. And his breeches,' he added on afterthought. Cathal was wearing saffron velvet.

'A man of genius.'

Jud helped him to undress the body and exchange the clothes. 'What now?' he pondered.

'How is your lovely sister? How is Lucy?'

'Eh? Oh, she's well. She has a son now. Robert.'

'Ah, indeed? I did not know that.'

Jud had forgotten how beautiful his soft voice could be. 'We must think what you must do,' he insisted, worrying. 'You cannot hope to pass as one of us for long. When the sack is over, the accounting will begin. You'll have to run for it somehow. Not yet.'

'Jesu, I was never good at sitting still and waiting to be snared,' moaned Cathal. 'I'd rather make a fight of it than that. And better still, I'd rather be at home, where I belong. Your devils will be marching our way soon, and it's there I should be, not here.' He fell silent, thinking.

'Listen,' he said after a space, 'I think I have it. If I can pass as English for a time, perhaps march south a way with the Army, I can get away when we are down the coast. There is a harbour there where I have friends. I'll find a boat to take me near to Dalkey, and win home from there.'

'Eureka!' said Jud, inspired again. 'Put a bandage round your throat; I'll say a ball took you there; the nearest thing I ever saw! Then you've no need to talk at all!'

'Miraculous! But you don't know the miracle it will take for me to keep quiet!'

It seemed to be the only way, however.

It even worked. Cathal was introduced as Charles Corner, a

long-lost friend of Jud's youth. His wound was marvelled over and he was kindly treated by the troopers, who had returned to their usual pleasant selves and would say nothing of what happened to Drogheda, except that it was the will of God.

That will had been so bloody, so brutal and so extreme that Jud, talking among the soldiers so that he might send an accurate account of what he did not see at first hand, was as nauseated by the description as he might have been by the sights. It was the old, old tale of churches desecrated, virgins raped, priests riven, old men and women spitted, children gored. All these things had been done by men who had become his friends. It hurt him to hear it, and to remember that he had taken part in its beginning.

They were marching now for Wexford, where it would happen all over again.

When Cathal left the army, Jud, on an impulse of homesickness and war sickness, went with him.

London, Autumn 1649

Lucy was alone that afternoon. Will had ridden up to Warwick to try, if he could, to unravel some of the strands that knit him too tightly into his uncle's business. He was beginning to wonder which of them owned several of his ships. He owed a great deal to Warwick, but he did not intend to pay back more than he owed. Cissie had taken Robert into the garden where he was staggering about in his new walking-pen. Lucy, relishing the freedom, went into the library to continue her discoveries among Will's books. She weakly chose Thomas Wyatt's poetry in preference to Bacon's essays and settled upon the ottoman with the book and some dried figs. She had been there about half an hour when there was some sort of commotion out in the hall. Then the library door flew open and there was Jud.

'You're back! You're safe! Oh, thank heavens!'

She ran to embrace him.

'Of course I'm safe. You can trust me to keep out of trouble. Listen Lucy, I've brought you a friend with me.'

'Oh? Who is that?'

Her eyes went to the door.

She thought afterwards that this had been the longest second of her life. There had been so much contained in it. The fact that he was there, the acceptance of that fact and then, ringing like a deafening carillon in her celebrant mind, the knowledge that, for both of them, nothing had changed. Nothing. O dear God. Nothing at all. She stood, wooden, unable to speak.

Cathal, recovering first because he had known how it would be, was able to help her.

'I think your brother has saved my life, Lucy. We have a long, tall tale to tell you. How good it is to see you, and you as beautiful still as the corn at noon.'

'Cathal,' she said quietly, thanking him silently for his ease, 'you will have to give me a little time to get used to this. I did not expect to see you again – so soon.'

Nor ever, my heart, nor ever again.

'The Lord has moved in his most mysterious way,' he said lightly. 'By rights I should be in Wicklow, as you shall hear. But seemingly my fate is here in London.' He lingered on the words and she felt her whole body flame.

'Well sit down, for Godssake, and we'll tell her everything,' Jud said. 'Let's have some wine, Lucy, to loosen our tongues.'

At least she could laugh without feeling that she betrayed herself. She gave the order and became a willing listener.

They took the tale in turns, Jud beginning. He was as terse as possible over Drogheda. She would read the truth soon enough, though he very much doubted if he would be allowed to print all of it. That bloody carnage might have been God's holy will to Oliver Cromwell but the ordinary citizens of England could not be expected to understand this. They might be foolish enough to see it as unnecessary cruelty. Or was this naivete? His countrymen considered Cathal's to be a dangerous species of wild beast. Was not the best thing to do with such to destroy them? Well, the Ironsides had made a good job of their destruction. They would come home heroes, he may as well make up his mind to it. But could he, in all conscience, make up his columns to it?

When Cathal took over, what had been accurate description of events became the stuff of adventure and fantasy. The courage and derring-do of himself, his family, his wife, his clansmen had been legendary and full of wit. They had outmanoeuvred the Protestants at every turn. He was full of praise for their leader,

Ormonde, whom he called 'the last honest man', and for the dead Aston, who had given his life in the Irish cause.

'But would he not have been better to surrender and thus save lives?' asked Lucy, sorrowing over the terrible losses.

'Sir Arthur was one of us enough to know that freedom is the only worth there is for us,' said Cathal grandly.

'I wonder how many of the grieving women of Drogheda would agree with you.' She was ignored and they went on with their tale, turning it to laughter as they described Cathal's dumb Englishman, who had developed a very definite character as they had marched down the coast, a droll and effete gentleman, so spoiled by family and servants that he couldn't lift a finger for himself, his air of complete helplessness combined with open good-fellowship had won the honest troopers over to the point where they had made themselves his slaves, so that he was fed, valeted, cosseted and kept comfortable every waking moment until they made their escape.

This had been swiftly done, and all according to plan, except that Cathal had delayed in the darkness for perhaps ten minutes. When Jud had asked him where he had been, he had replied that he had made a grave man of the man who had murdered Sir Arthur. They had reached the busy harbour of Dalkey and Cathal had tracked down his friend with the boat. He was out in it, doing mischief among the English Navy at present, and so they had waited. He had agreed to take them down the few miles of coast to a spot near the O'Connor lands.

'But weren't the tricksy English waiting for us out in their own little boats? And didn't they chase poor Padraic clear away from Irish waters and out into the deeps? So, didn't we consult and confer and decide we may as well win for England as go back to Wicklow and be sunk or shot?'

'Well, I am very glad you did,' said Lucy, her smile steady now. 'And will you stay awhile? Is it safe for you here? You can hardly keep up your dumb-show for long without breaking down.'

'Will you hear the impudence! Indeed I can. But I've heard enough of the English by now to be able to mimic efficiently. I'll be as safe as I was when I stayed with you at Chelsea; safer. Charles Corner has a good life to lead yet. He is to take up the trade of a printer and publisher.'

'You'll work with Jud?'

'I will. I'll take pleasure in it.'

She did not ask for how long. She would spoil the gift.

He left with Jud that day, for he was to stay at his house, but she knew he would come back to her alone. She both wanted it and feared it. He came the next day. She was pacing the garden when he found her. 'I was thinking of you.'

'Of course.'

They looked at each other. It was a long look, full of remembering. She broke it, shaking her head.

'We must not—'

'Must we not? Very well, then, we will not, if that is your wish.' He made it sound simple. She knew he did it to show her that it could not be simple.

'Your husband is still away. Is he often away?'

'Yes. I suppose he is. Lately he has taken more interest in his ships and their merchandise, and less in Parliament. He travels frequently, and spends much of his time in his offices or at the quay.'

'So you are alone a good deal, then. I am glad.'

She tried not to be glad also. The attempt made her angry with him. 'What you think – what you propose, is not honest.'

'You will hardly condemn me. But you may send me away – if you wish. But remember, I wanted you for my wife and I could not have you. You wanted it too. This time will be all we will have. Can you send me away, knowing this? Or am I mistaken? Have you changed?'

She made a small, unformed sound.

'I'm sorry,' he said. 'I should not speak to you so, I know it. But I would not have evasion between us. I know what is the case with us – and I see that you know it too. Is that not so?'

She turned away from him.

'If it is, what good does it do to say so?'

'If I could hope for any other good, I should not need it said.'

Relief flooded her. She faced him again.

'Then I will say this to you. It is with me as it has always been. I cannot alter that. But I wish that I could. I have been happy in my marriage. I have not thought of you often, and I did not expect that you would ever be anything more to me than a gradually diminishing memory.' He grimaced at this. 'I cannot say that I am not glad to see you; the very words are ridiculous; but there is sorrow in it too, as you must know.'

'I have not had time to feel sorrow. I am not so quick as you to see how things will be. When fate took a hand and pushed our ship towards you, I did not argue with it; I was simply happy.'

'And do you expect to go on being so?'

'In your presence, yes. I will try not to ask for more than I may honourably have.'

'And I,' she said with a trace of humour, 'will try not to give it.'

'We were never lovers,' he reminded her.

'We did not know the difference.'

'But now we do.'

'Yes. Now we do.'

'Love is no more a physical thing now than it was then,' he suggested.

'I am not sure.'

'Ah. I see. You make me damnably jealous of Will Staunton.'

The name brought her up with a sudden sense of shock. She was standing here, in her husband's garden, discussing the act of love with the only man she had ever chosen for herself. She was betraying Will in her very conversation. She hated the feeling of it. She was heavy with guilt.

'If we are to see each other at all,' she said slowly and with gathering purpose, 'we must act, even when we are alone, as if all that had never happened. It will be as well if we are not alone too often.'

'Lucy! You can't do that to yourself, never mind to me!'

'Our ways have already been chosen for us. And for myself, I have already suffered all the sorrow I need on your account. All those months of letters and waiting; and then Orla McDonagh at the end of it! And what about her, your lady wife? Have you no sense of loyalty towards her, that you can sail away on a wind of chance and turn your back on her – and your face towards me?'

He did not look ashamed. 'Orla will understand. We are good friends.'

'There – you see. Your life is with her. You know it. She *will* understand. Why don't you go back now, right away, before you have caused me to dislike myself even more than I do at this moment?'

'Lucy, don't be angry. I came because I love you. I always will.'

'It isn't love; it's legends; unreal, without future.'

'Why does a woman always think of the future? We have *now*. I am standing here, looking at you; you call it chance; I call it fate. The pattern of our existence has brought us together again. Don't spit at it! Take it. Enjoy it. Why should you feel guilt over it? You didn't make it happen.'

'Oh, Cathal, you make me feel old! Will you ever grow up?'

'Probably not. There doesn't seem much to be gained from it.

Now let's you and I kiss and be friends, for I mean to stay, and I mean to see you as much as I am able.'

She sighed. He was hopeless. He made her angry and tender at once. Was it just a habit that she had, of loving him? If so, she did not think she could break it, however bold her words and intentions.

'We are friends; we will always be that. But we will not kiss,' she said firmly.

He laughed. 'Perhaps not today,' he said.

She shivered. The words were lightly spoken but there was both threat and promise in them all the same.

After he had gone she was able to tell herself that all would be well, that she was worrying for no reason. She would, after all, be persuaded to do nothing that she did not wish to do. And had Cathal not promised, too, not to ask for more than honour allowed? It was only her own thoughts and desires that were distressing her so. And she had the control of them in her own hands. And Will would soon be home.

She tried to think what she would say to him, how she would explain Cathal's appearance. And Will himself, how would he take it? He had shared her agonies over Cathal's absence too often not to feel some doubts of her constancy, in thought, if not in deed. She wished that she could talk to him about it, now, as openly as she had been able to do when he was her friend and confident and she Cathal's dreamsick correspondent.

When she wept that night, her tears were neither for herself nor for Cathal, but only for Will.

If only he would return quickly. She would find a way to make it all come together. If she did not, then Cathal must not come here. Could she bear that? She did not know.

She wore out the night awake, wishing he had not come at all, that he had never left at all, that he were here now, warm in her bed and in her body.

When the morning dragged itself over the threshold, it brought the worst of news.

The letter was from Will, written in haste.

'Dearest one, I am most confoundedly sorry about this, but it seems I shall not be home yet awhile. Warwick has got into the most serpentine difficulties with the Signory over the "Belladonna" and the "Dragon" and their cargoes. They are impounded and it seems my own signature, in situ, is the only thing that will get them out. To my mind I'll come back from Venice short of a few thousand livres into the bargain. Italy did not produce a

Machiavelli out of nothing. I'll not see you till I return, my heart's darling, and God knows how much I regret it, but we sail from Deeside in one of Warwick's ships, with a naval escort as far as we need it – and no doubt a few arguments with the Dutch on the way. I shall take good care, my bird, and hope to be back with you before six months are over—'

Six months! Mother of God, how could she weather six months of Cathal without Will to keep her strong?

And yet, if Will were there, what test would that be of her strength? And why, indeed, should she feel so little trust in her own powers of restraint? Wasn't it true, what Cathal had said, that love was a matter of the spirit, not of the body and its carnal desires? Ah, but wasn't it she, who now knew how fierce the joy of the body could be, who had answered him that she was not sure?

'I must not be alone with him,' she swore determinedly, 'There must always be Jud, or Robert, or Cissie with us.'

But when he came again, after a space of two whole days, she dismissed Cissie from her side. Robert was sleeping in his cradle.

Cathal looked down at the boy with a mixture of sadness and interest. 'He is a handsome little creature; he has the best of both of you. I wish that I had got him on you.'

Weakness and wanting were liquid in her veins.

'Please. Don't think of it.'

'I am ashamed to say I think of little else. Your brother finds me a hamfisted pupil, I think, for my mind is always here with you.'

'Then let us find some other food for it,' she said with sudden energy. 'Come. We are going out. We will walk about London as we did so long ago. You will find it much changed.'

He sighed. 'If I must. I had sooner stay here.'

'No. I feel caged, in a room with you.'

'It is your true desires that are caged. If you were to let them loose, then you would feel quite delightful, in a room with me.' He spoke with humour, but he spoke, as he well knew, the truth.

Lucy did not think she was going to be able to handle him. 'We shall take Robert. The air will be good for him. I'll call Cissie.'

'Oh, take the whole household and be damned, why don't you? We shall all go down the Strand in a grand procession and no doubt the citizens will fall in behind us, thinking it's a state occasion. And all just to avoid being alone with me for half an hour.' Nevertheless, she made him walk.

And Cissie walked behind them, carrying Robert.

By the time they returned, Cathal had admired the work of Inigo Jones, deplored the diminution of gaiety in the streets, given her a vivid picture of the personality of the new young King, third-hand at least, in exchange for details of Cromwell's difficulties with his curtailed Parliament, and given Cissie a hair-raising description of Irish life which was quite untrue and very mischievous. He also carried Robert for the greater part of the way. He was charm itself to Cissie and Lucy could see the girl's heart begin to slip in his direction.

'You are not to torment her,' she told him, when on his next visit, she saw him throw Cissie a languishing glance in caricature.

'Why not? If *you* won't have me – I dare swear *she* would, as soon as you like! Ah no, now, I don't mean it, you know I don't.'

Lucy did not know which was the worse to bear; his teasing and flirting with ideas of love, which merely built up the tension between them, in the face of the knowledge that teasing was all they must have; or the moments when he became serious and let her see how deep was his need of her, how true, despite all the teasing, was his love. Sometimes, as they roamed together in one of the parks, or rode out into the countryside in the coach, they seemed to forget the years in between and felt themselves back at that first Christmas-tide, when everyone had thought of them as children, and only they had known that they were not.

The innocence was still there when, for long periods Lucy forgot, entranced by his words and his dark eyes on hers, that she was a wife and a mother, and listened to him with the same fluttering hope that had been hers then, her whole heart open to him. And then she would go home and take off the mask that she always wore about the streets, not now for fashion's sake, and as she removed that small symbol of mystery belonging to the unreal world of the stage, she was conscious that she too had just been treading the boards of unreality, playing her part in an old Romance that should never have been revived.

At night, alone, with all the hours until dawn in which to think, she knew precisely how much danger she was in, how accustomed she was becoming to her part, how little there was of acting in it. She would force herself to think of Will and not of Cathal. There was no difficulty in this. She had discovered almost immediately that her longing for Cathal, her inebriate's necessity for his presence, had done nothing to alter or damage her love for Will. It should not be the case, she was sure. It made no sense; but it was so.

She loved Will and she missed him when she thought of him.

When she thought of Cathal, or he was with her, she was all his. Indeed, this unseemly duality was so novel to her that she wished there were someone to whom she could speak about it. But who was there, who would understand her experience? She could hardly ask her mother. And Martha was unlikely to have shared such difficulties, though she might sympathize. But Martha was at Heron and Lucy would not write of such things. Cleo, if she told her, might well tell Jud, and she did not want that. Jud, if he recalled her earlier interest in Cathal, had by now dismissed it as a childish infatuation. He saw Cathal as a dear family friend, and as a link between himself and the rest of them; she was sure of that.

No; the only woman she could think of who might conceivably have loved two men at once, if love were the proper term for it, was, most uncomfortably, Mistress Nan Whittaker. And if *that* was the way she was going, Lucy might as well set up her establishment in Shoreditch right away!

Considerations of this sort, and the continuous employ of her own sense of humour enabled her more or less to keep her head throughout the passing weeks. She turned every dangerous passage to laughter, and Cathal, who saw clearly enough what she was at, made, surprisingly, no complaint, but joined in on every occasion. If their laughter was a little desperate sometimes, there was no one to hear the false notes except themselves. Laughter, of any kind, was better than the tears of remorse that would follow if they allowed themselves too much seriousness.

Their meetings could not be as many or as spontaneously joyous as they could wish. At Staunton House there were servants to be considered. In Jud's company there was the pretence of mere friendship to be kept up. Lucy in particular lived under a strain that made her quick to tears and given to sudden, equally swift, exhaustion. There were days when she wished that he would see that they were not the fabled protagonists of any high romance, but two ordinary mortals, without hope, whose fate did not lie with each other. And then there were the other days, far worse, when his nearness, the catch of his voice, the turn of his head, were such a torment to her that she would think she could not live another sane minute if he did not touch her.

It was at the end of such a day, when Lucy lay, dry-eyed and feverish with longing, upon her bed, alternately praying and cursing herself for her weakness, when there came a letter which broke through the door of selfishness that she had closed against the world.

It was from Tom. He was in Scotland.

He had been there since the early spring. Montrose, baulked by the success of Cromwell's invasion of his original plan to land and call up the Royalists in Ireland, was sent by his young master to test the loyalty of those who remained in Scotland.

'We were a pathetically small force, held together in hope by the passionate desire of James Graham to do service to the son as he had done to the father. You could not but love Montrose, could you but meet him. A sweeter nature and a higher spirit has not lived. Impossible not to follow him; impossible not to feel a resurgence of that great determination that took us out in '42 and after. And so, we sailed in January for the Orkneys and landed at Kirkwall. It is a bleak and bitter place but we hardly marked the cold. We were hot with our cause. If we could raise fair support for the King on the mainland, it would give him a far higher hand in his dealings with the Covenanters. Argyll and Montrose, although irrevocably enemies, might one day join hands on paper, as equal servants of the King. If Charles was to bargain with the Covenanters while they still held so much power, he would get little, and that not what he wanted. Montrose was sure that he could even the balance.

'We spent the winter raising troops. We were still too few when we crossed and marched into Sutherland. Before the clansmen could join us we were ambushed. It was a rout. Those who were not killed, got away over the moors. Some of us tried to keep together and to find Montrose, whom we knew to have escaped. We searched that godforsaken countryside for days. One by one, the Scots amongst us melted back to their homes; they would not stay without the marquis.

'At last we met with a man who said Montrose had been captured, betrayed by one of the McLeods, and taken to Edinburgh.

'I followed with my companions, now only two, John Dowson who has been my friend since Naseby, and Fergus Graham, a clansman of Montrose. We heard more of our leader as we came nearer to the capital, for now we were travelling in his footsteps. The McLeod, not content with his betrayal, had sent him off in a common cart, bound hand and foot, though he was too ill, they said, to notice where he was. Later, it seems, he had not even the comfort of the cart, for our informant had seen him led through his village on a horse with no saddle, his feet bound beneath its belly. He was still sick and pale, but such was his courage and dignified bearing in this adversity that the people who watched him pass found him an object of pity and admiration rather than scorn, as his tormentors had hoped.

'In Edinburgh, we saw him for ourselves. It was in the third week of May. All the folk of the town were out on the streets, hoping to catch a glimpse of the most famous man in Scotland. The mob in Edinburgh can be the most uncouth of any town, and that day they had been paid to be that and more. But as James Graham of Montrose was driven down the Canongate, tied to the seat of the hangman's cart, they held their tongues and were turned to stone. When they did speak it was to call out blessings and prayers to him. I managed to get near to the cart and speak to him. I don't know what I said. But I will hold his reply in my heart as the best part of my son's inheritance: "Tell my prince, when you see him, that I count it the highest honour to die, as I have lived, in his service."

'I said that I would, and indeed I will speak those words to the King with my own lips, and in such a way as will make it clear to him that such a servant is deserving of a better prince! For even as his father betrayed Stafford – yes, even I will say that now – so Charles has betrayed his most gallant soldier. It is part of his pact with Argyll. He will give up Montrose and he will take the Covenant – that is what they say here, and I believe it will happen – and then Argyll and Leslie will take back his throne for him. I tell you Lucy, if Charles were not my christened King, with a duty to his throne which must prevail above all else, I would leave him now as others are doing, for I swear that what is left of my heart is worn ragged for Montrose. I loved him and I honoured him. I wish I could say either of my King.

'I went to the hanging. He was splendid. He had dressed in scarlet and silver lace, with an embroidered shirt and ribbons in his shoes. As he came to die he said, "I leave my soul to God, my service to my prince, my goodwill to my friends, my love and charity to you all." His last words were for Scotland. "God have mercy on this afflicted land," he cried out as he ascended the ladder. As the hangman pushed him into space I saw that he was weeping like the rest of us.

'When the King rides into Edinburgh to take the Covenant which he will later forswear, Montrose will grin at him in greeting from where they have fixed his head to the walls of the Tolbooth. God help His Majesty, for there are no more like him.

'I feel hollow, Lucy. I wish I might just come home and look to my own pastures.'

There was little more, and all of it so despairing that Lucy wished that she had him here with her, to take him in her arms and tell him that she understood so very well, that he was right, that the honour had all gone out of it, out of all of them.

When Cathal came to take her riding next day she instinctively made for the forest, out beyond Chelsea, seeking the deep, mysterious protection that she had always gained from trees, taking them Tom's trouble and her own. 'If this were Ireland, we'd be dead or taken for ransom within twenty minutes.' Cathal raked both sides of the track as they rode.

'We are more civilized. There are highwaymen, but they do not come in so close to the city. We are only half a mile from the inn we passed, after all.'

'Nonetheless, it's well I have my pistols.'

The trees were mostly the short, stout mushrooming oaks, evergreen, occasionally interspersed with the darker yew. They tethered the horses in a small clearing and sat down to drink the wine they had brought with them.

Lucy drank silently, her eyes far away. 'You are distracted today. What is it? Why are you sad?'

She told him. Even she was surprised at the passion of his reaction. 'Will they betray and murder every true spirit that gives reason to these wars? I am surprised the little King did not throw Ormonde into his murky bargain! Your brother is right; we are all drained hollow of any goodness that was in us.'

'But you will fight again, for the King, if you have the chance?'

'Only because he will give us back what we have lost – if he does not become a Covenanted King,' he finished contemptuously.

'*No one* can ever give us back what we have lost, and those whom we have lost,' she said with a stabbing resentment.

'Why, you are weeping. You must not do that—'

He moved across and took her in his arms. So long, very many weeks had they been together, and this was the first time she had shed tears before him, and the first time, therefore, that he let slip his bridle of control. They both shivered as he held her. She half pulled away but he did not let her go.

They embraced without moving for a long, healing time. Then she looked up at him and their lips met, cool at first, as though their mouths were not part of them but messengers sent ahead to test the path.

And then suddenly it was all real. They were living, breathing in each other's arms, flesh to flesh, the storybooks thrown down, the impediments swept away. Each said the other's name, over and over, making the reality stronger with every note.

And when each had the sense of the other's presence to an aching degree, they became aware of the separation between them, of fate and time, and their own prohibition. It had been ridiculous. Every movement of their hands and lips told them how ridiculous it had been. Once more she felt the singing touch of his hands upon her breasts, the first who had ever touched them. .He laid her back upon the soft moss and she felt the fluttering in her belly that had teased and tortured her lonely nights. He undressed her slowly, his hands worshipping every curve. When she was quite naked he kissed every inch of her body, so that the fluttering became a throbbing ache and her eyes filled again with tears. He removed his own clothes quickly and lay down on his stomach beside her, his hand between her thighs. He gazed at her transfigured face for a moment, the nearest he would come to a question, and then, since she made no signal, he fitted his body to hers as they had always known it must fit and entered her as a prince might enter his kingdom.

At first their movements were almost reverent. They had waited so long that the thing seemed sacred. But soon they lost the first carefulness and began to bring each other to gradually increasing peaks of delight. Their eyes blazed, open and locked in wonder and joy. Their limbs weaved and caressed, never apart. They knew themselves to be at their most human and vulnerable, yet there was a soaring in it that brought them up into some heady region far above the earth, so they looked down and pitied it; they were man and woman, but they were also as the gods.

When it was over they lay close still, he covering her, their eyes closing at last. 'You are mine now. Forever. You will come back with me to Ireland,' he murmured into her hair.

'Forever,' she said, neither conscious nor unconscious. They lay like that for as long as it was necessary to them, then they dressed quietly and made themselves tidy and kissed in a manner that set the seal on their act.

'We will go to the inn,' he said, with his arm proudly about her. 'And look at other people and know that we are different and blessed and happy.'

'And you will tell me the story of Nieve all over again.'

'Kiss me again before we leave.'

'Your lips taste of mine.'

They walked to the inn, their horses trailing behind them, like two people who have been very sick and have not walked for a long time. It was wonder at what had happened that made them unsteady. They were under a spell of their own making as they moved beneath birdsong in the green shade.

At the inn they drank cider, for its sparkle and its taste of the Garden of Eden. They sat very close upon a bench in front of a barrel that served as a table, placed among others outside the windows where purple geraniums shared the sills with abandoned pewter.

As she had asked, Cathal told Lucy the legend of Nieve and Oisin and she listened with as breathless an interest as she had done that first Christmas of their meeting. And as she listened, there came the knowledge to her, creeping cold and slowly like the serpent, that their lives could never be as they had spoken of them, that today must be a gift from the gods and they must not ask for more. She said nothing to him, only bit her lip and did not allow herself to weep when he changed the ending of the legend so that all was well for the poet and his enchantress.

Still she said nothing. She would not spoil this day for him, although she herself could already taste ashes. She sat near to him and held his hand and loved him with her eyes.

They saw no one, not even the potboy, though the place was filled with thirsty customers enjoying the sun. But they themselves did not go unobserved.

When a tall, laughing woman came by, escorted by three gallants, who commandeered benches and called for wine, she checked at the sight of the two obvious love-birds beneath the geraniums. She drew in her breath and took a long look, to make sure that she was not mistaken. Then she whistled, very low.

'Damn it, Eliza, you look as if you'd just come into a fortune! What's making you so pleased with yourself?'

'Oh nothing, my dear Playfair, just life and love and the twists and turns of fate!'

When Lucy and Cathal arrived at Staunton House her heart began to knock and her head to feel taut and strange. She felt cold as they went through the door. He seemed unaware of any difference, and although he did not touch her, now that they were in sight of others, his glow of happiness seemed to her a very public thing. She did not know how she was going to be able to say what she must say to him. Perhaps, today, she would not even try. Let him have one night of that glorious sleeplessness, followed by the deepest sleep of all, that follows complete happiness.

As she tossed her straw hat to Cissie to take upstairs, the grave major-domo presented himself. 'There is a lady waiting for you, madam, in the withdrawing room.'

'Oh, who is that? I was expecting no one.'

'She gave the opinion that her name was no concern of mine, madam.'

'Indeed? Then we had better see if it is any of mine. Will you come with me, Cathal, to see the mysterious stranger?' There was no particular misgiving in her as she led the way. If she had any thoughts at all on the matter, they were vaguely connected with the Whittaker family, all of whom were pert enough to speak in that way to a servant.

The girl who was waiting for her, her dark head held proudly upon her long neck, her hands quiet in her lap, was unknown to Lucy. She had great beauty and also an appearance of strength of character that brought Valora to mind. She went towards her, a smile of welcome and enquiry on her lips.

Behind her, as Cathal entered the room, she heard him gasp. 'What in the name of God brings you here?'

'I do not come in the name of God, but in that of O'Connor,' the girl said precisely. 'Cathal, will you not introduce me to Mistress Staunton?'

The dismay on his face would have been comic had he not been so pale. 'Yes. Yes, of course. Lucy, this is Orla O'Connor. This is my wife.'

It was as if a great surge of warning music rose up inside Lucy's head, like the interlude before a masque. Her smile died, but she managed to nod in Orla's direction. Words were out of place. She sat down. Cathal, without hesitation stood at her back.

Mistress Orla looked hard at the two of them. 'I see how it is with you. I am sorry for it.' Since they gave her no answer, she continued, with no appreciable emotion, 'Cathal, you will know very well how difficult it has been for me to make this journey. The seas are dangerous, and the land not much less so. Therefore you will understand that it was not lightly undertaken, and will not be for nothing.' She rested here, to allow him to be sure she meant it. Still he would not speak. 'I have come to bring you home. Your people are fighting and dying on the plain and in the hills above us. Your place is with them, and with me. You bring shame to us all if you stay here with your English paramour while your brothers and your clansmen spill their blood into the heather in your name and for your lands and fame.' His cheeks had flamed at the word 'paramour' but he looked stubborn not ashamed. 'Your father is old. His wounds trouble him and he is slow in the fight. Soon he will be killed. You are the leader. Do not make us cast you out from your home and your inheritance.'

The silence was heavy when she had done. Lucy sat and looked at her, unable to avoid admiration for the pride that would not beg, the determination that would not bend. The girl sat before them like the figure of judgement, and Lucy, at least, could only feel that she was judged. She could say nothing and did not. Neither did Cathal answer his wife. The silence stretched about them until it seemed to crack and rend with the strain between them.

When it was long past being unbearable, he spoke softly. 'What will you tell me if I say to you that I do not care for my heritage, nor for the battle? If I say that my brother Carráig may have my place? If I ask you to break with me forever, and to forget that you were ever married to Cathal O'Connor?'

Her black eyes did not flicker once as she listened, nor did they ever leave his face. 'I would say that I would kill you, here and now, or elsewhere, with my own hands that have killed before, rather than let you bring yourself, your family and your wife to such dishonour. As for your heritage, it is not a question of whether you care for it; it is yours; it is around your neck and you must wear it. It does not, nor cannot belong to your brother, unless after your death. And for our marriage, well, that is a thing that cannot be broken. We are not Protestants to sink to the blasphemy of divorce. God has joined us together, and together we belong, no matter what romance you have woven about the yellow head of this woman.'

She knows him very well, Lucy thought wryly. And he is right; she is his friend, although she does not sound like one just now. She is right to recall him to his duty, to his place in the world, to himself also, for all I can know, who have had so little of him. Orla was right, and she herself had no place in this contention. Quietly she rose and left the room.

She heard a motion behind her as Cathal sought to follow her, then Orla's voice rang out 'No!' At the same time Lucy closed the door behind her.

In twenty minutes he found her in the library, looking blindly out across the sun-drenched gardens. Robert was careering about on his new-found legs in company with Cissie and a spaniel pup at much the same stage of development. She said without turning, 'I hope you have come to tell me that you must leave.'

His voice was close to her ear, very soft. 'Is that what you hope?'

She was near to breaking. 'It is what must happen.'

'I have told her; it rests with you. I will only go if you send me.'

'Then I do send you. Go with her. Go now.'

'Lucy, will you not look at me?'

'It only makes it harder.' But she turned and came into his arms. 'Kiss me once and then go. Please, let us not draw it out. It will not hurt less, but at least we shall not see each other's hurt.'

'Very well. But we will write again; you'll give me that much? I won't bear the complete loss of you; I must have your words.'

'I will write, but not often.' She drew his face down to hers and they kissed. There was nothing in it, no joy, no savour, because it was for the last time.

'My lips will always taste of yours,' he said. He smiled at her before he left, so that he should not leave her the memory of sadness in his face.

She rose to it and smiled proudly in return. He hesitated in the doorway. 'The white horse is waiting,' she said.

It would be the end of summer before Will came home. The weeks dragged. Lucy spent them in alternate moods of philosophy and despair. Apart from the terrible emptiness that surrounded her days, nothing, again, had changed. When she thought of her husband she missed him and wished him safe home; when she thought of Cathal she wanted him and was in pain at his loss. She knew that she must gain full control of her thoughts, and if possible, her emotions, before Will's return. He would know at once if there were anything new in her manner.

She had made her decision. She must expect to suffer on its account but by no mistake of hers must he be made to suspect either her suffering or the reason for it. They had made a happy marriage. That need not change, if she was careful and gave him what was easy to give; God knows he was lovable enough and she had not ceased to love him, not in any way. She was fascinated and subdued by the strangeness of this fact.

She began to practise looking forward all the while, thinking and planning for Will's reappearance in her life, firmly pushing back the intruder, memory. She had not yet written to Cathal, nor he to her. She sensed that he, like her, would wait first for the reverberations of pain to die away.

She was beginning to do well enough in her new strategy to find genuine enjoyment again in her everyday world. Robert was just starting to try to talk now, and that was sufficient enchantment to hold her almost completely. He called himself 'Wobbit', and also the pup, whom he hardly seemed to differentiate from himself. She taught him as much as he would listen to, which was very little as he was an active child who liked best to find out things for himself. She was delighted when he became attached to a model of the *Lady* that one of the sailors had made for Will. She would show him that he had a hopeful seaman for a son.

Her new calm pervaded the whole household. If no one in it had known the cause of her previous tension, they had been aware of it. She had been happy enough but she had not been at peace. Now she seemed restored to tranquillity and the house with her. And then, not in a single hour, but over the leaden course of several days, slowly and chillingly counted, that tranquillity was utterly destroyed.

At first she chose not to believe it. Time passed and gave her the lie. She believed it at last because she must. She was carrying Cathal's child. There was no doubt. She had missed two of her courses. And Will would be home at any time now.

She began to pray desperately, begging for a miscarriage. Then, realizing what she was doing, she begged forgiveness for that sin.

For the other sin, that had brought her to this conclusion, she could not ask forgiveness. She could not regret it. She had thrown away her peace, and Will's happiness, in the hour that had conceived this child, and yet she could not regret it. But she began to dread his return, knowing what she must tell him.

Cissie found her one morning, curled up in her bed, weeping and sick with nausea. 'It is something I've eaten,' she gasped, grabbing the bowl the girl held out. 'I'll be all right presently.'

Cissie regarded her, in two minds. Then she decided. 'Not yet awhile, you won't,' she said directly. 'That is a complaint that reckons to last nine months, if I'm not mistaken.'

'Sweet Jesus. How do you know? Is it so easy to tell?'

'Only if you've seen as much of it as I have, or many women. I've four married sisters, and my mother bore eleven times.'

'Oh Cissie, what'll I do? What'll I *do*?' She was in a blind panic.

Cissie ruminated. Then she said hesitantly, 'I don't know as you'd think of it, Mistress Lucy, but there is a way to be rid of it, if you have a mind to it. I'm no expert myself mind, but I know someone who is. There's a woman in Holborn—'

Lucy looked at her with dull hope. 'I don't know. I'll think about it. Oh Mother of God, what am I saying? Of course I can't murder Cathal's child! My child! No. No, Cissie, not that.'

'Then,' suggested the girl delicately, 'perhaps you may be able to pass it off as a seven months' child. Master Will should be home any of these days now – if you get my drift?'

Lucy groaned. 'O God, I don't know. How could I do that?'

'Well, how long do you reckon you are gone?' asked Cissie practically.

'About two months I suppose. Perhaps less.'

'Then it's a near thing, or will be if master doesn't look sharp. But he'll not think anything of it, if you can carry it off.'

Lucy looked at her miserably. 'I don't know, Cissie. I'm not sure that I *want* to carry it off. Heaven help me, what a mess! I don't know what to do for the best. If there *is* a best!'

'Well, you just rest and think on it. I'll help you all I can, trust me. No one need know of the sickness, save me. It won't come on you until you raise your head, and you never did get up before the master. As for the rest, 'tis warm enough still and we can dress you in loose things. Later, I'll just have to lace you a bit tighter. It can be done. Easily. Men don't enquire into these matters. They don't much want to know.'

'But Will took a great interest when Robert was born.'

'That was because he was the first. Mark my words, he'll not take such an interest in this one.'

'I'll think it over, Cissie,' Lucy sighed. 'I'll let you know.'

Will came home a week later. He was bronzed and bleached like a corsair and carried Lucy at once to the bedroom for a rapturous reunion.

And it was rapturous, as much for her as for him. As with her emotions, so it was with her senses. She discovered how much she had missed him and the bed was a place for loving and laughter again. As she basked in his pleasure and her own, everything seemed possible again. She would not do anything about the baby, not yet. She did not have to make up her mind for at least another six weeks. She would forget it, and simply enjoy her husband's presence.

He had bought her so many presents that she looked, she said when he had festooned them all over her naked body, like a houri. 'Houris are the delightful creatures the Musselman is given after death, if he had deserved them. You seem very much mortal.'

'A plain, straight whore, then! I don't care.' For a hair's breadth her security prepared to drain away, surprised by her own careless

641

words, but she got her balance again, almost at once, and he noticed nothing.

'And what did you do, all by yourself, while I was out-Shylocking Shylock?' he asked her lazily, leaning on his elbow and looking at her out of slitted, satisfied eyes.

She had prepared for this; there was no escaping it. 'I was showing the sights of London to Cathal O'Connor.'

His eyes widened. 'Were you so? And where, in the name of all that is windy and wordy, did *he* spring from?'

She forced a grin. 'From Dogheda, with Jud.' She told the story, making it as amusing as she could.

He listened, chuckling from time to time, but at the end of it all he said thoughtfully, 'And how did you find him now, the flower of your youth and first darling of your innocent heart? Was he much changed, or did he still strike a flame in your pretty white breast?'

Was the question as idle as it sounded? Of course it was not. 'He was changed a little,' she said slowly. 'His wife came here also.'

'With him?'

'No,' she said reluctantly, 'to fetch him home.'

Will's roar of laughter rose to the ceiling. 'And did he go?'

'Like a lamb,' she said, begging Cathal's forgiveness in her heart. 'He was good company,' she added. 'And yes, I still find him attractive. He *is* attractive, no matter how you may make fun of him.'

There, that would do it. She was safe now from anything but teasing. But that was enough now; she must not protest too much. She wondered afterwards, when they had got up and dressed and gone out into the garden to find Robert, if this meant that she had made up her mind that the child she carried was to be the seven months' product of Cissie's suggestion.

It was a week before Will would bother to plunge into the work that awaited him, both in his warehouses and at Westminster. The Commons were in a turmoil of excitement over Cromwell's invasion of Scotland, whither he had gone to meet the combined challenge of Argyll in the Estates and Leslie in the field.

He knew Leslie of old; he had fought beside him at Marston Moor. He was wary, wily and steady as rock. A month of tempting manoeuvres would not draw him into battle with the Ironsides on unfavourable ground, and the Lord General had been forced to withdraw to the plain near Dunbar, his men suffering greatly from dysentry and a kind of malarial fever that was common in camps. Leslie, taking this for his opportunity, marched quickly to cut off the English from the border, between the mountains and the sea, drawing up his battle lines in a good position on the hillside.

Now it was Cromwell who would not be drawn. He stayed on the plain. If Leslie wanted a fight he would have to come and get it. Knowing his army to outnumber the English by more than half, he did so with some confidence. What he did not consider, or not seriously enough, was that his men were mostly new recruits while Cromwell's were the legendary Ironsides. John Lambert's cavalry began the lesson. It was a very brief one.

Will listened with respect as the Speaker read Cromwell's despatch to the House. 'The best of the enemy's horse being broken through and through in less than an hour's dispute, their whole army being put into confusion, it became a total rout; our men having the chase and execution of them near eight miles.' It had been perhaps his greatest victory, perfect in its timing and performance, but all that the hero of the hour would say of it was that it was 'one of the most signal mercies God hath done for England, and His people, in this war.' His war cry had been 'The Lord of Hosts' and once more he had not been disappointed.

The young King's army did not surrender, but it had taken a hard knock. Charles would not be crowned in London *this* year. The rest of Parliament's business was of a sufficiently legal and administrative nature to bore Will for the moment. Accordingly, he allowed himself to devote much of his time to his various company interests. It was in the execution of one of these that he called one morning on his cousin Eliza.

His habit and her *déshabille* being what they were, it was not long before he found himself in her familiar bed, doing familiar things to her familiar body. 'Mmm! That was delicious. I *have* missed you,' she sighed appreciatively afterwards.

'But have not spent your days or nights pining,' he suggested, running his fingers over the pleasant incline of her thigh.

She rolled over so that she was looking into his face. She did not want to miss a flicker of his eyelid. 'Neither more, nor less,' she drawled, smiling nastily, 'than has your lady wife.'

He waited; he would not run at her cart-tail.

She smiled. 'Your Lucy has become loose. She has been showing her paces to that chestnut-haired young Irishman of hers. I believe you know him? He has grown up most personable.'

He gave her a crack across the face that sent her reeling. 'A poor price for the truth!' she gasped, pulling the sheet around her and glaring at him.

'Can you prove it to be the truth?'

'Yes, I can. I saw them together, at the Stag out beyond Chelsea. They were incontrovertibly lovers. I'd say they had just been at it. That's what Playfair said when he saw them.'

'So he's your proof?' Will swore softly.

'Yes, if you like. You can ask him yourself.'

'That will not be necessary. But mark me, Eliza, if I hear, from any direction at all, that my wife's name is being bandied about as you have described, I shall not merely mark your false-witness' face but also your whore's body, and in a very unpleasant fashion.'

'You are unfair, Will,' Eliza said flatly.

He left the bed and dressed with unusual carelessness. He probably *had* been unfair. He had hated her for what she had said. He had not altogether believed Lucy's blithe assurances about O'Connor. It was possible that so much of a young girl's emotion could be poured into such a splendid vessel as she had fashioned for that early love, only to be knocked idly off the shelf after two years of marriage to another man; it was possible, and with some women, very probable, but Lucy was not one of those women. He had accepted her words because she wanted to say them and he, damn it, had wanted to accept them. It was better so.

The boy was gone. He himself had returned. They would pick up where they had left off. That was, in fact, what they had done, and they were perfectly happy with it. Why then, did Madam Mischief have to open her poisonous mouth?

Eliza watched him dress, sitting quiet, soberly clad in her sheet. She wished she had not made him quite so angry. 'I'm sorry,' she said peaceably, 'I suppose no man likes to know he has been cuckolded.'

He tugged at the lace of his collar. 'Don't you think you are hazarding rather a lot upon the flight of your own imagination? Two people sitting together over a jug of cider hardly amounts to adultery.'

'If you had but seen *how* they sat. The world well lost. Oh Will, be reasonable. Why should I lie?'

'We will not go into that. It is you who would suffer most, not I.'

'As you will. I suppose you would rather I had not told you?'

'It is of no consequence – like your tale.'

'Then you must not hold it against me. You know my only care is for your contentment.'

'I thank you for that. If I were you I'd put a cold compress on your cheek. I wish you good morning, Eliza.'

She sighed, looking after him. This meant that she might not see him for some time. But he would come back eventually. He always did. And she had sown some thriving seeds, she was sure.

As Will strode away from St James' he had already made up his mind to say nothing further to Lucy. By the time he reached Tower Dock he had changed it. If there *had* been something between them – but even if there had, it was over; why not let it rest? Far wiser. His mind was set again.

As he sat in his cabin aboard the *Lady*, gently swaying on her hawsers, he destroyed his own reasonable arguments again. There must be truth between Lucy and himself; there was no honour in a marriage of concealment and distrust. No, if this thing were true, best to know it, to talk of it with her, and then to forgive her and get it over with. If he could forgive her. God knows how deep it had gone. He could not bear it if – God damn it, he had to know!

He thrust back the bundle of bills he had supposedly been studying into the arms of a startled clerk, and hurried back to land. He fished his bargemen out of the tavern and was home on the tide in twenty minutes.

Lucy was supervising the cleaning of the dining and withdrawing rooms, her hair tied up in a scarf to keep the dust out of it. Two of the maids were up a ladder, taking down curtains in a coughing cloud. 'Why Will, I had not expected you. This is nice. I will give up this doubtfully useful occupation. The girls are just as well without me. Shall we find Robert? You must hear him say Jacob Astley's prayer. He has it off pat, now, with no mistakes.'

'Later. I want to talk to you.'

'Very well.'

He led her into the library and closed the door. She was quick to sense his unrest. She could only hope it was the result of ill news from the sea or the Parliament. 'Sit down.'

She did so. He did not. He roamed the shelves as though seeking a volume, stopped and stared at the gilt lettering on a cover, moved on again, then stopped at last and faced her. 'I have heard it said – it is being put about that you have been closer than you should be to Cathal O'Connor.'

The truth was in her face at once. She had been too much

645

shocked to conceal it. Not that she had even planned to conceal it. She had made no reservations for such an event. 'I see,' he said dully.

'Oh Will—'

'Then I am not misinformed?'

She shook her head. She felt sick with self-loathing. He saw how pale she had become and pitied her. 'Then had you not better tell me all about it?' he asked gently.

All. Yes, now it would have to be all. Perhaps it was better so. The truth will out, they say, and perhaps it should. 'It is worse than you think,' she began, looking at him steadily, 'You should know that I am to have Cathal's child.'

His cry pierced her through. He turned away from her, marshalling his control. He had the soft desire to weep at her feet. When he thought he could, he faced her again. 'I would not have believed this of you. That you were close, yes, lovers, perhaps; but this!'

'It was only once, that we were lovers,' she said, more in rueful appreciation of ill luck than in extenuation.

'Surely you do not expect me to believe that.' He was cold now.

'But it is true. I will tell you nothing but the truth.'

'Indeed. But you were not about to tell me anything at all, were you, madam?' His voice cracked dangerously. 'You were going to pass your bastard off as my own, were you not?'

'No! I – don't know. We were so content together. I didn't want to spoil it.' It sounded lame, she knew.

'It's no use, Lucy. I can't believe you. We had best think what to do, or rather, *I* had.'

'There is nothing *I* can do. If only there was. Because I am a woman, I am trapped. The child exists. I can't unmake it, though I wish it with all my heart.'

'Though not half so dearly, no doubt, as you wished to make it!' he said crudely, glad to see her flinch. 'I wish you would leave me for an hour,' he decided then. 'I can't think clearly with your great eyes watching me.'

'Will. If only I might—' He had once said she would always be forgiven.

'Please. Do as I say.' She obeyed him and went up to her room.

It was a little less than the hour when she returned to the library. She had counted each lingering second, it seemed, and her nerve would not stretch any further.

He was seated in his favourite chair, beneath the row of books upon maritime matters. He looked tired and more than his age.

He gestured her onto a settle opposite. 'I have come to a decision that I think to be best for all of us. There is Robert to consider, as well as ourselves – and the – other infant, when it comes to be born. I do not feel that I wish to go on living with you as my wife—' Lucy gave a small moan. '—But my responsibilities to you will not change. As for our son, I think he should remain with you while he is very young, and come to me later for his education. The other will of course remain with you.'

'But Will—?'

'Yes?'

She swallowed. 'Where am I to go?'

He looked surprised. 'Why back to Heron, of course. Where else should you go. You cannot remain in London. I'll not have you flaunt your bastard beneath my windows.'

'Don't.'

'I beg your pardon. That was uncivil. But oh Lucy, you have been unkind! I had not expected to love a woman as I had come to love you. I find I hardly know how to deal with this. I only know it – diminishes me as a man, and that I can no longer be your husband.'

'God knows I am as sorry for it as you are,' Lucy said sadly. 'Can you tell me – is this to be forever – or will you, perhaps, one day—?'

He shook his head. 'I don't know. I don't think so.'

'Do you wish for a divorce?'

'No. We will leave it as it is. For Robert's sake. You will hear from me at intervals, and I shall hope to hear from you. Perhaps one day we shall be what we once were – simple friends.' He tried to smile. 'And now, I think it would be as well if you were to make your arrangements as soon as possible. I shall be out of the house for the next two weeks or so.'

She gave a little gasp and her hand flew to her cheek. 'But I love you!' she cried out dismally.

'And I you,' he said ironically. 'It is sad, is it not?' He left her then, and she did not see him again.

Heron 1650

Mary had written, 'Since you have nowhere else where you might go, you must perforce come here. But I may as well tell you, Lucy, you have broken my heart. You have brought to this family its greatest shame. I thank God your father is not here to suffer it.'

Her mother's letter, more than the midnight agonies, more even than the knowledge of the great hurt she had caused to Will, shocked Lucy into a new state of awareness of herself. She looked into her mirror and saw a new and different person from the one she had looked at for twenty-three years.

Until now, she had never questioned her own morality. She had been taught what was goodness and how to achieve it and had done her wavering best to walk in that path. Even when she had been punished for some misdemeanour she had never thought of herself as wicked, only foolish or selfish or disobedient. Now she must see herself as a woman who had ruined lives, caused the death of hearts, and would bring further sorrow into the world with her second child. She felt old and tired and full of a dull despair. She was without honour among her own people.

Her homecoming had been an unimaginable ordeal. She had been unable to prevent herself from feeling the old sense of relief and pleasure, beneath the apprehension that amounted to nausea, when she had crossed the border in to her own shire and, a little later, into Heron land.

They had sent John Coachman for her. She had sat beside him on the box, prefering the air to the dim carriage, and he had smiled at her and clicked the reins and said, 'We'll soon be home now, Mistress Lucy,' as he always did when they topped the hill just past Northleach. She had been so swamped with sudden gladness that she had forgotten why she was coming home.

A reminder was not long in coming. When they reached the brow of the driveway and hurried on down to the wide sweep before the front steps, there was no one to greet her. Normally every member of the household who was not most urgently occupied would race out at the sound of the coach. She understood.

'Never mind your things, mistress. I'll see to them,' John said quietly. She heard the pity in his voice and had to bite her tongue not to weep, as she had done when a child.

Those first few days had been a daylight nightmare. Her mother gave out that she did not wish to have any commerce with her other than the necessary meetings at table, or to discuss domestic tasks, when servants would also be present. Lucy, who had longed to throw herself on Mary's breast and be forgiven, found it a hard blow to bear.

The twins seemed embarrassed by her presence, and kept out of her way, she thought, although they could not be said to have been unfriendly. Kit had even given her a shy smile of welcome, at supper on her first night. It had wavered, however, as his mother threw him a severe look.

Julia, now a serenely pretty sixteen, and very devout, had blushed distressingly when she first met her sister, and, muttering that she would pray for her, had run off out of the room. Since then they had hardly spoken. Julia, who had once snuggled her round little body next to Lucy's every night, now melted away whenever she came near.

The presence of her elder sister, Jane, on a long visit from Oxford, where she had left James to the hopeless and perhaps ill-advised task of trying to prevent the election of Oliver Cromwell as Chancellor, had at first seemed an added rod for her back; but Jane's forthright character did not permit her to keep silent when her conscience called her to duty, so that she was at least bound to speak to Lucy. 'Well, you have made a rare mess of things, and no mistake. I should've thought you would have had more sense. Still, there's no use crying over spilt milk. The child is with you and must be welcome in the world, as is every child's right.' She had sighed then. 'Though I must say I think it queer in the Good Lord that he should see fit to give an unwanted child where it can only cause trouble and sorrow and deny that precious gift to those who are at him, night and day, on their knees for it.'

Jane's lack of children looked now as though it must be permanent. She was thirty and had never yet conceived. She had said no more about Lucy's condition after that and now treated her with the slightly asperitive goodwill which she dealt indiscriminately to all the world, so long as it were Royalist.

The one person who seemed not to wish to judge Lucy at all, nor in any way to restrain the natural affection that flowed between them, was Martha. 'Oh my poor sweet, I so wanted to come out and greet you, but your mother would not have it. I have tried to show her that what has happened was without prevention, but she cannot see it so. My dear Lucy, I am so happy to see you. We will make all things well, in time. And I will be with you, and Robert and young Thomas. We will enjoy them together and for much of the time you will forget your trouble.'

'Oh Martha, how could I manage without you? I seem always to have been saying this. It has always been true.'

'I could say the same. There are two twists to a skein of friendship.'

'But you have always seemed to be so strong; as though you did not need anyone. Perhaps it is because you are without Tom for so long at a time.'

Martha smiled. 'No, it is because my mother was who she was. I learned the habit of loneliness early. But that does not mean I do not need my friends. As for Tom, as long as there is a Stewart without a throne, want must be my master.'

Gradually, largely through Martha's careful tutelage, Lucy came to realize that it was only her mother and Julia who were implacable in their disapproval. Her brothers, once they had got over their initial embarrassment, soon treated her like one of themselves again, and whispered to her their secret plans to become soldiers again.

'Do you ever think of anything else?' she asked Humpty, amused.

'*Is* there anything else? Do you *want* gloomy Noll preaching to you for the rest of your life? Of course we must go. Only I'm not sure whether we should ask Mother's permission. After all, we're twenty-one now. And she's – not in the best of moods.'

'We'd best just go, like we did the first time – if you can manage to get away from Isabella,' teased Kit.

'I know how to deal with Isabella,' said Humpty smugly.

Lucy had observed that the young lady was doing very nicely with her reluctant swain. She was much in evidence, but she no longer ran after her quarry as she used to; she even had other suitors. Her cousin was mad for her. He was a very personable young man and she let herself be seen with him often. Humpty had been heard to say that Jude Stratton was all wind and waistcoat and would never make more than half a man. He had said this in Isabella's presence and she had simply smiled her maddening smile and looked as if she knew better.

The most senior member of the Stratton family was also still malevolently active. The old lady had herself carried everywhere on a red velvet litter, from which she ordered everyone's lives to her own satisfaction and their fulmination.

She had posted over at once when she had heard that Lucy was home. 'Well, miss, you've got yourself into a fine pickle, haven't you? I'll be interested to see if you can get out of it! I only hope the brat won't have cloven hooves; they say all the Irish are descendants of Satan. What will you do with it, sell it as horsemeat?'

'No, I'll have it dressed and delivered at your doorstep. The world will take it for your own late by-blow,' Lucy had snapped, losing patience.

The beldame had cackled like a gorse fire, hugely pleased. 'Well, I wish you well,' she said, eyes twinkling. 'You may not have the luck, just at the moment, but you still have your wits about you, and you have a high stomach in more ways than one. I like it! Your luck will return. Mine always did. Did I ever tell you about the time Stratton found me with young Handsworth—?'

It took all afternoon, but by the time Lucy had heard all, she knew she still had a friend in the craggy old woman. Nothing could console her for the loss of her mother's affection, but she was astonished to find how much sympathy she generated in such unlikely bosoms as that of old Lady Stratton, and even that of her great-granddaughter.

Isabella, as Lucy herself would once have done, viewed the circumstance as a great and tragic romance. 'You are lucky, to have had so much of love,' she told Lucy enviously. This was not a moral attitude but it was very endearing. And indeed Lucy herself, in her long and private moments, however deeply she castigated herself for the harm she had done to those she loved, could not, in the light of the truth of her own nature, bring herself to regret a single moment of Cathal's company, nor even the deed which had brought her to so much contumely. She would not deny love, now or ever. And, no matter what her mother, or the chaplain, or the rest of the judgmental world might say, there was an arrogant certainty in her that she was right.

Nieve was born in an hour of perfect spring sunlight and showers, at eventide on the first day of April. Margery, her loving midwife, was the first to chuckle and call her April Fool. The birth was a long and difficult one, so different an experience from the triumphant bearing of Robert that Lucy was determined, for many hours of sweating, agonizing pain without cease, that this was her punishment for her unsanctioned love and that she was doomed to die of it.

She heard Martha, Margery and Alice murmuring round her and was conscious of their gentle movements outside, the hazy net of her pain. The labour had gone on since five o'clock that morning. The waters had long since broken and there were contractions in plenty, but the child would not be born. Margery pummelled and wheedled. Martha brought dark, strong-tasting infusions and Alice incessantly prayed, while Lucy reared and tossed and streamed with sweat and tears. She no longer felt herself to be a woman, nor any sentient creature. She was at the mercy of nature at its most cruel, an uncaring force which selects the strongest and disposes of the weak with grim efficiency. She had become one of the weak. She had sinned and could not be forgiven. She deserved to die.

Above the tormented figure upon the wringing sheets, eyes met and agreed. Martha squared her thin shoulders and left the room.

A little later, Lucy became aware of another hovering shape outside her thickening net. A cool hand stroked her forehead. 'My dearest child. It is you who are preventing it; you must do as your body bids you. The child wants to see the light. It is you who keep it in darkness. Lie back and do not fight. You must let yourself relax except at those times when you feel you should push. Come on now, Lucy. We will all help you.' There was a pause, then the soft voice continued, 'We all love you.'

She reached through the web and found her mother's hand. After that there was a brief interval of tears, and then they all applied themselves to the work.

Nieve was born with a comical tonsure of dark chestnut hair, and eyes as deep brown as peat. There was no question as to what her name should be, although nobody knew how to spell it. She was born at that time when the production of young is prodigal and prodigious. Heron abounded with young lambs, young calves, piglets, pups, chickens, ducklings, kittens, and of course the horses. Calliopes's daughter, Echo, gave birth to a splendid chestnut filly about half an hour before Nieve came into this noisy world of spring babies. True to an old mischievous impulse, Lucy named her *Areopagitica*, with mental apologies to Cromwell's talented Latin Secretary, John Milton. By the time Nieve was able to pronounce her name, she should also be old enough to learn to ride her.

Lucy's first task after the little girl was born, one which made her tremble a little, was to try to send news of the event to Cathal. She had decided against telling him of her pregnancy in case she should lose the child prematurely. Now that all was safely accomplished, he had a right to know that he had a healthy and beautiful daughter.

She wrote hesitantly, expecting and fearing the flood of love that would wash her back into the limbo from which she had slowly redeemed herself during the months of waiting. In the end she was brief and factual, almost curt. She would do nothing that would bring him to her, nothing that would prevent, one day, the renewal of Will's need for her. She would live in the truth that she intended to follow. Cathal must become the dream-memory he was always meant to be; he could not be a part of her life, not ever again.

She gave the carrier precise instructions, but she did not have much faith in the arrival of her letter. Ireland was still under the sword, and Cathal a rebel in arms. For all she knew, he might be dead. She prayed for him, but tried not to think of him otherwise.

She found this increasingly hard as Nieve grew older. The child was more like her father every day. Her hair maintained its rich chestnut colour and her eyes soon developed an enquiring and irreverent sparkle that was all too recognizable to anyone who had ever met Cathal. She learned to laugh before she learned anything else, and seemed disinclined to cry except on rare occasions of physical discomfort. Even her grandmother, though still a little reserved with Lucy, now that the drama of birth was over, fell instantly in love with her, and thus she began at once to justify her borrowing of the name of an enchantress.

At the end of that summer the King's army entered England, or rather, what was left of it, after Cromwell had harried it through the Lowlands of Scotland into one untenable situation after another. He was behind them now, an untiring Nemesis, as they hounded across Lancashire towards Wales, hoping to increase the pack in these old Royalist chases. True to their word, Kit and Humpty rode out to join them, leaving Lucy to explain to Mary, who took it with a curse and a sigh.

The day after their departure Lucy received her first real letter from Will. Until now he had merely sent a regular enquiry as to her health and needs, couched every time in the same formula of words. He could have found no more obvious way to show her that he did not wish for anything more intimate between them. She had written, then, with less hope than ever, of Nieve's birth, thinking that she might well not hear from him again for a very long time.

She was surprised, therefore, to receive his letter, when her daughter was just over five months old. There was a parcel with it. She laid that aside until she had read his words. 'My dear Lucy, so you have a daughter. I am glad to hear that she is a healthy child that and that you are well and want for nothing.' Except you, my husband, except you. 'My news, if I were to give it, would be all of the sea and ships, for I am afraid I make a poor showing in the Commons these days. They manage their quarrels well enough without me. I find more profit in the Exchange than at Westminster. I have voyaged a good deal, these last months, and have seen the Serene Porte of Istanbul again, always a sight for a sailor's sore eyes. I thank you for your news of Robert. His progress is what I would expect of him. I shall ask to have him with me for a visit one of these days, though not yet as I am still much from home. You will easily tell which of the small gifts I send is for him. Pray continue your good care of him, and speak to him sometimes of his father, lest he forget.' He signed himself simply 'William Staunton'.

Sadly, Lucy unwrapped the package. It contained a tiny scimitar, its blade harmless as its appearance was fierce. Robert would menace Mary's shrubbery with it and be as happy as any boy could be who no longer had his father to play with him. Not that he lacked for male companionship. The twins had taken him about with them much as though he were another parrot or pup, and Dickon Stable had an especially soft spot for him, especially now that he was courting Doll in the dairy and might soon hope for children of his own. Even Tibbett, who was getting old and crusty, would sometimes give him a ride on his giant's shoulders, so that the boy would feel he owned the world and could touch the sky.

When Lucy looked at the other contents of the parcel, her heart gave a great lurch of awakening hope. There was a new book of music; it was entitled *Parthenia* and was a collection of the compositions of the three great masters of the virginals, William Byrd, Dr John Bull, and Orlando Gibbons, who were uncompromisingly described on the title page as 'Gentlemen of His Majesty's Chapel'.

So he did not hate her. She kissed the music. She would play it right away. She ran up to the gallery and began to skim the keys with a lighter heart than she had known for a year. But she soon fell to remembering how music had always been an emblem of the harmony of their relationship. She could play the melodies but she could not bear the sound of her single voice, without his to encircle it round and lift it up. The gladness left her as suddenly as it had come and she closed the instrument in a deep regret.

*

Only three weeks after their latest defection, Kit and Humpty returned home. They rode upon a single horse and were part of a brief, bedraggled cavalcade, consisting of themselves, their brother Tom, and that reluctant warfarer, Josh Pye. They had been seen by the field workers five miles back and the word of their coming had spread faster than they could ride. The household, therefore, assembled in front of the door according to custom, excitement buzzing among them as they quizzed each other as to whether they were there to cheer a victory or bewail a defeat. Had they a King again, or was old Noll still in command? It was not long before they knew.

The three horsemen rode neatly abreast as they came over the brow of the hill. They were slow and composed. None of them waved a hat or a sword, and there was no sound from them other than that made by the horses.

'The poor young King is lost, then,' said Tibbett, sighing.

'God bless him,' other voices said sadly.

'Perhaps they are just tired?' suggested Alice, hopefully.

Heads were shaken. Humpty, at least, would have to have been *dead* before he would give up the chance to roar a victory. Tibbett and Dickon went forward to take the bridles as the dusty little party drew up before them.

There were quiet nods of greeting. Tom laid his head for a moment upon Mary's shoulder. 'I am glad, at least, that you are together,' she said softly, 'and whole, as far as I can see?'

'Kit has a chest wound; superficial. I have a few cuts and bruises. Humpty has a whole skin, though the devil knows how.'

'Come inside at once, all of you; you look exhausted.' She raised her voice. 'Back to your tasks, everyone; you shall hear all their news in due course.'

Tom held up a delaying hand as they turned to go. 'It is such news as cannot improve with keeping, I'm afraid. Your King was defeated, fighting like Hector himself beneath impossible odds, in defence of the city of Worcester.'

'He wasn't taken, the poor young man?' asked Margery fearfully.

'No. We know that he escaped after the battle; but we do not know where he is. I imagine he will make again for France. Now, if you will forgive me—' His face was ashen, the bones showing plainly as they always did when he was at his lowest. He swayed

655

a little and suddenly Martha was beside him, her own frail shoulder beneath his, her arms about him, drawing him into the house. Everyone dispersed in a dull quiet, looking at each other and shaking their heads.

In the hall, Lucy was waiting, with Nieve in her arms. She had been taking an afternoon rest and the sound of their coming had only just broken through her summer drowsiness. Her smile was filled with her pleasure in seeing them all safe home together, and was particularly for Tom whom they had not seen for so long.

He checked as he caught sight of her and stood straight, eluding Martha's arm. 'I wonder, madam, that you have the gall to present me with *that*, on my very doorstep, as soon as I enter my house!' Lucy stood shocked, her arms tightening around her child.

'Tom, that is cruel!' It was Martha who cried out, with more admonition in her voice than they had ever heard from her. Tom took no notice of her but thrust past them and strode heavily towards the small drawing room.

'I'm sorry Lucy,' said Mary levelly, 'but I'm sure you must have expected something of the sort. You had best keep out of Tom's way until matters can be made easier.'

'I'll be damned if I will creep about the house with my head hung because Tom cannot scrape an ounce of charity from his miser's soul! And I'll not have him speak of Nieve like that. She is his flesh and blood, not a parcel of offal, like it how he may!'

'You cannot expect him to *like* it,' said Mary coldly. 'But you are right; the child is innocent and must not be made to suffer.'

'He will have accepted her long before she can understand what he says of her,' said Martha firmly. 'I shall look after that.' She went after him, a frown between her brows.

'Oh the devil!' Humpty had caught up with them, his face comic with dismay. 'Perhaps I shouldn't have told him, but I thought it better to get it over; have him prepared, don't y'know? He burnt his fuse pretty well to the quick *then*. I supposed that would be the end of it.'

Lucy reached to kiss his cheek. 'You did kindly. And it might have been worse. He might have thrown us both down the steps and bidden us never darken his door again!'

'Oh I say, you know,' said Kit with awkward affection, 'we wouldn't have put up with that, would we Humpty?'

'I should think not. But you have to make allowances,' he added. 'He's been through a lot recently.'

'No more than us,' said Kit, to be fair.

'Well, we're younger. We can take it,' grinned Humpty.

Lucy laughed. 'Go on; take yourselves off and clean yourselves up. A bath wouldn't hurt you! It's high summer. Then sleep till supper; you look worn out. We'll hear it all later.'

Humpty pulled a wry face. 'It don't make such good hearing. Bit of a blow, Worcester, eh Kit?'

Kit nodded. 'A death blow, I think.' They wandered sombrely off to the chamber that they had always shared, where Sam Hudson's blood was still a welcoming stain.

When later, rested, bathed and gratefully fed, they came to give their account of the battle that had seen the demolition of the King's army, it was not, as had been promised, happy listening. They settled, as they had always done on such occasions, about an unnecessary fire in the small parlour, with Tibbett and Margery present as the accredited ears of the household at large. Tom, who did not look any more cheerful than he had on arrival, sat close to Martha and declined to be the narrator. Humpty, when appealed to, swallowed hard and said he'd rather not, and anyway Kit would do it better.

Responsibility having come his way, Kit accepted it and began to speak in his light, hesitant voice. 'Well, we joined the army on the road just before Shrewsbury. They were glad to see us. Glad to see anyone. The recruits just weren't coming in, I don't know why—'

'Because,' Tom interrupted, his expression hard, 'they have lost their stomach for fighting. They knew of Cromwell's successes in Scotland, and saw no point in joining up just to be defeated again. We Royalists have become cowards.'

'I don't see that. I'd say it was distrust of the Scots as much as anything else that kept them away. They didn't want to fight alongside Covenanters; they still think of them as the enemy.'

'Then how do you account for the lack of support in the south? What became of the hundred and one risings that were supposed to flame up the minute His Majesty crossed the border?'

Kit shrugged. 'Perhaps they thought better of it after the executions in Norfolk.' The Council of State had awarded this end to the plans of certain would-be insurrectionists back in the spring.

'So, what were your numbers, when you entered Worcester?' asked Lucy, ignoring Tom's repressive glare.

'I heard 12,000. I'd say it was near enough.'

'And the Ironsides?' Mary asked.

'At least 30,000.'

'Lord have mercy on us!' ejaculated Margery.

'None the less, we made a good beginning,' said Kit, goaded by too much sympathy. 'We had hoped to make our stand at Shrewsbury, since it was obvious there was no hope of a march on London – but the good burghers declined the honour of dying for their King, as they thought certain, God rot their mean minds – and so we went on to Worcester. It was the first city to rise for the King in '41, and it did not fail his son.' There was a murmur of approval for the loyal city.

'We'd not long to raise our defences. The scouts had told us Lambert and Harrison were about four days behind us, and Cromwell himself coming down in the east at the devil's own pace. He marched his foot twenty miles a day in their shirt sleeves! But at least they had boots; which is more than most of our poor lads had, after their slog down from the north.'

'But how can a man march, without shoe-leather?' marvelled Julia, almost in tears at the thought of such privation.

Humpty threw her a smile. 'His *feet* turn into shoe-leather, after a while, like a dog's or a wild pony's. Go on, Kit.'

'As I said, the start of it was quite hopeful, despite our lack of numbers. Worcester is a good city to defend. It stands on one river, the Severn, and is protected by another, the Teme, southeast of the town, before the hills beyond which lies the Vale of Evesham; then there are the Malverns to the west; all natural defences. Of course the city walls were a bit battered, from last time – but the Scots soon got up some earthworks. We managed to blow up the bridges, too, all but one, where Cromwell ambushed our guard and repaired it. A pity, that.'

Kit scratched his head reminiscently and looked about the intent circle in bafflement. 'How shall I describe it to you? Perhaps the best thing is for you to imagine yourselves on top of the tower of the cathedral; that's where His Majesty viewed the opening of the battle, through a spy-glass, on the morning of September 3rd. You can see for miles up there. It's the prettiest sight imaginable. Except for the enemy, of course; they were not so pretty. Their main body was drawn up in the south and east, across the road to London. If you looked to the southwest you'd have seen our own Scots infantry defending the north bank of Teme. You would have seen them the first to come under attack from Fleetwood's regiments and fight back with courage and vigour. You would also have seen what they could not; that Cromwell had taken a detachment and begun to build a bridge of boats to cross the Severn below where the Teme flows into it, and take them in the rear. They were game, Covenanters or not, but they hadn't enough ammunition to hold out against such punishing numbers. It was about now that the King, upstairs, got the idea that might have won us the day, if we'd had the luck. He saw how Cromwell was pouring his men across the river and decided it was the moment for us to try a bold sally through the Sudbury Gate – the one that commands the London road – and charge the Ironsides while their numbers were down.

'You should have seen Charles, all of you! He is fine! He has all of his father's courage and a heap more humour. Don't growl so, Tom; it's true! He sat his horse in a buff coat and boots, like any common trooper, with his scarlet sash, and only the George on his breast – and that black, gipsy's face of his – to show he was the King. He had a word for all of us, before the attack; he seemed to *remember* everyone. When we'd tracked down Tom, during those first days, and made him present us, he called us "Castor and Pollux", and laughed and asked if we had a fair Helen at home. Humpty said you, Lucy, were a thousand times more fair and would launch a whole navy with no trouble at all! Charles gave us a wicked look and said we must be sure to bring you to court – when he had got himself a court to bring you to.'

There were indulgent chuckles. Tom pursed his lips.

'He said he had a liking for women named Lucy,' Humpty added, grinning. 'He must have been thinking of Lucy Walter, who bore him James Crofts in '49. They say she is a cracking piece!'

'She is a whore,' said Tom coldly. There was a silence.

Kit cleared his throat and continued brightly. 'We made a brave charge, though it was uphill all the way. It looked so hopeful then—' He stopped and gave an apologetic smile to preface what must follow. 'And who knows, perhaps, if Leslie had had the sense to send us his cavalry, who had not yet entered the scene, we might have held the day. But he did not. Instead, Cromwell saw what we were doing and recalled the regiments who were by now pursuing our Scots foot back into the city. They turned and came after us and cut us to pieces. We had to give way or die where we stood; many of us did simply that. They beat us back into the town, as their comrades were beating back the infantry on the other side of it.

'I wonder if you can catch any notion of what it was like; thousands upon thousands of raging men running through those narrow streets, pursued and pursuing. There were horses as well, dead or dying, blocking our path at every turn, their guts spilling onto the road, making it slimy and treacherous. The very conduits ran with blood. We had to hack our way through, with no real idea of where we were going, and often, I fear, of whom we killed to get there.'

'You mean you might have murdered your own men?' asked Julia, her startled eyes showing this to be a new horror to the list which she had heard before and hated to hear again.

'Well, they do not always wear a distinguishing mark, and unless they explain themselves, sharpish, they are like to have no windpipe left to do it with. There was one fellow I got into an argument with – couldn't have been more than sixteen, keen as mustard. He let me open up his belly from his navel to his ribs before he thought to cry "God save the King!" It was too late then, of course, poor young bugger! Oh, I say, I'm sorry Julia. But this *is* war we're talking about. The next bit is more cheerful, I promise.'

But Julia fled the room and ran to pour out her distress in the chapel. She wanted to dedicate her life to God, but God continued to allow such dreadful things to happen that she was not sure He deserved it.

'We tried to keep near the King, at this time. Derby and Buckingham stuck close too. We attempted to tell each other, between the maddest bouts of sword-play you've ever seen, that we had to get His Majesty away! We decided to make for the north gate. There was a bit more mud and blood before we reached it, but it worked out all right in the end. It was just before we got out that I got this swipe across the breast – bled a lot, but didn't amount to much, though I didn't know it then. Tom fought them off me like a veritable tiger!'

Tom frowned and drained his glass. 'Go on, Kit, for God's sake!'

'Well, there's not much more, really. We were all for staying with His Majesty, but he thought it best to remain as small a party as possible. There was talk of disguising him as some sort of servant, or even as a woman! He seemed to like all that. In fact we pretty soon got lost. It was pitch black on the road. But Derby thought if they kept on north they should hit Boscobel wood, where he'd once hidden out himself, and he'd vouch for the loyalty of the area. We parted then, and, as far as we know, they went to Boscobel wood. God keep His Majesty and send him to safety.'

'Amen,' said his audience.

'But what will he do, supposing he escapes the net they will throw out for him? Where will he go?' asked Mary.

Tom answered her. 'Back to France,' he said, his voice rising, 'to plan what he will do next.' An unmistakable emptiness greeted his words.

'So then, Tom,' said Lucy quietly, 'you have made your peace with your King?'

He met her eyes, but without affection. 'He spoke to me of Montrose,' he said. 'I will never think well of him in that particular – but I am prepared to think better in the future. He fought bravely at Worcester. He was an inspiration to us. No soldier could have asked more.'

'Then it is more battles that you want for him, my son?' Mary said.

'Yes, Mother. If that is what is necessary.'

'And you; what will *you* do next?' asked Martha softly, as they prepared for bed in her chamber that night.

He came to her and kissed her and stroked her hair. 'Ah. I do not need to ask,' she said, with her small smile. 'And will you take me with you, this time. I am lonely for you, when you are so far away.'

'And I for you, believe me.' He began to undress her, his thin, over-disciplined body famished for her.

'That is not what I mean,' she said, resisting as he cupped one hand upon a breast and began to hoist her towards the bed with the other hooked between her thighs. 'That is not all it means, to be a man's wife. I want to be *with* you, Tom.'

He heard her. But he had taken a wife with him once before. 'You are with me now, and you are wasting precious time,' he murmured, taking her shift from her. She saw that he would not listen, not yet, and came naked into his arms.

When at last he had to listen, being too exhausted by war and love to be able to escape her question, he was honest with her at once. 'My life is with the King, as it has always been. I do not know what sort of life that will be. I must go abroad quickly, for I'm a proscribed man, as you must know. Kit and Humpty escape that honour; they are not known, though they do their best to *become* known! I want you with me – no, do not hope, not yet – for I won't take you now. You would only be a burden to a man on the run. But I will send for you, as I did before. Now, will that content you?'

'When will you send?'

'As soon as I think there is a possibility of a life together.'

Martha smiled and talked of other things. She did not feel any the less lonely, she found now, when he was with her, than she did when he was away.

Before he left Heron, Tom sent to ask Lucy if she would speak with him. He was in Sir George's old study, as he had been when they had first talked of her marriage to Will.

His expression showed her that he recalled that occasion and had no such willing taste for this one. 'I'll not waste time, madam, for we have nothing to say to each other outside the matter which concerns us.'

He said nothing and he went straight on. 'Your sister Jane has come to me with a proposal which she wishes me to consider. You also. I must confess I myself find it most sensible and attractive, in the circumstances. It is this; that to all intents and purposes your bastard daughter should be become the child of James and herself—'

He was brought up by Lucy's gasp of incredulity. 'You can't mean it!'

'Assuredly, I do. It would be most fitting, and most kind of James and Jane to take on the responsibility. It would relieve this family of a great embarrassment, and give the child the best of homes at the same time.'

'Tom, be careful; I am probably going to hit you.'

'Then you will soon wish you had not. The world has been too kind to you, Lucy; it is kind to you now, though it seems you won't see it—'

'Kind! To take my child away from me as though I were the most degraded of criminals!'

'You are an adultress. Adultery is a crime. Thank your stars you are wed and do not go at the cart's tail.'

'Where *you* would gladly see me! No, Tom. Your answer is no. I'll have none of this. There is no way you can make me.'

His eyes narrowed. 'I do not attempt to force you. Only to ask you to consider your mother. To consider the child. To consider Jane, if you like, who would as soon take in one of her own blood, in part, as any other. And last of all, consider, and deeply, your husband. If Will were to know the child were well out of the way, do you not think he would come to you again? He loved you more than commonly. Think about it. It is in all our interests.'

She escaped from him then, and she did not see him again before he had gone, hidden behind a brand new beard and muffled in the rough cloak of an itinerant packman, leaving Martha too quiet and without serenity, and herself driven almost to distraction by the tantalizing question in those last words.

London, New Year 1652

Regina Staunton had commanded her son to be at home, as she intended to pay him a visit. She had announced that the time of her arrival would be half-past three. Since he had never known his mother to be anything other than prompt, Will handed his cousin Eliza into her handsome equippage at precisely ten minutes past the same hour.

Eliza had been staying with him, on and off for several weeks, or he with her. He had avoided her in the early days of his separation from Lucy. The fact that she had, against all his hopes, been right, had placed her beyond some sort of protective pale he had raised for himself, behind which he suffered, and made attempts to assimilate that suffering into his everyday life.

But soon they had met, as they must, at the house of a mutual friend. Eliza had come quietly to his side and spoken of old things, common to them both, never mentioning Lucy. She had not mentioned Lucy to this day, and Will had not encouraged her to do so. With this one prohibition unspoken between them, they managed more or less well together, as they had done in the past. It was not marriage, but it was all Eliza was likely to get, just at present, and she took it gratefully, making herself as pleasant and loving a companion as she could, and carefully starving herself of all greedy hope of a divorce. Though there might come a time for such hope.

'My love and duty to your mother,' she called as her coachman cracked his whip. Unfortunately she did not get on very comfortably with Regina, who had always had her measure and had never approved of her as a consort for Will.

'She will be delighted,' he replied automatically, raising his hand to wave and hoping the two vehicles would not pass each other *too* near his gates. His mother had spoken to him rather acidly about Eliza the last time they had met.

But when Regina arrived, she did not speak of Eliza. She seemed rather subdued, Will thought, as he ensconced her before the leaping flames of his study grate. 'Well, my dear, has it been a good Christmas at Staunton St Paul? Or was all jollity suppressed by the local killjoys?'

'There were no services – unless you call those dreary Puritan meetings by the name. But we managed a certain amount of merrymaking ourselves. You should have come to us.'

'Oh. I've been too busy, lately, to mark the seasons. But it's good to see you now, Mother. You look superb, as ever.'

'I do not. I look tired and distressed, which is as it should be, for I am both. However, it is in your hands to alter these unsatisfactory conditions, if you will.'

Will looked puzzled. 'I attribute the tiredness to your journey. An hour or two's rest will see to that. But I am sorry to hear of the distress. That is far more grave. How may I help you?'

His look of genuine concern told her that he had no idea of what she was going to say to him. Well, that was all to the good. She would not have wanted him prepared. 'You may help me, my son, by helping yourself.'

'How so?'

She sighed. 'I feel old today. It is inevitable that one should do so upon some occasions, but I could wish I had more energy for this.'

'For what, Mother? It is not like you to be mysterious.'

'I am not being mysterious. I am simply giving myself time. Be patient. And get me some aqua vitae. I need it.' When she had drunk a few sips she brightened.

'I have come here expressly to speak to you about a certain matter, so I will get it over with, and then take the rest you so kindly offer me. Now then – you will have noticed that I have made no comment, other than at first expressing my regret at the circumstance, upon the present condition of your marriage to Lucy.'

Will's brow clouded. 'Yes, and I hope—'

Her raised hand silenced him. 'That was because I hoped I had made a good enough job of your education to be sure that you would reflect wisely upon your impulsive action, and restore your wife and child to their proper place. Here.'

'Mother, I would rather you did not—'

'I do not care for your wishes. You are not the person about whom I am most concerned. Lucy has, apart from this one lapse, been an excellent wife to you. She made you happier than I have ever seen you—'

'And that is precisely why her unforgivable behaviour had the power to make me so *unhappy*!'

'Unforgivable? That is a hard word, Will.'

'It is adequately descriptive, I think.'

'For what, exactly, can you not forgive her?'

'You know as well as I!'

'For her adultery? For making you a cuckold? Or for the love she had for another man. An old love, not a new. It makes a difference.'

'Not to me,' he muttered.

'Then it should. You have old loves of your own, if I am not mistaken. The trollops I discount. Every man of spirit, it seems, must express himself in that way from time to time. But your cousin is not a trollop; or at least her name and station prevent her from being known as such.' She stopped, her look challenging him.

Will groaned. 'Mother. We have had this before. Eliza is old enough to do as she pleases.'

'She was not old enough when you destroyed her reputation as a girl.'

He shrugged. 'I do not think I was alone in that exercise. Leave Eliza alone, Regina. She manages her life very well.'

'She has thrown her life at your feet and you have kicked it into the gutter,' Regina said angrily. 'It is the most shameful thing in your life; or was, until now. Now you are proposing to do the same thing with the life of Lucy Heron. She deserves better of you! Even Eliza, whose morals I do not condone, deserves better.'

'Lucy deserves nothing more or less than what she has. She has nothing less, for having lived with me. She has a considerable amount more of money. And she has our son.'

'You talk like a fool. Who are you to sit in judgement on her?'

'I am her husband, whom she has betrayed!' His eyes glinted.

'And have you not betrayed her? Can't you see that this is what I am showing you? I don't speak of your own adulteries, though I'd be amazed to hear you swear there were none – but of your betrayal of her trust and of her spirit.'

He stared at her in astonishment. 'How can you say that? It is Lucy who bedded with the Irishman, not I!'

'Once only, from what she has written. Oh yes, did you not know that we correspond? I let it lie for a while, as I did with you, and then, when Nieve was six months old, I sent her my love and silver bracelet.'

'How could you? I count that a fresh betrayal!'

'What nonsense. A six months' child. You should be ashamed!'

'For God's sake, will you have done with this! I want to hear no more! Mind your business, Mother, and leave me to mind mine!'

'You are my business. And you shall not stop my mouth. I am nicely warmed up now and may go on for hours yet! Now listen to me, and let my words sink well into that cannon ball you call a head! Yes, do fill my glass; this is thirsty work.'

She settled herself more comfortably in her high-backed chair, encouraged by his sour and unwilling expression. 'Lucy, like every romantic young girl, fell in love for the first time. Nothing unusual. What *was* unusual was that she was able to express that love and to have it reciprocated. What's more, it was not the everyday kind of love that can come to its consummation in marriage, proud parents beaming on either side the church; no, it was cursed by the separation of miles of water, centuries of culture and the added prohibitions of blood and of war! Romeo and Juliet themselves had less between them. Therefore your Lucy was engaged not in a simple romance, but in a high tragedy. She is a girl who loved books, and must have been hard put to it not to have been utterly swamped by the character of the thing. And yet, she was able, somehow – by instinct rather than reason, to my own mind – to face up to the impossibility of the relationship, and to open herself to the possibility of the one she attained with you.'

'You make me out a very secondary bargain,' Will said bitterly.

'Not at all. I admire Lucy for being able, so quickly, to adjust from the impossible to the real; to what could be made *good*.'

'And if I were to accept all this,' said her son mutinously, 'it does not lead to an acceptance of her looseness.'

Regina tried not to feel tired. 'I am going to tell you something,' she said slowly. 'I did not really wish to speak of it; but it will serve, I hope, as an illustration and a lesson.'

Will controlled the desire to tell her he was past being grateful for lessons, and schooled himself to listen.

'When I was a very young girl, as young as Lucy was when she first met Cathal O'Connor, I too fell in love, as suddenly as tears, with the wrong young man. Oh, he was not so far wrong as Cathal; we had a nation in common, a religion – further than that, we had blood in common. Nevertheless, the separate parts of that family to which we both belonged did not deem it desirable that we should marry. We could not bear it at the time; we were young and hot and wanted our own way. But older and colder wills prevailed, and in quite a short time they had married him to the woman they thought suitable. She brought fine blood and an excellent name to the family and I do not believe she has ever given him cause to regret their choice. In time, I came to accept it, though I never forgot him. We met, quite frequently, you see. It was not easy for us. And then I met your father. I liked and admired him as soon as I came to know him. That liking grew into a love I think even you can vouch for. All the happiness in our house came out of it—'

'So much so that I can never think of that house as mine, only as his and yours.'

She nodded. 'You will feel it to be yours when you have invested something of yourself in it,' she said absently. 'We were happy then. It was a priceless happiness and I would have thought that nothing could have touched it. Then one day your father went away; it was for some time. Like you, he had a personal care for his ships and his people. The man who had been my first love came to see me—'

'Please – don't go on, not if you are going to say what I fear to hear.'

She smiled. 'So squeamish? I do not speak of blood and death, of sickness or cruelty, only of love. Is that so bad? Cover your ears then, my hypocrite, because, yes – I am going to tell you that I took that man into my bed while your father was away, that I gave him my body and my love, that I had never taken back from him. In that I gave him nothing that was your father's, nothing that was not all his, as it had ever been.'

'Sweet Christ!' Will bowed his head and would not look at her.

'I was very lucky,' Regina went on steadily. 'We were able to love only briefly and wildly. We both knew that our lives were already fixed – and I, at least, loved that life, and your father, too much to jeopardize it then. But my dear, you do see how infinitely lucky I was. We bedded only twice, and on neither occasion did I conceive a child. That is the only difference between myself and Lucy.' She finished quietly and waited for him.

She would never forget the face he raised to her. He stared at her without expression, his body very still. 'I wish I might never have heard this,' he whispered at last.

Then he let her know the hurt and the contempt she had given him. 'Are all women whores?' he cried viciously. 'My wife! My mother! My cousin! Thanks be to God I have no daughter.'

'Will!' she said sharply. 'You demean yourself. How dare you judge me? Or Lucy? Are you without sin yourself? You will not say so, because I know it to be untrue.'

'You know nothing,' he growled, 'or if you do, you have become very meddlesome in your old age. I am a man,' he added, as if this explained any sin of which he might be accused.

Regina smiled. 'And therefore, weak. And Lucy is a woman and therefore may conceive. Be damned to you Will, you are not the man your father was!'

His eyes narrowed. 'I'll lay odds you took good care *he* should never know of your transgression. He would have had the hide off you. And deservedly.'

'You think so?' She regarded him with grim distaste. 'You are wrong. I did tell him – as Lucy would have told you, in time, if I know her as well as I think – it was not until several months afterwards that I found the courage. Do you want to know what he said to me? He said, "Well, my dear, I am glad to hear that at last you have closed your old account." It was never spoken of between us again.'

'Then my father was a fool!' roared Will. 'And you make the mistake of thinking me the same.' He got up and made as if to leave the room, turning before he reached the door. 'Why, oh why, Mother, could you not leave well alone?' he asked, his anger quietening. 'This has nothing to do with me.'

She straightened, touching a hand to her dark coronet of hair. 'Has it not?' she demanded, with calculated interest. 'You have not asked me who it was that I so loved when I was young.'

'Why should I care to know?' he asked suspiciously. 'It cannot affect me. I had as soon remain ignorant.'

'Ah, but it does affect you. *He* has affected you, your life, your livelihood. You are not his child, but you might have been, and he has watched over you for my sake, ever since you were born. He had no right to give *me* anything; he could give you – and has given you – a great deal.'

His face was ashen. 'Warwick.'

She inclined her head. 'So you see, you are involved. Lives are not as simple as their owners would like them to be. You could be to Nieve what Robert Rich has been to you. You could be more. You could be a father to her.'

He threw out his hand as though to fling the idea from him. 'Never. I will see that the child lacks for nothing. I am not cruel. But that is all.' He looked at Regina a little more kindly. 'I suppose you have meant well by this, Mother, but it is of no use.

I shall not take Lucy back. And now, I have work to do, if you will excuse me. We will meet at supper.'

Sitting before the waning fire, after he had left her, Regina counted over what she had lost during the last half hour, and found it to be more than she had expected to lose. She began to wonder whether it had been worth it. Only time would tell.

Sadly, she began to compose, in her mind, the letter she must write to Lucy. For she must let her know that she had tried, on her behalf, to influence her son, using the only means that came to her hand. She must say that she had tried in all good faith, hoping for more from him than, it seemed, he could give, and that she had failed.

She would not give up the attempt. She was convinced that one day these two could make a splendid marriage, building up a core of strength and trust such as her own had possessed. But she would not press upon the wound now; she had discovered, to her cost, that it was still far too raw.

She sympathized deeply with her daughter-in-law, but her son was the one for whom she reserved her pity. Will was a victim of his own pride and of the world's conventions. She had thought he would have found more independence in himself. Perhaps he would find it in the future. There was little she could do to help him. Meanwhile she could see that his suffering was greater than his anger, and it was because of this that she pitied him.

As the few days passed that she had engaged to spend with him, she awarded a certain amount of regret to herself, also, for she had sacrificed the easy, loving and mutually respectful relations she had had always enjoyed with Will. He had become a stiff, polite stranger, who moved her chair for her, fetched her shawl, poured her wine, all with the carved expression of the butler at a Guildhall dinner. She had often felt sorry for parents whose offspring treated them so.

When she had left his house – she did not stay long – Will, too, was full of regrets. He wished he could forgive her as easily as his father had apparently been able to do. He wished, even, that he could find that forgiveness to have been fine in his father, but he could only think it weakness. He wanted no more of women, for the moment. When Eliza called, he said to her that he had business to attend to; he would wait on her at a later date.

He began to long for the sea, for an extended voyage, to stay away from shore for a long time. The sea was clean and cruel and he understood it. What he needed was a tremendous voyage of exploration or a carnival of piracy, or a war. It was not long before the government, in company with his brother sea dogs, some of them wolves, combined to give him what he wanted.

In the autumn of the past year, Parliament had passed the Navigation Act. This stated that the produce of British colonies must be carried only in British or Colonial ships, while goods from Europe must come in English vessels or in those of their country of origin. The resistance to this high-handedness had brought fierce contention on the high seas which evolved, over the months, into full scale war with Holland.

It seemed to Will that the best place for him was at the helm of one of his ships in the service of the navy. He thought sourly that his connection with Warwick would ensure him a good commission. He would lend them the *Lady*, the *Eliza* and the *Regina*; three whores well fitted for the use of mariners. The army were now the true representatives of the nation, in general, and the eleven-year-old Rump would soon find Cromwell's boot applied to it. He was sick of their eternal argument and had no desire to be involved in it further. He made his careful preparations and, more soberly than ever before, turned his mind towards the sea.

Before he embarked, he called on Jud, whom he had not seen for some time. They had avoided each other since Lucy had left. But it was an old friendship, and war recommends leave-takings more seriously than simple merchant voyaging.

He found Jud in a state of high excitement, in the process of setting up new type. 'I'm thinking of – well, I *am* going into book production! There is so much being written that is excellent. Have you seen this?' He held out a thick volume.

'*Leviathan*. Thomas Hobbes. Yes, I have it, but have not had time to read it yet. I gather it marches well with Oliver's government.'

'If you want to look at it that way,' Jud chuckled. 'Though Hobbes would have given short shrift to their calendar of "saints" His view of life is startling, unpleasant to most minds. But what fascinates me is that he can shelter both the divine right of Majesty *and* the conquistador rule that Oliver would impose, under the roof of his one theory. If the civil order *is* to be justified by conquest alone, and held by the persuasion of the sword alone, then it may as well be King Cromwell as King Charles.'

'That is as much as to say, if two or more contend, that we should live in a state of continuous war.'

'No. Only till one side is stronger. Then it prevails until it is toppled. It's true. It's the history of mankind.'

'Is it? Well, I'm weary of it for a while. I'm off to topple a few mynheers off their quarterdecks.' Will had heard enough of political theory, mad, bad and indifferent, in the last few months.

'What? You're going back to privateering?'

'No. This should please you and Master Hobbes. To war.'

'Good Lord!' Jud was flummoxed. 'Why? You're doing so well on dry land these days.'

'I want a change, that's all. Now, is there any service I may do for you before I haul up my anchors?'

'Well, yes, since you mention it. But first, there's something I'd like to say to you—' He stopped, wondering awkwardly how to go on. Will stiffened, fearing yet another repetition of unwelcome marital advice.

'Very well then what is it?' he said curtly.

'It's this.' Jud plunged in. 'You've been a good friend to me, Will, and it has seemed to me that I have repaid you in foul coin for that friendship—'

'What on earth—?'

'No; listen. When I brought Cathal O'Connor back with me from Ireland – not that I had any choice, you understand; it was England or be sunk – well, if I had entertained even the faintest notion of what would come of it, I'd have put him overboard without a second thought. I just wanted you to know that. I had no idea in the world that Lucy – that he would – well, you know what I'm trying to say,' he finished, beet-red.

Will produced a wintery smile. 'I think you have said it. It does you credit. I quite understand. I hold nothing against you, nor have I ever thought of doing so. Now, please, if you wish our friendship to prosper, do not mention the subject again.'

Jud glowed with relief. 'No. No I won't. But I just want to say how sorry I am that—'

'Not ever again!' prevented Will firmly. 'What was it you wanted me to do for you?'

'Oh. Yes, that. It's a little of an embarrassment really. You must not think anything of it. It's just an idea,' he said with unusual shyness. 'I just thought that you might like to invest a small sum in the publishing company. On the book side, that is. I really think it will grow, and fast. There is so much I want to do. There is Rene Descartes, in France, if you don't like Hobbes. And then there is John Milton and Andrew Marvell, scribbling fine verse in the secretariat. And I might do Harvey's "*De Motu Cordis et Sanguinis*"—'

' 'S'wounds! A hefty list! Are you to become an intellect, after so long in the pugilistic lists of the broadsheets?'

'I don't necessarily have to comprehend all that I print,' replied Jud, grinning, 'any more than my readers will comprehend all that they read. The thing is that a man of the world must show a good bookshelf. All I want to do is to give him every assistance. If I can get my hands on the properties; and if I can sell at the right price. That is; lower than anyone else's.'

Will considered quickly. 'You have an excellent notion there,' he decided. 'I'll take a chance or two with you. You'll have no trouble with licences?'

'I know where to go.'

'Good. Then, on Tuesday, at my house?'

'Perfect. Oh, and won't Robin be green! He still longs after the Leveller dream. He has got himself into trouble for corresponding with Lilburne in Bruges. He'll never change. He was born to revolt and revolution. I only hope it won't one day be the death of him.'

'Are you reconciled, then?' asked Will, amused.

'We converse. We argue, rather. But Cleo keeps us sweet as best she can. Will you not come and see her? She was asking for you lately.'

'Before I leave, I promise. And how is your hopeful son?'

'Oh Ned is a fine young rascal. How's Robert?' His voice died away and he flushed.

Will smiled kindly. 'Don't choose your words too carefully, or you'll end up in silence. Robert is well, a clever lad, your sister says, and leads young Thomas a sad dance.'

'I should dearly love to see them all,' said Jud, ambushed by a wave of family feeling.

'So should I,' said Will. He had not intended to say anything of the sort, and if asked, would have sworn it was not true. Jud, wise for once, held his peace.

When Will got home he sat down and wrote to Lucy. He told her of his decision to take ship, and of the provisions he had made for her in his absence. 'If I should die in this conflict, which God forbid, I should like you to know that I have made all arrangements for Robert's education. He is to come to Staunton House when he is seven, where he will have the best of tutors and of care. I shall also take care that he has companions of his own age, for a lonely child makes a sad man.'

What should he say to her? If he *should* lose his life, it would be his last message to her. He thought for a long time. Then he wrote, 'I expect to come back whole, and it is likely that one day we will meet. If not, know that I loved you dearly, and that no other could take your place.'

Heron, Spring 1653

When Lucy had received Will's letter telling her of his intention to go to war, her chief reaction had been one of anger. He had never before committed himself so strongly to the Parliament as to give over his own autonomy for it. She could not imagine him accepting any man's orders, even an admiral's. She sensed, because she knew him, the combination of pride and ennui that had led him to it, and it made her irritated with him. If he 'had loved her' as his letter claimed, why wait for the expectation of death to let her know it? Why, indeed, seek that death? He was running away from himself. It was as simple as that. Rather than stay and face the exact nature of his feelings for her, he had told himself some comfortable story or other and made for the sea as a spoiled child makes for an over-indulgent mother. He was a fool to waste what they might have made together. He was cruel, both to her and to himself, to cause the continuance of this unnecessary unhappiness.

Six months ago, if he had told her how much he had once loved her, she would have dissolved into feeble, self-accusing tears; but now she could be detached enough to analyze the emotions that motivated him. Because of this, she began to think that there would be a way that she might get him back. Or could be, if only it weren't for this thrice-accursed Dutch war.

She had written to him in return, thanking him for his sentiments and trusting that he would indeed 'return whole'. She expressed herself in an unexcited tone, pronouncing herself happy to see him at any date in the future, giving further news of his son, commenting on the harvest, assuring him that the household would pray for his safe return. At the end, her carefully measured courtesy took flight and she wrote, 'If you must know, Will, I think you are a great ninny to go to war. It will not suit you.' Then she sanded, folded and sealed the paper before she could change her mind. She did not know if he received the letter. In six months she had had no reply.

After he had set sail, Lucy also heard from Regina Staunton. This letter had caused her even deeper anger than the one from her husband. She felt the resonance in her own woman's pride and privacy of the effect of Will's ignorant and impulsive spurning of the gift that his mother must have found it so very difficult to make. Even more furiously, she wished she had him at the end of her tongue. She put the two letters away in the drawer that already contained the only other communication of any importance that she had received since her homecoming.

It was a worn and ragged parchment from Ireland, stained with sea water, and even, she imagined, in one corner, with blood. It was months late.

As soon as she had seen it, she had known that she had longed for it. She put away this knowledge as being of no possible consequence. She had opened it with a fragile hesitation, trying not to make it too important to herself.

'Asthore – there is no way of knowing if this will ever come to you. I have copied it half a dozen times, so one may win through. First, I love you. I will always love you. There can be no other. My wife is my dear friend, that is all, and it is much, in these troubling times. Second, you have turned my heart entirely over with your news. Oh my singing bird, my love, myself, you will think me foolish but I never thought of it. Never once, in all the hours and days of hours that I have dreamed and remembered, did it come to me that we might have made a child together. The knowledge of it is a joy to me such as only the angels in heaven can know else. And you have called her Nieve. Is it she then, who will at last bring me to my old age and my loneliness, sick with the want and lack of her?

'As for you and I, our story is not ended. Never think it. It may quiet your conscience to do so but it is not the truth. What can I send you, in return for such a gift as this? I would clothe you in jewels if I could, but I have none to give you. Every precious thing which I owned has gone to buy arms for my men.

'The time has changed with me, my Lucy; it has become very grave. My father, the great chieftain, is dead. He lost his life in defence of his lands and his people as he wished. I am the O'Connor now. It is a heavy thing to take on the yoke of my history. I must forge myself into an iron man such as was my father and all his forefathers. I will have Orla's help in this. I would make a sorry attempt without it, for she is stronger than I, and her blood runs high for Ireland.

'Tell my daughter, when she is old enough, all you can read and recall of our history, for I shall come to claim her one day. Part of me, and part of you, she is the most holy thing in my life, and will be set in my mind like the grail itself as I continue the struggle for freedom. I do not know when we shall meet, you and I and my daughter Nieve, but I am sure that God will allow it to be. Until then I leave you both my love and my blessing. Pray for me, Lucy. I am much in need of it if I am to succeed.'

The seriousness and sobriety of his mood impressed her deeply. The wild poetry and the careless egotism had all gone. He was no longer the boy she had first known, nor the young man who had thrown over all his responsibilities and sailed across to her in Jud's keeping. Cathal had become a man, and was trying to become a strong man and a good one, so that he might prove a worthy successor to Cathal of the Red Hand. He had never spoken much of God to her, but now he asked for prayers in all humility. He was changed. She feared for him, but she was also joyously proud for him.

She fell to dreaming of him again, dreaming and remembering as he did himself. She knew she must not let it last, but she indulged herself, just for a little, before exiling his image in prayers for his safety, and also, at decent intervals, for Will's whole return. She prayed also to be able to love her husband with a whole heart, and so to deserve his forgiveness.

Her life had settled into its old accustomed pattern once again. Perhaps her relations with her mother would never quite recover from the blow dealt by her daughter's birth, but they had improved considerably and there was no longer any question of her losing Nieve – she had fought to win her right in that. Jane had been saddened by the loss of what she had regarded as a God-given chance, but Lucy had shown her how much she had asked, and in the end she had been content with the status of aunt. Tom, when told of this, had expressed cold disapproval, but Lucy no longer cared what Tom thought. He would not put them out of the house, she was certain, and that was all that mattered.

Indeed her only interest in her elder brother now was as Martha's husband. He had been well over a year in Paris before he had begun to write of sending for her, and she had come to feel that missing him was to be the manner of their marriage. 'To love Tom is simply a lesson in learning to do without him,' she had said, not bitterly, to Lucy.

675

'If you ask me, it is Tom who needs the lesson – in learning to value what he has.'

'You have talked like this before; it does no good,' said Martha gently.

And then in the spring, he sent for her. She could hardly believe it. She blossomed like a suddenly forced flower and her conversation became almost giddy with delight. Tom was coming to fetch her himself. He would be at Heron in just another month!

'The waiting seems nothing now,' she said, her grey eyes shining like the moon. 'It is just as though he left me yesterday.'

Lucy spent a good deal of time that day marvelling at Martha's gift for the positive. Soon she began to enter into her friend's pleasure. They planned a new wardrobe for the traveller, and practised the fashionable ways of dressing her hair.

Lucy had never before known Martha to be frivolous. 'It is relief, that is all. I think that perhaps, underneath, I thought I might never see him again,' she confessed, smiling now at her lack of faith.

One Thursday afternoon she went on her own to see Catherine Lacemaker, a seamstress who was making up two new gowns for her. When she did not come back at the expected hour, Lucy sauntered off to meet her. There was a sharp March wind but she enjoyed the walk all the better for its stirring of her blood. She did not meet Martha on the road and when she arrived in the village, Catherine said that she had left nearly an hour since.

Mystified, Lucy made her way home again. When she did not find Martha in the house, she sent Dickon to look for her. He came back later, to report that she was apparently nowhere in the house or grounds. Lucy waited for a while, apprehension turning to fear in a great knot in her chest, and then alerted the household and sent out a proper search party to comb the entire demesne. They too came back empty-handed.

As the day drew into evening, and the family came together instinctively in their concern for Martha, Lucy voiced at last the nagging suspicion that had lay beneath her worry for the past few hours. 'I know you will think me foolish, after all this time,' she said, looking at her mother, 'but I think it is Nehemiah who has taken her. He wanted once before to take her away from Tom. Now, I think he has done it.'

'My dear Lucy!' Mary's protest was disbelieving. 'You can't be serious.'

'But I am. It is a feeling I have. I am sure of it.'

'He could not. He wouldn't dare. He would be afraid of the

law,' Mary said roundly. 'Only think of his position. A Member of the House to engage in the criminal abduction of another man's wife; the scandal would ruin him! Besides, Martha has been a married woman long enough, surely, for Ne'miah to forget his foolish notions about her.'

Lucy bit her lip. It did sound ludicrous. She knew it. But her instinct that she was right increased with every second that passed.

They all looked at each other, questioning. Then Humpty, who had listened with a frown gathering, suddenly brought down his fist on his thigh with the bruising thud that indicated he had made up his mind. 'By Hades, she's right, Mother! It's got to be Ne'miah. Well, hasn't it? Women don't just disappear from their own villages in the middle of the afternoon. And you can't tell me the man isn't mad enough. You know what he is like; once he gets hold of a plan for mischief he rides it till it falls down dead beneath him! I'm with Lucy.'

'I don't understand,' cried Julia, who had sat staring in pure bewilderment at their talk. 'What has that horrible man to do with Martha now? He was the one who tried to have her burned!'

'Hush. He also tried to save her,' said Kit, smiling reassuringly. 'It is too complex to explain. I don't think I *could* explain. Perhaps even Nehemiah couldn't. He is a strange, and I think, a sorrowful man. But yes, Humpty, I believe you are right; he could have taken Martha. Perhaps the best thing to do is to assume that he has – for want of any better ideas, Mother – and decide what we should do about it.'

'Well, firstly, it is obvious, we shall have to *find* him,' said Humpty, a light in his eye at the thought of any kind of action. 'Then God help him!' He eyed Kit. 'Sorrowful indeed!'

'I think you are all quite skull-struck,' Mary complained. 'For my part I shall continue to have the countryside scoured for Martha – though I shall be most surprised if, in the event, she does not walk in herself before midnight. There are any number of explanations, perfectly normal ones, that you have not considered. She may well have heard in the village of some poor soul who needed her skill most pressingly, and ridden up into the hills to attend to him.'

'She was on foot,' said Lucy.

'She could have borrowed a horse at the inn.'

'She would have sent a message home; you know that; she is too considerate to go off without letting us know.'

Mary had to admit that this was true. 'Then she may have started out upon a shorter journey, thinking to get home before supper, and had some sort of accident; her horse could be lame, or she might have broken an ankle.'

'Mother, I hope above everything that you are right. But if she does not come home tonight, nor tomorrow, nor the next night, we must continue to search nearby, certainly; but we must also pursue Nehemiah. I insist.' Mary heard the vibration in her voice and lowered her head in agreement.

'You can leave that to us, eh Kit?' said Humpty determinedly.

Kit nodded in confirmation. 'Yes. We should start our search at Westminster, for that is where we *ought* to find him, if he is doing his duty as a member of the Parliament. We'll go on from there. If he has gone, he'll have left a clue to guide us.'

Lucy's mouth twisted in frustration. 'It is all you *can* do. If only Will were still in London! He would have him flushed out for you in a couple of days. But perhaps Jud may be able to help almost as much. He has not such power to command, but he does have many and varied sources of information. If I might go with you myself—'

Her look begged Mary. Her hope was small. 'No, Lucy. Your place is here.' Her mother's eyes killed it.

'Very well.' Lucy accepted this without a murmur. It was one of her penances. 'It is all up to you two, then,' she said with a warm smile for her brothers. 'But you will promise us, will you not, most faithfully, to let us have your news, every day, of how your search progress – even if there *is* no progress. Please.'

'I promise,' said Kit without hesitation. 'I'll write a journal every night and send it to you every morning.'

'Thank you,' she said simply. She knew she could trust him to do it.

Martha did not come back that night, nor yet the next night, nor the one after it. Accordingly, the twins packed their saddlebags and set out for what they could only view as an adventure. They were on the trail of the hated Nehemiah, and he had again put himself in the wrong where the family was concerned. And this time, Cromwell's law would support them if he were found out. They welcomed the opportunity as they had not welcomed anything since last they had rode out to fight.

It was hard for Lucy, as they set off, scarcely hiding their exhilaration at the prospect before them, to wave them farewell and herself turn meekly back towards the house. She knew that no amount of work, nor her music, nor the company of her children, could lessen the terrible suspense she would feel until

Martha was found. She had never known the full story of that first imprisonment in Nehemiah's house, but she had suspected far more than she had ever allowed Martha to see. What she did know was that Martha had been painfully grateful not to be questioned.

London, Autumn 1653

Nehemiah Owerby strolled down a seamy street in Southwark. It was known as Damnation Lane, it being the Puritan's solemn opinion that this was because it was damnably hard to find. This could not have suited him better. Even so, he had followed a very circuitous route towards it.

He stopped to look about him, though hardly to admire the view, which was almost as repulsive to the eye as was the stench to the nose. Mysteriously satisfied, he took out a key and opened the door of an insignificant dwelling next door to an abandoned building successfully occupied in falling down.

Once inside, he locked himself there and made his swift way through other doors and openings until he reached the heart of the property and of his life. She was waiting for him. She had heard him come in. She was sitting neatly on a chair, reading. He had seen that she had plenty of books.

'My dear.' His harsh voice softened like crumpled canvas when he spoke to her. 'How are you today?'

'The same,' Martha said. She had begun to speak to him again. She would not, at first, but after the length of time that she had been here, and after the thing he had done to her, more than once, it seemed foolish to attempt to deny his existence. She did not loathe him any the less, but she accepted him. It prevented her, she thought, from becoming mad with melancholy.

She asked him now, as she did every time he came to her, 'When will you set me free, and let me be with my child, as it is only right that I should be?'

Usually, he gave her no reply, only smiled, rather sweetly; it seemed to her almost blasphemous how sweet his smile for her could be. Today he said, 'I think you must have understood by now that God has punished you for your sin in bearing a child to the man whom he did not choose to be your husband. This separation is good. Learn to bear it in humility.'

'As I must learn to bear *you*?' Her hatred lanced him.

He winced. 'Martha, you have come to know both my mind and my body in the time you have spent with me. Have you not come just a little nearer to accepting God's will?'

'You have forced both upon me. I accept nothing but the fact of my situation.' She would never let him see her anything but cold and controlled. The pillow soaked in her midnight tears lay beneath the warm woollen coverlet. Sometimes, because she would not feel anything for him, other than the occasional shaft of pure horror, she thought that, in the end, he might kill her.

But he seemed to be cheerful today. He ignored her words. He brought her wine and food. He always served her himself when he visited her. On other days the old, dumb servant looked after her needs. She had tried many times to suborn him, but he was as deaf to her pleas as he was speechless. His face was lined and impassive and he kept his thoughts to himself, except on one occasion when he had smiled suddenly at the sight and size of a lamb cutlet he had brought her.

'I shall have more time for you now,' Nehemiah said, as though it would be an equal treat for them both. 'Cromwell has dismissed the Rump at last. He made a fine performance of it. "The Lord has done with you," he thundered at us, then roared at Speaker Lenthall to step down and swept the mace from the table. "Take away this bauble," he cried in fine contempt!' Nehemiah grinned at the memory. 'Then he spoiled it somewhat. He noticed Sir Harry Vane slinking off to the door, and called out after him, like a rude schoolboy, "Sir Harry Vane! Sir Harry Vane! May the Lord deliver me from Sir Harry Vane!" '

'Apparently he has done so,' said Martha dryly.

'We shall see,' said Nehemiah noncommittally. 'Certainly he was about the Lord's work in the early days, and perhaps may continue in it – but I should like to see the consistency of the *next* Parliament before I am content to follow him.'

'And will you be a member of it?' She rarely questioned him. He was encouraged. But she wished merely to know how long he would 'have more time for her'.

'I trust so. It is said it will be a nominated House, of godly men, now that we are rid of those who only served themselves. But I am known to have certain sympathies with the Republican design, and it is possible that Cromwell may wish to rid himself of such.'

Martha questioned him further. If she could keep him occupied with his passion for politics, perhaps he would not touch her today. He did not do so often, only when he could not prevent himself. She hardly knew what she should do to prevent it. It seemed to make no difference to him whether she displayed utter revulsion and horror, or mere cold distaste, whether she wept or prayed, fought or remained an unmoving lump of flesh. If he wished to take her he did so, his lust always renewed, and its sickening outcome always the same; he would fall on the floor at her feet and beg God's forgiveness. Then he would beg her to come and live with him as his wife and thus prevent these shameful occasions. If she tried to argue with his hideous logic, he would leave her abruptly, bidding her to read the Bible and take it to heart. On his next visit he would be stern with her, as though she were a temptress who had schemed to seduce him. He had not used her last time.

Nor, it appeared, was he inspired to do so today. She thanked Cromwell for that. With what seemed to Martha a lunatic unreality, they sat and discussed the new breadth of Oliver's power; whether he would remain the mere steward of the land, as he professed himself to be, beneath the aegis of the newly composed Council of State, or whether, feeling the great force of the army behind, he might not adventure for greater things. Such talk between them was a black parody of normality, but Martha was willing to talk until sunset, if it would keep him away from her.

She did not have to do so, however, for he left her after perhaps two hours, regretting that he had an appointment with a man named Praise-God Barbon, who had some influence in the city and might use it on Nehemiah's behalf. When he had gone, she took up her book very quickly, as she always did. She never allowed herself to dwell on his presence, or what had, or had not, happened during his visits. Nor did she ever, except when she woke in dread before dawn, ask herself how long this way of life could continue. If she thought of her loved ones, it was as though they were part of quite another person's life. That way, she could more easily bear to think of them at all.

When Nehemiah stepped out into the street, it was as empty as it usually was, except for a scruffy urchin bouncing a ball against a wall. The Puritan pissed companionably against the same wall, and then took his same serpentine route back to the respectable side of the river.

Behind him the urchin, who had spat upon the spot where he had pissed, whistled sharply between his fingers. Three shapes materialized from behind broken doors and windows. 'Charlie? You're *sure* we're in the clear?' asked Humphrey Heron, shaking something nasty off his leg.

'Certin! Ee'll not come back till termorrer, an' the old man's gorn orf t'see 'is sister. Ee generally stays there orl nite.'

'My God, they're quick. Will you look at that!' Kit, who had just climbed out of a nearby midden and was wishing he'd found some less dramatic place of concealment, directed his brother's attention to the portly figure of Podge, and the slender one of Ettamaria, who were sharing the activity of picking the lock of the insignificant dwelling, with an address that suggested they had done it many times before. As his brother had once admired her sister before him, Kit found himself irrelevantly approving the delicate hour-glass of Ettamaria's half-stooped body, and the autumn flame in her ebulliently curling hair.

'They're in!' cried 'Humpty and was at the door before him. 'Now, Etta – you stay outside and keep cave, just in case.'

'If you don't mind?' said Kit, giving her an awkward smile.

'Why should I?' Henrietta Maria tossed the curls. This one fancied her, if she was any judge. She didn't mind. He was a good-looking young man, and a gentleman, being Jud's brother. 'I'll sing like I'm drunk if there's any danger,' she said, somehow making it a delicious promise.

Inside the house there was nothing. Literally nothing. There was no furnishing of any kind, and nobody in any of the empty rooms. Nor was there any sign of recent habitation. They could not believe it. It just wasn't true.

The young Whittakers had been watching the place for weeks. They had established the habits of both Nehemiah and the servant. There was no question but that he was visiting someone here. They had followed him from his lodgings near Westminster time after time.

They searched again. There was really nothing. There were no cellars and no attics. Nothing. They tapped on all the walls. Most of them were hollow; it was a very poor sort of a house.

Behind one of them, which was tapped upon more than once, Martha, worn out with the weight of Nehemiah's company, and cradled in relief at his departure, slept the sleep of the dead. Nothing short of an explosion could have woken her.

Kit and Humpty had been members of the extended Whittaker household for some weeks. When they had first explained their problem to Jud, they had been rather put out at his suggestion that their best means of detection was the selection of lovable, if doubtfully motivated, urchins who surrounded them. However, when, after only a fortnight's dogging of Nehemiah's footsteps between Westminster and anywhere else he happened to go, they announced that they were pretty sure of his nefarious use of an address not so very far distant from their own, the twins had to admit that they knew their business. And they certainly cost less than an agent would have done; though they were professional enough to insist on some payment.

The brothers soon found themselves very much at home in the odd establishment, and were content to help Jud with his books when they were not out making themselves more familiar with London, an opportunity not to be missed. They had been almost sorry when Podge had made his first confident report. The rescue of Martha, however deeply desired, would mean their instant return to Heron.

Now, paradoxically, they were even more disappointed to find no trace of her. They mulled over the enigma, while Podge and Charlie kept their watch on Nehemiah, who did not change his habits, though he did visit the empty house more frequently.

They were doing their own particular type of mulling over, in the snug parlour of the Bear, when Jud, who had stayed at home to look over a manuscript, heard a knock of abnormal authority upon his outer door. Not all the curiosity with which he opened it could have prepared him to find his brother Tom outside it. 'My God. It's you.'

They stared at each other. 'Yes. I'd like to come in, if I may.'

'Of course. I'm sorry.' Jud moved clumsily out of the way. 'It's just – the surprise.'

'You must know why I am here.'

'Well, no. At least – I can guess. But I thought you were to know nothing, until we had tried our chances.'

Tom stooped and entered. He scarcely glanced round, refusing the chair Jud offered him with an impatient shake of the head. 'I *would* have known nothing,' he said tersely. 'Only I came home earlier than I had planned. I found her gone and – they told me about your damn fool scheme.'

The suppressed violence in him warned Jud to be careful. 'It's not so foolish. We thought we had found her. I still think there is something we haven't fathomed.'

'Well, tell me! What *is* it, for God's sake?'

Rapidly, he brought Tom up to date. His brother ranged about the room as he listened, the confined space bringing him up every now and then against the walls. 'Then, let us go and speak with Kit and Humpty,' Tom said as soon as he had done. 'I must see this place for myself. I must confront Nehemiah! I can't think why none of you have done so.'

'Because we thought it best to do it this way. If we are wrong, we have not risked frightening him off.'

'Oh I suppose so! But in Christ's name let us go now.'

As they stumbled round to the inn, it did not occur to either of them that this was the first time they had spoken for several years, or that the last time they had met they had each wanted to spill the other's blood. There simply wasn't time.

Tom made no time, either, for a vinous reunion with the twins. They were sober in seconds when they saw his face. His whole being, with a depth of concentration they had never seen in any man, was thrown towards Martha.

'You are right. It has to be where you think. You have missed something. Somehow, I don't know. We must try again.'

They exchanged hopeless looks, but agreed, in pity for his suffering and suspense. 'We can go now, tonight, if you like. The manservant will not come back, I think. We can check with Podge.' It was so. No one had returned.

The four brothers moved through the thick blanket of the London dark, with Podge close ahead, carrying a lantern. They had all become part of Tom's unbearable waiting, and what had yesterday been an adventure now became the most urgent matter of their lives. It was not that they had not been committed in their previous attempt, but they had felt nothing like this utter involvement and necessity for success. If Martha had not been in that building when they had searched for her, her husband's sheer determination to find her would put her in it now.

The lane was black and soft underfoot and stank no less than usual. Their boots soughed liquidly as they walked. There was no need for stealth; no one in their right senses would be in such a place at night.

Podge had a little more trouble with the lock, lacking his sister's sensitivity to its movement, but he was not long, and Tom was first over the threshold, the light swinging before him. Now that they were inside, Kit and Humpty also lit lanterns. Nobody would investigate if they were seen from outside, which was very unlikely. Systematically they began to repeat their search. Again there was nothing. But they went over every inch once more. They could feel Tom's mounting rage; it was as though it would blow the building apart.

He stood swinging the lantern over a mess of footprints on the filthy floor, as if trying to discern a path from them. 'The walls,' he said harshly. 'We'll tap them again.'

They went over them obediently as they had before, knocking with their hands, tapping with the heel of a dagger or the butt of a pistol. From behind one of the ground floor rooms, Jud caught a hesitant echo. He knocked again. Again there was a delayed echo of his fist. He pounded and called Martha's name. This time he heard a shriek.

And now he was the echo, as he bellowed joyfully for Tom. There was a flurry of thuds and curses as his brother fumbled down from upstairs, crying 'What? What is it?' in a lather of expectation.

'There's something here. Listen.' He called 'Martha?' There was a definite reply, muffled, but unmistakably human.

'Oh my God,' moaned Tom, weak with relief. 'How do we get to her?'

'It's no use feeling about for false panels in the dark,' suggested Humpty, who needed a physical outlet for all this nervous tension. 'I vote we tear down the walls!'

'Hurrah!' cried Kit, in the same spirit.

'What with?' asked Jud practically. This nonplussed them all.

Then Kit suggested, 'What about that derelict place next door? There's bound to be a lot of rubbish about. An iron fender or something,' he added hopefully.

'No, hang on a bit. If you please, sirs,' said Podge who was feeling his way across the wall. 'I shall find it soon, I shouldn't wonder. Five livres if I do?'

'Fifty!' said Tom, with a spurt of laughter. Then he began to bang on the wall again, shouting to Martha that it was he, and that she would soon be safe.

'I only 'opes as it's 'er,' said Podge, worrying about his fifty livres.

They let him work in silence, controlling the desire to hurry his carefully searching fingers. When Tom thought he could wait no longer there was a sudden loud click that was almost familiar, so often had they imagined it already. A gap yawned before them and they plunged through, only to be faced with yet another door.

But this was an ordinary door like any other, and from behind it there came a shaking voice. 'Who is it? Is anyone there? Please—'

'Martha!' cried Tom exultantly. 'It's me! It's Tom. Oh thank God. Are you well? Oh, Martha, my dear!'

They heard the sound of weeping. Very shortly, the door opened to Podge's accustomed touch. Only Tom went in.

Behind him, an importunate hand tugged at Jud's coat. 'Ee did say fifty. You heard 'im, didn't you?'

Later, when they were alone in Jud's upper room, Tom tried to hold Martha so that she would know that it was different with him now, that he could *see* her, that she was the only thing of value in his life, that he could not do without her. He could not *tell* her these things – his was not a speaking nature – but he tried with all his will to make her feel them. He treated her with great gentleness. He could see that she was in no condition for too much emotion, even of happiness. A pure, sweet, righteous anger burned in him when he thought of Nehemiah.

Martha was very thin, though she assured him that she had been given plenty to eat. She had always had a translucent look, as though light shone through her, but now it was a transparency without light; there was no warmth to her, no substance. She shook continually when he spoke of her ordeal. It was a long time before he questioned her, but it was something he wanted to be over, put away from them into the past. 'Was it – the same as before?'

'The same.'

'Oh my dear. Forgive me.' She laid her hand upon his head. He could not feel it. 'If only I had come for you before!' he lacerated himself.

She smiled and shook her head. 'I won't come with you, not just yet, if you will not mind. I think I need to be alone, for a little.'

'No! I must have you with me. How else can I be sure you are safe? You *must* come.'

'What I should like, above all things,' she said, as though he had not spoken, 'is to go back to my cottage at Heron for a time. It is a place I love, perhaps best of all. I should feel safe there, and I would soon come to you afterwards.'

'But I can't—'

She was shaking again. 'Please. I have had to work so hard to keep my self, these last weeks. I *must* have time to set myself free. I wonder, can you understand?'

'No.' He was wounded by her lack of need for him. 'But you must do whatever you wish, of course.'

'You'll not be angry, or distressed?'

He smiled. 'I'll try not to miss you too much, that is all. Oh Martha,' he sighed ruefully, 'it seems that as soon as I have learned one hard lesson, fate must teach me another. Though I'm damned if I know what this one can mean. Must I learn how to miss you in two different ways?'

Martha actually chuckled. 'It is a hard lesson,' she agreed. She did not add that she had been a long time perfecting it herself. Tom's emotional selfishness was part of what she loved; it was so very childlike.

The next morning the brothers and the young Whittakers were again secluded in their various unsalubrious hiding-places in Damnation Lane. They stiffened in agonies of suspense when Charlie's whistle warned them of an approach. 'Dear Christ, if you ever loved this poor sinner, let it be Nehemiah!' prayed Tom, his lips bitten bloody.

Shuffling steps came nearer. The alley was not easy to negotiate. A wheezing breath was heard and all their hearts sank. Nehemiah was an excessively healthy man. He did not wheeze. Tom peered out between broken boards. Yes, it was the old manservant, carrying a covered basket. They watched him let himself in.

A minute later, they heard his stertorous and panic-stricken progress out of the house. He made distressing animal sounds as he went. Doubtless he was wondering what Nehemiah would do to him when he communicated his news.

When he was clear of the street they climbed out of concealment. 'What shall we do? Stay, to see whether Nehemiah comes back?' asked Kit.

'Or go to his house and drag him out of it?' Humpty was fiercer.

'We should have done that in the first place,' said Jud. 'It would have done no harm if half of us had waited there.'

'No,' Tom said. His mind was astoundingly cool, now that vengeance was near. 'We needed proof, if the law was to do our work for us. The only proof was the connection with the servant and this house. Nehemiah may deny them both if he likes, and he has enough influence, now, to get away with it. He has only to swear we are a gang of malcontents who hold a grudge over Heron.'

'So now we manage our affair without the law,' said Humpty in pleasurable anticipation.

'Yes. Or rather, *I* do,' Tom said firmly.

'But we have a score to settle too,' Humpty began again.

Tom's look scorched him. 'You know nothing of *my* score,' he said. 'Nor will. But you may believe me when I say that it comes higher than yours. The man is mine.'

'Leave it, Humpty,' said Kit quietly.

Humpty shrugged. It was a pity. He had been looking forward to some excellent sport. But if Tom wanted to play the lone hunter, let him. Why did he always have to be so tense about everything?

It was agreed that they should all converge on Nehemiah's lodgings; the rest of them could at least lend their aid as guards and lookouts. But when they reached their destination, a quiet street behind Westminster, they found that their bird had flown. 'No one of that name here, nor ever was,' said the Puritan woman who opened the door.

'Be careful. It is a sin to lie,' cautioned Jud.

'Indeed it is, and a shame to slander,' said the woman virtuously.

'You will not mind,' said Tom, and it was an order, 'if we search your premises?'

'I shall mind indeed, but I am only a poor woman, and my servants are two maids. You must do as you will.' It was obvious that they would find no trace of Nehemiah, but they searched diligently in case he should have left any clue. There was nothing.

As they left, Tom suddenly turned and wrenched the woman round by her arm. 'How would it be,' he murmured, close to her ear, 'if we were to take you away with us and begin to tear out your abominably backward tongue with hot pincers?'

'Then I should tell you all I could,' she said simply. 'But it would not help you. You do not wish to know who was here; you wish to know where he has gone. And even hot pincers could not drag out of me what I do not know.' Tom cast her away from him in disgust.

'So now,' said Humpty, his spirits rising, 'the search really does begin. You'll not refuse our help now, eh, Tom?'

Tom leaned against a wall. He looked drained and defeated. 'No, I won't,' he said. 'That man must die.'

In another part of the city, where he was making the last arrangements to take ship for a specified destination, Nehemiah Owerby had come to precisely the same conclusion about Tom Heron.

There was one thing which Tom had to do, before he took Martha

688

up to Heron, where he must try to bring himself to leave her for a time. It was something he had known even before she had expressed it to him, hesitantly, still fearing his displeasure, so long had it reigned. He had to make his peace, at last, with his brother Jud.

Now that the only thing which mattered to him was Martha's safety, he wondered tiredly what all that had been about, between himself and Jud. Had he really felt so inimically that his brother was a traitor to his King and his house? That King had betrayed them all, many times over, though he might never have seen it so. As for the family, Jud loved them dearly; that was clear to anyone with half an eye. Could he really have hated him so much?

He felt ashamed. He hardly knew himself any longer. On the evening before they left, he asked Cleo, whom he always treated with a courtesy that took her breath, if she would very much mind keeping Martha company while he talked to Jud.

Her face shone. 'Bless you, no, sir.' She could not call him Tom. 'There is nothing I'd like better.'

He knew she did not refer to Martha's company. He smiled and gently kissed her cheek. It was the first such impulsive gesture of his life. He was astonished at how easy it was.

Jud was upstairs, looking for a particular book among the piles in the chests in the bedchamber. He found it and came down, humming in his tuneless fashion. He checked when he saw Tom, sitting alone at the table. 'Deserted?' he asked with awkward bonhomie. They had not been alone together before this.

'No. I gave everyone marching orders.' Jud saw that his smile was encouraging, and was intensely relieved.

Wine was offered and accepted, and Jud settled into his grandfatherly chair, with its wooden back and flat, comforting cushion, sewn by Cleo. He nodded cheerfully. He would wait for Tom to say whatever it was he had in mind.

Tom felt his heart pounding. He thought it rather ridiculous. He brought a parchment out of his pocket. 'I wanted to give you this,' he said, holding it out.

Jud took it, interested. It had many seals and looked important.

'And simply to say,' Tom went on, trying not to grit his teeth, 'that I am sorry for what has passed between us.'

'Oh the devil!' Jud scratched his head in embarrassment. 'Don't think of that. What is this, anyway?' He was glad of the scroll in his hands to help him through the moment. Tom! Actually apologizing! To him! He had once told Will Staunton that he would not forgive his brother until he went on his knees. That had been the most unlikely event that it had been possible to imagine. And now this! It was positively indecent.

'Look at it. It is yours. Should have been long ago. I have tried, as you'll see, to make up for the time past. You have not lost by it.'

Intrigued, Jud unrolled the document. It was signed and sealed by Tom and by Heron's Gloucester solicitor, Jeremy Deeds. 'God's truth! It's my portion.'

'The accrued rents and interest that is due. It is less than it would have been, were it not for the sequestration, of course; but I think you'll agree it is a useful sum.'

'Useful!' Jud leaped up and threw the parchment in the air, narrowly missing the fire. 'You can't know how much this means to me right now. It couldn't have come at a better time! God bless you, Tom! You have made me one of the best publishers in London!' If he had dared, he would have kissed his brother. As it was, he poured him more wine and howled excitedly for Cleo to return from next door.

'Good Lord, whatever is it?' she cried, running in with Martha behind her. 'Is anyone hurt?'

'No, not at all,' Tom said light-heartedly. 'Someone is beginning to be healed.'

'Cleo,' cried Jud, picking her up and swinging her around, 'I'm a rich man now; will you marry me?'

'Certainly not,' she said, outraged. 'As if I'd marry any man for 'is money! But we *could* do with some new plates and things, when you've done buying books.'

The next day, as he watched Martha and his brothers set off for Heron, Jud wished he might go with them. His new and unexpected friendship with Tom made him greedy to develop it· further. They had not been gone half an hour, however, when he received a visitation that reminded him that he was all London's now. It was Rob, and he was excited, too much so to bother to be cool or polite, as he often was nowadays, to mark the disfavour between them. 'You have to help us, Jud! It's an emergency. You can't refuse, for old friendship's sake.' The foxy face was serious.

'I'm sure I can't.' Jud was still bathed in loving kindness to all the world. 'How can I help you, Rob?'

'Not me. It's John Lilburne.'

'But he's in France. Does he lack money?'

Rob shook his head energetically. 'He's back. He has come

home to stand trial. He is weary of exile and thinks he might win back.'

'Christ! There's no stopping the man. On what grounds does he think he could get his sentence revoked?'

'His chief defence will be that since he was condemned by the Rump, which was dissolved for its injustice and poor administration, its sentence cannot be upheld by a righteous court.'

Jud laughed affectionately. 'I wish him success,' he cried. 'I'm no Leveller, but I love the man. I am glad he is home.'

'Then show your gladness by printing these.' Rob extricated some papers from his coat.

'What's this? *A Juryman's Judgement* – Let's hope it comes before the right pairs of eyes! *A Plea in Law* – Lilburne's own, eh? I must read that at once.'

'Never mind *reading* them. Will you print them? As many as you can. We want them all over London tomorrow.'

For a very brief time, Jud deliberated. For him the Leveller cause had died before it could properly be born. But he had much to thank John Lilburne for; his interest had given him the start he had needed, both in print and in political thinking. It was time to show his gratitude. 'I'll take these round to the Lion myself. And anything more you want – just send them round. I'll leave instructions.' A thought struck him. 'If he *can't* convince them—' he began.

Rob nodded. 'He dies. They have only to prove that he has returned from a sentenced exile.'

'Then we must work hard.'

Rob grinned and pressed his hand for a second. 'Like old times, eh?'

'Very like. Except that now we can afford it!'

'Speak for yourself! I'm about on my last legs. It's no joke being below the law all the time. I've a mind to go back to thieving; it was steady – and I was far less likely to be arrested!'

Jud decided that this was not the time to reveal his own good fortune. Rob had been sailing very near to the wind lately, flooding the city with entertaining and mischievous literature comparing Cromwell to such well-known regicides as Macbeth and Richard III. It had been Jud who had introduced him to Shakespeare, in an hour of sentimental drunkenness in his father's memory. By now, he heartily wished he had not, as Rob was apt to make Will do much of his work for him. 'Within the hollow crown, will be Oliver's hollow noddle!' had been one of his most popular headlines.

Robin had twice been in the Fleet, from whence Will Staunton had once retrieved him and himself, in careful secrecy, once. He supposed there would be a next time. He did not, however, care for the mud that might stick to his own growing business. But just this once, for old times' sake, he would do all he could.

He printed thousands of the pamphlets; he was surprised to be offered payment, which he refused, assuming that the hard-pressed Lilburne had borrowed it. Perhaps it was this earnest of good faith which led him to swing the weight of the *Intelligencer* into the contest. 'Legislative Lilburne Appeals to Justice' ran his leader. He followed with a day-by-day account of the trial, which he attended himself.

There had been no such stir in the streets in many a month. The Old Bailey was packed to capacity, and outside an excited crowd soon took up the rhythm of a text which had appeared amongst them.

> *And what, shall then honest John Lilburne die?*
> *Three-score thousand will know the reason why!*

It was indeed like old times.

Certainly Oliver Cromwell must have thought so as the court struggled and sank in Lilburne's toils for six argumentative weeks. In the end, although they would not demean themselves to accept his reasoning, they could not find a means to defeat it. He was pronounced not guilty of any crime worthy of death. The roar of triumph which went up from the courtroom was even taken up by the soldiers who were there to guard it, and they beat their drums and blew their trumpets with the rest.

Cromwell took the lesson close to heart. Republicanism was by no means dead beneath his governance. Lilburne's influence could be as strong again as it had been when the King was alive. 'For the peace of this nation', he put Lilburne back in jail.

He had high hopes of the godliness and honesty of his new Parliament, chosen by the sectarian congregations throughout the country, with the approval or alteration of his own council. It was to be the rule of the saints. 'You are called with a high call,' he had exhorted them in his opening speech. 'And why should we be afraid to say or think that this may be the door to usher in the things that God has promised?'

It was, alas, far from saintly behaviour that kept the *Intelligencer* on the streets for the rest of that year. It was known as Barebones' Parliament. 'Barebones, they are named, and bare bones they will leave, when they have done picking the flesh from our poor state,' proclaimed Jud in editorial contempt.

Unfortunately for Cromwell, his method of nominating its membership had resulted not in a majority of responsible men who were guided by principles of toleration and brotherly love, but in one of extreme sectaries, who settled down to picking bones with the moderate men almost at once. Their disagreement came to a head over the vexed question of the abolition of tithes, that portion of his income which a man was required to give towards the support of his Christian minister. The sectaries, who did not all congregate in churches, and some of whom did not even have ministers, were violently against this forced stipend. But since tithes had been bound up with rents since doomsday, landlords became understandably testy at the idea of their withdrawal, especially as in many cases the tithes had passed into their own hands after the dissolution of the monasteries.

Part of Jud's own recent settlement came from just such a devolvement. On this question, therefore, he stood assertively with Cromwell. 'Rent and tithe must stand together! The country's fabric threatened!' cried the *Intelligencer*.

Exactly five statute months after he had called it into being, Oliver Ironside got up very early one morning, together with those MPs who still had their heads on their shoulders, and voted it into thin air. 'A Crown to Sit on the Laurels?' wondered the *Intelligencer* wistfully. But this was not to be the next step.

Instead 'Oliver Protector!' it screamed one day in December, 'Cromwell presides over the Constitution and a Council of the Wise.' That the wise men were all officers of the army might have seemed menacing to some, but since they all proved to be the sung heroes of the wars, their popularity was certain. As for the constitution, that was contained in a lengthy and often abstruse document called the 'Instrument of Government', which Jud was required by the Council to print.

It cost him a great deal and he was never paid, which laid him open to considerable ribaldry on the part of Rob. He and Jud were fast friends again, and if they did not work together, they spent a good deal of their brief spare time together, either at home, in contented argument, or over a cannikin or six at the Bear.

In January Jud had another piece of good fortune. He acquired the right to print an edition of Isaak Walton's delightful work, *The Compleat Angler*. It had already enjoyed a great success and this cheaper edition promised to repay his effort. It was a pleasant change from politics, philosophy or any other branch of mental effort; a book for a country gentleman, such as Jud might be one day, if he could ever tear himself away from London.

Into the middle of his enjoyment of this congenial task, there blew in through the door of his print shop, in a bluster of wind and sleet, two unappointed persons, heavily cloaked. Jud closed the door on the presses and prepared to be polite.

One of the sodden bundles stepped forward and threw back a clinging hood. 'What the devil! Cathal! Is it really you?'

'I hope so, or this lady has lost her reputation. Orla, this is my good friend, Jud Heron. Jud, here is my wife.'

Courtesy sprang to the aid of surprise and Orla was welcomed, relieved of her cloak and seated beside a good fire with a jug of hot wine. Jud was astonished by her beauty and by her evident nobility. He had, he realized, expected her to be something wild and elemental, a woman of the sword, a Boadicea. This quiet, dark, commanding girl would have graced any court in Europe. He spared his blushes and tried to make up for his mistake by his careful treatment of her.

There was another reason for his concentration to be, at first, upon the woman rather than the man. It had been a great shock to see Cathal again. The knowledge of his relations with Lucy weighed heavily on him. When she had first told him of their love he had been sorry for them. When he had thought, instead, of Will Staunton's disappointment in her, his sympathy had turned into anger. He had felt some part of the guilt to be his, for bringing Cathal to London. When it had all ended so sorrowfully, he had hoped never to see him again. And now here he stood, as at home in the world as ever, with his boots in Jud's fireplace and his beautiful wife at his side.

Jud no longer knew how he felt. In front of Orla, he could not speak freely, which was a pity, as his instinct was, as always in such situations, to have a rumpus and get it over with. He spoke guardedly to Cathal, then, and devoted all his attention to the young woman.

'I am grateful for your wine and your warmth,' she told him with a smile which he felt as a gift. 'It was a long journey, as you know, and not a comfortable one. We sailed on a cockle-shell, moved only by the captain's faith in the bottles of brandy wine that would be waiting for him on the shores of Devon.'

'He was a drinking man, your captain?'

'A smuggler. There are still some in Ireland, most of them English, who can afford good French wine.' Her voice was cool and shared Cathal's cursive music. She had Cleo's dark hair, and eyes that were darker still, and looked out as though they had the measure of the world. Why, when he was married to this queen of the night, wondered the mystified and admiring Jud, did he need to go loving Lucy?

Cathal let them talk until they were used to one another and to the fact of their being there. He wondered about the premises, examining what was new since he was last there, and exclaiming enviously over the *Angler*. But it was obvious that his mind was not half on what he did, and at last Jud took pity on him and asked him what, apart from friendship, had brought them both here.

'It gives me no pleasure to relate.' Cathal looked at him with a weary sadness that Jud had never seen in him. He was years older without his merriment. 'Cromwell is killing Ireland,' he said softly. 'He began it when he came as a conqueror; he continues it more slowly now. The suffering is measureless. For she and I, the choice was to stay, to fight and to be slaughtered without meaning, or to leave and become a part of the phoenix bird, to find our way among those who will work so that, one day, a new Ireland may arise.'

'So you will go to King Charles, in France,' Jud hazarded, 'in the hope that he will remember your loyalty to his father?'

Cathal nodded. 'Cromwell is fifty-five. He will not live forever, perhaps not for a decade. I have even heard he is ill?'

'Oh, the stone, gout, a boil on his breast that troubles him. He will live long enough yet.' Jud was embarrassed. Cromwell stood before him like Achilles, and these two, who had some claim on him, were showing him the heel.

Cathal nodded, understanding. 'We will not talk of it. It has taken us too long to build up what tiny store of hope we need for this terrible wrenching from our own skins that is the leaving of our land; you must not shake that hope. It will crumble at your touch.'

'No. I am sorry.' Jud bent his head. 'Was it very dreadful?'

The Irishman's eyes were full of an unwanted knowledge. 'Well, I will tell you.' He faced away from Jud, as though he could not trust his own countenance. 'Of course you'll know that Ireland is to be part of England now,' he began, controlling the bitterness in his tone. 'We may sit at Westminster, if we will not wear frieze and gnaw bones in public. Unity, it is called. And the chief characteristic of this unity is that Oliver Ironheart will take every inch of Irish ground for England, and will graciously give us back less than one-tenth of it! We are all, little and great, to leave our castles, our cottages and our lands, and we may live, if we like, in the "plantations" of Connaught and Clare, where you would be lucky could you plant a lichen and have it grow. Our faith is proscribed and its priests are hunted and killed. The whole land weeps with widowed women and fatherless children, turned out of their houses with nowhere to go.'

A stone was forming in Jud's chest. He put out a hand towards the man who would not look at him and made some sort of strangled sound.

'As for us, we are wealthy still, if you were to make comparisons; we live, we are young. We may choose to go beyond seas. When they killed my father, they fired our castle, but it is granite and nothing of it which is important will burn. We threw the English down our hills that day and their blood enriches our fields. And now, when they came again and said that we should leave, I brought my people into the hall and I said to them that there would be no profit in their dying. It is no gift to Ireland to bring her more deaths. What they should do was to stay and work the land as they had always done, and to take no heed of the Englishman who sits in my father's chair; to do his bidding and never to look at his face. And then, when we are ready, I shall come back to them, and they will rise up like free souls on the Day of Judgement and smite him to the ground. They shall cut off his head, as my father's was cut off, and set it over our gates, and his body will go down into our earth with his fellows who wait for him. They were sorry at first, for they longed to fight once more, but I persuaded them, and that is what we did. So you see, for us, it was not so very dreadful, not in the way you mean – but more dreadful than anything previously, all the same.' Suddenly aware of his tremendous tiredness, Cathal sat down beside his wife and took her hand in his.

Oh these Irish, thought Jud, swamped with emotions not his own, how they worshipped the bloodsoaked soil of that turbulent island! He wondered if he felt a quarter of such a fierce love for England? A tenth? At any rate, he had never had occasion to discover it, if he did. 'I will help you all I can,' he said.

'It is a passage to France that we need. Ormonde has given us letters for the King and for our people in Paris. I do not know whom else to ask,' he said delicately, 'and I am aware that your own maritime connections are – scarcely suitable—' He meant Will.

Jud shook his head. 'Never fear. I have more than one friend in the city.'

'If you should have difficulty – I have papers of introduction to a member of a society dedicated to the Royalist cause – though perhaps I should not say so to *you*.' He smiled.

'Tell me no more, at least,' said Jud hurriedly. 'I do not want John Thurloe on my tail.'

'John Thurloe? Who is that?'

'His official title is that of Secretary to the Council of State. Unofficially he is Cromwell's master spy. He has his agents in every nook and cranny of the kingdom, in France, and in Ireland too, I shouldn't wonder. If I were to start to meddle with Cavalier secret societies, my livelihood would not be worth a button.'

'Then forget that I spoke of the gentleman. There is one thing I have to do, before I leave—' He sounded hesitant. Orla flashed him a look of encouragement.

'Which is?' Jud asked.

'I wish to see my daughter. And to take leave of your sister.'

Jud glanced awkwardly at Orla who appeared unperturbed. 'I thought you had already done so; finally,' he said levelly.

'I did not know then that I *had* a daughter. We will discuss it no further, if you please. But I should like to leave Orla in your care while I make a swift journey to Heron.'

Again Jud looked towards Orla's averted head, his mouth dry. 'But will you be welcome there?' he asked doubtfully.

'I shall not cross the threshold, I assure you,' Cathal said bleakly. 'I may speak my words to Lucy, and to my child, in any field or wood. It is no matter.'

Jud sighed. Another romantic meeting 'in any field or wood' was exactly what he would not have wished for Lucy. He hoped that she was more strongly armed against her lover than before, or it would go ill with her. 'Of course, I shall be honoured to entertain Mistress Orla,' he said gallantly. And he meant it. She was magnificent. Cathal did not deserve her.

Heron, Winter 1653

As it had been with Jud, so at Heron the effects of his reconciliation with Tom had spread their largesse. There was a lightness in the household that affected everyone in it and prayers of thanks aspired both night and morning.

Tom had remained as long as he dared, which was not long, since he was now twice an exile, and had then made his unnoticeable way back to France aboard the vessel of a small wool merchant who owed them past favours, and whose Stuart loyalty was firm. The high spirits continued after he had gone. Young Thomas, Robert and Nieve indulged in no more childish games than their elders and the whole parcel of them were whipped to a frenzy of foolishness by Edward, who threatened to be more of a handful, alone, than both his twin brothers had ever been. It was as though they had been given back the world before the war.

When one day Lucy found Martha crying her heart out in the apple loft, she was therefore taken aback. True, Martha was never exactly rowdy, but she had given out her own intense little glow while Tom had been with her, and it had been clear from his concentrated care of her that he had come to value her more than ever before. 'Are you missing him? Is it that?' Lucy thought she had it.

Martha wiped her eyes neatly on her kerchief and sat up amid the rich warm scent of apples. 'No. It is something that – well, that I never thought of.'

Lucy wrinkled her nose, puzzled. 'What, then?'

Martha met her eyes. 'Can you not guess? You, above all? Look at me.'

'I see you, but that doesn't tell me very much. You look very well; rosier than usual, if anything, and definitely fa— oh, *that* is it! Well, for heaven's sake, what is there to cry about? You were delighted when young Thomas was born!'

'The comparison is not with Thomas,' said Martha resignedly, 'but rather, I am very much afraid, with Nieve.'

At first Lucy did not understand. Then she saw that there was shame in Martha. 'No. No it mustn't be; it cannot be – that man's child?'

'I think so. I suppose I cannot be absolutely certain, but – oh, I *know*, somehow, and the time would be right for the way I am at present. It is Nehemiah's child.' She wanted to speak the name. She would be less afraid of it. She saw Lucy looking at her in horror and pity. 'I'm sorry. I did not tell you of – that side of matters, because I did not wish anyone to know of it. Tom knows, of course. He had to.'

'But not about the child? *You* didn't know, while he was still here?' She was beginning to recover. Something pressed urgently into the slow working of her thoughts.

'No. It was just after he left that I missed my second course. I did not mark the first one. I suppose I put that down to – my captivity. Oh Lucy, it is such a terrible thing! I think we could have weathered the rest of it – given this time for healing, and Tom's blessed goodwill to me. But how are we to survive this? I cannot let him see me with that man's child in my arms.' Her grey eyes were wide and tearless, as empty as a traveller's over snow.

'Wait. Wait a moment,' commanded Lucy. 'I must think. And so must you.'

'There is nothing to think. I have already decided what I must do. I shall leave Heron and go back to my cottage. I won't go away altogether, for I need the protection of Tom's small force, in case Nehemiah should come back. But I forfeit the right to be Heron's mistress, or Tom's wife.'

'Martha!' Lucy was horrified.

'No, be still a moment. I can't raise my bastard at Heron, how can I? It is not like you; you are a daughter of the house and have a right to its shelter. I was born at its gates and am content to return there. But it will be very hard with Tom. You must help me, Lucy,' she appealed.

'No. Not like that I won't,' said Lucy angrily. 'Listen to me. Your reasoning is all wrong. *Think* of what happened to me! How many are unhappy because I have been sent home? Think how many will be unhappy if you do as you say. And what, by the way, did you propose to do with young Thomas, or had you not considered him?'

'I should leave him here, of course. He is the heir.'

'If you wanted to sacrifice yourself, Martha, you should have let them burn you when they wanted to! No, do not look so damaged. Your foolishness makes me forthright, not cruel.'

She knelt in the straw beside Martha, scattering apples. 'When I first discovered I was carrying Nieve, Cissie said I should not tell Will it was Cathal's child, but pass it off as his, a seven-months' birth. I did not do that. Some *demon* of honesty drove me to tell him the truth. And see what I have for it? Do you think, now that I have lost my husband's love and our life together, that there has not been a day passed when I have not regretted that honesty with every part of myself?' She finished on such a note of savage bitterness that Martha was shaken.

'Why, Lucy. I had no idea. I am so sorry,' she said, conscious of ineffectuality.

'We are speaking of *you*,' said Lucy brutally. 'Do you want to live out your life – sitting at your own gates like Patient Griselda, forsooth – with nothing to warm you but a similar regret? Will that make you happy? Will it make Tom happy, who is only just learning to be barely human? Will it make young Thomas happy, to see his mother leave him and live in a cottage with a child who has usurped all her attention? And the rest of us? Are we not to care what becomes of you, but pretend you never left the wretched hovel? God's holy patience, Martha! I think you are as fit for Bedlam as for a lying-in! The whole thing is the artistry of madness! And I am not going to let you begin to dream of it. If you do not write at once to Tom, and tell him you are to have his child, and are delighted, I shall do it myself.'

'Lucy. You would not!' Martha said weakly.

'I *will*,' Lucy made her certain.

Martha began to sob. She did not bother to turn away, but let the tears fall into her lap, her face a mask of pain. Hoping she had gone far enough, Lucy leaned to stroke the silver hair out of her eyes. 'You know I am right,' she murmured. 'There are things that are more important than plain honesty. I know it. I want you to know it too, but in the opposite manner from mine.'

Martha did not weep for long. She sat and was silent for a long period afterwards. Lucy examined the apples on the racks and did not disturb her. She rubbed a glorious scarlet pippin against her cheek. It smelled like childhood and innocence.

When Martha turned at last towards her she knew what she would say. Lucy smiled and nodded her head. 'You are as wise as ever,' she said, tossing her the apple.

'Oh, as Eve,' said Martha sadly. 'Like her, I will have to live with my knowledge.' She made one last small stand against her preserver. 'What shall I do if the infant turns out the spit of Nehemiah?'

'You will point out, with no end of pride, how much like Tom is its dark hair, its brown eyes and its lugubrious expression! Heaven help it if it should be a girl, poor thing!'

The next months were not easy for Martha, who could hardly recall ever having lied to anyone in her life. When Lucy told her that she did not know for certain that she *was* lying, she was reprimanded for casuistry.

Mary's pleasure in the expectation, and Tom's, when it came, by letter, did much to uphold her resolve, as did the daily sight of her young son's cheerful development. He was somewhat in the shadow of his two idols, tearaway Robert and madcap Ned, but positive and fearless – and in his own way, which was quieter than theirs, sure of himself. She would not now think of how she had once decided to threaten that assurance. Perhaps, as Lucy had said, she had been a little mad.

The baby, when it came, *was* a girl. There were no divine punishments in the form of difficult labour, and even more wonderful to relate, there was not the vestige of dark colouring anywhere on the tiny, delicately formed body. The child was simply Martha made small. Her limbs were long, and slender enough to have Mary muttering about a really good, strong wet-nurse. Her face was a minute caricature of her mother's, with the same fathomless grey eyes and sweet mouth. Her oval head was crowned with a pure white fluff resembling swan's down, and her expression was serious.

'What did I tell you?' whispered Lucy, as she leaned over mother and child after Margery had done her work. 'Perfect, quite perfect.'

'Yes, she is,' said Martha proudly, gazing at her daughter's face. Lucy did not bother to explain what she had meant. Tom had expressed his wish that a girl should be called Caroline, as a fitting tribute from a cavalier household at this time. Martha would have preferred something less grand, the name of one of her favourite herbs for example, such as Sage or Rosemary. 'Let us be thankful there is no need to christen her "Rue",' Lucy remarked saucily and was rebuked for her levity. 'Ah no, don't frown at me. It is good to be able to laugh a little, now that it is all well over. I only wish there were anything amusing in my own situation. And now that Caroline is here, Martha, I want to hear you tell me that I was right.'

'You ask a great deal,' said Martha slowly. Only she would ever know the effort concealment had cost her. 'But, very well. You were right. It must be the best for the most to be content. And as for you,' she added with her loving smile, 'perhaps matters will mend, in time. You are young still and there is so much time. I don't believe that Will no longer loves you; it is pride that keeps him away. You may perhaps be able to break that pride at the price of your own. Perhaps you should try.'

'He always spoke of that kind of pride as foolish and useless,' said Lucy in the slow voice of memory. 'Oh God, I miss him so.'

'Then ask him to come here, to visit his son, when he comes home.'

'Do you think he would?'

'I believe he might. It is worth the attempt.'

'Then I will.' There was no knowing when he would read her letter, but the English navy was successfully harrying the Dutch off the seas with the astonishing Admiral Blake as her chief helmsman. The Dutch were said to be prepared to come to terms, therefore peace might be established by the spring. Then Will would come back ashore. If only she could make him stay – and with her.

Later that week she sat in the small parlour with Nieve playing busily at her feet with a collection of birds' eggs that Ned had given her. She had her little writing desk on her knee and was chewing her quill and trying to find the words that would possess the magic to bring Will to Heron, where he had not been since their wedding.

She had begun again for the third time when Robert raced into the room, his coat open and his yellow hair flying. 'I was told to give you this.' Breathlessly he tossed a packet into her lap.

A letter? Her heart leaped. If only, by one of those strange correspondences of fate that seem almost like an instinct, it would be from Will. It must be. He had been so much in her thoughts.

'How did you come by it?' she asked Robert, beginning to open it. She did not recognize the hand, but he had most likely left the addressing to his secretary.

'A man in the park,' said Robert, already on his way out again. Young Thomas was preparing an ambush for him in the Italian Garden. They were Rupert and Cromwell. It was Thomas's turn to be Rupert. But Oliver's intelligence was better than he knew; he had a surprise for Rupert . . . Behind him he heard his mother, another victim of surprise, make an unintelligible sound which he felt free to ignore.

Lucy's first reaction, when she saw the old, bold, monkishly beautiful script, was to fold up the paper and put it from her. She did not want to read it. The instincts of fate were mischievous and contrary. She did not have to heed them. She sat with the letter in her hands for a time, one part of her mind waiting and watching while the other went through the series of mountebank

702

tumbles demanded by the jester who appeared to control her emotions.

At last, with a curiously empty sensation, she began to read. She did not know what she might have expected. Not this. A letter was one thing; it required only a little private courage. But to see him. Tonight. That would take more. It would take a perfect self-government, the abrupt and final dismissal of the jester. He had asked to see Nieve. He had a right to know his daughter.

If they should not keep the appointment, would he seek them out at the house? It was obvious that it had not occurred to him that she might not wish to see him. And he was right. She had to admit it; she did wish it. She was proud of Nieve and she wanted him to see her, to know hat so much good had come out of their love and that she regretted nothing, still.

He asked her to meet him, after dark, at a place in the park not far from where she had once found the slaughtered deer. Nieve was sleeping heavily and did not wake when Lucy lifted her from her bed and wrapped her well against the night cold. She murmured a little and burrowed into her mother's arms, as content to sleep there as anywhere. She was heavy and Lucy was tired by the time she had crossed the park and identified the particular oak tree under which Cathal would be standing. The moon was almost full and the sky clear and starry, the air tingling and aware of April's feet on the grass.

'It is a treacherous night for people with a history such as ours.' His voice set her thought to music almost before it was formed. It was as close and familiar as yesterday. She caught her breath at the nearness of it.

He was leaning against the bole of the tree, a part of its dark silhouette. He moved away from it and towards her, his arms held out. She wondered would he embrace her and would she let him? But he knew her difficulty and his arms were for the child. 'Let me take her. She is too old for you to be carrying.'

Nieve stirred as she was relinquished but did not wake. 'She could not walk so far, at this late hour.'

Such flat and irrelevant words and the two of them sharing the same yard of ground. He felt it too and smiled to tell her so. 'Let me get the light of the stars upon her. I know she must be beautiful.'

'Her hair is not golden.' Lucy's throat trembled. 'It is red.'

'Is it so? Yes, I see it is.' He chuckled, an intimate sound in the great space surrounding them. 'Well, in the old days, you know, when the legend of Niamh was in the making, the colour of gold had a ruddier tinge than it has now.'

'Had it so?' she echoed him. 'Well, I would as soon she did not grow up to think herself a princess of legend. It does not make for contented days.'

He stood very close to her, the child resting over one shoulder. 'And you wish her contentment rather than what we have had?' Her eyes were commanded by his and she looked into them and could not answer.

'When I first saw you, you looked into my eyes from the top of the stairs, do you remember?'

'I remember.' He would kiss her soon and she would be lost. But he only touched her cheek, as though a leaf brushed it.

'You have given me a beautiful child and I thank you,' he said with grave courtesy. 'Will you tell her about me? When will you tell her?'

'When she is strong enough to take no harm from the telling.'

'That is good. Yes. But when you wish her contentment merely, remember that we are the ones who have made her. Do not try, my bird, in the long future which I may not share, to bend her nature where perhaps it cannot turn.'

'I would never do that.'

'I wish I might watch her grow.' There was nothing she could say.

'And now tell me of yourself,' he said softly, his eyes and his mind touching every part of her. 'Have you no word from your husband? Does he speak of a return to you?'

'No. Never.'

'And is that what you most want?'

She left a space. 'Yes. It is.'

'Then I am sorry. But there is this I must say to you, only the once more, and then I have done. Will you come with me now, and bring the child, and we will go to France and live together as God must have intended that we should?'

She could not fend off the sudden stab of pain. 'Did you say to your wife that you would ask me this?'

It was a challenge, to remind him he had no such right. 'I did. How could I not? You would not wish to be the subject of my lying to her. She is too fine for that. As you are.'

'Mother of God. And does she love you, your Orla?'

'She does. Ah, don't turn away. I am not a monster. It was she who wanted our marriage. She has always suffered the truth from me. She would not take me on any other grounds.'

'To live with you must be like a knife in her belly.'

'You don't know her. You do not understand how she is. She is not like you.'

Lucy shook her head violently. 'No, indeed.'

'And you are forgetting Ireland,' he added gently. 'There is a bond between us on behalf of our fair land, that is as strong in its fashion as that between you and I.'

They stood apart still, and his words, instead of bringing her to him, make her take a step backward. 'There must be no such bond. No longer. The only thing between us now is this child. If there is a bond, I break it now. Do you understand me, Cathal? Nieve is yours, I freely admit it. I am glad of it, for in her I shall always have you with me. But there must be no tie of love to keep us longing for each other. You should give yourself to your wife, for she must feel a great loneliness in your company. As for myself, I belong to Will. It makes no matter whether or not he wants me. I love him. And my duty is his.'

'Ah Lucy, it is a brave speech to be making. You have no love left for me, then?' That was cruel.

'I don't say that. I don't deny the past. But I am willing to see that it *must* be the past. Can you not let it go, as I do?'

He stretched out his hand and drew it down her cheek as he had used to do when he was first beginning to know the curves of her face. A tear followed its line.

She shook it roughly away. 'It is best. Believe me. Like you, I want only truth between us.'

'Will you kiss me?'

'Are you even listening to me?'

'I will not see you again for a very long time. Perhaps never. I think your talk is foolish and your fears unnecessary. Now kiss me and bid me fare well. I have need of your kisses.'

There was nothing more she could do. Perhaps he was right. She no longer cared. Her body wanted to melt into his. She came into the circle of his arm and put up her hands to his face. 'Oh my dear.'

'My singing bird.' They stood together, the three of them close and warm and removed from time, until the sky began to lighten. The child was like the sword of chastity between them. She woke once and looked at Cathal with wondering eyes which crinkled into a delighted smile when he whispered to her. Then she slept again, her russet curls tangling with his, as though she slept every night of her life against his shoulder.

They talked very little, and all of old, far-off things; of the day they had gone skating and he had first begun to sense what she would become to him; of Christmas and her father's Shakespearian speeches; of the duel at St James'; of their joyous capture of the city of London for themselves. They did not speak of the last time they had met.

Their kissing was tremulous and half sorrowful as they tried to keep passion at bay. They succeeded better than they deserved but the price was paid in want and sacrifice. When the time came for him to leave her, she was dry-eyed, beyond tears.

His last kiss was for his daughter. 'You'll send her to me, for a time, one day when she is grown, and the world a better one?'

'I will. If that world ever comes.'

'It must. The worst will always pass. The wheel must turn; it can do no other.'

She looked down.

'We *will* meet again, my love. Won't you believe it? I must believe it or I cannot live.'

She met the words bravely, with silence. Then she took the child from him and turned away across the park. She walked very quickly, with brief, listening steps. She heard him call her name, just once.

Lucy had been mistaken in an earlier judgement; naval warfare had suited Will Staunton very well. He had found it much the same, give or take a few courtesies, as privateering, except that, theoretically at least, one was also paid for it. He had profited considerably from the discomfort of several Dutch vessels and had enjoyed the company of his fellow officers. He had been an excellent captain and a shrewd strategist, and better still he had made a name for being lucky. He had kept his own three ships, among others, close under his command and had lost none of them. The *Regina* was badly holed just above the waterline; the *Elizabeth* had lost one of her masts and most of her upper deck; his flagship, the *Lady* holed like a colander and streaming like a moving waterfall, drew the shreds of her sails about the splinters of her masts and hove into the Thames like the Old Queen on a progress. Will listened appreciatively to the cheers from the dockside as she came in and felt himself to be in a better humour than he had been when he left.

It was not until after he had spent several days sleeping and several nights regaling scores of eager interlocutors with salt tales of gun thunder and lightning sword-play that he discovered, one afternoon when he awoke with his head on his desk where he had collapsed the night before, that Lucy had written him a letter. He had opened one experimental eye and there, in the midst of the fuzz of sunlight, was her handwriting, forward and clear. Its contents sobered him quite quickly and he ordered his breakfast to be brought where he sat, so that he could eat while he thought about it.

When his cousin Eliza entered the room in her peignoir to drink coffee with him, it was clear from her moody expression that she had not been best pleased with his sleeping arrangements. She was even less well impressed when he ran a hand through his tousled hair and announced, as though it were the most delightful inspiration, 'I do believe I will post up to Heron for a few days, and see what my wife is making of my son.' An old hand, Eliza confined her outward reaction to the earnest hope that he would not be gone long as there were a thousand interesting invitations waiting his pleasure.

As for herself, she had not waited out the war in vain, and certainly not alone. But she was by no means satisfied yet. She wondered if she dared to introduce the delicate subject of divorce, but decided that, on the whole, she did not. She prayed instead, as Will packed, that Lucy would disport herself in her old fashion with some lusty squire and cook her own goose twice over.

Before Will left she gave him a night the memory of which he would most certainly take with him. It was quite extraordinary, even to such experienced performers in the lists of lust as themselves. It had all turned upon the crushed bodies of some insignificant insects called cantharids, which you powdered and added to your wine. Playfair had got them for her. He had said they came from Spain.

At Heron, Will was embarrassed by his welcome. He was treated, much as he had always been, except on the occasion of his wedding, as the greatest possible friend of the family. He was given his old chamber as casually as though that occasion had never taken place. Everyone he encountered, whether family or servant, seemed equally glad to see him and unaware that there was anything in the least way out of the ordinary in his domestic arrangements.

In the first couple of hours, however, it appeared that he had encountered everyone except Lucy herself. Not wishing to be heard to ask where she was, he stated that he would take a short walk in the gardens, just to take the stiffness out of his legs after the ride. He went at once to the sunken garden. The Quickenberry had finished flowering and was beginning to think about its berries, its green leaves grinning at the insistent reds around it. But Lucy was not there. 'The deuce!' Will muttered, foolishly put out.

He walked to the edge of the park and gazed out across the green with his sea eyes. There were deer again, he was glad to see, and several men working among the trees, but there was no sign of his wife.

He found her, when he had decided he had given up and just wanted to stroll and stretch his legs alone, in the Italian garden. She was sitting on a bench near to one of the statues, reading. He noticed with a quirk of his lip as he strode towards her that the identity of the sculpture was Aphrodite.

Her eyes were on the book but she had known of his approach from the moment he had turned into the avenue. She did not wish him to think she was looking out for him. There were shrieks behind her in the shrubbery and she looked up as if this was all that could concern her. 'Why, Will,' she said in the low voice of warm, but unexcited welcome she had practised, 'you have made good time. I am very glad to see you.'

'And I you.'

They stared at each other in unashamed curiosity. 'The sea has sharpened your features a little. You look more dangerous. You are very brown. It suits you.'

'It is easier to judge the differences in a woman if she is standing up. I may tell you that your face is as lovely as ever; perhaps also a little thinner. But how do you compare with the lady behind you?'

He had taken a chance, but it was the right note. Seriousness between them was not yet possible, but they had always been able to rub along on the ground of mutual raillery.

'Rather well, I should suppose,' Lucy said coolly. 'I would certainly require a smaller yardage of drapery were I to display myself about the grounds in her style.'

'A captivating thought, I am sure,' he answered politely, inclining a fraction at the waist.

'And how was the war?' she asked, as though enquiring about a garden party.

'It was very well, for a war. We won, you know.'

'I had heard. And were you wounded at all?'

'Nothing obvious, as you see. A few cutlass stripes and the odd musket burn to go with them. I was lucky.'

'Tell me about it,' she said quietly, the teasing gone for the moment. He took her at her word and gave her a terse resumé of the story he had told in a dozen taverns and twenty houses since his return.

'So, taken all in all, this conflict has been good for England?' Lucy inferred when he had finished.

'It has indeed. To begin with, it was good for the navy. New ships, nearly thirty of them; new men, new money. We've a fighting force to be reckoned with now, as we have in the army. The rest of Europe no longer sniggers up its satin sleeves at poor ungovernable Britannia. They take us, and they take Cromwell, seriously, and they are right to do so! And it has been good for trade too, which means good for the house of Staunton.' There was a very slight hesitation as the human condition of that house occurred to him. 'The Dutch will do as we tell them now, and we have made sound commercial treaties with Sweden and Portugal, and will make more. Oliver has an instinct for trade that the King never had; I've a feeling it will serve us well.'

Lucy, with Ireland in her thoughts, was not disposed to praise Cromwell just then. At that point their conversation was interrupted; not without some relief on both sides, for the pretence of a complete lack of strain was beginning to wear thin. The interruption came in the form of the advance from the bushes behind them of what seemed like a very long column of children.

It was led by Lucy's youngest brother, Ned, marching in strict time and carrying one of the twins' old swords. Behind him, loosely bound together at the wrists by long tendrils of ivy, stumbling dolefully one behind the other, were young Thomas, Robert Staunton, John Coachman's daughter Daisy, whose conception had cost her mother a black eye, and Lucy's daughter Nieve, who had cost more. Bringing up the rear with his father's horsewhip was the coachman's first-born son, Jake, only a little younger than Ned. The prisoners were marched solemnly onto the path and marshalled in front of Lucy and Will.

'Party of Indians, sir,' Ned reported, straightfaced, to Will. 'Caught firing the settlement. And the women were stealing. What is to be done with them?'

Ned saluted smartly and stepped back. Jake prodded the male Indians with the handle of his whip, just for the look of the thing. Daisy gave a convincing moan of fear, and Nieve, by far the smallest, giggled richly.

Lucy saw Will's eyes flash to her freckled face. She felt a second's fear, but he said nothing, only rose and stalked up and down the thin rank, frowning as horribly as he could. Then he pulled his beard and scratched his head and frowned again. 'What tribe do these misbegotten creatures represent?' he asked. Lucy deeply suspected his choice of adjective.

'They are Aztecs, your honour, except for this one.' Ned pointed to Nieve. 'She is a Mixtec, and swears her father is a king.'

'Does she indeed?' murmured Will at his most silken. 'Is it true? D'you reckon she'd fetch a tidy ransom, Captain?'

'Captain Aquila Gomez y Hernandez.' Ned clicked his heels.

'Quite so. At ease, Captain.'

'Well, I don't know sir. She seems very grubby, for a princess.' This was true, alas.

'It'th a dithguise!' declared Nieve, much offended. 'I didn't tell you who my father wath until you thaid you'd kill me!'

'Can we stop playing now?' asked Robert, unable to keep silent any longer. 'That's *my* father, in case you didn't know!' He broke his ivy bonds with a swift tug and came to stand before Will. 'You *are* my father aren't you, sir?' he asked shyly.

Will reached for the boy and hugged him strongly. 'I most certainly am,' he said. Then he turned quickly to Nieve. 'And who is this young lady?' he asked cheerfully, ruffling her chestnut curls.

'I'm Nieve,' said the child automatically. 'And I *am* a princess,' she insisted.

Will kissed her hand gravely. 'The captain is a boor if he cannot see beneath the dirt,' he said. 'I shall ransom her personally. Send the others to my tent. I'll decide what to do with them later.' He waved a dismissive hand and Ned drove them all off up the avenue with the help of Jake's whip and a few Spanish-sounding curses.

'A princess, eh?' mused Will, as they disappeared round the corner. 'Is that what you will tell her, when she asks?'

'No,' she said, hating him. 'I'll tell her the truth.'

'She will ask very soon. She sees now that Robert has a father—'

'And will think him hers also. I know it.' The friendliness of banter had all gone now. He was taking a mean delight in her dilemma. 'It is she who will suffer,' she burst out, full of contempt. 'A mere child of four. Does that content you so much?'

'No.' His voice was quiet and level. 'It does not content me at all. I would wish it otherwise. She is a charming child and has character, if I'm not mistaken. I wish she were also mine. Does *that* content *you*?' The last sentence was spoken with controlled bitterness.

She shook her head, suddenly awash with misery. 'Jesu! What a desperate mess!'

Having caused her unhappiness, Will was surprised by the guilt for it. She deserved it right enough, but he found he did not like to be her punishment so directly.

'It's not so bad as you think,' he said roughly. 'Children of that age do not dwell on anything for long. Nieve will not care who is her father, so long as her life remains secure and she has her playmates about her.'

That was true. Lucy began to recover. 'It may be so now,' she said, sighing, 'but later, when she is grown, it will be a different tale.'

'Ah, later—' He looked at her sidelong, as if to ask who knows what might happen later. She found it very irritating. He saw that they would get no further today. He rose and held out his hand. 'Come along,' he said, 'let us go in and behave in whatever manner it has been ordained that we shall. I promise you, Nieve shall know no difference from Robert in my treatment of her. I like the little rogue.'

'Thank you. That is kind,' said Lucy, avoiding his hand.

'I hear that Martha has added another to Heron's private army. Tom must be pleased.'

'Yes, he is. Very,' said Lucy brightly.

Caroline was at the stage of being passed from hand to hand and exclaimed over. Will joined in with the faintly bemused air that large men are apt to wear on such occasions and gave her his finger to chew. 'What a very delicate creature,' he admired, smiling at Martha. 'If I did not know better I'd say she was sired by the King of the Fairies!'

Martha blushed raspberry red and Will was conscious of a *faux pas*. He had always known the girl to be of a retiring nature, but to colour up at the very suggestion that a child must have a father was carrying modesty too far.

'Just look at those children,' said Martha fiercely to Lucy, later, as Captain Hernandez force-marched his captives over the fearful mountains of the sunken garden. 'Do you realize that if I were to add Caro to their number, there would be more bastards than legitimates? What is wrong with all of us, that we can't get our children in our marriage beds?'

Lucy chuckled. 'Wait until Jud brings Cleo into the family fold,' she said gleefully. 'Then we shall have to start a society. We shall hold intellectual gatherings, after the fashion of Lady

Ranelagh in town, and dispute that question as the Dominicans do, with inalienable logic.'

'Logic!' Martha practically spat. 'There's no logic in human behaviour, only momentary madness and ill luck. Well, very occasionally good luck too,' she added, more sweetly, thinking of Tom.

'I wish you might trouble to remember the good luck more often,' Lucy snapped, tired of being controlled. 'That child is just as likely to be Tom's as anyone's; why dwell on anything else?'

She left Martha abruptly, to lock herself in her own lonely chamber for a time. She was suddenly exhausted. She had strung herself to such a pitch to be able to meet Will that now she felt as though all her strings had loosened and could give no note of truth.

She still loved Will. She had known that as soon as she had seen him. Worse, she wanted him, with a shaming hunger. But there would always be that spark of enmity between them, that might catch at any time and cause a conflagration. It had been lit long ago, on a quayside in May, and had remained the constant accompaniment of their relations ever since. If she wanted him back she knew she must dampen down that spark so that it could not fly and ruin her efforts to govern herself.

But did he want her back? This was the question that now tormented her. She simply could not tell. He had been courteous, urbane, teasing, charming, and had preserved absolute distance. If his eyes had suggested that he found her attractive, then he had found Aphrodite equally so. If his words had intimated that he missed family life, they had given no clue that she was any part of what he missed. She wondered how long he would stay with them. He had stated no limit as yet. She could be thankful, at least, that he had taken to Nieve, though that had been predictable enough, if you thought about it; Will was not one to take out his difficulties on a child, and Nieve charmed every creature, human and animal, who came within her reach. She was a wholly joyful spirit, filling her small world with her deep laughter and a thoughtfulness for others far more developed than in most children of her age. As far as she was concerned, there was no question but that Will was her father. Lucy, her heart full of her, was only glad that custom insisted that she address him as 'sir'.

As for Robert, it was as though he and Will had never been parted. He had simply picked up the old cameraderie of the garden at Staunton House and was more than content to be the son of the man who held them all spellbound with his stories of the sea and ships. He and Will spent long hours walking or gently riding together and Lucy felt that at least her husband could not fault her there. She had always spoken of him as a man whose absence was on account of his duty elsewhere, and this was a common enough occurrence to be accepted without question by his son.

Lucy could not make out whether or not Will ever actually sought her company. She would come upon him during her own movements about the house or gardens, and he upon her, but she had no idea if it were by design or otherwise. When they did meet they were pleasant and inconsequential with one another, never reaching either the cheerful badinage or the tense recrimination of the first meeting. As the days passed she began to feel that she must make an effort to bring this empty phase to a close or they would make no progress at all.

She had hoped at first to draw him to her by the intercession of music. She had invited him to play and sing with her, knowing that this must conjure a hundred happy memories. But if it did so, he gave no sign. He sang as charmingly as ever, standing at a little distance behind her, following the score with perfect musicianship, executing every note exactly as the composer might have wished; but his voice did not swoop and hover about hers, courting and caressing as it had in the past. They were as pure and separate as choristers.

Lucy began to lose heart. 'It is no good,' she told Martha in despair. 'He no longer cares for me at all.'

But Martha would not believe it. 'He is wearing a mask,' she said. 'It is cunningly wrought and a perfect fit, but there will be a way to make him discard it. Your work is to find that way.'

'But what can I do?' Lucy cried. 'I can hardly throw myself at the man!'

'Can you not? Perhaps not. But I would be disposed to try—'
Could she, Lucy asked herself, abandon all her pride and pretence and simply beg him to take her back? Surely that was more than even God could expect of her!

But if it should be the answer? She did not exactly resolve to make the attempt, but neither did she rule it out altogether.

She began to look for him on purpose, and to give him little attentions of the sort a wife gives to a husband, securing him his favourite cuts at table, pouring his wine herself, playing his best loved songs. If he noted them he did not remark upon it, but continued to treat her with the same, slightly removed pleasantness, as though she were someone else's wife, not his.

One afternoon it had been decided that there should be a harvest picnic, according to their old custom. Margery and Tibbett had organized luncheon in the chosen field with all the application of quartermasters to a bivouac. All the family and most of the immediate tenants were present, and the sun shone mightily upon a mountain of food and drink. Kit, Humpty and Ned strummed guitars and sang dirty songs about roundheads and maidenheads, and the field-workers capered about in the stubble with much wagging of elbows and flirting of skirts.

Lucy settled herself next to Will beneath a hedge and offered him a pasty from her basket. He took it, tasted it, nodded and polished off half of it before saying lazily, looking at her from under his lids, 'I seem to remember sitting with you like this once before.'

'Oh, on many occasions, surely? Will you have cider or wine?'

'Wine if you please. I was thinking of a particular day. You had reason, if you recall, to be sad.'

'Oh? I don't think I—'

'Oh? You have no recollection? And I'd swear, at the time, you thought your heart was broken.' His tone was quite casual.

'I see.' Her voice was low. She remembered now.

'And I, in my conceit, had, even then, the notion that I might do something about that unfortunate situation.' He was not casual now; there was no mistaking the bitterness of his words.

'Will, please. There is no use—'

'But I *wish* to discuss it. There is one thing I would have clear. I don't like to live in ignorance. Tell me, since the time when you took the Irishman to your bed and let him get his child upon you – have you seen him, or corresponded with him? You must tell me Lucy. I need to know.'

Lucy sat quite still and quiet. She had not expected a shock such as this. None of their conversations had led her to fear such an outright assault. She thought quickly. She had not planned to tell him of Cathal's secret visit, though she thought he would hardly jib at their brief exchange of letters. But now, faced with the immediate prospect of Will's newly obvious hurt and distrust of her, she remembered what Cathal himself had said to her about his own wife – 'I would not have anything less than the truth between us. She is too fine. So are you.' Oh no, I'm not, I'm not! If I tell the truth now I may lose him forever.

She drank a little cider, to give her courage, then turned to meet his waiting gaze. 'I wrote to him once, to tell him of his daughter's birth,' she said slowly. 'It was his right.'

'And?' He knew there was more.

'And I have seen him. Once. Here. For a few hours.'

'When?'

'In March.'

'Of this year?'

'Yes.'

He said nothing. She looked beseechingly at him, willing him to understand, and to pity her a little.

He sighed. Then he smiled sadly and reached out a finger to her lips, the first time he had touched her since he had sent her away from him. Then he said softly, 'Lucy, I had better leave tomorrow. And you must have guessed already why I came here. Please have Robert packed and ready. I shall take him with me to London.'

She was on her feet. 'But you can't! He is only a child still. He is too young to—'

'I hope you will not cause an unpleasant scene here. It has always been my plan to take him when he was seven. You have known that as well as I. Please do not demean yourself by making difficulties now.

'This is to punish me, isn't it?' she asked, her voice harsh and hateful. 'You think I am still in love with Cathal. Well, it is not true. I want—'

'Lucy! Will you never learn? I do not want to hear.'

'But we must—'

'I am going to speak with Robert. I shall tell him he is to be ready to ride with me tomorrow.'

'He *can't* ride all that way!'

'I have a coach waiting at Faringdon.'

He slipped away before she could say any more, and she watched him pick his smiling path through the harvesters. He had a kind word and a smile for everyone. He looked as if he were leaving an occasion which he had greatly enjoyed.

Perhaps he had, Lucy thought mournfully, watching the sun strike his head to a gold brighter than the corn. Perhaps he had.

When he had gone, with an excited Robert chattering non-stop at his side, so keen to leave that he had scarcely given Lucy a proper farewell, there was a feeling of looseness about the house, as though everyone had held their breath in expectation and had now been disappointed. There was a tendency to treat Lucy as an invalid.

Only Martha still stubbornly held out hope. 'He loves you still. It is plain to me. And love must triumph, or the world is mad.'

'Tell that to Nehemiah Owerby!' cried Lucy unforgivably, rushing headlong away from any comfort.

London 1654

Every time he wished to work undisturbed, thought Jud, he could be sure he would be interrupted. Who was it this time? He laid down the pen with which he was writing an editorial article of great length and, he hoped, some influence, and scowled at the opening door.

'It's only me.' Rob pushed past a protesting Endymion.

'I'm terribly busy, old friend. Can't it wait?'

' 'Fraid not. Got a problem.'

'Not John Lilburne again?'

'No. John is safe and sound behind bars, I'm sorry to say. He'll not escape from Jersey. A pity. He is needed now as he was never needed before.'

'You mean the Levellers have lost their cause with their leader?' Jud provoked.

Robin sighed. 'I will admit to a certain lack of cohesion,' he said. 'Jud, my press has broken down. It's the third time in two months.'

'The old girl has lasted well past her time already; you can't expect miracles. She was old when we first had her.' Rob still worked from their original premises in the rose alley.

'Well, I have my hopes. I've one of Richard Overton's men working on her. But there's something I want to get out right away. Will you let me use one of your presses, as soon as you've one free?'

'Oh damn it, Rob. I wish you wouldn't put me in this position. You know I don't like to refuse you—'

'Then you won't. Excellent! When can I start?'

Jud groaned. 'Well, perhaps. What is it you want to print?'

716

'Here. Read it!' He tossed a wad of paper across Jud's desk. 'I'll read what you're doing, if you like.'

Jud grinned. '*You* won't like; it hardly represents *your* opinions.'

What Rob read was a concise approbatory summary of the good deeds of the Protectorate to date. It covered Cromwell's many social reforms; it applauded his vigorous attempts to reform the law; it warmly recommended him for his tolerance both of those who followed the Episcopal or Catholic religions (except the Irish, of course). It praised him too for his thorough prosecution of the Dutch war and his intelligent trade-cum-religious pacts with other Protestant nations that had made the name of Cromwell respected deeply enough to expunge that of Stewart forever. There was also a strongly worded paragraph of distaste for the present behaviour of the House of Commons.

'Why, you arse-licking, piss-drinking toady!' shouted Rob, flinging the article across the floor. 'Why don't you go and sue for a job on the *Mercurius Politicus* if this is all you have to say? Or perhaps old Ironside would let you polish up his warts on Sundays!' He farted roundly to endorse his opinion.

'Did you finish it?'

'Not I! I'd had enough of this weevil-headed balderdash.'

'And I suppose you think *this* will serve the country better?' Jud tapped Rob's papers with lofty contempt. 'This is nothing less than a call for revolution.'

'It is not,' declared Rob with passionate conviction. 'It is a call for the restoration of the proper privileges of Parliament – so that we may be governed by them as the true representatives of the people – not by a tyrant dictator with the power of the sword at his back!'

'When you speak of Parliament, you speak only for the Republicans and those head-in-the-cloud fools who think to rule by "the agreement of the people". We have moved on since then.'

'Aye – to the "instrument of government" and Oliver aping King Charles! Look, you know as well as I do, Jud, Parliament cannot be said to rule unless it has control of the army. And do you think Cromwell will ever give it that?'

'Oh, hold your peace for a minute; you're not at Paul's Cross now. If only you'd stop working from naive first principles and look at what has actually *happened*! I seem to recall you were hot enough, and loud enough in praise of Oliver when he was first set fair on the course that has brought him where he is today. And you cried "traitor" even louder when you thought he had let down the army at Saffron Walden!'

'That was before he had begun to use the army as his own personal threat.'

'What else is he to do? He rose *from* the army, *of* the army, and the army has supported his policies throughout, apart from the disaffected extremists. But his true commitment is to parliamentary government—'

'Then why does he not let the Parliament govern?'

'Oh God, you are as subtle as a turnip! If he gives Parliament its way and puts it in control of the militia, then the militia will not obey the Parliament but will look to Cromwell. Such a split would be disastrous.'

'He may get himself out of that dilemma by sanctioning "the agreement of the people" and declaring a republic.'

'That would be as good as to declare another war, you turd-brain. The majority do not share your lunacy.'

'Then they must be taught otherwise.'

'Not on my presses! I'm sorry, Rob, but I won't print this criminal incitement to trouble. You have become a short-sighted fool. If Cromwell were to fall, we should have anarchy, that's all. And none knows that better than he!'

There was a polite cough at the conclusion of this speech. It was emitted by Will Staunton who stood grinning in the doorway. 'At last. Rescue! Thank the Lord!' Jud was expecting him.

'Endymion thought you would not mind if I came in. I gather nothing has changed in these parts. Still happily at each other's throats!'

'If you were to cut off Rob's head, he'd grow two more,' said Jud disparagingly, 'both bleating for the agreement of the people!'

'Ah, that old song,' said Will shrewdly. 'If they sing that one too loudly in the House, we shall all find ourselves without a job again.' Will had managed to scrape into the new Parliament by reason of his good service in the navy, rather than any inclination to the godliness after which Cromwell idealistically hankered.

'He'll never dismiss this session; they haven't yet voted his supplies and he is in dire need of money,' jeered Rob.

'King Charles found other ways,' said Will quietly. 'I daresay the Lord Protector may do likewise.'

'The Lord protect us!' prayed Rob disgustedly.

'Oh, go home, if you can't talk sense,' Jud told him. 'And take your arse-wipers with you!'

718

Robin retrieved his pamphlet with as much dignity as possible and prepared to depart. 'I was just going anyway,' he said stiffly.

'I should have drowned him when I had the chance,' said Will when his ex-apprentice had gone. 'Now Jud, I've not much time; I'm due back in committee this afternoon. So I'll give you the broad outline of the thing, and to save time I'll not say anything you can't print. How's that?'

'Suits me. D'you want to read the rest of it first?'

'I don't think I need to. It didn't seem to take Robin's fancy, did it? What is it, a chorus of "Good old Noll! Look what he's done for us! Think what he'll do for us yet!" '

'More or less. But your contribution will be the crowning glory – if you'll forgive such a controversial expression – it'll take some of the stodge out of it. Remind people of Drake and the singeing of Philip's beard.'

'Do we *always* have to look back to Bess's day to be satisfied with ourselves as Englishmen?' asked Will, somewhat wistfully, knowing himself guilty of the same.

'So it would seem. And to my mind, Oliver has far more in common with her than he has with Charles Stuart, if only enough of us could be got to see it.'

'Well, you are doing your best to lend us spectacles for the task. Here you are, then, I have prepared some notes on the Western Design. We should prefer it if you did not publish until the end of next week. As you know, the expedition has been made ready in secrecy.'

'Thank you, Will. You are a good friend. But don't you wish you were to sail with Penn and Venables instead of being a boardroom admiral?'

Will shrugged. 'Perhaps. But one cannot supervise the education of a small boy – two small boys – from the West Indies. I have had my share of sailing. Though I must confess the expedition appeals to me. It's a most ambitious scheme. Even Elizabeth never considered anything quite so unambiguous.'

The Western Design, according to the brief given to its naval commander, Admiral William Penn, which Will had in part helped to compose, was 'in general to gain an interest in that part of the West Indies in the possession of the Spaniard'. It was to be an unequivocal attempt to occupy and permanently colonize a base from which profitable trade might take place. The objective was the island of Hispaniola. From there England would break the Spanish monopoly of South American trade, the enviable silver trade in particular. She would begin by pirating the silver fleets on their way out of port. Will would have enjoyed that. But he had other responsibilities now that he had Robert to look after, not to mention Jud's own son, Edmund, who had been invited to Staunton House to provide what Will thought would be stimulating companionship for both boys.

They had at first, predictably, loathed each other, but that had soon ended after several scuffles in the stableyard, some of them quite bloody. They had at last declared themselves well-matched and taken an even bloodier oath of friendship that Ned had got from a sailor in the Bear, where he was, naturally, forbidden to go. The sailor swore he had it from a Turk whose lifelong passion was to avenge the death of his own blood-brother.

Jud finished reading Will's notes with an air of great satisfaction. 'This is splendid. Just what I need. But I hope you don't mind if I go easy on the conversion-of-the-poor-benighted-heathen, and play up the discomfort of Spain?'

'If you could manage both?' Will's smile was disarming.

'Oh, very well. We serve a hard master.'

'But an honest one, I think. I'll forgive him a great deal of psalm-singing for that.'

'I too. I wish Rob could see it, before it's too late. He'll fall into deep trouble one of these days.'

Will frowned. 'That reminds me. I saw a fellow hanging about in the street as I was coming here. I thought I'd seen him before. You don't think Rob already has a follower?'

'It's possible. He makes little secret of his sympathies, though he tries to keep the whereabouts of his press to himself, not very successfully, I should guess.'

'Well, take heed for yourself, that's all.'

'Oh, I'm safe enough; how could I be otherwise when I print articles like this?'

'All the same, I'm glad to know you won't print his ranting. Look, I didn't come only for the Design. I have another scheme in mind which I'd like your advice about. Not so grandiose, but perhaps more personally important, to both of us.'

'What is it? If it's money that's needed, I'm a single-minded man. Every groat goes back into the business.'

'It isn't that. It's Tom. I have been wondering lately, now that there is a milder climate towards the Royalists, whether I might not try to get a pardon for him.'

Jud's eyes lit. 'Have his exile quashed, you mean, so that he could come home?'

'If it's possible. I believe there *have* been a number of such cases.'

'It almost happened for poor John Lilburne, but not quite.'

'Tom Heron is no such dangerous animal as Lilburne; at least, I trust he is not. I have no notion of how he comports himself in Paris. Whether he is a simple courtier, whether he does any work for the King that the present dispensation might take exception to? I was hoping he might have confided in you.'

'No. We did not discuss anything like that. Certainly he works for King Charles, but in what capacity I can't say.'

'That is a pity. I was hoping to claim that he was simply living his own quiet life and longed more than anything to get back to his home and his wife and children, which would be worth more to him than all the kings in Christendom.'

Jud grinned. 'You may try it if you will. It is certainly worth the chance. Have you written to Tom about it?'

'Not yet. I wished to establish first whether there might be some sort of chance.'

'And you have?'

'I think so. I won't be more precise at present. But you don't think Tom is a spy or a potential assassin?'

'God, no! He's too straight for that.'

'Good. Then I'll pursue my enquiries further.'

Looking back, later, on this particular period of time, Will was to curse himself for his lack of foresight. He, above all people, was well placed to be able to predict the events which in the early part of the next year were to have such a decisive effect on the fortunes of the family with which he had become so inextricably involved.

Firstly, in January, exactly five lunar months after he had called it, Cromwell dismissed the Parliament which might have been willed to him by the sardonic ghost of the king he had killed. Rather than be content to pull together under the paternal authority of the Protector, it had shown an increasing unhealthy interest in its own prerogative and self-perpetuation and a nasty tendency towards financial blackmail. There was far too much discussion of the relationship between the House and the Protector. Open criticism is not good for a regime which is still building its power. Oliver therefore removed the public platform from under his most vociferous critics and reluctantly, for he would have preferred their cooperation, took up the reins of personal government once again.

Will was rather dashed by this outcome. He had hoped great

things of the Parliament and had begun to make quite a name for himself in matters of shipping and trade. Now he looked restively after the West Indian expedition and toyed with the idea of trying to catch it up.

Before he could translate the notion into action, however, his attention was caught by the unrest that followed the dismissal of the House. In February one of Secretary Thurloe's agents arrested the Leveller leader John Wildman in the very act of dictating a pamphlet reviling the Protector.

As Wildman wielded considerable influence among the army, the incident alarmed Oliver, and Thurloe became busier than ever.

Even more alarming was what happened in March, when there was a Royalist rising in the West Country, a pitiful affair, ill-organized and easily put down. But it was a sign of the times, and as Will was to learn from an unimpeachable source, a sign of rather larger things than its poor showing suggested.

It was now some six months or more since Will had begun to make tentative enquiries on Tom Heron's behalf. He had received some encouragement right away. Oliver had been in a forgiving mood. He had given him a note for John Thurloe and Will had been extensively interviewed upon Tom's character and activities during the wars. It was Thurloe's opinion that there might be a case for a pardon, simply as the munificent gift of the Protector, if it could be established that Tom was not now engaged in nefarious commerce for 'the young man', as Cromwell called Charles Stewart, and would give his word never so to engage should he be permitted to return.

Will had written to Tom of his hopes and the conditions thereof. Tom had not yet replied, which was typical of his usual slowness to react, or to know that he should react, to any situation he had not thought of himself.

When Will found himself summoned one day to Thurloe's office, he saw no reason not to be hopeful. He felt sure that the man's network would have completed its investigation by now.

John Thurloe was the Protector's protector. Originally in the service of Oliver St John, he had been close to Cromwell since his entry into politics, and had been Secretary to the Council of State under the Rump and Barebones' Parliaments. His loyalty to his master was as intense as his mind was clear and farseeking.

He was a thin man with a look of ascetic concentration. He welcomed Will from behind an immense desk upon which papers were arranged in obvious order of urgency. He wasted no time.

He did not have enough of it. 'My dear Staunton, it seems we have reason to be grateful to you.'

'I was rather hoping it might be the other way round,' Will said, looking for clues in the fine-boned face and finding none.

'Ah, I am afraid not. I will not pretend that I am not disappointed, on our own behalf as well as yours. It is pleasant sometimes for this office to uncover the rosy face of innocence in place of the black countenance of deceit.'

'And Tom Heron?'

'Is not innocent.'

'I see. I am very sorry. Might I know—?'

'How he is guilty? Certainly. He has been discovered by one of our agents in Paris, a most industrious and thorough gentleman, to be a member of that so-called secret society known as the "Sealed Knot". It is a network of Royalist sympathizers both in England and in Europe whose sole aim is the restoration of the man they regard as the King.'

'Oh, secret societies – every cavalier I know has tinkered with them at one time or another – and most let them drop, if they are sensible. I can't see Tom Heron—'

'If I might finish. I agree that, for the most part, these societies are mere child's play, and do more to keep their member *out* of mischief than to cause it, but the Sealed Knot has been rather more adventurous. It will perhaps surprise you to know that the late rising in the West, under the incompetent Penruddock, was only the mistimed offshoot of a much larger plan, very sensibly postponed after our scooping up of the Leveller fraternity. The rebellion was planned to take place in six different areas, locally organized to come under the command of Lord Rochester who would land from France to take control. Our speedy despatch of the Leveller conspiracies persuaded our friends that this was not the time. This news, however, did not, apparently, reach poor Colonel Penruddock. He died bravely, I am told, but quite unnecessarily.'

Will was surprised. He had known of the feeling coming back into the cavaliers, in the wake of Cromwell's Parliamentary problems, but he had not gauged it to be so strong. About Tom's activities, he was not so surprised. He had not, on the whole, expected to find him a member of quite so large-scale an operation, but he supposed that, at bottom he had known Tom would never give up. There were probably a million like him by now. But it had been worth a try.

He returned Thurloe's regretful gaze with a shake of his head.

'I am very sorry to have troubled you over this,' he said quietly. 'It appears I have mistaken my man.'

'A human failing,' said Thurloe briskly. 'But you must see that there can be no question of a return to England. If Sir Thomas Heron were to fall within our English sphere of influence we should find ourselves very delicately placed, very delicately indeed.'

Will understood him perfectly. 'That is unlikely to happen now,' he said ruefully.

'There is one more thing—' The secretary gave a dry little cough.

'Yes?'

'You will be aware of the measures that the Lord Protector has had to take after these plots and rebellions – not to mention the unfortunate occurrence of the assassination attempt—?'

'The major-generals? Not his most popular move.'

'Perhaps not, but you will agree, a wise one in the circumstances.'

Will shrugged. He was not at all sure that he did agree. In placing the country under the rule of eleven major-generals, whose power extended not only over their own troops and all local militia but over the day-to-day workings of local government as well, Cromwell had proclaimed martial law. He had acknowledged the source of his power in the most obvious possible way. It was what the land had once feared from Strafford, and many of them remembered this.

'I refer in particular to the decimation tax.' Thurloe repeated his dry little scourge of a cough.

'Ah.' Will guessed what was coming. Unable to raise money for his government by the vote of his intractable Parliament, Oliver had, after its dismissal, set about getting it elsewhere. There were confiscations of cavalier property and other civil penalties, among them the levy of one-tenth, the 'decimation' of their income, which would help to defray the cost of his new military rule.

'I know that Sir Thomas's Gloucestershire family have been quiet enough in their behaviour of late – there have been one or two anomalies, but we need not go into that—' The twins, Will supposed, had been up to their old tricks. 'So you may think it a little hard, but it has been decided that Heron must pay its dues.'

Will sighed. 'I suppose you must punish its master, though his misdeeds take place beyond the sea. As for his family, I daresay they'll weather it well enough. They've known worse.'

'I repeat, I regret the necessity. It was not my decision.'

'Of course. I quite understand. And I offer you my best thanks for all that you have done. I am only sorry that my efforts would seem to have done more damage than good to Sir Thomas's fortunes.'

Thurloe spread out his hands. 'It is not so rare an occurrence as you might think,' he said. 'It is surprising, when one begins to monitor the pattern of one man's behaviour, into how many other, often quite disparate lives, one is led; some of them extraordinarily unexpected.'

'I can well believe it,' said Will politely. It was obvious that the efficiency of his web gave this industrious little spider the utmost satisfaction.

He left shortly after that, his hopeful mood turned cautious. He walked home, as he often liked to do, mentally preparing his next letter to Tom.

Behind him, John Thurloe consulted the file marked with the code-mark meaning 'Heron'. It was in several sections. He wrote a few sentences in the one which pertained to 'Heron, Major Sir Thomas, Bart'. Then he took up another division, reread it carefully and added a query at the end. To the file marked 'Staunton William Rich', which was slender but well-thumbed, he gave an affectionate pat.

Heron, Summer 1655

Nehemiah Owerby had been a sick man. After he had lost Martha once again he had suffered most horribly. His whole being, physical and spiritual, had seemed to collapse in on itself in a terrifying crisis that he had endured alone, with only the most basic help from servants who were strange to him. When he had been forced to flee London he had gone to The Hague, expecting he would be able to pick up Tom Heron's trail there. He knew enough of his movements by then to be sure he would go either there or straight to Paris. John Thurloe's agents were most accommodating when he wanted information.

But he had lost Tom when the sickness came upon him. He had

lost himself. For months he lay, neither conscious nor otherwise, upon a narrow bed in some undistinguished lodging, and thought, when he was capable of thought, that he had also lost God. He was in hell.

Then, gradually, as the bodily part of his affliction lessened, he came to realize that God had not abandoned him. It was only that he was once more being put to the test. To those whom God loved most dearly He sent the most arduous trials.

There came a day when Nehemiah came out of the darkness and knew himself still to be one of the elect, his immortal soul and its salvation triumphantly intact. He felt very weak, and rather light in the head, but that did not trouble him; in fact it was quite pleasant.

He began to smile at his Dutch servants, who had looked after him faithfully throughout his raving and vomiting, and to make plans again. With the help of Colonel John Bampfylde, Thurloe's most trusted Paris agent, he would soon find Tom Heron again. He knew he must kill him before the Lord would let him have Martha.

That was where he had been wrong before. He should have attended to Tom first. Because he had not done so, the Lord had chastised him by taking her away from him, and by allowing him to suffer the cruel illness. This time, all would go well. He was very slow and careful in Paris. He knew that he had all the time he needed and he used it generously to establish an intricate picture of Heron's daily life.

It would not be easy to assassinate a member of the false King's court. Tom stayed very close to his master in St Germain. He was rarely alone, always attended by servants in the daytime, and he never went out alone at night. The figure of the young King made a cynosure for the eyes of murder, so that it was constantly in the minds of his followers, for themselves as well as for him. Tom kept himself well guarded.

But Nehemiah had patience. He had the certainty of success within him like grace. He took his time. He planned. He followed.

And then, unbelievably, he lost Tom. One day he was there, tracing his slightly irregular pattern of movements between the court and a rather seamy part of the city where the lesser sort of spies wove their complex existence. The next day he was not.

Two days before Will Staunton's discouraging information was placed in reliable hands on the quayside at Calais, Tom Heron was tossing among sturdily playful waves on his way to a certain little-frequented cove in Devon, aboard the merchant vessel in which he had sailed before. He might have been seasick had he not felt so cheerful. He was conscious of unusually impulsive behaviour and it made him feel unusually carefree. It was not that he set much store in Will's hope of a pardon; he was too realistic to think his present way of life unknown to Cromwell's agents. But he did think he had managed to give them the slip. He did not have many secrets; it was not worth the trouble when one was followed everywhere one went, but he was pretty certain that no one had yet discovered his relations with Captain Pascoe. Tom, when he chose, was a master of disguise, and the scrofulous, quarrelsome and noisomely drunken sailor who had been dragged aboard the *Pretty Priscilla* by courtesy of a blow on the head from the mate's truncheon, was unlikely to have stirred a connection, in even the most suspicious mind, with the curled and perfumed cavalier who had gone upstairs with Mistress Nelly of the Green Dragon and might not be expected down again until dawn.

He was not going home because he would be safe in England; he was going in spite of his lack of safety, on a pure inspiration, simply because he wanted to see his wife, his house and lands, and his family, especially the new daughter upon whom he had never laid eyes. Now that he had determined to do it, *was* doing it, by God – he could not understand why he had not done it long before this.

When he reached the shore, in a longboat with its rowlocks well muffled, moving across black waters under a black cliff hanging beneath a near-black, starless, moon-dark sky, he was no longer a jug-hugging tar, but a travelling preacher of the Calvinist persuasion, one of the saints like Cromwell himself, with a Bible beneath his belt and fire and brimstone in his eyes. His story, should anyone be so forward as to require it of him, was that he had been travelling in Holland and Germany, deepening his faith, and had come home to deliver the benefits he had derived to his fellow men. Should anyone demand a sermon, he was capable of delivering it, though he fervently hoped this would not be the case. He journeyed as fast as he could and hoped that his plain, humble figure would excite no interest.

He did well enough, at any rate, to provoke a groan of distaste as he trotted, on the execrable hack he had acquired at a posting inn, up his own carriageway at Heron. 'Lord save us, here be one of them God-bothering sermonizers, or my name's not Margery

727

Wormit,' said that dame, astounding her first employer, who had forgotten that it was.

Mary Heron peered through the newly clean glass of the oriel. She was supervising the shining of the house for summer, an annual occasion full of dust and polish and complaints of aching backs and stiff fingers. 'Give him a crust in the kitchen and send him on his way,' she said, disparagingly. 'You would think someone in the village would have told him he would waste his time here.'

'Not if they thought they'd be rid of 'im the sooner,' chuckled wise Margery, quite agreeable to dropping her window cloth.

'No! Do not trouble!' Mary cried then, in quite another tone. She shook off her mob-cap and ran from the room like a girl. The black-clad visitor with the severe white bands had just got down from his horse. If you are a woman who has raised a houseful of men you know exactly how each one gets off a horse. In Tom's case it had been with a slight stiffness ever since Marston Moor.

When he had unfastened his meagre saddlebags and turned around, his mother was halfway down the steps to meet him. 'My dear boy! This is nothing short of a miracle!' Their embrace was hard and strong.

'Oh Mother! And I thought it was such a superb disguise. I needn't have bothered with all this extra hair, not to mention the pesky flax stuffed in my cheeks. I am most disheartened.'

'Don't be,' she laughed. 'It is very good, I assure you. And if you intend to stay for any length of time, perhaps you had best stay this way.'

Tom's ears pricked up. 'Oh? Why, what's the matter?'

'Just that we have a regular visit from the Major-General; a certain Captain Ashe, who comes to relieve us of a tenth of our income. It is quite like old times.'

Tom ground his teeth. 'I had heard of the levy. Like old times indeed. Old times under King Charles.' He grinned, cheering. 'Poor Oliver, how he must hate the comparison!' Then his face changed. He took Mary's hands and said urgently, 'Mother, where is Martha?'

'I think you will find her in the still-room. She has invented a new recipe for raspberry cordial—' She was talking to thin air.

When Tom first saw his wife he thought he could have been in Holland still, looking at one of those pictures of their ordinary lives that they liked to have, composed of stillness and light and peace that takes the breath. Martha stood, in a honey-coloured dress, upon cool grey flags, the light from a small square window

728

falling upon her hair, her face and the lucid glass jug she held up to it, to see the ruby beauty of the liquid in it. The foolishness of their being apart stabbed behind his eyes. He was not aware of making any sound, but she turned and saw him, the jug shaking in her hand.

Then she set it carefully down and came into his arms. 'Oh my beloved. I have not even dared to pray for this.' She placed a cool hand at each side of his face and kissed him with her sweet remembered gravity. 'I am very sure you should not have come, but so very glad that you did. You must not leave me again. I am a poor thing without you.'

'And I without you. And such a fool to remain so.' They kissed like very young lovers, with the desperation that hears time at its heels for no reason.

After a while he asked her to show him the child. Martha did not pale, or redden, or betray in any manner the sudden curdling of all her joy. She smiled and took his hand and led him to the room where Caroline lay sleeping. He knew her too well, and cared for her now, too deeply, not to be aware of what she was feeling then. He had often wondered how he himself would react when this moment came. Now he realized that it did not matter. He cared only how she must feel. He had never loved her as much.

He bent over the fair, bright head of the sleeping baby and turned her cheek towards him with a gentle finger. Caroline's eyes flickered revealing a shaft of clear grey, then she turned over and burrowed into her pillow, putting her thumb in her mouth. Martha leaned to take it out, her face hidden in her hair.

'She is a joy,' said Tom deliberately. 'You have given me the loveliest daughter in England.' He felt as light as air. He did not know how it was that now he was able to think kindly of a child perhaps conceived out of wedlock, to understand that the welfare of that child was a matter of no small importance in the world, and that the fabric of a true marriage must be strong enough to withstand the strain imposed upon it by the birth of such a child. He was even surprised at himself.

Perhaps the vision of working happiness that was Jud's unconventional home had something to do with it. He had no idea. What he did know was that he would never be sure, and that probably Martha herself did not know, whether he or Nehemiah was Caroline's father, and that it did not matter a jot. He made a pact with himself, there and then, as he stroked the fine, silken head, that he would never ask the question, either of her or of himself. The loveliest daughter in England, that was what Caroline was going to be for him.

He said nothing of this to Martha, but she sensed it as easily as if he had spoken. Her happiness flooded back and she seemed to exude as much of a glow as her jewel-coloured cordial had done. 'I never thought that God would be so good to me,' she confided in Lucy with that humility that always put her listener a little on edge.

'You must get used to expecting an average amount of contentment in your life. You brought yourself up badly; to expect nothing, or worse. Now you see that this is not what was intended for you.'

Lucy, happy for Martha as she was, did not herself expect to reap any particular benefit from it, apart from the satisfaction of knowing that Caroline's future was assured and that Tom was becoming more human every day. She was quite taken aback, therefore, when her brother sought her out one day, after he had been home for more than a week, and told her that he thought he owed her an apology. 'Great Heavens, what for?' Could this be Tom?

'I have treated you abominably with regard to Nieve. I should like you to think better of me in the future.'

'Oh! I can think of nothing to say. Except that I thank you.' She was embarrassed. She wished she knew what had happened to bring about this startling speech. Had Martha been foolish and told him more than she should?

'We have made our peace, then?' asked Tom, who liked ends to be tied when possible.

'Yes, of course. Though I am so used to your being stern and unyielding that I may not easily attune to *too* much peace.'

He gave a funny, efficient little nod and hurried off, in obvious relief to have got the interview over. Lucy laughed over him when he had gone, but it was the laughter of release. She had hated his disapproval.

But if Lucy was content simply to dismiss past quarrels from her mind, Tom was resolved, if he could, to do more. He took up the subject of his sister with Mary. 'She looks well, but I can see she is not happy. Has there been no word from Will, in all this time?'

'Not the kind of word you mean. He writes, each month, to report on Robert. The boy writes too. It is clear that he misses his mother, though he has everything he could wish for in London.'

'He has not been home since Will took him?'

'No. Lucy wanted him to come for Christmas, but Will thought it would unsettle him, so soon after leaving.'

'Poor Lucy. I am sorry for it, all of it. I would dearly like to see him return to her. In fact I believe I will try to engage him about it—'

'Do not, if you value his friendship,' Mary interrupted crisply. 'He will not brook interference. I myself have made the attempt, in writing. The epistle I received in return would have seared your eyeballs. Even his own mother has no influence in this matter. It seems there is nothing we who love them may do except watch them suffer.'

'You think that Will suffers?'

'Regina assures me that he does. He won't show it, of course, or thinks that he does not. He is grindingly busy, keeps an old mistress and a new one, and has the social life of an established *roué*, she says.'

'Sounds as though the poor fellow requires rescuing.'

'Perhaps. But I should advise you to leave well alone.'

It was shortly after this that Will's second letter to Tom caught up with him. He sent a copy of it within one of his factual budgets to Lucy about Robert. 'Send this to Tom, if you can. I have sent it once already, but am not answered.' He had added a resumé of its contents.

'We must leave soon, then,' Tom told Martha. 'They will know I have left France. They are bound to look for me here before long.'

Martha looked grave. 'We are ready, Caroline and I.' She hesitated. She did not want to ask: 'And young Thomas? Is he to go with us?'

Tom shook his head. 'His place is here. If anything should happen to us—'

'Yes. I see. Then – in that case, just a little longer, Tom? It is so quiet here, and Captain Ashe suspects nothing. Let us stay just a little longer.'

He could refuse her nothing, though his instincts were all against it. Not that he was averse to spending a longer time with his son. He had just begun to know young Thomas. He found him a child he could understand for he saw in him many of his own characteristics. He was more hesitant, felt his way more carefully than the ebullient Robert, though he exhibited greater sureness now that the mischievous influence had departed. He did not laugh as much as the other children, although he sometimes smiled at more adult jokes than they could comprehend. Nieve could always make him laugh. He was excessively fond of her and was her champion whenever she needed one.

Often he was to be found puzzling his way through some book in the library that was far too difficult for him. 'It is no fun if it is easy,' was his reply when Tom taxed him on this. Tom sighed and ruffled the boy's dark hair. He hoped that he had not passed on too much of his saturnine disposition. Martha, too, had never been disposed to take life easily. But surely, with what they had learned between them, they would be able to smooth the path for young Thomas?

Meanwhile he occupied himself in making a friend of his son. He succeeded so well in this aim that he began to dread the day when he must explain to Thomas that he and his mother and sister must leave him and go to France.

When the time came he was astonished at the boy's reaction. 'That's all right. Everyone's father goes away – except John Coachman, who only goes for a day or two. When I am older, will you send for me, as Silken Will did for Robert?'

'Perhaps. Or we may come back. Who knows? A lot of things can happen in the next few years.' How did he explain to a child that Oliver Cromwell could not live for ever, that his popularity was waning with a speed that made it unlikely it would wax again, that the succession to power was a mystery not yet unfolded, but that there was a young King waiting in France who had a right to take England for his own, and would do so whenever he was given the faintest possible chance?

'Can I go to London, while you are away, and stay with Robert and Ned?' Young Thomas worked on a shorter time scale.

'I don't see why not. I'll see if it can be arranged.'

Ned. So Robert wrote of Ned, did he? Yes. Indeed. Well, it was time something was done about Ned. When the crowd of young ruffians that seemed permanently to infest the gardens made off with Thomas, he went in search of his mother. He hoped he would not give her too much of a shock.

'Edmund? Oh, I know all about Edmund,' Mary said, her attention hardly straying from the roses she was beheading and trying to train up the chapel wall. 'Lucy told me about him, let me see – oh, a long time ago. She said I may as well have the full story of all my children's children, as far as she knew it.'

Tom sat down on the low wall that bordered the chapel walk. The wind was knocked out of his well-intentioned sails. He was annoyed at first. Then he relaxed, realizing that it was all to the good. 'Didn't you mind?' he enquired, curious.

'Mind? No. I didn't – well a little at first, perhaps, but Cleo does sound such a sensible girl that I decided Jud was very well off – and knows it, by all accounts.' She put down her pruning shears and looked at her son with exasperated affection. 'Poor Tom. Did you want to surprise me? Surely you have learned by now that the world doesn't wait for you to come back and run it? I am hoping to see Jud and his little family here one day soon,' she said serenely. 'I have asked him to come, commanded him almost; but he always writes that he is so dreadfully busy, and Cleo won't come without him. Apparently she is afraid of what sort of an old dragon she is going to meet. I do wish you would persuade her, if you have any influence, that I am quite a harmless individual and have no desire to breathe fire over her. I have written as much, but perhaps I did not strike the right note.'

'I will do what I can,' Tom promised.

Good, that has given him another little task to take care of, Mary thought. He seemed to wish to go round putting the world to rights these days. If only he could like gardening! Tom, having promised, realized that it was unlikely he would see either Jud or Cleo, or even the twins, who were in London at this very moment, for some time. When he and Martha left England, they must go again by the back door.

It was hard to leave. They kept putting it off. He knew they should not. They had been much blessed. If they should be too greedy for blessings, they would be withdrawn.

London, 1656

Jud and Robin were eating, drinking and arguing. There was nothing new in this except the occasion for it, which was that Jud had just published the first edition of the *Intelligencer* in which he had been openly critical of the Protector; Rob had read it and had come round to congratulate his sparring partner upon his sudden access to good sense. He had also brought their lunch, which Cleo had packed with the hope of keeping them out of the tavern. There was cold fowl, sausage and honey cake, with a bottle of her mother's French sailor's wine.

Jud's criticism had been aimed at the new confiscations imposed on Royalists, the notorious 'decimation' among them. There had already been enough punishment. These new taxes were outrageously unfair.

What Rob was trying to make him see was that *all* taxation was not only unfair, but illegal, under the present system. 'There can be no taxation without consent of Parliament!' he cried again and again. Jud tried earnestly to make out a case for Cromwell. He would dearly love to call another Parliament, but how could he? All he would get would be another Houseful of argument and schism. First kill the argument; the major-generals were making an excellent job of that; *then*, when the noise had died down, call a new Parliament.

'The people will not follow Oliver while he holds a gun to their necks!'

'Oliver cannot listen to the people while they raise one idiotic plot after another!'

'Oh Christ! Have another drink!'

'Right! Now listen – you remember Lord Justice Rolle?'

'Would you ever let me forget?' The lord justice had refused to prosecute the case of a man accused of refusing to pay his customs dues, denying the legality of the present constitution. He had resigned over it. 'Would you ever admit that he, above anyone, must know the right of the law—'

'A King may levy such duties when he will, so why not—'

'Aaargh! Now we have it! You'd crown the bastard!'

'Oh for God's sake – well, Endymion, what is it?'

The boy had slipped in unheard. He looked disturbed. 'There are some men at the door—'

'What men?'

'They say they are to do with the Council of State.' Endymion visibly trembled. He did not like the law.

'Chickens come home to roost, eh?' grinned Rob, who did not like them either, but had learned to keep a place for them in his busy little life.

'Tosh! Someone wants something printing, that's all. Show the gentlemen in, 'Dymion.'

The gentlemen had not waited to be shown. There were four of them, two soberly dressed and official-looking and two bruisers.

'You are George Heron.' Jud caught their mood at once.

'Is that a question or an accusation?'

734

They ignored him. 'And you are Robin Whittaker.'

'If it's me you want I should inform you that these are not my premises.'

One of the dark-clad men sighed. 'We know that, sir. Now, Mr Heron, if you do not object, we intend to search these offices.'

'And if I do mind?'

'We shall search them anyway.' He thumbed at the two Goliaths behind him.

'I thought so. You had better go ahead. Might I first ask on whose authority you do this?' He heard Rob snigger.

'On the authority of the Lord Oliver Cromwell, Lord Protector of England,' the man intoned with deep boredom.

The search was quick, efficient and surprisingly tidy. Within half an hour the senior of the two officials was seated behind Jud's desk with a sheaf of printed paper in front of him. 'If you would just look at each one of these and tell me whether they are your work.' The man frowned. 'I might add that we know they are. This is a formality.'

'Of course. Let us be formal, by all means.'

'First, the edition of the *London Intelligencer* for 15 June 1655.' This was the number that contained the article of which Jud and Robin had been speaking.

'You see? Chickens,' offered Rob smugly. 'Oliver may be many things, but you cannot call him a grateful man. One single iota of critical matter in all that inky-minded miasma of afflated respect, and this is what you get!'

'Oh be quiet, will you! What else?' Jud demanded tersely of the man at his desk. To his horror he saw the pamphlet he had printed, two years ago, before Lilburne's last trial.

'Is this your work?'

'Yes, but—'

Robin said quickly, 'In fact it is mine. I merely borrowed the use of the press.'

'But you knew what was in it?' the man said to Jud.

'I did, yes.'

Sober-sides shuffled his papers. 'And what about this?'

'What is it? I don't think I recognize it.'

'Please examine it if you wish.'

He did so. It was a copy of John Wildman's army petition. 'This is not mine.'

'Then why is it here?'

'I have no idea.'

'I see.' The man tapped on the desk with a clean fingernail.

Robin felt the pricking of dilemma horns. The pamphlet was his, but there was no evidence of it at his own shop, he knew. He did *not* know how the devil it got here. He decided to keep quiet, for the moment.

'Perhaps you would care to glance through the rest of these.' The official handed Jud the pile. One or two he recognized as Rob's.

'Exactly whereabouts did you find these?' he asked.

'They were all under the large cabinet, through yonder.' The cabinet did hold old stock, for the most part, but never any of these.

'I see. Then I suggest that whichever of you "found" them also concealed them there. Not one of them is mine. I am prepared to swear to that.'

The world-weary crow behind his desk heaved a deep sigh of ennui. 'Those are not the methods of this office, sir. We have never found them necessary.' He held out his hand and Jud angrily slapped the papers back into it.

'Thank you, sir.' The man rose and put on an even more official expression. 'I'm afraid I must ask both of you gentlemen to accompany me. There will be further questions. Mr Thurloe himself has an interest, I believe.'

Jud bit his lip. He could see no obvious way out. Of course it was a mistake, and would all be cleared up soon enough. Or so he hoped. He turned to Rob and made a single appeal. 'You did not leave these here, did you, and simply forget them?'

Rob shook his head. 'I never forget such things. No.'

Jud believed him. It was a matter of common policy that all such remnants would be burned immediately after their publication.

There was, it occurred to him, one other possibility. 'Endymion!' he called sharply.

The boy appeared, dragging his feet. 'I assume you have been listening at the door. These pamphlets; do you know anything about them?' Endymion shook his tousled curls. He seemed curiously interested in the floor.

'Look at me when you speak.' Jud heard a sniff. Endymion raised his head and reluctantly met his eye. 'Oh my God, so that's it, is it? But what on earth were you doing with them? They can be of no use to you.'

The boy stabbed at a tear on his cheek. 'I used to sell them, Mr Jud, sir; you can still get some sort of a price for most of 'em; not much, but—'

'But worth selling my reputation for? You ungrateful, mercenary, thieving little gallows-bait! I'll have your tripes for this, believe me!'

'If I don't get to you first,' said his brother venomously.

'This is all very touching, gentlemen – but the offensive articles *were* printed; and you two *do* seem to enjoy a particularly close relationship, both business and personal. So, if you would be so good as to follow me?'

'In just one moment,' said Jud murderously. He took one step across the room, seized the quivering Endymion by the front of his inky shirt and cudgelled his skull as if it were a moor's head at a fair. 'That is just an advance on your future reward,' he promised the miserable youth resonantly.

There had been a time, reflected Will Staunton grimly, seated in his carriage on his way to John Thurloe's office, quite a recent time, when England had been content. She had scarcely noticed it, as is the way when one is content. But now there was a new feeling prevalent, which was that times were bad and getting worse. As far as his personal life was concerned, Will shared this feeling. It was as arid as the sands of Jamaica where he might have been at this moment were it not for the duty he owed to his son. The Western Design expedition had miscalculated somewhat and had ended up taking that island instead of Hispaniola, but equally great things were expected of it economically. Had he been in a more reasonable frame of mind, Will might also have recalled that the expedition which he had so lovingly and enviously helped to structure had not only gone completely wide of her mark but had involved the decimation of her forces by the combined enemies of disease and near-starvation. Perhaps Will had been luckier than he knew in his position as 'boardroom admiral'.

He was not a man to be pleased by mere negative aspects, however, and try as he could, the only positive thing of worth in his life at present was Robert's evident happiness and the intelligent progress he made. Ned too; the boy was as sharp as Robert, too sharp in some ways, but that was only to be expected when you considered his heritage. The two boys spent their days learning and playing and making discoveries together, accepting everyone and everything that came their way. He looked at them with something akin to jealousy sometimes, wishing he could share their freshness.

His own days rolled and rattled on like this damnable coach, along the same well-travelled ruts. There was no House to sit in, of course, but he still had his work at the Admiralty, monitoring the various activities and needs of England's ships. At home there was usually Eliza. He had tried to make the break with her a short time ago, by the blunt method of introducing a young and very attractive lady named Maria Hawthorne to the house. He had met her one night at a play at the Red Bull Theatre which continued to give delightful illicit performances, despite the habit of the military of marching in and onto the stage to arrest all the actors. Maria was the daughter of a country squire, come up to town to lose her virtue and find a husband. When Will encountered her she had done the first but not the second. She was plump, easy-going and much inclined to laughter. Will enjoyed her and her company. Eliza, understandably, did not. However, she was more than equal to the situation. She dashed off a letter to Miss Maria's father, telling him where and in what state of physical grace he could find his daughter, and sat back to attend the result. It was swift and, for poor Maria, painful. Even Will was made to feel a certain amount of discomfort; it was scarcely dignified to be confronted by an angry father at his age and station. He was furious with Eliza. He was not seeing her at present.

To tell the truth, he brooded as they bounded through St James', there was not a woman on earth he ever wanted to see again except Lucy. He had known that for a long time now. He knew it before he had last seen her. He had intended to let *her* know it too, on that occasion, until she had turned his hopes to ashes with the name of Cathal O'Connor. He could have forgiven her the past. He had come that far towards her. But to find that she was still as bound up as ever in that fatal relationship, still unfaithful after all this time, still ready to risk all for a moonlight tryst with her lover – he could not pass over all that. He had been more deeply hurt by it than he would ever have thought possible. He had sat there in the sunlit field and known how much he loved her, and longed to tell her so again at last, and then she'd done him this great hurt all over again.

He had not recovered. He would not recover. He only wished her blasted relatives would leave him alone. Lady Heron had written him a most unnecessary letter, and lately there had been a queer, hinting epistle from Tom, full of the joys of perfect marriage. Well, for himself, there could be no such thing, he thought savagely.

The carriage had stopped. He had arrived. He wondered what the hell Thurloe wanted with him this time. It had better be important; he had work of his own to attend to. He jumped down from the coach without waiting for his driver to let down the steps. He nodded at the soldier who guarded the door and followed another towards the sanctum of the man who, they said, was closer to Cromwell than any other, on the grounds of necessity as much as of friendship.

As he entered the dark-panelled room he was met by the same burning gaze from behind the same spacious table, crowded, no doubt, with different papers. 'Master Will. Do me the honour to sit down.' The soldier placed a comfortable chair for Will and departed.

'You will forgive me for not coming to you. Time presses in this office in a manner you would scarcely credit. It has seemed to me lately that you might be of inestimable assistance to us, if you would be so kind as to consider the answers to a few questions I might put to you.'

'On the subject of Tom Heron?'

'Partly, perhaps. Not altogether. Those investigations most certainly have to do with it; but my interest now is a little wider than Sir Thomas's affairs.'

'Indeed? Then how can I serve you?'

'Not myself. The Lord Protector. Perhaps the nation.'

'You amaze me.'

'Firstly let me give you my personal assurance that nothing you say will go beyond these walls.' Will raised his brows.

'The matter is a delicate one for you. I would not wish to make it more so.' He delivered his small, dry cough. 'And I need hardly say that there is no question whatsoever of our entertaining any suspicions regarding yourself, none whatsoever.'

'I should imagine not,' said Will, startled.

'Very well, then. If you will bear with me. You may not see much sense in my queries at the beginning, but you will soon catch my drift, I am sure.'

'Fire away.'

Thurloe coughed again to make himself comfortable, and fired. 'Perhaps you would tell me what you know of a gentleman named Cathal O'Connor. He *is* known to you, is he not?'

This was a salvo that caught Will broad amidships. 'Yes, I – he was an old friend of my wife's family. His parents, I think, had connections with her mother, Lady Heron.' What in God's name was this about?

'Did you know that Mr O'Connor was in London towards the end of the Irish Rebellion?'

'I did.'

'You were out of the country yourself at the time?'

'I was.'

'Did you know that Mr O'Connor had visited your wife upon numerous occasions at that time?'

Do *you* know that you are visiting a kind of refined torture on a man whose old wounds will not close? 'I learned of that on my return, yes.'

'Were you also aware that Mr O'Connor has paid a more recent visit to your wife, at Heronscourt House where she now resides, if I am not mistaken. This visit would be, let's see, somewhat over a year ago.'

'I was aware of it, yes.'

'Thank you. You will also know, doubtless, that Mr O'Connor's host, while he was in London, was your good-brother, Mr George Heron?'

'I knew that, yes.' At least they had got away from Lucy.

'And did you know that Sir Thomas Heron also stayed with his brother, let me see, about two years ago?'

No one was supposed to have known of that. 'I was at sea at the time.'

Thurloe seemed to accept that for an answer. He scoured his throat, more quickly than usual, and continued, 'You know, of course, that Sir Thomas is a member of the Sealed Knot. What you may not know is that Cathal O'Connor is also a member of that organization, thanks to contacts he made at the time of his stay with George Heron.'

'I did not know. But I am not surprised.'

'Has Sir Thomas ever mentioned Mr O'Connor to you, in that particular reference?'

'Never.'

'In word or in writing? Never?'

'He has not,' said Will firmly.

'Upon what sort of terms, would you say, is Sir Thomas with his brother George?'

'Upon good terms.'

'And has this always been the case?'

'I imagine you know already that it has not.'

'But they have been on good terms since the occasion of Sir Thomas' visit, about two years ago?'

'Yes, I suppose so.' Will was beginning to lose patience. The fellow was so confoundedly labyrinthine that he had absolutely no notion what he was getting at.

'How would you describe George Heron's relations with one Robin Whittaker, a one-time apprentice of yours, I think.'

This was more obvious country. He must be careful for Jud. 'They are good friends who disagree about almost everything except that they are good friends.'

'Or so you judge it.'

'I have said so.'

'Very well. Now listen to me carefully, Master Will, and tell me, when I have done, how my words strike you.' A brief cough was purely introductory. 'It seems to me that, in the Herons of Heronscourt, we have an interesting and most resourceful family. On the one hand we have Sir Thomas, like his father a dyed-in-the-wool cavalier, a member of the Sealed Knot, as is the family friend Mr Cathal O'Connor, as so too, perhaps, is your own lady, from whom you are separated, and who has corresponded with both Sir Thomas and with Cathal O'Connor—'

'Just what are you—'

'Please. If you will let me finish. On the one hand, as I say, we have these three. On the other we have George Heron and Robin Whittaker, a known Leveller who has already served sentences for sedition. And we have the fact that both Sir Thomas and Cathal O'Connor have lodged with George Heron at different times.' He paused, watching with a small amount of satisfaction as enlightenment spread over the bronzed, authoritative face before him.

'What you are suggesting,' said Will slowly, wondering even now if he had believed his ears, 'is that the Heron brothers and Rob Whittaker, with my wife and Cathal O'Connor thrown in for good measure, are involved in some extensive, subterranean plot in which Leveller and Royalist make common ground against the Protectorate!'

Thurloe beamed. 'You *have* caught my drift. I knew you would.'

'But that is absurd!'

'Is it? I am glad to know that it seems so to you who know them all so much better than I. But I would advise you to consider it a little more carefully before you dismiss it as absurd. The findings of this office are rarely mistaken.'

'What, then, have you found?' asked Will abruptly.

'It might interest you to know that George Heron and Robin Whittaker are at this moment under arrest and detention for publishing seditious articles.'

'Jud is! But that's nonsense. He's Cromwell's man to his bare bones and beyond! Rob – now that's a different matter.'

'Well, if this is so, the truth will no doubt reveal itself in questioning. There remains the connection with Sir Thomas and with O'Connor.'

'Are you trying to make a Leveller out of Jud, or a Royalist. You can't have it both ways. You can't have it either way, in fact. I will go into any witness box you like and swear to his good character as far as the Protectorate is concerned.'

'He has admitted to publishing a criticism of the recent new taxes on Royalists.'

'One article! In a whole career of loyalty!' He sounded passionate.

Thurloe was impressed. 'If there were any other explanation of these relationships. I would be prepared to believe that the Heron brothers might differ, *do* differ, in their loyalties; but the advent of Mr O'Connor puts a different complexion on the matter.'

'Ah. Mr O'Connor!' Will said between closed teeth. 'If that is what chiefly troubles you, I can tell you very easily where Mr O'Connor comes into the story. I am surprised that your busybodies have not worked it out for themselves, but I suppose the drawback of having one's nose constantly in manure is that one does not notice when it has changed from cowshit to pigshit! If you think it will be of any help to Jud Heron, I will tell you all about Cathal O'Connor.'

'I think it could be. If you will be so kind.' Thurloe ignored his visitor's thunderous looks and settled back to listen.

Without any colour in his voice, but with a face like the crack of doom, Will described the exact particulars of Cathal O'Connor's relationship with the Heron family. He then reiterated his knowledge of Jud and Rob in so far as they had ever worked together and the reasons why they no longer did so. He finished by signing a written testimony on Jud's behalf. After this he asked if he might leave.

'Of course, of course. It only remains for me to thank you once again, and to offer you my most—'

'Thanks are not necessary. I would not have spoken were there any other way. You will of course have your people check my statements, in so far as they are able. Kindly instruct them to keep out of *my* way. That is all. Good day to you, sir.'

'Good day, Mr Staunton,' said John Thurloe gently. But he could see that it was not. He was sorry. He liked Will.

But he had had to know. Even now, it was by no means certain that his fears were mistaken. Not certain, but on the whole he was disposed to think that Will was right. He had told the truth. That was something Thurloe could still recognize though he did not meet it often. If there were no more to it than that truth, then George Heron, at least, might go free, more or less.

Far too soon after the preceding interview for Will Staunton's nervous system, he received a troubling letter from Stanton St Paul. 'What does it say? Is my grandmother well?' asked Robert who was eating breakfast with him.

'No. I'm afraid she is not. I shall have to go up there at once. You'll be master of the house while I am gone. Don't burn it down between you, you and Ned.'

Robert ignored this elephantine wit. His father usually did better than that. 'Is Grandmother *very* ill?' he asked curiously. Old people died. He hoped she would not die. He had not thought she was quite old *enough*. And he was very fond of her.

'It seems so.' Will sighed. He felt tired suddenly. 'When sorrows come, they come not single spies,' he began ruefully to quote for his own benefit and perhaps Thurloe's.

'But in battalions,' finished Robert triumphantly. 'That comes in *Hamlet*.'

'How do you know?'

'Master Faversham read it with us, sir.' Faversham was the boys' tutor, the impoverished younger son of a cavalier who had died at Naseby. His education was excellent and his tastes, which Will considered almost equally important, matched those of his employer in most respects. He was a good speaker and a fine musician and gave cheerful company when Will desired it.

'You like Shakespeare, then, Rob?'

'Oh yes, sir. Very much, sir. Especially the fights!'

'Your grandfather Heron would have been pleased by that.'

'Is that the one who was a pirate?'

'No, but he was the one who was a hero in the wars. He used to go into battle with Shakespeare on his lips.'

'Do you have to die to be a hero?'

'No. But it is universally considered to be the swiftest way of doing it, by and large, should it be your aim.'

Robert grinned. His grin was very like Will's own, and a lot readier these days. 'I think I'd rather stay alive. Give my best love to my Grandmother, and tell her I hope she is soon well.' He left the room as he left every room, as if there were a fire behind him.

'For some people,' he said softly, 'it can be a matter of heroism simply to *be* alive.' He was feeling remarkably sorry for himself.

At Stanton the servants all wore long faces and went about on tiptoe. His mother's room was shrouded in darkness, the curtains drawn over the windows and only a single candelabra burning beside the bed. Regina lay on her pillows in an attitude of defeat. He had never before seen her like this. It frightened him as much as though he were still a child at her knee. 'My dear. What is this? You, laid low? I don't trust my eyes.'

She reached towards him. Her hand trembled. He had never noticed before how thick and knotted were its veins. 'Will? How nice. I am glad you have come too.'

Too? He wondered who else was in the house. Then he realized that there was someone else already in the room, sitting in the shadow of the curtain on the other side of the bed. A female figure, wearing dark clothes and holding herself very still. It was Lucy.

'Good day, Will.'

He was glad of the darkness then. It would cover him decently while he got himself in control. It would have been a shock to see her in any case; to do so so soon after Thurloe's little diversion was almost more than he could face. 'Lucy. Are you well?' he asked feebly.

She nodded.

'But I, alas, am not,' Regina reminded him gently. Her voice was as wasted as her looks. 'I do not know how much time God will allot to me, but I should like to make the most of it. I have very little to say, but it is important to me—'

'But what is it?' Will burst out, clutching at her hand. 'How can you be so ill, when last month, no, less, I saw you so well? What is wrong with you? Have you no doctors?'

'Oh, yes. Dozens of them, if I wish. But they can do no good. Now, if you will please listen—'

'Not until I know just what is wrong with you and who there is who knows the most about it! Is it a fever, or a wasting disease, or the cough, or an ailment of the stomach, or what is it?'

Regina sighed like a leaf falling. 'Oh dear. I can see you are going to be difficult. I told Lucy you would be. Now why cannot you sit quiet as she does and let me speak when I want to. It is not kind to make me waste what may be some of my last breath.'

'Oh Mother! You were always a dirty fighter.'

'I had to be,' she said grimly.

'Have *you* spoken to a doctor?' Will suddenly asked Lucy.

'There does not seem to be one in the house,' she said. Her voice troubled him with its low music, even now. 'They say he will return tomorrow. A doctor – Scrope, wasn't it, Regina?'

'Yes. Linus Scrope. I've known him all my life. You remember him, Will?'

'I'm not sure. I don't think so. What happened to Dr Jarvis?'

'He died, God rest him. Now Will, you must just believe that I am in good hands and—' she stopped and got her breath again with some difficulty, 'stop *fussing*. You know how I detest *fuss*. As for the disease – it is something in the heart, it is thought. A disorder of the heart. They are often fatal, I'm told.'

'Regina. My dear. Are you in much pain?'

Lucy's heart went out as much to him as to Regina herself as she saw the thought that he might lose her crease his brow in agony.

Regina moved her head. 'Not at all,' she said.

Will took her hand. 'You are as brave as ever my father was.'

'Nonsense!' she said quite strongly. She pulled herself up a little. Lucy helped her. 'Good. Now come round here, next to Will, where I can see you, child. You are like death waiting, sitting there in the shadows. That is better. You may sit on the bed. There is a chair there for you, Will. Do as you are told.'

He relinquished her hand and drew up the chair. He felt Lucy's skirt brush against him as he sat down.

'That is better. Now hear me, both of you. I have had a very happy life. It has been full of all kinds of felicity, but the greatest happiness has come from my marriage. No, Will, don't speak. I do not give either of you permission to speak. My marriage to Richard Staunton was a happy one not simply because we found each other pleasing and compatible in the early stages. Even monkeys can probably manage that! It was because we saw that we had good material with which to work and we were both determined to make a success of it. I do not pretend we had no troubles. You are both aware of at least one of them. There are others, irrelevant here. But we allowed none of them to sadden us beyond the limit from which a loving effort could pull us back; and we did not let anything lessen our respect for each other. Respect of this kind is not an empty word, taught to us by our grandmothers or a bored tutor; it implies first of all a true understanding of the other person, or an attempt to build towards such an understanding. I do not think you, Will, and perhaps not you either, Lucy, have ever begun to make that attempt. If either of you thought at all, which I sometimes doubt, you both thought that you had done something so fine by entering into this marriage, that you need do no more work on it for a month of twelvemonths. Well, you have proved yourselves wrong. Now I would like to know that you are about to try to prove *me* right. I want you to take Lucy back into your house and your bed, Will. That you love her, I am certain or I would not ask it. That she loves you, I am equally sure, for I have asked her and she swears it.' She looked towards Lucy, who bowed her head.

It seemed to all of them as if the world had stopped with the breathless, sometimes amazingly strong voice. 'You may speak now, my son,' Regina finished with a glint of humour.

Will did not know whether he was more appalled by the fact of his mother's blackmail, or the truth contained in what she had said. He felt as though she had tied him up like a hog for slaughter. He got up and stretched his arms, then went to the window and pulled back the heavy curtain, leaning into the slightly open casement and sucking in great lungfuls of air.

'Oh Regina,' whispered Lucy, crying a little. 'Should you have?'

'Why not?' asked the unrepentant invalid. 'What have I to lose? As for you – things could not well be worse than they have been between you. We shall see. Give me a drink, there's a good girl.' She drank watered wine and called Will back to the bedside. 'Have you considered what I have said?'

'I am considering it. You are using your illness to force me.'

She was angry. 'You fool. I am using my last strength to persuade you to reach for your own happiness.'

Lucy saw how he was trapped. 'I'm sorry for this,' she said. 'I did not expect it. And do not approve it,' she added gently to Regina.

'Oh, do not think I blame you. I know her of old,' he said, smiling sardonically.

Regina suddenly drooped on her pillow. 'I think – if you don't mind – I should like to sleep a little now,' she said faintly. 'Come back – at suppertime.' She appeared to fall asleep instantly.

Will and Lucy crept out of the room, neither knowing quite what they felt about anything.

'It is terrible to see her so ill,' said Lucy nervously outside in the gallery. 'She must have kept it to herself for so very long.'

'She sent for you?'

'Yes. Two days ago.'

'I must speak to that doctor,' he fretted.

'Tomorrow. He will come tomorrow.' They looked at each other. What was there to say?

Cowardice overtook him. 'I think I shall take a stroll in the gardens. We will go in again, as she wishes, at supper.'

'Very well.' Her voice was forlorn.

He saw instantly that she felt rejected. Even had she been a stranger he would have asked her to walk with him at such a time. 'Forgive me. Will you come with me? I am not quite myself. I think Regina has made me shy of you.'

She smiled. 'That is not quite what she intended.'

'No.'

He did not speak again until they were outside in the grounds, and then she was able to make it easier for him by talking of the house and the gardens. 'It has great beauty and dignity. It was built at about the same time as Heron, I should think – or at least, *most* of Heron; the earlier part.'

'Yes. But its fortunes did not go up in the world like Heron's. It was built as a fairly well-to-do manor house, and that is what it has remained.'

It was a long, low, gabled house, in a soft grey stone that was turning to rose and lavender as the sun declined. The gardens were full of misty colours, each one sinking into the next in perfect harmony. The trees, the oaks, the elms, the beech, the sycamores were all very old and stood singly, very often, as if aware of their respected state. Will gave Lucy its history as they walked in the dusk, and as she began to question him and to offer comparisons with Heron, they found that they could talk to each other again almost naturally.

It was as they moved back towards the open door that he suddenly found his mind made up and waiting for release. 'Lucy—' he stopped and called her back.

She turned. 'Yes?'

But now he was thinking no; it is too important. I must not let Regina influence me. This is not the time. 'Oh, it doesn't matter. Later,' he said. They went back into Regina's room.

She was awake again and sitting up against her pillows in a bedgown hung with icicles of white lace. 'You're back. Good. We'll have supper.'

Noiseless servants brought trays of food and wine. Regina seemed to be the only one who could eat. She examined their faces shrewdly as they picked at bits of bread and meat and Will drank quantities of wine because his stomach wanted filling with something.

'Come on. Eat up. I am not dead yet,' she observed sharply. 'I do think you might make an effort, for my sake,' They did so, though neither wanted food.

When she had finished her own meal Regina lay back and sipped at her wine, still studying them with her disconcerting gaze. 'Well, have you anything to tell me?' she suddenly rapped at Will. 'You were out in the twilight long enough to have come to some conclusion.'

Will had already prepared himself for this. 'You go too fast for me, Mother. But I shall take Lucy back to Heron after this visit. We shall go on from there.' Lucy could not prevent the hope from entering her as she looked at him, surprised.

Regina did not know whether to be satisfied. She sighed. She looked as if she were in pain. 'I wish you would promise me—' she began.

'No more tonight. You are tired. We'll talk again tomorrow.'

She stared at him. He was not going to be trapped again. She prepared for her last throw. She let her head fall back, her eyes closing and her mouth puckering as though she were going to cry. Then she pushed herself up again and smiled at them in a bright, resolved manner, the unshed tears bright in her still fine eyes. Then she shook her head. 'No.'

'No what, Regina?' Will was puzzled.

'No tomorrow. I don't want to see you again. Not either of you. I mean it, Will. I have no desire for an audience when I depart this world. My death will be entertaining to no one but myself.'

'You can't mean it. And who says that you are going to die?'

'I think one knows,' she said with heavy sarcasm, 'when one is going to die.'

'Oh Regina.' Will fell on his knees beside the bed and took her in his arms.

She had not bargained for this. She must stop this or she would lose it all. 'You are fussing,' she told Will irritably. 'I told you not to fuss.' She detached his arms and pulled her bedclothes about her shoulders instead.

'Come and kiss me, Lucy,' she ordered. Lucy did so, hugging her straight form very close. 'Now you may go.' She was obeyed.

'Will,' Regina said, fixing her son with an unsentimental eye that he would never forget, 'try not to be a bigger fool than you can help.' She allowed him to kiss her, just once, and then he too was ordered from the room.

In the morning, as she had promised, Regina refused to see either of them. Will was brought a brief note ordering him to

748

leave with Lucy at once. 'I have done things in my own fashion all my life. I will arrange its ending to suit myself. I cannot help it if you think me selfish. My love to you. Regina.'

They travelled to Heron in Lucy's coach. As they left Stanton, Will thought he caught the sound of a girl singing in one of the upper rooms. He must have been wrong, of course. They did not talk much during the journey, except when they stopped to rest, when John Coachman became voluble in his pleasure at seeing Will again. When they retrieved Heron's horses at the inn in the Worcester he entered into a long conversation about the upbringing of boys. His opinion seemed to be, in the main, that they 'wanted a lot of whip, like horses, and then they would go sweet as you like'.

'I trust you do not agree with John,' Lucy observed when they were back inside the rumbling vehicle.

'I've never had much cause,' Will confessed cheerfully. 'Robert, though as full of mischief as he is of energy, is really not a child who would respond to the whip. It would simply strengthen his inborn resistance to absolute intractability.'

'He resists, then? Yes, I suppose, by now, that is what you would call it. He used just to go off quietly and do what he wished and hang the consequences.'

'You can see where he gets it all from,' said Will darkly.

'Oh, yes,' said Lucy. She was not thinking of Regina.

They arrived at Heron to find a full house. Kit and Humpty had returned from their assault on London. Isabella, naturally, happened to be staying, and Tom and Martha had as yet been unable to tear themselves away, knowing that when they did so it would perhaps be for a very long period.

Lucy, giving swift orders to Margery to get his old chamber ready, yes *again*, listened wryly to the excess of welcome that her husband always excited in her family. When it died down a little she thought he must be telling them of Regina's illness and was saddened again herself as she pictured the slight, straight, determined woman in the bed, overruling every convention by the outrageous strength of indomitable character. She thought that Will had found her harsh; she had found her magnificent. She was lovingly grateful for what she had tried to do. The outcome, she saw now, was left up to her. Regina had got Will to Heron for her. Somehow, now, she had to get him to *her*. This time she would make no mistakes. 'You will stay awhile?' she asked him shyly.

He shrugged. 'I must. Regina told me she would send no messages to any other address.' Lucy thought he might be angry, but his eyes crinkled.

'Your childhood must have been rather a restricted one?'

'Not at all. She left me to my own devices *then*.'

It seemed to Lucy that Will spent most of his time with Tom, or with the twins, or with the children, and very little with her. Perhaps it was because she counted every minute as precious after so long without him. There was a good deal of catching up to do, she knew. A lot of the masculine talk concerned Jud. He had written that he was to serve a six-month sentence for his 'seditious' criticism of the new taxes and his 'mischievous' involvement with Robin. 'And the poor *Intelligencer* is to lose its licence, along with every other free-thinking newssheet in London. Only the lickspittle *Mercurius Politicus* and the pathetic *Public Intelligencer* are to remain, both edited under the direction of that busy man, John Thurloe, who keeps the wheels of England oiled while Oliver cracks the whip. What has sickened both Rob and me to our souls, is that it is now revealed to have been Richard Overton who was our undoing! Overton, who taught me how to print, and was my best guide along so many thorny paths; now a poxy government spy! It is no good sign for the times if such an honest man can turn his honesty in such twisted directions. And while I dwell on this subject, ask Tom, if you are in contact with him, what he knows of a certain Colonel Bampfylde, a supposed cavalier, living in Paris, I have heard his name mentioned here in the Fleet as one who may also be taking double pay.'

'Bampfylde!' Tom groaned. 'I know the name. It's an honest one, or so I thought. But I will write to Paris—'

'My son,' said Mary firmly, fixing Tom with the eye she kept for slugs and aphids, 'we shall all feel far more secure when you *go* to Paris. You let day after day go by, and you say "tomorrow". I warn you, you will leave it until the wrong day.'

'Secure!' Tom protested. 'You have more security now than you had throughout the entire war. Every man on the place has a weapon close to hand and knows how to use it.' It was true. The twins had amused themselves by raising a private army among the servants and loyal tenants, 'Just in case' as Humpty wistfully put it.

Nevertheless, the wrong day came.

Lucy had done her best to avoid picnics, not wishing Will to be reminded of things she would rather he might forget, but she had been overruled today and had to make the best of it as they all trooped out into the park to eat dinner beneath the trees. The boys took their guitars and someone brought Lucy's virginals and they settled down to make a lazy afternoon of it.

Lucy kept well in the background, careful to sit nowhere near Will. It so happened, because of this, that she was the first to see the running harvester who was coming towards the party, stumbling with haste and shouting something incomprehensible. But by the time he had reached them they could all see what it was he had been trying to tell them.

A party of horse was moving down the driveway at the trot. 'Oh Lord, it must be Captain Ashe,' said Kit, shading his eyes. 'He don't usually bring his friends, though. Perhaps the dues have gone up, and he thinks we'll need persuasion!'

'Captain Ashe wears a uniform,' remarked Julia, blushing prettily. 'None of those men do.'

'By Gad, she's right,' said Tom. 'Well, at least I don't have to race off to make myself scarce.' He looked at Julia with distaste. To the great embarrassment of the whole family, she had shown an astonishing predilection for the pleasant-faced young officer who came fortnightly to collect their taxes. What was worse, Mary had forbidden everyone to comment upon this. Until lately, Julia had given out that she intended to enter a convent when she came of age; even a Roundhead captain, in her mother's opinion, was better than that mournful possibility. Martha smiled at Julia to sweeten her husband's scowl.

'Well if it isn't Ashe, damme, who is it?' asked Humpty, standing up in order to see better. Then he breathed, 'Oh, the sweet devil! I do not, I cannot, I won't believe it! Tom. Look here!'

They saw Tom go white. He too stood up. Gradually all the men rose and looked where he looked. He moved his hand. There was a metallic clatter as they found their pistols. With his small party of riders behind him, all better dressed and far more confident than in earlier days, Nehemiah left the road and spurred across the grass to meet them.

Tom moved closer to Martha and placed his hand on her shoulder. 'Tom, I – I *can't*,' she gasped. She was in pure terror.

'Lucy, take Martha and Caroline into the house,' said Tom quietly. She nodded and picked up the child. 'Mother, Julia, will you go too? All the women.' They began to obey.

Martha hesitated, torn between her own panic at the sight of Nehemiah and a desperate concern for Tom. He gave her a little push towards Lucy, and she followed her then, not daring to look back. She expected every second to hear his horse's hooves behind her and to be swept up into that nightmare of unreason once again.

But they reached the house, where they locked themselves into Martha's bedroom. It was no use looking out of any window. They could not see the park from the house.

'Well, Nehemiah,' Tom greeted the man as he came up and reined his black horse, 'have you come to beg your punishment of me, for that is all that you will find here.'

'No,' said Nehemiah levelly. His eyes glittered as if with a high fever, but neither his hands nor his body were restless. 'I have come to take away my wife and my child.'

There was a gasp from the men about Tom. He stood frozen. When he spoke, after what seemed a long interval, it was very softly. But he sounded most dangerous. 'It is your madness that brings you here. I see that. But I do not speak to madness when I say that you are outnumbered here, and that if you seek to prevail by force, you will not succeed.'

Nehemiah looked about him speculatively. 'We are twenty. You are four men, one boy and a mess of servants. Certainly you all hold pistols, but so do we. But I have not come to do violence, only for Martha and the child.'

Tom felt as though his heart would burst with hatred. It filled him with nausea to hear him claim Caroline. He longed to put a simple bullet through his head and stop it all for ever. But he could not; not because Nehemiah did not deserve it, but because he himself was a cavalier. He could no more put a bullet through the head of a man who did not oppose him in battle than he could give up his wife and child. He saw Humpty raise his pistol to the aim. 'No! Not that way. It is my quarrel!'

'It was ours first,' grumbled his brother, lowering the weapon.

Tom wondered seriously if he was up to what he was about to suggest. He felt so damnably shaky. His limbs would not obey him. He had not felt like this since the days of his early warfare. But there was nothing else for it. They could not have a bloodbath all over the park. 'Get down from your horse, Nehemiah,' he said wearily. 'If you want to take Martha, you will have to kill me first. You know that. I wish to kill you. You know that too. There is only one possible solution that I can see. A duel. You and I will fight, to the death. Does that satisfy you?'

Nehemiah considered. He did not need to do so for long. For this was better than his wildest dreams. God had delivered the evil-doer into his hands. He wanted him to kill Tom Heron and here He gave him to His servant to be offered as a sacrifice. There would be no other bloodshed. He felt himself washed through with joy. He bowed his head in an ecstasy of thankful prayer. When he raised his head he said, 'It satisfies me.' They all wondered at the brilliance of his face. He got down from his horse.

'Will it be swords, or pistols?' asked Humpty, taking it upon himself to be Tom's second.

'Swords,' said both men. Pistols were far too chancy. You were lucky if your aim was true.

'Now?' asked Will, moving forward to stand beside Humpty. Tom nodded. Nehemiah too. 'Then, gentlemen, will you all please retire your horses and place yourselves in two lines, a good twenty yards apart.' Humpty had seen duels before.

'Someone should go in and tell them what is up,' Kit thought.

'No. They will only come running out to try and stop us,' Tom snapped. He was less of a jelly now, he felt, but he could wish he had kept up a little more practice lately. He had once been one of the best swordsmen in London or Paris, but now he knew himself to be slower and less sure. As for duels, the last one he had fought had been that ridiculous affair with Horatio Bulmer, that Valora had been so hot about. Valora. He fancied he could hear her sardonic shade now; not in reproof, but bold approval. Yes, this time, you are right; a duel should always be between the principles of good and evil – but do you think you are quite strong enough to take up the arms of the good?

Say a prayer for me; you are better placed than I, my dear, he thought. We shall soon see, shall we not?

They were waiting only for Tibbett, who was fetching his sword. 'You said nothing?' he asked nervously when the giant returned.

'I met only Margery. She will not tell.'

'Good. Then – let us begin.' He did not speak to Nehemiah again. He did not want to think of him as a man, to whom words might be addressed and be understood, but as the embodiment of evil in a shape that could be killed.

The men divided into their two lines and moved apart. As he walked into the centre he saw faces that he had known all his life. Foolish Sam Hudson and his partner, Straightways Sawyer, Nehemiah's men as they had been his father, Andrew's men, following where he led and never questioning, sharing his faith as they had shared the produce of his land. He looked at them all, all the silly, sheep-like faces that stood on Nehemiah's side, some grinning, some doubtful, some expecting pleasure as if they were at the play-cart. Were the faces on his own side equally silly and sheep-like? Probably. They were his tenants, as the others were Nehemiah's tenants now, and tenants thought what their landlords thought and always would, though smaller men were landlords now and more of them had the vote. He didn't think their faces were foolish, not hard-working Dickon Stable, or precise Ninian Ffoulkes or William Blacksmith or bluff Walter Rollins. The faces belonged to him and he loved them all. He had never known before, never stopped to discover how much he loved them. They were all encouraging him now. They had always known Nehemiah for an enemy. He had been theirs too. Well, now Tom would be their champion. Theirs and Martha's and Caroline's and Dominic's and Valora's and Heron's and the King's – and for God and for all of them, he would stand the winner!

Both men had reached the centre. Humpty and Sam Hudson measured out the paces. They could begin.

Each one put everything out of his mind save the desire to kill. They circled slowly, deciding whether they would watch the eyes or the hand, trying to judge each other's fitness and possible speed. Nehemiah exuded a superb confidence. He was glossy with it, his eyes as bright as a new colt's. And as Tom very soon discovered, he *had* been in practice.

He began with a strong lunge towards Tom's shoulder, touching it but drawing no blood. Tom parried his next strokes with a thoughtful regard for his own skin. He had always thought of Nehemiah as a stolid man, a useful fighter perhaps, but one who would not be quick to move. He was mistaken. The Puritan was as lithe as a tiger. His sword glittered in his hand and his hand was never still. Tom began to wake up. He remembered the words of his teachers; De Treille in London, Trintignant in France. He remembered his faults, his tendency to present more of his left side than was wise, and a certain slowness of the left foot. He fought with careful economy, preserving his strength, avoiding unnecessary movement. Let Nehemiah wear himself out, dancing round him like a devil round Satan's fire; he would let himself be the centre and fight outwards, parrying more than he thrust, waiting for the split second that could surely come, when Nehemiah made his first mistake.

But Nehemiah did not make any mistakes. He seemed tireless and continuously inventive as he forced his adversary to wheel and turn and guard his back and his breast and his side all, it seemed, in the same eyeblink. Tom realized that he had better cease to fight from the centre. He was like a bear baited by dogs; Nehemiah was the whole pack of them, and Tom was beginning to feel their nips.

He saw blood on his sleeve. That left shoulder again! De Treille had been right! *Eh bien*, so long as it was not the right one! His enemy's sword suddenly flashed close to his eyes. Damnation! That had been too close and now he was – devil take him, he had drawn blood from beneath his right arm! It was only a prick, but the warning was strong. Tom leaped sideways, then forward with a mighty lunge to Nehemiah's side where the sword arm was just coming up to parry him. Amazed, he found his own sword knocked downward and almost out of his hand.

Before he could bring it up again he felt the other's blade enter his chest. There was the slightest hesitation of resistant flesh, then a strange tearing that was sensation not sound, and a rush of heat to his breast. He staggered, surprised and wondering why, and fell headlong to the ground.

Nehemiah held up his sword like a cross. There was absolute silence, and then pandemonium as too many men rushed forward with a babble of admiration and advice. Tom, hearing, thought that the noise was the blood gushing from him, and then, ceasing to hear, thought no more.

'Get back out of it, you fools!' Will Staunton raised an angry voice; it was just enough to calm them. Most of them moved backward, leaving Will, Tibbett and the Heron brothers facing Nehemiah.

'It is a death wound,' said the latter with grave certainty. 'If he still lives, it will not be for long.'

Kit was bending with his ear to Tom's heart. 'Be silent!' he begged.

'Well?' asked Will when they could bear it no longer.

'He lives, but the beat is faint; not altogether regular. We must send for Dr Grace. Dickon, will you ride for him?'

The young man edged out of the crowd, tears in his eyes. Kit and Humpty both leaned close to Tom, trying to make him hear them, asking him to come back to consciousness.

Nehemiah regarded them with a casual sympathy. They seemed to have forgotten he was there. He addressed himself to Will. 'I shall not trouble this house any longer for the moment. There will be time later to finish my business here.'

The twins looked up at that. Humpty's hand flew to his pistol.

'No.' It was a weak voice but it was Tom's. 'Can't you see?' He gasped out the words, punctuated by pain. 'If you do that – makes it all pointless. Guard Martha. Leave him go.' He was silent again, his eyes closing.

Humpty stood up and came very close to Nehemiah. 'You heard what he said. Go. Go now. But do not think to escape me, or my brother Kit, as you have escaped Tom. Perhaps his was the greater grudge against you – but we have held ours since we were little more than babes, and we have not given it up for this. Go now, before we all forget that Tom wants us to be gentlemen of honour; but we'll find you, when we want you!'

Nehemiah sighed. To tell the truth he was a little confused. He knew he had won. He had known that he would. But he also knew he must not take Martha now. The Lord did not want this, or else he would have made it easily possible. He would have to come back yet again. It was all very wearisome. The ways of God were sometimes hard to understand. He had felt such a glory about him while he fought. Now it was all dissipated into the foolishness of those ignorant boys. For a moment he thought he might kill one of them too, just for the lesson, but it didn't matter. He was tired. He would leave it for now. He did not answer Humpty at all, but turned and walked to his horse, his men trailing after him.

'He seems mazed,' said Sam Hudson to Straightways.

The sawyer shook his head. 'He never did think nor speak nor do like other men. I always thought 'twas his wisdom.'

Will Staunton, gazing after Nehemiah with a look of utter incomprehension, suddenly focused on the truth. 'He is a madman,' he said. 'We should put him in Bedlam.'

Kit looked up from Tom's side. His brother lay quite still now, his breathing shallow, the bleeding spreading through the bandage they had made of his shirt. 'He'll soon be a murderer,' he said with soft viciousness. 'Then we shall put him to death.'

'Were we mad too, to let him go, do you reckon?' asked Tibbett.

'No. His men would have fought for him. Tom didn't want that, and he was right.'

'But if he dies—' Humpty began wildly.

Will looked at Tom. There did not appear, sadly, to be any question about that. It would be just a matter of time. They made a stretcher of boards and carried him into his house.

'And to think,' Kit said bemusedly to no one in particular, 'that when we were children, we used to *laugh* at Nehemiah!'

When they brought him into the house they did not need to

explain anything to Martha. She already knew. When Kit tried to form some sort of apology, she stopped him at once. 'It is something that had to happen. It was where they had both been aiming. Take him to our chamber and lay him on the bed. I will look after him myself. Send the doctor to me when he comes.'

She could see that he was dying but she would not have it. If her skills and instincts had been given to her for any purpose, it was for this. She kept everyone away from him except for Dr Grace, whom she knew and trusted.

She fed him infusions of her own making, changed his dressings, and kept him as comfortable as she could without any help. She wanted no other will to interfere in that room. She felt her own expand and take the place of the very air he breathed so reluctantly. She did not pray. Prayer had nothing to do with this. If it was God who aided her efforts He did so for his own reasons, not hers. For many days she sat behind that closed door while they all thought she was watching him die.

Tom knew that he must be dying. He felt nothing at all; no pain, no sensation of the existence of his body at all, almost no thoughts. His mind sat up in the corner of the ceiling reflecting every now and then that he was taking a very long time about this. He had done with that sloughed-off carapace on the bed. Why then, was he still here? He had a sense that there was somewhere else he should go.

It was a long time before he noticed that there was anyone in the room, other than his non-self. Once he thought it was Valora. And then there came a time when he knew it was Martha.

She did not want him to go. She would not let him go. He began to feel pain after that.

He came down from his corner. His body was not comfortable. It would not obey him in any way at all. He thought Martha must be very foolish to wish him to stay with it.

One day he tried to tell her so, but he did not get beyond her name. There was happiness in the room after that. He didn't understand it.

The pain grew stronger and with it grew the claim of his wretched body upon him. In the end he gave in to it; it was easier. They were one again, confoundedly weak and profoundly disadvantaged, but an entity; somebody; himself. Tom Heron.

And this was Martha leaning over him. Martha whom he loved. When he reached for the first time, uncertainly, to try to kiss her, she knew she had won. Now she was able to pray. Thanks are easy to say.

'Do you think Nehemiah will come back?' said Kit to Humpty who was making a swing for Isabella in one of the smaller oaks, while she stood by holding a parasol and looking extraordinarily pretty.

'I think we shouldn't wait for that. When Sturges sends his report we should go and make sure of him. This thing must finish. If he comes back, who knows what hare-brained scheme Tom and his honour will think of next? He'll probably want the devil legally hung at the assizes! We can't have that.'

'I wish you would not go after him. The man is evil. I hate to think of you in danger from him,' Isabella said, looking only at Kit.

'Good Lord, what danger?' demanded Humpty. 'There are two of us, and we are both sane.'

'Comparatively,' she supposed.

'Well then, there is no need to worry. Sturges won't lose him; he was our best tracker in the old days with the captain. I must confess I'm glad to have found a use for him.' Sturges had turned up at Heron half-starved and barely clothed, and had been eating his way to overweight ever since.

'I hope you won't be away *too* long,' Isabella said casually. 'I would not like you to miss my wedding.'

'Your what?' Humpty was knocked half into next week.

She fluttered her lashes. 'Well – I *may* not accept him – my cousin Jude you know – you may have noticed—'

'That mincing, primping frog-brain! What do you want to wed *him* for?' He couldn't believe it. He was mortally offended. Hadn't she shared *his* company, on and off, for – well a considerable long time. 'I'm disappointed in you Bella,' he said, shaking his head sadly.

'We must all learn to bear life's disappointments,' she replied primly. Then she gave them a little wave of the hand and set off across the park. Jude, she said, was coming to fetch her home.

'Well of all the ungrateful hussies!'

'Why, what have you given her, apart from hard words and the occasional kiss?'

'Well, I – what do you mean?' Humpty stood with his legs apart like an angry bull which is puzzled as to which way to charge.

'I mean, my purblind, slow-witted twin – why don't you ask for her yourself? Or do you *want* her to marry Jude Stratton and have to watch her grow big with his children and sad with his company?'

'No,' said Humpty, suddenly deadly serious. 'No, I don't believe I do. But marriage!'

'It needn't change everything in life. One can leave them at home and take one's pleasures occasionally.'

'Yes, but—'

'Well, why don't you put your mark on her,' suggested Kit. 'Give some encouragement *now*, so that she doesn't rush off and wed Jude – and then sort it out properly after we have come back from killing Nehemiah?'

That might be a very long time. Sufficient unto the day – 'That sounds like sense,' said Humpty more cheerfully. He started across the grass after Isabella.

Like Tom, Will Staunton remained at Heron far longer than would have been his intention; but since his mother had refused to send news of her progress in any other direction, his intentions were not his own. He would have stayed, anyway, on Tom's account. By now, it was clear that a miracle had occurred and that Tom would recover completely. The old story that Martha was a witch had more in it, Will thought now, than he had ever given credence.

There was no use denying, too, that he was comfortable here. He was fond of the house and of everyone in it and had always felt more welcome here than anywhere else. He was developing a new, strange relationship with Lucy. They had not yet spoken together about their marriage. Each held back, as though they dare not spoil this new chance by reaching for it too quickly. But both of them knew it was there. Though Will could not exactly thank Regina for it, he understood that she had been right to throw them together. He would not have come to Lucy any other way, not just now.

So far they had received only one short bulletin from Regina. 'Nothing has changed with me. I am still with you.' Even now, he could not give himself to the idea that she might, would, die. She had never been ill in her life. And this sickness had come upon her so swiftly; he had not known of it until its course was almost run. That was like her; she never could abide deathbed scenes. She had avoided them in others and did not intend to play one herself. If she went against the tenor of the time in this, it was not the first time she had done that.

The knowledge of her lying at Stanton, determined to die alone, made him weak with pity and love for her. He tried to put the love in a letter. He left it incomplete, for he knew that there was something else she would want him to put into it. Well, she had won. She had the right to hear it. Now that he was with Lucy often, he knew that he did not want to be parted from her again. That was enough. He could forget the rest and begin from there.

One day he looked for her again beside the Quickenberry tree. This time she was there. 'What are you reading?'

She looked up and smiled. 'Prayers for the sick.'

'Thank you for that.'

'There is no need. She is very dear to me also.'

They talked of Regina for a time while Will realized that, now that he had determined to speak out, he had lost his hard-won ease with her again. 'You always look well in green,' he told her awkwardly, for want of better inspiration.

'And you in gold,' she said gravely. 'You wore gold the first day I saw you. I thought you were Sir Galahad.'

He laughed roughly. 'I'm afraid I have been somewhat of a disappointment in that respect.'

'No, I don't think so,' she said thoughtfully. 'It is I who have been the disappointment. To myself as well. You must understand that.'

'I understand you have no regrets?' he said gently. They were almost there now. They needed to say these things, though the experience was not comfortable.

She looked at him directly. 'I think that is what disappoints me. I know I should have regrets. All my teaching tells me so. And yet I can't. Is that not strange and perverse?'

He smiled. 'Yes, it is. You are. But I like you strange and perverse. I chose you for it. I must not complain if the perversity is sometimes turned against me.'

It was a great deal to allow. She caught her breath. 'I can't regret Nieve,' she said then bluntly. Nieve was the heart of their trouble.

'Don't,' he said. 'I don't. I have come to love her – and I will be her father, if you want no other for her.'

She stood up with a cry of joy. But there was still one thing she must say. 'But one day, she must know. And if he – if Cathal writes, I must reply. It is his right and hers.'

So, nothing had changed. Well, he must learn to accept it as it was. He judged himself capable of keeping 'Mr O'Connor' away from his wife, should John Thurloe not do it for him. 'I agree to that,' he said firmly.

'You do?' A bird flew up in her heart.

'I do.'

They stood apart one second longer, savouring the grace of the fact that nothing now was between them except what they wished there to be. Then they converged and were united in a kiss that was both a seal and a greeting.

'It has been a hard, long time without you,' he said. He took her up and sat down with her upon Mary's bench.

'That was not what I had heard,' she said with a mischievous frown.

'But it is quite true!' he protested.

She saw that, whatever she, or the rest of the world might think, Will firmly believed what he said. She decided not to enquire after Cousin Eliza. 'Will we go home soon, all of us?' she asked, rubbing her cheek against his golden beard.

'We will. As soon as—'

'Ah, yes. God forgive me, I had forgotten. I was so happy.'

'That is what she wanted,' he said. Then, 'And by God I know what *I* want! Have you any idea, Lucy, how long it is since you and I were in bed together?'

It was while they were in bed together, at an indiscreet hour in the afternoon, that they received the next message from Regina. It requested them to finish what they were doing and to come downstairs.

'What the devil is this?' cried Will to Margery, who had brought the note.

'I don't know, sir. You'd best come down and see,' shrugged Margery with the air of one who has work to do.

They came down some twenty minutes later. Not even curiosity could take him away from her *before* they had finished what they were doing. When they appeared, looking rosy and both rather young, Margery, who was hovering in the hall now, said laconically, 'In the parlour.'

In the parlour Mary Heron was taking coffee, an unusual concession to a new trend. Beside her, splendidly gowned and in the rudest of health sat Regina Staunton.

'Ah, here you are.' She put down her cup and regarded them closely. 'I see you have taken my advice.'

At once, for he knew her, Will was rocking with horrible suspicions. Lucy only with shock. 'So, you also have made a miraculous recovery, have you?' he said with patent sarcasm. Regina flushed a little.

'Will!' Lucy reproved. But she began to wonder.

'Yes, wasn't I lucky?' Regina responded brightly. 'It was that excellent Dr Scrope who was responsible.' She crossed her fingers and asked forgiveness for the lie. It was poor Dr Jarvis who had cured her – of a most unpleasant bout of colic – and who had agreed to keep out of the way and be a party to her little scheme. He had even given her some white powder for her face. And since she had not slept for several nights, she *had* looked quite ill. Oh dear, she could see that Will was not going to forgive her. A little more blackmail was required. It was a terrible thing to have come to in one's old age, but then what else was one to do with it, but be useful to the young, whether they could see it, or not?

'Did *you* know about this?' Will asked Lucy sternly.

'Certainly not!' She was offended.

'Now – you must not put yourselves at odds over it,' Regina ordered. 'I was quite sick, if you must know. I was in great pain. But I am quite recovered now, I am glad to say. Quite restored.'

'But if it was your heart—' Will began, worried again.

'Well, no, perhaps *that* bit was just a small untruth – though not really, when you think of it. Your happiness *is*, after all, a matter that touches my heart. But tell me, my son, are you not glad to see me well? Or would you prefer, as your frowning countenance suggests, that I were flat on my back and making out my will?'

'Oh Regina,' he said disgustedly. 'You know I would not. But it has been a monstrous fraud!'

'That is very well,' she replied equably. 'Now I wish to relax and drink my coffee and talk with Mary.' She waved a regal hand and they were dismissed.

They went upstairs to the gallery, shaking with laughter and relief. 'Your mother is a terrible woman!'

'Yes, indeed. Pray don't make too close a study of her methods. I should hate to see them repeated.'

'Not by me. I am too blunt for subterfuge.'

'And too honest for your own good,' he said softly, kissing separately each honest lip.

They stood in front of the oriel and looked out over Heron. They leaned against each other. They had gone about in these last few days drunk with the intoxication of being able to touch each other again.

'Would we have come together without Regina, do you think?' asked Lucy, raising his warm hand to her mouth.

'Yes,' he answered certainly, turning to bring her to him. 'But it would not have been *now*, and I would have missed too many hours of you. But I *would* have come to you at last, wretched with pride and loneliness, and I should probably have mishandled it in my stupidity, and you might have sent me away again.'

'Oh no!' She kissed him three times, quickly, as though to stop his mouth of such notions. 'I could never have done that. I have wanted you too much and too long. *I* would have come to *you*. I think I would have begged you to take me, in the end. My pride had all gone. I was just gathering my courage. Before this happened, I had nearly enough. It would not have been long.'

'Let us by all means fight over who would have come to whom the first!' he said laughing. 'Whatever the case, Regina has made us the gift of a few precious months or weeks or hours and we must use them joyfully as one should always use a gift – especially one so thoughtfully made!'

Lucy laughed too. Then she turned and drew him with her to the harpsichord. The instrument had been the companion of so much of their happiness. It was right that it should share it now.

'Then so that she shall hear she is forgiven for her gift,' she said, pressing a few tentative chords, 'let us make very joyful music together. I have longed for the sound of our two voices twining.'

He kissed her once more then stood behind her, his hands resting on her shoulders, caressing, while she played. She began an old love-song of Dowland's and their voices rose above the strings in a voluntary of pure joy.

Beyond the gallery, the whole house heard it and was renewed.

THE BLACK MOUNTAINS

Janet Tanner

Black mountains dominate the Somerset town of Hillsbridge, and beneath their brooding shadow the Hall family – Charlotte, James and their seven children – carry on an earthy, turbulent existence. Independent spirits, the Halls are united by strong family values, divided by the conflicts of a community caught up in the changing patterns of industrial progress. Then the darker shadows of impending war fall upon this vivid family canvas, and the Halls are forced to reaffirm their most basic beliefs.

Janet Tanner has created a memorable and moving saga of love, hate, happiness and heartbreak on the slopes of THE BLACK MOUNTAINS.

'Sensitive and exceptionally polished' – *Manchester Evening News*

Futura Publications
Fiction
0 7088 2278 9

COLLA'S CHILDREN

Alanna Knight

Morag Macdonald is a child of the Hebrides, spirited, strong, and steeped in the magic and the traditions of the windswept, ancient isles.

A true daughter of Clan Donald, 'Colla's Children', Morag makes her way to the Isle of Lewis and there embarks on a loveless marriage and the rigours of a crofting life, as unchanging as the surrounding hills. Until Sergei Svenson, a Norwegian sea captain, sweeps briefly, but tempestuously into her life . . .

Alanna Knight has created a haunting and powerful tale of the Hebrides and its rich, turbulent history – and of Morag, who seeks the key to her own history, a woman before her time.

Futura Publications
Fiction
0 7088 1813 7

THE FLOWERS OF THE FIELD

Sarah Harrison

From London and the fields of Kent to Paris, Vienna and the Western Front, the lives of three very different women are changed irrevocably by love, ambition and the First World War.

Dorothea, Dulcie and Primmy. Their dreams and aspirations found a voice above history's most horrifying conflict. Their triumphs and tragedies were shared by a generation. Their unforgettable story unfolds in the epic novel of our time.

'Smashing . . . a story which hurried you along from page to page at breakneck pace' – *Daily Mirror*

'A stirring tale of love, loss and loyalty' – *Publishers Weekly*

Futura Publications
Fiction
0 7088 1812 9

DYNASTY 1: THE FOUNDING

Cynthia Harrod-Eagles

Triumphantly heralding the mighty Morland Dynasty — an epic saga of one family's fortune and fate through five hundred years of history. A story as absorbing and richly diverse as the history of the English-speaking people themselves.

THE FOUNDING

Power and prestige are the burning ambitions of Edward Morland, rich sheep farmer and landowner.

He arranges a marriage. A marriage that will be the first giant step in the founding of the Morland Dynasty.

A dynasty that will be forged by his son Robert, more poet than soldier. And Eleanor, ward of the powerful Beaufort family. Proud and aloof, and consumed by her secret love for Richard, Duke of York.

And so with THE FOUNDING, The Morland Dynasty begins — with a story of fierce hatred and war, love and desire, running through the turbulent years of the Wars of the Roses.

Futura Publications
Fiction
0 7088 1728 9

All Futura Books are available at your bookshop or newsagent, or can be ordered from the following address:
Futura Books, Cash Sales Department,
P.O. Box 11, Falmouth, Cornwall.

Please send cheque or postal order (no currency), and allow 45p for postage and packing for the first book plus 20p for the second book and 14p for each additional book ordered up to a maximum charge of £1.63 in U.K.

Customers in Eire and B.F.P.O. please allow 45p for the first book, 20p for the second book plus 14p per copy for the next 7 books, thereafter 8p per book.

Overseas customers please allow 75p for postage and packing for the first book and 21p per copy for each additional book.